...SOME PEOPLE
WILL DO
ANYTHING.

How Far Would She Go?

"I've got to tell you the truth," Paul said. "The Jaguar was repossessed. I couldn't make the payments. My trust fund check hasn't come. I'm not taking very good care of you," he said shyly, looking at Beth Carol from under his curly lashes.

Oh, he was so sweet, Beth Carol thought.

"There's only one possibility," he said, taking a few steps toward her, taking her hand. "I hate to do this, Beth Carol. I don't know what you'll think of me, but I have to ask you. It's our only chance."

"Ask me, Paul," she begged. "Ask me anything. Nobody's ever treated me the way you have. You've been wonderful."

"Well, there's this guy," he said. "He wants some action tonight."

Also by Barbara Wilkins

Elements of Chance

Published by
HarperPaperbacks

BARBARA WILKINS

IN NAME ONLY

HarperPaperbacks

A Division of HarperCollinsPublishers

HarperPaperbacks   *A Division of* HarperCollins*Publishers*
10 East 53rd Street, New York, N.Y. 10022

Copyright © 1992 by Barbara Wilkins
All rights reserved. No part of this book may be used or reproduced in any manner whatsoever without written permission of the publisher, except in the case of brief quotations embodied in critical articles and reviews. For information address HarperCollins*Publishers*,
10 East 53rd Street, New York, N.Y. 10022.

A hardcover edition of this book was published in 1992 by HarperCollins*Publishers*.

Cover photography by Herman Estevez

First HarperPaperbacks printing: February 1993

Printed in the United States of America

HarperPaperbacks and colophon are trademarks of HarperCollins*Publishers*

❖ 10 9 8 7 6 5 4 3 2 1

For the memory of my mother

And for my dearest friend, Gerry Brown

CHAPTER 1

*J*eers, catcalls and long, low wolf whistles shocked Beth Carol awake as she sat dozing on the seat of the Greyhound bus, three rows behind the driver. The bus had stopped, she realized. They must be in California now. In Crescent City, just across the border from Oregon. She shook herself to clear her head and looked towards the front of the bus, at the center of all of this sudden energy and attention.

The girl who stood there was so blond her hair was almost white. It towered over her small face in an elaborate mass of curls. Even through the cloud of stale, acrid cigarette smoke that hung in the air, Beth Carol could see the long, black, false eyelashes, the eyelids painted bright blue, the red cupid's bow mouth. On the girl's cheeks were two blobs of rouge. She wore long, dangling earrings of some kind of metal that glittered in the artificial light. They were so long that when she moved they hit the shoulders of her white angora sweater. That sweater, Beth Carol thought, amazed. Oh, golly. The girl's enormous breasts were bursting out of it. Her waist was tiny, tightly belted to show it off. Her hips and thighs were voluptuous in the tightest pair of capri pants Beth Carol had ever seen. Her shoes were plastic, backless, frontless, with high, high heels. Around one ankle Beth Carol caught the glint of metal. An

1

ankle bracelet. The girl's handbag by itself would have riveted everybody's attention. It was pink, huge, with a white poodle appliqué, a rhinestone collar around its neck and a chain draped across its surface that snaked up to the top.

Beth Carol's eyes widened at the sight of her. The girl was impossible, an apparition. Beth Carol had never seen anybody who looked like that in her life, not even in the movies. Unconsciously, she pushed the sleeves of her white blouse down over her wrists to be sure that the scars, still red and angry, were covered. She smoothed the lap of the blue cotton skirt she had bought at the department store in Spokane.

"Well, ladies and gentlemen," the driver announced over his loudspeaker, "as you can see, we're now in California."

Two soldiers sitting together across the aisle from Beth Carol beat on the back of the seats in front of them with their fists. More whistles, snickers. "Her mother ought to take that child into the bathroom and scrub her face." It was a woman's voice, floating from the row behind Beth Carol. Then there was another sound. "Tsk. Tsk."

Golly, if the girls in California look like that, Beth Carol thought, it sure isn't much like home. She glanced out of the window at Crescent City. It was pretty much the same as Coeur D'Alene, where she came from. The bus depot, well, it was like all the rest of them. The sign with the sleek racing dog, the storefront windows. A couple of the town loafers sitting on the bench out in front of it, watching the people who were traveling. Their excitement for the day. There was a greasy spoon next door, a sign propped in the corner of a window advertising a long-past church bazaar. Then the dime store. That was probably the bank down there. It was around ten o'clock in the morning, and the sky was a dead gray, threatening rain. Beth Carol lit a cigarette, wishing she had a cup of coffee to go with it, and sighed.

First came the perfume, sickeningly sweet, and then came the girl, sauntering down the aisle. She's going to sit next to me, Beth Carol realized as the cheap fragrance enveloped her, made her long to open the window even though she knew it would be too cold and the biddies in the row behind would be tapping her on the shoulder, telling her in no uncertain terms to close it.

"Is this seat taken?" the blond girl asked in a breathy, baby girl voice. Beth Carol looked up, saw the girl's big smile, her tiny teeth, like a kid's before they fell out, was aware of one chubby hand with long red nails on the seat in front of her.

"No, it isn't," she said, smiling back.

The girl looked around, making sure she still had every eye upon her. Then she daintily lowered herself onto the seat, squirmed into a comfortable position, and started to fumble around in her huge handbag. The cloying scent of her perfume was unbearable. Beth Carol took a long drag on her cigarette, hoping it would help. The girl flicked open a fresh pack of Lucky Strikes and pushed one into a long cigarette holder. She leaned into the aisle to accept a light from the soldier sitting across from her.

The bus driver flicked the lever closing the door, and started the engine. He dropped the transmission into first gear, and in a moment they were lumbering slowly out of the depot, joining the trucks, Fords, and a Chevrolet in the light flow of traffic down the main street of the town. On the sidewalk, a small boy holding his mother's hand smiled at them and waved.

Beth Carol smiled and waved back at him.

"Good-bye to nothing," the blond girl said contemptuously, leaning over Beth Carol and looking out of the window as the stores, offices, a Mobil station slowly transmogrified into rolling green fields where black and white cows contentedly grazed. The bus shook as a pair of monstrous semis sped by in the opposite direction. An imperceptible mist beaded droplets of water on the windows. The blond girl intently maneuvered her cigarette holder while she examined her face in the mirror of a large compact studded with colored stones. She practiced an enticing smile, keeping her upper lip down over those little teeth, a frown. She looked immensely pleased with herself as she snapped the compact shut and dropped it back into her handbag, ignoring the young soldier across the aisle who was trying to get her attention.

"I'll be back, though," the girl said under her breath. To herself, Beth Carol realized. Still, she was going to be a talker. Beth Carol could almost feel the words bursting out of her. Well, let her talk. It wouldn't be too bad, especially after some of the sex maniacs who had sat next to Beth Carol since she had gotten on the bus in Spokane. That was two days ago. It seemed longer, though. It seemed as if she had been on this bus forever.

She had been so scared at first, cowering in a stall in the ladies' room of the bus station at six o'clock in the morning, a scarf tied over her hair, dark glasses even, as if somebody were coming after her. Her mouth had been so dry, and her heart was beating so fast, that it had been as if her father, or one of the people who worked for him, or her sisters were hot on her trail, as if they would burst into the stall and find her sitting there on the lid of the toilet.

"Oh, come home, Beth Carol," they would beg and sob. "We love you. It'll be all right, just the way it was before. It's all gone away. It never happened."

Beth Carol had the whole scene outlined in her mind. Whoever it was who played the leading role would tell her how everything was going to be wonderful. More wonderful than it had ever been. If it were her father in the scene, he would kiss her gravely on the forehead and tell her over and over again how everybody in town had forgotten all about it. That he, personally, had asked them, and that they had just looked at him blankly. That he had forgotten about it, which was really what mattered.

"Are you sure, Daddy?" she would ask, looking up into his gray eyes, always so distracted in real life, but now, here, warm and loving, which made her heart swell with joy. Then he would put out his hand to her, and she would take it. Stand. Together they would walk out of the bus station while all the passengers would clap, the women smiling and misty-eyed, the men murmuring to each other that they wished they had a daughter like that, to love the way that father obviously loved his little girl.

Fat chance, Beth Carol thought, with a tight, bitter smile. Good riddance was what they probably really thought. All of them. Her father probably saw that she had only taken four hundred dollars from the hollowed-out edition of one of the leather-bound classics he kept among the books on the shelves in the library, the ones just behind his big oak desk that was always cluttered with all kinds of files and papers and had thought, Only four hundred dollars to get rid of her. What a bargain.

She had been so anxious about missing the bus that she kept rushing out of the ladies' room. It still sat there in the terminal with all the other buses. It was empty, its doors closed. Above its windshield was its destination: Los Angeles. With the tips of her fingers, Beth Carol touched the racing dog painted on its side.

Then the anxiety, the exhaustion, the terror that would well up in her, making her want to scream and scream, would send her scrambling back to the safety of the ladies' room, where she would lean against the coolness of the tiled wall, her eyes closed as she fought to get her breath, to get control of herself. Every few minutes, she would cautiously approach the long bank of mirrors over the row of washbasins, pull the dark glasses away from her eyes, assuring herself at the sight of her reflection that she was still there. Leaning closer, she would examine her face to see if she looked different, tainted in some way. But no. There was the pale, rounded forehead, the dreamy, blue eyes. Her short, straight nose, a family characteristic. The full lips. Too full, she sometimes thought. Not quite ladylike. Her chin was rounded, too, a baby's chin, her face a baby's unformed face. She had a nice complexion, glowing a healthy pink even in the constant rain. Even her sister Luanne, the prettiest of all the girls, grudgingly admitted that Beth Carol had the nicest complexion. She was sixteen years old, and she had never even had a pimple.

Then the door to the ladies' room would swing open and

Beth Carol would jam the dark glasses back over her eyes and drop her head. But it would be just another woman sweeping past her, usually carrying a leather overnight case like her own, closing the door of the toilet stall, locking it behind her.

When it was announced over the loudspeaker that the bus for Los Angeles was ready for loading, Beth Carol was the first one to board. She hurried frantically down the aisle to the very back and crouched in a seat by the window. She darted glances toward the front door as if even now, at the last moment before her escape, somebody, her father, would be standing there, would have come for her. She was barely aware of the man who sat down next to her until she smelled the body odor, the after-shave, the cigar smoke stinking up his brown suit. She glanced at him out of the corner of her eye. Old enough to be her grandfather, she thought fleetingly. Down on his luck, if he'd ever had any. Then the bus was on its way, rolling through the gloomy, rain-filled streets of Spokane with its dowdy, gray office buildings squatting in an endless row.

She was aware of her own beating heart, her breath coming in little pants, the feeling of relief as the bus inched along, the changing of gears at red lights, at green lights, the slowing before it edged around a corner, gained speed, slowed again. Except for Beth Carol and the man sitting next to her, the entire back of the bus was empty. She could feel his eyes on her and shuddered with disgust as she realized that even though it was just past dawn, the smell on his breath was alcohol. He was breathing hard, too. Hot, rasping gasps. Beth Carol huddled against the window, concentrating on the view, the buildings, thinning out now, the occasional pedestrian under an umbrella, the sheets of rain blurring everything. The man was saying something to her. She ignored him, closed her eyes as she prayed he would just leave her alone. She almost jumped out of her seat as she felt his hand on her arm.

"I'm sorry?" she said in her polite, little girl's voice, ter-rified now as she partially turned toward him. Oh, he was horrible, with his watery eyes, a gray stubble on his cheeks, his chin. His smell. The predator.

"Twenty dollars," he whispered. "Nobody can see us back here, honey. I'll just take it out, and you kiss it a little."

This can't be happening, Beth Carol thought wildly as she shrank away from him. He had one gnarled hand locked on her forearm, the other massaging himself down there. All of these people on the bus, the driver. She opened her mouth to scream, willed herself to scream.

"Just you kiss it, baby, and I'll give you that twenty dollars," he whispered, his voice soothing, conspiratorial.

Scream, scream, Beth Carol told herself as visions of rabbits caught in the headlights of trucks froze in her mind. All she could do was make little mewling sounds, the tears spurting, coursing down her cheeks. The man looked at her with dismay.

"Okay, okay," he muttered, pulling himself out of his seat and moving up the aisle.

Beth Carol sat there, frozen. Crying silently, but with relief now. She counted to a hundred, then five hundred. A thousand. Taking a deep breath, she grabbed her overnight case, her handbag, and scurried up the aisle, looking straight ahead, until she found a seat as close to the bus driver as she could get. My fault, she thought, feeling a little sick. Sitting way back there all by myself, that was dumb. Dumb. But nothing had happened. The realization made her feel better, more in control. No more hiding, she decided. It wasn't necessary, anyway. Nobody was coming after her. She knew that by now. Only four hundred dollars. Good riddance. Cheap at twice the price. Tears of self-pity filled her eyes and she wished she had taken it all.

The bus droned through the forests of northeast Washington, the sky dark with thunderheads. A sudden flurry of raindrops pounded on the window next to her, making her start for a moment in her sleep.

She was dreaming of Buddy. She could almost see his face, the serious blue eyes, his long lashes, the blond hair cut short, but his curls springing up anyway, the wonderful way his mouth curved up when he smiled, which touched her. That wonderful smile. Those nice teeth. You didn't often see teeth like that in a boy from Buddy's class.

White trash, her father called people like Buddy and the family he came from. And the other families that lived in Deadman's Gulch, where the little kids ate dirt and got sick, and nobody seemed to have any idea that there was more to life than working all week at the mines and getting roaring drunk on Saturday night and punching each other out. Beth Carol cringed when she even thought of those people, Buddy's family in particular. His father was one of the worst drunks, his mother a harridan, and the family, in their falling-down shack, was one of the ones to whom she and her sisters delivered Christmas baskets in the Packard with her father's chauffeur driving. Well, they *were* white trash. There just wasn't any other way to think about them.

Buddy was different. Buddy was handsome, and he was the quarterback of the Lakeside High School football team. His crimson and white letterman's jacket was the great equalizer, and Beth Carol was only one of the rich girls who felt a little rush of something, attraction, whatever, when he sauntered down the hall, or when the team had won and he trotted off the field with all the other guys slapping him on the back, the kids in the stands screaming their heads off for him.

No matter what anyone said, it was very special between her and Buddy. They talked and talked when they could sneak away to be together, and he told her all about how he was going to be a big success. About how he was going to join the army when he graduated because he might as well. He'd just get drafted if he didn't, and maybe it would give him some brownie points. Then Korea, probably. But he was covering that possibility, too. He was taking typing so, with any luck, he'd be a clerk. Then college on the GI Bill, because, face it, he was a good quarterback, but there were better, and none of the colleges was exactly beating his door down with offers of a scholarship.

"Oh, Buddy," she whispered, "you're going to be a big

sucess. I just know it." She could almost see him a few years down the line in his office, in a nice suit. His new car outside. A Lincoln, maybe, or a Cadillac. She was thrilled at his ambition, at his vision of himself. At her own vision of herself at his side.

And oh, how she loved it when he touched her, murmured her name over and over as they lay together on the piles of tarps in the boathouse while the speedboats below them in the water rocked and moaned. Buddy. Oh, she hadn't thought of him in so many days now. Not since all of it had happened, and she had so much else to think about. It was wonderful to think about him again the way she had done every minute that they weren't together. Think about his words. "Baby, when I'm with you, I know I can do anything. You make me feel so good."

Think about his touch. About the way he made her feel when he had his hand between her legs, his fingers prodding under her panties, in there. Getting her so hot. She stirred in her sleep, feeling wet down there. Smiled.

Abruptly, she woke, sitting up straight in her seat, as the bus droned on through another sudden storm and bolts of lightning crackled through the black sky. The soldier sitting next to her jerked his hand out from under her skirt.

"I'm sorry," he mumbled, flushing crimson.

Beth Carol sat, staring at him.

"Don't say anything, okay?" he begged. "He'll throw me off the bus, and I've got to get back to camp. I'll be AWOL. I've just got to get back."

She brushed her skirt into place, her lower lip trembling. What was the matter with these people? she wondered. Why did they think they could do these things? What gave them the right?

"Please," he implored, tears starting in his worried brown eyes. "Look, I'll move," he added, starting to rise. "Just don't say anything."

Then he was gone, loping off down the aisle toward the back of the bus. Beth Carol sat there, knowing she should say something to the bus driver, thinking about it for a

while until she realized she didn't have the heart to do it.
But there was something really wrong about the whole
thing. That he could do anything he wanted because she
was asleep and vulnerable, and then she was the one who
had to be big about it. A couple of hours later, she saw him
get off at Bellingham. He rushed by, his eyes straight
ahead. It was at Bellingham that she'd gotten the chatty
grandmother with her pictures of prolific sons and daughters, their sons and daughters, dogs and cats, friends sitting
around, all smiles, at picnics, in front of Christmas trees.
The chatty grandmother had really been mind-numbing.
But at least she didn't want anything except Beth Carol's
smiles and little exclamations of approval at her kids and
their kids and all.

And now this girl.

Beth Carol could feel her getting ready, could almost
feel the girl's vocal chords tuning up.

CHAPTER 2

T'm Fern Darling," the girl said in that stupid baby voice of hers that she must have practiced because nobody in the real world talked like that.

"I'm Beth Carol Barnes."

Sitting there next to her, Beth Carol got past the effect the girl created and really looked at her for the first time. She did have nice eyes, Beth Carol saw. They were light blue, and the whites were very white, although Beth Carol had to wonder how she kept them open, what with the weight of those false eyelashes. But she wasn't even really pretty. Her nose was narrow, her face sort of pinched and unhappy looking. The mouth wasn't a cupid's bow. It was just painted on thin lips. And she had added a beauty mark, too, a black dot on one cheek. There was such a pall of smoke hanging in the air in the bus that it wasn't easy to make out actual details, but there was a good possibility that her neck was dirty. The expression on her face had been friendly, anticipating something from Beth Carol that she evidently hadn't gotten. The garish mouth dropped in disappointment.

"You don't like it," she said.

"Like what?" asked Beth Carol, wondering what she'd missed.

11

"The name." The girl frowned. "Fern Darling. You don't like the name."

"I don't understand," Beth Carol said.

"Well, don't you think it sounds like a movie star's name?" the girl asked. "I mean, can't you just see it on a marquee? Fern Darling, up there in lights?"

"Well, sure," Beth Carol said. "I guess so."

"Well, do you guess so, or do you know so?" the girl demanded crossly. "You can't imagine how long it took me to come up with that name. I stayed awake at nights for months trying to come up with the right one, once I'd decided."

"Decided?" asked Beth Carol, bewildered. The two of them had exchanged about sixteen words, she calculated, and she was hopelessly lost.

"Once I decided to go to Hollywood and become a movie star," the girl said. "You have to have the right name, you know. I ran through hundreds, thousands, even. Oh, all the usual ones. And wouldn't you know it? Most of the good ones are already taken. I mean, Rita. Lana. Ava. Marilyn, of course. Her real name is Norma Jean Baker. I read that in a movie magazine." The girl's expression was suddenly serious, beseeching. "Do you think Rose would be better?" she asked. "Rose Darling?"

"No, no," said Beth Carol. "I think Fern Darling is a perfect name. I think you've made just the right choice."

"Are you sure?" the girl asked. "Because now's the time."

"I'm positive," Beth Carol said. She wondered how she was going to get through two whole days of this. Even the chatty grandmother was starting to look good.

"I'll bet you're wondering what made me decide to become a movie star." Fern's whole attitude implied that nothing else could possibly be on Beth Carol's mind.

"Sure," said Beth Carol, her stomach growling. She blushed, wished she had gotten something to eat in Crescent City, hoped the other girl hadn't heard. It was so embarrassing to make awful noises like that. "Tell me," she said quickly. "I'd like to hear. I really would."

"Well, it all started when I was a baby," Fern began, savoring every word, every vowel, as Beth Carol inwardly groaned and wished that she could have started maybe a little later, say at the age of ten. "You know how little babies are so ugly and red?" She was leaning into Beth Carol now, almost whispering in her ear as if she were sharing a major secret. "Well, I wasn't. I was all pink and rosy from the very beginning, and I had a full head of blond curls."

"What do you use now?" Beth Carol asked, getting into it with Fern, deciding she should be happy for the chance to think about something other than herself and her problems. "At home, some of the gals use peroxide." No reason to add that those were the cheap gals, the ones the other gals looked down on. The ones the boys snickered about with each other, but nonetheless ran after like a bunch of dogs.

Crimson flushed Fern's cheeks under the dots of rouge, and mottled her neck, which still looked kind of gray to Beth Carol, even close up like this. "This is my natural color," she sputtered indignantly, shaking her head a little, as if she just couldn't believe that Beth Carol could think anything else.

"Gee, you're lucky," Beth Carol said lamely, thinking, yeah, and I'm Dwight Eisenhower, the President of the United States.

"I won all of the beautiful baby contests," Fern began again. "Mama would have me dolled up so cute in little ruffled dresses and bows in my curls to match. Pink and yellow and powder blue." She batted her eyes at Beth Carol. Just practicing, Beth Carol decided. Seeing how she was going over. "Well, the first one was at a market near where we lived when I was just a few months old," Fern continued. "Then a photographer on Main Street had a contest, and I won that one, too." She widened her eyes and added, her voice filled with wonder, "Why, do you know what? That picture is still in his window, after all these years!"

"That's great," Beth Carol enthused.

"Then it was the Elks and the Masons," Fern recited.

"Then the whole town. The county fair. Then the state fair. Every year there were more. After the beautiful baby contests, there were all of the beautiful child contests. I won them, too. All of them. People said I put Shirley Temple to shame."

"That must have kept your mom busy," Beth Carol said. "Taking you around everywhere and all."

"Oh, she was happy to do it," Fern said solemnly. "All she ever thought about was me. I'm her life."

"So how come she's letting you go off by yourself to Hollywood?" asked Beth Carol. Sitting next to her like this, Beth Carol could see that Fern was young. Maybe not even sixteen.

"Oh, well, she wants the world for me," Fern said vaguely. "When I get settled, Mama will walk out just like I did. She'll be there with bells on."

"That's great," said Beth Carol again, wondering how much of what Fern was telling her was true, if anything. Wondering if Fern's mother even knew she was gone.

"Mama saw to it that I took up baton twirling in the third grade," Fern continued. "Don't you just love baton twirling? There I was, in my little white skirt and my hat with all of the gold braid on it, and my white boots with the tassels in front. Oh, how I loved those boots. I really loved them."

She lowered her eyes, dug into her handbag, and Beth Carol's heart sank. Here come the pictures, she thought. Instead, Fern unwrapped a piece of spearmint gum and popped it into her mouth.

"And there would be the whole parade behind me," she went on. "The floats and the bands. The old farts from Rotary and the Jaycees on their horses, and the horses plopping turds into the street."

Old farts? She'd really said it. Old farts. Beth Carol was shocked for an instant, and then she giggled. They *were* old farts. It was just like home. At home they had those parades, too, with the marching bands and the floats and the old farts on their horses thinking they looked so great with their paunches hanging out and wheezing away and their faces getting redder and redder from the exertion, and hardly able to hold up their American flags. And everybody looking away discreetly when the horses plopped all over the street.

Of course, she and her sisters were never a part of the parades. No, the Barnes girls were too good for that, above it all. Luanne, Patricia Jane, and Maggie, with their cool, blond good looks. Beth Carol was the fourth, not as pretty, as the older girls always told her. Not as vivid, either, with her brown hair. The baby, little Linda Marie, was almost ignored.

So many girls.

Why, when she was born, her father hadn't even come to the hospital. It was one of those family legends that Beth Carol must have heard sixteen thousand million times, as if it were something wonderful. He had been so disgusted when Maggie turned out to be another girl, he had just about given up. Then, a few years later when she was born, he hadn't come to the hospital, and a year later when Linda Marie was born, he didn't go to the hospital, either. So their mother had given up and died out of disappointment. That's what she and Linda Marie were told, anyway. She'd just died because there was no boy. Nobody to be groomed to take over the mines and the plants, and all the rest of the stuff. Linda Marie and Beth Carol used to talk about it sometimes. It seemed to them that the older girls and the aunts and everybody almost approved of her dying, as if it were the honorable thing for her to have done. Like the Jap kamikaze pilots they would hear about during World War II when they were little, who would just dive into ships and die for honor. Golly, it was really creepy. There were other rumors, too, that never seemed to have been said in so many words, but that were just there. That she'd taken her own life. Beth Carol and Linda Marie never said the words, either, but the thought was there.

Neither of them remembered their mother, so they didn't know what she had been like. Her maiden name was

Alice McNealy and she came from a very good family in Wilmington, Delaware. She had met their father at some hunt ball when he was east at the university. Oh, she had been beautiful in her wedding pictures in her white satin gown, its bodice embroidered with pearls, a crown of pearls holding her veil on her fair hair that shone in the light the photographer had set up. And Beth Carol's father had looked so handsome, even though it was only the flush of pride and happiness, because he wasn't handsome. His eyes were small and his face was kind of fleshy even then. There was something wet and sensual about his mouth. No, he had something better than good looks. He had this almost overwhelming masculinity, like animal magnetism. And money. He was looking at his bride as if he had won the greatest prize in the world.

The honeymoon pictures were nice, too. After their wedding at the church, where her mother's family had gone to worship for generations, and the reception at the country club, they had gone to New York, where they had spent the first night of their married life at the Plaza Hotel. Another photograph on the deck of the ocean liner, all smiles and looking blissfully happy. Her mother standing on the first step of the Orient Express, her father, one step up, his arm around her shoulders, protecting her. Cherishing her. Big, big smiles, both of them.

Even the pictures of them holding Luanne when she was a baby showed a happy couple, delighted with their beautiful little daughter. They still seemed to be happy in the pictures when Patricia Jane was born. After that, there were no more posed, formal pictures, as if making a record of Maggie, Beth Carol and Linda Marie wasn't even worth bothering about. Her parents hadn't even named Linda Marie. They had left it to the three older girls. It was strange, really. It was almost as if the older girls were in one family, a happy one, and the younger girls were in another family, a miserable one.

"I developed early, too," Fern was saying. "I had these big tits by the time I was in the fifth grade. All through junior high and high school, I won all the beauty contests there were. I was homecoming queen, and the queen of the senior prom. I wore a white satin dress and I had my hair up on top of my head and everybody told me that I looked just like the angel on the top of the Christmas tree. Even the principal asked me to dance."

Beth Carol looked at Fern quizzically for a moment and thought about what she was saying. Narrowing her eyes, she thought about it for a couple of minutes more. Maybe the beauty contest stuff and the parades were true and maybe not. But Fern Darling, or whatever her name was, would never, never have been elected homecoming queen, or queen of the senior prom. As Luanne would put it in her two favorite words, Fern was common and vulgar, and no matter how small the town, or maybe even because the town was so small, there was always a hierarchy. Some family was always richer and more respected and had more status than any of the others, and it was the daughters of that family who were elected to things like that.

Luanne, for instance, who was now a senior at the University of Idaho, majoring in education—a degree she would never use because the only reason to go to college was to be able to say you did, and to meet the right kind of boys—really had been the homecoming queen at Lakeside High School, and also queen of the senior prom. Then Patricia Jane. Then Maggie. Beth Carol's own turn would have been next, two years from now.

Beth Carol sighed, wondering if she could have made it, putting aside the scandal for a moment. Probably she wouldn't have, she decided, and neither would Linda Marie. There was just something too wounded about the two of them, too neglected, despite the private island, the house that rambled on and on all over the place, the swimming pool, the tennis court, the green, velvety lawn rolling gently for an acre or so down to the edge of the lake, and the boathouse with all the speedboats.

But the point about the three older girls being elected homecoming queen and queen of the senior prom wasn't that they were pretty, which they were, or popular, which they also were. It was that their father, R. Millard Barnes, the *R.* standing for Raleigh, a family name, owned the Barnes Mining Company and a number of related businesses, and employed more than half the people in town.

Beth Carol could almost see her father in his office in the plant with the tinny light and all the workers swarming around and the smokestacks belching out those lethal gray clouds of lead that made all the kids downwind sick, which the company denied. Her father was a little paunchy now, at least compared to those early pictures of him and her mother. His wavy, brownish hair was a little thin on top, and his face was etched in a permanent scowl. His little eyes were cold, his mouth frightening, and his earlobes had gotten longer as he got older, sort of like the natives in *National Geographic* who did it on purpose as a sign of beauty. He worked with his tie loosened, his coat off, and his sleeves rolled up to just below his elbows. Everybody in the plant was scared to death of him. Once she had heard somebody whisper when he passed, "There he goes, striding like doom."

Now she was making herself anxious again, Beth Carol saw, as her hands started to shake and an awful feeling of weakness made her lean against the seat. Oh, golly, ever since it happened, she had been so scared, so tired of thinking, that she just couldn't do it anymore. When she tried to get two thoughts straight in a row, her mind just turned and turned and the cogs didn't connect.

Next to her, Fern pushed another cigarette into her holder and lit it with a gold lighter.

"You know where I'm going to live when I get to Hollywood?" she asked brightly.

Where to live, Beth Carol thought, a spasm of anxiety grabbing at her insides. See what a mess you are? she said to herself. You haven't even thought of that. "Where?" she asked.

"The Studio Club," Fern announced triumphantly. "That's where all the stars live at first. Even Marilyn

Monroe lived there before she got so rich and famous. Did
you see her in *The Asphalt Jungle?* Or, *Niagara?* Well, I've
seen every movie she's ever been in. Some of them ten,
even fifteen times. You know what I did? I'd cut the last
class at school and I'd go to the theater when the movie was
half over and I wouldn't have to pay. I think she's the most
beautiful gal I've ever seen in my life."

"Yes, she's pretty," agreed Beth Carol, although her own
tastes ran more to Grace Kelly, Ava Gardner, and Elizabeth
Taylor. Boy, the first time she'd ever seen Elizabeth Taylor
in a movie, she'd really been depressed. It just didn't seem
possible that anybody could be that pretty.

"In fact," confided Fern, "it's because of Marilyn
Monroe that I decided to become a big movie star. You
know, everybody in Crescent City thought I looked just like
her. Why, people stopped me on the street all the time to
tell me about our amazing resemblance." She looked anxiously at Beth Carol. "You think so, too, don't you?" she
asked, her eyes beseeching.

"Oh, yes," said Beth Carol. "You look just like her. You
could be twins."

"Well, there's one difference," Fern said, her voice
dropping to a whisper. "You see this beauty mark? Well, it's
not real. I just put it there with an eyebrow pencil because
she has one there."

"Maybe she puts hers on with an eyebrow pencil, too,"
said Beth Carol.

"I've never thought of that," said Fern.

The bus driver announced over the loudspeaker that
they would be arriving in Ukiah in ten minutes. One of the
soldiers across the aisle from them shook the other awake.
A woman carrying a baby and a diaper bag hurried down
the aisle to the rest room at the back of the bus. People
began to stir in their seats, straightening their clothes, lighting cigarettes. Beth Carol thought of food. An American
cheese sandwich with lots and lots of mayonnaise. A glass of
milk. Her mouth watered.

"I have a whole plan of action to be discovered," said

Fern, snapping open her compact and examining her face with adoration. "I'm going to that drugstore in the middle of Sunset Boulevard. You know, where all the nightclubs are, like Ciro's and the Mocambo. Schwab's. All the movie stars go there. I'm just going to sit down at the counter there. I'll go every day until it happens."

"That's all?" asked Beth Carol, disappointed.

"Well, that's how they found Lana Turner. I read it in a movie magazine. Don't you just love movie magazines, and reading about all the stars?"

"I'm not permitted to read them," said Beth Carol.

"Why? Doesn't your mom like them?" asked Fern.

Now, that was really interesting when she thought about it, Beth Carol realized. Who was it exactly that wouldn't permit her to read movie magazines? They sure had them all at the newsstand. *Silver Screen. Modern Screen.* All of them. Every month the new ones were there. And she would have loved to read them, would have loved, even, to be waiting for the truck when it arrived. But she didn't. Somehow she just knew that one of the Barnes girls wouldn't read movie magazines. It would be noticed, commented on. There wasn't a whole lot of privacy in a town the size of Coeur D'Alene.

"It's my big sister, Luanne," said Beth Carol. "She thinks they're common."

"Oh," said Fern, ice fringing her voice at the implied disapproval.

"Oh, she doesn't know anything," Beth Carol said. "She thinks everything is common. That's just how she is."

"Anyway, it's going to be so wonderful to be rich and famous," Fern continued, mollified. "Everybody will look at me wherever I go, and they'll say, 'There's Fern Darling, the most beautiful gal in the world.'"

"They look at you now," Beth Carol said.

"That's different," said Fern. "When I'm rich and famous, they'll respect me. They'll want to be like me. They'll want to know what I wear to bed, and what perfume I wear. Things like that." Her face hardened, and her mouth under her lipstick was a narrow, bitter line. "I've even planned how it's going to be when I go back for the first time. I'll be sitting in the backseat of a black Cadillac convertible with the top down, and I'll be wearing a mink coat and I'll have two little dogs with bows, poodles, and I'll wave to everybody, and they'll all be lined up on the sidewalk, and they'll all be so jealous they'll be shitting in their pants." She crushed her compact closed. "I know I'll be a star," she vowed. "I know I will. That'll show them, all of them."

Beth Carol just stared at her. Golly, Fern was so intense. Beth Carol didn't know that she had ever met anybody who wanted anything as much as Fern wanted to be a star. Oh, when it came to ambition, sometimes Beth Carol thought about the poems she wrote that her English teacher liked. A couple of them had even been published in the junior high school yearbook. But really, all of the gals she knew, herself included, just thought about falling in love, getting married in a beautiful bridal gown, having a nice home. A couple of wonderful kids. And the way Fern talked—all that profanity. Beth Carol had never heard anybody, gal or guy, talk like that. Fern was really extraordinary.

The bus slowed as the driver downshifted, came to a stop at the bus depot. Next door was the usual greasy spoon. The hand-lettered sign in its window announced that chili was the special of the day.

"Twenty minutes," the driver said.

The door swung open, welcoming them to Ukiah, California.

CHAPTER 3

*I*n front of them, everybody seemed to be as anxious to get off the bus as Beth Carol, and they pushed against each other, hurrying down the stairs. Behind them, though, everybody seemed to be in a state of suspended animation.

Fern finished fussing with her towering hairdo and pushed her feet with their bright red toenails into her high-heeled shoes. Her ankle bracelet shone in the pale sunlight framed by the window of the bus. The ankle itself was grimy. Then she stood, took a deep breath as she tightened the belt around her tiny waist, and wiggled out into the aisle. The soldiers came alive, bumping against each other as they flocked after her.

Beth Carol stood, pushing the sleeves of her blouse down over her wrists, while she waited for a break in the flow of passengers. Smells of stale smoke, old food, and unwashed bodies hung in the air. A baby had been sick. As she picked her way down the steps, Beth Carol saw Fern's blond head, a bright spot in the sea of khaki as the soldiers fought to open the door of the restaurant for her. By the time Beth Carol entered the restaurant, there was only one seat left at the counter. The waitresses were rushing around like crazy, screeching orders to the cooks.

The sandwich the waitress eventually slammed down in front of Beth Carol was everything she had been dreaming about. Three slices of American cheese, lots of mayonnaise, a piece of lettuce. There was a pickle, a bag of potato chips. Boy, does this taste good, she thought, gulping it down, all the while watching Fern at a table across the room. Look at her over there, pushing out her chest and batting her eyes and all, while all of those guys blush and stammer, and would almost kill each other to get at her. It must be nice to be like that. To have that kind of confidence. To know what you wanted to do and where to go to get it done. Fern Darling had courage. That was what it was. Beth Carol wondered what that would feel like as she caught the waitress's eye and ordered a piece of lemon meringue pie.

"It's been sitting there for a couple of days," the waitress said doubtfully.

"That's okay," said Beth Carol, deciding that the woman just didn't want to change the total on the check.

"Well, don't blame me if you don't like it," the waitress said breezily.

A peal of laughter from the table where Fern sat with her swains caused heads to snap in that direction. Beth Carol could see Fern shaking her finger at one of the boys while her body language said the opposite. Such white trash, Beth Carol thought, smiling to herself. That's what her sisters would have to say about Fern. Her father, too, if he could be bothered. In truth, she had to admit to herself, she thought Fern was white trash, too. Still, having courage was a wonderful thing. And what about you? she asked herself as she chewed on a piece of the pie. The waitress was right. It was awful. What you did, she told herself, was run away. That's the opposite of courage. It would have taken courage to stay. What she was doing was cowardice.

In clumps, the passengers from the bus started to file out of the restaurant. Hurriedly, Beth Carol scanned her check, put down some change, added a ten-cent tip. There were some new people, she saw, as she pushed open the door to the restaurant. A mom, carrying a baby in one arm, stooping to take the hand of a toddler and help him up the steps. That must be hard, Beth Carol thought. Traveling with two little kids. Behind them was an elderly couple, the woman in a flowered summer dress and a white straw hat with some fake fruit on the side, the man in a suit and tie. There were a couple of kids in jeans who looked to be about twelve. They had no luggage. Probably getting off at the next little town. They all did that at home, too. They just got on the Greyhound and took it down the highway to wherever they were going.

Fern, standing at the door to the bus, ignoring the two soldiers who were crowding her, was looking anxiously around. Beth Carol caught her eye and gave a little wave.

"Oh, there you are," Fern said crossly. She reached out her hand and put it on Beth Carol's shoulder.

Beth Carol smiled at her, feeling warm and unexpectedly pleased.

"Don't leave me." Fern giggled into Beth Carol's ear. "Have you ever seen anything like this? They're just like a bunch of dogs."

And you're just like the bitch they're panting after, Beth Carol thought, but, of course, she didn't say it. They took their seats again as the bus started.

"Where were you?" Fern asked, reaching into her handbag again, finding a cigarette. "I thought you'd come over. I would have ordered a steak, but in a hick town like that they didn't have one. Just hamburgers. So I had a hamburger with everything on it and a chocolate malt and a piece of pie. It was all I had time for." She sighed triumphantly. "They were fighting to pay for me," she added in a confidential voice. "That's why I was looking for you. So they could pay for you, too."

"Well, thanks," said Beth Carol, charmed. "That's nice of you."

"Well, you know," Fern said, poking her in the side, a smile on her face, "we gals have got to stick together, don't we? It's us against them."

"Us against them," Beth Carol agreed, her voice hearty.

Maybe they could be friends, she thought. Maybe they could team up when they got to Hollywood. United we stand, and divided we fall, and all that. Funny, she hadn't even thought about what she would do with her life after she left Coeur D'Alene. It had all been in the leaving. Creeping down the stairs in the middle of the night. Stealing the four hundred dollars from her father's library. Hurrying down to the dock and casting off one of the rowboats. She hadn't dared to take one of the speedboats because she was sure the noise would wake the dogs. Then they would go crazy, rushing around and barking their heads off and waking everybody on the island.

She'd sat in the rowboat, her heart trying to beat its way out of her chest, and sort of let it glide onto the lake before she even started to row. Crossing the lake always terrified her, and she knew why, too. She didn't know how to swim. Nobody had ever taken the time to teach her. Oh, it had been so black that night. The water, the sky, even though there was a sliver of moon, the pines, the fir trees, so tall and foreboding, the rustle of animals. An owl hooted, and she was so scared there for a moment she thought it was the end of her.

Being caught would have been worse than the way things were, with the psychiatric hospital the next stop. The Menninger Clinic in Topeka, Kansas. Well, that was one thing you could say about being rich. You could pay for the very best in the way of nuthouses. Beth Carol closed her eyes, remembering that awful day that Luanne had picked her up at the Coeur D'Alene hospital in her little white Ford convertible with the red leather interior that their father had bought for her when she went away to college.

Beth Carol had sat in one of the chairs in the reception area of the hospital, a long-sleeved cardigan sweater over the bandages on her wrists. Boy, was it ever embarrassing. The nurse behind the desk not looking at her, the people trickling in and out the front door not looking at her. But everybody knowing that she was sitting there. Everybody. That's the way it was in small towns. She could just hear them talking about her.

Leave it to Luanne to keep her waiting, punishing her some more. Beth Carol kept her eyes on the floor, counting the squares of pale yellow linoleum with their alternating streaks of gray and white.

It seemed like three days before the door to the hospital opened and it actually was Luanne, gesturing for Beth Carol to step on it with an impatient shake of her blond hair in its perfect flip.

Unless it was actually snowing, or raining so hard that people started to joke about Noah's Ark, Luanne always kept the top of her convertible down—to show off, Beth Carol knew. So that all the people in the town could see Luanne Barnes, the oldest Barnes girl, and the prettiest, home from college. If only they knew the contempt she felt for them and their corny, small-town ways.

But it doesn't even come close to the contempt she feels for me, Beth Carol had thought as she shuffled along in the wake of Luanne's splendor. Long, tanned legs in tennis shorts. The latest boyfriend's fraternity pin on the collar of her blouse. That golden hair with never a strand out of place.

The car was parked way around in back where nobody could see it. Beth Carol's cheeks burned when she saw the top was up.

"Get in," Luanne ordered, her eyes flashing angrily.

Beth Carol did as she was told, closing the door very carefully. Luanne hated it when anybody slammed the door. Beth Carol just sat there as Luanne drove, her eyes looking straight ahead, her mouth set.

On the main street, which they couldn't avoid, kids were coming out of the malt shop, shoppers were examining the displays in the windows of Angel's Department Store. The windows of the laundry, the cleaners, the dime store, the market, all looking fresh and clean from a recent rain, the nearby pine forests stretching toward a pale blue sky dappled with clouds.

"You see all those people?" Luanne said, not looking at her. "Every single one of them is talking about you."

Beth Carol shuddered from the icy chill of her sister's disdain.

"You know what I heard somebody say?" she continued. "That it was a blessing that Alice Barnes wasn't alive, so she wouldn't have to know that Beth Carol had come to this."

Beth Carol felt so sick inside she wondered if there were any way on earth that she could feel worse than she did at that moment. She shrank against the door, trying to get as far away from Luanne as she could.

"I begged Daddy not to make me go to get you," Luanne said. "I asked him over and over again. I must have called him at the office six times. 'Please Daddy,' I said. 'Send somebody else. The housekeeper can go. Anybody. I just don't want to see that slut. Not ever, ever again.'"

Beth Carol buried her chin in her neck.

"You've disgraced the family," Luanne said. "You've made us a laughingstock. You do know that, don't you?"

"I'm sorry," Beth Carol whispered, wishing she were dead, wishing that when she'd slashed her wrists with the broken Coke bottle that night that she'd made a better job of it.

"Buddy Hatcher!" Luanne spat the name. "People like us don't even let somebody like Buddy Hatcher speak to us." She shook her blond flip vigorously. "And there you were, Beth Carol Barnes, letting white trash like Buddy Hatcher hump you, touch you with his dirty, white trash hands." She stopped, fighting back angry tears.

"It wasn't like that," Beth Carol mumbled, wondering how Luanne could make what she and Buddy had together sound so dirty, so terrible. Nobody had ever made her feel as good as Buddy made her feel. All she had ever wanted was to love somebody, belong to him. Be loved back. She wanted to claw Luanne's face, scream at her to stop. Stop right now. Don't you say that, you bitch!

"He must have gotten a good laugh out of that," Luanne said, snickering a little. "White trash like him humping one of the Barnes girls. He must have had a lot to tell the other boys in the locker room about how he was getting nooky from Beth Carol Barnes. Yes, Millard Barnes's daughter. Oh, that must have made him a big man, all right." Luanne turned and Beth Carol could feel those cold blue eyes boring through her. "Are you listening to me, Beth Carol?" she asked savagely.

Beth Carol nodded miserably, thinking that, yes, this was worse than anything, worse than that night in the boat house with Buddy. She'd been wrapped in his arms as they made love on top of a couple of boat covers. Oh, he had felt so good inside her, making her cry out in pleasure. Her eyes were tightly closed, her breath was coming fast, and she was calling out his name. Saying, "I love you." And then her father was there, looming above them, beating on Buddy's naked back with his big fists, knocking him off her, while Buddy struggled to get up, to grab his pants. Buddy ran, with Daddy right after him, and the dogs, ecstatic at all of the excitement, chasing him, too, barking their fool heads off, while Beth Carol scrambled into her clothes, ready to die with shame.

"Buddy Hatcher wasn't the worst of it, though," Luanne reflected, as the dock came into view. A couple of speedboats from the island were rocking gently in the water, for use by everybody who came and went all the time. What more could there be, Beth Carol wondered as Luanne pulled into the parking place on the dock painted with her name and turned off the ignition. She was just being as cruel as she could be. Vindictive.

"The worst of it," Luanne continued—gleefully, it seemed—"was what you said about Daddy. That was what really did it."

"What did I say?" asked Beth Carol, startled.

"It was when you were in the hospital, right after they brought you in," said Luanne. "And nobody thought you had really tried to kill yourself, either. All the doctor had to do was look at what you'd done to see that they were just scratches. But they gave you a shot of something, and you said all of those things about Daddy."

"What things?" asked Beth Carol, pleading, and so

scared. "What did I say?" She tried desperately to remember lying in the hospital bed for those days, the IV dripping into her arm. Everything was white and hushed with the nurses padding in and out, the doctor stopping by, the whispered consultations. She had dreamed, she knew that. Sometimes about Buddy, sometimes Buddy with her father's face. Sometimes her father with Buddy's face. Sometimes she would scream, remembering the sight of the blood spurting from her wrists, the searing pain. "Tell me, Luanne," she said. "You've got to tell me."

"Oh, it's so sickening that I can't even talk about it," Luanne said. "I can't even say the words. It's too horrible."

"But what did I say?" she begged. "Oh, please, Luanne. You've got to tell me."

"He's sending you away, you know." Luanne smiled.

Well, Beth Carol had figured something like that would happen. That she would have to go away to give people time to forget. In fact, she had hoped her father would send her away. It had been so horrible just sitting in the hospital waiting for Luanne, with everybody pretending not to look at her. And the thought of going back to school made her want to die.

"You're going to a psychiatric hospital," Luanne said smugly. "They're going to lock you up forever because you're crazy. Really crazy." She reached over and gave Beth Carol a little punch on her arm. "The Menninger Clinic in Topeka. That's the right place for you, all right."

"He can't do that," Beth Carol whispered.

"Oh, really?" said Luanne. "Why not? What's going to stop him?"

Beth Carol just sat there, shaking her head.

"Aren't you interested to know how your boyfriend is?" Luanne said blithely. "Shame on you. You didn't even ask. That's how much you care."

Not a psychiatric hospital, Beth Carol thought. Oh, no.

"He's so loyal and faithful that he left town that night," Luanne said. "He's probably joined the army. Well, maybe he'll get killed in Korea, and that'll be that."

"When am I going?" Beth Carol had asked, her voice shaking.

"Tomorrow," Luanne had said.

So she had to leave that night. No matter what happened to her, it would be better than being locked up forever in a nuthouse.

Now she felt a hand on her shoulder, felt herself being shaken awake. Gagged a little at the scent of cheap perfume.

"Oh, I'm sorry," Beth Carol said, rubbing her eyes.

"You were grinding your teeth and making these little, sputtering sounds," Fern said, annoyed.

"I was dreaming," Beth Carol murmured. "It was awful."

"I was just thinking about how I'm going to miss my daddy," Fern said, leaning close to her. "Did I tell you that he's the biggest banker in Crescent City? Well, he is."

CHAPTER 4

*B*eth Carol smiled to herself, admiring Fern's resourcefulness. A beauty queen, a Marilyn Monroe look-alike, and now a banker's daughter. She thought of the biggest banker in Coeur D'Alene, with his beautifully tailored suits from the best men's stores in Seattle and New York, the highly polished wing-tip shoes. His daughter was a freshman at Vassar, his son a senior at Brown and a potential husband for one of the Barnes girls. She had met other bankers, too, the ones who would come from Boise, Spokane, Chicago, New York, to see her father about business deals he was putting together.

Fern was redoing her makeup again, frowning at herself in her mirror. There was no way Fern could be a banker's daughter, not even if you put her hair back to whatever color it really was, washed her face, dressed her in cashmere sweaters and pleated skirts. Couldn't Fern see the difference? Did she really think she could get away with a story like that in Hollywood? Would they believe anything?

Still, it was wonderful the way Fern was literally creating herself as the miles passed. Who could predict the glorious past she would have improvised for herself by the time they got to Hollywood? Maybe that was its attraction. That you could start fresh. Be anybody you wanted to be.

31

It was nice, too, that Fern had looked around for her at the bus depot, that she wanted to share the guys with her and have her lunch paid for, too. What could that mean to her? Beth Carol asked herself. So what if somebody else paid for you? Did that mean you won in some way? Still, it was generous, and Fern did seem to want to be her friend.

Another nice thing was that Fern didn't ask any questions. It was a relief just to forget about herself for a while and play along with Fern's fantasies. They were like two little girls playing with their dolls and making up stories about their lives, the way she and Linda Marie used to do all the time.

Beth Carol had been in such shock it hadn't even occurred to her that she might have to explain herself to anybody. What would she say? The truth? Well, my father caught me with a boy, and I cut my wrists with a Coke bottle. Then I said some terrible things about my father and he was going to commit me to a mental institution. I didn't want to do that, so I stole four hundred dollars and ran away.

Oh, if only it were Buddy sitting next to her and they were going away together. She felt the most awful twinge of longing for his arms, for the feeling that somebody really cared about her that she only got when she was with him. Some of it with the two of them was the hugging and kissing and going all the way. Sometimes she still couldn't believe that she had let Buddy do it. None of the girls she knew would do anything like that. Not until you were married. It just wasn't right.

But he was so sweet and he wanted her so much, and he had promised her it wouldn't hurt, so finally she said she would. He was wrong about it not hurting. He was so gentle, but it still hurt when he put it in her the first time, and there was all the blood that scared her. Her guilt was awful, but in a funny kind of way it made her feel they belonged to each other. And she loved to listen to his plans for the future, about how he was going to be a big man and take care of her and they would be married. She just couldn't stretch her imagination to see the families together, though. What would they talk about? The last time his father got drunk and ended up in jail? The last time he knocked out Buddy's mother's teeth?

Beth Carol still felt embarrassed when she thought about the time she and her sisters had gone in the Packard to Buddy's house in Deadman's Gulch with the Christmas basket that her father made them deliver each year to the families of the men who worked for him.

Deadman's Gulch wasn't really its name. That was just what everybody called it. It was a dirt road, actually, a few miles east of the lead processing plant. The houses were like the shacks in those pictures from the Depression, only they had indoor plumbing, heat, and electricity.

They couldn't have gotten through at all, but the chauffeur had put chains on the Packard's tires. The dirty snow that made the road so bad mostly covered the rusting cars, the discarded mattresses, and the rest of the garbage and debris in front of each shack. From a branch of a dead tree in front of Buddy's house an old tire hung from a rope, which all the little kids must have used as a swing. There were a lot of little kids, that was for sure. They all stood around in their shabby coats with the linings hanging down, looking at them as she and her sisters pulled up in the beautiful, shiny limousine. And the kids were so cute! All blond and blue-eyed like Buddy, even though they were sort of dirty looking and all sniffly and runny-nosed from winter colds.

Beth Carol stood with her sisters at the trunk of the car as the chauffeur handed them the basket, the presents, and wondered what those kids were doing outside. It was freezing cold, and the stench of the smoke from the lead processing plant hung in the winter air.

Luanne—the leader, as usual—marched up and knocked on the door. She certainly looked pretty that morning, Beth Carol remembered. She was wearing a black fur coat, her blond hair pushed up into an ermine hat that matched its ermine collar, while all of the rest of the girls in their furs and boots crowded around her, shivering and stamping their feet.

Afterwards Beth Carol wondered why it had been so

bad. After all, all the families knew they were coming. It happened every year. But Buddy's mother just went white when she saw them standing there, as if she were amazed to see them. Boy, did she look old. She could have been Buddy's great-grandmother. She had stringy hair and a lined face, and her mouth was all sunken in, so it was true what they said about her teeth. She wore a sweater with the elbows out, and her housedress was dirty. Her stockings were sagging and her house slippers had holes which showed her little toes. Really, it was as if she had sat up planning how to look pathetic.

Luanne swept past her like the Queen of the May carrying a present that she had wrapped with her own hands, and the rest of them followed with the basket and the other stuff.

By this time, Buddy's mother's face had gone from white to a mottled red, and Beth Carol really had to try hard not to react to the scene that lay before them. There had been a fight. There was a broken window that had been covered by a dingy sheet. There was glass all over the floor, and blood.

The linoleum was cracked and dirty. There were plates on the tables, rotting food. There were dirty clothes tossed everywhere. There was also the biggest, most beautiful television set in a fancy cabinet, a lot better than the one the Barneses had on the island. And there was a record player, too, in an expensive-looking contraption that also had space for hundreds of records. It was all the dried blood, though, that was so unexpected. None of them could stop looking at it.

Beth Carol was so embarrassed she just wanted to drop the stuff and get out of there. But no. Luanne was doing her grand lady number, asking about the children. Wishing everybody a Merry Christmas from their father and from each of the sisters. Buddy's mother mumbled something about would they like a cup of coffee, and the look of horror that crossed Luanne's face was really funny. Beth Carol had to concentrate to keep back the giggles. It seemed like a long time before they finally got out of there.

That was years before she started up with Buddy, and it was only that bad once. The other times they came the house was tidy and Buddy's mother was smiling at the door like all the other women. Beth Carol never told Buddy, either.

Buddy. Oh, what a sweet boy he was. Beth Carol blinked back tears.

"Do you want a hankie or something?" asked Fern, frowning, as if Beth Carol's tears were some kind of affront.

"I was just thinking about my boyfriend," said Beth Carol, drying her eyes with the palms of her hands.

"Oh, I know what you mean," Fern said sympathetically, her little baby voice breaking. "I've been thinking about my boyfriend, too. Oh, he was so upset when I told him I was going to Hollywood. He begged me not to go. He begged me to marry him instead. He said he couldn't stand the thought of sharing me with all my fans. 'I'll buy you a diamond ring and a fur coat,' he said. 'I'll take you to San Francisco for your honeymoon, and we'll stay in a big hotel, and we'll go to Fisherman's Wharf.'" She paused for a moment, a little smile on her face. "I thought he was going to cry when I told him I had to go, that I belonged to the world."

Beth Carol raised her eyebrows at that one, but she smiled, let Fern's words wash away all her own thoughts.

"His daddy is the town banker," she said. "The other town banker, that is. We have two banks. His daddy is almost as rich as my daddy, but not quite. Their house is almost as big as our house. It sits on a hill that looks down on the whole town. And they have lots of beautiful cars, and his mother goes up to Portland to buy her clothes. You should see his two sisters. They're so pretty. Both blondes, like I am. He was always telling me that what first attracted him to me was how much I look like his sisters. Julie and Emily, their names are. They go to Stanford. His name is Clark. Clark Johnson.

"Mine is Buddy Hatcher," said Beth Carol, feeling tender toward Fern because Fern had left Clark as she had left Buddy. Well, she would have left Buddy if he hadn't already been gone. They both missed their boyfriends. They were gals together, lonely for their guys. "His real name is Elroyd. My big sister, Luanne, is always saying how people in that class always give their kids funny names. Don't you think so?"

"Yeah, sure," said Fern, looking at her strangely.

"He joined the army," Beth Carol said. "He'll probably be killed in Korea."

"Oh, well, they're a dime a dozen," Fern said, patting her on the arm. "Clark's got a deferment. He goes to Stanford, too. I mean, all of the Johnsons have gone there for generations. They give a lot of money to the university. It's always in the paper, how much they give."

"Education is a wonderful thing," said Beth Carol, nodding and smiling.

"You'd think they could do something for the town, too," Fern said with a bitter tinge in her voice. "Those sisters of his, driving through town in their fancy cars, looking down on everybody. So snooty. They really are. You'd think they could give money to build a hospital or something. Do something for the people who've made them rich, instead of spending it out of town."

"Yeah, that's strange," said Beth Carol, thinking about her own father, about how he had built a hospital, a library, the park he had donated.

"You know what they do every year?" Fern said. "They have a big party, a carnival, on the Fourth of July. They bring in a Ferris wheel and rides, and there are all these booths where you can win prizes. Stuffed toys, goldfish in bowls. Stuff like that. There's a band that plays patriotic songs, and everything is decorated in red, white, and blue. There's lots and lots of food, hot dogs and hamburgers, cole slaw, potato salad, cakes and pies. There's beer in tubs of ice for the grown-ups and Coke and Seven-Up for the kids." She searched her memory for a minute, adding, "And balloons. Red, white, and blue balloons and some guy who writes your name on the one you want. Everything is free. Everything.

"And everybody bows and scrapes and says 'Thank you,'

and 'Oh, what a wonderful party,' and stuff like that. It's so awful and embarrassing that they do that. It's like the Johnsons are the kings and queens and everybody else is nothing. I mean, don't they think we know how to go to the market and buy some hot dogs? Don't they know how we feel when they do that?"

Beth Carol felt her cheeks burning, and squirmed miserably in her seat. She felt bad all over again about the Christmas baskets, even the library, the hospital, and the park. What she wanted to say to Fern was that they thought they were doing the right thing. That it wasn't so great as it looked to be rich. To be living in the big house on the private island, having lots of cars and clothes and servants. That you could feel just as lonely and neglected, just as much that there was nowhere you belonged and nobody who cared about you.

"You didn't have to go," she said.

"Oh, wrong," Fern sneered. "You did have to go."

"You didn't either," Beth Carol protested. "It's a free country, you know."

"Fine, you don't go," said Fern. "So then you go to the bank and you want a loan to buy a car or something. And everybody knows you didn't go, and you get these strange looks and why didn't you go. Or you go to the market and you need to charge something for a few days and the grocer looks at you and he's wondering why you didn't turn up, and you're not like everybody else anymore." She puffed furiously on her cigarette. "I hate small towns," she said. "Everybody knows every move you make. It's like being in prison."

"The others, do they like the party?" she asked.

"Yes, they love the party," Fern said, exasperated. "But you know what I'm going to do when I'm rich and famous?"

"What?"

"I'm going to go back to Crescent City and I'm going to shove that Ferris wheel right up their asses," she said.

Boy, the way Fern swore, Beth Carol thought, blushing again. It was disgusting, just like trash. She turned away from Fern and looked out of the window. The late afternoon sky was streaked with gray and a couple of stars glimmered dimly.

Empty fields loomed ahead, outlined by tumbled-down fences. It felt different from northern Idaho, Washington, Oregon. For one thing, they had gone a long way and the weather was nice. At home, it always snowed in the winter. The forbidding pine forests, the freezing snowdrifts, and that endless black lake just waiting for you to make a mistake so it could swallow you up. Those were the constants. Everything about home was so closed in, so claustrophobic. Here, though, there wasn't much of anything. Oh, there was a horse standing at the fence, gazing at them as they passed. In the distance was a farmhouse, a couple of cows. Other than that, there were just the endless fields, indistinct in the gathering dusk. It made Beth Carol feel funny, sort of as if she had nothing to hold on to.

In the bus, people started to snap on their reading lights and from somewhere a few rows back, a guy's voice said, "I'll raise you five."

Beth Carol started to visualize Fern and what she was going to do with the Ferris wheel and she started to giggle. She just couldn't help it. It was such a funny picture.

"And the hot dogs, too," Fern added, laughing, too.

Ahead of them, the lights of a small town beckoned.

"Fifteen minutes," said the bus driver into his loudspeaker when the bus was stopped at a diner on the main street.

"Come on," said Fern, taking Beth Carol's arm.

Being with Fern and all the soldiers while they had dinner was like being in the middle of a fistfight about to happen. The boys were showing off for Fern, trying to get her to smile. Anything. It was really amazing. Beth Carol just sat there, her eyes wide. When they were back on the bus, the boy who had picked up their check crouched in the aisle, talking to Fern, while the rest of them just sat down and went on with what they were doing.

"Come on to the back, okay?" Beth Carol heard him saying. She wondered why this one had won and the others had lost. He didn't seem to be any different. Just another soldier with his ears sticking out, hardly old enough to shave. But all guys were mysterious. Another species, really.

"No," said Fern.

"You're the most beautiful girl I've ever seen," he cajoled. "Come on, baby. Just for a minute or two."

"No."

"Listen, honey, I'm on my way to Fort Ord, and then I'll be shipped to Korea to fight the good fight. Maybe I'll even be killed."

"What's that to me?" Fern said.

"Oh, come on," he pleaded.

"So you can look like a big man to your buddies?" she asked. "Get lost."

"Oh, come on," he said, rocking with the bus as it turned.

Fern just looked straight ahead, ignoring him. Finally he left.

"Come and sit in back with me," Fern mimicked. "You're so beautiful." She turned to Beth Carol, her eyes hard. "You probably don't even know what this is about," she said in her breathy little voice. "You're probably a virgin and you and your boyfriend think it's hot shit to hold hands."

Beth Carol cringed.

"Fucking," Fern pronounced. "That's what it's about."

That word. Well, she knew it, of course. Everybody did. But this was the first time, ever, that she had actually heard somebody say it. She gasped, and giggled with embarrassment.

"All they want is one thing," she continued. "My mama told me that when I was only ten years old. What she said was, 'If a guy has the time, he'll fuck anything. He'll fuck mud. That's how they are.'"

"She said that? Your mother?"

"Well, I knew it anyway," Fern conceded. "From her and her boyfriends."

"She has boyfriends? Golly, what does your father say?"

"This was when they were separated," Fern said quickly, probably improvising. "See, in our house her bedroom was on one side, and then there was the bathroom, and then there was my bedroom." Her little pink tongue darted over her red lips, and her eyes in the dark were wet and glittery.

"All night long I would hear the toilet flushing. 'She's douching,' I would say to myself. You know, to get the guck out when he would come in her. All night it would go on. Three, maybe four times."

Beth Carol stared at her, enthralled.

"What else?" she whispered.

"Nothing else," said Fern. "All they did was fuck."

Fern did it all the time, too, starting at the age of twelve. She had gone to bed with her own grandfather, her male cousins, her dentist when he was filling her teeth.

"Weren't you afraid of getting pregnant?" Beth Carol asked, her eyes wide. Because that was the hitch, getting pregnant. Then your life was ruined forever, although sometimes she wondered why it was all so wonderful if you were married and so terrible if you weren't. Buddy had always been so careful about that, pulling out before he came.

"I did get pregnant," Fern said. "Twice."

"What did you do?"

"Two pregnancies, two abortions," said Fern, snapping her fingers. "Simple as that."

"What was it like?" Beth Carol asked. "Were you scared?"

"Sure, I was scared," admitted Fern. "Going to some old Mex in her dirty house who could have killed me? But she was okay. A couple of days later it was like it never happened."

"Didn't you feel bad?" Beth Carol asked.

"Well, I did, a little," Fern admitted. "I threw up some on the second one."

"I mean about the baby," said Beth Carol.

"The baby?" asked Fern. "Gee, I never thought of that."

Beth Carol was entranced as Fern went on and on. Reminisced about going down on the druggist in the back room of his drugstore for ten bucks. And she really had fucked Clark Johnson. Only once, though.

"It was like a conquest," Fern said. "You know, the big man in town. Well, I was walking down the street and he pulled up beside me. He was driving his dad's Caddy convertible, and he just opened the door and looked at me from under his eyebrows like he thought it was real sexy. Once we were out of town, he jumped me. I mean, he didn't even kiss me. It was about as big as my little finger, so it didn't matter, and it was less than a minute. What a letdown. I'd been sort of thinking about knocking him off for years. But what an asshole. Really ho-hum."

"Weren't you afraid he'd say something?" asked Beth Carol. Because guys talked, showed off. She remembered Luanne's pronouncement that Buddy probably bragged to all his friends about how he was going all the way with her. "Don't people talk?"

"Oh, sure," Fern said wearily. "Everybody talked. You know how it is. They don't have anything else to do, so they talk. I took care of that, though. I found out what they were hiding, and then I had that over them. Because everybody has something they don't want other people to know. Everybody has a skeleton in the closet."

Beth Carol stared at her, feeling about four years old. How could Fern know all these things? It just didn't seem possible, but there it was.

Fern reached into her handbag, pushed a cigarette into her holder, and handed Beth Carol her little lighter. "See that?" she said. "That's real gold. I got it from a guy I was with once, and I took it to a jeweler. Real gold, eighteen carat."

"It's beautiful," Beth Carol said, turning it over in her hand, giving it back.

"Every gal is sitting on a gold mine," she said. "That's where we get them. Every time."

"But if you take money for sex, you're a prostitute," Beth Carol murmured.

"Yeah, that's what guys say. So we'll give it to them for nothing. Then we're, what? Pure?" She snorted in the dark. "Suckers, that's what."

Fern was so cynical, so hard. She thought everybody was like she was. Just out for what he could get. It must be awful to look at life that way. Still, she would bet that nobody would ever be able to hurt Fern. Fern would never trust anybody enough to be let down. Was that good, or was that bad?

Glancing over, she saw that Fern had fallen asleep, her mouth open, her legs askew. Gradually, throughout the bus, the reading lights were snapped off. The headlights thrust into the inky blackness, and there were a zillion little stars twinkling in the sky. Beth Carol reached up and turned off the lights. She leaned back, tried to get comfortable, and closed her eyes. She willed herself to think about nothing. Not that nightmare that lay behind her. Not the emptiness that lay ahead. Later she realized that she must have fallen asleep, when she felt a hand on her arm, pulling her back to consciousness, a frantic whisper in her ear.

"I'm so scared," moaned Fern. "Oh, I'm so scared."

Beth Carol put her arms around the other girl, felt her body heaving as she sobbed. So it was bravado. Whistling in the dark. She felt her own tears hot on her cheeks, and surrendered to her terror of what lay ahead.

She felt better, though. Somehow, Fern's anxiety echoing her own, Fern's tears, made her feel that there was someone in the world who trusted her, who depended on her. She felt connected, no longer alone. They were friends.

After a while, Fern drifted off to sleep, and Beth Carol felt her eyes closing, too.

CHAPTER 5

$\mathcal{B}$eth Carol stirred at the morning sounds on the bus. The mothers dragging their kids, the old ladies, the khaki brigade, everybody was heading down the aisle for the rest room. There was the crinkle of waxed paper as sandwiches were unwrapped, popping sounds as Coke bottles were uncapped. At that hour of the morning. Unbelievable.

She gasped when she opened her eyes. Glittering in the dawn was San Francisco Bay, crisscrossed by bridges. Little sailboats rocked on its whitecaps and an ocean liner steamed out into the open sea. In the cloudless, pale blue sky, a silver dot grew larger. It was a passenger plane, she realized, coming in to land at San Francisco's airport. Her heart swelled, and for the first time she had a feeling of well-being, as if everything were going to be all right.

Fern gave a gasping little snore. Well, they were blood sisters now, Beth Carol thought tenderly. After last night, there was no turning back. She saw, though, that Fern was definitely one of those people who lost it in the morning. She looked as if she had melted. Her lipstick was all over her chin, the blue mascara like congealed grease on her eyelids. One furry false eyelash had come unglued and looked like a caterpillar crawling down one cheek. Her

43

hair, in the morning sunlight, was greasy looking with a greenish tinge. The white angora sweater looked as if it were molting. There were streaks of dirt on Fern's thin neck and on her ankles.

I probably don't look much better, Beth Carol thought, forgiving Fern. She dug in her purse for her compact and lit a cigarette before she dared to look at herself. Yes, not much better. Worse, even. Drained white, so pale she could even make out the sprinkling of freckles across her nose that should certainly be gone by now. A hint of grime on her own neck. The collar of her blouse was filthy. Still, she saw, there was a lively expression in her eyes. A sparkle, even, now that she felt some hope. My friend, she thought, surprised to feel her eyes misting with happiness. Two against the world. She thought ahead, to Hollywood, and the Studio Club where Fern was going to live.

It would be sort of like Luanne's sorority house at the University of Idaho. A lot of girls pinning up each other's hair and doing each other's nails, and running to the phone when someone's boyfriend called. Only at the Studio Club, the girls would be studying singing and tap dancing, and the boys who called would be Rory Calhoun or Robert Wagner. Ummm, so cute. She thought of Cary Grant, but that was silly. Too old, too sophisticated.

Well, Beth Carol couldn't live at the Studio Club. She couldn't even pretend she wanted to be an actress. Even the thought of standing up in front of class to read one of her own poems was enough to make her nearly die with fright. She shuddered, remembering. Everybody looking at her. The boys in the back contemptuous and bored, the girls hoping for her to fail because of who she was. Her own scarlet cheeks and shaking knees. Awful.

They were coming into San Francisco now, and it was adorable. There were lots of little houses in all different colors jammed against each other on a series of rolling hills. There were all kinds of cars and taxis barely clinging to the tops of the streets that slid away like the downside of a roller coaster. A darling little cable car clanged by, and the people in it waved. There were stalls blooming with a thousand bright flowers on every corner. Beside her, Fern stirred.

"Isn't it beautiful, Fern?" enthused Beth Carol, impetuously touching her friend's arm. "Look at all of the flowers. Look at the cable cars. Aren't they cute? They look like toys, don't they? Isn't it all wonderful?"

"Ummm," said Fern, shaking off Beth Carol's hand with a grimace of distaste, and pulling her compact out of her bag. "God, I look a wreck."

"Oh, not really," said Beth Carol vaguely.

Fern craned her neck and looked down the aisle. "It'll be a year before I can get to the bathroom," she muttered. "Shit, I need to pee, too." She pulled out a jar of Pond's, a wad of tissues, and started to wipe off her makeup. With the tips of her thumb and finger, she plucked off the false eyelash that had come unglued, then the other.

Beth Carol gazed into her vulnerable, plain, adolescent face.

"What are you looking at?" Fern snapped. "Haven't you ever seen anybody taking off her makeup before?"

"Well, pardon me," Beth Carol said huffily, turning to look out of the window again. Another one who was a big grouch in the morning, she thought. Just like Luanne. Nobody could get a word out of Luanne until she'd had a pot of coffee and a dozen cigarettes or so.

"Union Square, five minutes," the bus driver said over the loudspeaker. Around them, people started to gather their belongings. Fern sighed loudly and flounced down the aisle. Even at that hour of the morning, somebody gave a long, low wolf whistle and a couple of boys laughed.

Now, this was a real city, Beth Carol decided. It was just beautiful. There was a bright green patch of grass with trees, neat beds of flowers, benches, all tucked away among tall, white buildings. She pressed her forehead to the window, reading the names as the bus went by.

There was I. Magnin, a tall building with chic clothes on the mannequins in its windows. The City of Paris. Saks

Fifth Avenue. Gump's, its windows filled with lacquered tables, massive oriental vases. A black Cadillac limousine was parked in front of a building with a red canopy over its entrance. A doorman held open the back door and two beautifully dressed women in hats and gloves got out while the chauffeur dealt with their luggage. The St. Francis Hotel. It was so exciting that she could hardly believe she was here. She looked toward the sky and saw that the clouds were turning gray, threatening rain.

When the bus stopped in the enormous gloomy terminal, all the people started to file off, and Fern still hadn't come back from the rest room. Beth Carol glanced anxiously down the aisle, thinking that the thing to do was go and check to see if something had happened. Slowly she walked back, considering the possibilities. Well, Fern could have fainted, but that was really about it. Then it dawned on her. Fern and a guy. It had to be. She felt her face go red at the thought that she was about to knock on the door and interrupt them. Boy, that would have really been embarrassing, she thought, hurrying off the bus, looking around for the ladies' room.

She stood in one of the stalls, her blouse off, sponging off some of the grime with a wad of sodden paper towels. What an unlikely couple she and Fern were, she thought. Fern a slut. . .and Beth Carol? She winced as she looked at the ugly red scars on her wrists. Well, practically an escapee from a mental institution. A loser until now. I just won't tell her about what I tried to do to myself, she decided. She'll never understand. Her father beating on Buddy as if they were dogs in heat. How it made her cringe with shame to think about it.

Fifteen minutes before the bus was scheduled to leave, Beth Carol was already on the platform, looking up and down. Trying to find Fern, and not seeing her. Not seeing any little cluster of guys that would have signaled Fern in its center. Nearly every seat was already filled, and the motor of the bus was revving up. The bus driver was just about ready to close the door, and Fern still wasn't there. Golly, what could have happened to her? Beth Carol worried as she darted onto the bus. But there it was—Fern's overnight case, right under the seat just where she had left it. Maybe she just never got off. Leave it to Fern, she thought, smiling to herself. What an operator.

And then Fern was there, standing at the front of the bus, whispering earnestly to a tall soldier who had to lean down to hear what she was saying. She'd changed her sweater. The new one was pink, clinging, with a low-cut neck that showed a lot of tit. She strutted down the aisle, this time leading a parade of one soldier. She didn't even glance at Beth Carol as she passed, not even a smile of complicity.

So she'd found somebody to get some money from, Beth Carol reasoned. That was the way Fern looked at things. Those were her very words. What would they think about that at the Studio Club? she wondered. Beth Carol didn't believe for a minute that they'd put up with Fern doing it with guys for money. I mean, the name. Like, it was a club, after all. Well, that could be an argument to get Fern to share an apartment. Beth Carol wouldn't care. Fern could do anything she wanted and it would be okay with her. Still, it made Beth Carol feel a little funny. She had to admit it. But you had to get used to things in this life, she supposed.

Before long, San Francisco with all of its adorable little houses nestled on the hills faded in the mist behind them. They were on the open highway now, the traffic heavier, the fields on either side greener, lush. For a few minutes, a train streaked along beside them. In the dining car, Beth Carol saw roses in silver vases, a woman in a smart hat leaning forward so that the well-dressed man across from her could light her cigarette.

At Monterey, most of the soldiers swarmed off the bus to make their connection to Fort Ord. Beth Carol looked around for Fern, but she didn't see her. Another bunch of soldiers got on board, and they were off again, the big, bright Pacific Ocean a looping ribbon of blue, patches of its sandy beaches crowded with sunbathers, children splashing in the foaming waves. She dozed for a while and dreamed about Buddy holding her. Only he had her father's face.

It was the vague awareness that Fern still hadn't come back that jarred her awake. What would a friend do now? Walk back to see where Fern was sitting? Ask her if everything were all right? A breathy laugh from somewhere reassured her. That was Fern. She was fine, having a good time. She slept again, a long exhausted sleep.

When she woke, the traffic was heavier. Many of the cars were convertibles with the tops down, the kids in them around her own age. They were really great looking, too. Mostly blond and tanned. Beach shacks teetered on stilts or leaned against each other for support. Through the open window, she watched the sea gulls as they dived and dipped, heard the roar of the waves as they broke and foamed on the white sand.

Something felt very different.

It was the air. It was getting lighter and lighter. And the sun was blindingly bright, painting the water gold. It was all so extravagantly lovely that it made Beth Carol feel almost giddy, as if she were about to float away. It scared her, sort of. She shrank away from the open window of the bus and grabbed the top of the seat in front of her.

Things just got brighter and emptier as the bus rumbled through the fringes of Los Angeles. There were a lot of vacant lots choked with weeds, and little cottages with tiled roofs and arches. The bushes were all white and pink, the roses every imaginable color. Palm trees punctuated the bright, blue sky, and the perfume from the orange blossoms was intoxicating. It was sort of like paradise around the time of Adam and Eve. There were people in the cars, of course. But, nobody on the streets.

The sign overhead said they were on the Hollywood Freeway, and they were gaining speed. The little houses with their tiled roofs dotted the bright green hills. And there was the sign she had seen so many times in movies, newsreels, magazines.

HOLLYWOOD.

It was enormous, unreal. Like a banner flying across the top of an entire mountain.

Beth Carol turned away, unable to bear to look at it. She felt miserable and panicked as she tried to remember what had made her decide to come here. It was just that she had to go somewhere, anywhere else but Coeur d'Alene, and Hollywood was just about as far as she could go without ending up in the ocean. Just the thought made her feel light-headed again. Don't think about it, she told herself over and over. Think about Fern. Your friend. Think about the things that have to be done. Finding a place, for one thing.

Beth Carol didn't even look up when the bus driver announced over the loudspeaker that they were at Hollywood and Vine. If she didn't see it, it wouldn't be real. She willed the bus to go on forever and ever. San Diego. Mexico. In a couple of minutes, it lumbered into the terminal and came to a stop.

"Hollywood," the bus driver said. "Thank you for riding Greyhound."

The passengers in the seats around her gathered up their belongings, started to trickle through the open door. Outside, the driver had already opened the baggage compartment and was helping them with their suitcases and packages. Inside the terminal, Beth Carol could see a lot of people waiting, a couple of the kids with their faces pressed against the glass doors. Their expressions were smiling, eager.

"There's Grandma," squeaked a small voice as a woman and child hurried down the steps. Then it was soldiers, a whirl of khaki. Beth Carol sat there, waiting for Fern.

She felt almost weak with relief when that awful perfume wafted up the aisle. And there she was. Fern. Sashaying up the aisle, laughing. The last of the soldiers trailed after her. He was pitching her hard, talking fast. Beth Carol could imagine what he was asking her to do. Fern whispered something into his ear, and he nodded. Beth Carol clutched her handbag as the soldier leaned down and picked up Fern's overnight case.

"Fern," she said, reaching out and putting her hand on the other girl's arm.

"What?" Fern demanded, scowling. She jerked her arm away.

"Well, I thought. . ." She was faltering now, embarrassed, as she tried to remember what she had thought, and why she had thought it.

"Oh, I know what you thought, honey," Fern said with a sneer, turning to the soldier. "Do I look like a bull dyke to you, baby?" she asked him.

The sudden heat that shot through her made Beth Carol feel as if she were going to faint. She grabbed the top of the seat in front of her. But you're my friend, she thought wildly. We cried in each other's arms.

"No, thanks," Fern snapped, wiggling past. The soldier followed her, looking sheepish and uncomfortable.

It took Beth Carol a couple of minutes to get herself together before she could even move. She was the last one off the bus. She saw her suitcase sitting by itself on the loading dock in the golden, early evening sunlight.

CHAPTER 6

*B*eth Carol stumbled through the double doors leading into the bus terminal, blinded by tears of rage and humiliation. What happened? she asked herself. What did I do wrong? One minute Fern had really opened up to her, and she had done everything she could to make it okay. And the next minute, that awful rejection. Those insults. A bull dyke. Beth Carol had never heard that before, but she knew at once what it meant. Girls who liked girls. Is that what she deserved because she had been nice? She stood there, feeling shamed and dirty and so betrayed by what had happened.

And without Fern, she felt so alone, so defenseless. She looked around and saw that everybody in the world had decided to come to Hollywood at the same time. The bus station was jammed, the overhead speakers droning out arrivals and departures. Hordes of soldiers clamored around the ticket counter. Little children, their eyes wide with wonder, their mouths edged in chocolate, held tightly to their mothers' hands. Sauntering through the front door was a huge black man in a white suit, a white panama hat, a black shirt that looked as if it must be silk. A black handkerchief peeped from his breast pocket. Beth Carol's eyes widened. He was the first Negro she had ever seen in person and she thought he looked exotic and wonderful.

A really good-looking man in a terrific suit stood talking intently to some blond kid in jeans who had been on the bus. Beth Carol looked hard at him. He was in the movies, she realized. Not a big lead, but sometimes the lead's best friend. The kid couldn't have been more than fourteen, and he really looked scared. Now, what could that be about? she wondered. What could those two people possibly have to talk about? She was even more confused when she saw the boy nod, and the two of them walk out together.

She jumped as somebody touched her arm.

Fern, she thought joyously, turning. It was just some drunk, asking her if she had any change.

"No, no," she said, shaking him off.

And the girls. There were so many of them, all in tight blouses and capri pants, high heels and a lot of makeup. The old bags were done up the same way. On the bus, Fern had seemed extraordinary. Here, everybody looked like that. How did they know? she wondered. Was there some kind of dress code that got passed out at the California border that only she hadn't gotten? Boy, she thought, this is like landing on the moon.

There was music, too, coming through a doorway that led into the bar. "Come on-a My House." It was Rosemary Clooney, singing here just the way she did on the jukebox in the malt shop at home. There was laughter, the tinkle of glasses. A man in a plaid jacket asked if he could buy her a drink.

He was really old. Maybe fifty. And she was sixteen and probably didn't even look that old. What was the matter with these people? she wondered.

"No, thank you," she mumbled, shaking her head. As she found an empty seat on a bench and sat down, it crossed her mind that she wasn't going to be all right in Hollywood. It was too different. Then she thought about the Menninger Clinic, a padded cell. Herself in a straitjacket. Crying. She shook her head and lit a cigarette, wishing that Fern were there. Wondering what had gone wrong.

It wasn't that she'd told Beth Carol about all the guys she'd been with. No, she was proud of that, proud of the power it gave her over them. She guessed it was that Fern had said she was scared and that she'd cried. That was weakness, and somebody like Fern didn't want to be reminded that she had been weak.

Weak. Strong. Well, she was past all that, she thought, smoking another cigarette. She was right where her imagination had taken her. She was sitting here in the Hollywood bus station. But what would she do now? Where would she go?

It was dark outside, so she had been sitting here for hours. She felt strange and light-headed. Golly, I'm hungry, she said to herself. She wondered if she were going to pass out, and kind of wished she would.

"I've been watching you, dear," said a woman's voice next to her. "Are you all right?"

Beth Carol turned and looked at her. She was old and wrinkled, her hair a brassy blond. She was wearing a low-cut, bright pink blouse, green capri pants, and high-heeled shoes with no backs. In her arms, wrapped in a blue blanket, she held the ugliest baby Beth Carol had ever seen. Then Beth Carol looked again and saw that it wasn't a baby at all. It was a monkey.

I must be hallucinating, she thought.

The woman peered at her through heart-shaped glasses embedded with colored stones. "See that telephone over there?" She gestured. "You can pick it up and it's a direct line to Traveler's Aid. They have a list of places to stay. They'll help you."

Sure, and they'll want to know who I am and where I come from, and they'll be on the phone to my father in about twelve seconds, Beth Carol thought.

"My aunt is meeting me," she lied.

"Does she know you smoke?" asked the woman, shaking a bony, ringed finger at her. "A girl your age smoking the way you do, well, it's not right."

"I don't usually," Beth Carol said, wondering why she

was explaining anything to this apparition, but grateful for the human contact. "I mean, I'd just tried it a couple of times, and then I was nervous about traveling was what happened."

"Well, it isn't a habit for a nice girl," the woman admonished. "Certainly not in public." She sank into a reverie, while the monkey looked brightly around and squirmed in its blanket. "You have to be careful about the impression you make, especially in a place like this," she continued after a moment. "I live just down the street, across from the market. You know, that market never closes. People shop there all night long. Isn't that something? I come over here sometimes when there's nothing on television. Just to get out, you know. It gets lonely sometimes, just sitting there in the apartment. If I didn't have Shirley, here, I don't know what I'd do." She made little cooing noises at the monkey. "Isn't she a darling?"

"Yes, she is," said Beth Carol politely, hating the monkey, wishing the woman would just go away.

"I tell you, dear, Shirley is better company than anybody else in this town," the woman said. "Oh, I know what they say. Hollywood, where the streets are lined with gold, and you can be a star overnight. I believed it, too. But it's a lie. It's a terrible town, and this bus station is the most evil place of all. They come to prey, like a bunch of wild animals. The queers, they're here in droves. Old men looking for pretty young boys. You'd be surprised at some of them. They're famous, rich, and you read all the time about how they're in love with this actress or that actress. But that's just for appearances. The truth is that what they like are these boys. They take them away with them, and who knows what happens to them after that?"

The woman was really scaring her now, Beth Carol realized. She was even trembling.

"And the men come looking for young girls like you. Innocent young girls who don't know how evil the world can be."

Is she crazy? Beth Carol wondered, recoiling from her,

from the singsong voice, the funny smile.

"My aunt will be along any minute," Beth Carol said. "I called her. It's a surprise. For her birthday."

"Well, that's nice, dear," said the woman, rising, rocking the monkey in her arms. That awful, obscene monkey. "I hope you have a nice visit with her. And don't smoke in public. It gives the wrong impression."

Beth Carol watched her as she drifted away, crooning to her monkey. She breathed a sigh of relief.

After the madwoman left, time seemed to stop. Beth Carol managed to get to the ladies' room and back. All of those odd-looking people in their crazy clothes rushed around. Nobody bothering her, nobody even looking at her. Beth Carol had never felt so alone, so abandoned. She felt tears of self-pity welling up in her eyes, heard her stomach growl. She lit another cigarette and listened to Frank Sinatra from the jukebox in the bar.

Then she must have slept for a few minutes because she saw her father's face. He had the sweetest smile, and he told her that it was all right to come home now because everybody had forgotten. He had seen to that because he had given everybody an amnesia pill. "You know that you can always count on me," he said in this wonderful loving voice. "You're my favorite, Beth Carol. You're not stuck on yourself like your sisters. You're sweet and good and you're my favorite. I haven't told you before because I don't want your sisters to feel bad and be jealous. I love you."

She snapped awake, feeling very strange. Oh, she did want Daddy to love her so much, the way she loved him. Golly, the ways she had tried to make him love her. . .and nothing had worked. "I love you," he had said in her dream. That was the only place he had ever said that to her. It didn't seem fair, somehow. Weren't parents supposed to love their children? Wasn't that part of the deal? Boy, if I ever have a baby, will I ever love him, she vowed. But what came into her mind was that awful monkey in its blue blanket. I think maybe it's time, she told herself. I'd better get something to eat, because everything is kind of fading in and out. There was a boy sitting next to her who she was positive was a mirage, which was really scary. He couldn't be there because he looked like the last person on earth who would ever be sitting in the Hollywood bus station.

He was older than she was, about the age of somebody Luanne would be interested in. She could just see her big sister changing from the bitch she really was to the sweet, demure young thing she somehow became when there was a cute guy around. He had close-cropped, curly hair that was almost black. She got the impression that his eyes were dark, too, with long lashes. And he had a great tan. Very California. He wore a blue-and-white-striped seersucker jacket. Her father had one like that. He'd gotten it at Brooks Brothers in New York. His white shirt had a button-down collar, and he wore a narrow, black knit tie. His trousers were gray flannel with a sharp crease, and his black loafers had tassels on them. She could smell his shaving lotion. It was wonderful, vaguely familiar. She could hardly believe it when he turned and spoke to her.

"Pardon me," he said. "You probably don't remember me. I'm Paul Fournier. I'm a friend of your sister's. We met at her coming-out party last December. We danced. I even remember the song. You were the prettiest girl there."

"I beg your pardon?" she said.

"We met at Jane's party," he said. "It was terrific, I thought. One of the best of the season. Everybody thought so. Jane was going on to Vassar, wasn't she? Or was it Radcliffe?"

He has me confused with somebody else, she thought, disappointed. If only it were true. Beth Carol looked straight into his eyes and prayed for a miracle that would turn her into Jane's sister, whoever that was.

"I couldn't believe my eyes when I saw you," he said shyly. "This is the last place in the world I thought I would run into anybody I know, especially you."

"I'm really sorry," she said. "You have me mixed up with somebody else."

"Look, if you don't want to talk to me, just tell me," he said. "But I'll never forget dancing with you that night. It was the highlight for me. I was going to call, but you were so involved with somebody else that I thought, no, better not."

"No, really," she started to explain. "I'm Beth Carol Barnes. I just got here."

Her head was swimming again. The lights in the bus station were suddenly brighter, fringed with halos. Oh, this was so awful, so embarrassing. And on top of everything, she'd hurt his feelings.

"Are you all right?" he asked.

"I haven't eaten," she said faintly.

After that, things happened very fast.

He had his arm around her waist as he helped her through a door in the rear of the bus station that she hadn't even noticed. They were in a parking lot. He led her through a maze of cars to a beautiful black Jaguar roadster with the the top down. She gulped the fresh air as he helped her into the car and stowed her suitcase in the trunk.

"I'll just get my package and I'll be right back," he said. "Then I'll take you wherever you want to go."

"I don't want—"

"No, no," he said. "It's all right. It's my pleasure."

Boy, did he ever get more than he bargained for, Beth Carol thought ruefully as she watched him hurry away. But it was nice of him to help her out this way. The fresh air was making her feel better. She leaned her head against the seat and breathed deeply.

He'd found a Hershey bar for her. Now, wasn't that sweet of him. She ripped off the wrapper and gobbled it down. Her vision cleared, and she felt almost herself again.

"You've been very nice," she said. "Thank you very much."

"Oh, look, it's nothing," he said. "Now, where can I take you?"

"A hotel, I guess. Something inexpensive," she said, anxious again. "I was thinking maybe the YWCA. But I don't know. A girl I talked to told me about the Studio Club. But I guess that's for girls who want to be actresses."

"So you don't have any place to stay," he said.

"Well, anything will do. Really. I've got money."

He just sat there for a moment, looking thoughtful. Then he started the beautiful car. "I'll tell you what," he said. "Let's get you something to eat and I'll try to think of something."

"I don't want to impose," she said miserably. "Gee, you've been so nice and all."

"I'm glad to do it," he said, inching the car out of the parking space and turning onto a street in a neighborhood of little cottages and new apartment houses with palm trees in the front. "I don't think the YWCA is right, though. It's all the way downtown, and you'd just be stuck."

He turned onto a wide, busy street and Beth Carol saw the big market the crazy woman had talked about. It had a clock out in front with hands that kept going around, and a sign that said, WE NEVER CLOSE. Imagine that. Being able to shop anytime you wanted. She remembered, too, what the woman had said about guys who preyed on innocent girls. She glanced gratefully at Paul. She had been so lucky she could hardly believe it.

Paul stopped for a red light at an intersection. There was a large store with saxophones and clarinets and drum sets in the window, and a lot of people milling around inside. Wallach's Music City. And that imposing building across the street was the National Broadcasting Company. Beth Carol glanced up at the street sign. Sunset Boulevard. This was just like in the movies. She started to get excited. All of these new places, and this cute guy.

Paul was talking about how he'd gone east to prep at Choate and then to Yale. His dad wanted him to major in business, but he decided on psychology. After all, if you could figure people out you practically didn't need anything else. And he was taking a couple of classes at night in law school. Then he started to talk about the movie studios and what a mistake they were making about television. How they thought that if they just pretended it wasn't there, it would go away. That was idiotic. If people could stay home and get what they wanted for nothing, or if they had to go out and pay, which would they choose.

Half the time Beth Carol didn't know what he was talking about, but she nodded once in a while and made little sounds of interest, the way guys liked you to do.

He still believed in movies, though, only it was all going to be different. He was going to be a producer and control his own product. That was the way he put it.

"Golly, you're so ambitious," she said earnestly. "That's wonderful."

He sort of swelled up with pride at what she'd said. Gee, they loved to be complimented. It was almost as if hearing that you approved of something made it all right in their minds. Like the *Good Housekeeping* Seal of Approval.

"Bread and circuses," he said. "That's what people want."

Beth Carol didn't have the faintest idea what he meant. What she did was smile and nod and look as if she agreed with him.

"There's Ciro's," he said.

Well-dressed people were standing in front, talking and laughing. Parking lot attendants drove up in Lincolns, Cadillacs. Beth Carol gawked. It was so exciting to see the places you'd only heard about.

They drove past the Mocambo, the Crescendo, where the sign said Billy Eckstine was appearing. Among the nightclubs, the restaurants, the dress shops, the stores where custom-tailored shirts were sold, was . . . well, it was a castle. There was no other way to describe it. It had gables, towers and turrets. And in front of it, maybe a couple of stories high, was a revolving replica of a show girl in a skimpy costume advertising a hotel in Las Vegas. It was just like a circus here, only better.

"A lot of old-time stars lived there," said Paul. "It's a hotel. The Chateau Marmont. Jean Harlow. Greta Garbo."

Across the street from it was a collection of bungalows, another hotel called the Garden of Allah. She'd heard of that one.

"There's Clark Gable," said Paul.

And it was in the flesh, right across the street in front of a restaurant. He probably wasn't more than a hundred yards away. He was signing autographs and smiling, in a circle of fans. Then he took the arm of a beautiful blond woman and walked with her through the door.

Clark Gable. Just think of it. Beth Carol mouthed his name. A thousand lights twinkled in the hills above them, and the air was perfumed. It was like having the most beautiful dream ever and waking up to find it had all come true.

Ahead was a restaurant that was all curving arcs outlined in neon, a spaceship to take them into the next century. Paul pulled into a parking lot next to it and found a space between a little sports car with wire wheels and a yellow Studebaker.

"I can't go in there," Beth Carol said.

"Why not?"

"I'm not dressed," she said. "I wouldn't feel right."

"Nobody cares." He grinned. "That's the beauty of life here. Anything goes."

"Really?" she asked.

"Really," he promised.

The place was jammed, every booth overflowing, every seat at the counter taken, people standing and waiting. Everybody looked up when Paul pushed open the heavy glass door. Well, Paul could have been the biggest movie star who ever lived. Everybody knew him, and wanted him to come to sit with them. And she was on his arm. Beth Carol felt wonderful about that. The hostess with her menus said hello to him, and even a couple of the waitresses waved. He took Beth Carol's elbow and led her to a booth to join some of his friends.

She just sat there, scrunched in-between Paul and a pretty girl named Dru, taking it all in. Everybody was talking about auditions and contracts, acting classes and what their agents were telling them. They were the cutest kids Beth Carol had ever seen. The girls all looked like models and the boys looked like movie stars. And the energy they generated was amazing. Beth Carol wouldn't have been surprised if they had all jumped up right there and put on a show.

She wondered how they had gotten to be the way they were, so eager to perform, to strut their stuff. She would practically faint if the teacher even called on her in class. They were nice, too. Asking her about herself, and telling her she had a great figure. Cute hair. Things like that.

Paul ordered a steak for her, a cup of coffee for himself, which seemed to be what everybody else was having, too. From what everybody was saying, getting into show business sounded easy. Maybe Fern was right. Maybe all it took was sitting on a stool in a drugstore somewhere and somebody would come along and discover you.

Paul sat next to her, holding court. His arm was on the back of the booth. Beth Carol willed it to drop to her shoulders, to show everyone that she was with him. He was uncanny, he really was—he seemed to sense what she was thinking, and he leaned over.

"You have the most beautiful eyes," he whispered in her ear, his mouth just grazing her hair.

Beth Carol thought she was going to faint with pleasure at his words, at his nearness, the smell of his shaving lotion. He was wonderful. They all thought so. She could see it from the way they looked at him.

"I'll be right back," Paul murmured.

He disappeared through the thick glass doors as if he had never existed.

But he couldn't just do that, she thought to herself. He couldn't just extend the hand of friendship, of caring, and then walk off, leaving her here in the middle of nowhere. She felt terrible, knowing she was about to cry, knowing that everybody could see her lower lip trembling.

"What's wrong?" asked the girl next to her. Dru. That was her name.

"Nothing," she said.

"Don't worry about Paul," she said, with a look that made Beth Carol wonder how well she knew him. "He's just doing a little business. He'll be back."

She craned her neck, searched the parking lot. Dru was right. Paul was standing next to the Jaguar, talking to some guy. What a relief, she thought, as he turned, walked back toward the restaurant.

"I just had a brilliant idea," he said, crowding into the booth, his hip against hers. "My family is out of town right now. They're at our house in Jamaica. You can come and stay tonight. You can have my sister's room. It's getting a little late to find you someplace." His eyes crinkled as he smiled at her. "How does that sound to you?"

CHAPTER 7

*W*hen they got to Beverly Hills, all that seemed to be there was the sign welcoming them and an island running down the middle of Sunset Boulevard planted with flowers and blooming bushes. There was hardly any traffic, either. They could have been on a country road, except that everything was so neat and pretty. Paul hit the accelerator and the Jaguar roared through the perfumed night.

Paul was giving her a little history, telling her that the island with the flowers used to be a bridle path and that it might look as if there were nothing here, but there were mansions behind all the tall hedges along the boulevard.

"There's the Beverly Hills Hotel," he said.

It was big and pink, with its name spelled out in pale green, sitting back from the street with tall, skinny palm trees, bushes blooming with white flowers. Flower beds in pinks, reds, and purples. It didn't seem real, though. It was more like a postcard.

She just looked at him, her face full of wonder.

"We'll have brunch there some Sunday," he said. "Everybody goes there for brunch. In the Polo Lounge. All the guys used to go there after polo. That's how it got its name."

Beth Carol just smiled and nodded, her head whirling as she tried to make sense of things. She hoped she had made the right decision to stay at his house tonight. He'd really been thrilled when she agreed, as if she were doing him the favor. He'd said it was great, and that it would be just like having his kid sister, Diana, home, and how the two of them got along and how much he missed her.

"She's really pretty, like you are," he said. "And she's a little spoiled. I've got to say that. My parents can hardly stand to let her out of their sight, especially my father."

"Aren't you jealous?" she asked.

"Oh, it's different with boys," he said. "It's carrying on the tradition, taking over the family business. Take school. I wanted to go to school here. It's where I live. But no. It had to be Choate and then Yale because my father went there."

"Is your father in the movie business, too?" she asked.

"He's in oil and gas leases, real estate development. There's a big marble building on Wilshire Boulevard with his name on it. I'll show you."

"He can't be very happy about your plans."

"He's not. He rants and raves and threatens to disinherit me. He thinks people in the movie business are nouveau riche, show-offs."

"Well, gee, you don't want to get disinherited," Beth Carol said.

"You have to go your own way," Paul said, more to himself than to her.

One minute they had been in civilization, and the next they were in the wilds. Other than the occasional light in a window of one of the big houses they passed, it was mostly vacant lots and silence.

Paul looked different now, with only the light from the crescent moon, the lonely streetlights that sort of sprang up from the bushes. Beth Carol clenched her fists as she wondered where he was taking her. They hadn't even passed another car. Paul seemed to realize that she was scared.

"We're almost there," he said.

He downshifted into second, then first, crawling up to the entrance to a driveway behind a high, wrought-iron gate with a brick wall that must have been ten feet high, and covered with ivy. He put the car into neutral and sprinted out, did something near the mailbox to make the gates start to open.

"Home, sweet home," he said, as they creaked open.

At first Beth Carol thought that what she was looking at was the moon reflecting on the grass. Then she realized it was a lake. An actual lake, right here, only a couple of miles from Sunset Boulevard. Ahead of them was a huge stone mansion, three stories high, with clusters of chimneys, that looked as if it would have been right at home in the French countryside. It was enormous, a palace. Nobody lived in a place like that. She looked at Paul with new respect as he parked the Jaguar in an eight-car garage.

Beth Carol glanced around, and saw a sea of tarps covering the other cars. It was all so desolate and sad. Paul helped her out of the car and opened the trunk to get her suitcase. Beth Carol looked out at the grounds, the groves of trees. Listened to the crickets singing. What have I done? she wondered. Getting in a car with a boy I don't know. Coming to this deserted place.

Paul flipped on a light just inside the door leading off the garage.

"Come on," he said.

Docilely, she followed him into the house.

There was a service area, and then a kitchen, all stainless steel with a stove that could have served a hotel. The entry hall was really spooky. The floor was white marble and the walls were white, too, with elaborate molding on the ceilings. But everything was draped with dust sheets. The furniture, even the paintings on the walls. Through the arches of a doorway leading into what was probably the drawing room, there were more dust covers. Motes of dust floated on the light from the moon that spilled through the windows. She swallowed a couple of times. Did people really go through all this just for a little trip to Jamaica?

"How long did you say your family is going to be gone?" she asked in a choked voice.

"Oh, for the season," he said vaguely. "Come on. I'll show you something you've never seen before."

"I want to get out of here," she said. "Please. Just take me back. Okay?"

Her breath was coming fast and she knew he could see how frightened she was. He could probably smell it. She could smell it herself.

"What's wrong?" he asked, looking so sweet, like a kid who had done something wrong. "I don't know what you're thinking, Beth Carol. Am I Jack the Ripper? No. Do I want to hurt you, or something? No." He picked up her suitcase and started to walk back in the direction from which they'd come. "Come on," he said. "We'll find you a hotel."

"I didn't mean anything," she mumbled.

"Well, what's it going to be?" he asked.

"No, no. It's okay."

"God, women," he said, shaking his head. "Come on. You'll like this. Really."

Beth Carol looked at him, at his open face. His nice smile. He really was trying to please her.

"Okay," she agreed.

She trailed after him, looking at his back. The dark hair, the coat perfectly tailored over his broad shoulders. He had an athletic walk. Very graceful. He stopped in front of a huge, arched doorway with carved mahogany doors and golden handles.

"Close your eyes," he said.

She sensed a blaze of light.

"Now," he said.

There were two glittering crystal chandeliers, crystal sconces along the paneled walls. It seemed to Beth Carol there must have been an acre of highly polished parquet floor. Way at the end there was a raised area where an orchestra would play. On either side of it there were banks of French doors. She could almost see beautiful women in fabulous gowns, men in tuxedos. Waiters passing things. She could almost hear a waltz.

"Oh, my," she murmured.

"It's something, isn't it?" Paul said proudly. "There aren't many ballrooms in a private home, even here in the land of wretched excess. It's used, too, all the time. For charity balls.

My mother's sorority has its rummage sale here to raise money."

"It's just like in the movies," she said. "Why, I can just see Vivien Leigh and Clark Gable. Or Bette Davis when she shocked everybody when she wore a red dress."

"Oh, they'd like that," Paul acknowledged. "The studios ask all the time. But we won't let them. Do you know how much equipment it takes to make a movie? You can imagine what it would do to this floor." He gave her shoulder a brotherly pat. "You must be really tired," he said. "Come on. I'll take you to Diana's room."

She was tired and she needed a bath. She felt intimidated by everything Paul was showing her. Intimidated by Paul himself. Beth Carol followed him up a wide, winding marble staircase, then down a wide hall that seemed to go on forever. Then Paul opened the door and they were in Diana's room.

There were dolls everywhere. Marie Antoinette dolls. Oriental dolls. Dolls in costumes from every land. They lined shelves or were displayed in glass cases. There were dollhouses, a small city of them. There was miniature furniture, tiny tea sets of real china. Utensils that looked like real silver. There was a child-sized carousel with a unicorn, a Cheshire cat, and a coach shaped like a pumpkin. Paul flipped a switch and calliope music played, the unicorn and the cat moved up and down. He flipped it off.

"One of my father's business associates gave her that when she was three," he said. "The dolls, too. They all came from business associates of my father's when she was a kid."

I wanted a childhood like this, Beth Carol thought, tears of self-pity welling in her eyes.

"How old is she now?" she asked.

"Sixteen," he said. "The same age that you are."

"Oh, no," she protested. "I'm eighteen and a half."

"Oh, I'm sorry," he said. "You look a lot younger."

They were in the bedroom, which was all pale pink and white. The single, four-poster bed had a white canopy. White curtains hung at the windows. There was a pretty antique desk. There were crystal sconces on the walls here, too. There was even a built-in television set. Golly, it must be nice to be loved like this, she thought. A mother, a father who wouldn't let her out of their sight. A big brother to depend on.

"It's like a dream," she said.

"The bathroom is just through there." He gestured. "It's late, and I have to be on my way first thing in the morning."

He was saying good night, she realized at last. He was going to leave her. But he couldn't do that.

"I'm just down the hall," he said kindly. "Three doors, to the left. Okay?"

"Okay," she said with a brave smile.

He gave a little wave, and then he was gone.

Beth Carol ran water into the tub, her head swirling as she tried to sort out the events of a day that seemed to have gone on for at least a year. She could hardly remember Fern Darling and the way it had seemed as if they could team up, be friends. Then Paul, and all of his friends at the restaurant with all of their compliments, admiring her. Why, it was just like a fairy tale.

Gratefully, she lowered herself into the tub, saw again the brutal scars etching her wrists. Fairy tale. Whatever. There was no way to go back.

CHAPTER 8

For a moment, Beth Carol didn't know where she was. The light was blinding, and everything was pink and white.

The knock on the door was impatient. The second time somebody had knocked. She remembered now.

"Come in," she called, sitting up and pulling the covers around her shoulders.

It was Paul, carrying a tray.

She stared at him, hardly able to believe he was there. Hardly able to believe that the night before hadn't just been a dream.

"I've brought you some coffee and toast," he said with a big smile.

He was even cuter than she remembered. Nothing threatening about him now in the California sunshine streaming through the windows. He was wearing chinos and a pale blue polo shirt, and there was a little glob of soap on his cheek that he had missed when he shaved.

"Gee, thanks," she said. "Nobody's ever brought me breakfast in bed before."

And he was saying that he had to get going and that he'd be back later. That he hoped she had slept well. Then he was gone. Beth Carol scurried to the window and watched through the trees as Paul in the beautiful black Jaguar sped down the drive. It was such a beautiful day that she felt as light as air. The sky was a bright blue and she could even see a corner of the lake, glistening in the sun.

She snuggled in the bed, sipping coffee and wanting to pinch herself to see if all of this was really true. After a while, she got out of bed and switched on the television set. At home there wasn't anything on at this time of day. Fifteen minutes of news at six. Then the variety shows. Milton Berle. Lucille Ball. Gosh, she was funny. She even made Beth Carol's father laugh.

Fuzzy images flickered onto the small screen, and Beth Carol saw a girl in her twenties telling a man in a tuxedo that her husband had been killed in Korea and that it was what would have been their first anniversary and so that was why she thought she should win. It upset the master of ceremonies to hear that. He looked pained, and he patted her shoulder as if he shared her grief. Then there was an older, fat lady who had been named Mother of the Year in Iowa somewhere. She had twelve children, all living, and every one of them a success. There was another girl who was crying as she told the master of ceremonies that she had a little boy who had lost the use of his legs because he had polio. The master of ceremonies was practically crying with her. So was Beth Carol. She felt the sudden tears in her eyes. Oh, I hope she wins, she thought, sobbing. It's so sad.

The girl with the little boy won, and Beth Carol felt better right away. A smiling blond assistant in a rhinestone-covered swimsuit and high heels appeared, draped a cape with a fur collar around the girl's shoulders, put a crown on her head, and handed her a bouquet of roses. The audience roared as the girl's husband appeared, pushing the little boy in his wheelchair. Both of them waved to the audience, and you could just see that the little boy was very brave. The camera showed the audience, mostly middle-aged ladies, but some men, too, and kids on vacation. They were all crying.

And, boy, did she win a lot of prizes! First of all, there was a visit to Max Factor to have her makeup done. There were all kinds of gift certificates, and dinner for the whole family at a place called Sugie's Tropics in Beverly Hills where the stars go to dine. They got to go on a tour of Metro-Goldwyn-Mayer and have lunch in the commissary, all in the company of that hot new star, Cory McIntyre. The audience screamed and clapped as Cory McIntyre trotted onto the stage. He was a big, good-looking guy who looked a little like John Derek. He grinned and waved to the audience, and when he got next to the winner, he leaned over and gave her a little kiss on the cheek. The audience screamed some more. He shook hands with the husband and the little boy in his wheelchair. Then the big prize was announced. It was an Admiral refrigerator-freezer. A couple of guys wheeled it onto the stage and the girl had her hands to her face, roses and all, and the tears of joy were just streaming down her cheeks.

It was all so wonderful, Beth Carol thought. One day you were just going along like everybody else, and then you were singled out and all of these special things happened. It was sort of like her own story, only what had come along was Paul.

By the time *Auntie Emily's Cooking Hour* came on, Beth Carol had drawn all the shades so she could get a better picture. It was a nice idea to be able to watch from bed, but the screen was so small, and the set was kind of old, one of the first sold, she decided. She sat cross-legged on the floor in front of it, licking her fingers and picking at the last crumbs of the toast Paul had brought her. That was hours ago. He'd been gone a long time.

Auntie Emily had a big, sweet face. She wore rimless glasses and her hair was pulled back in a bun. She stood behind a table with all her ingredients neatly arranged in a row. "Now, today we're going to make a very special luncheon dish," she cooed, her fingers fluttering over the ingredients. She wore a pretty summer dress and a darling apron that said KISS THE COOK.

Beth Carol leaned closer as Auntie Emily faded out and then reappeared on the screen.

"This is called Shrimp Eggs Foo Young," she said brightly, "and as you can tell from the name, ladies, it has a touch of the Orient."

I'll be able to do all of that someday, Beth Carol told herself. It was all about practice, like everything else. She saw herself in a big, sunny, all-electric kitchen. She was wearing a pretty dress, high heels, a little apron like Auntie Emily's. She flipped her own Shrimp Eggs Foo Young onto a plate. She heard the front door open.

"I'm home, honey."

It was her husband. She smiled as she arranged the sprigs of parsley.

"I'm in here, dear," she called, fluffing her hair. "Lunch is ready."

He stood behind her, his arms around her waist.

She turned and looked into his blue eyes, saw his smile.

It was Buddy, of course.

He was wearing a nice suit and he had a briefcase in one hand. And his expression—that look of love. Still, it certainly hadn't been very nice of him to leave town like that, leaving her in the lurch. That had been a cowardly thing to do, she had to admit. And besides, there was something disloyal in thinking about Buddy, when here she was, the guest in another boy's house.

Auntie Emily was doing something marvelous with a lemon pie mix and whipped cream. Boy, was this making her hungry. And she was feeling strange and disoriented, too, because Paul hadn't come back.

She quickly showered and dressed, then hurried out of Diana's room, trying to remember the direction in which they had come the night before. This place was so big it was almost worse than being outside with no protection at all. Even her echoing footsteps sounded lonely as she scurried down the stairs. In the white marble hallway, a jillion particles of dust hung in the sunlight that was blazing through the windows. And it was so quiet. You'd think a phone would ring, or a doorbell. Something.

In the refrigerator there was a can of coffee, the end of

a loaf of bread, congealed streaks of butter on a dinner plate. Nothing in the freezer except ice cubes and a quart of vodka. Well, Paul was so popular he probably never ate at home. She gobbled down the bread as she foraged through the shelves. There were some canned goods. A package of macaroni. An opened box of Wheaties. It was stale, but she scooped handfuls of it into her mouth.

Oh, where was he? she agonized. He couldn't just leave her here. Back in Diana's room, she flipped on the television set. Something had happened to the reception and she couldn't make out what was going on. She looked at Diana's books. *Nancy Drew and the Vanishing Staircase. Dr. Doolittle. Heidi.* All of them for little kids. She wandered over to the bureau and looked at all of the pictures of Diana in their tarnished frames. Such a pretty little girl, with her long, fair curls, her beautiful dresses. And there were her parents. A really attractive blond woman, a handsome man. There were also pictures of Diana with a blond boy a few years older than she was. None of Paul, though. No, here he was, with the blond boy.

Huddling miserably on the bed, Beth Carol smoked her last cigarette. Now she didn't even have that to do. It was getting dark outside. She could see the shadows laying across the floor, filling the room. Even if he'd forgotten that she was there, she rationalized, he would still have to come home sometime. Closing her eyes, she started to count. First to a hundred, then a thousand.

In her dream, she was in a rowboat in the middle of the lake. It was night and the sky was black. There was no moon, and without it she wasn't quite sure which way to go. She sat there, listening intently, hoping for a sound that would guide her to shore. There was no sound. Arbitrarily, she decided on a direction and reached for the oars. They weren't there. She couldn't go forward and she couldn't go back. Silently, she started to scream. A hand reached out to her. She was dying.

It was Paul, leaning over and shaking her awake.

"You were having a nightmare," he said, his expression

tender and full of concern. "I knocked and you didn't hear."

"Oh, you're here," she gasped.

"I'm sorry," he said, looking flustered. "I thought about you all day, and how we had to get you settled. I got tied up. I kept trying to get away, and I was so worried about you." He looked away, his beautiful long lashes brushing his cheeks. "I was so afraid you wouldn't be here."

Why, he really was feeling guilty, she thought, feeling waves of warmth toward him. He couldn't even look at her.

"Oh, that's all right," she said, the whole miserable day fading from her mind.

"Well, listen. I've got some places I have to go to and some people to see. Do you want to come?"

"I'd love to," she said.

"I picked up some Chinese food." He smiled shyly. "We can eat it in the car."

"I'll be just a minute," she said.

CHAPTER 9

$\mathscr{N}$ow she knew what they meant when they said that you're on top of the world, Beth Carol thought. Below them, the city was like a black velvet quilt embroidered with thousands of pinpoints of light. The stars were so bright, so close, it seemed to her that all she had to do was reach up her hands and pluck one for her own.

Paul downshifted into second and handed her one of the cartons of Chinese food. He had changed to a white button-down shirt and a black cashmere sweater.

"Sweet and sour pork," he said.

"It's wonderful," she said.

When the mountain road ahead of them was straight, Beth Carol took the wheel of the car while Paul ate. They drove along, passing the cartons back and forth. The gentle, warm night seemed to caress her cheeks. Nearby, an owl hooted and the bushes rustled with the movement of small creatures. The road started to wind downward, and Paul took the wheel back from her. She glanced at his profile, thinking that he was so in command of everything, so sophisticated.

The traffic signal, its red light, here in the middle of nowhere, seemed like an apparition. Paul drew up to it slowly, put the Jaguar in neutral, and dipped again into one of the cartons.

Theirs had been the only car on the road for so long that Beth Carol jumped a little when she heard the hurumphing engine of another one as it pulled alongside them. It was sleek and gleaming red with a thousand coats of lacquer, a hot rod with no top. Its nose was inches above the asphalt, and there were huge tires in back. There were a couple of boys in it. The driver leaned forward and caught Paul's eye, raised an eyebrow. Smiled.

Paul looked straight ahead, his jaw set, his body tense. Oh, no, Beth Carol thought, dismayed, her own body tensing, as Paul casually dropped the Jaguar into first gear.

The light flashed green.

Tires squealed in a stench of burning rubber, great belches of exhaust burned her eyes as Paul threw the Jaguar through its gears, the speedometer climbing, climbing. The hot rod was just beside them, a few inches ahead. A couple of feet. Paul dropped the Jaguar back into second, spurted ahead. They were flying along, the hot rod right beside them, crossing and recrossing the double line, winding around the looming mountains. Beth Carol felt the wind cracking against her face, squeezing the tears from her eyes, her hair tangling, standing up on her head. Her heart was going as fast as the speeding car. Ahead was a sign indicating a sharp curve. Paul dropped the Jaguar into second again. Wheels seemed to leave the road. The hot rod was just beside them, inching ahead.

The road was straight now, Paul's foot on the accelerator pushed to the floor. The speedometer read 100, 110, 120. Next to them, the boy driving the hot rod slowed, shifted. Then he flew past them as if they were standing still.

A couple of hundred feet ahead, he must have touched the brakes. The red taillights blinked a couple of times, and then there was only the darkness again, the song of the crickets, the whispered sounds of the night. Beth Carol started to breath again as Paul slowed the car.

"I didn't have a chance," He laughed.

Trembling like a leaf, Beth Carol closed her eyes.

"A chopped and channeled '32 Ford," he murmured.

"Not bad. Kid must have a fortune in it."

Beth Carol opened her mouth to speak, but no words came. She tried to decide how she felt. It hadn't been fear. No, it had been so far beyond fear that there weren't even the words in her vocabulary to describe it.

"There isn't a stock car on the road that could have taken him," he said, explaining his loss. But to himself, Beth Carol thought, her breathing returning to normal. Not to her.

In a couple of minutes, Paul pulled off the curving highway onto a flat area with a view of the city.

"How about this for a picnic site?" he asked, holding out one of the cartons of Chinese food.

With shaking hands, the city only an impression in her peripheral vision, Beth Carol took the carton and dipped into it with the wooden fork. She looked down and saw Los Angeles spread out beneath them, an endless, undifferentiated sea of tiny lights stretching on forever.

Where were the landmarks? she wondered, feeling her anxiety rising. It was all the same. How did you tell where you were? There was nothing down there to hold on to. Nothing. Even that red light in the sky was moving. A plane about to land. Beside her, she could hear Paul breathing. He wasn't all that calm, either.

"If you knew you couldn't win, why did you race him?" Beth Carol asked.

"You have to try," Paul said, surprised. "The only failure is not to try."

Beth Carol thought about that. It made a lot of sense to her. But try what?

"You know something?" Paul said as he started the car. "I like you. You're a good sport."

"Thank you," she said, a note of doubt in her voice. Here he'd told her that she had beautiful eyes, and that the girl he had mistaken her for at that coming-out party had been a really big deal to him, and all she was was a good sport? Boy, that made her sound like a mascot. Like on a football team, or something.

Within a couple of minutes they were in civilization again, dropping down into a pass carved out of a mountain range and joining the stream of cars on the Hollywood freeway. Paul eased the car onto the Cahuenga exit off ramp and then onto Hollywood Boulevard.

But it couldn't be, she told herself, as she glanced from the street sign to the street itself. Hollywood was glamorous and luxurious, with movie stars in open convertibles waving to the fans. Strolling with greyhounds on jeweled leads. Things like that.

But this was a lot of tacky stores advertising sales. A drugstore at the corner of Hollywood and Vine. A department store called the Broadway. It was a big gray building that would have been right at home in Spokane. Even the clothes on the mannequins in its windows were dumb and dowdy. The trash baskets on every corner were overflowing. There were a lot of soldiers and cheap-looking girls milling around on the sidewalks, waiting in line in front of the movie theaters every couple of blocks, pushing through the doors of a thousand bars. A drunk slept on a bus bench. Big buses belched exhaust, and every other car seemed to be the police.

In fact, the only glamorous thing about Hollywood Boulevard was the Jaguar, Paul, herself at his side. People were actually tapping each other on the shoulder so that they would turn around to look at them. Beth Carol felt like a celebrity herself to be at Paul's side. She glanced shyly over at him, and he gave her a big smile and patted her hand.

He really was cute, she decided as she thought fleetingly of Buddy and what a hick he was next to Paul Fournier.

The nightclub when they got there was already jammed, bursting to the seams with people and noise. The lights were so low that Beth Carol had to guess that the gray haze was cigarette smoke. Paul took her elbow as the guy at the door gave her a questioning look and then led them to a tiny table near the stage. The din was something, the laughter and conversation so loud she could hardly hear the jukebox playing some African-sounding record. When her eyes adjusted, Beth Carol saw that there were as many as four people crowded around each tiny table. The people were a lot older, many of them Negroes. The women wore cocktail gowns with glittery earrings and necklaces. The men were in suits and ties. Soldiers crowded the bar, with its neon signs advertising Seagram's, Dewar's White Label, Budweiser. The bartender wore a white shirt and a black bow tie. He was laughing with a customer as he poured a drink into a stemmed glass, popped in an olive. The waitress slinking up to them was older, too, her hair an unlikely red, a mouth to match, heavy makeup. She was wearing tight shorts that practically showed part of her bottom, fishnet stockings, and a low-cut blouse that made her breasts look like watermelons.

"Well, long time, no see, baby," she said, bending to kiss Paul's ear.

Beth Carol could hardly believe it when he grabbed her and pulled her down to whisper something. She gave a short laugh and licked her lips. For a moment it had seemed to her that she and Paul were out of place, babes in the woods, and now it seemed that Paul and this cheap-looking gal were the best of friends. No wonder Paul and his father didn't get along, Beth Carol thought. His father probably didn't even know that Paul came to a place like this. He'd have a heart attack for sure. She felt a stab of jealousy as she heard Paul ordering a Coke for her, a Dewar's and water for himself.

Later, the place got very still when a beautiful Negro lady got up and sang with the live band. She had very pale skin, golden sort of, and she wore a white, beaded evening gown. A white gardenia was tucked into her hair, which she wore in a chignon. She was wonderful, not at all like any singer Beth Carol had ever heard before. She had a little baby voice and everything she sang sounded so sad, as if she were taking out her broken heart and sharing it. And the words to the songs were all about losing love and feeling alone, and longing for her lover to come back to her.

Things that seemed to be the story of Beth Carol's life. Only Paul was there and he wasn't her lover. Not yet.

She sat there, tears in her eyes, but somehow it made her feel better to know that she wasn't alone in what she felt. That other girls felt the way she did. That they wanted love, wanted to belong to somebody. When the Negro lady finished, there was so much screaming and applause that Beth Carol realized that a lot of other people must feel the same way. That whatever this was, it struck a universal chord.

When Paul went off to the men's room, some guys from the bar came over to flirt. Beth Carol kind of hoped that Paul would mind, but he didn't. He threw some bills on the table and, with some other people he knew, they left.

They were all crowded into a big new Oldsmobile, just driving along. Paul was one of those in the front seat and Beth Carol was in back with four, maybe five guys and gals. They were all half sitting on each other, and what they were doing was passing around little hand-rolled cigarettes that they smoked by taking really deep drags and holding the smoke in their lungs. Even the smell was different from anything Beth Carol had ever experienced, almost nauseatingly sweet and harsh at the same time.

For some reason, Beth Carol felt an inexplicable affection toward the girl who was half sitting on her lap. She started to brag to her how rich her family was, and about her sisters and the island, and everything. She really felt strange, though. Her eyes were smarting, the lights on the streets outside, the oncoming headlights, were all so clear and lovely, and everything anybody said seemed so funny to her that she got the giggles and just couldn't stop. Then somebody else started to giggle, too.

They just drove around, stopping at nightclubs here and there. Somewhere along the line, Beth Carol staggered off to the ladies' room. There was a Negro lady wearing a maid's uniform sitting in there, working a crossword puzzle. On the counter with some little folded towels, soaps, combs, and tiny bottles of perfume, there was a bowl filled with quarters.

Beth Carol looked at herself in the mirror. Her eyes were all red, and her hair was going every which way. Boy, she was a mess. Awful. The worst. She started to giggle again at her reflection as she let the cold water from the tap run over the backs of her hands.

"You shouldn't be smoking that shit at your age, honey," the woman said, handing her a towel. "You're going to get in big trouble doing that."

"I'm eighteen and a half," she said in a slurred voice, "so it's legal." She fumbled with her purse, spilled its contents out on the counter. The pack of Herbert Tareytons. A lipstick, a couple of tissues.

"I don't care what you say, girl," the woman sniffed. "You're doped up."

"No, I'm not," Beth Carol said, staggering against the counter, stuffing things back in her purse. "But thank you for the towel." She groped around inside her purse again, looking for her wallet, for the tip. A quarter it was. But her wallet wasn't there. That was funny. She must have dropped it in the car.

"I don't seem to have my wallet," she said. "I'll have to get a tip for you from my escort. He's from one of Los Angeles' oldest families, you know. His home is so big that they even have a lake on the grounds. He's a wonderful boy and he's going to be the head of a movie studio soon."

"Why don't you just let me call your mama and have her come to get you, honey?" the woman suggested. "You're, what? Sixteen? Fifteen? Somebody's doing a snow job on you."

"My mama's dead," Beth Carol said, slumping onto one of the little vanity stools in front of the mirror. "How could she do that to me? How could she leave me all alone in the world this way?"

She was crying, she realized, and the woman was looking worried and upset.

"Get me next time," she said, her eyes wide with dismay. "And you take care, hear?"

Back in the car, everybody was starving. They stopped at

an all-night market and bought a lot of donuts and cupcakes, all kinds of candy bars. Beth Carol thought she had never tasted anything so good in her life.

A couple of places later, it was really feeling late. Everybody was drinking out of coffee cups, but Beth Carol knew they were full of whiskey like the ones at their table. Somehow the whole group had changed except for her and Paul. Where had the others gone, she wondered vaguely, and who were these new ones? Guys wandered into the club with instrument cases and they sat in with the band on the stage. Then they would drift out, and others would arrive. Another big Negro lady sang. She was great, too. Not like the other one, though, the one with the gardenia in her hair. This one had the most exquisite voice, like a silver bell, but what she sang didn't make Beth Carol feel as if there were somebody on this earth who knew exactly how she felt, exactly what she needed. Which was to be loved, to belong.

It was light when they walked out of there, and somehow it was just the two of them again, back in the Jaguar, drinking in the crisp new day with a sun that was just beginning to warm the street. There were only a few cars, fewer pedestrians strolling into coffee shops, papers under their arms. Paul looked just as fresh as he had when they had left the house the night before. Beth Carol could only remember how horrible she had looked in the mirror in the ladies' room with her red eyes, her hair all over the place. And there was something else that had happened in the ladies' room. She tried to concentrate, to remember, but it skirted away, out of her consciousness.

She didn't know how she felt, either. She wasn't tired, but then she wasn't exactly as fresh as a daisy, either. She'd had, what, a few Cokes, a couple of candy bars. How she felt was the way she imagined a hangover would feel. Maybe it had been the excitement, all the new people, the new places.

When she woke later, her eyelids felt as if they were glued together. A blanket covered her, and except for her shoes, which were beside the bed, she still wore what she'd been wearing the night before. The shades in Diana's room were drawn, but she could tell it was afternoon. She had never been so hungry. Beth Carol got up and stumbled out of the room and down the stairs. She seemed to be moving in slow motion. By the time she got to the kitchen, she felt as if she had been walking for hours. The cartons of leftover Chinese food were in the refrigerator. She ate it cold with her hands.

The house was still and empty as she made her way back up the stairs. Something was really funny about her time perception. Everything seemed to take forever. And something else was wrong, too. Something was nagging at the corners of her mind. Her wallet. It was gone, with every cent she had. She sat on the bed, her face buried in her hands, wondering what she was going to do. Wondering how she was going to tell Paul.

CHAPTER 10

The coffeehouse was perched on a hill out in Malibu with a view of the ocean, its white froth like plumes at the hem of a dress, trickling onto the sand. The full moon cut a golden swath across the ocean's surface, and the stars seemed very close. Candles flickered on the tables, and the walls were covered with posters from World War II. LOOSE LIPS SINK SHIPS. UNCLE SAM WANTS YOU. Classical music played over the speakers. Beth Carol sipped her espresso and idly watched the boys next to her at their chess game. A girl at another table in a black leotard was frowning and moving her lips as she read a book of poetry. The conversation here was only a low hum. They were beats, existentialists, Paul had tried to explain. What they said was that life had no meaning, but frankly, Paul told her, his personal opinion was that they just didn't believe they could make it in any meaningful way.

She looked up as the door opened, expecting Paul to be back. It was just a couple of kids in turtlenecks, jeans, and corduroy jackets. She felt a twinge of disappointment.

Their evenings and nights were always like this. When Paul got home, it was into the Jaguar and off on his rounds. To the mansions on the Beverly Hills flats, where a Moroccan palace sat next to an English country cottage.

And next to it, a Mediterranean villa. A French chateau. A modern ranch house without the ranch and with the house larger by a factor of ten. It was all higgledy-piggledy, making no sense at all, with only the width of a driveway separating one fantasy from the next. Most unnerving of all to Beth Carol was that they all looked so insubstantial, mere facades that a child could push over with one hand. It was impossible for her to believe that people actually lived in those houses. That they loved and fought, that children woke up in the bedrooms and went down those stairs to eat breakfast and go off to school.

They drove the winding curves of Laurel Canyon. It was chaos to Beth Carol's eyes, with lean-to shacks next to graceful residences; rusting cars and empty, broken swimming pools abutting manicured parks, shiny new Cadillacs and Packards. There was a mansion, with a turntable in the courtyard for the cars, which had been broken up into apartments and studios. One of them belonged to a friend of Paul's who was a fashion photographer. Beth Carol felt kind of sorry for him the first time she met him when she saw that he wore a black eye patch, and she wondered what had happened, and if it were permanent. Then it crossed her mind that maybe he was just emulating the Hathaway man in the magazine ads. He had that air about him. His pictures were wonderful, though. Huge black and white blowups of the most beautiful girls, a couple of them posed with leopards, panthers.

They visited pretty houses in hidden canyons in the hills above Sunset Boulevard at four o'clock in the morning when Beth Carol would have thought that everybody in the world would be asleep. But no. These guys were screenwriters, musicians, composers. This was the time when they worked, entertained. Academy Awards lined their mantelpieces. Plaques, trophies of all kinds, lined walls, sat in glass cases.

They went to restaurants and nightclubs, once in the Negro section way downtown where Beth Carol was afraid to go to the ladies' room and where a Negro stood on the bar itself playing a saxophone that drove everybody wild, and everybody was shouting and stamping on the floor with their feet. They went to artists' shacks in Venice on the beach down the highway, apartments shared by students near UCLA and USC, appearances at the Palladium by Woody Herman and Stan Kenton, concerts at the Shrine Auditorium by Duke Ellington and his Orchestra. Count Basie. Jazz at the Philharmonic.

The thing Beth Carol found absolutely astonishing was that they never seemed to see the same people twice. At home everybody, rich or poor or in-between, saw everybody else all the time, several times a day. And if you didn't see them, you heard about them, what they were doing. Who was sick. Who was arguing with whom, who had made up. Why, just think about the scandal between her and Buddy. People would still be talking about it years from now. It wasn't just the reaction of her father, her family, that had shamed her so. No, it was bigger than that. She'd let them down, sure. But she had let everybody else down, too. The approval or disapproval of the community let her know how she was doing, and the way she felt she was doing told her who she was, how to think about herself that day, that week.

Here in Los Angeles, nobody would remember her and Buddy after a couple of days. It was what Paul had said that first night. That it didn't matter what she wore or what she did because anything went. And anything went because everybody had just gotten to town, had just made themselves up, decided who they wanted to be and tried to be it. They didn't share memories. Every morning when they got out of bed, it was a whole new world. A blank page.

It was true that you always had a second chance the way things were here. But it was scary, too, because there was never any you from yesterday. You were always out there on the wire, but you hadn't learned how to do it. You had nothing to fall back on. No values that defined who you were or what was okay for you to do.

Or maybe it was just Paul and the way he always liked to

hang out with different people, different sets. Of course, he came from a solid base. His family and its standing in the community. The mansion on its grounds, still there when they got back each night or morning, and always such a surprise to her that it hadn't just vanished while they'd been gone. Paul knew who he was. Everything in his life told him. His education, his goals. The words he lived by. "If you're going to do anything, you might as well do everything." "The only failure is not to try." "You've only got to get it right once." "This isn't the dress rehearsal."

So Paul was okay, and when Beth Carol was with him, so was she. She knew exactly who she was. She'd heard people say it. "You know, that cute girl Paul Fournier hangs out with." Things like that. But when Paul was off somewhere and she was alone, she sometimes had the feeling that she would just float off into space.

That attendant in the ladies' room that night had been right. Beth Carol had been on dope and she hadn't even known it. What they'd all been smoking in that car with the windows up was marijuana—grass, they called it. Or shit. She'd been contact high, as high as any of them. And it had happened again and again. She'd gotten a lot of condescending looks when she kept asking for Cokes at the nightclubs, so finally she tried a drink somebody told her really tasted good. A vodka gimlet. It did taste good, too. And she liked the way it made her feel. All happy and high, and one of the crowd, whichever crowd they happened to be with at the moment.

Still, sometimes Beth Carol would wake up in the morning in the little bed in Diana's room so ashamed of what she had done the night before she wished she were dead. The higher she would have gotten, the more things would get out of hand. There would be touching and kissing. Worse. At least she would go in the bedroom, but couples would be doing it right there. Girls and girls even. Or a guy with two girls. And since she never saw any of them again, there were no furtive looks the next day, there was no social price that had to be paid. Maybe they knew about it, too.

Maybe they woke up the next morning and said, "Oh, God. What did I do?" But the only reactions Beth Carol knew about for sure were her own and Paul's.

What happened the night before made her feel like dirt. Worse than she had felt when her father caught her with Buddy.

And Paul?

He didn't even seem to notice, didn't care. Didn't judge. He treated her with the same respect he had from the moment they had met. As if they'd been at a church social. There was the brotherly kiss on the cheek at the door. A little wave as he said good night.

It had taken her two days to get up the nerve to tell him she had lost her wallet.

"Oh, no," he said, and Beth Carol saw the concern etched on his face. "You poor kid." He seemed to be lost in thought for a second or two, as if trying to find the words to reassure her, to make her feel better. "I'll look in the car," he said at last. "Maybe it's there. I'll call around. Somebody might have turned it in."

It wasn't in the car, and Beth Carol didn't know if he phoned to see if it had been turned in. It just wasn't mentioned again. Instead, he took her shopping at a fashionable store on Wilshire Boulevard called Jax and bought her a lot of new clothes, paying for them with a wad of hundred-dollar bills. The salesgirls loved it. That cute, elegant guy, all that money. He was like the cock of the walk, preening in front of them as they batted their eyes. Looked from him to her, trying to figure out who she was to him. What was going on.

Beth Carol stood in the tiny dressing room, looking at her reflection once, twice, three times in all the mirrors. She wore a sleeveless linen dress in pale blue with a low waistline that sat on the top of her hips. At the waist there were a couple of tabs in the same pale blue, ornamented with flat mother-of-pearl buttons. The blue brought out the color of her eyes. She twirled, posed, looked at herself over her shoulder. Oh, she looked so smart, so sophisticated, she saw. Oh, I'm so pretty, she thought to herself, a blazing smile on her lips. How could I have ever thought that I was the plain one? Seeing herself in the dress made her feel like a million dollars, like a queen.

"Gorgeous," exclaimed Paul when she stepped out of the dressing room. "Now, let's see some more."

And it was more, more, until they could hardly find room for all the packages in the Jaguar when they got out of there.

He must care for me, she told herself in a daze of happiness, or he wouldn't buy me all these things, take me everywhere. And he was a perfect gentleman, too. Oh, she was crazy about him, thought about him all the time. It really made her feel guilty when she thought about the things she'd let Buddy do to her. She'd even thought what she had felt for Buddy was love when, of course, it wasn't anything of the kind. They had just been a couple of kids fooling around.

"Now, nothing too different, okay?" Paul said, a hand on the steering wheel, the other arm leaning on the door of the Jaguar. "I don't want to come back to find Joan Crawford as Sadie Thompson."

"Okay," she said, feeling a little strange as she stood on the sidewalk, looking at him sitting in the car. Of course, he couldn't very well come into the beauty salon with her and sit there holding her hand while she had her hair done, her nails. But still, flutters of anxiety twanged her nerves. For a couple of weeks since they had met, they'd been sort of semi-attached. She waited at the mansion when he was out, knowing he would be back, and if they were out on his rounds, even if she didn't see him, she knew he was somewhere in the vicinity.

"And not too short," he added. "Just give it some shape."

"Okay," she said, a tremor in her voice this time.

He glanced in the rearview mirror, then over his shoulder, gauging the instant when he could join the flow of traffic on Sunset Boulevard. Beth Carol stood there watching him ease the Jaguar into the stream. He tapped the horn and gave her a big grin as he dropped into second and drove off.

She turned, took a deep breath, looked up at the name of the salon on the white marble facade. SECRETS, it said. The best, Paul had told her. Everybody went there. Movie starlets, models, society ladies. His mother went there. Rich girls. Like Diana. She went there, too.

Inside there was a lot more white marble, hanging plants, crystal chandeliers. There was a lot of bustle, with skinny, cute boys in tight pants and Negro girls in white uniforms rushing around. Three women in lavender smocks, their hair in pin curls, their foreheads swathed in tissue, hairnets tied over it all, sat on a curving, lavender sofa, drinking coffee from china cups and chatting together in hushed tones. They all wore sheer stockings and pretty, high-heeled shoes. One of them, Beth Carol saw, wore a huge diamond ring with her wedding band. The biggest diamond ring Beth Carol had ever seen. In front of them on the coffee table were stacks of magazines. *Vogue. Harper's Bazaar. Redbook. The Ladies' Home Journal.*

Beth Carol felt intimidated as she took the few steps toward the reception desk, where a haughty blonde with perfect makeup was giving change to a woman who looked as if she had just stepped off a magazine cover herself. Beth Carol's heart was beating fast as she gave her name to the woman, who scanned the appointment sheet.

"Ummm," she said, looking through Beth Carol as if she weren't there. "He's running late. We'll call you."

Thumbing through a magazine, Beth Carol didn't mean to eavesdrop on the three women who were talking together in low tones. She really didn't, but once she caught the drift of the conversation, that the husband of the lady in the middle, the one with the huge diamond, was having an affair with his secretary and that the other two were her best girlfriends and that what they were actually doing was having a strategy meeting, she just couldn't shut out their words.

"I say, ignore it," one of the other women said. "You know how it is, Dolly. They get to be forty and they think they're losing it, and so what they need to make them feel young again is some little chick who'll spread her legs for them, and listen to their crap, and make them feel like they're hot stuff."

"Oh, I don't know," the woman said, shaking her head, her mouth a tight line of crimson. "What he's doing is charging things for her on our Saks account. And, of course, the bill comes to the house, so he wants me to know. After all, I know I haven't been shopping for peignoirs and nightgowns in their lingerie department."

"She's right," the third woman said. "You can't do anything. You remember when my Larry went through this and it was the manicurist at his barbershop? And it wasn't lingerie, honey, it was a fur coat. A mink, just like the one he gave me for Christmas. God, I was so insulted that he would give that little tramp the same coat he gave me. I cried. How I cried."

The two other women nodded grimly, remembering.

"And it was my dad who sent him through medical school. The perfect son-in-law, that's what my mother and father thought he was. And I couldn't face them, couldn't look my mother in the eye. And the kids? Well, they must have known something was wrong. All I did was cry. Menopause. That's what I told them it was."

"But she went too far," the woman with the diamond said. "'Get a divorce, Larry,' she told him. 'Get a divorce or I won't see you anymore.'"

"That was her mistake," the other woman said. "She pushed too hard, too soon. You can't do that. You've got to let them think that everything is their idea. So, what happened? He came crawling back, all apologies. All 'I'll never do it again.'"

"They don't like change," the third woman said. "And they don't want to give up the money, the alimony, half of everything."

"Well, it's still just lingerie," the woman with the diamond said, doubt in her voice. "But he's absolutely rejuvenated. He even whistles."

The three of them sat there sipping their coffee, shrouded in gloom.

"Beth Carol?" said a soft voice in front of her. "I'm ready for you now."

"Oh, thank you," she said breathlessly, looking up at Bobby Prise. He was the best, Paul had told her after checking around. He stood in front of her with a shy smile, a tan, brown hair and eyes. He was one of the cutest boys she'd ever seen. She looked with regret at the three women as he took her elbow and led her into the beauty salon. Now she'd never hear how the story came out.

Inside it was enormous, with marble counters in the same white, a thousand mirrors edged with lights. And women, women everywhere, old, middle-aged, young. Women in hair nets, their nails being done. Women with their feet in soapy water, attendants manicuring their toenails. Women holding up hand mirrors, examining the backs of their heads. Women drinking coffee, watching their reflections while boys rolled their hair onto curlers, combed them out. And everywhere the low hum of conspiratorial voices, hushed, secretive.

"I had someone who just had to come in." Bobby smiled at her as he handed her a smock. "They were going to New York and they had to have their roots bleached. Really, they didn't need it, not for a couple of weeks."

"Oh, I see," said Beth Carol shyly.

"I said to them, 'You don't need to do this,' but they're very particular and they needed a manicure and a make-up."

Beth Carol just stood there.

"Their husband is very rich and he likes them to look perfect," he said. "They're the second wife, of course."

"Golly," she said.

"I'm Bobby," he said.

"I'm Beth Carol."

"You can change in there," he said, gesturing to a row of dressing rooms along one wall.

One of the pretty Negro girls took over after that, leading her to a row of washbasins where she washed her hair, massaged her scalp, even massaged her shoulders. Oh, it felt wonderful to be pampered like this, to be made over, Beth Carol thought when she was sitting in Bobby's chair, looking at herself. Bobby looked at her reflection, too, his eye critical, as he decided what he was going to do. While he clipped, he talked in his soft, sweet voice, pointing out this woman, that woman. She's the model in the Chesterfield ads. She just got a contract at Fox. She's married to the biggest Cadillac dealer in Los Angeles. She's some gangster's girlfriend. Bugsy Siegel, or was he the one who's killed? Some gangster, anyway. She's married to Slim Taylor, the guy who's developing all that property in the Valley. She's married to the guy who owns the Mocambo. She's a hooker. One of the three most expensive in town. A thousand dollars a night.

"You know everything," she said, looking into his eyes in the mirror. He was looking into her eyes, too. Flirting. She could tell it. But how could that be? They were all queers, beauty operators. Paul said so.

"Don't make it too short," she said.

"You have good hair." He lifted a lock. "And beautiful eyes. You know that, don't you? Everybody must tell you."

"Yes," she said, blushing, as his fingers touched her shoulder. Maybe they weren't all queer, she decided. Maybe he was just trying to get into movies, or something.

"I'm staying with a friend whose mother comes here," she said. "Mrs. Fournier. And his sister comes here, too. Diana."

"Fournier, Fournier," he said. "Sounds familiar, but I don't know her."

"And here I thought you knew everything," she said with a little smile.

"I know one thing," he said, leaning close to her ear. "I know you've got something special. An innocence, a vulnerability. You're going to be a big success in this town. I can just feel it."

Did he say that to everybody? she wondered. Was it part

of his beauty operator line? This was all so new, everything was all so new. She just didn't have any way to evaluate things anymore. Beth Carol watched him while she sat under the dryer, the manicurist picking at her cuticles with a little metal implement. She watched the other operators flitting around, posing. Her eyes widened as she saw one of them pat another on his rear end. The manicurist was saying something to her.

"What did you say?" she asked, pushing up the hair dryer.

"You've got good nails," the woman said. She had bleached blond hair, a lot of wrinkles, and very red lipstick.

"Thank you," Beth Carol said, pulling down the hair dryer again, feeling its heat frying her scalp. Good nails. Was that good? Well, maybe it was if you looked at nails all day. Bobby was talking to a very pretty girl with a pale brown flip. Their heads were close together. No, he wasn't like the others.

"We're going to be great friends," he whispered to her as he combed her hair out. "I can just feel it."

And that sent a little shiver through her because he was definitely flirting with her. She just knew it.

Paul was thrilled when he saw her, and she was thrilled for him, too, when he told her he had a job in the story department at a studio. His first big break. She could have cried. And they had to celebrate. He just had to take her to Romanoff's for dinner, and that was the most exciting thing that had happened since she'd come to town.

Beth Carol had been a little nervous when they got there, even though she was wearing a really pretty dress Paul had bought her. It was black taffeta with a full skirt and black netting dotted with rhinestones covering the swell of her breasts. Thanks to Bobby, her hair was perfect. It was smooth on top with a half bang covering part of her forehead and it turned under at the bottom. Paul looked great, of course. He was wearing a black suit, a gray silk tie, gold cuff links. The owner was a Russian prince who had escaped with nothing, a short, kind of ugly guy, but so nice.

He greeted Paul as if Paul were a long-lost friend, and he actually kissed Beth Carol's hand, which made her blush.

The restaurant itself was pretty, all bathed in pale pink light that made everybody look beautiful. The prince led them to one of the banquettes along the wall, and everybody in the other booths and at the tables in the center of the room looked up, expecting to see somebody famous. The maître d'hotel didn't even raise an eyebrow when Paul ordered martinis for the two of them.

"Very good, sir," was what he said, just like in the movies.

Beth Carol hoped she didn't look as excited as she felt as she looked around the room. It was crowded, and every face was familiar. She swallowed hard when she recognized Humphrey Bogart and Lauren Bacall, Robert Wagner and Natalie Wood, Janet Leigh and Tony Curtis. They were all so beautiful that it didn't seem possible that they were real. But there they were, talking and laughing, eating and drinking. Just like anybody else.

Paul ordered oysters Rockefeller, beef Stroganoff, asparagus so tender it practically melted in her mouth, a bottle of wine with dinner. It was such a wonderful evening that Beth Carol was sure that this would be the night. Paul would sweep her into his arms. He would hold her, kiss her. Tell her that he loved her and that he wanted her to be his wife.

It was just as well that it didn't happen.

Beth Carol was throwing up all night because she wasn't used to drinking, wasn't used to all that rich food. And the next day it turned out that he didn't have the job after all. After that, they just didn't mention the evening at Romanoff's. In fact, he had been in a terrible mood ever since. She could barely open her mouth without Paul snapping her head off. She had the feeling that she couldn't do anything right, that she would never be able to please him again, no matter how hard she tried. They still rushed around, though, every night. But it wasn't much fun anymore. There was something almost desperate in the way Paul kept going, going, and she with him.

He'd been gone for so long this time, she realized, sipping the last, bitter dregs of her espresso. It must be twenty minutes, maybe a half an hour. Where did he go, anyway, whenever they were out? What did he do for those minutes, and with whom? And why didn't she have the nerve to just come out and ask him?

"Can I get you anything?" the waitress asked, wafting over in her leotard, looking as if she should be in her ballet class rather than here in this coffeehouse carrying a tray. Beth Carol did want another espresso, but then Paul was sure to come back, and he would want to leave right that minute. He always did.

"No, thank you," she said.

So she sat and sat, and it wasn't until the kids from a string quartet were lugging their instruments onto the tiny stage that the door opened and, finally, it was Paul. Beth Carol felt weak with relief and started to rise. Then she saw the expression on Paul's face. It was black as thunder, horrible. Oh, no, she thought, sitting down again. Something was wrong. Terribly, terribly wrong. And maybe what was most wrong was that she didn't even dare to ask him what it was. Just sit there, quiet. Wait to see what would happen next. On the stage the kids started to play, and all around them people looked up from their chess games, closed their books. Paul sat, looking at them, too. Every muscle in his body was so tense that she wondered if he would just spring right through the ceiling. The only thing she knew for sure was that whatever it was, it wasn't anything she had done. He'd even smiled and petted her shoulder when he'd left her this time. But then, maybe it was. Maybe after he was out doing whatever he did, some offense she'd committed had occurred to him. But what? If only he would say something. The kids must have played for nearly an hour and Beth Carol didn't hear a note. All she was aware of was Paul, looking straight ahead. Or glancing at the door. He was expecting somebody.

"Come on," he said at last, throwing a couple of dollars on the table.

Beth Carol rose, looked at the door.

The boy who was standing there had a big head with tight blond curls. An eye patch. Oh, no, she thought guiltily. It was that fashion photographer she had done it with that one time when she was so drunk. Darby something. Darby Hicks. That was it. She trailed after Paul as he caught up with Darby, who was holding open the door. Glanced at her and didn't even acknowledge her presence.

It was a gorgeous night, hot and still. Ahead of her the boys were sauntering along, talking. Beth Carol strained to pick up their words.

"You couldn't talk them out of it, huh?" Darby asked. "Did you offer them money? Sometimes that'll work."

"Well, I did, and it wasn't enough," Paul snapped.

Gee, he was being mean to Darby, too, Beth Carol realized. So it wasn't just her. That made her feel better somehow.

"Maybe if you would have offered them some grass. . ." Darby persisted.

"Oh, knock it off, will you? You know how things are right now."

"Well, how did they find you?"

"I don't know," Paul said. "I guess they followed me from the house."

Something was different, Beth Carol realized as she looked around the parking lot. The Jaguar was gone. Oh, no. It had been stolen. That was what must have happened. That was why Paul was in such a fury, why Darby Hicks was here. Other ramifications flooded her mind. Paul could have been hurt. He could have been killed. Then where would she be? What would she do? Her legs almost went out from under her at the thought.

They were waiting for her now at Darby's car, a really wonderful old European sedan with caned sides. She slid into the backseat, hoping they would just forget she was there. Hoping that they would say more about Paul's car.

"I never could figure out why you did it in the first place," Darby said as they wound down the narrow road leading to Pacific Coast Highway. "You've got, what? Six, eight cars at the house? Packards, Cadillacs, a Lincoln. So you go out and buy a Jaguar roadster? What kind of sense does that make?"

"Lay off it, will you?" Paul said, a note of exasperation in his voice. "I don't need you to tell me how to run my life."

"Well, just tell me," said Darby, turning onto the highway, dropping into second gear, then third.

"Okay. I'll tell you. I bought it because I wanted it," Paul said. "I've always wanted it, ever since the first ones came out."

"But you knew things were getting tight, that it was the last for a while. Everybody knew it. And you did it anyway."

"Well, old buddy," said Paul. "It's what I always say. My own personal words to live by. The only failure is not to try."

Beth Carol tried to decipher what they were talking about, but she couldn't make head nor tail of any of it. They could have been speaking in Chinese, Swahili. But she relaxed anyway, leaning against the seat, looked at the beach houses holding each other up, the froth of the waves as they broke on the beach. The moon. Paul's tone had changed. The urgency, the anger, had just dribbled out of it. The irony was back, the hinted laughter. He wasn't mad anymore.

CHAPTER 11

*B*eth Carol almost went mad with anxiety in the two days before she saw Paul again. It had been so easy just to go along. Not to think about anything much except when Paul would get home and where they would go that night. She sat, shifting the fragments of conversation between Paul and Darby on the way home from Malibu the other night. The problem was money. The Jaguar roadster hadn't been stolen. It had been repossessed because Paul couldn't make the payments. But how could that be? What could have happened? The only thing she could think was that he must have gone over his allowance. She knew what that was like. It had been one of the ways she had used to get her father's attention.

She lived on the opened packages of macaroni and rice in the cupboards. During the day she wandered the grounds, eating the oranges and peaches she picked from the fruit trees. She checked her watch, saw that it took her eighteen minutes to walk from the house to the front gates. She stood there, looking at the button that would swing them open, wondering where she would go if she left. The driveway curved up-hill to the house. Twenty-two minutes to get back. She toured the house, lifting the dust sheets to examine the furniture, pawed through the drawers.

99

Twenty-six, maybe twenty-seven hours had passed before she finally got up the nerve to try the door to Paul's bedroom. It was locked.

Beth Carol sat cross-legged on the floor in front of the television set, watching John Cameron Swayze and the news while she picked off the last of the pink nail polish. Oh, she longed to go back to Secrets, to have all of those wonderful things done to her. To be pampered, to have her head massaged, her shoulders. To have the manicurist shaping her nails. Good nails, the woman had said. Beth Carol raised her hands, spread her fingers, and examined them. They were nice, she decided. Strong and pink, with white half-moons. On the screen, John Cameron Swayze was saying that another atom bomb had been exploded. There was a grainy, gray picture of a huge cloud billowing in the sky, a hundred times bigger than the newsreel pictures she had seen of the other bombs exploding. Oh, no, she thought. The world is coming to an end. It was awful, the apocalypse. And here she was, alone, hungry. Penniless. And Paul was dead somewhere. He must be dead, or he would have come home by now.

She heard what she thought was a sound, held her breath to hear it better. There were footsteps in the hall outside. Not Paul's, though. Not all light and springy, the way he walked, an athlete's walk. Beth Carol dashed into the bathroom, and locked the door behind her. Her heart was racing in her chest as she stood, her head against the door, listening.

"Beth Carol? Beth Carol, are you in here?"

She felt all of the tension drain out of her as she recognized Paul's voice. But what had happened? He sounded so different, so weary. She unlocked the door and slowly opened it. He was standing in the entrance to the room, his shoulders slumped. There was a Texaco commercial on the television set.

"I've been trying to work things out," he said quietly. "I'm sorry."

"I thought you were dead," she whispered.

"I've got to tell you the truth," he said. "The Jaguar was repossessed. I couldn't make the payments. My trust fund check hasn't come."

So that was it, Beth Carol thought. Everything had an explanation.

"The guy who takes care of the transfer at the bank is on vacation. Nobody else has the authority to do anything about it. I've been beside myself."

"What about your parents—" she began.

"I tried to call. They're out on a yacht somewhere. Nobody can get in touch with them."

This just couldn't be happening, she thought. But it was, of course. Paul was telling her it was happening, turning to her. Opening up to her for the first time. Her thoughts careened off each other. He had been so good to her, done so much. How could she help him? What could she do?

"I'm not taking very good care of you," he said shyly, looking at her from under his long lashes. Looking like a little boy. Oh, he was so sweet, in spite of his temper, his bursts of anger that seemed to come from nowhere. Here he was, after all, with his problems, and what was he thinking about? Not taking good care of her.

"There's only one possibility," he said, taking a few steps toward her, taking her hand. "I hate to ask you this, Beth Carol. I don't know what you'll think of me, but I have to ask you. It's our only chance."

"Ask me, Paul," she begged. "Ask me anything. Nobody's ever treated me the way you have. Golly, you have taken care of me. You've been wonderful. You took me in."

"Well, there's this guy," he said. "He wants some action tonight. A bartender friend of mine happened to mention it, and I jumped at it. 'Beth Carol will understand,' I told myself. 'She'll realize how desperate things are for us.' I told him to set it up."

"What?" she asked blankly.

"The best part is that all he wants to do is watch. They're the easy ones. I've got to find another girl, though. I'll have to make a couple of calls."

"I don't know what you're talking about," she said slowly, but slowly she was beginning to know exactly what he was talking about.

"It's thirty dollars each," he said, his eyes imploring.

"Oh, no," she blurted. "I can't."

"Oh, don't give me this bullshit," he said angrily. "It's okay for you to do it for nothing, but when we need the money to survive, suddenly it isn't."

"That was different," she pleaded. "I had some drinks. I wasn't used to them. I didn't even know what was happening."

"Different," he spat.

"But I didn't even know," she wailed. "It was all a blur, like a dream."

He stood, looking at her, his hands thrust into the pockets of his trousers. His face was livid.

"I'm not a whore," she whispered.

"Okay, you're not a whore," he said quietly, a hideous smile plucking at the corners of his mouth. "So what are you?"

Beth Carol averted her eyes, her legs trembling, as she realized her situation. He would make her leave. He was so furious she would never be able to face him again. And here she was, without a cent. Worse, without Paul. Her lower lip started to quiver and she grabbed the back of a chair for support.

"You don't seem to have much to say," he said, his voice casual, but not at all casual, she realized. She stared, fascinated, at the white spots at the corners of his mouth. "Okay, let me tell you what you are. You're a runaway with scars on your wrists, that's who you are."

"Don't do this to me," she mumbled. "Please."

"What was it?" he said with a sneer. "Some boy? Or worse? You certainly can't claim inexperience, baby."

"Here's my watch," she said, unclasping it with shaky hands, holding it out to him. "You can sell it."

He wouldn't look at her. He just stood there, stiff with fury, as if he were holding himself in so that he wouldn't turn on her, really lash out at her.

"All right," she said. "I'll do it."

Then she was where she had wanted to be all these days since they had met. In his arms. He kissed her hair, her lips. He held her close, stroking her back, her hips.

"Oh, thank you," he whispered. "Thank you, baby. I knew you wouldn't let me down. I knew it."

Beth Carol felt Paul glancing at her as they drove along in one of the Cadillacs. She knew he was embarrassed at what he was asking her to do—ashamed, even. Well, he should be, she thought miserably. Here she loved him with all of her heart, and she knew he loved her, too. So how could he even suggest such a thing, no matter how tight things were without his trust fund check? And that had really hurt, when he'd told her she was just another runaway with scars on her wrists. But, of course, he'd been so mad when he'd said it. That was why. And as awful as it was that he'd asked her to do this, well, what were their options? She gazed morosely out of the window as she reminded herself that they did have to eat, after all. That nobody could live just on love alone, not even the two of them.

Paul took a right onto Ventura Boulevard in the Valley, going slowly now, trying to find the right motel in a veritable city of motels. Just tell him to stop the car and get out and walk away, she told herself, knowing she wouldn't.

"I'll be right in the parking lot," he said anxiously. "Don't worry, really. It'll be all right." And then more of Paul Fournier's famous words to live by. "It's only your body, not your soul. Don't let him come in you unless he's wearing a rubber."

The other girl Paul had gotten was Dru, the pretty brunette who had told Beth Carol she was an actress that first night at the coffee shop on Sunset Boulevard where everybody looked as if they had just walked out of an MGM musical. Beth Carol felt her eyes widen with surprise as Dru closed the door behind her.

It was just an anonymous room in a motel. There was a double bed, a couple of chairs with a table between them.

A bureau with a bottle of scotch, some glasses and an ice bucket. A mirror over it in which she could see her reflection. What's a nice girl like you doing in a place like this? she asked it. She looked about twelve years old and ready to fall on her face.

"He's in the bathroom," Dru said. "You want a drink?"

Beth Carol nodded, nearly dead with fear, as she heard a toilet flush. There wouldn't be anything funny, Paul had told her. The guy just wanted to see her and the other girl go down on each other. Then maybe he'd fuck them. That would be another twenty each. Maybe not. He liked watching better.

"Well, hello, baby," the man said. "I'm glad you could make it."

Beth Carol tried to smile at him, wanting to turn and run out of there. He seemed so ordinary. Just another guy, around forty years old, zipping up his fly, doing up his belt over a little paunch. He had a receding hairline, the beginning of jowls. He wore glasses, a white dress shirt open at the collar to show his undershirt, gray trousers. He sat down on the bed, and Dru sat down beside him. She started to massage his shoulders as she unbuttoned his shirt.

Beth Carol took a gulp of the drink, her eyes wide. I can't do this, she thought as Dru reached up, took her hand, and pulled her down on the bed with the two of them. Hands—his, Dru's—were fumbling at her clothes, peeling off her blouse, her bra. Dru, her mouth open, was kissing her, moaning, as the man took off her panties, then her skirt. Dru was nude now, forcing Beth Carol's head down between her legs, writhing, as the man sucked on her nipples, her mouth. The man prodded inside her with his fingers. Now he was nude, too. Perspiration gleamed on his chest with its scanty hair covering almost womanly breasts, his hairy stomach. He had a little, tiny thing that stuck straight out.

This isn't me, Beth Carol thought, her head whirling, as she pulled herself up and took a long drink of the scotch. The man pulled her down, his wet mouth covering hers, his nails digging into her back. The sheets were a sodden mess, smelled of sweat and sex, spilled scotch. The man was half sitting against the pillows, jerking off, making funny little sounds. Mewing. He jerked Dru's head around, pushed his thing into her mouth, screamed as he came. Beth Carol lay on her stomach, her elbows, panting as she watched them, unable to believe that she was doing this, unable to believe that it would ever end.

An hour passed. Maybe two.

"Thanks for coming, kids," he said when they were at the door. It was fifty for each of them.

Even as she stumbled down the stairs, Beth Carol saw the lights of Paul's car flash on, heard him hit the horn a couple of times. Beth Carol didn't even look at him as she slid into the passenger's side, trying to figure out how she felt. Dirty. Used. It seemed to Beth Carol that even if she lived a million years, she would never forget the feel of the fingers and hands of strangers on her body. Wet mouths all over her.

How could Paul have put her through this? she asked herself as she slumped against the door of the car. Nothing was worth the way this had made her feel. Not even being with Paul.

Still the car didn't move. Beth Carol knew Paul was looking at her, felt him willing her to turn and look at him. But she wouldn't. She sat there, wanting to be sick.

She felt him move toward her, felt his arm around her shoulders, his breath in her hair. With his hand, he turned her face toward him and kissed her, while he stroked her breasts, the curve of her hips, her thighs.

Beth Carol felt her breath coming faster as she opened her mouth to his tongue, licked his lips, grabbed him hard around the waist.

"How could you have made me do that?" she whispered, running her hands over his shoulders, his face. "I love you so. You know that."

"Oh, baby," he crooned, holding her, caressing her thighs, pushing her legs apart. "God, it made me so hot to think of you in there."

He had his fingers in her panties now, fondling her. Beth Carol was so hot she didn't think that she could stand it for a moment more. She dropped her hand onto his fly, felt his thing, so hard to her touch. She unzipped his fly, grabbed it. It was big, so big.

Then he was pulling her panties off, pushing her skirt up to her waist. He switched off the ignition, turned off the headlights, as he dropped his trousers down over his buttocks, started to mount her.

Beth Carol pulled him toward her, found his mouth with her own, wound her legs tightly around his as he pushed into her.

"Yes, yes," he sobbed, his breath coming fast.

He was calling her names, a bitch, a whore. Telling her how hot she made him. And she was calling him names. Darling. My angel. She could taste him in her mouth, the scotch, she didn't know what. She didn't know where she stopped and where he started, or whether they were really one and the same.

"Now. Now," he said, his voice starting as a growling whisper, rising to a scream, as Beth Carol felt him shudder, felt him spurting into her in spasms.

Oh, how she had wanted him, yearned for this. Oh, Paul, she thought, dazed, lying back against the seat of the car, her legs, her arms still wrapped around him as he lay gasping. You'll love me. I'll make you love me.

CHAPTER 12

*T*he hardest thing, Beth Carol found, was going up and knocking on the door. There was always that look of surprise on the guy's face, as if she could have been any-body. A Girl Scout waiting to whip out an order form for cookies. Somebody who had the wrong address. A messen-ger from the lobby downstairs.

She was as discomfited as they were.

"I'm sorry, I seem to have the wrong room," was what she wanted to say. Something like that. But there was always Paul, sitting nervously at the bar downstairs waiting for her to come back, or parked down the street some-where.

Even when she was inside the room, the guy was usually as embarrassed as she was. "Would you like a drink?" was always the first thing, and then there didn't seem to be anyplace much to go for a while. After all, she couldn't exactly ask him why he was in town, ask after the wife and kids, or anything. And what could he say to her? How's business?

What she did was develop a little line of patter. Like she was a student at UCLA, and that she was only doing this to help pay for her tuition. And that the more she looked at him the more attractive she thought he was. He had something, she would say. Something different. Not like the others, although there were only a few. She was so new at this. She was going to get out of it as soon as she could, and how nice it was to meet a nice person like him, and how he couldn't imagine how scary it was, not knowing who was going to be on the other side of the door.

They were all embarrassed about their bodies. Laughed at the little roll of fat they had around their waists. They were all embarrassed because they were losing their hair. "Oh, I love bald men," she would say shyly. "It's so masculine." To a man, they were all embarrassed about the size of their things. It's so small, they would say doubtfully, looking at it as if they had never seen it before. "Oh, no," she would reassure them. "Look, I'm a working girl, and I've seen my share. You're right up there with the best of them." Still, when she'd get down there to take it in her mouth, sometimes she wasn't quite sure she was on target. And they were all so lonely. It was terrible. Five minutes of sex, and two hours of conversation. Nearly every time. Beth Carol felt as if she were collecting unhappy life stories. All these guys in unhappy marriages, with rotten kids, parents who were either recently dead or dying hideous deaths. Stuck in jobs they hated, going nowhere, sure they were going to be fired. And then what? And, truthfully, it did sound sad to her. They all seemed so trapped.

She tapped on one door at a little house on a side street in Hollywood and when it opened, some big guy reeking of after-shave lotion looked down at her. His expression turned from welcome to dismay. Then to anger. "What is this?" he demanded. "Entrapment? You're jailbait."

Then he slammed the door in her face, and she could hear him cursing like crazy as she walked slowly back to the car where Paul had just settled in for a couple of hours with his schoolbooks. Yeah, he did go to school. It wasn't a lie. She'd found out from Darby. He was taking just enough classes so he wouldn't be drafted for Korea. And Darby was the best source on it. He was doing the same thing.

The birthday cake had been awful. Somebody's stag party, and there she was crouched inside it in a little G-string and pasties, sweating like a pig because it was so hot. She felt like a contortionist in that position and it occurred to her that if her cue didn't come soon, she would probably just pass out from the heat, and when the cake opened, she would be lying there unconscious. Finally she heard the strains of "A Pretty Girl Is Like a Melody," and she pushed open the top of the cake and rose to her feet, her arms out, a big smile on her face, while all those yo-yos hooted and screamed and applauded, and the groom-to-be looked as if he would like to fall through the floor with embarrassment. She did a little dance she had practiced to the radio at the house, and smiled and smiled, while the guys cheered and laughed and had a great old time.

She'd really earned her money that night, though, and a bonus, too. They all but attacked her, right there in the private dining room of one of the best restaurants in town. They were pulling at the G-string and pushing her down, and some guy had his head between her legs, going down on her, while all of his buddies cheered him on, and Beth Carol struggled to get free. That hadn't been part of the deal, and she was on the verge of making a big scene when she thought, Oh, well, why ruin it for everybody?

What she did love was the admiration, the fact that all these guys not only wanted her, but were willing to pay for it. And not just for the sex. To talk. To confide in her because nobody else in their lives would listen to them. Because they were supposed to be big and strong, and to know it all. Because to be unsure, afraid, was to be weak, and that wasn't what a man was supposed to be.

"Beth Carol," said a voice, as she sat in Bobby's chair, having her hair combed out one day. "I didn't know you came here."

Beth Carol turned and saw that it was Dru, the girl she had been with at that motel with the guy. Dru had a big smile on her face, as she slid into the chair next to Beth Carol where the customers waiting for Bobby always sat. Talk about wanting to drop through the floor! Golly, she just about died.

"Hi," she said weakly.

"So what's new?" Dru asked brightly, looking at her own expression in the mirror, narrowing her eyes as she leaned forward. "Bobby, I've been thinking about becoming a redhead," she said. "What do you think?"

"The new Susan Hayward," Bobby said in that soft voice of his, a hint of amusement. "I like it. What a terrific idea." He looked at Beth Carol in the mirror. "What do you think? Don't you think it's a wonderful idea?"

"Yes, it's great," said Beth Carol in this little voice.

But then they were all talking and laughing together like old friends who saw each other all the time, and Bobby was telling them about Hedda Hopper, his newest client, who didn't wash her hair for three months at a time, and how it was all wound up in a lot of rats, so she wore those hats because if she didn't, it would probably all fall out. And there had been the awful scene in the salon a couple of days earlier when a handsome movie star who lived in the neighborhood, but was such a drunk, had somehow gotten into the supply room and had rampaged through the place, wrapping everything in rolls of toilet paper—the plants, the chairs, the lamps, the customers. Everything.

"Of course, wouldn't you know that it would be a Saturday," Bobby said. "Our busiest day."

Nobody had called the cops, though. That would have made it even worse. After a while, he got bored and left.

Beth Carol kept glancing at Dru's reflection in the mirror as Dru prattled away about a great audition she'd been on for a fifteen-minute soap that would run five days a week. Dru was wearing a sleeveless dress of dusty rose with a chiffon scarf tied around the neck. She looked so fresh and pretty that she could have stepped right off the front of a bottle of Breck shampoo.

"It's the ingenue," she said. "Only they want a redhead."

"Gosh, that's terrific," Beth Carol said, but all she could see was the two of them in that motel room out on Ventura Boulevard with that guy.

One of the cute little colored girls who worked there came up and took Dru off to have her hair washed, and Bobby leaned over, lit a cigarette with a gold lighter as thin as a half-dollar.

"You're getting a reputation, Beth Carol," he said in that confidential voice of his. "You've got to be more careful."

Chills shot through her and all the hairs on her arms stood up straight. She was so upset she could hardly speak.

"Oh, no," she whispered.

"And that boyfriend of yours, the dark kid who brings you. He's supposed to be some kind of drug dealer."

"No, Bobby," she said firmly. "That's not true. He's rich. You've got to come up and see the house, the grounds. Golly, there's even a lake. So why would he do something like that?"

"I don't know. But that's what they say."

It started off the same way all of them did. The address this time was just off the Sunset Strip, up the street a few hundred feet from Restaurant LaRue, one of the most elegant restaurants in town. It was in a cluster of smart little houses staggered on landscaped lots around an Olympic-sized swimming pool and two championship tennis courts, where a couple of girls were batting balls across the net under the lights.

The guy who opened the door promptly at nine o'clock was really cute, Beth Carol saw with surprise. He couldn't have been much over thirty, with sandy hair, a great smile, and a terrific tan. So sophisticated, too, in a smoking jacket, his cigarette in an ebony holder.

"I'm Don," he said, stepping aside so that she could go in.

"I'm Jane," she said.

"Can I fix you a drink?" he asked. "How about a vodka gimlet?"

"That's fine," she said, looking around.

It was a charming room, with Danish modern furniture, all blond and sleek looking. One whole wall was a window, looking out on hibiscus bushes, oleanders, the swimming pool. There was a baby grand piano in one corner, open sheets of music. Something classical on the stereo. Great-looking guy, great place. Why did he have to pay for it? she wondered. Golly, he could have anybody. She was surprised he wasn't beating them off.

"I hope this is okay," he said, handing her the drink in a pretty crystal glass. Modern, too, with the skinniest stem that looked as if it would break if she held it too hard.

"It looks fine," she said. "Thanks."

"Would you like to sit down?" he asked.

"Oh, yes, thanks," she said, moving toward the sofa.

And then she saw them. Two balls of fur that separated, yawned, stretched. Siamese kittens that couldn't have been more than three or four months old.

"Oh," she exclaimed. "They're so cute. Adorable."

"Mahler and Mozart." He grinned. "I'm a musician."

"Oh, they're so cute," she repeated, dropping to her knees to pet them, to hold them, to caress their silky fur. Oh, how good they felt against her skin, their little tongues scraping at her hands.

"You're quite a surprise," he said, sitting down beside her.

She looked at him expectantly, cradling one of the kittens to her cheek, hearing its purr.

"You're so pretty, for one thing," he said. "And you look like a high school girl."

"Oh, I'm not," she assured him.

"But you look like one," he said. "That makes it even better."

He touched her glass with his own and smiled at her. "Drink up," he said. "We're going to have a lot of fun."

Usually Beth Carol just nursed one drink through an entire evening, but Don was urging her to finish it, pouring her another one, smiling as he handed it to her. She took a sip, feeling a little strange. Her eyes weren't quite focusing, her thoughts seemed confused. Absently she petted one of the kittens as it batted at her hand. She was hardly aware of it when Don picked her up, pushed open a door, and laid her down on a double bed. She tried to sit up, looked at him. Two of him, now. Don One, and Don Two, kind of weaving in and out of each other. Oh, golly, she thought, her mind a blur. This wasn't right, couldn't be right. He'd put something in her drink. That had to be it.

Her head dropped to the pillow as he moved her around like a rag doll undressing her, then stepping out of his own clothes. He—they—had their things in their hands, moving them back and forth, making them hard. Deftly, he flipped her over, whipped cords around her wrists, cords around her ankles, spread-eagling her on the bed.

"No, you can't do this—" she started to say, but he shoved something into her mouth, tied it in place. He's a madman, she thought, her mind trying to form the letters into a word. I'm going to die. Murdered. She gasped, tried to scream against the gag, nearly passing out at the excruciating pain as he thrust something into her sex, something big and smooth. Like glass. Desperately she tried to raise her head, tried to make the sounds come. I'm dying now, she thought with wonder. And then, unconsciousness. Blessed unconsciousness.

Paul was sitting on the bed next to her, bathing her face with a warm cloth, when she fought her way back to consciousness. The cords that had bound her lay on the floor.

"That fucker," Paul muttered, holding her in his arms, his breath coming fast. "And in his own house, too. He didn't even get a motel room, didn't even use a phony name."

Beth Carol whimpered with pain, heard something new in Paul's voice. Why, he's scared, she thought. He's out of control. Just a kid.

"He leaves the door unlocked," he said to himself. "He just goes out and gets in his car and drives away, leaving you here like this."

He was wiping the inside of her thighs, her buttocks.

The bottom of the bedspread was spattered with blood. My blood, she realized. Oh, no. This couldn't have happened.

Paul found her clothes, awkwardly dressed her as she lay on the bed, moaning. As Paul carried her through the living room, she was vaguely aware that everything was neat and tidy again. The glasses had been washed, the ashtrays emptied. In the corner, the kittens played, batting each other with their paws.

"Isn't it beautiful?" asked Bobby, holding out his hand, his wrist. There was something triumphant in his voice.

Beth Carol started, looked at his reflection in the mirror. Golly, would she ever stop feeling so shaky? Oh, she had been so scared, and so had Paul. He'd hovered over her, brought her soup. He looked so worried all the time, beside himself. But it hadn't been anything much. Not physically, anyway. It was the way it had made her feel that was the problem. So vulnerable, as if anybody could do anything they wanted to her at any time, anywhere.

"If it was going to be rough sex," Paul said indignantly, "he had to say so. I never would have let you go in there. Never."

Beth Carol had lain there, wondering whether Paul was so solicitous because he'd be implicated in some way if she were really hurt. That was an awful thing to think, though, after the way he had taken her in, the good times they'd had together before his trust fund check hadn't come. But there were other things that were starting to bother her about the whole situation. That rumor Bobby had told her that Paul was a drug dealer. All those places they had gone where Paul had disappeared into the parking lot or the men's room. She even remembered Dru's words that first night, that Paul was out there doing business.

Beth Carol looked at the beautiful identification bracelet on Bobby's wrist, looked up into his handsome face, his twinkling eyes.

"This is white gold," he said, fingering the heavy links,

"and this is, well, I guess you'd call it gold gold, wouldn't you?"

"Maybe just gold," she suggested. "It's really beautiful."

"It's from Bulgari," he said happily. "Bulgari's the best. They took me to New York last weekend, and we stayed at the Plaza. Well, they know how much I love presents. So they took me to Bulgari and they said I could have anything I wanted."

It was funny how Bobby always said *they* when Beth Carol was pretty sure he meant *he*. She guessed that it was because he didn't want anybody to know he was queer, although he didn't have to bother. Not really. After all, all the other boys in the shop were, and, who cared? He picked up a wet tendril and wound it quickly around a pink curler, then another.

"You never should have gone up there," he whispered, close to her ear. "Everybody knows about him. It's always rough sex. He really hurt a girl a couple of months ago. He put her in the hospital. One of these days he'll do worse than that."

"What are you talking about?" she asked.

"That boyfriend of yours knew," he said. "He gets around. He let you walk right in there."

A shiver went through her.

"I don't know what you mean," she said.

"You should have asked me," Bobby said. "I would have told you, Beth Carol. I want to help you, I want to be your friend. You're not like these other girls, hard as nails. Harder. There's something so soft about you, so sweet. Men like that. We have to take care of each other, don't you see? Use them before they use us."

CHAPTER 13

$\mathcal{I}$t was another perfect day, Beth Carol saw, as Paul backed the big Packard out of the garage. The sky was an even pale blue, like a kid would do in a coloring book. The sun made what looked like golden crowns on the tops of all of the trees, made the lake all shimmery and magical. The flowers in their beds were all so bright and lovely that it didn't seem possible they were real flowers. No, they must be an illusion, like everything else here in Los Angeles that looked so splendid on the surface, and which was so corrupt and dangerous underneath. She thought of the joke everybody was always telling about it here, how underneath the fake tinsel there was the real tinsel. But even that wasn't the way it was. Nothing here was the way it seemed to be.

She glanced over at Paul, saw the curve of his cheek, the way his hair sort of feathered around his ears, well shaped and close to his head. She hadn't been able to believe it a few nights after that horrible incident with Don when Paul had come in and said that there was someone for that night, but that it was okay. A repeat who had especially asked for her. Beth Carol sat there, staring at him, realizing that nothing had changed. Oh, maybe he would be more careful about who she went with, but that was all.

"Listen," she said after a couple of minutes, "there's something I want to ask you."

"You better get dressed, baby." He grinned. "This guy is waiting for you. He really likes you."

"Paul, did you really think you knew me that night we met?"

She watched with a sinking feeling as all of the blood drained out of his face. He looked stricken, so hurt she might as well have stabbed him with a knife.

"How can you even ask me such a thing?" he asked finally, his voice choked. "Look, if you don't believe in me, Beth Carol, we don't have anything."

She sat there, shifting uncomfortably in the chair, asking herself if she believed in him. Well, of course she did. It was just that there were all of these little inconsistencies that tugged at the corners of her mind. Things that didn't quite add up somehow.

"Oh, Paul," she said unhappily. "Don't be upset. Please. I believe in you. I do."

"You've got to, baby," he said, pulling her up, holding her close. "You're the girl I love. You know that."

And she knew he meant it, that he loved her. Because nobody would say such an important thing unless it were true.

Beth Carol never had any trouble in the hotels with house detectives or elevator operators. As Paul told her, she was just too young looking, too well-bred looking, and too well dressed to be anything other than a guest. That night, though, the elevator operator in his uniform and white gloves was really looking at her in a funny way. Beth Carol knew why, too. She was so scared, shaking so much that she knew she looked as if she were about to faint.

"Are you all right, miss?" he asked as the door swung open on her floor.

"I think it was too much sun at the pool today," she said, trying to smile. "The sun is so beautiful here in California."

"Well, I hope you enjoy the rest of your stay, miss," he said, smiling back at her. "If I may suggest it, you might think about wearing a hat when you go out tomorrow."

"Thank you," she said, stepping out of the car. "Good night."

She didn't know how she made it, but there she was,

actually at the room. She must have stood there for a couple of minutes, trying to get up the nerve to knock. Behind the door was somebody she sort of remembered as young and sweet and well mannered, and downstairs, waiting, was Paul.

The man who opened the door was still in his late twenties, even though he was going bald. He had big blue eyes, a turned-up nose, and a mouth like a Kewpie doll. He was tall, too, and the hand he extended to her had long, sensitive fingers. He didn't look at all like a businessman, which was the first thing Beth Carol remembered when Paul told her who it was. No, he looked more like a gentleman, with the same sort of refined air that Paul had. He was smiling at her, really glad to see her, Beth Carol thought, pleased.

"Come in," he said shyly.

It was the living room of a suite, with sofas facing each other across a coffee table, good prints on the wall. There were vases of roses, a bottle of champagne cooling in an ice bucket. Beth Carol stood uncertainly, looking around, wondering if he had gone to all of this trouble for her.

"I'm really happy you were able to come," he said. "I've been thinking about you. All the time, in fact."

"Well, thank you," she said, blushing, trying to remember what had happened between them. Nothing special, she remembered. Quick sex, no more than a couple of minutes. And then he had wanted to talk and so she had listened to him for hours.

And it turned out that he had gone to all this trouble just for her. It made her feel terrific. He watched her anxiously as she sipped the champagne, waiting for her approval, almost relieved when it came. She tried to describe to herself how all of this was making her feel and finally, she got it. Powerful. In control.

Later, after they were through, he went over to the dresser and took out a little box, gift-wrapped, dripping with ribbons. It was a gold bracelet with a charm, a rainbow with tiny sapphires, rubies, and topazes.

"Golly, thanks," she said as he put it on her wrist, swelling with pride as she realized this was her first gift from a guy who was smitten with her. "That's so sweet of you."

"Do you really like it?" he asked, and this time he was the one blushing.

"Oh, yes," she said, barely able to wait for the next time she went to the beauty salon so she could show it to Bobby, show him that he wasn't the only one who got great presents for services rendered.

Then he told her he would like to take her out to dinner, and she said that she couldn't because she was, well, going with someone. And she thought that must have sounded pretty dumb to him because it wasn't twenty minutes ago that they had been writhing around together and he was in her, and now she was telling him she couldn't have dinner with him.

"But you'll see me again?" he said, looking hurt.

"Oh, sure," she said, kissing his cheek as she left, thanking him again for the adorable bracelet.

He wasn't the only one, either. There were other special requests for her, other gifts. A guy said he'd like to set her up in an apartment and give her a car and an allowance. But he was married and unattractive. Still, she was flattered. By him. By all of them. By the attention, the presents. By the big tips that were just for her and which Paul didn't know about. And what he didn't know wouldn't hurt him.

Whenever she was alone, she counted the money. Nearly four hundred dollars now, more than she had lost with her wallet. She pretty much knew what she could get for the bits of jewelry, too. Thanks to Bobby. He would hold the trinkets up to the lights surrounding the mirror, half close his eyes, think for a moment, and pronounce the price. Honestly, you'd think sometimes he could be a jeweler the way he did it. And that was nearly three hundred dollars more if she pawned it, nearly a thousand if she sold it. Trophies. That was the way she thought about things. More trophies. That was the way she thought about the compliments, the admiring looks, the words she heard so often. "You're the only one who has ever listened to me." It was sort of like money in the bank.

Anyway, the things were nice to have. Just in case. A little buffer, something of her own in case she found herself out on the street one fine day. At least it would get her started in an apartment. Of course, she didn't know what she would do. She didn't know how to make the contacts to keep on doing what she was doing, and besides, without someone to intercede for her, it would be too dangerous, anyway. She'd considered Bobby, but that wouldn't do. He was too involved with himself, with feathering his own nest.

So she just didn't know. Sometimes it would be great between her and Paul. There would be money from somewhere. Not the trust fund, though. He never mentioned that anymore. They would rush around and go to dinner and have fun and he would buy her clothes, lavish her with compliments. Then he would get all gloomy again and start to whine about how they didn't have any money and they couldn't even eat. Well, they could eat with what she brought in, but they couldn't eat on the level Paul was talking about. At Frascati's. Scandia. Perino's. The places he liked to go.

Then he'd start coming up with all of these crazy ideas to make money. It wasn't what he did when he was flush, with money, which, she was pretty sure, was from drug dealing. That had been why they met, why he had been at the Hollywood bus station. That was where the drug dealers picked up the marijuana that came in from wherever it was grown. And then supplies had dried up, and that was when he'd turned her out. Turned her into a whore. But, of course, he hadn't turned her into anything. If she hadn't wanted to do it, she could have left. But she wanted to stay with him, so there it was. But if it was the marijuana that gave them the money to go to the terrific places, what about the trust fund? Was there a trust fund, or was it just that there wasn't enough? Now he was talking about getting another Jaguar on the proceeds of this new scheme. A movie. Not dirty, not really. Not just some grainy film of a guy and girl making it for a couple of minutes, but a movie with a real story, taste, good lighting, production values. Darby would shoot it, of course. The point was to get away from piecework. She'd smiled at that in spite of herself. No, the thing was to make money while you slept, to have your product out there all the time producing revenue while you went on to other projects to produce more revenue.

"I won't do it," she said, shaking her head. "You can't ask me to do this, Paul. I mean, golly, what if somebody recognizes me?"

"Nobody will recognize you," he assured her, his eyes glittering in that way they did when he was really manic. "You'll wear a wig, Cleopatra makeup, chiffon. It's all part of the plot."

"What about the guy?" she asked.

"He's just some kid. Cute. He works in a gas station on Hollywood Boulevard. We have to give him a hundred. He's being thrown out of his room."

"What about you?" she asked. "Will you be there?"

"Well, of course I'll be there," he said. "I'm the producer, for God's sake."

"Then I'm not going to do it. Not if you're there."

So they'd agreed on that. He could be there for all the setting up, fine. But not for the actual filming. She didn't even think about Darby. That she would be making it with some guy and Darby would be there, filming it. Darby, with his superiority problem and his phony black patch because he thought it was so chic.

It was going to be filmed in the big stone room in the Houdini mansion where Darby had his apartment. It had been a ballroom at one time, and now some of the other kids who lived there used it on New Year's Eve for parties, or, once, when somebody got married. It was very private during the week, though, with everybody off at work, doing whatever it was they did while they tried to break into show business.

Beth Carol had expected, maybe, Darby and a camera, the guy, the other girl who was going to be in it with her. The two girls, that was what was important, Paul said. You had to let guys who would watch it have their fantasies about girls who just wanted to do it all the time, and how, if only they were in the right place at the right time, the girls would do it with them, although in real life nobody would even be seen with them on the street. So it was the two girls, Beth Carol, in a long blond wig, playing the wood sprite, and the other girl, in a long brown wig, playing her attendant in the forest. That was important, too, Paul had said—the color of the hair. Guys responded to blondes. He would have made the other girl blond, too, but at least the brown would be some contrast so there wouldn't be any question about who was who. The guy would just come in at the end for a minute or two, made up like a satyr with horns. He was the surrogate for all of those guys out there who couldn't get a date. So he didn't matter. It was just the girls.

Paul and his psychology, she thought bitterly as they walked through the open door into the entryway leading down to the stone room. Paul, who could only get it off with her just after she'd been with somebody else. Boy, if anybody needed to go to see a psychiatrist, which it seemed that everybody was doing these days, it was Paul.

Excited voices drifted up the stairs, one of them Darby's barking an order about some lights. Oh, golly, Beth Carol thought with a sinking feeling in her stomach, everybody in town is going to be here. There were maybe six, seven guys rushing around, adjusting lights on the set, which did look like a meadow with the backdrop somebody had painted, the fake grass, the rocks somebody had lugged in, a few trees in disguised pots. It looked so realistic Beth Carol was startled for a moment. They were all arguing, too, about how the sequences should go, and what effect they were after in this shot, that shot. You'd think they were shooting *Citizen Kane*, the way they were going on. A guy took her arm and led her over to a makeshift makeup table. And look at Darby, she thought, smiling. A cravat. Men, she thought. They were such show-offs, such babies. She looked at the other guys, wondering which of them was going to be in the movie. They all looked pretty much alike. Maybe he wasn't here yet.

Beth Carol saw in the mirror that the other girl was picking her way down the stairs into the glare of the lights set up all over the place. It was Myra, some stripper Paul knew who worked at the Pink Pussycat down on Santa Monica Boulevard. She was nice. Beth Carol had been with her before with some businessmen from Chicago who had wanted to party. The makeup guy handed Beth Carol a smock and she looked around for someplace to change. No pantie girdle or stockings today. Not even a bra under her dress. So there wouldn't be any lines, Paul said. Well, it was fine for her. She didn't have all that much anyway. Beth Carol smiled as she wondered how Myra felt about it. Myra was really voluptuous. She could knock a guy over with her boobs. Beth Carol and Myra said hi to each other as Myra went to change into a robe, too, and the makeup guy started to work on Beth Carol. A major motion picture production, Beth Carol thought with amazement. It was incredible.

The makeup guy was patting on foundation, smudging Beth Carol's eyelids with sooty gray eye shadow, slathering on black eyeliner, gluing on curly black fake eyelashes. Beth Carol watched him work in the mirror. She was starting to look just like Cleopatra, she saw. It felt good, as if she were wearing a mask, as if she were hidden from everybody but could still see everything that was going on. Two of the guys were standing in for them on the set Beth Carol saw, as Darby barked directions and Paul stood, his hands in his pockets, nodding approval. Somebody brought Beth Carol a cup of coffee just as the makeup guy was painting on her new mouth. She wiggled her fingers and rolled her eyes to thank him. The makeup guy was on his knees, painting her toenails. Finally he was pinning the blond wig in place. From Western Costume down on Melrose next to Paramount Studios, Beth Carol knew, where the movie studios rented stuff.

She looked at herself in the mirror, at the soft blond waves around her face, at the blue eyes emphasized by the dark makeup, at the vivid mouth. Paul was right. Her own father wouldn't have recognized her.

"Let's do a run-through," Darby called in his usual

officious voice, and the two of them sauntered to the back of the set where they were supposed to make their entrance, clutching their smocks around them.

The plot was simple enough. Beth Carol was supposed to glide onto the set with her arms outstretched, looking ethereal, with Myra floating along just behind her. They would sort of dance around in their gauzy costumes and then Beth Carol would swoon onto the grass and Myra would kneel, looking solicitous. Slowly Myra would undress her, start to caress her and the rest, and she was supposed to look as if she were getting hot, and then she would undress Myra. Then the guy would come in and they would do a threesome, and that would be that. It was only going to be eight minutes, after all, and there wasn't even any sound. That would be dubbed in later. A lot of moaning, and classical music so the guys watching it would be able to feel they had seen something uplifting instead of just another blue movie with three people doing it.

Beth Carol could barely make out the guys watching because the lights were so strong, so bright as she glided onto the set, but she knew the whole crew was paying strict attention as she sank to the fake grass, picked at a fake flower, and felt Myra folding away the gauze that covered her boobs. There were little titters of embarrassed laughter from around the room, for one thing. So they were really getting off on it.

Myra mimed going down on her, and at the end of it the guy came in, wearing jockey shorts, a T-shirt, and short brown socks that just covered his ankles. He was just another guy, Beth Carol saw. Around twenty, and looking embarrassed.

The whole thing was taking forever, she thought as the hours passed. Something was always wrong. The lights. The poses. She looked like a cow when she made her entrance.

"Glide!" Darby shouted. "Keep your arms up, for God's sake."

When he came over to position her, to show her what he wanted, she felt the impatience in his touch, saw it in the set of his jaw, smelled his after-shave lotion as he leaned close to her. Did she want him to see her doing it? Beth Carol wondered. Did she want to tempt him into making another run at her so she could say no, tell Paul his best boyfriend was betraying him? But Darby was strictly professional, she realized, disappointed. He could have been moving around an inanimate object.

After a while, it really got tedious. The crew lost interest, too. Everything was strictly business, especially with Darby. Beth Carol wondered if Paul had kept his word and left the room while the actual shoot was going on. He could tell her anything and she wouldn't know the difference. It was the lights. They were so hot, so bright, she couldn't see anything. The makeup guy came over to dry her off with a towel, pat on more makeup. Somebody brought in sandwiches from Greenblatt's down at the bottom of the hill and they broke for lunch.

It was late afternoon before they finally started to shoot the last scene with the guy making it with the two of them. It was really awful, too, because he just couldn't manage to get his thing up, no matter how he diddled it. He just kept trying while Beth Carol and Myra sat there, and Darby tried to be encouraging and patient, and the crew smoked cigarettes and waited for the magical moment when it would work. She could understand, though, why he couldn't. When they had started, all those hours ago, probably every guy in the crew wished he were this guy, wished he could be the one who could make it with these two girls. But then there was the reality. The lights. Having to get it up in front of the girls, all the other guys who were probably feeling as embarrassed for him as Beth Carol was. Even Darby was looking as if he didn't quite know what he was going to do about it. They had to have the scene, after all, or there was no movie.

Myra was sucking on him now, while he stood there, looking as if he was just going to die of humiliation. Then Beth Carol gave it a try, and it worked, sort of. He got hard enough to put it in her, with the camera in close, and she closed her eyes and tried to look ecstatic. But just about as soon as he had it in, he lost it. It was soft. You just had to feel so sorry for guys sometimes. They never knew what it would do, never knew that it would work. No wonder they had so much to prove all the time.

The big finale was supposed to be when the guy pulled it out of her and came all over her stomach, her breasts, her face. Well, finally he managed to get it about half hard again, and at last he managed to milk a few globs on her breasts, and Darby said it was a wrap.

With a john, it was so different. He would admire her, tell her how pretty she was, but this made her feel just ghastly, like a side of beef in a butcher shop. And the crew had been so excited, but after a while they might as well have been shooting a documentary on potash mining, or something. Usually after she'd been with somebody, Paul couldn't wait to get her home and make it with her. Not this time, though. He seemed so preoccupied as they drove back home that he might as well have been in Arizona.

"It's going to look great when it's put together," he said at last. "The guy was a disappointment, but all of the elements are there. A little editing, the sound track. We'll do fine with it."

Now he was going to say something about her, she realized. She could feel it coming. She didn't believe for a minute that he had kept his promise. That he had left when she was being filmed. Oh, he had been there, all right. Back behind the lights where she couldn't see him.

"That was disgusting," he said, "you swinging on that guy's cock, trying to get him hard."

So it was just the way she had known it would be if Paul actually saw her with somebody, how he would feel about it. That she was dirt. Here he was, always saying that it was only her body, and he didn't believe it any more than she did. She did what he wanted and he hated her for it. That was the truth of the matter. Damned if I do, damned if I don't, she thought miserably. If only I didn't love him. But there was no point to even think about that. Because she did love him. She really did.

CHAPTER 14

*B*eth Carol sensed the difference in the atmosphere in Secrets the moment she stepped through the front door. Usually there would be a buzz of excitement because some movie star had just come in. Like Barbara Payton, that pretty blonde who was going with Franchot Tone and Sonny Tufts, too, and they had had a big fight over her in some nightclub on the Strip. She was really something, strutting around with her smock open and nothing under it, showing everybody all she had, although Beth Carol couldn't really figure out why. The boys who worked there either didn't care or they were terrified, and the other girls just thought it was sort of common. She'd seen Shelly Winters, too, and Claire Trevor. She'd even seen Hedy Lamarr one day, just as she was getting out of Bobby's chair. That was a thrill and a surprise, too, because usually Bobby went up to her house and did her there.

Or there were the girls who ran around with gangsters like that Mickey Cohen, who had wonderful jewelry and wore beautiful clothes and who all looked like show girls. There were other girls who got a lot of envy, the ones who were kept by rich guys, who had those guys wrapped around their little fingers. Then there were the hookers, like Dru, who said they were actresses or models. The other hookers who didn't pretend.

127

Everybody seemed to have a story, especially the girls who weren't gangster's molls, movie stars, kept women, or hookers. Their conversations were about their kids, their clothes, their diets and vacations, their servants, psychiatrists, and their interior decorators. Mostly, though, they talked about the guys in their lives. If it was an ex-husband, it would be about the fights they were having to get their alimony, and how the child support wasn't enough and how the husbands never saw the kids, or when they did, how they took them out and bought them a lot of stuff to make the mom look bad.

And the way they talked about the husbands, the boyfriends, was as if they were these jerks who had to be led around by the nose so they'd go to work and make the money so these girls could sit around with their friends and have their hair done and everything, and brag about what they had.

But there was something else that Beth Carol heard in their voices, too. Yes, the contempt was there and it was real, as if these girls were asking what kind of a sucker would let himself be used this way. But there was also fear. She'd overheard people who worked for her father talk about him in the same tone of voice. Yes, the contempt. Even loathing. But they were scared because they were at his pleasure. He could fire them and he didn't even have to have a reason. Well, maybe it was like that with these wives and girlfriends, too. All the guy had to do was find another girl, and they were out. Then the wife would slide into the company of the divorced girls whose only hope was to find another guy to marry so he could take care of them.

So there they all were, being dyed and combed and massaged, preening and practicing their wiles, comparing strategies, trying to stay ahead of the game, trying to keep the guy off balance, interested. Beth Carol would watch them, trying to learn what worked, as they would hold the hand of the boy lighting their cigarette, looking up at him from under their lashes. Stuff like that. She tried it and the guys really got unnerved, flustered. So it worked.

Beth Carol decided that she wanted to be like the girls who really could wrap a guy around their little fingers, so she watched them most. But she also wanted to be married, to belong to someone who would love her and take care of her. And, in time, she wanted a baby of her own, someone who would belong to her, whom she could take care of forever. Sometimes she even dreamed of walking down the aisle of a beautiful church beside her father, the most beautiful bride in the world. One of the girls would have done her makeup, another her nails. Bobby was there, too. Combing out her hair, helping to adjust her long veil. Her dress was *peau de soie* with a high collar and hand-embroidered antique lace around her throat and at the cuffs of its long sleeves. And it had a long train, a very long train. She could almost hear the organ music, visualize the white bows tied on every pew, see the well-dressed guests. Paul, waiting for her at the altar in gray-striped trousers, a black tailcoat with a sprig of baby's breath from her bouquet as a boutonniere, his gray silk cravat. His best man next to him, nervous about finding the ring at the right time. She tried to keep the face of Paul's best man vague, to be filled in later, when the time came. But Darby's face kept attaching itself to the best man's body. It was inevitable, she supposed. A guy's best friend was always his best man.

When the nurse put the baby into her arms for the first time, he was wrapped in a blue blanket. She would look down into his face and his blue eyes would open, his dimples would dance. She would stroke his blond head, and he would clutch her finger with one of his tiny, perfect hands. She would push down the top of her pretty nightgown and feel him suckling at her breast with his rosebud mouth, while Paul stood beside the bed with a proud, possessive look on his darkly handsome face.

All of these hard times without the trust fund check would be behind them. Paul's parents would be there. So proud of him, of her. Of their first grandson. And Diana. She would be there, too. Smiling down at her baby nephew, tears misting her eyes. Sometimes it was even Diana who was the maid of honor in the wedding party. That made Beth Carol feel guilty, though, because it should really be her sister Linda Marie, because they had been so close and all growing up. But whoever she picked as her maid of honor, everything would be all right and the important thing was that nobody would be mad and they would all live happily ever after.

That was what everybody had in mind here at Secrets, all these girls, all the people who worked there. They were all trying to find the key so they could live happily ever after, trying to find the formula so they would be loved. It seemed to Beth Carol that voices were never raised at Secrets. No, it was like a temple of women, and conversations were murmured—whispered, even.

Today, though, it was so quiet it was almost eerie, and the lady paying her bill at the reservation desk was sobbing into a little lace handkerchief.

"What's the matter?" Beth Carol asked the girl behind the desk, her voice loud to her ears. The girl looked strange. Her face under her makeup was pale and her eyes looked as if she'd been crying, too. Beth Carol felt a little chill of foreboding run down her spine.

"It's Norman. There's been an accident. He's dead."

But Norman was the cute one who was always mincing around and putting everybody on and saying bitchy things that you couldn't help but laugh at. Shirley Booth went to him. He couldn't be dead.

"Oh, no," Beth Carol said. "Was it a car accident?"

"He was murdered," the girl said in a choked voice, tears standing in the corners of her eyes.

Murdered. But people only got murdered in the movies. It was unthinkable.

And then the colored girl washed her hair and Beth Carol was in Bobby's chair and he was telling her all about what happened in that feathery voice of his, but gleeful in a way, as if he were sort of enjoying the excitement. Norman, he told her, had been into rough trade and he was always cruising Hollywood Boulevard, or Ivar, down from that big newsstand, or the men's rooms in drive-ins. This time, though, he'd picked up the wrong kids. Soldiers, probably, who were out for a good time. Not that the cops knew they were soldiers. What they did know was that there had been four of them, because there were five glasses that had been used. Maybe things had just gotten out of hand, because Norman liked to be tied up and beaten. Anyway, they'd beaten him to death with one of those things from a fireplace. An andiron, that was it.

They'd robbed the house, too. They always did. They'd taken all the good silver that Norman's mother had left him, his six watches, all his gold cuff links. Oh, and they'd stolen the car, which was stupid.

"I mean, who would be dumb enough to steal a 1948 MG-TC roadster with wire wheels?" Bobby asked. "The cops will find it in a minute."

"I don't see why you think they could have been soldiers," Beth Carol said. "Don't they have rules about that in the army?"

And then Bobby was explaining how they didn't like boys, how they really liked girls. But maybe you didn't have the money to pay for a girl, or maybe you didn't even have the money to buy a girl a drink and hope. A queer would pay you, and he'd give you liquor and drugs if there were any around, and, face it. Sex was sex. It was just too bad when it got out of hand, like with Norman.

"Well, they'll find them," Beth Carol said. "They'll go to the gas chamber."

"Oh, the cops won't do anything," Bobby said. "It's just another fag murder. It happens all the time."

"Oh, Bobby," Beth Carol said. "That can't be true."

"You know the cops who care about fags?" Bobby said. "The cops on the vice squad. You know what they do? They stand around in men's rooms at the urinal and they have it in their hands. Then they wait for someone to make a pass. Then they bust them. They do it in the fag bars, too. And in the men's rooms at drive-ins."

"Why do they care?" Beth Carol asked, feeling a little uncomfortable—guilty, even—at some of the things she had done. "Why can't people just do what they want? Who are they hurting?"

"Well, it's illegal," Bobby said, looking puzzled. "It's soliciting."

"Well, still," she said lamely.

Then Bobby was prattling on, telling her about some of the other things that went on. About the holes in the walls between the stalls in some of the men's rooms where one guy would put his thing through it and the guy on the other side would suck it and they never saw each other. Or how on weekends they were all lined up on Santa Monica Boulevard behind that Safeway near Robertson, and how they made it on people's lawns, in the alleys, and how it drove all the neighbors crazy and they were always on the phone to the police.

The more Bobby told her, the more nauseated Beth Carol felt. Looking at him in the mirror, she just couldn't believe he would be capable of doing such things. But he had to be talking about himself, she decided, or how would he know?

Bobby's eyes met hers.

"You've got the wrong idea about me," he said, flushing.

"I wasn't thinking anything," she said quickly, her face burning, too. "I was just wondering why they did it, what they're looking for."

"True love," he said.

"Like that?" she asked.

"Yes," he said.

That night Beth Carol was still thinking about how awful it was about Norman as she knocked on the door at the house in the Hollywood Hills. Poor Norman, all bloody, his head crushed in with an andiron. And she was thinking, too, about all the other guys Bobby had told her were really fags, the movie stars the studios had to protect. Rock Hudson, Bobby had said. She just couldn't believe that. Why, he was so tall and handsome and masculine. He'd even been a truck driver, she'd read somewhere. The boys in the shop, well, some of them were as feminine as she was, as feminine as the most feminine of the girls who went there. But Rock Hudson? And there were rumors about others. Randolph Scott and Cary Grant. Tyrone Power. James Dean, who Bobby said liked to have lighted cigarettes snuffed out on his skin. Wally Cox and Marlon Brando. And all the horrible things they did to each

other, the things they put into each other. How did they even
know to do those things? Where did they find out? Even the
thought of two guys kissing each other was enough to make
her want to throw up.

Of course, she had kissed girls and they had kissed her, but
that was just when the guys wanted to see them do it, and
somehow with girls it wasn't as serious. True love. That was
what Bobby said they were looking for. That was the most
amazing thing of all. Golly, it was all so confusing, so complicated, so different from the world where she had grown up, where
a guy and girl got married, settled down, raised a family.

As the door was opened for her, Beth Carol heard the
music blaring from the hi-fi. The smoke in the room was so
dense it made her eyes water. The eight, maybe ten people
in the room were in various stages of undress, various
stages of getting loaded, too. Whoops of laughter filled the
room, and a drink was thrust into her hand.

A guy was kissing a girl, his hand stuck down the front of
her dress. On the sofa, a guy was sitting with his trousers
undone, with a girl on her knees in front of him giving him
head. Through the bedroom door, moans and screams added
to the din. A girl was spread-eagled on the coffee table, and
another girl had her head between the legs in their black,
fishnet stockings, the black garter belt, black suede, high-
heeled shoes. The girl on the table pushed herself up on her
elbows, flaunting her enormous breasts with their brown
nipples. A few guys stood watching them, fascinated. Beth
Carol saw the contemptuous curl of her thin lips, the glittering eyes scanning the room. The peroxide hair piled high on
her head. It was Fern Darling, the girl from the bus.

Beth Carol felt her face burning as Fern's eyes met hers.
She saw Fern's puzzled look as she searched her memory,
saw her subtract Beth Carol's new hairdo, the subtle makeup, the smart dress. She cringed with embarrassment at the
disbelief on Fern's face as she remembered who Beth
Carol was. Then the sneering smile as she pushed the other
girl's head away, raised and lowered her buttocks on the
table as she offered her sex to Beth Carol. Her pubic hair

was shaved into the shape of a heart and dyed pink.

Somebody changed the record. A man cursed as he stumbled against a wall, dropping his glass, its shards tinkling on the floor. Beth Carol turned, ran through the open door and into the Southern California night with its manicured flower beds, its skinny palm trees, its wide, clean streets and its air perfumed by orange blossoms.

CHAPTER 15

*W*hen she thought about it, Beth Carol knew she was looking better and better, more as if she belonged. As the days passed, though, she was feeling more and more disoriented. Nothing was what it seemed here, everything was illusion. People could say that black was white, up was down, and they didn't even know that what they were saying wasn't the way it was. They didn't even know they were lying. It was as if everybody was living on dreams, on what would be. That there was no present, no now. And no past, either, when they had been ordinary kids with moms and dads, sisters and brothers, growing up in little houses in Platte, Nebraska, or Des Moines, Iowa, or, yes, Coeur D'Alene, Idaho, going to school and worrying about grades, worrying about what the other kids thought of them. Worrying about pleasing, belonging.

The Miltowns were what was getting her through. She was only supposed to take four of them a day, but sometimes she couldn't quite remember how long it had been and she would be feeling sort of anxious so she'd take another one. That and the daquiris, and the vodka gimlets. She loved them. They really tasted good, gave her a false courage.

She stumbled as she got out of the car, grabbed the door to stop her fall.

"Are you all right?" Paul asked sharply.

"I'm fine," she said with dignity, straightening her shoulders.

"I'll be back after class," he said, looking at his watch. Not the expensive gold one that he had been wearing when they met. That had disappeared along with the Jaguar. A cheaper one, second best. Well, it was this money thing. Poor Paul. He was always so worried, and no matter how she tried to please him, his mood was always black. "If I'm a little late, go sit in the lobby and look like a tourist," he added.

"I know, I know," she said, turning, trying to avoid the pain she always felt when she watched him drive away, the anxiety that he was abandoning her to whatever guy was waiting behind the door. It was sure getting harder to do, she decided as she trudged up to the door of the bungalow behind the Beverly Hills Hotel. But she couldn't tell Paul because it would just make him mad.

It was a gorgeous night with a big moon and a swirl of stars that cut across the black sky. And there was the Big Dipper, just as if it were printed on a page in a book at school. She listened to the crickets singing until she got up her nerve to ring the bell.

Beth Carol felt better right away when she saw the look on the guy's face when he opened the door. It was as if he hadn't known what to expect and then he'd gotten a wonderful, beautiful present wrapped in silver ribbons. And she was the present. He'd ordered champagne, too. She saw it across the room, cooling in its ice bucket.

"I'm Jane," she said shyly.

"I'm Wilbur," he said, taking her hand. "I just can't believe this. You're the prettiest girl I've ever seen."

"Thank you," she said, feeling really wonderful now. How she loved to hear those words, how she loved to be admired. It made her feel so powerful, so in control, as if she could make a guy do anything for her. Conquer the world and lay it at her feet.

He was rushing around now, asking her to sit down, and

trying to open the champagne. He was really nervous, she saw, and it made her wonder if he'd ever paid for sex before and that it was kind of sweet if he hadn't. He finally got the cork out of the champagne bottle with a loud pop and it was foaming all over the place, but he got it poured and presented the glass to her as if it were a trophy.

"Thank you," she said, tossing it off, putting out her glass so that he could fill it again. She'd had, what, three daquiris before she'd come, or was it four? Anyway, the alcohol really helped, calmed her down.

Then he was telling her how he was a recent widower and that he lived in the San Diego area, where he was in defense contracting, and maybe she would like to come down sometime and he would show her through his plant. He had a thousand employees, he said.

"What about you?" he asked, sitting very close to her now, his breath coming just a bit faster than normal.

"I'm putting myself through UCLA," she said earnestly, her hand on his forearm, stroking it, feeling a little bit high from the champagne on top of the drinks at home, the pills.

"That's terrible that Baby has to do this," he said, the tone of his voice dropping, as he put his arm around her, pulled her close to him, and started to run his lips over her cheek, her hair. "It doesn't seem right that Baby has to let all of these nasty old men put their things in her so that she can pay for her education."

"Oh, but you're nice," Beth Carol said, leaning back against the sofa, closing her eyes, her head swimming, as she felt his hand on her thigh, pushing up the skirt of her dress. "And you're so attractive, and important, with all of your employees and everything." Her breath was coming faster now as he guided her hand to his trousers, unzipped his fly so that she could take it out and hold it.

It was already hard, she saw as he peeled off her panties.

"Come and sit on my lap now," he said huskily, his trousers dropping around his ankles on the rug. "Come and sit on Daddy's big dick."

He was pulling her over on top of him, spreading her

legs, helping to guide it into her with his hand. Beth Carol felt it way up inside of her, rode it up and down, watched his face as he took off her blouse, unfastened her bra, dropped his head to suck on her nipples.

"Does Baby like that?" he crooned.

"Yes, yes," she panted as he slid it out of her, stood up and carried her into the bedroom, where he put her gently down on the double bed.

She lay there and watched him undressing. Fumbling with his cuff links, his shirt. It was funny how guys all got to look the same after a while, all balding, all with glasses, the little paunch. Then he was looming over her, sucking on her lips, licking her eyelids while she groaned and stroked his thing.

"Now I want you to ask me for it," he murmured.

"Yes, yes," she whispered.

"But we mustn't let Mommy see us, or she'll get mad, won't she? No, we can't let Mommy know what Daddy is doing to Baby, or she'll be very, very mad." Now say it, Baby. Tell me. 'Daddy, please fuck me. I won't tell Mommy what you do to me. I promise.'"

And she tried, tried to say the words as he prodded her, poked her, kissed her, sucked on her toes, her nipples.

"Tell me, Baby," he whispered, his breath hot in her ear. "Tell me now."

The guy's face was all fuzzy and indistinct in the thread of light coming from the living room, and his words, those awful things he wanted her to say, were harsh whispers in her ears.

"Daddy," she murmured, holding onto his shoulders, looking up into his face. "Oh, Daddy," she said as his face blurred in front of her eyes, rearranged itself into the one so adored with its small gray eyes, the sensuous mouth, even the long earlobes. Her father's face. And, oh, he was acquiescing finally, after all of her longing for him to notice her, to validate her, to accept her, love her. He was going to do to her what she had always secretly yearned for, and it was so simple. All she had to do was ask for it. Say it.

Give him permission. "Daddy, I want you to fuck me." That was all it would take.

"Now, you little bitch," the guy was saying. "Tell Daddy to fuck you. Say it. Say it."

"Daddy," she whimpered, but his patience was gone, and he pushed his thing into her, way in, while she tried to focus on his face, on her father's face. And somewhere in the back of her mind she knew this was wrong, that it wasn't the way a daddy proved that he loved his baby. That this wasn't what she had meant, wasn't what she wanted. But she was impaled on his thing, and he clutched her, held her against him as she tried to push him away, tried to squirm free.

From somewhere there was a hideous scream, a scream of such pain, such loss and betrayal, that Beth Carol could hardly stand to hear it, could hardly bear to admit that it was her own.

Red lights were flashing and sirens wailed. People were standing stock-still on the street, watching the ambulance with her in it streaking past. As she drifted in and out of consciousness, Beth Carol, strapped to the gurney, could almost hear them thinking how happy they were that it wasn't one of them in there. Everything was all fuzzy like on a television screen, and then it went to white.

Opening her eyes, she saw the white walls, the ceiling, the white sheet covering her. She winced as she saw the needle taped into a vein on the back of her hand, the tube leading to the IV bag hanging overhead. Paul sat in a chair by the window, his face buried in his hands. Oh, he was going to be so mad, Beth Carol thought dreamily. She closed her eyes again, trying to remember what had happened. Remembering her father's face above her own, his arms urgently holding her against him, asking her to say something. But that couldn't be, she thought. He didn't even like her, and besides, he was so mad at her about what had happened with Buddy, but still, it seemed so real. That he had been holding her, asking her for something. A favor. But what? she wondered, opening her eyes again. Paul was staring at her, his face livid under his tan. He was wearing that seersucker jacket she liked so much, the one he was wearing the night they met.

"How could you do this to me?" he asked.

What could he mean? She frowned, trying to process what he was saying. She was in a hospital bed with an IV dripping into her arm, and he was sitting over there in a chair, and she had done something to him. She glanced over at him, felt a wave of tenderness as she saw the terror in his eyes.

"Where am I?" she asked.

"You're in the psycho ward at Mount Sinai Hospital," he said, as if he were unable to believe it. "The third floor, the one they lock."

"Why?" she asked.

"You went nuts, that's why," he said. "And you're dehydrated, you have malnutrition." He ran his hand through his hair, almost sobbed as he looked at her with a helpless expression on his face. "I'm only twenty-two years old," he added, his voice trailing off into a strangled sigh.

Beth Carol lay there, wondering what that could mean. He didn't have to tell her that. She knew how old he was. She looked at him quizzically.

"They want to keep you here for a few days," he said. "They want to build your strength up, run some tests. They want you to talk to someone, a shrink. You know how it is with doctors. Once they get hold of you, they won't let go."

Beth Carol felt almost relieved. She could just lie here, and nurses would bring her things to eat. They would cluck over her and take her temperature and she would be safe and she wouldn't have to do anything. So they wanted her to talk to a shrink. Well, she'd listened to all the girls at Secrets talk about their shrinks, and she'd wondered what it would be like to talk to one, to have a guy you could tell anything, a guy who would listen to you and take you seriously instead of the way it usually was. Oh, they'd listen to you, but it was just the warm-up so they could talk about themselves. And, really, the only time they cared about what you were saying was when you were telling them how wonderful they were. That might be fun, to talk to someone who listened. She watched Paul, who was pacing now, looking out of the window. He should try to calm down. He was going to make himself sick, going on this way.

"How am I going to pay for this?" he said to himself. "What am I going to do?"

Beth Carol thought about the money, the trinkets she had hidden in the pages of Diana's books, in the folds of the dresses of Diana's dolls sitting on their shelves that she played with sometimes, composing little stories of their lives the way she and Linda Marie had done with their dolls when she was a kid.

She stared at him, shaking her head.

"If only I could get at my trust fund," he said, exasperation in his voice. "If only I could reach my parents."

"Paul, that guy who handles your trust fund at the bank was supposed to be back from vacation in two weeks. It's been almost two months. What bank gives a two-month vacation? It doesn't make sense."

He looked away, crimson staining his cheeks, the back of his neck.

"You know, I don't even think you have a trust fund," she said thoughtfully. "I think what Bobby told me way back is true. That you're a drug dealer, and that's why we went so many places and you were always in the men's room or out in the parking lot. And all those cheap girls we were always seeing and those dangerous-looking guys, and you were always right at home with them. I told Bobby that he was wrong, that you couldn't be a drug dealer. Not living at your parents' estate with a lake and all the cars and the cleaning crew that comes in and everything."

"Well, ask yourself this, baby," he snarled. "If I'm a drug dealer, why am I worried sick about how I'm going to get you out of here? I'd just sell some drugs, wouldn't I?"

"There isn't anything to sell," she said patiently. "Oh, I

know you and Darby didn't think I knew what you were talking about, and maybe at first I didn't. But then at Secrets I started to hear there wasn't anything around and everybody was sort of laughing about it, and kidding that maybe they should ask Bob Mitchum, see if he had anything left after his bust. Or maybe Mickey Cohen, because, after all, he's a neighbor with his men's shop just down the street, and it would be the neighborly thing to do. You know, the trouble with you is that you don't think girls know anything. But after a while I just put two and two together, and it's like Bobby said. You're a drug dealer."

He stared at her, hatred in his eyes, his mouth a tight line.

"You're going to have a big career, be head of a studio," she said. "But people will remember."

"I don't have to put up with this bullshit," he said abruptly, "and what happens to you isn't my problem, either." He said with scorn, "Don't call me, baby. I'll call you."

"That's why you were at the Hollywood bus station that night," she said. "Drugs, that was what was in that package you were picking up."

He stood looking at her, his hands jammed into the pockets of his trousers. Then he adjusted his tie, his shirt, turned, and strode toward the door as if he'd done some mind thing and had erased her from his life. As if she weren't lying in this bed, as if she weren't even there. But he couldn't do this, she thought wildly. He couldn't just walk out and leave her. She loved him. He loved her.

"I'm going to tell on you," she shrieked. "You'll see, you criminal."

He stopped in his tracks, one hand on the door, his back to her. "You don't have to threaten me, Beth Carol," he said as he turned. There was something defeated in his voice. "I wasn't going to leave."

"I love you, Paul," she said.

"I love you, too." He sighed, slowly walking toward her, sitting beside her on the bed, gingerly putting his arms around her.

Beth Carol nestled in his arms, felt his presence, smelled his shaving lotion, felt something else. Triumph. I've won, she thought.

"You're right," he said, rocking her. "I have been selling drugs. Nothing to hurt anybody, though. Just marijuana."

"But why?" she whispered.

"It's my father," he said. "He's cut me off. He's putting on the pressure so I'll give up on the movies. So I'll agree to go on to the Wharton School of Business, join the family firm when I get out."

"Oh, no," she said. "How awful."

"You do see that I can't do that, don't you, baby?" he murmured, his lips against her hair. "I'd rather be dead than do that."

"Oh, I do see, darling," she said. "Of course I understand. Of course I do." With tentative fingers, she wiped away the tears on his cheeks, the tears on her own. Oh, he was so dedicated, so committed, so strong. He really was everything wonderful that she had thought he was in the first place, before all the things started to happen that made her doubt him.

"So you were picking up marijuana that night we met," she said. "A shipment of marijuana."

"Yeah, that was it," he said, his voice a little shaky. "And what a bonus. Meeting you. I couldn't believe it when I saw you sitting there. It was like a dream."

"I thought so, too," she said. "Did you really think you knew me, darling? Because sometimes I've thought—"

"Of course I thought I knew you, my baby girl," he said. "Of course I did."

"Once, when you were mad, you said you knew I was a run-away," she said. "You'd seen my scars."

"That was a lot later," he soothed, putting a finger under her chin, looking into her eyes, making her feel so full of him, as if they were the only two people in the world. "You know, you're not the only one who can put two and two together."

"Oh, darling." She sighed.

"You're wrong about one thing, though," he said into her hair. "People won't remember. That's this town. It doesn't have a memory."

A nurse in starched white carrying a tray pushed open the door with her shoulder and smiled when she saw the two of them.

"You'll have to leave now, young man," she said, putting the tray down on the table beside Beth Carol's bed. "Visiting hours are over."

Paul flashed a disarming smile, leaned over, and kissed Beth Carol lightly on the mouth.

"I'm glad you know," he murmured. "It's a relief to have it out in the open."

"I love you," she said.

After the nurse had taken samples of her blood, her urine, Beth Carol switched off the light in the room and lay back against the pillow, wondering how she had managed to get up the nerve to confront Paul, to threaten him. But oh, she was so happy that she had been able to do it. So happy to know the truth at last. It explained his family's endless trip to Jamaica. They were just waiting him out, waiting for him to break. So there were no more doubts. No pieces of a puzzle that couldn't be made to fit. She was even glad to be in the hospital, glad there were no pills, no booze, no guys to paw her and exploit her.

But, of course, she really couldn't blame them. If anybody was exploiting her, it was Paul. But it was all right now between them. They loved each other. Beth Carol thought of how tender she had felt toward him as he sat holding her on the bed, the tears wet on his face, the feel of those tears on her fingertips. Paul Fournier, crying over her. Oh, he was so sweet, so very sweet.

In the moonlight filtering through the window, she could practically conjure him up. He was nude, coming toward her, a look of incredible love and yearning on his face. She could almost reconstruct his wonderful athlete's walk, his broad shoulders, the dark hair matting his chest, curling down his stomach toward his thing. It was hard, standing out from his furry balls, the heavy curling hair inside his upper thighs. She had to be ready before he got there, had to be all wet from some other guy. That was what turned him on so much that they never got home before he had to have her. Never even got more than a block from where she'd been with a guy before he was at her, tearing off her panties, pushing up her skirt, biting at her nipples, shoving it into her and screaming as if he were being killed when he unloaded into her. It got her so hot, the way he wanted her, that she would be moaning, maybe even making more noise than that. She felt herself blushing at the thought.

Beth Carol thought of the guys she'd been with over the past couple of months. Their admiring looks, their appreciation of her, the way it made her feel so good that they were willing to pay money for her company, the big tips because they loved to talk to her, to listen to themselves saying the things they couldn't say to anybody else in their lives. The young, balding guy who was a regular who treated her as if she were a queen. Why, she wouldn't be surprised if he weren't a little bit in love with her. She could feel it. Every time they saw each other, she expected him to make an offer. An apartment, security. Some of the others, too.

None of them mattered, though. Nothing compared to the way she came alive when she felt Paul's mouth on her own, her whole body tingling at his touch. Nothing even came close.

Still, tiny doubts began to tug at her mind about Paul, about what he had told her. After all, he had told her so many lies. Why should she believe him now?

CHAPTER 16

$\mathscr{P}$aul sure wasn't kidding when he said that the third floor at Mount Sinai was a locked ward. The Negro orderly who was pushing her wheelchair had to use two keys to the locks to get the door open, and even the little window in it had wire mesh embedded in the glass. Beth Carol decided that the wire was there so that nobody could pick up a chair and break it, but maybe that wasn't it, because even if somebody did break it, it was too small to get through. Finally she decided it must be so that the psychiatrists could look in as they passed in the hall outside and see how everybody was doing, and the wire was just there to remind everybody that they couldn't get out.

Not that any of the other patients seemed inclined to do so, to do much of anything. Whenever she was wheeled out for some test, most of them would just be sitting around in their robes, staring into space. Those were all the new medications they were being given, the nurses told her. A couple of times she had been awakened by screams in the night, by the running footsteps as the orderlies and nurses rushed down the hall outside her room. But this was the exception now, not the rule. Padded walls, straitjackets, all of that stuff was becoming obsolete, the nurses told her with relief.

146

Mostly the other patients were women, and mostly, the nurses told her, they were there for anxiety or depression. Oh, the nurses were so nice, maybe because she was the youngest patient there. They brushed her hair, did her nails, pampered her. And they just loved to gossip about the other patients who were just coming in. A couple of the patients were older girls who had had babies and who were suffering from something called postpartum depression, or even postpartum psychosis. That was something that happened when the hormones sort of got confused and the girl couldn't take care of her baby and she cried all the time and even wanted to kill it. Beth Carol just shook her head at that. Kill a baby? She even thought the nurses were kidding her in some macabre way, but then she realized they would never do that, so it must be true. A couple of the other girls had tried to commit suicide, and of course Beth Carol could relate to that. Could understand the despair and shame, the feelings of worthlessness that took them to that point.

What really got the nurses excited was when a patient would be admitted to one of the special rooms. That was where they put the movie stars who went crazy on booze and smashed up restaurants or went after their wives with a gun, or who gulped down a whole bottle of sleeping pills over a broken romance with some other movie star. Golly, the nurses were just like fans over the patients in the special rooms.

But, really, what got them most excited of all was when the psychiatrist was admitted. He was this handsome guy with a big practice on Bedford Drive, which was where all of the shrinks had their practices. Couch Canyon, the nurses would call it, and laugh. So here was this shrink with a great office, and a lot of movie stars in his practice, plus some directors and producers and community leaders and the usual rich ladies who went to shrinks between their appointments to have their hair done and lunch, and a nice wife, too, and two kids, and a house in Beverly Hills with a swimming pool. One of his patients happened to prop himself up and look behind him from the couch, and there this shrink was, sitting in his big leather chair, crying.

Well, the patient was touched because he felt the guy was really empathizing with him. But then it happened again, and with some other patients, too. And this shrink was just sitting there, crying through everybody's sessions. Finally the psychiatric society started to get all of these complaints, or maybe it was concern. And so the shrink had ended up here.

The nurses were ecstatic. It was all they could talk about. What it was, they said, was that the shrinks treated them like dirt. That the nurses had to stand up when one of them would walk into a room, hold the door open for them, all of that kind of demeaning stuff. So their joy was sort of revenge for the awful way they were treated, but it made Beth Carol really nervous, because psychiatrists were like gods. Everybody knew that. They shouldn't fall apart like normal people. It upset the order of things.

Whatever, it was great to be feeling this good. She hadn't even realized how bad she had been feeling until she compared it to the way she felt now that she was eating properly, sleeping well. She was gaining weight. Her breasts were filling out, her hips, her thighs. Her eyes were clear, and when she looked at her reflection in the mirror she saw something new there. A zest for life, maybe. Something.

Paul saw it, too. Oh, he was being so attentive. He came to see her every evening just after dinner, and he'd brought long-stemmed roses that the nurses had oohed and aahed over and kidded her about. He told her that she wasn't to worry about anything because he had the money to get her out. Well, that sent chills through her because it probably meant that he was selling dope again. But he could have borrowed it from Darby. Maybe Darby, because he really seemed to be doing well.

There were these volunteers who came by every day with a cart with magazines and newspapers to hand out to the patients. They were called candy stripers because they wore these bibbed aprons that were in pink-and-white stripes. Some of them were older society ladies and some of them were young society girls. When it was an older lady, Beth Carol was happy to see her because she could feel her sympathy, feel that she knew it could just as easily be one of her own daughters cooped up like this. But when it was one of the society girls, who were all from some group called the Spinsters and who were the daughters of old, established families like Paul's, and who gave charity balls for worthy causes and who gave a few hours a week to hospitals so they would have something to do when they weren't shopping for beautiful evening dresses or going riding or something, Beth Carol was really embarrassed to be there.

Anyway, she started to get interested in the fashion magazines these candy stripers brought her, and one day, when she was sitting in a chair next to the window, she found a two-page layout that Darby had taken. And, as jealous as she was of Darby's friendship with Paul, she had to admit to herself that it was the best layout of all. She got interested in reading the newspapers, too. Especially the society columns. She would mouth the names. Doheny. Dockweiler. Hotchkis. Douglas. Chandler. Memorizing them.

She liked to just sit and look out the window. Right down below, there was a little park with a pony ride for the kids, a Ferris wheel and some other rides, and a stand where the moms and dads could buy hot dogs, hamburgers, Cokes, pink cotton candy, and balloons.

It was funny, Beth Carol thought, as the orderly pushed her down the hall. Here she had run away from home so she wouldn't end up in a place like this, and she was here anyway. And it wasn't so bad, either. The nurses were nice. The interns and residents dropped by all the time to talk to her. And one of the residents was even a girl, which sort of seemed strange, not only to Beth Carol, but to the nurses, too, who seemed a little uncomfortable when they came along with her. And the good food, and everybody taking care of her. The nurses told her that there were patients who would just check themselves in when they were feeling that life on the outside was getting to be a bit too much for them. So, in a way, it was like being part of a really caring family, and not scary at all, the way she had thought it would be. Sometimes she thought it wouldn't be all that bad to just stay here forever.

The orderly was slowing now, stopping in front of an office where the name MARK ROSS, M.D. was painted on the frosted glass in gold-leaf letters. This was it, the office of the chief resident, and her first meeting with him. Beth Carol swallowed hard, felt queasy in her stomach. What would he think of her? she wondered. One of the nurses had brushed her hair and tied it with a pink bow. Her lips were painted the same pink. She was wearing the pretty pink nightgown and the matching lacy peignoir that Paul had brought her. Her nails were the same pink as her lipstick, and it was only at the last moment, when it was too late to do anything about it, that Beth Carol saw with a sinking feeling that somehow she'd broken her thumbnail. She couldn't believe it after all the care she had taken, and she was so distracted at the sight of it that she hadn't even had the presence of mind to bring along a nail file so she could at least shape it, even if it were shorter than all the others. So there it was, jagged and hideous. She tucked it under her fingers, reminded herself to keep it there, unnoticed.

It was a big corner office with six windows, three of them facing the Hollywood Hills. There were a lot of leather-covered medical books jammed in the shelves, and medical journals were scattered all over the low, modern Danish coffee table and the desk. There was a sofa, a little arrangement of chairs around another modern table, rows of medical degrees in frames on the wall above it. The late morning sun streaming through the windows almost blinded Beth Carol, and all she could see of the guy standing in front of them was a kind of black outline. He turned, took a couple of steps, sat down in the big leather chair behind the desk, and gave her a big smile. Behind her, Beth Carol heard the door close.

She looked at him warily, saw his gentle, open expression, felt the kindness and acceptance radiating from him, saw the twinkle in his blue eyes. She warmed to him as if she had known him all her life, as if they had been through a zillion different situations together and he had always been there for her.

"I'm Dr. Ross," he said, his elbows on the desk, his fingers making a little steeple as they touched each other. He was wearing a white coat, a white shirt, and a maroon tie with diagonal stripes.

"I'm Beth Carol Barnes," she said shyly, taking the hand he offered her, wanting to hold on to it forever, hoping against hope he wasn't aware of her broken nail.

"You've been here, what, five days?" he said, thumbing through the file in front of him. The file was huge, with all kinds of forms in different colors stacked on top of one another. Golly, there must have been fifty, sixty pages in there, reporting every word she said, every time she ate a soft-boiled egg. She felt her mouth go dry again, wondering what else it said in there about her.

"How do you feel?" he asked, his eyes meeting hers.

"A lot better, thank you," she murmured.

"You've been through a rough spell," he said, his voice neutral.

Beth Carol tensed, sat there frozen as he glanced over the papers, waiting for her to speak.

"You've heard about a doctor-patient relationship, haven't you, Beth Carol?" he asked, his voice so nice, so kind. She could hardly stand the kindness. It made her want to cry.

Slowly she shook her head.

"Well, anything a patient tells a doctor is confidential," he said, smiling, willing her to talk to him, tell him everything. "Even in court, we don't have to talk about anything a patient tells us. Do you understand?"

"Yes," she said.

"Now, you were found nude and unconscious in a bungalow behind the Beverly Hills Hotel," he said, reading from one of the reports. "Somebody had made an anonymous call to the police."

"Oh," she said.

"When you were examined in the emergency room, you had had recent consensual intercourse."

She nodded.

"Do you want to talk about that?" he asked.

"Well, I met this guy and he seemed nice," she said. "And so when he said why didn't I stop by for a glass of champagne, I didn't see why not." She looked at him imploringly. "He was very respectable," she added. "He has a big plant in San Diego with a thousand employees. He asked me to come down to see it sometime."

"Did he pay you to have sexual intercourse with him?" he asked gently.

"Oh, no," she protested indignantly. "He was just a nice guy. I liked him, so when he asked me if I wanted to make it with him, I said okay."

"Well, what happened, do you think?" he asked. "Was this an unusual occurrence for you?"

"What do you mean?" she asked blankly.

"Well, have you ever fainted before when you've been having intercourse?"

"There had been a lot of parties," she said vaguely. "You know how it is. You have a drink or two. You stay up late. You forget to eat."

"So that's what happened?" he asked, making little notes.

"I guess so," she said. "It's all I can think of."

"Are your parents here in Los Angeles?" he asked.

Beth Carol froze, that feeling of panic in the pit of her stomach again.

"It's up to you," he reminded her. "You can tell me, you know."

"I'm staying at my boyfriend's house," she said. "He's from an old California family and they're out of town."

"So you're not from Los Angeles?" he prompted.

"No, no," she admitted. "I'm from Idaho."

"Do your parents know where you are?" he asked.

She shook her head.

"Well, don't you think you should get in touch with them?" he suggested. "They're probably very worried."

"They're not," she said.

"How can you be so sure of that, Beth Carol?" he asked.

"I just know," she said sullenly.

"Does that have anything to do with the scars on your wrists?" he asked. "What happened that made you do that?"

"I wasn't trying to kill myself, if that's what you mean," she muttered. "It was just spur of the moment. I heard the doctors talking up there when they thought I was asleep. 'Just superficial.' That's what they said."

"Well, what happened?" he asked. "You know, something can seem very bad at the time, but before too long, it falls into perspective. Then it isn't so bad after all."

"Oh, yes, it was," she said.

"Was it a boy?" he asked.

She nodded.

"You were caught with him?"

"Yes," she said in a strangled voice.

"Well, that happens with adolescents," he said. "More often than you can imagine. And after a while, the parents begin to understand that it isn't such a terrible thing. A parent has a lot of forgiveness in his heart."

"If a parent loves you, I guess," she said.

"And you don't think your parents love you?"

"There's just my father," she said. "And I don't think he doesn't love me. I know it."

"Oh, so many men become so involved in their work," he said with regret. "They spend so many hours making a living that it often seems to the child as if he, or she, isn't loved. But it isn't that at all. It's just the order of a father's priorities. He feels that if he makes a living for his family, he's fulfilled his role."

"Look," she said, "that's not my father. He doesn't love me."

"Why are you so certain, Beth Carol?"

"Because I was supposed to be a boy." She sighed. "I let him down. He can't forgive me for that."

"Well, perhaps you'll have to be the one to find forgiveness in your heart," he said.

She stared at him, wondering what he was talking about. It must be some shrink thing, she decided. Some grownup thing. Nobody could love her father as much as she loved hers. What did she have to forgive? It didn't make any sense to her.

"You've gained four pounds since you've been here," he murmured, looking at the papers in her file again. "And you've been sleeping well."

"Yes, it's been wonderful," she said.

"And you've been eating well, too. You're responsive to what goes on around you. You're interested in the other patients. You read magazines and newspapers. You've been watching television in the lounge."

"That's right," she said, feeling proud of herself, hearing in his voice that everything the nurses, the residents, the interns had reported sounded normal, sane. She felt a little shiver of dismay as she realized what his next words were going to be. That she was going to be released. That she was just fine. And then it would be back to, well, whatever it was. It wouldn't be back to what she was doing. She'd find some other way to help out while Paul waited out his father. There had to be something. Still, just the thought of leaving this place, this wonderful, secure place, made the anxiety well up in her. Looking over at Dr. Ross, she wondered if she could ask him to get her a Miltown. Just one.

Now it was his turn to sigh, to lean back in his chair with his arms behind his head. He glanced out of the window as the fear crept through her veins, made her scalp crawl.

"I don't know how to put this," he said slowly after what seemed to Beth Carol to have been minutes.

What could it be? she thought wildly. Did she have some terrible disease? Was she going to die? She grabbed the arms of the chair, dug her fingers into the soft leather.

Whatever awful thing it was, she didn't want to know. Don't tell me, she wanted to scream. Please don't tell me.

"Do you realize you're pregnant, Beth Carol?" he asked, his expression gentle as he looked into her eyes.

All of the blood drained out of Beth Carol's head and she was suddenly so dizzy she thought she would faint. But she couldn't be pregnant, she couldn't be. That was what happened to white trash, the girls the people at home talked about in whispers, snickered at when they hurried by, their heads down with shame. Beth Carol knew what being pregnant and unmarried meant. That your life was ruined forever. That you were an outcast and you could never go home.

In spite of herself, she started to smile, to almost laugh out loud with joy. A baby, her very own baby. The one she had always wanted, dreamed of holding. Oh, how she would love him, care for him. Unconsciously, she moved her hand toward her breast, as if cradling him there. Someone to belong to her, who would never betray her. Someone she could love who would never hurt her. She could almost feel his silky blond curls, feel her hands supporting the back of his little neck. She was happy, and she didn't care who knew it. Who cared about being an outcast? That didn't count here. She could be anybody, anything. A war widow whose husband had been killed in Korea. She could just hear herself telling people that she was so sad because his father had died before he could see him, almost see their quick looks of pity for the brave young mother.

"Are you all right?" he asked anxiously. "Would you like something? How about a cup of tea?"

"You're sure?" she asked, noticing that her hands were shaking, her breath coming in short little pants.

"Yes, we're sure," he said.

"Well, you know," she began slowly, "I really want to have a baby. I've always wanted one. And I'll be such a great mom, I know I will. But you see, my boyfriend isn't settled yet. He's going to be the head of a studio, but that takes a lot of time, and so far he's only produced one film, and, well, I don't think he'll marry me until he's further along in his career."

"I'm sure this gives you a lot of things to think about," the doctor said. "I understand."

"I couldn't take care of him by myself," she mused. "I mean, if I were on my own, I could only get some dinky little job that wouldn't pay much, and for my baby it has to be the best of everything."

"I see." He nodded.

"I mean, he has to have a beautiful nursery, all lace and everything, and a lot of toys." She looked at him, wondering if he did know what she meant, but then he probably did. Shrinks heard it all. "I've thought about his room," she continued. "Pale blue walls, pale blue blankets. Then, when he's a little older, those Merry Mites the little boys are wearing now. Oh, they're so cute, with the little straps that button over the shoulders, the little white shirts with the Peter Pan collars. Maybe a giraffe on the pocket. And white shoes, high tops to support his ankles, and white socks."

"Yes, yes, Beth Carol. I understand."

"And I can't do anything even near that," she pleaded.

"Do you know who the father is?" he asked.

The father. Oh, God. She hadn't even thought about that. Oh, she'd just die if it was one of the guys she'd gone with for money. She'd just die. It was such a shock it was hard to think, but she started to count them off in her mind. Who had come in her, who hadn't. Who'd used protection. Who hadn't. Well, it had to be Paul, that was all. He never used anything, and she'd done it more with him than with anyone. He'd have to marry her, that was all there was to it. Then his father would come around. He'd have to come around when Paul had the responsibility of a wife and child.

"He won't marry me," she whispered. "I know he won't."

"Well, perhaps the two of you can work something out,"

the doctor said. "After all, if you have a firm, loving relationship it wouldn't be the first time a couple got married when a baby was on the way."

"No, no. It won't work. I know it won't."

"Well, what about adoption?" he suggested. "There are several good agencies who have wonderful, secure couples who have been waiting for years to adopt a baby."

"You mean have my baby and give him away?" she asked slowly.

"You know, I might even have a solution," he said with a big smile. "I have friends who want to adopt. They're a wonderful couple, Beth Carol. Both educated people, very refined. He's a psychiatrist, too, on the staff at the medical school at UCLA with a private practice on the side in Beverly Hills. And she's a marvelous woman, very sympathetic, very nurturing. She was a cellist before they got married."

She sat dumbly, staring at him. Unconsciously, she started to bite her broken thumbnail.

"I'm sure they would pay all your expenses during the remainder of your pregnancy," he said warmly. "And, of course, your hospital bills as well."

"Dr. Ross, I'm not going to have my baby and give him away." Her voice in her ears was strong and firm. He must have thought so, too. He sat up straight and stared at her. "I'm not going to give away my flesh and blood."

"Well, Beth Carol," he said. "As you know, there are only so many options."

"I'm only sixteen years old," she said.

"I wish I could help you," he said, closing his eyes as if he were in pain.

CHAPTER 17

$\mathcal{B}$eth Carol sat erectly, her back against the chair, her feet together, every muscle in her body tense. She picked at a cuticle as she looked at the other girls sitting around the reception room. There were a few boys, too, holding their girlfriends' hands. Behind the admitting desk, a nurse was looking at a chart, pointing out something on it to another nurse. They could have been the nurses at Mount Sinai, nurses anywhere.

"Tammy, we're ready for you now," she said, looking around the room.

A blond girl with a ponytail and bangs got up, looking scared. She was maybe twenty, Beth Carol decided. All the girls in the room were real young, except one across the way who had a scarf over her head, dark glasses, her face buried in a tattered copy of *Time*. She was older, maybe thirty.

Beth Carol's eyes were wide as she watched Tammy walk stiffly up to the nurse, saw the nurse pat her on the shoulder, hold open the door for her as if she were just going back there, say, to have a tooth filled or something. That was kind of what it was like. Everybody was calm, looking at magazines, this and that, but there was an underlying feeling, too. Dread. Not bad dread. Dentist-

158

office dread. Waiting-to-be-called-on-in-class dread.

Beth Carol, all the rest of them, started when the front door swung open. Real dread this time, terror. But it wasn't the cops, come to take them off to jail and close the place down. It was just another teenage girl looking doubtful, as if she had wandered into the wrong place. Into a real dentist's office like the sign outside said. Then she walked across the room to the admitting desk and the other girls went back to their magazines, to grasping their boyfriends' hands, to staring straight ahead, smoking.

It was all happening so fast. Only a few days ago Beth Carol had been sitting in that doctor's office and he was telling her, and then Paul was walking beside her wheelchair to his car parked right outside and helping her into it, saying good-bye to the nurse, Beth Carol thanking her for everything. It was a glorious morning, with clear blue skies, the slightest breeze touching her cheeks. Another day in paradise, as Paul was always saying. In front of Chasen's, a workman was hosing down the sidewalk.

She looked out of the car window at apartment houses where gardeners were already mowing the little lawns out front, trimming the bushes. A woman in capri pants and flats was hurrying to keep up with a German shepherd that was straining at its leash. What she kept seeing was the doctor in his chair behind his desk, herself looking over at him. The smoke from his pipe curling into the air.

Three months pregnant.

Had she even been in town for three months?

It must be Buddy's baby, her sweet, beautiful Buddy, who had loved her and who had wanted to marry her and take care of her forever. She sat there with her eyes closed for a moment, picturing a miniature version of Buddy curled up inside her stomach. Still, he had always been so careful, always pulling it out before he came. There was only that last night that it could have been, with all the chaos and everything, and Buddy way inside her with his thing when her Dad had come in.

Paul had been so nice, treating her as if she were made

of glass. When they got back to the estate, she went to sit by the swimming pool and every couple of minutes, it seemed, there was Paul, asking if she wanted anything. He even asked her if she wanted to go to a movie that night, a real first. Just like other young couples in love.

Beth Carol stood in the courtyard of Grauman's Chinese while Paul waited in line to get the tickets. Surreptitiously, she put her feet in the outlines of Janet Gaynor's shoes. Norma Shearer's. Not Joan Crawford's—she had the tiniest feet. Inside, the theater was really luxurious. Everything was all red and gold, and black lacquer, too, in keeping with the oriental theme.

The movie was good, too. It had Burt Lancaster and some new girl.

"Didn't you think that girl was cute?" she asked Paul as they sauntered back to the parking lot next to the theater after the movie and found the Packard gleaming under a light.

"Yes," he agreed, opening the door for her, helping her in.

"She's going to be a big star, I'll bet," Beth Carol said.

"I don't think so," he said. "Every movie that comes out these days has some new girl, and you never hear of her again."

Why, he was right, she realized, as they drove to the restaurant where they were going for dinner. She'd noticed that, that all the movies had these new girls and you never heard of them again. Paul was so smart. He really was. What she didn't know was how he was going to react when she told him she was going to have a baby. And that was a funny feeling, too. Paul was talking to her as if it were just the two of them, and it was really the three of them, and she was the only one who knew it. Or maybe the baby knew it, too. She didn't even know how aware they were at three months. Golly, three months. Only six to go. She could just kick herself that she hadn't even known she was pregnant. But she'd only gotten her period two years ago, and sometimes she'd gone for a couple of months without one. Why, she hadn't even noticed she hadn't had one with all of the other things that were going on. Coming to Los Angeles, the new places. Then the guys. She winced, thinking of all those guys who had put their things in her, in there with her baby. Oh, how could she have let them, she agonized, with him in her stomach, growing, trusting her? And, of course, the fact that she was going to have a baby explained a lot of other things, too. Like the throwing up in the morning, and always feeling kind of sick, and the tenderness in her breasts. She'd just thought it was the way she'd been living. The pills. The booze. The guys always sucking on her nipples, even biting sometimes.

Paul found a parking place right in front of the restaurant. Beth Carol looked at it, a little disappointed. It was just a storefront with a sign over it that said, THE FOGCUTTERS. It was really cute inside, though, and once they were in their booth, the waiter brought the menu, and what it was was a platter with different cuts of steaks, because that was all they served.

"I'll have a martini," Paul told him. "Just a couple of drops of vermouth. What do you want, baby?" he asked, turning to Beth Carol.

"Milk," she said.

"Thank you, miss," the waiter said, making a note on his order pad.

"Milk?" Paul had asked. "Is that what you were drinking in the hospital?"

"We're going to have a baby," she had blurted.

The door where all of the girls had been going in with the nurse opened slowly, and Beth Carol looked up, feeling the tension in the entire reception area. A girl stood there. She was a little pale, true, but there she was. The first one to reappear since Beth Carol had been there. Every eye in the place was on her as she walked gingerly by them, opened the door, and was gone. Everybody in the reception room relaxed, and Beth Carol let out a sigh of relief. She opened an old copy of *Seventeen* and started to read the letters to the editor.

"You, too, huh?" said a weary voice next to her. "It's really the shits, I'll tell you."

Beth Carol turned and looked at the girl who was just sitting down. At the blond hair pulled back in a ponytail by a rubberband, the thin neck that didn't look quite clean. The blue eyes, the thin lips. The enormous breasts in a pale green jersey top, the cinched-in waist, the full white skirt, the high heels, the glint of an ankle bracelet on a bare white leg. Fern Darling. Beth Carol's stomach clenched, and she turned away. Well, if Fern thought that her being here was anything like Fern Darling being here, she had another think coming.

"Look, I'm sorry about the other night," she said, touching Beth Carol's arm. "I was just so surprised that you were there. When I met you on the bus, you didn't seem the type."

"What type is that?" Beth Carol asked icily.

"The type to be hooking. I didn't think you would do something like that. I thought you were real refined, you know?"

"I wasn't hooking," Beth Carol whispered angrily.

"Then why were you there?"

"I had the wrong address," she whispered.

Fern started to laugh, threw back her head. Everybody in the place was looking at her. The door opened. Another girl came out, walked stiffly through the reception area to the front door. Disappeared.

Beth Carol sat there, her cheeks burning.

"So what happened?" Fern asked, her shoulders still shaking a little.

"I don't want to talk to you," Beth Carol said.

"Oh, come on," Fern said. "What happened?"

"Oh, I met a guy."

"So what kind of a guy?" Fern asked.

"Well, he's really cute," Beth Carol said, warming to the notion of telling Fern all about her great catch. "And he lives on this huge estate with a real lake, and the house is enormous, and there are all these antiques and paintings and things. There are eight cars."

"Golly," Fern said, looking at her with admiration.

"But his father is mad at him because he wants to go into the movie business and his father doesn't want him to, so he won't give him any money unless he agrees to go to the Wharton School of Business and then, when he graduates from there, to go into the family business."

"The Wharton School of Business," Fern said. "I've never heard of it."

"It's in Pennsylvania," Beth Carol said. "He's from one of the oldest families in California. They're very rich and very social."

"So he's got you out hooking?" Fern said.

"Yeah, I suppose so," Beth Carol said, slumping in the chair.

"Was he the one who knocked you up?" Fern offered her a cigarette from her pack of Luckies.

Beth Carol took one and leaned over as Fern lit it for her.

"No, it was the boy I told you about," she said. "The boy from back home."

Fern looked at her, admiration still on her face.

"Jesus," she said, "and I thought butter wouldn't melt in your mouth."

"What about you?" Beth Carol asked. "How's the Studio Club?"

"Oh, man," Fern sighed, a bitter smile on her lips, "I wasn't even at the front door before some asshole was there, sweet-talking the shit out of me."

"So do you go to Schwab's and sit at the counter, like you said?"

"Yeah, I do," she said. "Sometimes."

"So?"

"So I get a lot of assholes hitting on me."

"That's all?" Beth Carol asked, thinking about it. Thinking about the town and what they said it was in the magazines and newspapers and how they showed it in the movies, and how it really was. Whatever it really was, because the whole place was like sand. It shifted all the time. You just couldn't get a grasp of any kind.

"Just about," murmured Fern. "So I'm doing something else. Besides, well, you know."

"What?"

"I'm a reporter," Fern said.

"You're a what?" Beth Carol asked, her eyes wide.

"Well, sort of," Fern said, leaning toward Beth Carol, speaking in a low voice. "See, what I do is sell information to this magazine. It's called *Confidential* and it publishes stuff on all the movie stars. Dirt. You know. And I call them up and give them this information. Items, they call them. And I get paid."

"Golly," said Beth Carol, amazed at Fern's ingenuity.

"Yeah," she said, "it's okay. Like which big male movie star likes to wear ladies' panties. Or which happily married newlywed is already paying for it after only six weeks of wedlock. Or which all-American boy movie star really likes to be tied up and beaten, or peed on. You know."

"Do you make those things up?" Beth Carol asked.

"Of course not, man," Fern said indignantly. "It's all true. I'm, like, the one doing it, so I know it's true."

"I'd be scared," whispered Beth Carol. "I mean, don't they get mad?"

"Oh, who cares if they get mad?" Fern sniffed. "If they don't want this stuff to be printed, then they shouldn't do it. What are they going to say? That it's a lie? And I keep records, too. Names, dates, places. The works." In her eyes, there was a malevolent look, one that Beth Carol remembered from the bus. "Sometimes," she added, "I can make more if it's not printed, if you know what I mean."

"Blackmail," Beth Carol said.

"Call it anything you want," said Fern, blowing a smoke ring, then another.

"So how come you're here?" Beth Carol asked.

"Shit, I don't know," said Fern. "Like the first thing this

guy did was take me to a doctor and get me fitted for a diaphragm, and he showed me how to grease it with this jelly to kill all the stuff, and how to insert it and make sure it's hanging off that little bone in there. So I don't know."

"Do you know whose it is?" Beth Carol asked.

"Man, I don't have a clue," Fern said. "So what I did was tell three johns it was theirs, so I collected three times."

"Weren't they mad?" Beth Carol asked.

"Who cares if they were mad or if they weren't mad, or what they were?" Fern said, snuffing out the cigarette in the nearly full ashtray. "I mean, nobody is going to shove a knife up their cunt, after all."

She really was the limit, Beth Carol thought, wondering how she ever could have thought she and Fern could be friends.

"Say, this place isn't bad," Fern was saying, looking around at the other girls sitting in the leather chairs, at the curtains on the windows, at the top of the nurses' heads behind the admitting desk, at the tired plant that sat on the counter. "It sure beats some old Mex in Crescent City with a knitting needle. And it's right here, too. In the middle of everything."

Oh, let her rave on, Beth Carol thought, disgusted. Such white trash. Why it had to be Fern who sat down next to her this particular morning, she would never know. She sat there, almost wishing her name would be called. But not really wishing it.

"You see that girl sitting over there in the dark glasses and the scarf?" Fern whispered. "That's Cara Conway."

"Oh, it is not," Beth Carol said. "Cara Conway is a movie star. What would she be doing here?"

"Just what we're doing here," Fern whispered. "Getting an abortion."

"Oh, stop it," Beth Carol said. "She wouldn't come here. That's just ridiculous."

"Why not?" Fern whispered. "This isn't like having your hair done, you know. You can't just have someone come to the house."

Despite herself, Beth Carol glanced furtively at the girl. It sure did look like Cara Conway, she decided.

"I'll be right back," said Fern, springing up. "Save my seat, okay?"

Beth Carol watched as Fern sauntered across the room, dropped to her knees beside the girl's chair. Watched the girl start, surprised, lean down to hear what Fern was saying. In a couple of minutes Fern was back, triumph etched on her face.

"It's her, all right," she said, sinking back into the chair. "This'll make me two hundred bucks, at least."

"Oh, Fern," said Beth Carol. "You wouldn't."

"Oh, yes, I would," she said. "This is a big story."

"You'll get her in trouble," Beth Carol said.

"So what do I care?" Fern said. "This is a tough town. You've got to survive."

The girls were a steady stream now. Coming in. Disappearing through the door. Coming out, disappearing onto Santa Monica Boulevard, back into their own lives.

"Beth Carol," the nurse said, looking around the crowded room.

Beth Carol started to get up, a shiver of fear shooting through her.

"Say, what's your phone number?" Fern said, fumbling around in her handbag and pulling out a grimy address book. "Maybe I'll call you sometime."

Beth Carol glanced down, saw Fern turning pages blotched with purple and red ink, with crossed-out names, with names printed in large letters, others starred in various shades of ink.

"It's Crestview 88731," Beth Carol said.

"Crestview," Fern said, looking at her with admiration again. "That's Beverly Hills."

"Yes." Beth Carol nodded. "And listen, if you do call, ring once and then hang up and call again. Okay? Because he doesn't let me answer the phone if it's for him."

"Okay," Fern said.

"Well, here goes nothing," Beth Carol said.

"Hey, wait," Fern said.

"What?" asked Beth Carol, turning.

"What's your name?" she asked.

"Beth Carol. Beth Carol Barnes."

"Oh, okay," Fern said.

She was turning the pages of her address book as Beth Carol walked tentatively toward the smiling nurse.

"Isn't it a pretty morning, dear?" the nurse said, patting Beth Carol on the shoulder, putting her arm loosely around her waist as she pushed open the door.

Inside, it was like any doctor's office with some doors and charts in holders outside each one. Inside one of the little rooms, it was like a doctor's examining room, too. There was a leather-covered examining table, covered by a fresh sheet of paper, stirrups at the foot of it.

Well, good-bye, my little baby, Beth Carol thought, her mouth dry as she looked around the tiny room, looked with dread at the table.

"I'm sure the doctor explained the procedure when you met with him, dear," the nurse said in the kindest voice. "You can get undressed now, and you can put on that smock." She looked at Beth Carol expectantly. "Did you bring a belt and a sanitary napkin?" she asked.

"They're in my handbag," she muttered in a strangled voice.

"Put on the belt, too, dear," the nurse said, patting her shoulder again. "But, when you put on the napkin, you just attach it to the back."

"Okay," she said.

"Then you just hop onto the table and put your feet in the stirrups, and I'll be back in a minute or two to give you a shot."

"Okay," she said.

"Don't worry, dear," the nurse said. "It's the simplest procedure in the world, even as far along as you are. In a couple of hours, you won't even know anything happened."

"Okay," Beth Carol said as the nurse opened the door, gave Beth Carol another smile, and closed it behind her.

Well, here it is, the moment of truth, she thought, paralyzed with fear. Scrape, scrape, and it would all be over. She would be just the way she had been, only a bit wiser. No stupid stories about how she was a war widow, or some of the other stuff she'd thought up. No nothing. No beautiful baby, either, to love her and trust her and know that she would do anything in the world to take care of him.

"Oh, you can have a baby anytime," Paul had said. "This isn't the end of the world."

She was still standing there, clutching her handbag, when the nurse pushed open the door a few minutes later.

"Is something wrong?" she asked in that gentle voice of hers.

"I've changed my mind," Beth Carol whispered, her nails digging into her handbag now, her breath coming in little gasps.

"Have you really thought about this, dear?" the nurse asked. "I know it's a big decision."

"Yes," Beth Carol said.

"Well, if you're sure you know what you're doing . . ." she said slowly.

"Yes."

"Well, all right," the nurse said. "I wish you the best, dear."

"Thank you," Beth Carol said, pulling back her shoulders.

"You do understand that we can't return your money," she added.

"I don't care about that," she stammered.

Every eye in the reception room was riveted on her when she pushed open the door. She glanced over at where Fern had been sitting and saw that she was gone.

CHAPTER 18

*R*ockabye baby, on the tree top,
When the wind blows, the cradle will rock . . ."

Beth Carol knew she had never had much of a voice. She sang the words softly to herself, trying to stay on key, trying to sound very, very loving as she stroked her silken stomach under her nightgown. She imagined the baby somehow absorbing all of the love she was sending toward him. She could almost feel him in there now, awakening. Yawning, turning over. But it was probably too early for that. She stroked her breasts, felt them swelling under her fingers. Getting ready for his mouth. Should she breast-feed? she wondered, frowning, as she lay in Diana's narrow bed. Nobody was doing it now. She knew that from what the girls said at the beauty shop. It ruined your breasts, they said. Made them sag like some old cow in a pasture.

She decided she would. To hell with how her breasts would look. She had a picture of herself in a rocking chair by a window with the sunlight streaming into the room. He was nursing, and she was gazing adoringly at the top of his blond head. One of his little hands was curled around her finger. She hummed softly to him as she rocked back and forth. She was wearing something pale blue, with a lacy white shawl around her shoulders. There were other people there, too. Bringing gifts.

"When the bough breaks, the cradle will fall,
And down will come baby, cradle and all."

She sang louder now, at the top of her voice. There was nobody to hear, after all. Nobody to disturb. They were there alone, just Beth Carol and her baby. Her secret still.

Hot tears filled her eyes as she thought about Paul, and how he had disappeared again. Well, she should have known it, she told herself bleakly. He'd been scared when she had to be locked up at Mount Sinai, all right. She knew that was true. So he'd been there all the time, and when she got home, too. He hadn't been able to do enough for her. Beth Carol remembered how great that had made her feel, as if she'd struck some protective chord in him and, bingo, he'd turned over a new leaf. And then when she'd told him she was going to have his baby, he'd been shocked at first, but concerned. Really concerned about what they should do. There was almost a longing in his expression, some deep-seated yearning to see his son, the mirror image of himself. She looked at him intently, feeling a little guilty about how it would be when the baby was born. He'd started to make it with her when she'd been in town for a month or so, so that part of it was all right. The baby was just a little early. That happened all the time. But what would he think when he saw the baby? It would be blond and blue-eyed. It couldn't be anything else, so maybe he would know, and that would be awful. She'd worry about that when the time came.

"You can have a baby anytime. This isn't the end of the world."

That was what he had said. Even now she remembered the sudden hurt, her disappointment, the tears. She had cried and cried.

And he had been right there when she had walked out of the abortionist's office, parked right in front. He was staring straight ahead when she saw him, smoking furiously. When she approached the car, he had turned, seen her, and gone dead white.

"Are you okay?" he stuttered.

"I'm fine," she said.

"Did it hurt?" he asked, starting the car.

"No."

"We've got to get you home," he said. "Get you into bed."

She sat silently beside him, wondering what she was going to do when he found out she hadn't gone through with it. He'd really been nervous about it. There were maybe twenty cigarettes in the ashtray. More, even.

He'd helped her up the stairs, making her stop every couple, to be sure she was okay. When she'd gotten into bed, he'd sat with her, the television set on. The only time he left was to go downstairs to heat up some soup he'd picked up at Greenblatt's. And every time she glanced over at him, he was glancing over at her, too. Reassuring himself that she was okay, and that she wasn't going to die on him.

Maybe that was why he was so attentive, she thought angrily. If she died on him, he could get in trouble. Terminal trouble for his career, no matter what he said. Or maybe it was because of what she had said in the hospital that first night. That she would tell on him.

He hadn't gotten restless until around seven o'clock the night before. Then she saw him twisting in his chair, glancing at his watch.

"Where are you going?" she asked as he stood up, stretched. She heard the anxiety in her voice. The disappointment.

"I've got to see someone," he said. "Just for an hour or so."

Well, she should have known. He was just the way he always was. Why would anything that was happening to her make him turn into somebody else? She didn't want him to know how disappointed she was, though. She turned her head away so he couldn't see her tears.

"You're okay, aren't you?" he asked. "No twinges or anything?"

"I'm fine," she said.

When he'd come back from changing in his room, she

saw that he was wearing a new pink shirt with his black knit tie, a new pale blue denim jacket.

"I won't be long," he said, kissing her hair. "I promise."

Paul and his promises, she thought, wiping away her tears with the back of her hand. About an hour, he had said, and here it was, nearly dawn. The room was pink with its coming. Another beautiful day. What was it going to take, she wondered, before he started to act the way she wanted him to act? What key was she going to have to find in him? Turn. Change him.

A sound from down the hall startled her. The ringing of the phone. A ring. Silence. And then it rang again. It was his signal that she was to answer. Oh, he does care, she thought happily as she glanced at the little clock on the table next to her bed. Here it was, not even six o'clock in the morning, and wherever he was, whoever he was with, at least he was thinking of her. Beth Carol jumped out of bed, rushed down the hall, was panting a little as she grabbed the receiver and said hello.

"Beth Carol?"

Oh, no, she thought, her whole body sagging with disappointment as she heard the breathy little voice. She should have known that Fern would turn out to be a pest. Imagine calling somebody at this hour.

"Oh, hi," she muttered.

"I was just wondering how it went for you," Fern said.

"Do you know what time it is, Fern?" Beth Carol demanded. "Fern, it isn't even six o'clock. It isn't even light out."

"Well, it's sort of light here," the voice said. It was weary, a frightened child's voice. Beth Carol felt the fine hairs on her arms stand on end. "I waited." The voice trailed off apologetically.

"What's the matter?" Beth Carol asked.

"I don't know, man," Fern said. "It's never been like this. I mean, I think something's wrong."

"Well, what? What?" Beth Carol demanded.

"Oh, man," Fern said in a barely audible voice, "I've

been hurting a lot. And so I took some aspirin and everything and I thought, well, okay, so it's not like the other times. So it'll take a little longer and then it'll be okay." She stopped, sighed. "So now I'm bleeding. A lot."

"Oh, golly," Beth Carol said. "Did you call the doctor? His number's right there, on that slip they gave us when they said what we were to bring, and how we weren't to have anything to eat. That slip."

"All I got was the answering service," she said. "He can't be reached."

"Oh, no," Beth Carol said. "Well, I'm really sorry, Fern. I really am."

"But you're okay, man?" she asked.

"Yeah, I'm fine."

"Well, that's good. So I'll talk to you sometime."

"Fern, Fern," Beth Carol cried. "Is the doctor going to call you back? Did you tell the answering service to have him call you?"

"Yeah," she said in the same tired voice. "But I don't know. The bleeding's pretty bad."

"Fern, Fern, I don't know what to do," Beth Carol sputtered. "I don't know how to drive. What am I going to do?"

"Oh, it's okay," she said. "I'll be okay. Like, I just wanted to—"

"I know," Beth Carol said. "I'll take a cab. I've got money. Where are you?"

"Well, I don't want to bother you," Fern said, her voice a whisper.

"Oh, stop it," Beth Carol screamed, hysterical now. "Just tell me where you are. I'm on my way."

East of the Strip, Sunset Boulevard was a mélange of markets, gas stations, and courtyards built in the twenties, framed by the omnipresent palm trees with their tousled heads, the bushes massed with enormous hibiscus blossoms in white and yellow. The cab stopped at a light. Beth Carol glanced at Tiny Naylor's, the drive-in with its soaring wings that always looked to her as if it were about to head for outer space. Everything was quiet, with only a few guys hosing down parking lots, preparing for the day. On the right was the Café de Paris with its pretty outdoor terrace, its awning in red, white, and blue. It was even too early for school, Beth Carol realized. Hollywood High was just squatting there. Catty-corner was Stan's Drive-In, the place Bobby had told her about where the fags put their things in holes. Maybe it was even too early to be out looking for true love, she thought. Still, it was her favorite time of day, before the sun really came out, when the sky was kind of navy blue tinged with pink, when everything was fresh again. Reborn.

"I had a hard time finding your house," the cab driver said. "I'm new here, and I'd never been up that way before. It's gorgeous."

He pronounced *hard* as if it were spelled "hahd," *gorgeous* as if it were spelled "gawjess." New York. She knew things like that now. Good-looking, too, in a flashy kind of way, with a big smile, lively eyes.

"Could you go a little faster?" she asked.

"I just got here three weeks ago, from New York," he said. "Yeah, good old New York. Great town, but Hollywood's the place. I know it already."

The Crossroads of the World, a collection of offices and stores. A Catholic church next to it. Shiny cars behind the plate-glass window of a Chevrolet dealer. Coffee shops and doctor's offices, and driveways leading to the parking behind everything.

"Say, listen," he said. "Do you like Stan Kenton? He's playing at the Balboa Ballroom for two weeks. How'd you like to go with me some night?"

Beth Carol's eyes darted from the addresses on the buildings to the one she had scribbled down. Golly, she could hardly read it herself and it was her own handwriting.

"I'm not really a cab driver, you know," he said. "I'm an actor. So it's not as if you'd be going out with a cab driver."

"Would you do something for me?" Beth Carol asked.

"Would you mind putting out that cigarette? I'm going to have a baby, and the smoke is making me kind of sick."

She really almost gagged as she pushed open the door of the motel room and got the full blast of Fern's cheap perfume. That, and clothes that hadn't been washed, and something worse. Sickness. The draperies were closed and Beth Carol could hardly make out the figure in a tangle of sheets on the double bed.

Fern moaned, and Beth Carol froze, wondering what she was doing there. Hoping that the baby would forgive her for bringing him to such a squalid place. She picked her way across the room, stepping over piles of clothes dropped on the floor. She fumbled around for the lamp she knew was always on a table next to the bed in a motel room and switched it on.

Fern lay there, her pale hair plastered to her forehead with perspiration, her eyes closed in her little, white face. She tossed and turned, moaned again as she clutched the blood-spattered sheet around her. On the floor was a crumpled heap of red towels. Red with Fern's blood, Beth Carol saw with horror, wondering why she didn't faint. She put her hand on Fern's forehead, felt the heat. She's burning up, Beth Carol thought, shaking. What am I going to do?

"Fern," she said hoarsely. "Fern, I'm here."

The girl's eyes flickered open, unseeing. She shook her head, trying to focus.

"You came," she whispered.

Her voice was harsh, guttural, not even caring about anything anymore, Beth Carol realized as she picked up the phone, waited until someone in the office in front gave her an outside line. She dialed the other number she had scrawled before she'd left the house.

"Good morning, Mount Sinai Hospital."

"Dr. Ross, please," she said, trying to control the hysteria in her voice.

"I'm sorry. Dr. Ross won't be in until eight o'clock. Would you care to try back?"

"I have to reach him now," she said. "This is Beth Carol Barnes, and I'm a patient of his. It's an emergency. It's a matter of life or death."

"One moment, please. I'll put you through, Miss Barnes."

"Yes, Beth Carol."

Beth Carol felt so relieved to hear his voice she had to sit down. "I'm here with a girlfriend," she said. "She's very sick. She's burning up, and she's hemmorrhaging. It's really bad. I've never seen so much blood."

"Did she say what happened?" he asked urgently.

A warning clicked in her brain. If she told him the truth, would Dr. Ross just let her die?

"I don't know," she said.

"Well, what did she say when she called you, Beth Carol? I know you're upset, but try to remember."

"She didn't say anything," she said stubbornly. "I swear it."

"Give me the address there," he said. "I'll send an ambulance. I'll meet you in emergency. Try to stay calm, Beth Carol. It won't be long."

She really lived like a pig, Beth Carol thought with disgust as she scurried into the bathroom to get a cold cloth for Fern's forehead. Spilled powder, and open jars of makeup, hairpins all over the place. And the blood, drops, rivulets, all over the rug, all over the bathroom floor. In what seemed like no time at all, there was a tap on the door, the ambulance guys were there, loading Fern onto a gurney. The pink baby doll nightie she was wearing was sodden, too. Her legs sprawled lifelessly as they covered her with a sheet, strapped her down. Outside, Beth Carol could see the other tenants of the motel, standing near the ambulance. Standing at their own open doors.

A guy in a brown bathrobe who had to be the motel

manager was standing right at the rear of the ambulance. This was embarrassing, Beth Carol thought as she walked along beside the gurney. She saw Fern's eyes flicker open.

"Beth Carol," Fern said weakly.

"Don't talk," Beth Carol told her. "You're going to be fine. Honest."

"I won't forget this," Fern said. "You'll see. When I'm a movie star, I'll make it up to you."

Oh, sure, she thought. When you're a movie star and when I'm the Queen of the May.

"Don't even think about it," she said awkwardly.

"Are you coming, miss?" one of the ambulance attendants asked her.

"No, no. I'm not," she said.

Then the doors were banged shut and there was the snarl of the ambulance's siren as it gathered volume. Beth Carol felt a little lonely as she watched it go, and then the motel manager was there, asking who was going to pay the bill for the room. Stuff like that. He was even grabbing at her arm, looking intimidating. "What if she dies?" he said. "What am I supposed to do with all her things?"

"Listen," Beth Carol said, shaking off his hand, backing away. "I don't even know that girl. I've just met her a couple of times. Okay?"

And then she started to trot out of the motel's parking lot, looked around for a phone booth, and called a cab.

"That could have been us, baby," she whispered to her stomach as she sat in the backseat. "Oh, we're so lucky. So lucky."

CHAPTER 19

*I*t was always a shock to Beth Carol to see the mansion in the daylight, to get the full impact of that great stone house with its twelve chimneys sitting there like something that should have been in the French countryside. Or maybe it was more like San Simeon up north a little that that publisher who had died not long ago had built. It was enormous, too, and you had to get to it by train. It didn't have a lake, though, or she hadn't seen one in the newsreel pictures. It was one of the days that the gardeners came. There must have been ten of them, swarming all over the place.

She crossed and uncrossed her legs, squirmed a little on the seat, getting a little nervous now that they were almost at the entrance to the house. Please, God, she said to herself. Let him still be away. Don't let me have to explain where I've been, what I've been doing.

She wrinkled her nose with disgust as she pictured that awful hole Fern was living in, the awful scent of her perfume, and the dirty clothes and the spilled cosmetics, and Fern herself. The perfect resident for a dive like that. It was a million miles away from a glorious place like this, the home she shared with Paul. The perfect place where she would raise her baby. Oh, what a close call it had been, she thought, seeing Fern in front of her again. Seeing all that blood. She hadn't really considered it until just this minute, but there was a good possibility that Fern was dead. How much blood could you lose, after all? It didn't seem that she could have had even a drop left inside her.

And the nerve of that ambulance attendant thinking that she would go along in the ambulance with Fern. As if somebody as refined as she was would know somebody like Fern well enough to do something like that. And that motel manager, thinking she was going to pay Fern's bill. What did she look like? Lady Bountiful, or somebody? No, she had just done what she had to do. And it was funny in a way, because doing what she had to do really made her feel good about herself. It had probably been shock, of course, but she had done it. Gotten through to Dr. Ross, been there until Fern had been taken away.

She glanced over at the garage, at the sea of tarps. At the one empty space.

"Right here," she said to the driver, relief flooding through her that Paul wasn't home.

"Thank you," he said as she counted out his fare, added a tip.

"Don't worry about the gate when you leave," she said. "I'll close it from the house."

"Thank you, miss," he said again.

So where was he? Beth Carol wondered unhappily, as she let herself in the back door, sauntered slowly into the silent kitchen, where she opened the refrigerator and poured herself a glass of orange juice. Well, at least he'd thought of orange juice, she told herself, although it wasn't any big deal. It was the least he could do, considering. He'd put her in the psycho ward, after all. And he'd tried to make her abort their baby, too. His own son. How could he have been so insensitive? For all he cared, she could be dead now, too, just like Fern. Tears of self-pity filled her eyes as she scrambled eggs, fried bacon, put a couple of pieces of toast in the toaster. Poured herself a glass of milk. Could almost see the baby getting ready for breakfast, too.

Beth Carol hated to admit it, but there was no reason for Paul to be out all night like this unless he were with another girl. It was the first time she'd even said it to herself. And she knew just the type of girl it would be, too. Common, vulgar, with big boobs. Oh, she'd seen him look at those girls often enough, seen the speculative look in his eyes. One of those waitresses of his, or a stripper like that Myra she'd done the movie with. That would be sort of funny. If they'd both had the same girl. You have to stop thinking about things like that, she told herself firmly. You have to think pure thoughts, good thoughts. For the baby. Everything for the baby.

Well, she was just going to force herself not to care what Paul did, or who he did it with, either. Oh, she loved him, more than life itself. But she had to think about the baby, the future the three of them would have as a family. So she'd have to be strong. She just had to be.

She breathed in the odor of the sizzling bacon, wondered if it was such a good idea. Actually, it was making her feel a little sick. Maybe just the scrambled eggs, she decided as she stood still, listened. Heard a car outside.

Paul had a furtive look on his face as he let himself in through the back door and saw her standing there in the kitchen.

"I thought you'd still be asleep," he said apologetically. "Do you feel all right?"

"Where have you been all night?" she shrieked, the tears coming as she started to beat on his arm with both of her fists. "How dare you come home at this hour? I could have been dying, for all you knew."

"Oh, for Christ's sake," he exclaimed, grasping her hands, holding her away. "Pull yourself together, will you? I'm going to bed."

"Who were you with?" she screamed. "Some cheap floozy, I know that. Who? Who?"

"Look, I'll see you later," he muttered as he pushed past her.

Beth Carol sat down at the table, put her head on her arms, and cried until there were no more tears.

o   o   o

"Dahlber, Felix, Beloved husband of . . ."

No.

"Darnell, Bertha, aged ninety-seven, orginal settler of the Bunker Hill district . . ."

No.

So maybe she wasn't dead, Beth Carol decided as she sat at the kitchen table the next morning, scanning the obituary notices in the paper. Or maybe she was, and the hospital knew her real name, and it was under that. Maybe if I look at the ages, she thought. Forty-seven, seventy-three, eighty-one. Oh, here was one that could be it. "Saunders, Joanne, age twenty-four. Beloved daughter of Herman and Claire Saunders, adored sister of Debbie and Brian Saunders. In an automobile accident on . . ."

Oh, it was hopeless, she thought, flinging the paper onto the floor. Calling the hospital had been hopeless, too.

"I'd like to inquire about a patient," she had said when she'd called.

"Who would you like to know about?"

"Fern Darling."

"Are you a relative?"

"No, I'm not. Just a friend."

"I'm sorry, we can only give out information on patients to a relative."

"Well, is she okay?"

"I'm sorry."

The only thing she could think of was to call Dr. Ross and see if he would tell her anything. She wouldn't do that, of course. It had been one thing to bother an important doctor like Dr. Ross when it was a matter of life or death. But she couldn't just call him to ask how somebody was, or even *if* somebody still was. It wouldn't be right. So that left getting in a cab and going down there, and wild horses wouldn't get her to do that. Admit she knew someone like Fern Darling in front of all those nurses and everybody? Never.

Oh, who cares anyway? she thought crossly, picking up the paper again, opening it to the society section, her favorite thing to do in the whole world. Oh, here was something about the Spinsters. That was the group all of those candy stripers at the hospital belonged to. They had given a charity ball at the Huntington Hotel in Pasadena. She scanned the row of smiling faces, not recognizing any of them. Read the names. Phyllis Babbitt. Alice Fenton. Patricia Nation.

Real names. Not the made-up ones of all of the girls and guys she had met with Paul. His sister, Diana, would probably have been at that ball, too, if she weren't in Jamaica with her parents. But probably not. These girls were older. Eighteen, probably. Nineteen, even.

She tried her own name there, too.

Alice Fenton. Patricia Nation. Beth Carol Barnes.

It would never happen now, she thought with a sinking feeling. Maybe I've made a mistake, she thought, stroking her stomach. Maybe this wasn't such a good idea after all. And then she reminded herself that Paul's family was right up there with the best of those society families. That she herself was a Barnes, of the Idaho Barneses. That it would all be fine after a while. Of course, Paul would have to go to the Wharton School of Business. He would have to go into the family business. Well, everybody had dreams. And most of them had to be put aside for the realities of life.

Beth Carol sighed and turned her attention back to the society pages. She read those names, started to get the drift, finally. None of the people in these pages had anything to do with the movie business or the television business. In all of the lists of names at all of the parties, there was never the name of a movie star, never the name of a director, or even of the heads of studios that Paul practically genuflected in front of. It was as if she and Paul and all the kids they knew were living in one world that they thought was the best and most important world that could ever be, and the paper was reporting on stuff that happened in some other world completely, a world that could have been on the moon. So which was the real one? she asked herself as she scanned the blurry pictures. It had to be the one the paper was talking about, she decided. The one that wasn't built on sand where everything shifted from moment to moment.

She stopped at one of the pictures, read the caption underneath it. Roger Horton, Jr., his charming wife, Bitsy, the former Felicity Cunningham, and their two-year-old son, Roger II, enjoying a tailgate luncheon at the polo matches in Santa Barbara. The Hortons, well, they were one of the biggest of all those society names. Maybe the biggest because they owned the paper. Had owned it for generations. Taking the paper, she walked over to the window, looked at it again in the morning sunlight streaming into the room. Her eyes widened as she looked into Roger Horton, Jr.'s face, his pleasant expression, his receding hairline, the way he was holding Roger II in the crook of one arm, the way he had his other arm around Bitsy's waist. It was that guy she had been with so many times, the one who had given her jewelry and tips. The one she was so sure was half in love with her, and who she sort of had the feeling would like to set her up in a place of her own. Her cheeks burned as she recognized him. Well, thank heaven she was away from all that, and if she and Paul ever ran into him after they were married, well, she'd think of something. She knew she would.

"I was worried about you," Bobby said, his hands on her shoulders as he stood behind her, his eyes meeting hers in the mirror. "You should have called me."

"Oh, I didn't think. . ." she began, flustered at his words, and pleased, too. It was funny how she never expected anybody to notice her, never expected anybody to care.

"Did it go all right?" he asked, leaning close to her, almost whispering in her ear. "The name of the doctor I gave you?"

"Oh, it was fine," she said, nodding, remembering what Paul

had said. "Ask your beauty operator. They always know of somebody. Those girls they do are in and out all the time." He'd been right. Bobby hadn't even hesitated. He'd just reached for his big, fat address book and turned right to the page.

"Everything's over now." He offered her a cigarette and lit it, lit one of his own, with a gold Dunhill lighter. "They got raided yesterday, closed down."

"Oh, no," she said, the fine hairs on her arms rising as she realized she could have been sitting there and looked up to see the cops storming in.

Yes, it's terrible," he said, and again there was that look he got when something exciting was going on, as if he were enjoying the sheer awfulness of whatever it was. "There was a story in *Confidential*, you know, that terrible paper everybody says they don't read but they do, and it said that there was this abortion mill down on Santa Monica Boulevard and that they were running all of these girls through and killing them or botching everything and sending them to the hospital. And you know who they said was there? Cara Conway." He sighed, took a sip of his coffee, another puff of his cigarette. "And she's been going with, oh, I forget his name, the head of the studio who's married to one of the movie daughters. Warner? Mayer? Oh, one of them. I never can remember names."

So Fern was alive, Beth Carol thought reflectively. And she'd done just what she said she was going to do. Made her two hundred dollars. Closed down the abortion place in the process.

"So she's suspended," Bobby continued. "And she's in hiding somewhere."

"What'll happen to her?" Beth Carol murmured, aware of her own shock as she saw how pale her face was in the mirror. "Will they put her in jail?"

"No, not jail," Bobby said. "The doctor, he's the one who'll go to jail. But Cara? How would they prove it?"

"Well, the doctor should go to jail," Beth Carol said self-righteously. "I know for a fact that he's a butcher, Bobby. He almost killed a friend of mine."

"Well, I don't know," Bobby murmured, combing her wet hair, squinting at her in the mirror. "I've known so many girls who've gone to him. Fifty, maybe. A hundred. And it's been fine with every one of them."

"Well, my friend—" Beth Carol began.

"So everybody will just have to find someone else," he said. "And I hope Cara's gotten a bundle of dough from that boyfriend of hers. She'll never work again, not after this."

"But Bobby, if they can't prove it—"

"They don't have to prove it," he said. "The rumors are enough. She's over."

That was really terrible, Beth Carol thought. Something that couldn't even be proved, and it could ruin a career. Just like that.

"So you can see why I was worried about you," he said, brushing her face with his fingers. "I hadn't been able to sleep because I was thinking about you. When I heard you'd made an appointment, I was really relieved."

"Bobby," she said, looking up at him. "I didn't do it."

"What do you mean?" he asked, frowning.

"I didn't go through with it. When I got in there, I decided I was making a mistake. I'm going to have my baby."

He stared at her for a moment, then dropped into the chair next to hers.

"Are you crazy?" he whispered savagely. "You'll ruin your life. And now, with all of this happening, you don't even have a second chance. There's no place to go yet."

That made her scared, the thought that now she didn't have any alternatives. That, like it or not, she was committed.

"I've never heard of anything like this," he said. "Tying yourself down like this."

"But it's my baby," she whispered. "I couldn't kill him, Bobby. I just couldn't."

"Beth Carol, no guy wants to be stuck with some other guy's kid," he said, holding both her hands in his own. "Haven't you heard these girls talk around here? Don't you know how things really are out there?"

"I don't care," she said desperately.

"How are you going to take care of it?" he asked.

"I-I'm going to marry Paul," she stuttered. "He'll take care of the baby, take care of me."

Bobby sighed, got slowly to his feet, picked up a tendril of wet hair and wound it around a curler. "A customer of mine was there when the cops broke in," he said conversationally. "They were just sitting there, minding their own business, and they looked up and here were all these cops swarming through the place. And the worst thing was that they were supposed to go to New York in a couple of weeks with their husband on some really important business trip and the last thing they wanted was to be throwing up and all."

"Did they arrest her?" Beth Carol asked.

"They just let her go," Bobby said, shaking his head. "But they've already got a boy and a girl. They don't want any more kids."

"Well, I'm sure they'll love it when it's born," Beth Carol said.

"Oh, maybe," Bobby said morosely.

"What did you think of my idea?" she asked.

"Which idea?"

"Marrying Paul," she said. "That idea."

"I think it's the craziest thing I've ever heard," he said with a quick smile.

"Oh, you don't know Paul," she said. "He's not what you think."

"Say, I wanted to ask you something else," he said, as if he'd just remembered. Probably *had* just remembered whatever it was, because Bobby could be a little vague. "Do you know somebody over at *Confidential?*"

"Of course not," Beth Carol said indignantly. "Why would I know anybody at a place like that?"

"Well, there was a little mention of you in that same issue, the one with Cara in it. That Beth Carol Barnes, the beautiful debutante, had just blown into town and was breaking hearts among all of the most eligible bachelors."

Oh, no, she thought, with an awful sinking feeling in the pit of her stomach. It had to be Fern, thinking she was doing something nice for Beth Carol to thank her, and having her name printed in the worst place in the world. What am I going to do? she wondered.

"Well, I don't know anybody there," she muttered. "It must be a coincidence."

"Yeah, that's what I thought, too," Bobby said.

When Beth Carol let herself in the back door of the mansion, she heard the phone ring once. Stop. Then ring again, twice. She picked it up on the third ring, breathing hard after running down the hall.

"Beth Carol? Hi, it's Fern."

"Fern," she panted. "Where are you?"

"I'm still in the hospital," Fern said. "That fucker perforated my uterus, my bowel. That's what went wrong."

"So you're okay?"

"Yeah, now I am," she said. "And shit, I was hardly out of surgery when the cops came. A couple of detectives and a couple of cops in uniform, as if I was going to escape, or something."

"What did they want?"

"Well, they wanted to know what happened. What else would they want?" she asked. "After all, it was pretty clear that something had happened, and so I told them."

"They closed the abortion place," Beth Carol said. "The cops went in and busted it. They arrested the doctor."

"Oh, yeah?" said Fern indifferently.

"And Cara Conway, she's been suspended by the studio. And my beauty operator says she's through, that her career is over because of this."

"I've got something really funny to tell you about that Cara Conway item, man," Fern said. "You're not going to believe this."

"What?" Beth Carol asked.

"Yeah, well, what happened was that it got a lot of attention,"

Fern said, her voice almost a purr. "You know who called, wanting me to go to work for them?"

"Who?"

"How about Hedda Hopper? Louella Parsons?" Fern said triumphantly. "And Sir George Dean, that English guy who's on the network news a few times a week."

"Golly, Sir George Dean," Beth Carol breathed, feeling a tingle of jealousy. "He's been knighted by the king. That's why he's Sir George Dean."

"Oh, yeah?" said Fern. "I just thought it was his name."

"I tried to call you, too," said Beth Carol. "I couldn't get through. They wouldn't tell me anything, either."

"Well, you have to know how," Fern said vaguely. "I mean, there are ways and ways. You can find out anything, if you know how to do it."

"So are you going to go to work for one of them?" Beth Carol asked.

"Yeah," Fern said. "Sir George Dean. I'm having a meeting with him as soon as I get out of here, and I'm going to work for him. A leg girl, is what he calls it. Someone who goes around and gets items for him."

"Why him, and not Louella Parsons or Hedda Hopper?" Beth Carol asked, her lips pursed. "I mean, they're more famous."

"Yeah, I guess so," Fern said. "But he's going to pay me more money. And guess what? I'm supposed to call him when I'm ready to get out, and he's going to send his limousine for me. Isn't that hysterical?"

"Hysterical," Beth Carol said through clenched teeth.

"Yeah, man, he said he was going to send his car and driver for me and I said to him, 'Say, Sir George, do you mean a limousine?' and he said yes, so I guess it's kind of vulgar to call it a limousine, or something."

"I guess," Beth Carol said.

"What I was wondering," Fern said, "was if you saw that item I had them run about you. The one where I called you a glamorous debutante."

"I heard about it," Beth Carol said.

"Well, did you like it?" Fern asked.

"Sure, it was fine. Thank you."

"See, man, I wanted to thank you for coming down that morning and calling that doctor, and everything. You didn't have to, you know. I didn't expect it."

"I was glad I could help," Beth Carol said stiffly. "Are you going back to the same place?"

"No, I'm not," Fern said. "I told Sir George Dean that I didn't have any place to stay right now, that I was just kind of living here and there, and he said he'd fix something up for me."

"The manager wanted to know who was going to pay the bill," Beth Carol said.

"Oh, fuck the manager," Fern said. "So look, I just wanted to be sure you knew about what I had them write about you."

"Okay, Fern," she said. "Thanks again."

"I've got to go, man," she said. "You know how it is here. All these people wandering in all the time. So I'll call you when I'm settled and give you my new number, okay?"

"Great," Beth Carol said. "And congratulations. I'm really happy for you."

"Yeah, it's about time," Fern said with a little laugh.

After she hung up, Beth Carol sat at the kitchen table for a long time, wondering how she really felt about Fern's big break. Wondering how she really felt about the baby growing in her stomach, so sweet and trusting. The one she couldn't get rid of now, even if she changed her mind. Wondering what Paul was going to say when he found out she hadn't had the abortion. But she kind of knew what that would be. He'd tell her to get out, and then what was she going to do?

CHAPTER 20

$\mathscr{G}$lamorous Lana Turner, one of our personal favorites in this town of glamorous ladies, and the star so far this year of three of the top blockbuster films, is on the verge of throwing away a brilliant career," Sir George Dean said, a look of distaste on his patrician face as if there were something that smelled bad right there on the desk in front of him instead of the stack of pages he turned as he read them. He wore what Beth Carol knew was an impeccably tailored pinstriped suit, a tie handsome even on the tiny screen, and what was clearly a flower in his buttonhole. His hands, on the pages, were long and tapered, and on the little finger of his left hand he wore a ring. Probably a signet ring, Beth Carol thought, because the only rings for men were class rings, like the one Paul wore from Yale, or signet rings, which English guys wore. The only other rings were diamond pinky rings, but the guys who wore those were gangsters or maîtres d'hotel at Italian restaurants.

"Yes, our own little birdie has once again flown in with a twig of news to truly dismay lovely Lana's most dedicated fans, and that is her infatuation with one of our fair city's most notorious philanderers. Doesn't lovely Lana know that this aviation whiz and pathetic, amateur film-maker has gals stashed in bungalows and apartments from one end of town to the other? You're better than that, pretty lady. Don't just be another face in the crowd."

Oh, no, thought Beth Carol as she stood behind the iron-ing board, one of Paul's long, black socks in front of her. He had to mean Howard Hughes, and everybody knew about him. Why, he changed girls as if they were, well, socks. Oh, Lana Turner would never be that dumb. She could have anybody. Beth Carol crinkled her nose, smelled something burning, and, guiltily, grabbed the iron off the sock.

"And that's our news from Hollywood tonight," Sir George Dean said, his hands clasped together on the desk in front of him, a tight smile on his narrow mouth. "Bless you, and we'll see you next time."

Well, she had to admit there was something very grand about him, Beth Carol thought, reaching behind her, lowering the zipper on her capri pants another few inches. The pants were really getting tight, she realized, lumbering over to a chair, putting the sock she had just ironed on top of the others, grabbing a handful of Paul's white boxer shorts and testing them with her hand, seeing that they were properly damp, ready to be stroked by her into wrinkle-free perfection.

Of course, part of what made Sir George Dean seem so grand was that English accent of his. Beth Carol just loved that. And then the way he looked down his nose at every-thing. And those wonderful clothes. Even Paul had said he'd never seen such suits and said they probably came from Saville Row, which was just about the only place you could get suits handmade like that. And those shirts. The way the collar fit, the way just the right amount of cuff showed, no matter how many papers he turned, or how he moved. Of course, Paul's shirts were still ready-made, but they all came from Brooks Brothers, like all his other clothes, and he was very particular about the way they looked. He'd been grateful when she had offered to iron them for him, but he said that the Chinese laundry did such a good job. So she'd had to beg, and finally, just before he got so exasperated that he was ready to storm out the door, he'd said that she could try to do a couple of the older ones if it would make her happy and give her something to do.

From what she'd read about him, Sir George Dean was out every night at all the best nightclubs and restaurants and he was driven in an antique silver Bentley, which was a kind of a Rolls-Royce in every way, except the grill was different and it had a *B* where the Rolls-Royce's emblem was. And to complete the picture, his chauffeur was this little Oriental guy in a gray uniform with puttees and high black boots.

Beth Carol stretched, feeling that sharp pain in her lower back again, wishing she could figure out some way to iron sitting down. Wondering what she was going to wear in about three weeks, when she knew she wouldn't be able to get into one thing that hung in her closet. Well, at least Paul hadn't noticed yet. Didn't have the time to notice since he was so busy and so happy. She'd never seen him as happy as he'd been since he'd decided to take that class at film school. He was making a documentary as his class project. "How To Make a Movie," his documentary was called, and it was a terrific idea, really, because what they were doing was shooting the documentary at Metro-Goldwyn-Mayer, the best studio of them all, and they were shooting everybody while they made the real movie.

"Think of the contacts," Paul had said, looking so bright-eyed, bursting with joy that he had finally figured out a way to get into a studio, to get his career started, as he saw it.

Hot tears of pity filled her eyes as she folded a pair of shorts and walked over to put them on the stack of finished underwear. Poor Paul, she thought. Because it would all come to nothing. He would have to go to business school. It was inevitable. He wouldn't be able to support her and the baby with any movie he made, for a long, long time. He wasn't even being paid to make this one. In fact, he was paying them to go to the school. Men, she thought, shaking her head. They really were just a bunch of little boys, just the way the girls at Secrets talked about them, treated them.

He'd come around, though, she promised herself. She'd

see to it. All the care she was taking of him, the ironing, the darling little snacks she would leave for him in the kitchen, so no matter what time he got home, there would be something. A reminder of her, of her love for him, her devotion. Beth Carol's eyes widened with dismay as she looked at the yellow stain on the white boxer shorts she was pressing. Oh, golly, she thought, wiping the tears away. The iron was too hot. They were ruined. Oh, it was all so sad. So hopeless. And these pants, they were really killing her now. She could hardly breathe. She reached behind her, pushed down the rest of the zipper, sighed with relief as she pushed them down to her thighs in front, letting her stomach hang out. All she'd done so far were his socks and about half of the shorts, and already she was so tired all she wanted to do was lie down and sleep until morning. She felt a little stiff-legged as she picked her way across the room to Diana's bed, flopped down on top of it with another great sigh. Her bra was killing her, too. Cutting into her back. She unbuttoned her blouse, squirmed around to unhook it in back, let her breasts fall loose. She lay panting with exertion, looking down at them, at her stomach bursting out of the elastic of her panties. She pushed them down, too. Gazed down at the length of herself. Smiled with satisfaction at what she saw.

She had boobs for the first time, after all those years of being jealous of the girls who had them. And hips, too. And, of course, her tummy, but that didn't show when she was wearing a pair of tight pants, like these, to hold it in. And it was funny how even more guys came on to her than before she'd started to bloat up this way. She'd be waiting for a bus when she was through at Secrets, and all of these guys in their Caddies and Lincolns would come screeching up to the light, offering her a ride. Or when she got off the bus and started to walk up the hill to the house, they were always stopping then, too. It was interesting that they really did like voluptuous girls better. Like Fern. The little birdie that Sir George Dean had talked about might be Fern. Or maybe it wasn't. Probably not, because once Sir George Dean got a look at Fern, he must have realized what a terrible,

terrible mistake he'd made to offer her a job.

Poor Fern. Nobody would want anybody who looked like a slut around. No guy would ever want to have anything to do with her except to make it with her. Nobody like Sir George Dean, or anybody else, would hire her to do anything. So about the only thing Beth Carol could see ahead for Fern was that she would just keep on hooking until she was too old, and then she would be a streetwalker, and then, finally, she would be a waitress at a coffee shop, if she were lucky and her insolent attitude didn't get her fired the first day on the job.

Beth Carol pulled herself up, feeling ravenous again. All she seemed to do these days was eat or sleep, she realized. She just seemed to go along with what the baby wanted her to do, what the baby needed, as if she were a puppet and the baby was sitting inside her stomach, pulling the strings. He was starting to take up a lot of space inside her, too. Pushing everything aside and taking the room for himself. Why, she could hardly get her breath anymore, and she didn't even show yet. At least not in clothes. And she barely had the energy to lift her arms. She undressed and lumbered over to the closet to hang up her blouse, her pants.

Her spirits lifted as she examined her reflection in the full-length mirror on the back of the bathroom door. My baby, she thought proudly, running her hands over her stomach, which was hard with his presence, then over her breasts, which were all swollen with tiny blue veins, the nipples enlarged, getting ready for his mouth. What she figured was that there was only one thing she owed the baby that she wasn't already giving him. And that was going to be hard, because it was getting the man she loved to marry her before he was born. Because she wasn't going to have her baby be illegitimate. A bastard. No, he had to have a proper mommy and daddy on his birth certificate, and somehow she was going to have to find a way to make that happen.

She stared at herself in the mirror, thought again of all those guys who hit on her because she looked like this now. Thought about all the money she could have made from those guys. Money Paul wouldn't have had to know about. But she'd stuck to her decision not to have anything to do with any of them, not even accepting a ride on the last part of the street where it was really uphill and she would have to stop and rest for a couple of minutes before going on. No, the only people she'd accepted rides from were some of the ladies who lived on the street who always gave rides to the kids coming home from school, and they thought she was just another kid. They all assumed that she went to the Westlake School for Girls, which was a few blocks away, and then they always started to ask if she knew this girl or that girl. Sometimes, did she know their daughter, stuff like that. Beth Carol would nod and smile and try to be vague about exactly which of the mansions was the one where she lived, who her family was.

She turned, posing in front of the mirror, thinking that she should have a quick shower, put on her robe, go downstairs, and have a nutritious supper, like what was on the list of stuff the obstetrician had given her, the stuff she got from the market that delivered.

She stood on tiptoe, raised her arms above her head, gave herself a big smile in the mirror. A spurt of fear ran through her and she dropped her arms, as she became aware of something different in the room behind her.

It was Paul, his face white, the remains of a smile still frozen on his face.

Beth Carol froze, too, her eyes darting to meet Paul's in his reflection in the mirror. What was he doing here? she thought indignantly, guilt coupled with fear sending tremors through her legs. He was supposed to be in school, shooting his movie. Somewhere. In the mirror, she saw him close his eyes as if in pain. She stood there, feeling like an idiot, one hand clasped over her pubic hair, the other at her swollen breasts.

"Just tell me what you were thinking about," he said, his voice husky, quivering with rage. "I really want to know."

"I couldn't kill our baby," she said, her voice catching in a little sob.

"You what?" he demanded, his voice strangled, a vein throbbing on his forehead, his eyes bright with fury. "I get down on my knees, beg people for the money, and you didn't go through with it?"

She turned to face him, her lips trembling, feeling vulnerable and afraid as she stood there naked. She'd known this moment would come, but she'd put it out of her mind. The actuality of it, this awful feeling that she'd betrayed him, everything.

"What about the money?" he asked.

"They kept it," she said.

"So what was going to happen when I found out?" he asked, perplexed. He really was trying to understand, she saw. Paul and his psychology.

"I thought you'd come around," she mumbled.

"Come around how?" he asked. "What are you talking about?"

She stood there, feeling like a trapped animal, not knowing what to say.

"Put something on, will you?" he snapped, exasperated.

"We love each other," she said as she scurried to the closet, wrestled her arms into a robe. "I love you. You love me."

"Oh, shit." He sighed, burying his face in his hands.

"We can get married," she said hopelessly.

"You really do live in a dream world," he said.

"Other people do it," she said, creeping over to where he sat, perching gingerly on the edge of a chair so that their knees were almost touching.

"I suppose it's too late to do anything now," he said.

Miserably, she nodded, trying to remember how she had seen this going. That Paul would take her in his arms, probably. Reach into his pocket and produce a diamond ring. Call in an announcement of their engagement to the newspapers with the other hand.

"You really must think you're something. Here you are, just out of a psycho ward. You've tried to commit suicide. And you think I'd marry you?"

Her head jerked as if he had slapped her. She felt tears stinging the corners of her eyes.

"You love me," she muttered. "You've told me."

"That isn't enough," he said.

"I thought if we got married, and the baby and all, that your father would come around."

"Come around." He snorted. "That would really do it. He'd disown me."

"You'll go to business school, just the way he wants," she begged.

"Oh, shit," he muttered. "I just don't believe this."

"It'll be all right," she said, pleading. "You'll see. I'll stand by you. I'll be everything to you. You won't be sorry."

"I'm not going to marry you, Beth Carol," he said. "You can forget about that. I'm not going to ruin my life."

"I'll make you so happy, Paul," she said, closer to him now, stroking his leg, her robe falling away from her breasts. He was looking at them, she saw, in spite of himself. And she recognized the look in his eyes, too. He wants me, she thought. Right here in Diana's room, and, for once he wants me. In spite of everything.

Still, she was astonished when he leaned over suddenly, and took one of her nipples in his mouth.

"You look different," he said, his voice husky.

"Not that different," she breathed, pressing her luck now, her hand flat on the fly of his trousers, gauging his reaction. He was getting hard, she realized, satisfied. If she could get him to make it with her now, if they could merge their bodies, she could just forget about everything he'd said. All the mean things, all the awful rejection. What you did was what mattered, not what you said. That was another one of Paul's mottoes, too. More words to live by. Beth Carol leaned over and gently kissed his mouth, felt his breath coming faster as he put his arm around her and drew her onto his lap.

His tongue was pushing her lips apart as she started to unbutton his tattersall shirt. She ran her hand over the black fur matting his chest. He was stroking her hair now, running his tongue over her lips, holding her firmly as he dropped his mouth to her breast, held it as he sucked on her nipple. Beth Carol felt a little guilty as she looked ahead to what was going to happen, knew that he would be putting his thing inside her when she had promised the baby that he wouldn't be disturbed, that inside her body was his territory. He probably didn't even like this, she thought, feeling that her vaginal fluid was starting to really flow now, feeling her pulse racing, her mounting excitement at the thought of Paul. Beth Carol could almost see the baby frowning and she felt so bad about it, but there was no turning back now. This was going to prove something important for both of them, this time with Paul, and the baby was just going to have to forgive her because she was fighting for their whole future as a family.

Paul pushed the robe off her shoulders, stroked them while he suckled at her breast, started to stroke her pubic hair as she stroked his bare chest now, leaned to lick his nipples. Sliding off his lap, she unzipped his trousers, knelt at his feet, and took it in her mouth. He really was hard, she realized with a little shudder of pleasure. Above her, she could hear him panting, feel his hands in her hair.

Oh, it was so thrilling, ecstasy, to be making love with someone she loved, who loved her, she thought as Paul lifted her in his arms and carried her to Diana's bed. Put her down as he quickly took off his clothes, dropping them on the floor in his eagerness to take her into his arms. Really, it transcended everything, made her feel as if she were alive for the first time as he held her against him, kissing her mouth, her eyelids. And here, too, she realized. On his sister's bed, in their home. So that meant a lot, too.

Beth Carol cringed with embarrassment when she realized that Paul was kissing her there, sucking on her just like one of the guys she did it with for money, and here she had been ironing, and it had been such a hot day, and she had been just about to jump in the shower when he had walked into the room and surprised her. And he was so good at it, too, she thought, nearly swooning as she felt his tongue, felt his hands grasping her buttocks. And then he was taking her hand, putting it on his thing, telling her in a hoarse whisper what he was going to do to her, telling her to put it inside of her, his hand on top of her own as, together, they guided it into her.

She gasped as he entered her, then wound her legs around his waist, felt herself leap to another plane of consciousness as he pushed into her, whispering all those dirty things she couldn't separate from each other. Usually when he took her, it was just a couple of thrusts. Not this time, though. No, it was going on and on, taking her physical places she had never been before.

"Give it to me, baby. Give it to me," he commanded, his face above her contorted, his eyes glittering.

"I love you," she whispered. Over and over, as she wound her legs more tightly around his waist, her arms around his shoulders, consuming him as he was consuming her. Seeing little flashes of light as she felt herself explode, praying for one instant that whatever it was that was happening to her wouldn't make the baby explode, too. Hoping that the baby was all right.

Her first orgasm, she realized a couple moments later. Now she knew what they were talking about. Then Paul was thrusting faster, faster, screaming, his head thrown back as she felt him spurt into her. She lay there, holding him, waiting for him to push her away, get up the way he always did.

She was in his arms, his head buried in her neck, their bodies, dripping with perspiration, locked together as she listened to his even breathing. Realized he was asleep. In her arms. In Diana's bed.

It's going to be all right, she thought, her eyelids fluttering closed as she drifted off to sleep. I don't know what happened, but I've won.

CHAPTER 21

"I didn't know you were going away," Bobby said, combing her wet hair as the colored girl put a cup of coffee on the counter in front of her. He really had a great tan today, she saw. He must have been with his friends in Malibu this weekend, the ones with the big house right on the beach in the colony. And that was a new watch, too. Solid gold. She would bet on it.

"I'm not going away," she protested, wondering what he was talking about. It was so good between her and Paul these days that she barely wanted to leave the house even to come here. But, of course, she had to come here to be pampered and perfected so it would go on being as good as it was between her and Paul. He couldn't keep his hands off her these days. All he had to do was look at her before he had his hands all over her, before they were making it. She could hardly believe it, but she had a sneaking feeling she knew why. She had been looking at herself in the full-length mirror one afternoon, admiring herself, admiring the way the baby was pushing out her stomach, when she realized that she looked just like those waitresses, those strippers, that Paul really liked. With her breasts the way they were now, the hips, she could have gotten right up on the stage of the Pink Pussycat and strutted her stuff, and

Paul would have been right in the front row, applauding like crazy and stuffing ten-dollar bills into her . . . well, into her G-string, she guessed.

"Well, I read it," Bobby said stubbornly. "That you were off to your family's villa in the south of France."

"Huh?" She looked at him blankly in the mirror.

"In Sir George Dean's column, that's where I read it," Bobby said. "Glamorous deb Beth Carol Barnes, off to her family's villa in the south of France for a short stay, after breaking hearts in Hollywood wherever she goes."

"Oh, Sir George Dean," she said. Oh, Fern, she told herself with a smile.

"Lady George Dean, we call him," Bobby said, leaning toward her, his voice low, confidential.

"Bobby, you say that about everybody," she complained. "If everybody in the world is a fag, why are all these girls here getting their hair done, and everything? I mean, what's the point?"

"Well, not everybody," Bobby admitted. "I never said that. But Sir George Dean, yes. I know it for sure."

"There's only one way you can know it for sure, Bobby," she said, looking at him in the mirror. It was funny, but now that she wasn't drinking or taking pills or anything, she could tell when somebody else was. Bobby was really out of it this morning. His hand was even shaking, and when he would stop for a moment and say he'd be right back, she could smell liquor on his breath. She was sure of it.

"Well, I don't know it firsthand," he said. "But these friends of mine took me up there and it was pretty obvious. I mean, I got real close and I could swear that Lady George was wearing a little eyeshadow and mascara. I'd put money on it."

"Oh, Bobby." She giggled.

"The house is wonderful," he went on, flushing. "Great antiques, rugs. Right above the Sunset Strip, up from the Sunset Towers. And he has a lot of Oriental boys running around serving things."

"Are you okay?" she asked.

"Sure," he said. "And he wears a smoking jacket, and a cravat, too."

"I have a girlfriend who works for him," Beth Carol said. "I guess that's why my name was in his column."

"You're getting famous," Bobby said with admiration. "Everybody will know who you are."

"I guess so," she said, wondering how she felt about it. It sort of made her embarrassed, actually, but still, when she and Paul got married, maybe she would give Fern a call and see if she'd run something. Glamorous deb Beth Carol Barnes marries prominent scion Paul Fournier in an elaborate church wedding with sixteen attendants. Something like that. It couldn't be long now. Paul was so sweet these days, so attentive. He was even taking her to dinner tonight with friends of his. Another young couple who lived in Brentwood whom he was sure she would like. That was a first, too. Another first.

It was just past dusk that evening when Paul and Beth Carol pulled into the driveway of Joycie and Eddie Newfeld's two-story house in Brentwood, a neighborhood just west of Westwood and the University of California at Los Angeles. It was really a pretty house, Beth Carol saw, white clapboard with dark green shutters, and a lot of fruit trees in the front yard. The fragrance of orange blossoms hit her as Paul came around to open the door to the car.

"Nice neighborhood, huh?" Paul said, smiling, as he took her arm. "Lots of room between the houses. Churches, schools, a great shopping center just a few blocks away. The works."

"It's lovely," Beth Carol said, licking her lips, trying to remember all of the things Paul had said about his friends. That Eddie Newfeld had been a football star at USC and was now a big insurance agent. That Joycie was a Kappa Kappa Phi, a real sweetheart. It was Eddie who opened the front door almost as soon as Paul rang the bell. He looked like a nice enough guy, tall and big-shouldered, carrying a little weight around his middle. Joycie was a little blonde, peering out from behind her husband.

It was Paul who made the introductions in a new, hearty voice, while Beth Carol smiled and smiled, hoping it didn't look as if she were absolutely bursting out of her dress. It was tangerine linen, a sheath, with three fishes in yellow and the same shade of tangerine sewn to the front. Its belt was at its last notch. Maternity clothes were going to be next, she had thought gloomily when she was dressing. Oh, how she hated the thought of that. She was practically waddling now and feeling so unattractive. But it was going to be worth it, she reminded herself, patting her stomach, thinking about the baby, not thinking anymore about how all of the sex she and Paul were having these days might be affecting him. After all, even the doctor said it was okay. Just the last few weeks were when they weren't supposed to do it. She was already planning for that, for what she could do to keep Paul satisfied so he wouldn't be tempted to go back to his floozies.

"What a lovely home you have," she said, feeling Joycie Newfeld's bony little hand in her own.

"Oh, do you like it?" Joycie asked tremulously. "Here, I want to show you around."

Beth Carol let herself be led into the large living room with its fireplace, its chintz-covered furniture, its coffee table neatly stacked with copies of *House Beautiful*, and *Good Housekeeping*. The French doors leading into the back garden were still open. There was a brick terrace, a lighted swimming pool, more fragrant fruit trees, flowering bushes, flower beds. The dining room was pretty, too, the table already set with gaily colored place mats, stoneware plates, crystal wineglasses with skinny stems.

"And this is my pride and joy," Joycie said, standing aside to let Beth Carol step into the kitchen.

"Oh, it's beautiful," Beth Carol said, a stab of envy rushing through her as she saw all the electric appliances. The stove, the refrigerator. It was a dream kitchen, the one she was going to have, too. Someday soon.

When they joined the guys back in the living room, Eddie had already gotten Paul a drink and the two of them were standing at one of the open French doors. Beth Carol caught the drift of the conversation as Eddie told Paul how involved it had been to have the swimming pool built, and how the next step was to have it fenced in so there wouldn't be any accidents.

"What can I get you, Beth Carol?" he asked, taking one of her hands and leading her to the sofa.

"Just some orange juice, if you have it," she said apologetically.

"Oh, of course we have it," said Joycie, her eyes meeting her husband's. "I'll just be a sec. You make yourself comfortable, Beth Carol."

And then she was back and they were all sitting around, talking like old friends. Well, maybe not like old friends. Joycie kept talking about the neighborhood and how nice it was, and stuff like that. And her family. A lot about her family. Her parents who lived in Arcadia, and how they had come to California around the turn of the century and about how her dad was a developer, in a small way, of course, and how he was retired now and spent a lot of time with his roses.

Then Eddie was talking about his family, too. About his dad, who had a wholesale hardware business, but how Eddie hadn't wanted to go into it. When he'd gotten out of USC, there had been all of these offers because of football and all, and he was pretty much of a people person, and he loved selling insurance because that way the widow and children were protected when a man died, and how he felt as if he were actually performing a public service in a way, and didn't she agree.

"Oh, yes, that's wonderful," Beth Carol said as she thought that, nice as they were, Joycie and Eddie didn't really seem much like people Paul would know. In fact, usually Paul laughed at people like Joycie and Eddie. Squares, he called them.

"Now, Beth Carol, you must tell us all about yourself,"

said Joycie, looking at her with bright, wet eyes.

"There isn't much to tell," she said, self-conscious now because it was almost as if they were all applying for a job or something with all of these personal details.

"What about your folks?" Eddie prompted heartily. "Why not start there?"

"Well, my father is head of a mining company in the Northwest," she said, wondering why that made Eddie so happy, wondering why the look he gave Joycie had a hint of triumph in it. I mean, after all, she said to herself, what difference does it make to them?

"And your mother?" Eddie asked. "What about her?"

"She died when I was very small," Beth Carol said, feeling uncomfortable now, wishing, really, that they had never come.

"Oh, that's terrible," Joycie said quickly, her eyes filling with tears as she petted Beth Carol's arm. "What was it?"

"Look, Joycie," Beth Carol said. "I really don't want to talk about it."

"Oh, my dear," Joycie said. "I'm sorry if you're upset. I understand. It must have been terrible, to lose your mother when you were just a baby yourself."

Beth Carol bit her lip and tried to catch Paul's eye, but he was just looking from Joycie to Eddie, a little smile on his lips.

Dinner was good, beef Stroganoff and rice, and a salad. But Eddie and Joycie had a million questions. About her sisters and more family history, and was there any insanity in the family. "Only me," she was close to saying just to shut them up, but then Paul jumped in, talking about his film that he was making and how well it was going, and how the brass at MGM were so impressed that they had offered him a job in the story department, reading scripts.

Well, that was the first she had heard of a job offer, Beth Carol thought, shaking off Joycie and the salad she was passing around again. She bowed her head over her plate, feeling a stab of anxiety at the thought. That would put off business school, put off their whole future. But, of course, it probably wasn't true. Just Paul, trying to impress them. He was such a liar, just like everybody else in this town. Only Paul didn't have to do it. He was rich. Still, he did it anyway.

Joycie was fluttering around, serving lemon pie she had made herself.

"Coffee?" she asked Beth Carol.

She practically beamed when Beth Carol said no.

After the three of them had finished their coffee, Joycie said she really wanted to show Beth Carol the upstairs and what they had done with it, and Paul, too, so why didn't they take a look?

"Oh, how nice," Beth Carol said, her pantie girdle cutting into her waist and the tops of her thighs, her bra feeling like a razor cutting across the top of her ribs. Maybe if we just look at this we can go, she told herself as Joycie took her hand again and led her up the stairs, with Eddie and Paul just behind them. Honestly, she couldn't imagine why Paul knew these people. They were the worst show-offs, talking about the money they had invested in stocks and bonds and insurance policies, of course, and how bright their future was, and how secure they were, and everything. And, golly, the personal questions! It was really rude. She didn't like to admit it, even to herself, but she actually hated Joycie and Eddie Newfeld and if she never saw them again it would be too soon. She was going to tell Paul, too. The minute they got out of here. Let him be upset. She didn't care.

As Joycie put her hand on a doorknob off the hallway, a vagrant thought crept across Beth Carol's mind. Could they be Paul's customers? she wondered. Did they buy grass from him? Or maybe this was some kind of a sex thing Paul wanted the four of them to do. She felt her stomach lurch at the thought.

Warily, she let Joycie drag her into the master bedroom, stood there as Joycie flicked on the lights. She glanced over at the king-sized bed with its pretty spread embroidered with birds and flowers, ready to turn and run.

"I embroidered this myself," Joycie said shyly.

"It's very pretty," Beth Carol said, looking at the painstaking work, wondering how long it had taken. Forever, she decided, but it was really nice. The whole room was nice, with its pale green walls, just the right shade, the diaphanous curtains at the windows, the early American furniture that was probably real.

Then Joycie was dragging her into the bathroom, which was in the same green, and all the towels and washcloths were embroidered, too, while Eddie and Paul sort of lurked behind them, looking a little bored and impatient with all of these girl things.

"And this is the pièce de résistance," Joycie said dramatically when they were all standing in the hall again. She flung open a door, switched on the lights, and stood back for Beth Carol to take a look.

Beth Carol gasped with surprise as she realized what she was seeing. It was a nursery with pale yellow walls, white curtains, shiny floors, a white wicker crib, a bassinet, already in place. There were toy chests painted white, teddy bears, clowns, alphabet blocks, a hundred other toys sitting around the room. There was a rocking chair, its cushion in the same pale yellow, a night-light, shaped like an elf, in an outlet just above the floor.

"Oh, you're going to have a baby," she blurted. "How wonderful."

"There's a room just through the bathroom for the maid," Joycie was saying breathlessly. "Of course, she'll be here full-time. And then, in a couple of years, we thought we'd get a dog. A cocker spaniel. They're supposed to be very good with children."

"When are you due?" Beth Carol asked, looking at Joycie fondly now, understanding everything. The self-consciousness, the nervousness. All the conversation about security, the future.

She saw Joycie's face go white, her eyes flutter over to meet her husband's. Paul, she saw, was looking away.

Beth Carol sighed, felt herself trembling as she leaned

against the top of the crib with its decals of a cow jumping over the moon, its mobile of miniature horns and drums and other musical instruments.

"How much are you planning to pay for our baby?" Beth Carol asked trying to keep her voice steady, as she realized what was going on. Not succeeding very well. She could feel her tears, hear them in her words.

"It isn't like that, honey," Eddie said, his face red, reaching out his hand to her. Joycie, she saw, was looking stricken, as if she were about to collapse, too.

"It's no sale," Beth Carol cried, and she turned, rushed blindly down the stairs and out of the pretty house where Joycie was sobbing in her husband's arms.

Blinded by her tears, Beth Carol started to run down the country lane. Stumbled on a pebble or something, almost cursed as one of those stupid three-inch heels on her shoes snapped, throwing her onto the street. She wrenched it off, then the other, and ran again, her lungs feeling as if they would burst, the taste of phelgm in her mouth, the eternal, oppressive stench of the orange blossoms like an added weight, holding her back. In front of her, she was vaguely aware of her shadow, outlined in the headlights of a car. And then Paul was there, wrestling her into the passenger side of the car, cursing her, shouting as she screamed, screamed as if she were being killed.

"Ten thousand dollars," he kept saying over and over again as she sobbed, the tears streaming down her face. "We would have had ten grand. Ten grand."

The car veered wildly, the headlights picked up a stand of eucalyptus trees, the tires screeched as Paul fought to control the car. He's going to kill us both, she thought.

"You whore," he shouted. "You cunt. You bitch."

"Let me out!" she screamed, beating on his arm, his shoulder, grabbing at the wheel as he tried to push away her hands. "Stop the car!"

"I know what you're trying to do," he said, ducking away from her blows, trying to grab at her hands as she rained blows on him. "You're trying to trap me, trying to give your bastard a name. Trying to give your bastard my social position."

"Don't you call our baby that name!" she shrieked, hysterical now, rising out of her seat as she punched ineffectually at his face, his chest. "Don't you dare, you monster, you animal!"

"Don't you think I know that kid isn't mine?" he said, almost hysterical, too. "You've been dicked by everybody in town, and you try to pin it on me. Well, you've got another think coming, honey."

Sobbing, Beth Carol fell back against the seat. She covered her eyes as the car careened around curves, barely in Paul's control.

He was driving more slowly now, Beth Carol realized. They were on a main thoroughfare, Olympic Boulevard, going by occasional apartment houses with turrets, courtyards, schools, gas stations, small businesses closed for the night, coffee shops advertised with neon signs, cars in rows in their parking lots. She sat there, trying to catch her breath, her hands on her stomach.

"It's our baby, Paul," she said, trying to put conviction into her mumbled words. "I used protection with the others, just like you told me. You're the only one who never used anything. That's how I know."

He stared straight ahead, his mouth set, his eyes dead in the lights from the oncoming cars, the streetlights.

They were in downtown Los Angeles now, she saw. He was stopping in front of an old brick building with light gleaming from its foyer. Etched into the facade over the doorway was the legend, YOUNG WOMEN'S CHRISTIAN ASSOCIATION.

A stab of fear coursed through her, the fine hairs on her arms rose as she saw Paul fumbling around in his pocket, saw him take out his wallet.

"Here's twenty dollars," he said, handing her a bill. "It's all I have."

Beth Carol sat there, her mouth open, staring at him.

"I'll bring your stuff down tomorrow," he said gruffly,

not looking at her. "I've done the best I can. I just don't know what else to do."

"Paul, don't do this," she begged. "We'll get money. I promise. My father will give it to us. He's rich, you know that. He won't let anything happen to his grandson. I know him. I swear."

He sighed, slumped back against the seat, still holding the bill limply in his hand.

"What if it's a girl?" he asked at last.

"Joycie and Eddie can adopt her," she said.

"You're lying."

"You can call and tell them right now," she said. "Find a telephone booth. I'll tell them myself."

He was looking at her now, his eyes wary.

"I swear on the baby's life," she said earnestly.

"Oh, shit," he said as he started the car.

Beth Carol looked out the window, watched the occasional pedestrian on the street, a cop car now and then, wondering idly whether Paul was the bigger con artist of the two of them, or whether she was.

CHAPTER 22

*S*o you've got to come over and see my place," Fern was saying on the other end of the line. "It's this little guest house at the back of Sir George Dean's place, and it's real cute."

"I can't, Fern," Beth Carol said, still panting with the effort of getting to the phone. She sat in a chair next to it on its table, her belly huge in front of her, her legs apart.

"Ah, come on, man," Fern said. "Like, I haven't seen you in so long I won't even know you."

"You're right about that," Beth Carol said gloomily, "but I can't. I really can't."

"Well, you've got to tell me why," Fern insisted.

"I'm pregnant," Beth Carol whispered. "That's why."

"Oh, not again," Fern said, her voice filled with dismay. "God, let me think for a sec. Everybody's going to Tijuana now, but I hear it's okay. Clean, and everything."

"It's not like that," Beth Carol said. "I'm going to have a baby, Fern. Any time now, the doctor says."

"You mean you didn't have the abortion?" Fern asked, incredulous.

"I couldn't kill my baby," Beth Carol said with dignity.

"Oh, that's hysterical." Fern laughed. "And here I'm writing about you all over town with all these eligible guys and I've got you going to New York and Europe, and all, and you're going to have a baby."

"Oh, don't," Beth Carol said, trying to get comfortable on the chair, really feeling as if she no longer existed, that she was just a thing now. Hideous, bloated. Eaten up alive. Why, she couldn't take two steps without sitting down to recover, her back killed her all the time, and she slept so much that sometimes she wondered if she weren't more dead than alive.

"So are you married?" Fern asked.

"Not yet," Beth Carol admitted.

"Well, you'd better get married," Fern said.

"That's easy for you to say," Beth Carol panted, running a hand through her stringy hair. "Paul can't even stand to look at me. He doesn't talk to me. The only time he's home is when he has scripts to read for his job, and then he locks himself in his bedroom and I don't see him. He's got some-one else. I'm sure of it. Some floozy. That's his type. And here I am, about to have his child."

"I thought you told me it was that guy back home," Fern said, puzzled.

"Well, yes," Beth Carol said lamely, flushing. She should have remembered that Fern was a gossip columnist's leg girl now, that she was bound to remember every little thing she was told. "But he doesn't know it. What I've told him is that it's his. You can see that, can't you, Fern?"

"Oh, sure," Fern said. "It's the only thing to do. I dig it. So why don't I come and see you? You can tell me all about it, man. Maybe come up with a plan."

And it was tempting, Beth Carol thought. It really would be fun to see somebody. Other than Bobby, of course, who came every couple of weeks to do her hair when she just couldn't stand it anymore. He was so impressed with the estate, sure that she could get Paul to marry her before the baby came. Well, he said that was what he thought, and he'd really been great in a lot of other ways, too. He'd been the one who'd gone out and bought her maternity clothes, who came every time with stuff for the baby. Clothes and things. Even a crib. But it would be fun to see another girl and try to work out a strategy about Paul. Bobby wasn't much good for that. He was too busy with his own plans, the new house that "they" had rented for him and were furnishing with beautiful English and French antiques, the expensive trips that they took him on, all of those gorgeous presents they gave him. And his moods swung a lot. One minute he was all elated, and the next minute it was all this stuff about suicide and tears. It was booze, probably pills, too. Beth Carol was sure of it.

And besides, the bigger she got, the more horrified Bobby seemed to be when he looked at her. It really made Beth Carol feel bad to know that she looked so unattractive, even if it was Bobby, and what did he care?

"I'll pick up some sandwiches at Greenblatt's," Fern was saying. "So why don't I come up in about an hour? Okay?"

"Not today," Beth Carol said hastily. "Friday, and I'll make lunch."

"But, man," Fern complained, "it's only Monday."

"Friday," Beth Carol said. "I'll see you then."

Now, why did I do that? she asked herself when she had gotten off the phone. I don't even have the strength to stand up. Still, it would be something different, something to look forward to. That little room off the swimming pool with the great view of the gardens. Yes, that's where they would eat. She'd have to take the dust covers off the furniture in there. Find some china. That would be easy. Golly, there were twelve different patterns in the cupboards, each with service for twenty-four. And which silver pattern? Oh, and crystal bowls for the flowers. She could pick the flowers right from the garden. She'd have to order wine. Fern would want wine. Or would she? Maybe she'd want a vodka gimlet, or a rum and Coke. Well, she'd order everything. And what else? Oh, of course. The food. What was she going to serve? It was funny, she thought. She didn't feel nearly as tired as she usually did, and here she was, with all of these things to do.

*   *   *

When the buzzer sounded from the street, Beth Carol hit the button that opened the gates and waddled through the house, opened the front door, and posed at the entrance the way she had been planning ever since Fern had called. Heat shimmered in the bright blue sky, and she wiped away beads of perspiration that were gathering on her upper lip. She felt wet under her arms, too, wet under the band of her maternity bra. Even the insides of her thighs slid against each other when she moved. Still, she looked as good as she could under the circumstances. She had put in an emergency call to Bobby, and he had come to do her hair. She had done her nails, and she was wearing this sort of flowing, flowered maternity thing that could have been a beach cover-up if you didn't look too close.

Her pulse quickened as she saw a hint of silver way down on the driveway, just rounding the lake, which looked so pretty glittering in the midsummer sun. The flowers in their beds looked a little wilted, and there were even patches of brown on the rolling lawn. Still, she thought smugly, it was all pretty impressive.

And there it was, Sir George Dean's antique silver Bentley, just like she'd read about in the stories on him, and the Oriental chauffeur driving, and Fern's improbably blond head towering in the backseat. Beth Carol stood there, transfixed, as the car stopped and the chauffeur hurried around to help Fern out of the car.

"Hi, Fern," she called.

Fern stood, staring up at the three stories of the mansion, her eyes round with amazement.

Beth Carol had to admit to herself that she felt a little disappointed at the way Fern looked. What had she expected? she asked herself, examining Fern. Probably that in the months since they had seen each other, the new job would have turned Fern into a whole new girl. Like Rosalind Russell, maybe, in a smart suit. But no.

Fern was wearing a low-cut, sleeveless powder blue top with silver threads running through it, her boobs practically hanging out. Her capri pants in the same color were embedded with silver studs. There were the high, high heels, the shoes with no fronts, no backs, the gold ankle bracelet. Even her makeup was plastered on the way Beth Carol remembered it, and her neck had that same gray look.

Fern undulated toward Beth Carol, taking her arm, smiling at her. Something had changed, Beth Carol realized. The perfume. It was Joy, the most expensive perfume in the world.

"Say, it's great to see you, man," Fern said. "And what a house. You know, all this time I thought you were bullshitting me."

Good old Fern, Beth Carol thought, feeling a rush of tenderness toward her as she led the way through the front door, down the wide marble hall to the pretty little room off the swimming pool with its table set with flowers, the finest china and silver, the embroidered linen napkins she had ironed the night before. She was really happy that she had ordered all different kinds of liquor because, wouldn't you know it, what Fern asked for was a double Beefeater martini with two olives.

"So, what's new, Fern?" she asked, panting a little as she slid gratefully into a chair opposite her. The baby seemed to be happy to have company, too. He was kicking and rolling around to the point where Beth Carol was feeling a little seasick.

"Well, let me see," Fern said, taking a dainty sip of her martini, licking her lips. "Barbara Stanwyck and Robert Taylor are getting a divorce."

"Oh, no," Beth Carol said unhappily. "Not Barbara Stanwyck and Robert Taylor!"

"Yeah, well, I always thought he was kind of an asshole," Fern said. "You know what I thought? That it would kind of be like being married to an eight-by-ten glossy."

"Yeah, I can see what you mean," Beth Carol said, conjuring up Robert Taylor's face in her mind with its aquiline nose, that little pencil-thin mustache, the perfect widow's peak. "But what about you? What's going on with you?"

And then Fern was off, regaling her with tales of life working for Sir George Dean. She called him Lady George Dean, too, just the way Bobby did, and the stories were outrageous, with his screaming fits and throwing things, and blackmail, and threats of exposure, and the wonderful presents that streamed into the big house all the time, and all the little fags mincing in and out on the hour. Then there were the nightclubs they went to, the restaurants, the parties, the premieres at Grauman's Chinese, or the Egyptian, the Paramount, and all of the fans in the stands screaming their heads off, and everybody bowing and scraping, and all of them scared to death because Sir George Dean could ruin any of them in a minute. He often did, in fact, just for laughs.

"So, have you met anybody?" Beth Carol asked.

"Man, you've got to be kidding," Fern said, looking at her strangely as she lit another cigarette with a slim gold lighter. "Man, I've met everybody. Haven't you been hearing me?"

"I meant, well, you know. A guy."

"Oh, a romance," said Fern, giving her a big smile as she sat back in her chair, let the smoke curl up in front of her little, pinched face. "Oh, I've got a pack of them sniffing around. You know, like always."

"You're not still, well . . ." Beth Carol's voice drifted off.

"Hooking, you mean?" Fern grinned. "Oh, sure. Sir George Dean says my cunt is his secret weapon."

"It's time for lunch," Beth Carol said abruptly, her cheeks burning as she lumbered to her feet. She'd never get used to the way Fern talked, not if they knew each other for a thousand years.

She really felt good, though, when Fern seemed to like what she'd made. The big beef tomatoes stuffed with crab and lobster and the Thousand Island dressing she'd learned to make from one of the cooking shows she was always watching, the avocado slices arranged just so on the plates. The thick slices of French bread slathered with butter she had heated up in the oven. The pecan surprise with real whipped cream she had made for dessert. And Fern, looking at her with admiration, confessing with a laugh that what she usually did was open a can of spaghetti and eat it cold, or pig out on candy bars.

"He's a fool not to marry you, man," Fern said kindly, leaning back in her chair, patting her stomach. "You'll make a great wife."

After a while, it seemed to Beth Carol as if they had been sitting there for hours, with Fern smoking, looking thoughtful at all of the things Beth Carol was pouring out to her. About Paul and how the family was waiting him out until he agreed to go for his graduate degree in business, and how he had to marry her before the baby came, although time was sure running short on that score. But the baby had to be part of the Fournier family for his future, for his social position. And, well, for her social position, too. She had already been noticing the names of private schools that might do for the baby when she read about them in the society section. And Fern didn't seem to be bored at all. She had another martini, then another, and it was terrific to be sitting there, confiding in a girlfriend, giving her all the information available so that they could plot strategy, just the way the girls at Secrets did with their best girlfriends.

"So, you see how things stand," Beth Carol finished at last, her tone urgent.

"I want to ask you a question, man," Fern said, her eyes narrowing behind the veil of smoke. "But I don't want to hurt your feelings or anything."

"You won't," Beth Carol said anxiously.

"Do you really believe all this crap?"

"What do you mean?" Beth Carol asked, suddenly frightened.

"Well, it's crazy," Fern said. "His folks are away with his sister for, what, eight, nine months now. And first it's Jamaica, he says, and they won't give him any money. And how long can anybody stay in Jamaica, right? So then he tells you they've gone to England. And all of this is to pressure this guy into going to business school?"

Beth Carol nodded slowly.

"So he had you out hooking, and now he's selling grass and working at this kid's job at the studio which probably pays a hundred a week if he's lucky?"

Beth Carol nodded miserably.

"And the only reason he hasn't thrown you out is that you've told him your dad is going to come through with some bucks when the kid is born, and you don't know if he will?"

Beth Carol stared at Fern, felt her lower lip start to quiver.

"It doesn't make any sense," Fern said firmly, tapping her long, red fingernails on the glass-topped table. "What they'd do is be here, see? They'd throw his ass out on the street and they'd tell him to come back when he shaped up. That's what they'd do."

"I guess so," Beth Carol said weakly.

"So I say it's a bunch of bullshit," Fern pronounced, knocking back the rest of her martini. "Tell you what. Let's see what he has in his office."

"Oh, I couldn't do that," Beth Carol said breathlessly.

"Well, I could," said Fern. "You can find out anything about a guy's life in his office, from his papers. Believe me, I should know."

"Everything's in his bedroom," Beth Carol said, hearing the fear in her voice. "It's locked."

"Oh, that's nothing." Fern snickered. "Let's go."

It took Fern and her nail file, with Beth Carol looming above her, trying to catch her breath, about a minute before the lock on Paul's bedroom door clicked and Fern pushed it triumphantly open.

There was the room that Beth Carol had only glimpsed from the doorway, with its massive, four-poster bed with the wood-paneled canopy and headboard, the American primitive paintings on the pumpkin-colored walls, a gilt eagle over a highboy, the carpet, black and white rectangles. On a table there were neat piles of scripts, stacks of trade papers, a healthy-looking plant, its leaves lime green.

"Say, man," Fern called from Paul's walk-in closet. "Do you think this guy has enough clothes? And prissy, prissy, too. Shit, it's practically alphabetized in here."

Beth Carol stood at the doorway, licking her dry lips, feeling funny about this whole thing. Disloyal. She saw Fern reappear, undulate through another doorway.

"Come on, Beth Carol," she called. "All the stuff's in here. It's the office."

Hesitantly, she followed Fern's voice, found her sitting at a big, old-fashioned rolltop desk, her tongue between her teeth as she concentrated on picking its lock. Above the desk was a window that looked out onto the back garden with its statues of the Seven Graces clustered near the gazebo. The walls were lined with bookshelves filled with books.

"Eureka," Fern said with satisfaction as she rifled through the stacks of receipts, scanned sheafs of papers with a practiced eye. "Nothing here," she said cheerfully, putting a paper aside, another on top of it. "Nothing here."

Let there be nothing anywhere, Beth Carol prayed, watching Fern's lips moving as she read whatever it was, then tossed it aside.

Fern jerked open the middle drawer of the desk, fumbled around until she found the tiny key to the file cabinets.

"Here we go," she murmured, opening the first drawer, lifting out a couple of volumes that looked like oversize photograph albums bound in leather. Let them be family pictures, Beth Carol thought without hope. Even from where she stood, leaning against the door jamb, her arms folded over her bloated breasts, she could see that they were newspaper clippings, front-page stories with banner headlines.

"What is it?" she asked tremulously.

"Come and see for yourself," said Fern, thumbing through the papers.

CHAPTER 23

*W*ORST DISASTER IN COMMERCIAL AVIATION HISTORY KILLS 107, read the headline on the *New York Times*. AIR DISASTER! screamed the *New York Post*. CLEAR SKIES NO DETERRENT TO CRASH OF PASSENGER PLANE, read the headline on the *Herald Tribune*. PLANE CRASH KILLS ALL ABOARD NY/LA FLIGHT. And 107 DIE IN PLANE CRASH.

There were more clippings, page after page of them, all the papers in the country, it seemed to Beth Carol, all with the same smudged, gray photographs of the downed plane, its pieces scattered across the countryside.

The headlines in the *Los Angeles Times*, the *Mirror*, the *Examiner*, the *Herald* read, LOCAL FINANCIER VICTIM IN CRASH THAT KILLS 107. FINANCIER MARVIN KENDALL, WIFE, SON AMONG VICTIMS IN NATION'S WORST AIR DISASTER. There were different pictures, too. Pictures of the man Paul said was his father. Marvin Kendall. Pictures of the woman he said was his mother. A picture of the boy Beth Carol recognized from the pictures in Diana's room. Howard Kendall, twenty-one, a recent graduate of Yale University.

Pictures, taken from the air, of the house in which they were sitting, of the grounds, the lake. Biographies in every paper of Marvin Kendall, pictures of the office buildings he owned in downtown Los Angeles, of the one on Wilshire

Boulevard in Westwood. Lists of the boards of directors on which he sat. His schools, Choate and Yale. His clubs. The Los Angeles Country Club. The California Club. One of the richest men in America. A daughter, Diana, seven years old, survives.

Beth Carol stood, weaving as she leaned over Fern's shoulder, the words on the pages blurring in front of her eyes. The desk a blur. Fern, too.

"Oh, shit, don't faint on me," Fern said, grabbing her, helping her into a chair. Going back to the clippings, scanning them.

"Here it is," she said triumphantly. "Also killed in the disaster was Margaret Fournier, Kendall's secretary." She glanced at Beth Carol, making sure she understood. "So he's the secretary's kid. Margaret Fournier. That'll be his mom."

Gleefully, she opened another drawer and another. Glanced at the records, the accounts. The inventory of everything in the house, a thick bundle of papers, audited. Notarized. "So he's a kind of a caretaker here," Fern said. "He gets two hundred dollars a month."

Paul and all his airs, Beth Carol thought hopelessly as the baby kicked inside her. A secretary's son. A caretaker. What have I done? she asked herself, closing her eyes. God help me. Please.

"Hey, man, here's your file," Fern laughed, thumbing through it. "All the tricks you turned, all the money paid in, everything paid out for your clothes. Shit, he's even got your beauty salon charges here. Operating expenses, huh? Your hospital bills." She reached for another file, a big smile on her face. "I've got to hand it to him," she said. "He sure keeps great records."

Beth Carol saw her interest quicken as she flipped through the pages in the file. "Here are the dope customers," Fern murmured, running a fingernail down the list. "Say, man, it's practically a Who's Who in Hollywood. And these would be the codes, I guess." Casually, she closed the file, stuffed it into her huge purse, as Beth Carol looked into space, seeing the end of all of her dreams.

"So look," Fern was saying. "This is yours."

Beth Carol glanced at what Fern was holding, trying to comprehend what it was. It was her wallet, the one she had thought she'd lost way back in the beginning when she had first come to this house. With shaking hands, she took it from Fern. Opened it to see her own innocent face on her identification card from Lakeside High School, her identification card from the Poetry Club. Her season pass to the football games. All the money was gone. She had known it would be.

All a ploy, she thought, turning it over in her hands. Those tiny glimmers of doubt that had skirted around the corners of her mind all along were right.

"Here's some more stuff," Fern said, a little frown on her forehead. "Carbons of letters his mom wrote. Let's see, oh, they go way back, like right to the beginning of the time she went to work for this guy, this Marvin Kendall."

"I need a drink," Beth Carol whispered.

Fern stood up, stretched, as she glanced out the window over the desk.

"Yeah, so do I," she said. "I'll go get them. What do you want?"

"A martini. A double."

"Okay," Fern said, patting her on the shoulder. "You know what I think, Beth Carol? Well, what I think is that you've been too smart for your own good."

Too smart for your own good. Too smart for your own good. The words reverberated through Beth Carol's consciousness as she lay slumped in the chaise longue she had pulled over to the door of Diana's room. Oh, it had been such a lovely dream, she thought wistfully, her eyes welling with tears. Even now, all of these hours later, she couldn't believe it was over. Couldn't believe that it had never been. I was going to give you everything, baby, she thought as she caressed her belly, felt his outline inside her. The world on a silver platter, a silver spoon in your mouth. And now what?

She sat up straight at what seemed to be a sound from

outside the door. But it was nothing. Her mouth tasted awful from all the martinis, she realized. Maybe some water. That would help. She staggered into the bathroom, turned on the faucet, cupped her hands to gulp the water. Her face in the mirror was swollen from her tears, the expression in her eyes hopeless. Dead. Through the open window of the bedroom, she heard Paul's car. Finally. It was after two in the morning by now. But she'd made it. She was awake, ready for the confrontation. So mad she could kill him for what he had done to her. Would kill him if she had something to kill him with.

She waddled over to the bedroom door, jerked it open just as she heard his footsteps. He stopped when he saw her there, a flicker of distaste on his face.

"Is something wrong?" he asked without interest. "Is it time to go to the hospital? Have the pains started?"

She stood, holding on to the doorjamb, panting a little. He looked wonderful, fresh and scrubbed in his perfect summer coat, his trousers with their crisp crease, his tie impeccably knotted, his black loafers with their tassles all shiny and nice. She felt a wild surge of love for him, a joyous rush of pleasure at the sight of him. I must be crazy, she told herself. Either that or I just haven't realized it yet, the truth.

"I know everything," she said, her whole body shaking. "About Marvin Kendall, and how your mother was his secretary."

He frowned, and he looked pale under his tan.

That was good, Beth Carol thought savagely. Yes, that felt good.

"I read those copies of her letters, where she said she'd taken the job because she could have you with her. How the two of you could live here on the estate, have a home."

"So?" he said politely.

"Oh, you went to Choate, all right. And Yale, too. Because Mr. Kendall paid for it, that's why. Because you and Howard were friends for all those years. And your mom wrote that Mr. Kendall was going to provide for you in his will, too. That he would see that you had something to get a start in life."

"Yes, that's what he told her," Paul said.

"But he didn't, did he?" Beth Carol screamed. "So you had to improvise. So you sold dope. And not just grass like you told me, either. We saw, we broke the code. And so you ran girls. Me, the others. We saw the files, all of them." Through her tears, her fury, she looked right into his eyes. Saw his terror, saw him run his tongue over his lower lip, do that thing about patting his hair into place, what he did when he was buying time, trying to think. Golly, he was cute, she realized, hating herself for thinking it at a time like this. But he was. He really was, in spite of everything. And here she was, at such a disadvantage. The hideous bloat of her belly, the arms and legs sticks compared to it, her face swollen, red from her tears.

"What did you do?" he whispered. "Did you call the police? Did you go through my files with the police?"

"You stole my wallet," she sobbed. "You made sure I couldn't leave, that you could turn me into a whore whenever you wanted."

He was next to her now, his after-shave clouding her senses, his presence almost unbearable. He took her wrists, the expression in his eyes frantic.

"Who went through my files with you, Beth Carol?" he begged. "Who was it? You've got to tell me." He was walking her now, back into Diana's playroom with all its dolls, its cunning crystal figurines, the child-sized carousel with its unicorn, its Cheshire cat, its pumpkin. Into the bedroom itself, where he pushed her down onto the chaise longue, pulled over a chair, took her hands in his again. He looked half dead with fear, she saw, feeling a stab of triumph at the sight of his expression.

"Who went through my files?" he demanded, hurting her wrists as she lay there, her chin against her shoulder, strands of hair in her mouth. "Tell me. You've got to tell me."

She shook her head, her breath coming in pants, as she saw him raise his hand, saw with horror that he was going to hit her.

"She's got your file," she blurted. "The one with your customers."

"Who?" he screamed, his body all stiff, as if he had been shot.

"My girlfriend," she said.

"Your girlfriend?" he asked, incredulous. "What girlfriend?"

"You told me you loved me," she wailed. "Over and over you told me."

"Tell me her name, baby," he said, his voice soothing now, as he reached over, picked the strands of hair out of her mouth, patted her hair.

"Her name is Fern," she mumbled.

"What is she going to do with my file?" he asked, his voice calm now, insistent, but with that sweetness that she never had been able to resist.

"I don't know."

"Well, tell you what," he said. "First thing in the morning, we'll give her a call and then we'll go over and see her, get it back. We can make a day of it, baby. God, it's been a long time since we've gone anywhere. I'm sorry I've been neglecting you, sweetheart, and at a time like this. But, you know, my job. I've really been concentrating on getting ahead, for the two of us."

"You work in the mailroom," she said. "We found that out, too."

"I know what would be fun," he said, a flicker of something in his eyes, something she had never seen, something indescribable. "We'll drive to Santa Barbara for lunch, we'll go to the Biltmore. It's got a great view. You'll love it."

"Everything you've ever told me is a lie," she mumbled.

"Maybe we'll take your friend along. That's great that you have a girlfriend," he wheedled. "And she can just give me back the file, and we'll forget the whole thing."

"She won't," Beth Carol said.

"Sure she will." He grinned, his voice hearty. "What can she do with it?"

"Maybe a lot of things," Beth Carol said. "She works for Sir George Dean. She's his leg girl."

He sighed, a great big sigh, as if he were a balloon

deflating. He reached into his pocket, found a cigarette, lit it. Sat next to her, almost companionably, exhaling smoke in the gloom of the bedroom. Through the open window, Beth Carol could hear the crickets singing.

"How could you tell me all those lies, Paul?" she asked, her own voice little more than a sob. "I trusted you, I loved you. I would do anything in the world for you."

"Not everything was a lie," he said softly. "One thing was true. I love you, baby. I really do."

"Oh, you don't," she said. "You don't."

He put out the cigarette, pulled her to her feet, and took her in his arms as well as he could, with the baby and everything.

"It's late," he said. "I think it's time for you to go to bed, sweetheart. We can talk about all of this in the morning."

Beth Carol let herself be led to the bed, looked up at him imploringly as he covered her gently with a single sheet, felt his lips brush her own.

"I love you," he murmured. "It's the one thing that has always been the truth, baby. You have to believe me."

She lay there, clutching the top of the sheet with both hands as she watched him turn, walk hurriedly through the room with that great walk of his. Oh, he's so cute, she thought with regret, while at the same time she told herself that she was mad to think he was cute at a time like this, when she knew what he was, which was nothing. No, nothing was too mild. Worse than nothing. And yet, just seeing him made her so happy, made her come alive. It just hasn't sunk in yet, she thought, Yes, that had to be it. And as for telling her he loved her, that it was the one thing that was true, well, that's just what he would say. Still, would he say it, she wondered, if it weren't true?

CHAPTER 24

*B*eth Carol lay staring hopelessly at the ceiling, her hands folded over her enormous belly. She'd never get to sleep, she knew. Not if the night were a thousand years long. Her thoughts swirled aimlessly, colliding, dissipating into fragments, incoherence. Paul, the total rat. Oh, yeah. He'd been all lovey dovey. And when was that? Just after she told him that Fern had his dope file, that was when. His mom, a secretary. Paul, a caretaker. A servant. Tears squeezed out of the corners of her eyes.

It was so hot, so still. Night after night. Why, her night-gown was absolutely soaked, she realized as she wiped the perspiration from her forehead. And, of course, there was no way to get comfortable anyway, not with the baby taking up all the room inside her, scrunching all her own organs out of the way like he did. She watched, fascinated, as the sheet covering her stomach rose and fell, felt the baby as he woke, started that struggle to get out of her. To get on with it.

"Poor baby," she whispered, petting her stomach. "I tried to make it right for you, baby darling. I really did. I tried so hard."

Still, when she finally managed to doze off, she had the nicest dream, the best one she'd ever had. Her father was in it, of course. He was always in her good dreams. But the best part was that her mother was in it, too, and she couldn't remember ever having dreamed about her mother. Her father looked the way he'd looked the last time she'd seen him, and he was in Technicolor and her mother looked the way she did in their honeymoon pictures and she was in black and white, very chicly dressed, but in an old-fashioned way, with pearls. The thing about this dream was that she was the baby in her mother's arms, and she was looking at her father and then she was looking up into her mother's face and feeling very loved, very protected, as if nothing in the world could ever happen to her. Her mother was rocking her very gently and smiling, like in the pictures, and she started to sing a lullaby and there was even something accompanying her. The tinkle of crystal, miniature crystal bells, maybe, rung by elves who were her protectors, too.

Her mother was rocking her more vigorously now. "Stop, mommy, you're scaring me," she said in her dream. The gentle tinkle of crystal became the frightening sound of glass crashing into a thousand shards. The entire mansion shuddered on its foundations as Beth Carol bolted up in the bed, shaking with terror. Screaming.

It was so loud, the roar from outside. The whole world was splitting apart. She held on for dear life to the rocking bed. The room was swaying crazily. The bureau lurched and toppled forward, scattering the pictures of Diana, her dead family, onto the floor in a shower of broken glass. The crystal teardrops on the sconces rang dissonantly as they banged against each other. Beth Carol screamed and screamed, fell back against her pillows as an unbearable pain shot through her. The baby was coming. Right now, when the world was cracking into a million pieces.

For a moment, the hideous roar subsided, the swaying ceased. With a hand shaking so hard she had to fight to control it, Beth Carol reached for the switch on the lamp, turned it. Nothing. She dragged herself across the room to look out the window. Was anything left? she wondered as another pain made her gasp. She clung to the windowsill, barely able to comprehend that she was standing in a puddle of the water pouring from her body. The eucalyptus trees were swaying, waves crashed on the lake, and blue flashes of electricity rent the inky sky.

Somehow, Paul was there, holding her against him so that she could hear his heart racing, as fast as her own.

"The baby's coming," she whimpered. "Right now."

"The power's out," he muttered. "The gates won't open."

The mansion lurched violently, and Beth Carol screamed with fear, with the pains that were coming faster now, pains so intense nobody could survive them. And Paul was carrying her to the bed as she screamed again and the house rocked. Then candlelight was flickering in the room and she could see Paul's face, white and terrified, as he wiped her forehead with a warm cloth, winced as she dug her nails into his hand. It would be hours more of this, she realized, and she couldn't stand it. And the lights would come back on, and she could go to the hospital, and this was all a bad dream anyway. A nightmare. It would end. She would wake up.

"It's his head," Paul said. "I see the top of his head."

Not here. Not now. You don't want to do this, she told the baby dreamily. Despite herself, she pushed, pushed harder. Anything to stop the pain.

There was another aftershock.

A wail.

He was out of her, on his own.

Maybe a champagne bottle felt like this, after the cork was pulled.

"A perfect baby," Paul said, his voice shaking. "Well, we can call your father and give him the good news."

CHAPTER 25

he baby's name is Raleigh," Beth Carol said into the telephone as she lay in bed, idly fingering its cord. "For my father. Paul said that if we named the baby for him, it would be a selling point, so he'd be sure to send us some money." She glanced down the length of the single sheet that covered her. It was still such a shock to see that her stomach was flat. "Oh, Fern," she cooed, "I knew he'd be thrilled. I just knew it. And he wired money, too. Five hundred dollars, and he said he'd send more."

"Raleigh?" Fern said, a tinge of distaste in her voice. "That's sort of a dumb name, man. I mean, what about a real name? Timothy, or something. Anthony. Say, how about Christopher? That's a real cute name."

"But then it wouldn't be for my father," Beth Carol said, feeling a little annoyed at Fern. Sometimes she could be so dense. "And what a time for the baby to decide to come," she added. "Right in the middle of the earthquake, with everything falling over, and the power out."

"Yeah, how about that earthquake, man?" Fern giggled. "I've just got to tell you, it was such a scream. I was, like, humping this john and everything started to move, you know? And I thought to myself, 'Hey, this guy is it. Mr. Right. It's never been like this for me before,' and then I fell flat on my ass on the floor."

"I've never been so scared," Beth Carol whispered, feeling the fear clutch at her again. Golly, those first couple of days when the power was still out, the phone. All of Diana's dolls lay tumbled on the rug. The carousel had fallen, too. The unicorn had broken in pieces, the Cheshire cat. Downstairs, two of the china cabinets had crashed to the floor, which was carpeted with shards. Antique tables had lost legs, priceless vases destroyed. A portion of one of the chimneys had rained bricks on the grounds next to the mansion. For all she knew, she and Paul were the last people on earth. And the baby, of course, wailing lustily in his crib, sleeping for what seemed to Beth Carol only minutes before he was kicking and squirming again, eager to get on with things.

Finally, the power had come back on. The two of them sat in front of the television set, looking with fascinated horror at shattered boards that had once been buildings, at massive, old trees, uprooted, laying on their sides. At the grim, gaping fissure that had wrenched apart Sunset Boulevard near Schwab's. At the cars, mashed beyond recognition, flung crazily onto lawns, through plate-glass windows. Beth Carol rocked the baby, felt tears streaming down her cheeks as she listened to the interviews with the bewildered moms who had lost everything. And the quake hadn't even been centered here. It had been in Bakersfield, way up north. She couldn't even look at the film from there. It was too awful.

"I thought the world was coming to an end," she added, her voice hushed.

"Oh, yeah?" said Fern. "I thought it was fun. Shake, rattle, and roll. What a trip!"

"Fern, the baby, you've got to see him," Beth Carol said abruptly. "He's so cute. He has these huge blue eyes, and lashes, even this soon. And he has all of this blond fuzz all over his head. And a dimple. Just one, in his right cheek. Oh, he's so beautiful."

"I guess," Fern said vaguely.

"You won't believe this, but Paul's gotten him a job. He's going to be in a movie when he's fifteen days old. That's as soon as they can work, you know."

"Oh, yeah? So what's he going to play?"

"Well, a baby," Beth Carol said. "He's going to play the part of a baby."

"Oh, God," Fern said. "I know that, man. What else could he play? I mean, whose baby? I can get Sir George to do an item on it, see? 'A Star is Born.' Literally. He'll think it's cute. Sentimental things like that get to the old pervert. God knows why."

"It's the Susan Hayward movie," Beth Carol said.

"Right," said Fern, and Beth Carol could almost see her, the phone cradled between her shoulder and her ear, making notes in that barely literate handwriting of hers. "So it's Raleigh Barnes, and it's his first role, playing a baby. See how cute that is?"

"Yes, that's cute," Beth Carol agreed happily, thinking what fun it was that Raleigh would be in Sir George Dean's column, maybe even on his national television show, and here he was, only five days old. She felt heavy and uncomfortable now, realized her breasts were engorged with milk, leaking onto her nightgown, onto the sheet. Well, Paul was bound to know that it was time for Raleigh to nurse, that it was time to bring him home from whichever talent agent he had taken him to see. "Oh, Fern," she gushed, "you should see him when I'm breast-feeding him. He's so greedy I can't believe it. And he has the most adorable little mouth. Like a rosebud. You know, when he's sucking on me, it's the most wonderful feeling in the world. I feel so close to him, so tender. It's as if it was what I was born to do, to be Raleigh's mommy."

"Stop it, man," said Fern. "You're making me sick."

"Well, anyway, he's really cute," Beth Carol finished lamely.

"So how do you feel?" Fern asked.

"Kind of fragile, actually. Oh, it was awful, Fern. I've never hurt so much. Take the worst pain you've ever had and multiply it by a million times, and it still wouldn't be enough," she said. "I just can't describe it to you."

"Yeah, well, don't, okay?" Fern said. "You'll be all right in, what, a couple of weeks? So you'll be able to get out of there soon, huh? That's great that your old man sent some dough. You'll be able to count on that for a while. And then you can always get more."

"Oh, I couldn't call him," Beth Carol said hastily. "I'm too embarrassed."

"So you write to him, man. What's the dif?"

"Well, Paul arranged for the job for the baby. And there are things to do. I mean, he's got to have a Social Security number, he's got to have a work permit. That sort of thing. So I can't even think about leaving until after that's over, can I? And who knows? It could be a long job. Weeks, even."

"So what am I hearing?" Fern asked. "After all the lies that asshole laid on you about what a big man he is, after all the shit he put you through, you're telling me you're not going to leave?"

"He delivered Raleigh," Beth Carol said solemnly. "You should have seen his face when he held him for the first time. There was such wonder in his expression, such amazement. He just loves him, Fern. I know he does."

"Yeah, sure," Fern said. "He looked down at that darling little face and what he saw was another source of revenue. That's what he saw, and you know it."

"That's not true," Beth Carol said, shocked.

"I don't believe this," Fern said. "Like I'm not real sure you're playing with a full deck, man."

"But you'll come to see Raleigh, won't you?" she asked, flushing. "I mean, Fern, you're my best friend."

"Yeah, I guess so," Fern said.

"And when you do, would you do me a favor?" Beth Carol asked. "Would you bring that file back, the one you took from Paul's desk? He's been asking me and asking me. He's upset, Fern. He really is."

"You think I'd do that?" Fern asked incredulously, a laugh in her voice. "You take the cake, man. You really do. You know what you've got in your head, Beth Carol? Rocks. That's what you've got in your head."

* * *

Anybody who would go through this really did need to
have her head examined, Beth Carol thought glumly as she
looked around the enormous room. There must be three hundred babies here with their moms, and some others, too.
Toddlers, older kids, some of them reading comic books as
they slumped in their folding chairs, some playing tag, or just
kind of hitting each other. And a lot of them crying or whining. Most of the moms looked truly horrible, she decided.
Shabby clothes, a few of them with runs in their stockings.
Why, a couple of them even had their hair in pin curls with
scarves tied over them. Beth Carol could hardly believe it.
After all, what was more important than taking your baby to a
casting call? Wasn't that enough to get them to comb their
hair? There were even a couple of dads, looking self-conscious. They must really feel funny to be here, to try to charm
the casting director, who was only used to moms.

Surreptitiously, she examined the babies. The brunette
babies, the ones with olive skin, might as well go home right
now. The only ones who ever got work were like Raleigh, all
blond and pink with big blue eyes. Or the redheaded ones
sometimes. But mainly blond, blue eyes, pink. All-American
Babies. That was the way Beth Carol thought of them.

It had all seemed so exciting in the beginning when
Raleigh got that first job, playing Susan Hayward's baby. It
just hadn't occurred to her that she would be the one who
would have to sit there on the set all day, holding Raleigh,
feeding Raleigh, trying to amuse Raleigh when he was a little fretful. Still, it had been fun to meet Susan Hayward,
her first real movie star.

"How do you do?" Susan Hayward had said. "What a
beautiful baby."

Beth Carol had been so in awe of Susan Hayward that
she had just stuttered something that sounded okay. What
she had really noticed, though, was that up close Susan
Hayward was just as beautiful as she was in the movies.
Her hair was this wonderful, glistening auburn, and her
eyes were sort of auburn, too, and she had a deep dimple
in her chin. Beth Carol had hoped against hope that she

would meet Gregory Peck, who was co-starring. She never did, but he was really polite. He always smiled at her when he walked by. He was so good-looking. And really tall, too.

Mostly it was dull, watching them rehearse with a doll playing Raleigh's part, and then when they were trying for a take, the girl from the Division of Labor Standards Enforcement hovering around to make sure Raleigh didn't work for more than twenty minutes at a time.

Raleigh had really come through. He had a lot of personality, even at that age. He liked to look around at things and he didn't cry a lot. He had a great reputation and right away he was cast as Bette Davis's baby in a movie at Warner Brothers.

And right along, it seemed that Darby was always there, photographing Raleigh. Waiting for Raleigh to smile. Raleigh asleep. Raleigh, wide-eyed, a single tear running down his cheek. Darby was such a great photographer that Raleigh's composite for the casting directors, with a big picture of him in the middle, and four little ones surrounding it, was the best composite in town.

The funny thing, though, was that a new composite had to be done every two weeks to keep it current because little babies changed so much. Beth Carol always had to laugh when Darby would come tiptoeing over to look at Raleigh in his crib, as if he half expected him to have turned into a gargoyle or something. But Raleigh just kept on getting cuter and cuter. And brighter, too, and more outgoing.

Beth Carol looked down at the top of Raleigh's blond head as he slept, wrapped in a blanket, in her arms. He was such a sweet baby, too. So good-natured. He'd go to anybody. Why, even when he saw that awful Darby looming over him with his phony eye patch and that whole arrogant thing of his, Raleigh would reach up his little arms and start gurgling and cooing.

Oh, it had been rough in the beginning before Raleigh got on a schedule, when he would wake up all the time at night, wanting to nurse or play. She didn't know that she'd ever gotten a full night's sleep since his birth, what with keeping one ear cocked to hear every move he made, every sigh. Then there would be the days of sitting around the set for the two movies, and after that, the days like this one, the casting calls where he would be up against every baby in town to get a commercial, a role in television or a movie, a newspaper ad, or a catalog job.

Beth Carol just hated it when Raleigh was turned down. Her darling baby being rejected. Even the thought of it brought tears to her eyes. Once it had happened because he was too cute. "Nobody will look at the product," was what the casting director told her. That was dumb. Really.

Most of the time, though, Raleigh was the baby they picked. He got the Bullock's catalog, the Saks catalog, the Sears catalog, a newspaper ad for a diaper delivery service. There were the television commercials for talcum powder, cotton swabs, both national, which was great. In fact, with a hundred dollars here, a couple of hundred dollars there, what was sure to be thousands for the national commercials if they ran for a while, plus the money her father sent every month, Raleigh was on his way to supporting all of them in grand style. She felt a little guilty about that, bad when she couldn't stop herself from complaining about how tired she was all the time.

"I'll take him at night," Paul said.

Beth Carol just stood there, speechless.

But that was exactly what happened. Now Raleigh was living in the room next to Paul's, which Paul had set up as a gym with pads on the floor, rings, and bars. His sports equipment like his polo stuff, his tennis rackets, his fencing mask and rapiers. Here she'd had this dream baby's room in mind with a crib dripping with lace and organdy, and little lambs painted on the walls, and all. What Raleigh got instead were movies projected on one of the walls with the sound off all the time. Erroll Flynn movies. Douglas Fairbanks, Jr. Tyrone Power as Zorro. And Raleigh didn't have a crib. Just a playpen. So that he could see out in all directions all the time, Paul said.

Once when she'd gone into the gym, Paul was tossing Raleigh into the air like guys do. And Raleigh was just loving it, chortling and grinning and waving his arms and legs around. Then Paul tossed him through the air to Darby, who didn't look as if he were going to catch him.

Beth Carol let out a horrified scream, covered her eyes with both hands. Jerked her hands away to see Paul's white, shocked face. Darby's. In Darby's arms, Raleigh, looking terrified at her scream, started to cry.

"What are you doing to my baby?" she demanded hoarsely. "You could have dropped him!"

"We're teaching him to trust," Paul said coldly.

Trust Paul Fournier, she thought grimly. That's the laugh of the day. But she had to admit it. Whatever they were doing, Raleigh absolutely loved it. The one time he would fret was when they decided he had had enough conditioning for that session.

What Paul would do when Raleigh woke up during the night was bring him to her room so she could feed him. It was sort of companionable in a way, with Raleigh suckling at her breast and Paul sitting there talking with her.

"You've got to learn how to drive, baby," he would say.

"Oh, I can't, Paul. Don't ask me."

"Why not?"

"Because I'm scared."

"Well, why don't we try it?" he cajoled. "Just here, on the estate. Okay?"

"I can't," she said, tears filling her eyes.

"You've got to, baby. You can't live in Southern California if you don't know how to drive."

"Don't make me," she begged.

"Okay, okay." He laughed, throwing up his hands,

He could be so sweet, really. And he had so much to do these days. It seemed to her that the insurance adjusters were always there, going over the inventories with him, figuring out what had been destroyed in the earthquake. He was at the studio full-time, too, and even if it was in the mailroom, all of the guys there were actually in a training program to go on to bigger things. Then there was all the setting up of Raleigh's casting calls and other interviews, driving Beth Carol and Raleigh there, timing it so he was back for the actual interview because, as he told her, she couldn't sell a glass of water to a man dying of thirst in the desert, and then driving them home. Sometimes the thought flitted through her mind that maybe he was still selling dope, but she decided he wasn't. Raleigh was bringing in so much money Paul didn't need to, for one thing, and the other thing was that Fern still had that file of his, which he brought up all the time. Fern even thought Paul had broken into her house to try to get it back.

"I don't know why you think it was Paul," Beth Carol said when Fern called to tell her about it. "Gee, Fern, you've got so much stuff on so many people, there must be a thousand of them who would like to get it back."

"No, it was that asshole boyfriend of yours," Fern said, her breathy little voice quivering with rage. "Who else would, like, straighten up my stuff, man? I mean, there's only one person in the world who would leave the scene of a burglary neater than when he got there."

"That doesn't prove anything," Beth Carol said.

"Well, you just tell him that all that kind of stuff is in a safe in Sir George Dean's house. And you can also tell him that I've gotten a dog. A big, scary dog with real sharp teeth."

It was laughable, really, that Fern would think it was Paul. Besides, she hadn't done anything with the stuff in that file, even though it was a little like waiting for the other shoe to drop and knowing it was just a matter of time before it did.

In Beth Carol's arms, Raleigh's eyelids fluttered open. He stretched in his blanket and yawned. She looked down at him, into his big, blue eyes, felt a rush of nearly unbearable tenderness at his ecstatic smile.

My baby, she thought to herself, stroking his blond head. You're so beautiful. And that smile, well, it's worth anything.

"Raleigh Barnes," called the receptionist.

Oh, no, Beth Carol thought anxiously. Not yet. Paul wasn't here. Well, she'd just have to do it on her own this time. After all, he couldn't blame her if he hadn't managed to get here in time.

She scrambled to her feet, straightened Raleigh's blanket as he gazed adoringly up at her, and nearly stumbled as she avoided a baby crawling at her feet.

CHAPTER 26

*S*he was so nervous she didn't catch the name of the guy holding the door of the audition room open for her. He had sandy-colored hair, a nice, scrubbed look. He was wearing chinos, penny loafers, a pale blue oxford-cloth shirt with the collar open. He had a nice smile, too, Beth Carol thought.

"I'm Beth Carol Barnes," she said. "And this is Raleigh."

"Well, hello," the man said, smiling at Raleigh, wiggling a finger in front of him as Raleigh looked up, grabbed at the finger, chortled.

The room was cute, Beth Carol saw as she looked around. The walls were pale yellow, decorated with animal cartoons. Sitting around were hobbyhorses, dolls, toy telephones, blocks, stuffed toys, even a high chair covered in some green velveteen fabric. Lights and cameras surrounded a padded table, which was covered with a soft blanket. The casting director motioned her to a chair in front of his desk, smiled again as he slipped into his own. In front of her were stacks of cans of formula.

"Do you know about Similac?" he asked.

"Oh, yes," Beth Carol said. "I use Similac. Now, I mean. I breast-fed until he was just three months. That's supposed to be good for them. And then, well, it really wasn't very convenient because Raleigh would be off on some appointment, and I would be somewhere else, and Paul—that's my husband—said, 'Well, three months is fine according to the books,' and so we started on Similac, and Raleigh just loves it."

"Let's see," the man said, thumbing through some papers on his desk. "Your agent is . . ."

"Nell Garber," she said. "You see, Paul got him his first part. He's in an executive training program at MGM, and he heard about it. And the next one, too. But after that he knew we'd need somebody who would know what was going on, and everybody said Nell Garber."

"She's the best." He smiled, glancing through Raleigh's pictures. Holding up one of the rough proofs from the Saks catalog to the light, a couple of stills from the the cotton swab commercial. Smiled as he read the item from Sir George Dean's column.

"The camera sure loves you, little guy," he said.

Raleigh gazed at him, his mouth open.

"This is a national commercial," he said, getting up, coming around the desk, reaching down to take Raleigh from her arms. "I've already gotten the three backup babies, but I don't know, none of them is quite right. Now, this little guy has a lot of personality. He's just bursting with it."

Be careful with my baby, she wanted to scream as she watched the man walk toward a mirror on one wall. Raleigh leaned toward it, trying to touch his reflection. "Yeah, that's some boy, isn't it?" the casting director murmured. He took Raleigh over to the table with the lights and cameras, put him down as the blanket fell away.

Oh, he looks so cute, Beth Carol thought, her eyes misting as she watched Raleigh in his adorable little blue and white knit suit, his arms flailing, his feet in their little blue booties kicking vigorously, a big smile on his face. The casting director picked him up, swung him back and forth in his arms as Beth Carol gulped back a protest and Raleigh chortled with joy. Beth Carol thought she was going to die on the spot when the casting director tilted Raleigh upside down. But leave it to Raleigh. He screamed with laughter and waved his arms.

"You're some guy," the casting director said to the baby,

sweeping him into his arms, handing him back to Beth Carol. "That's the best kid I've ever seen." He grinned. "He's a natural." He flipped the intercom on his desk, asked the person on the other end to send Dick in to take some test shots. Held up the pictures of Raleigh again, smiling as he looked at them.

"The thing is," he said, "that you get a cute kid, but it's a whiner. Or it screams bloody murder if you try to take it out of its mother's arms."

"Oh, Raleigh isn't afraid of anything," she said. I am, though, she said to herself. I'm afraid of everything. "He even knows how to swim."

"Really?" the guy said, his eyes widening.

"Oh, yes," Beth Carol said. "My husband read somewhere about how babies can learn to swim as early as six weeks old, and so he taught him. Raleigh swims like a fish."

"You have a swimming pool at home?" he asked.

"Oh, yes," Beth Carol said with a little laugh. "We even have a lake."

"So why are you doing this? I mean, for most of these women, it's the money. If it weren't for what the kids can make, they'd be at the telephone company, or in some dead-end job folding sweaters in a department store. That's the trade-off. They drag the kids around to these casting calls, dig up the money for their pictures, scream at the agents, try to sell the kid to the casting director. So they feel the money the kid makes is money they've really earned."

"Oh, it isn't like that at all with me," Beth Carol protested.

"So, what, you want to be an actress, and it's a vicarious experience?"

"No, no. I could never do that. I'd just die if I had to stand in front of a camera."

"Well, tell me," he pressed. "After all, Beth Carol, you're the first mother who has ever come into this office who has a lake at home. I'm curious."

"It's for Raleigh," she said. "He loves it, loves the attention. He even loves the lights."

"He's how old?" the guy said, glancing down at Raleigh's

file. "Three months and two weeks old, and you say you're doing it for him? That you know this is what he wants?"

"Oh, yes," she said. "We're sure of it."

Actually, it was in the national commercial for the carpet cleaner that Beth Carol thought Raleigh was the cutest. He had all of this shining blond hair now, and he was on his hands and knees, crawling toward the camera like the little engine that could, and he had this big grin on his face and his eyes were bright. There was just a little bit of drool running from one corner of his mouth down his chin, but the guy directing just loved that. It looked so real, he said.

The thing about Raleigh in that commercial was that he was beginning to look sort of like Buddy's little brothers and sisters had looked when she and her sisters had gone to deliver those Christmas things. Buddy had probably looked something like that when he was little, too.

Beth Carol sighed, thinking about how it would have been if she and Buddy were together, if they were still up there in some other little Idaho town, and Raleigh had been born there. What would have happened to the three of them? she wondered. Not much, she thought. Would they have been happy? Maybe for a while, she decided. After all, when she was up there, she didn't know any better. And maybe after a while her father would have come around to some extent and there would have been money for Raleigh to go to college. But no. Under those circumstances, probably not. It was just because she was down here with Raleigh that it was all right. This way her father didn't have to deal with the situation up close, so he could justify sending her the money. To keep her away, maybe. He never even wrote as much as a line in response to the chatty little letters Paul made her write, enclosing copies of Raleigh's current pictures, stills from the commercials, copies of the print ads, and all.

What a portfolio he was building up now that he had started to crawl! That Similac commercial was really cute, and the one for Carnation dried milk. That one had run in newspapers, ladies' magazines, and on television, too. It was too bad about what had happened at the Jell-O audition, though. Beth Carol had to smile in spite of herself. There Raleigh had been, nestled in the casting director's arms, grinning and cooing as usual. So the casting director had spooned some of the new Jell-O flavor into Raleigh's mouth, and then what happened was really a surprise because Raleigh loved Jell-O, especially strawberry. But what he did was get this really thoughtful look on his face and then spit the Jell-O all over the casting director's shirt.

What Beth Carol really hated were those times when what they wanted was a baby who was crying, because they would do something to make sure it happened. Like on the orange juice commercial audition, where the casting director just pulled the nipple out of Raleigh's mouth. Well, most babies would have been hysterical. Not Raleigh, though. He just looked up at the guy as if he'd lost his senses, and then he scowled at him. The casting director had to laugh. It was such a cute expression.

But still, even though the money was really rolling in now, it just didn't seem right to Beth Carol that they were all virtually living off what a little baby was making. Even Darby, now that he'd moved in. They played foreign language records to Raleigh, Latin and Greek, because those were the root ones, Paul and Darby said, and those action movies were always going, too. They'd started Raleigh on the gymnastic rings, and Paul and Darby were always babbling away about Sparta, and ancient Greece, and the perfect marriage of mind and body.

Frankly, she just hated what they were doing to Raleigh. What was wrong with just letting Raleigh have a good time and be a baby? Of course, the thing was that Raleigh was having a good time. He was having a great time.

Raleigh. Raleigh.

Sometimes it seemed to Beth Carol that she didn't even exist anymore. In the beginning it had been fun that Raleigh was the center of attention. But sometimes she just wanted to say, Hey, how about me? Don't I count?

Raleigh's agent treated her as if she didn't even exist, and the other moms hated her guts because when she walked in with Raleigh, they knew that the best their babies could hope for was to be picked as a backup baby, and that only paid a hundred dollars with no residuals. So maybe it was all that animosity she felt from the moms that had made her start to take Miltowns again because she just hated sitting there and nobody would talk to her. She'd started smoking again, too, and having a couple of drinks in the evening because she was alone so much and the baby was always with Paul and Darby.

Darby had never paid any attention to her, so that hadn't changed. There had just been that one night during the months when she was still nursing Raleigh, and she had looked up, expecting Paul to bring him, and it had been Darby instead.

"Oh, I can't," she said. "Not in front of you. I'd be too embarrassed."

"You have a convenient memory," he said in that clipped, cold voice of his, and she had felt all flustered, remembering everything. At least they'd decided they weren't going to do anything with that movie they'd made. That on second thought they didn't want a dirty movie associated with their budding careers. That was a laugh, Beth Carol thought grimly. There was only one career that was budding that she could see, and that was the career of Raleigh Barnes.

She'd kind of hoped that by now, well, that she and Paul would be together again. It had been a long time. Nearly eight months. Oh, he was really nice to her, and all. He'd drive her down to Wilshire Boulevard so she could go shopping at Saks and I. Magnin, and Jax, and some of the other cute places. That made her feel good for a while, buying pretty new things and having the salesgirls pay attention to her. They were just about the only ones, she thought bitterly. Even Bobby seemed to like Raleigh better than he liked Beth Carol, and after all, Bobby had been her friend first.

It wasn't fair, she thought. It just wasn't fair.

CHAPTER 27

*T*his was really great, Beth Carol thought, her eyes shining as she looked out the window from the backseat of Sir George Dean's limousine. And everything looked so pretty today. There were the jacaranda trees with their lacy leaves, their lilac flowers, the magnolia trees with their white velvet blossoms, the other flowering trees in shades of pink and white. The beautifully manicured lawns were all in lime green and the beds of flowers were, well, it was like being in the middle of a fairy tale. Beth Carol smiled to herself, had to stop herself from bouncing up and down on the seat from sheer joy. Of course, she would feel that way today no matter where she happened to be. At the bottom of a cave. On Devil's Island, even.

"So it was like a bolt out of the blue, huh?" Fern said, squinting through the smoke from her cigarette.

"I just couldn't believe it." Beth Carol giggled, hugging her. Dear Fern. Who would have thought that two girls who were so different would be such great friends? And she looked so nice today, almost respectable in a black sheath dress, low-cut, of course, and a black cartwheel hat. "'Say it again, Paul,' was what I said."

"Say, lighten up, man," Fern said, squirming out of her grasp. "You're rumpling me."

"It's just that I'm so happy," Beth Carol whispered. "It's like a dream come true."

She leaned back against the seat, vaguely aware of that wonderful scent of fine leather, trying to remember every word Paul had said, every word she had said, and yes, every touch, too. Had it really only been the evening before when she had been sitting in front of the television set, crying as she watched *I Love Lucy*, feeling so sorry for herself that she would have been happy to just turn herself in on some new model? Erase herself, start over with a clean slate.

It had been so long since anybody had paid any attention to her that she thought she was hearing things when there was a tap at the door.

"Come in," she had called, a sob in her voice.

"Why, baby," Paul had said as he stepped into the room. "What's the matter?"

"I don't know," she muttered, wiping away her tears with the back of her hand. She felt him standing over her, felt the touch of his hand stroking her hair.

"Oh, you poor kid," he said sympathetically, kneeling in front of her, frowning with concern. "Now, come on, sweetheart," he pleaded. "I've got some great news. Let's see a smile."

"Okay," she said tremulously. Trying to smile, but starting to cry again, harder this time, as he took her in his arms, held her against his chest. "I thought it would be so different," she stuttered. "I mean, when Raleigh came, I thought I could be his mom and take care of him and everything. I never even get to see him anymore. You're the one who even takes him to his auditions now. You and Darby. And I just sit here, and nobody cares about me. Nobody loves me anymore."

"Oh, sweetheart," he soothed. "That's not true, and you know it. Raleigh loves you, you know that. And I love you. You know that, too."

"You haven't even been near me," she wailed. "It's been nearly eight months now since Raleigh was born, and you don't have to wait that long, Paul. It's okay in just six weeks. That's what the doctor said."

"Oh, darling." He sighed, kissing her hair now, running one of his hands along her forearm. "I know I've neglected you, and I'm sorry. But you know how it's been with Raleigh, with getting his career off in the right way, getting his life going in the right way."

"It isn't natural what you do with Raleigh," she sobbed. "All that physical conditioning, all those movies you play for him all the time, the records. He's just a baby. It isn't fair."

"I think I'm hearing something else." He smiled. "I think my girl needs some attention. That's what I think."

"I try so hard," she said.

"I know you do," he said, kissing her lightly on the mouth. "I appreciate it, baby. I really do."

"And that awful Darby," she added hopelessly. "Why does he have to live here? When is he going to go away, Paul? He thinks I'm dirt, you know. I can see it in his eyes every time he looks at me."

"Beth Carol, you're imagining things," he said. "He doesn't think you're dirt."

"Well, what is it with him?" she demanded, her voice rising. "Why does he think he's so much better than anybody else? That he's above it all?"

"He's just a very private person," Paul said.

"A private person," she scoffed. "You know what I think? I think he's in love with you. That's what I think. Why else would he be here? It sure isn't for me."

"Sweetheart, you're just a little jealous," he said. "Darby and I both spend a lot of time with Raleigh, and that makes you feel left out. Now, isn't that really what you're feeling?"

"I don't know," she said. "I just don't know anything anymore."

"It's all going to be different now, darling," he said, stroking her breasts now, her hips. "Something wonderful has happened at last. We can be married."

"Married," she gasped, wondering if he'd really said the words. Staring at him in disbelief.

"That is, if you want to," he said anxiously. "I couldn't ask you until now. But it finally happened. The big break. Raleigh's going to be the new Gerber baby. He'll be doing all their television ads, all their print ads. His face will be on every jar of Gerber's baby food, every piece of the point-of-purchase material in the markets. He'll be making personal appearances, too."

"That's fabulous," she exclaimed, feeling a surge of joy, of a heady pride in her beautiful baby, her wonderful, perfect baby. "But I don't see—"

"It's a one-year contract," Paul said proudly. "It's fifty thousand dollars."

"That's a lot of money," she said slowly.

"It's the big time, baby," he said. "And everything will be on the up and up. A judge has to approve it. Half of everything he earns from now on goes right into a trust fund for him. That takes care of his education. I'll start looking into investments for him. The court has to approve those, too. He'll be set for life."

"But I don't understand, Paul," she said in a small voice. "I mean, that's wonderful for Raleigh, but what does it have to do with the two of us getting married?"

"Darling, I didn't have anything to offer you until this happened," he whispered huskily. "Oh, I know. Raleigh has been bringing in money, but even when I added up all the jobs, it wasn't a career. It wasn't even the start of a career. He could have decided he didn't like doing it. A lot of kids are like that. He could have changed physically for the worst. A lot of kids do that, too. But with this, well, there's a future. We'll have security, we can start to build. Don't you see, baby?"

"I guess so," she said tentatively.

"What is it, Beth Carol?" he asked quietly. "Don't you want to marry me? Don't you love me?"

Did she love him? she wondered as she looked into his pleading brown eyes. Oh, she'd loved that fantasy of him that he'd created for her, but that was all a lie. But this Paul, the real Paul. How did she feel about him? Oh, she did love him. So much she could hardly bear it.

"I love you, Beth Carol," he said. "I want to take care of you forever. You and Raleigh."

"I love you, Paul," she whispered, burying her face in his neck. "I always have, ever since the first time I saw you."

"Oh, darling," he said.

"But there can't be any more lies," she said. "I've got to know how things really are."

"There won't be any more lies, dearest," he said, one of his hands on her breast, a finger massaging her nipple under her blouse. "Beth Carol Fournier. Mrs. Paul Fournier. How does that sound to you?"

Oh, what a wonderful name, she thought, savoring it, bursting with the wonder of it as Paul brushed her lips with his own, ran his tongue over her teeth.

"Paul, there's something I have to tell you," she said, her voice hoarse as she pulled away. "Raleigh . . . you're not his father. I just told you that so you'd love me and let me stay. It must have been the boy back home, the one my father caught me with."

"I suspected it," he said after a couple of minutes, his voice shaking. "The timing, it wasn't right. And Raleigh. Well, there isn't anything of me in Raleigh. I tried to see something, anything, but I couldn't make it work."

"I just can't lie anymore, Paul," she said wearily.

"It's okay, baby," he said, stroking her hair. "You know I love Raleigh. I couldn't love him more if he actually were mine."

"So it doesn't matter?" she asked.

"No, darling," he whispered. "It doesn't matter."

Oh, he was so wonderful to take it so calmly, she thought, feeling his mouth against hers, his breath coming faster while he stroked her breasts, started to unbutton her blouse. And she felt so relieved, clean again now that her terrible confession had been made.

He was sweeping her into his arms, and it felt so good to be there again. She clung to him, felt the muscles in his shoulders, his arms. Drank in the scent of his after-shave, his special masculine smell that she had been starving for all these months. She was almost weeping with shock, with gratitude, desire, as he put her on the bed. She watched him, panting, as he moved around the room, switching off lights, the television set, took off his clothes, folded them neatly over one of the chairs.

Then he was standing over her, outlined by the moonlight splashing white on his shoulders, his face.

"Let me look at you, darling," he said huskily as he undressed her, touched her breasts with reverent fingertips, her mouth. "My wife," he whispered as he took her in his arms, licked her lips, sucked at her nipples, exciting her as she felt the pull of his lips. She was shaking with desire as he spread her legs, buried his face in her wetness. I'm going to faint, she thought wildly as her heart danced in her chest. But he understood, she realized as he urgently thrust his thing into her body, filling the emptiness that had been there since Raleigh's birth. She wrapped her legs around his waist, her arms around his neck, screamed as he brought her to orgasm.

"We are one," he panted into her ear as she lay next to him, her body still shaking, her eyes closed.

"I love you," she moaned.

She could hardly believe it when she felt his presence next to her the next morning, opened her eyes to see him there. Oh, he was so handsome as he quietly slept. Those long, black lashes brushed his cheeks, his skin was so rosy. Oh, they'd talked for hours the night before. About how they were going to have to get Raleigh's birth certificate now that the court was involved, and that Paul would be listed on it as Raleigh's father. After all, he was the only father Raleigh would ever know. It made sense. And they would be married as soon as possible. My wife. He had called her that again. "I love you," she had told him, her eyes wide and solemn, when she looked up into his face as he penetrated her again. "I'll love you forever."

∘   ∘   ∘

"I'm having a little trouble following this guy's logic," Fern said, lighting another cigarette. "Like, it's hard for me to get from the kid getting this great contract to this guy suddenly having something to offer you."

"Oh, Fern," Beth Carol said, starting out of her reverie, "it would really be nice if you would give Paul the benefit of the doubt. Just once, you know?" She sighed with exasperation as she lit a cigarette and drew the smoke deep into her lungs. "Just think about it for a sec. Raleigh couldn't very well be the Gerber baby without Paul, could he? I couldn't do it. I don't know, when I'm around all those people I get so scared. I'd ruin everything. So it's Paul. Without Paul, there's nothing."

"So what you're telling me is that Paul is the Gerber baby?" said Fern, chortling. "That's, like, hysterical, man."

It was, kind of, Beth Carol thought, laughing, too.

"So where are you going to do it?" asked Fern.

"Golly, I don't know," said Beth Carol, blushing. "You know, with Raleigh being nearly eight months old, and us just getting married now, well, it's so embarrassing. I said to Paul, 'Why don't we go to Mexico? Nobody will be counting on their fingers if we do it there,' but he said he didn't want to do it there, that maybe it wouldn't be legal."

"Yeah, he'd want to be sure it's legal, all right," Fern said. "That's our boy."

"And I always wanted a beautiful church wedding," Beth Carol said wistfully. "Ever since I was a little girl, I've dreamed about it."

"Yeah, you would," said Fern.

"Well, everybody does," Beth Carol said defensively. "I'll bet even you want one."

"It's never crossed my mind," Fern said, a puzzled look on her face. "I mean, the chick is in this white dress, which is the guarantee that no guy has put it to her, and then her old man gives her to another guy. It's sort of gross when you think about it, man."

"I just don't know," Beth Carol said anxiously. "Maybe we could just drive to Ventura. Or Santa Barbara, maybe. I hear Santa Barbara is pretty." Turning, she put her hand on Fern's arm. "But wherever we get married," she said, "I want you to be in the wedding party, okay? I want you to be my maid of honor."

"Oh, you don't want me," Fern said. "Like, I'm not the maid of honor type, you know?"

"Of course I want you," Beth Carol said, incredulous, as she saw that Fern's face and neck had gone all red, that she didn't know where to look.

"Well, I'll think about it," Fern said at last.

"Well, if you don't say yes," Beth Carol said, "I'll never speak to you again."

"Gee, man," Fern said, "you're embarrassing me."

"You're my best friend, Fern," she said earnestly. "You always will be."

"God, if you don't knock it off, man," she said, "I'm going to get out of this car and walk." She puffed daintily on her cigarette for a moment before she added, "You want it to be nice, though. A good party. Pictures. Something you can look back on."

"Yes, I'd like that," Beth Carol said.

"Like, how about if I ask Sir George Dean to give the wedding for you?" Fern said. "He's got that great house, and if it's a nice day, we can get the tables set up on the terrace. He's got all those Orientals on the staff up there. They could put on a great spread. And, like, maybe there could be music, too. Something real dignified. A harp, maybe."

"But why would he do it?" Beth Carol frowned. "He doesn't even know us."

"Yeah, well, like I told you," Fern said. "He's got this big sentimental streak. Weddings, babies, all that crap. It really turns the old queen on."

CHAPTER 28

*F*ern kept coming up with all of these improbable people to invite to the wedding, and the two of them were laughing so hard that they almost drove right by Secrets.

"There it is, Kato," Fern shrieked into the speaking tube, and the chauffeur gently guided the limousine to the curb in front of it. A couple of girls who had never even acknowledged Beth Carol's presence before glanced at them with envy, Beth Carol saw with satisfaction as Kato helped them from the car.

"Thank you, Kato," Beth Carol said shyly.

"See you in a couple of hours," Fern said as he trotted ahead of them, held open the door to the salon. "Bye-bye, Kato," she added with a little wave. "That's not his name," she murmured into Beth Carol's ear. "I just call him that to drive him nuts."

"So who else should we have?" Beth Carol asked as she saw the three ladies sitting on one of the sofas glance up from their magazines, their eyes widening as they stared at Fern. "How about Greta Garbo?" she suggested. "And William Holden. We forgot William Holden."

"I know," Fern said triumphantly. "Queen Elizabeth. Wouldn't that just kill everybody? Sir George Dean can ask her. She's some kind of cousin of his, he says."

"Really?" Beth Carol asked.

"Oh, who knows?" Fern said, looking around. "You know how it is here. People will say that the man in the moon is their uncle, and then they're hurt if you don't believe them."

"We'll probably have to wait a few minutes," Beth Carol said as they approached the reception desk. "Bobby is always so busy, and there always seems to be some emergency or something."

"Yeah, so you said." Fern grinned. "Say, this is a cute place."

"Do you really like it?" Beth Carol asked anxiously. "It's got everything you could want. A massage room. A coffee shop. Everything."

Oh, she hoped she was doing the right thing by bringing Fern here. All those ladies were just gawking at her in that startled way, and a couple of the operators were giggling behind their hands. But finally, there was Bobby, gliding toward them, his eyes all rapt and shiny, the way they got sometimes. She scrambled to her feet, introduced Bobby and Fern, and in a second or two they were giggling and chatting about the wedding and how he had to come, and it was as if the three of them were old friends.

"So what do you think, man?" Fern asked, sitting in Bobby's chair, watching Bobby watching her in the mirror. "So the bride here wanted you to take a look at me and see what you think about my look, is what she calls it."

"Your look," he said blankly. "Oh, yes. Your look. It's perfect, your look. You're a masterpiece."

"You see?" she said triumphantly, turning to Beth Carol in the chair next to her.

"Maybe just the teeth," Bobby mused. "They're too small. You should get the teeth capped."

"Yeah, the teeth," Fern agreed. "Anything else, Bobby?"

"Nothing."

This had to be a joke, Beth Carol thought. How could he look at the way Fern was done up and see all of the whispers and giggles she was causing—and that was here, where they really had seen everything—and say that the only thing the matter with Fern was her teeth? She gazed at his face, searching for a hint of irony, anything. Golly, she thought with dismay. He really means it. He thought Fern looked just great the way she was.

"So what about this wedding, Bobby?" Fern was saying.

"I don't know what to wear," he said helplessly, a silly grin on his face.

"Yeah, that's right," Fern said, snapping her fingers. "What are we all going to wear to the wedding?"

Fern said why didn't they start to look at this place she'd found on Hollywood Boulevard that had some terrific stuff. Frederick's, it was called. And Bobby said maybe a little later, after they'd seen what the department stores had to offer. He'd even winced when Fern had said Frederick's, Beth Carol thought triumphantly. So much for Bobby and his new best friend. Fawning all over her like that. Really. It was a bit much, and all because Fern worked for Sir George Dean who Bobby was always laughing about.

"I get a lot of my things at Jax," Beth Carol ventured.

"Too casual," Bobby said, shaking his head as he wound Fern's stringy hair into pin curls. "We're going to have to do a little something to this hair," he said aloud, but not really to either of them. "Some conditioning. You've got some split ends."

"Well, I like Frederick's," Fern said firmly.

"I think I'll wear a gray suit," Bobby said dreamily. "Pearl gray. Double-breasted. What time will it be?"

He was already in the back seat of Sir George Dean's limousine with Fern the next day when they pulled up in front of the mansion to pick Beth Carol up, and when they got to the "Better Dresses" department at Saks Fifth Avenue, Bobby's favorite salesgirl already had all kinds of beautiful things picked out to show them. What Bobby had said about the salesgirl in the car was that she had been a rich lady with a big house in Bel-Air who used to spend most of her time shopping at Saks. Then, when her husband died and it turned out that there wasn't enough money, she would either have to get married again, or get a job. So she had gone to work at Saks, where she felt at home. She must have been there fifty years, Beth Carol thought, looking at all the fine lines on her patrician face, the smooth blond pageboy, the discreet navy blue dress with the obviously good piece of jewelry pinned to its lapel. Everybody went to her, Bobby had said. Everybody with taste, that is.

"Best wishes," she said in her finishing-school accent as she took both of Beth Carol's hands in her own. "You'll make a beautiful bride."

And then Beth Carol was crowded into the dressing room with Bobby and Fern, being helped into dresses, suits, in wonderful fabrics in soft beiges, grays, pale blues, ivory. The salesgirl was in and out carrying shoe boxes, handbags, scarves, hats as Beth Carol tried to absorb one version of herself after another through the cigarette smoke in the three-way mirror.

"The rose," Fern said.

"No, no," said Bobby.

"Which do you prefer, my dear?" the salesgirl asked.

Beth Carol's mind was reeling, as she tried to remember, tried to fathom her feelings of pure joy at what was happening, that she was getting married. She must be, because here they all were, picking out the dress. The right dress.

"I don't know," she said helplessly.

"We'll be back," Bobby said, and then they were sweeping out of the store, the limousine following them as they sauntered to I. Magnin, a block away, stopping every few feet to look at what was on display in the store windows, as the other pedestrians stopped in their tracks to stare at Fern, and the guys who had stopped for the red light at the corner honked their horns, trying to get her attention.

At I. Magnin, it was more of the same. A pale green cocktail suit in the most delicate crepe, a lace dress with a high neckline, the picture hat the salesgirl brought in from the millinery department.

"We'll think about it," Bobby said in his soft voice.

"I still like the rose," Fern said stubbornly as they crawled into the backseat of the limousine and were driven the three blocks to Frascati's, where they had a reservation for lunch.

"It's nice to see you, Miss Darling," the maître d'hotel said to Fern as he took her hand, brushed it with his lips. He nodded to Beth Carol and Bobby and led them through the jammed restaurant with its hum of conversation and bursts of laughter onto the covered terrace, where he ushered them to a table covered with a red-and-white-checked tablecloth. Beth Carol felt her mouth drop open when she saw the guys sitting next to them. Why, that was Tony Curtis, and there was Jack Lemmon. And the other one looked familiar, too.

"Hi, Fern," he called with a big smile, a wave of his hand, as the maître d'hotel fussed with her chair, asking her if she was comfortable, if this table was satisfactory, if everything was all right.

"Yeah, yeah, it's fine, Jacques," she said. "I'll have a martini. Up."

Then the busboy was there, bringing the basket of bread, and the waiter was bringing the drinks, and all of these guys, movie stars and everything, were stopping by to say hello to Fern, to give her items about whatever movie they were making or had just signed to do. And Bobby just sat there, drinking martini after martini, watching Fern with this big, dumb smile on his face. She was matching both of them drink for drink, and she had to admit it, when they got out of there a couple of hours later, she was staggering a little.

Frederick's was really funny, Beth Carol thought, giggling as she wandered from counter to counter while Fern and Bobby were looking at dresses in another department. She just couldn't believe that the bra she was holding didn't have any covering where the nipples would be, and that just about made her blush because the whole point of wearing a bra, after all, was so that nobody could see your nipples. And these black lace panties didn't have a crotch! Who bought these things? she wondered, really blushing now, embarrassed to even be in this place, as she realized what she was looking at. A false rear end.

It seemed to Beth Carol they had spent a couple of eternities at the department stores and they were at Frederick's of Hollywood for so long that any minute somebody was going to ask them to start paying rent. That was nothing, though, compared to Bobby once they started hitting Lew Ritter's on Wilshire, and some of the other places he liked where they sold clothes for guys.

They all had wood paneling and looked like libraries in the English country homes in movies. Bobby tried on every suit in his size, except the brown ones, in every store. Then there were the shirts, the ties, with the salesmen holding them up and making recommendations, and Bobby frowning as he shook his head. And then it was on to the shoes. This must be what forever feels like, Beth Carol thought as she and Fern just sat there smoking, bored to death. Finally, Bobby came over and said he thought he'd found something, but he'd have to bring them in to see if they liked it, too. They should have something to say, since they were going to pay for it.

Fern looked over at Beth Carol and winked.

It was closing time when they walked out of the store, so they had the chauffeur take them over to Romanoff's, where the cocktail hour was just getting under way. It was so late by the time she got home that Raleigh was already asleep. That made Beth Carol feel really guilty because she hadn't seen him at all that day. And what a shock it was to see Paul asleep in her bed when she crept into her room. Oh, he was going to be furious that she had come home so late, and drunk, too. All he did, though, was stir a little when she got in beside him. And once he realized she was there, he started to try to get her hot between her legs while he told her he loved her and called her his wife.

Oh, thank you, Gerber's, she thought, running her hands through his hair, drinking in the scent of his after-shave as he pushed into her. Thank you for making all of my dreams come true.

In the morning, her legs were shaking from all the love-making, and she was hungover, too. It was all she could do to get ready by the time the Bentley pulled up with Bobby and Fern in the backseat.

She wasn't the only one who looked like a wreck, she saw as she got in the car. Bobby was pale, and Fern looked as if she'd just plastered on more makeup over what she'd had on the day before. Still, it was a beautiful day and Beth Carol was in a daze of happiness.

The clouds were like great blobs of whipped cream slathered on a pale blue background as they drove slowly along Wilshire Boulevard, past vacant lots, a school of some sort, the gates that led to the estates in Fremont Place, the most exclusive street in all of Hancock Park. Acres of rolling lawn surrounded the bungalows, the main building of the Ambassador Hotel, with its nightclub, the Coconut Grove, where all the big stars like Marlene Dietrich, Lena Horne, and Harry Belafonte appeared. A courtyard with flowering trees and beds of flowers led to the ornate facade of the apartment building where that publisher, William Randolph Hearst, who had died a couple of years ago, had lived with Marion Davies sometimes when they weren't at San Simeon, and next to it was Perino's, the fanciest restaurant in town.

Bobby took a swig from a silver flask and offered it to the two of them as the towering green spire that topped Bullock's Wilshire came into view. It looked like a cathedral, Beth Carol thought. It was the most beautiful building she had ever seen.

It was like a cathedral inside, too, with its soaring vaulted ceilings, its hushed air of gentility and good taste. The scents of countless expensive perfumes mingled in the perfume department and the fashionable outfits were decorously displayed. The salesgirls looked really snooty, too, and the customers looked like those Junior Leaguers she saw in the pages of the society section of the newspaper.

"Shit, what a bunch of dogs, man," Fern muttered as they crowded into the elevator next to the uniformed attendant with his white gloves. "Like, where do they get their clothes? From the Salvation Army?"

"I think they look wonderful," Beth Carol whispered. "I mean, they're so refined, and all."

"Well, different strokes for different folks," Fern said, undulating off the elevator with Beth Carol and Bobby trailing after her onto the floor where better dresses were sold and where a smiling salesgirl hurried toward them to ask what she could do to help them.

"I'm looking for a dress for a special occasion," Beth Carol said.

"Yeah, she's getting married," Fern said.

"Oh, best wishes," the woman trilled. "I'll tell you, I have the most beautiful wedding gown I've ever seen. It just came in yesterday."

"I was thinking about something less formal," Beth Carol said, flushing.

"Why don't I just show it to you?" the woman suggested. "After all, it can't do any harm, can it?"

"Well . . ." Beth Carol said, a note of longing in the word.

It was a beautiful gown, Beth Carol thought as she stood in the enormous dressing room, looking at her reflection in the three mirrors. The delicate lace framed her jawline and dropped to the creamy white satin that hugged the bodice and flared into a full, white skirt with a long train. The sleeves of the gown were slightly puffed at the shoulders, and the satin crept to a meeting with the lace that fanned over each hand.

"That's reembroidered alençon lace, of course," the salesgirl said as she fastened each mother-of-pearl button on the back of the gown.

"Of course," Beth Carol whispered.

"Now this is *trés* dramatic," the woman said, lifting the veil into place and adjusting it.

It was really incredible, Beth Carol saw as she looked at her reflection. It was sort of like what the wicked step-mother wore in Snow White with a V descending onto her forehead, only white, of course. A silver band that looked like a crown held a cloud of tulle that fell behind her.

"Cathedral length is very popular these days," the salesgirl said, a satisfied smile on her face. "Now, what do you think?"

Yes, somewhere in the back of her mind from the time she was a little girl she had had a vision of herself looking kind of like this, Beth Carol thought as she turned and watched the way the train of the wedding gown moved in the mirror. But the reality looked better than the dream. She had never thought she would look so pretty. She'd never thought that a wedding gown this beautiful could exist.

"Perhaps a more conventional veil. . . ." the salesgirl said, a critical look furrowing her brow. "A crown of satin flowers holding it. Or a band of lace to carry out the lace motif on the gown."

"I've got to show my friends," Beth Carol said as she gathered up the skirt and floated into the next room.

"Oh, you're so beautiful," Bobby said, his eyes wet as he gazed at her.

"Hey, who's kidding who here?" Fern asked with a kind of a sneer. "Come on, you guys. Let's not get all carried away."

Beth Carol's lower lip was quivering. She plodded back to the dressing room. Oh, if only she could turn back the clock, she thought miserably as the salesgirl deftly unfastened a button, then another. If only there had been no Buddy. No Paul. None of the others. No Raleigh, most of all. How cheaply she had abandoned the right to wear this dress, the right to come to her wedding day the way she was supposed to come. But she couldn't be thinking these awful things about Raleigh, that she wished he had never been born. It was ghastly, the worst thought she had ever had.

"I'm so ashamed," she murmured as the salesgirl carefully lifted the glorious white gown over her head. "Oh, I'm so ashamed of myself."

"My dear child," said the woman, her face pale. "Please don't. Please."

To never be able to look like that, Beth Carol thought. To never finally see the pride on her father's face as he escorted her up the aisle where the man she loved was waiting to take possession of her. To never see the faces of her sisters, of her girlfriends from home, in her wedding party. It was almost more than she could bear, she thought as she trudged along behind Fern and Bobby and watched with distaste as the two of them examined one exquisite objet d'art after another. A Chinese vase. A perfect piece of porcelain. All the beautiful vases, bowls, sets of glasses perfectly lit in one hushed room after another in the gift section of the store, while the anxious eyes of the salespeople followed Bobby's and Fern's greedy fingers.

And she'd never have any of these as wedding presents, either, Beth Carol thought bitterly. No white boxes tied with white satin bows. No cards offering best wishes. No Steuben or Orrefors or Lalique nestled inside in white tissue to make her gasp with pleasure and surprise.

No white wedding gown.

No wedding presents.

It seemed to Beth Carol that what she'd done was throw away most of her life as a woman.

"Hey, look, Bobby," said Fern, tugging at his arm as she gazed at a flat alabaster bowl on a low teak stand sitting on one of the tables. "That's just like the one you have, man."

Now, how would she know what Bobby had or didn't have? Beth Carol wondered, staring at her. Slowly it dawned on her what must have happened as she looked over at Bobby.

His face was beet red, and he looked as guilty as she'd ever seen a person look.

Fern and Bobby, Beth Carol thought. Oh, this was too much. It really was.

"Oh, so what?" Fern said with a flicker of annoyance when they were in the ladies' room later repairing their makeup. "What's a lay between friends?"

"But he's a fag," Beth Carol said, her voice quivering.

"Oh, yeah?" Fern said. "Well, you couldn't prove it by me."

"Well, it just wasn't the right thing to do," Beth Carol insisted.

Fern turned and looked at her as they stood next to each other in front of the mirrors in the beautiful room with its marble floors, its marble walls. The colored girl in her black uniform and little white apron was humming as she folded towels into little squares.

"You know," Fern said, shaking her head, "sometimes I don't know where you're coming from, man."

CHAPTER 29

*T*he problem was that Beth Carol was too embarrassed to be married at Sir George Dean's house in front of all those people if Raleigh were there and that the only reason Sir George Dean had even agreed to give them the wedding at all was because he was so intrigued with Raleigh, the wonder baby.

"Don't make me do it," she begged Paul.

"We have to do it," he said, a pleading note in his voice. "Think what it can mean to Raleigh's career, baby. You know how it is with kids in this business. They're just a flash in the pan. But with Sir George Dean on his side, well, think about it."

"Can't you see my side of it for once?" she asked. "Here I am, getting married, and my baby is there?"

"You've got to stop worrying about what other people think, honey," he said, stroking her hair. "You've got to start getting used to the way it is here. Nobody cares. Nobody remembers."

"You're always saying that, Paul," Beth Carol mused, "but you know what? Sometimes I think you're just trying to convince yourself."

It was really nice that when the day actually came, Sir George Dean sent the car for them. With all the stuff they

were taking, all of Darby's camera equipment, and
Raleigh's stroller with the little steering wheel on the front,
his playpen for his nap, a diaper bag, and a couple of
changes of clothes just in case, it seemed to Beth Carol as
if they could have made it across darkest Africa for six
months. Then she had to fit in the car, and Raleigh. Darby
and Paul, of course, looking as handsome as she'd ever
seen him in what he called a lounge suit with a gray silk
cravat.

At the last minute, she remembered she'd left behind
the outfit she was going to wear when they went off to their
one-night honeymoon at the Hotel Bel-Air but finally they
were on their way.

She lay her head against the seat for a moment, exhausted from tossing and turning all night, trying to remember
everything she had to remember. Worrying that she'd do
everything wrong, make a fool of herself when she tried to
talk to all those people, and not believing any of it was happening, anyway.

But there they all were, driving grandly down Sunset
Boulevard in the late afternoon with the sinking sun turning the nightclubs, the restaurants, all of the smart shops a
glowing red, and all the tourists in the cars alongside them
looking at them curiously to see if they were movie stars—
so maybe it was true. Beth Carol turned the little diamond
ring that Paul had given her. My husband, she thought,
looking at him next to her. I'll try to make you so happy.

The limousine curved along a tall hedge for a few hundred feet until it came to a gate nearly hidden in the
foliage. Beth Carol watched the chauffeur holding the
phone at the gate, her mouth dry, her heart racing. Then
they were driving into a pretty courtyard, the hum of conversation, a piano, a man singing "Baubles, Bangles, and
Beads" filling the tranquil scene. Two or three Oriental
boys in white coats and black trousers surrounded the car,
helping them out, helping to unload, and then Beth Carol
was propelled into the entryway.

Sir George Dean was brushing her hand with his lips,

welcoming her, offering his best wishes, and in the background, Beth Carol was vaguely aware of clusters of attractive, well-dressed men and women chatting, of the fragrances of expensive perfumes, men's scents, the roses in the garden. And then Fern was there, clutching her arm with her hand, hurrying her down a wide hall hung with modern paintings to the room where they would wait, freshen up. Beth Carol's stomach clutched with anxiety as Fern closed the door behind them.

She was panting as she looked at her reflection in the full-length mirror on the back of one of the doors in what seemed to be a large dressing room with flowered wallpaper and the flower prints she had seen in rooms that weren't used very much. Self-consciously she smoothed the full skirt of her organdy dress which was called ecru by that first salesgirl at Saks Fifth Avenue, where they had finally bought it. The neckline was slightly décolleté, edged with matching lace, the sleeves puffed just above the elbow. She had taken her satin shoes back three times before the color was right, but they looked fine, she saw, pirouetting a little. She wore wrist-length gloves on her hands, which she raised to adjust her cartwheel hat with the ecru velvet ribbons hanging down the back.

Behind her in the mirror, she saw Fern, squinting as she lit a cigarette, dressed the same way, only in a delicate shade of mauve.

"I'm going to be sick," Beth Carol muttered, a stricken look on her face.

"Don't be a jerk," Fern said, impulsively hugging her. "Oh, man, you look just great. Your eyes are all shining. Hey, it's the happiest day of your life, right?"

"Right," said Beth Carol. Through the door she heard the piano playing the first strains of "The Wedding March."

"We're on," said Fern, thrusting a bouquet of cattleya orchids, white rosebuds, and baby's breath into her hand. "Now, don't fall down on me, okay?"

Beth Carol nodded tremulously as she followed Fern with measured steps out the door, down the short hallway to the drawing room. It was a blur of reds, wonderful fabrics, great sprays of floral arrangements. She smiled tightly at the pianist, who was grinning encouragingly from where he sat behind the grand piano. Through the open French doors, she could see the used brick patio, the elegant men and women perched on little red and golden chairs, the judge in a dark suit and a somber tie, standing under an arbor festooned with pink and white roses, carnations, interwoven with greenery. Darby in his dark suit, a white rose in his lapel, his jaw jutting forward, his body ramrod stiff. And Paul, her Paul, looking so handsome that it almost broke her heart as he frowned a little, his face as pale as she felt.

Then she was beside him, swallowing a couple of times to moisten her dry mouth, her hand shaking as he took it in his own shaking hand, vaguely aware of all of those eyes on the two of them, the eyes of all of those people they didn't know.

Beth Carol tried to focus on the judge's face, tried to comprehend what he was saying as she dug her fingers into Paul's hand.

"We are gathered here today to unite this man, Paul Andrew Fournier, and this woman, Beth Carol Barnes, in holy matrimony. . . ."

". . . take this man to be your lawful wedded husband, to love, honor, and obey, in sickness and in health . . ."

"I will," she whispered.

". . . this woman to be your lawful, wedded wife, to love and to cherish . . ."

"I will," muttered Paul, in a voice no more audible than her own.

Then Paul was fumbling with her glove, the wedding ring, a narrow gold band with tiny, chip diamonds, and the judge was saying something about by the authority vested in him by the state of California he now pronounced them man and wife.

"You may kiss the bride," he said, grinning at Paul.

Then Paul gathered her into his arms, and he kissed her

softly. And Fern grabbed her and gave her a big hug and a smack on the cheek. Darby kissed her on the cheek, and so did the judge, while the pianist rousingly played "Here Comes the Bride."

Oh, I'm so happy, Beth Carol thought in her daze as all the people she didn't know crowded around her, offering her their best wishes for her happiness, their cool, patrician cheeks briefly brushing her own. And there was Bobby, some girl clinging to his arm, looking impossibly handsome in the black suit he had finally decided to buy, wiping away a few tears and telling her in a soft voice choked with emotion that he hoped she would be happy, that everything had worked out after all.

"This is my friend," he said shyly. "This is Sandy."

"I hope you'll be very happy," the girl said, extending her hand.

"Thank you," Beth Carol said, taking it, trying not to look as shocked as she felt when she met her eyes and smiled. Why, the girl was absolutely beautiful, she realized with a stab of jealousy, with thick, blond-streaked hair in a bang over her forehead melding into a perfect pageboy. She had a fawn's soft, brown eyes, high cheekbones, a full, red mouth. Her sheath dress was a sort of teal blue, and instinctively Beth Carol knew that the necklace she wore was real diamonds and sapphires, the earrings, too. On the ring finger of the hand that held hers was the biggest, prettiest diamond ring Beth Carol had ever seen.

"Bobby has told me so much about you," the girl said. "He's so fond of you."

"He's told me a lot about you, too," Beth Carol said. "About all the fun you have, about all of the trips you're always taking."

"Oh, yes." The girl laughed. "We're always on the go."

"That must be nice," Beth Carol said stiffly.

"And the baby, Raleigh," the girl said. "Bobby just loves Raleigh."

"Thank you," Beth Carol said as other people crowded in to congratulate her. She watched Bobby lean down and kiss the girl on the mouth as the two of them, arm in arm, sauntered toward the bar where people were ordering drinks, chatting in small groups.

Somebody touched her shoulder, and she turned to see Darby motioning to her to join Paul, Fern, the judge. A camera was in his hand, another couple dangled from his neck. Happily, she trotted over to Paul's side, felt his arm around her waist as cameras clicked. Clicked again. From the corner of her eye she saw Raleigh sitting in his stroller wearing the adorable little outfit they had bought him with its white shirt with the Peter Pan collar, the little blue shorts with its bib that buttoned over the shoulders, his hair all golden in the late afternoon sun. His little hands clutched the steering wheel in front of him, and he was looking with wonder at Sir George Dean, who was kneeling in front of him, making those motions with his fingers that people always did with babies.

Oh, he was so cute, Beth Carol thought. They would all be so happy together.

"Kiss the bride, Paul," directed Darby, his one good eye on the viewfinder, one of the houseboys beside him with more equipment. And she saw Sir George Dean next to him now, his own camera to his eye.

They posed with arms locked, sipping from each other's champagne glasses. Darby set his camera, handed it to Sir George Dean, and trotted to his proper place at Paul's side in the wedding party. She and Paul posed under the arbor with the judge between them. Sir George Dean, smiling, one arm around each of them. Darby kissing her on the cheek. Fern leaning up to kiss Paul.

"Come, my dear," said Sir George Dean, "I want you to meet a few of my friends."

Beth Carol felt intimidated as Sir George Dean steered her from group to group. The guests seemed to her to be talking in all kinds of different languages as they approached, or were chattering in English-accented voices about the season in Gstaad, or St. Moritz, the Italian Riviera. Clucking about how Paris was still impossibly dowdy, almost as bad as

England, and here the war had been over for eight years, my dear, and wouldn't one think that by now things wouldn't be quite so primitive. Why, they still hadn't repaired the fifth column at the Crillon, for heaven's sake. "You know the story about that one, don't you, darling? Well, it was during the war, of course, and one of those Nazis said to the ranks that they would have to destroy the fifth column and so they fired a cannon at it. Can you imagine?"

Sir George Dean led her firmly into the laughter and they were really so nice, stopping what they were talking about at once and saying what a pretty bride she was, and how lovely the ceremony had been. One of the ladies in wonderful jewels of her own even took Beth Carol's hand to admire her ring.

Others were talking about a cocktail party, she thought, until it turned out that what they were talking about was a play called *The Cocktail Party* by someone named Mr. Eliot, who was an American who had moved to London and who had worked in a bank. And some others they approached were talking about Audrey Hepburn, a new actress in a movie called *Roman Holiday*.

Beth Carol could only smile and nod as Sir George Dean moved her firmly along, introducing her to this one, that one. Stopping in front of a wall of framed pictures of people in uniforms and sashes, seated in ball gowns, some with tiaras.

"My family," he said, his eyes misting. "You're lucky to have a family, dear. That beautiful little boy. I could cry, he's so beautiful."

"He said his first word the other day," announced Beth Carol, taking the glass of champagne one of the waiters was offering her. "And he's only eight months old."

"My heavens!" Sir George Dean said in his own clipped British accent, "That is young. What did he say?"

"Hi," said Beth Carol. "That's what he said."

"Oh, my dear," Sir George Dean, propelling her forward, "that is wonderful. I'll mention that in my column, I promise you."

The din of conversation, of laughter, all but drowned out the Cole Porter, the George Gershwin, the Vernon Duke as Sir George led her over to the main seating area, where dusk was seeping into the room behind it through the French doors, and where a bevy of young men sprang to their feet to be introduced to her.

And then Sir George was introducing them, rattling off a long list of names that Beth Carol couldn't begin to absorb, as she nodded and smiled and licked her lips. "And this wondrous creature here on the sofa is Lady Weyburn who has that magnificent villa in Acapulco that I'm sure you've read about."

"Of course," she lied, taking the older woman's hand, feeling a little blurry now with all the excitement, all the champagne. It had been a long time since she'd seen Paul, she worried, as Sir George Dean pointed to a chair and told her how the fabric was Aubusson, that he'd taken some old rugs and had this chair and that one over there covered with them, and didn't she think it was effective.

She nodded and smiled as she stumbled away from him, trying to remember which way she should go to get to that little powder room she thought she had seen. And Raleigh, she probably should check to see that he'd been put to bed in his playpen somewhere. Of course, that was the one thing she probably didn't have to worry about, she thought, and giggled to herself. There was always somebody there to take care of Raleigh, the wonder baby, just the way he was taking care of every last one of them.

CHAPTER 30

*E*ven as Beth Carol stepped out of the powder room, she could feel the urgency, the heat between the two figures standing close together in the shadows at the end of the hallway. It wasn't that they were doing anything. They weren't even touching. She took a couple of steps along the Oriental runner before her eyes adjusted to the gloom.

It was Paul, she realized with a sickening lurch in her stomach. He was leaning against the wall, his arm next to Fern's blond head.

"It's the bride," called Fern in that breathy little voice of hers, a big smile on her face as she looked toward where Beth Carol was standing. "So what do you think, man?" she asked, undulating toward Beth Carol. "So isn't this a great party?"

"It's wonderful," Beth Carol said, meeting Fern's eyes for an instant, searching Paul's face. He seemed as nonchalant about the whole thing as Fern was, but there was something else in his expression, too. Relief. Oh, she knew him so well, this husband of hers. "And here I was, so worried about whether you would get along," she said sweetly, with a hard edge to her words.

"Oh, we're getting along great," Fern said. "What I was doing was giving Mr. Hot Shot here a wedding present."

"A wedding present?" Beth Carol said blankly, noticing for the first time that Paul held a manila folder in his hand. "Oh, a wedding present," she said lamely.

"It's my file," Paul said huskily.

"Yeah," said Fern, grinning. "So the groom here says, 'Did you make any copies?' Now, is that gratitude for a really great gesture? I ask you."

"Did you make any copies?" asked Paul, and there it was again, Beth Carol realized. That urgency, that heat as he looked at Fern.

"What do you think?" Fern asked, licking her lips as she smiled up at him. "Don't you trust me?"

"No," said Paul, smiling now.

"Well, then, I guess we're just going to have to wait and see, aren't we?" Fern chuckled, locking Beth Carol's arm in her own, walking her back toward the din of the party with Paul a step behind them.

Beth Carol sat at Sir George Dean's right, glancing from time to time at the sea of heads at the other tables, at the waiters who poured the wine, deftly removed the plates. Paul, clasping her hand under the table, didn't make her feel any better. These women, for one thing. Oh, they were very smart looking, of course. But they were too massaged, too thin, too phony, somehow. Just masks, really. And the men, well, there were twice as many of them, maybe more. They were too well tailored, too smooth. Even with the young ones, there was something about them that was overripe, decadent. There was some awful quality about them that made the fags at the beauty salon seem as innocent as babies. Because they were all fags here. She was sure of it.

And the way the tables were decorated, well, she'd never seen anything like it, not even in magazines. The tablecloths were white shot with silver threads, the centerpiece was a tall facsimile of a palm tree. The tall candle holders were palm trees, too. There were all sorts of different porcelain birds grouped around, and the flowers were big, flat, red, shiny things with a long, yellow pistil that looked exactly like she knew what. With all of that, you'd think the plates would be plain. But no. They were white, but they had abstract blue trees all over them. And the wineglasses. There were three of them at each place in different shapes and sizes. Beth Carol watched what Sir George Dean was doing and did the same.

You'd think at a wedding reception the food would be kind of elegant, but the first course was just soup. Still, it didn't taste like any soup she'd ever tasted. It was delicious, and very light. The next thing the waiters brought around was some fish. Just a little bit, charmingly arranged. It was pretty good, she had to admit. But it didn't seem like enough, even for all of these skeletons, so it was a surprise when the next course was dessert, a kind of lemon sherbet. Well, finally it was over, she thought, sighing. What a sham. Well, she'd just never think about it again, and besides, she'd only agreed to it for Raleigh's career. Her eyes misted as she thought of the sacrifice she had made, when her sherbet was whisked away and one of the waiters was standing at her right, offering a huge silver platter with bloody slices of paper-thin meat, tiny potatoes, mushrooms, all kinds of cunning little vegetables.

"Thank you," she whispered, serving herself with trembling hands as another waiter glided by, filling one of her glasses with red wine. Watching these guys was like it must be at the ballet, she thought admiringly. They were really good.

After the chateaubriand, a salad was served. Just a few leaves of some wonderful lettuce she'd never tasted before. Beth Carol glanced at Sir George Dean with new respect. This whole meal was beyond belief. She sipped the white wine that had accompanied the salad, feeling a lot better about everything, even a little giddy again, from all of the different wines.

Silently the waiters removed plates, replaced them. Only candlelight illuminated expectant faces as a door was pushed open and the most beautiful wedding cake in the whole world was wheeled in to the gasps of appreciation of the guests. It was four tiers high, with white roses sculpted in frosting. Next to the groom on its pinnacle was a replica of Beth Carol in the outfit she was wearing on this, her wedding day, the happiest day of her life.

It was the most charming gesture she had ever seen, Beth Carol thought, tears trickling down her cheeks. How sweet of Sir George Dean to go to so much trouble. Why, he must have quizzed Fern about what she was going to wear. There was no other explanation. She met Fern's eyes across the room. Fern was smiling broadly.

"I would like to propose a toast," said Sir George Dean, his voice shaking with emotion as he rose to his feet. "To Mr. and Mrs. Paul Fournier, to their love, to their happiness on this, their day of days. To their continued happiness throughout their life together."

And all those people Beth Carol had thought were so jaded and laughing at her behind their hands were clapping, and she could see that some of them were wiping away their own tears, and a couple of the guys called for a speech.

"Thank you, all of you," said Paul huskily, standing. Pulling her to her feet, his arm around her waist. "I'm so thrilled you have all been here today to share our happiness. And Sir George Dean," he said, raising his glass, "well, there are no words to convey our gratitude for this beautiful party, for your unparalleled hospitality and graciousness toward us. And, of course, our special thanks for the kindness you have shown our little son, Raleigh, on your television show and in your newspaper and magazine columns. You've been wonderful.

"But most of all," he said, his arm tightening around her waist, "I want to thank Beth Carol for doing me the honor of agreeing to become my wife." He paused, and scattered applause filled the room. "Better late than never, as they say."

Everybody started to clap, and there was the warmest,

most understanding laughter. Beth Carol whispered her thanks, too, as the lights came up. Darby was there, snapping pictures. Sir George Dean was taking pictures, too. Everybody was hugging and crying. Together they cut the first slice of cake, and Beth Carol fed it to Paul, and he fed it to her as flashbulbs popped.

"I love you," Paul said, his eyes wet. "I'll always take care of the two of you, Beth Carol."

"I love you," she whispered. "I always will."

He took her in his arms and kissed her hard while the flashbulbs popped again.

Beth Carol was glowing as, arm in arm with Paul, she sauntered over the bridge leading to the entrance of the Bel-Air Hotel. In the meandering stream below, regal swans with arched necks rocked on the water. The pale moonlight played on the lush, tropical planting that adorned the grounds, the terra-cotta roofs of the rambling buildings. She hung back in the reception area with its polished wooden floors, the occasional Oriental carpets, the fine antiques, while Paul registered. Then the bellboy was unlocking the door of their bungalow, the bridal suite, and Paul was sweeping her up into his arms and carrying her across the threshhold.

It was so pretty, she saw, all in shades of peach and gray, with a sliding glass door leading onto its own garden. And there was a spray of pink rosebuds about to burst open, a bottle of champagne cooling in a silver ice bucket. She strolled over to the bureau, looked at her reflection in the mirror. Her face was flushed with happiness. The little hat and her going-away suit looked very smart, very appropriate. Beyond her own reflection, she saw Paul, trying to look sophisticated as he thrust a tip into the bellboy's hand.

"Well, here we are, Mrs. Fournier," he said as the bellboy silently closed the door behind him.

"Yes, Mr. Fournier," she whispered. "Isn't it wonderful? Isn't everything wonderful, darling?"

"I've never been happier," he said, pulling her into his arms, looking down into her face.

"I'm happy, too." She raised her mouth for his kiss.

"Well, I guess now the groom goes to the bar for a couple of drinks and the bride gets ready," he said with a little laugh, kissing her hair.

"Oh, I don't want you to leave, Paul," she said, clinging to him.

"But it's the way it's done, honey," he said.

"Well, all right," she said hesitantly. "Yes. Sure."

"Now, you make yourself beautiful for me," he said, at the door. "Even more beautiful, that is."

"Oh, I will, darling," she said, her eyes shining. "You can count on it."

"Just Paulie and me, and baby makes three," she hummed to herself as she sprang from the tub, grabbed one of the thick, white towels and started to pat away the drops of water. Oh, it was going to be so wonderful tonight when Paul came back, she thought dreamily, slipping the exquisite satin nightgown over her head, patting the lace inset over her breasts into place, straightening the spaghetti straps. Fern's special present to her, she thought happily, turning in front of the mirror. But, of course, Bobby must have picked it out for her because it was in such good taste. She was still humming as she applied just the faintest hint of eye shadow, powder. A touch of pale pink lipstick. Then she combed her hair, fluffed it out with her hands like a cloud around her face. She slipped on the matching peignoir, pushed her feet into the cute mules that went with it, and danced back into the main room, the bedroom, where the roses in their vase were already unfolding and the ice was melting in its bucket with the bottle of perfect French champagne.

Any minute now, and Paul would be walking through the door, she told herself excitedly as she switched lamps on and off, settled finally for just the single light on the table next to the biggest bed she had ever seen. Carefully she turned back the covers, got in wearing the peignoir.

Shaking her head, she got out of bed and took off the peignoir, which she arranged—artistically, she thought—over the back of a chair. Yes, just the nightgown, she decided, a happy smile on her face as she slipped back into bed.

Seconds flew by, then minutes. She must have been sitting here propped up against the pillows for nearly an hour, she thought with dismay. What could have happened to him? she worried as she crossed the room, turned on the television set, and tried to concentrate and be rational about all this. After all, nothing could have happened to him between the bridal suite and the bar. It was only a couple of hundred yards away. He was bound to be back at any moment.

Later, she thought she must have fallen asleep because she awoke with a start at Paul's voice.

"Honey?" he said. "Are you asleep?"

"No, no," she protested groggily, squinting against the light from the table next to the bed.

"I'm sorry I was so long," he said. "I really am. But you'll never guess who I ran into and who bought me a drink."

"Who?" she asked, pulling herself up on the pillows, watching him as he started to take off his tie, unbuttoned his shirt.

"Jack Warner," he said. "Can you believe it? And we started to talk, and, well, I couldn't just get up and walk away, could I? Not from Jack Warner, after all."

"I was getting worried," she muttered, stifling a yawn.

"Well, there's nothing to worry about anymore, baby," he said, slipping into bed next to her, sliding an arm behind her back and pulling her to him. "You know what I think?" he asked, kissing her hair. "I think we've both had a busy day. Tonight I'm just going to hold you. How does that sound to you?"

She lay in his arms, her face against his chest, her eyes wide open, breathing in his scent. It was Joy, the most expensive perfume in the world. Fern's perfume.

CHAPTER 31

$\mathscr{W}$ ell, what happened," Beth Carol began, clearing her throat as Bobby drew a comb through her wet hair, "was that a call came through from the publicity people. Raleigh was invited to a birthday party. Paul is so busy right now. There are all of these meetings with investors on the four movies he's planning to do, the ones where Raleigh will play the lead in *The Adventures of Robin Hood,* and *Zorro, Captain Blood,* and the other one I can never remember. And, a lot of times Paul takes Raleigh along, sort of to show him off, put him through his paces. Just the sort of thing that's a lot of fun for a five-year-old, right?"

In the mirror, Beth Carol saw Bobby's reflection, the barely perceptible way he shook his head.

"The call was from someone named Mrs. Wilding, and the party was for her little boy," Beth Carol continued. "And I thought it would be a wonderful idea because, you know, Raleigh only gets to play with other kids once in a while when they're working with him on the set or in an ad, or something. It's Paul. Paul and Darby. 'Oh, we don't want Raleigh to be corrupted.'" Her voice was singsong, mimicking them. "'Oh, we don't want Raleigh catching their brattiness.'

"So anyway, I asked Paul if it would be okay if Raleigh went, and he thought he'd heard of this Mr. Wilding. He thought he was an important producer, or something. And the address was right. It was in the Beverly Hills flats, so it had to be one of those big mansions there. Well, he didn't have anything he needed Raleigh to do. And neither did Darby, so Paul said maybe Raleigh had been working too hard. He said fine, that Raleigh could go.

"Well, Raleigh was all excited, too. I went to Saks and then I. Magnin and finally I went to FAO Schwarz, and I found the most perfect present. It was a little race car set, and the little race cars were all reproductions of some of the most famous race cars throughout history, and it had a track that was shaped like an eight and it ran on batteries. Then I had a talk with Raleigh and I told him that he had to give the present to the little boy who was having the birthday and that he couldn't keep it for himself." She gave a little laugh, remembering the conversation. "Well, Raleigh was so indignant! 'Do you think I'm a baby?' he asked me. 'I know that, Mommy. After all, I'm five years old.'"

"I used to hate that," Bobby murmured. "Giving them the presents. I'd cry."

"We got there," she went on, "and it was a really beautiful Mediterranean house. You know the ones just below Sunset. A red-tiled roof, and arched doorways, and a lot of exotic planting. Birds of Paradise, that kind of thing. The door was open, and there was a girl standing there. Raleigh ran out through the French doors because he could hear the other kids, and I went up to this girl and I said, 'How do you do, Mrs. Wilding. I'm Beth Carol Fournier. I'm Raleigh Barnes's mother. Thank you so much for inviting him.'

"Well, it wasn't Mrs. Wilding. It was one of the secretaries. Mrs. Wilding was outside with the children and the other mothers, and then she told me that if I went outside I would be sure to find her.

"It was really something," Beth Carol said. "There were about twenty or thirty kids running around, playing, and they'd had the swimming pool covered, and a real carousel brought in, and all kinds of rides. There was a magician, and some acrobats, and five or six clowns. There were all of these servants milling around, seeing that the kids were happy. The mothers were sitting under a canopy around tables that had flowered cloths and beautiful arrangements of flowers, and some of the other mothers were strolling around, looking after the kids and talking. Oh, and there was a real director and a real cameraman shooting movies of everything that was going on.

"I went over to the girls who were sitting under the canopy and I introduced myself, and they introduced themselves. And they're just the cutest girls, all married to important men, and so well dressed, and I even had seen a couple of them here at Secrets. I said I was trying to find Mrs. Wilding, and did any of them know where I could find her because we hadn't met."

"Oh, there she is," one of them said, pointing across the lawn. "The one in lavender."

"And I turned around, and I looked at the girl she meant, and Bobby, I nearly fainted. Guess who it was?"

"Who?" he asked.

"It was Elizabeth Taylor!"

"Elizabeth Taylor!" he breathed.

"And she's so beautiful, the most beautiful girl in the world. Those eyes, well, they really are violet, just the way they photograph in movies. And her skin is like porcelain. And her hair is so black, it's blue. I just couldn't believe it. And, of course, she's Mrs. Wilding because she's married to Michael Wilding, the actor.

"So it was wonderful, and Raleigh had the best time, and all the girls were saying how beautiful he was, and how jealous they were that he was mine. And the kids had such a good time going on all the rides and running around, and everything. We all sat under the canopy, and then all of these waiters brought us lunch. The most adorable little sandwiches with no crusts. Watercress, cucumber. And platters and platters of strawberries, and cantaloupe, pineapple, blueberries. It was all so pretty.

"And just when the kids were all getting a little bored and whiny, in came all of these Shetland ponies, prancing in with the marching music that was on the loudspeakers in the garden, and they had these little dogs sitting on their backs, wearing ruffles around their necks. Well, the kids were ecstatic, and all of us moms clapped and cheered. It was so cute, the cutest thing I've ever seen. The clowns helped all of the kids onto the ponies and started to lead them around. Very slowly, of course. And Raleigh was the only one who knew how to ride. I was just so proud of him, Bobby. It was wonderful.

"Then the cake came. It was three tiers, with clowns in all different colors of icing sort of tumbling down it, in keeping with the whole circus motif. And there were all of these candles and Elizabeth Taylor's little boy, Michael, Jr., I think his name is, blew them out.

"I really had fun," she went on. "Three of the girls asked me for my phone number and said we had to get together so that the children could play together, or why didn't we have lunch, and all. And Raleigh loved everything."

"What a great day," said Bobby, a touch of envy in his voice.

"It was," she said bitterly. "Then we got home, and it was one of those wonderful evenings. Paul was actually home for dinner, and Darby was off editing something. So it was the family, Paul and Raleigh and me. I set the table in the small dining room, and I whipped together something light. I was telling Paul all about it, and how wonderful it had been, and how excited I was when Mrs. Wilding turned out to be none other than Elizabeth Taylor, and Raleigh was bouncing around and so happy, and everything. And do you know what Paul said?"

"What?" asked Bobby.

"He said, 'Did you go like that?'

"And I said, 'Yes. Why?'

"And he said, 'Because you have your sweater on inside out,'" she whispered, the tears starting to trickle down her cheeks. "That was so mean."

Beth Carol reached for a Kleenex on the counter in front of her, brushed away her tears. Heard Bobby sigh, commiserating.

"He's still seeing your friend Fern, too," she said hopelessly. "Wednesday night, it was. He said he was working, of course. He always says he's working. But I know. What he doesn't realize is that he comes to bed absolutely reeking of that perfume of hers. She must bathe in it. You can smell her coming a mile away."

"You promised me you wouldn't put her down, Beth Carol." Bobby sighed.

"Well, you ought to tell her about loyalty," she said indignantly. "You should let her know that a girl shouldn't do that to her best friend. A girl should tell herself that it's strictly hands off."

"Well, Paul's doing it, too," Bobby said. "It takes two to tango."

"Oh, Bobby," Beth Carol said. "You realize, don't you, that the only reason Fern has her job with Sir George Dean is because she goes to bed with all of those men, and they tell her things, and so that's why Sir George Dean keeps her on." She lapsed into silence for a moment, brooding about Fern, about Paul. "It's a good thing for her, I guess," she said. "I mean, after all, can you see any man wanting to marry Fern, wanting to take care of her? It's laughable."

"I don't think she wants to get married," Bobby said mildly, putting a pink net over the pin curls, tying it in front.

"Well, of course she does," Beth Carol blurted, hearing the shock in her voice. "That's what every girl wants."

How could he have come up with such a thing? she wondered, frowning, and then slowly the light dawned. "Oh, I see," she said triumphantly. "You're still sleeping with her, too."

"You have a one-track mind," Bobby said, a little annoyed.

"All I want is a faithful husband who comes home at night," she said. "Is that too much to ask?"

"Well, from what I hear all day, maybe it is."

"And a home of our own, for the three of us," she said dreamily. "Oh, I know it's the thing to do to have a large, important house, but that isn't what I want. I want a home that's small and cozy. That's not good enough for Paul, of course. Oh, no. If he can pull off this movie deal for Raleigh, do you know what he's going to do? He's going to put in a bid for the mansion when probate is finally finished in a couple of months. The time is perfect, he says. Real estate is going for nothing."

"Yeah, all my customers say real estate is a good investment," Bobby agreed.

"That wouldn't be Paul's reason, though," Beth Carol said. "There's nothing in this world that would give Paul more satisfaction than owning the estate, because it belonged to the Kendalls and his mother was a servant there, and he was a servant's son, and he never forgets it, even with the wonderful education Mr. Kendall paid for Paul to have at Choate and Yale."

"Well, maybe the movie deal won't come through," Bobby said.

"And, of course, when you think about it," Beth Carol continued, ignoring him, her voice, low, harsh, "it isn't Paul who's become such a success that he can buy it. It's Raleigh."

"Raleigh wouldn't have a career without Paul."

"Yes, I know that," Beth Carol said. "But Raleigh has something to do with it, doesn't he? And what about what I want, for once?" She sighed, felt as if she were going to cry again. "You know, Bobby, I feel that I've done what I was supposed to do. I was raised to give myself away to a man, just like every other girl in this room, and that's just what I've done."

"Well?" said Bobby.

"But it didn't work out," she said. "I gave myself away, but I'm not gone. I still have myself."

"I've got an idea," Bobby said, "Why don't you have another baby? Then you'd have something to do."

"Paul won't hear of it," Beth Carol said. "Everything is Raleigh. He even checks my diaphragm before . . . well, he checks my diaphragm."

"Well, why don't you get involved with the stuff Raleigh does?"

"Paul won't let me," Beth Carol said.

"But he's your kid, too." Bobby frowned. "I don't mean negotiating the contracts or directing the movies, or anything. Just some little thing. Then, when he sees that he can count on you, he'll let you do more."

"Do you really think so?" she asked doubtfully, swinging around and looking up into Bobby's face.

"I don't see how it can hurt to try," he said. "After all, all he can say is no."

CHAPTER 32

*W*hat it turned out to be was an appearance at a supermarket in Brentwood, one of the last ones Raleigh would be making under his nonexclusive contract with Wheaties, Breakfast of Champions. And it wasn't even as if Beth Carol would be there alone with him. The account executive from the advertising agency and somebody from the client would be picking them up in a limousine to take them there. And the assistants, as usual, had been swarming all over the place for days, generating excitement, drumming up an audience for the promotion.

Still, she would have a lot of responsibility to be sure everything went smoothly, Beth Carol realized, glancing at Raleigh. He was sitting next to her by the window of the car, kicking the seat. He looked pensive, the way he always did when he was about to perform, as he focused his concentration on what he was going to have to do. On the jump seat across from her, the guy from the advertising agency, his elbows on his knees, smiled encouragingly at her. Brad Something, Beth Carol recalled, flushing as she smiled back at him. He was so nice looking, and he had a way with him that made even the guy from the client seem to defer to him. He was wearing a tan, lightweight suit, a tattersall shirt, and a black knit tie. He looked as if he had walked right off one of those fashionable Ivy League campuses a few years earlier. She loved guys who looked like that. They were just her type. She thought maybe she was just his type, too. What was that he had said when they had gotten in the car at the mansion? Something about if he had known she was going to be coming along with Raleigh, he wouldn't have tried so hard to get out of coming along himself. So that was fun, she thought, but business was business.

She fumbled in her handbag for the list of items to be checked that Paul had written out for her. The pennants fluttering over all the cars in the parking lot had to be the ones they used with Raleigh's picture on one side and the cereal on the other. The glass cases on the front of the store where they usually advertised the specials of the day had to display Raleigh's latest poster, where he was in his fencing outfit, with the name of the movie prominently featured. She had to check to be sure there was the latest point-of-purchase blowup right behind the area where Raleigh would sit to sign autographs on the eight-by-ten glossies that were the same as the one-sheet poster outside. Count the discount coupons people turned in. Raleigh was entitled to a percentage on each one. Count the Wheaties boxtops that went into the giant fishbowl so that Raleigh could pick the winner of the grand prize, a weekend for the entire family on Catalina Island and a trip on a real seaplane. A percentage there, too. Do an approximate crowd count, for comparative purposes with similar promotions.

Of course, everything would be checked and double-checked by Brad and the client guy and all the assistants. But still, somebody had to be there to represent Raleigh's interests, and this time she was it. Beth Carol was so excited that she felt as if she were the one who was going to be flying off the roof of the market on a wire and who would be performing on the rings and bars out in front for fifteen minutes before the autograph session, and all.

Ahead, she could see a lot of people—children, mostly—milling around in the parking lot. Somebody from the store was dishing up little cones of pink cotton candy, someone else was pumping compressed air into red, green, blue, yellow balloons. People certainly did have a good time when Raleigh turned up, Beth Carol thought, smiling proudly. It was always like a party, a carnival. Back when Raleigh had first gone to work, Paul had been all excited by every little thing, too. But somewhere along the line his attitude had changed. When Wheaties had wanted to renew Raleigh's contract, Paul wouldn't do it. No more commercials, either. No more small roles in movies, on television. With this four-movie deal he was putting together with Raleigh as the star, they would all be making a quantum leap. And if it didn't work out, well, Paul had enough producing experience now that he would be able to catch on somewhere. At one of the studios, which was a long shot the way things were going with them. But maybe an independent, or at a television network. If there was one person who would be all right, it was Darby. Everybody wanted him to come and direct feature films. And still he was there, living with them, functioning mainly as Raleigh's trainer. If she lived to be a hundred, Beth Carol didn't think she'd ever be able to figure out what made Darby tick.

It was mainly the moms and dads who clapped and cheered as Raleigh got out of the car, Beth Carol saw. The little girls looked tentative about what was going on, and the little boys looked either hostile or bored.

"Oh, he's so beautiful," Beth Carol heard one plump, elderly woman say to her friend. "I could kiss him to death, that one." And Beth Carol felt so proud of Raleigh. Of herself, if it came to it. A couple of assistants were hustling Raleigh into the store, and Beth Carol pushed into the crowd that was gathering, their eyes already on the roof of the store.

"He's quite a boy," said a voice just behind her, Brad's voice. She felt a little tingle of pleasure.

"Thank you," she said shyly.

"Is he an only child?" asked Brad.

"Yes, yes, he is," she said, looking up at him from under her lashes. "Do you have children?"

"Yes, we've hit our limit," he said, smiling pleasantly. "Our Kimmi has just turned four, and Kevin is two."

"A boy and a girl," said Beth Carol. "How nice."

"I'd like to see you sometime," he said, his smile still pleasant.

"What do you mean?" She frowned.

"Just what I said," he replied, his arm against hers as somebody pushed by him.

"I'm married," she said.

"So am I," he said.

"Well, I'm flattered," she said with a little laugh, "but I really can't."

He was laughing with her, and he took her elbow when Raleigh appeared at the edge of the roof of the market, and grabbed the wire in one small, strong hand. Beth Carol felt a stab of fear watching Raleigh swing off into space. She closed her eyes as Brad pulled her into his arms, buried her face in his neck, as he patted her hair.

"He's just fine," he whispered. The applause, the cheers filled the air, and the pennants flapped noisily in a sudden breeze. "What a boy. Better yet, what a mother."

Raleigh finished laboriously printing his name on the last glossy photograph and looked around. The crowd was pretty much gone. There were only a few people in the checkout lines. The assistants had started to pack up, and the Wheaties man was deep in conversation with the manager of the store. Mommy had made a new friend, Raleigh saw. There she was, up at the front of the store by the charcoal briquettes, talking to the man from the advertising agency. Their heads were close together.

Something was different, he realized, and then he knew what it was. Nobody was paying any attention to him. He was alone. So this is what it's like, he thought, smiling to himself. It feels nice. He stood up. One of the assistants smiled at him as he folded the legs of the table, whisked it away.

They sure have a lot of stuff here, Raleigh thought to himself as he sauntered down one of the shining aisles. There were all different kinds of laundry detergent. Tide, he read. Bold. All different kinds of kitchen cleanser. Ajax. Comet. There were a million cans with pictures of different vegetables on them. And here was the meat counter with neatly arranged rows of different kinds of meat, with little white things stuck into them that showed the price. There was a lot of fish, too, and beautiful pink shrimp on a bed of ice. The butcher in his white coat and cap smiled down at him. Raleigh smiled back.

Here were the real vegetables, hundreds of tomatoes, all kinds of different lettuces, cauliflowers, green peppers and red ones. Mushrooms. And here was the frozen food department with its fried chicken and Salisbury steak. And the dairy section, with its cartons of milk, its boxes of butter, the yellow containers of cottage cheese. And this was sour cream, he read. This was really, really fun, he decided. With all of the hundreds of appearances he had made in supermarkets, this was the very first time he had ever looked around to see what they had for sale.

When he went back to where the point-of-purchase display showing his picture was still standing, he saw that Mommy was still having a good time talking to her new friend. He didn't see the Wheaties man at all. Raleigh pushed open the front door to the store and stepped outside. There was the picture of him in his fencing outfit in the glass display case, he saw, wandering over to take a closer look. That was fun, the fencing. En garde, he said to himself, striking the classic pose in front of his poster.

"That's you, isn't it?" said a voice.

Raleigh turned around, saw a young man standing there. He had close-cropped blond hair and big blue eyes. He wore neatly pressed chinos, a checked sports shirt, an anxious smile.

"Yes, sir," Raleigh said. "It is."

"I saw you jump off the top of this building here," the man said. "Weren't you scared?"

"No, sir."

"So what is it?" he asked, coming a couple of steps closer. "Are you scared of anything?"

"Well, I'm not anymore," Raleigh said.

"But you were?"

"A little," Raleigh admitted.

"What of?"

"Well, I didn't want to go to sleep," he said. "I couldn't figure out where dreams came from. I'd wake up, and I'd be crying." This probably wasn't the right thing to be telling this man, Raleigh realized. But he was so nice, and he seemed so interested. "Of course, that was when I was little," he added hastily.

"So what happened?" the man persisted. "You just stopped being scared?"

"Well," Raleigh said, frowning, trying to get it right. "I decided that having a dream was just like going to the movies all by yourself. After that, it was all right."

"Say, that's great, you know?" the man chortled. "You're a smart kid."

"Thank you, sir," Raleigh said, pleased.

"Oh, you don't have to call me sir," the man said anxiously. "You can just call me Buddy, if you want to. Buddy. That's what all my friends call me."

"How do you do, Buddy?" Raleigh said as his hand was enthusiastically pumped up and down.

"You know who used to call me Buddy?" he asked. "This will really surprise you. Your mom. That's who."

"You know my mom?" Raleigh asked suspiciously.

"I sure do," he said. "We come from the same home-town up in Idaho. Beth Carol Barnes. That was her name before she got married."

"You could have read that," Raleigh said.

"Well, how about this, then?" the man said gleefully. "Your granddad's name is Raleigh Barnes, just like yours.

So how would I know that if I didn't know your mom?"

"Well, I guess so," said Raleigh. "You can say hello to her, you know. She's just right inside, talking to this man from the advertising agency."

"Oh, no," Buddy said. "I don't want to do that. I saw her standing there, watching for you to throw yourself off this building here, and she was so pretty, prettier than I even remembered. I tell you, Raleigh, it almost broke my heart to see her after all of the years when she's only been in my dreams every night, is all."

"I dream about her, too," Raleigh said.

"We were sweethearts back home," Buddy said with a little choke in his voice that worried Raleigh because he thought Buddy was going to cry. "I know, I know," he went on, "you don't believe me, and I can see why you don't. There she is, so beautiful, and back home her daddy was cock of the walk, and my daddy was so much white trash and drunk every night, too, just like yours truly—when my disability check comes, that is. And I've been sick, too. Real sick. They tell me they flew me home from Korea in a straitjacket strapped to a stretcher, raving crazy out of my mind, but you know what? I don't remember a minute of it. One minute I was there, and the next thing I knew I was in the Veteran's hospital, that big, gray place down the street, and they were pumping me full of tranquilizers, and all of these kid shrinks who looked to be about fourteen years old were sitting there with me and asking me to tell them what my problem was."

"That's terrible, Buddy," said Raleigh.

"Yeah, it was terrible, all right," Buddy agreed. "I'm better now. I've even got my own place. I still have to go back, though. Three times a week, sometimes four. It's a trial, they say, to see if I can make it on the outside."

"You seem fine to me, Buddy," Raleigh said doubtfully.

"Do I? Do I, really?" Buddy asked eagerly, a big smile on his face.

"Yes, Buddy. You really do."

"Say, Raleigh, I've got an idea," Buddy said. "You want a dog?"

"Pardon me?" Raleigh said blankly.

"A dog," Buddy said impatiently. "You see, I was here at the market a couple of weeks ago, and there was this little dog running around in the parking lot, real scared. No collar, no tags. Nothing like that. So I figured that somebody just didn't want him, and they dropped him off here, see? And I took him home. But it isn't right, Raleigh. He shouldn't be cooped up in a little apartment all day long. So I figure you can have him and he'll have a place to play outside. You do have a place for him to play outside, don't you?"

"Oh, yes," Raleigh said. "We have a hundred acres or so."

"A hundred acres!" Buddy exclaimed, his eyes wide. "Holy cow!"

"Well, it's not all level," Raleigh explained. "Some of it is ravines. Some of it you can't even get to. But it's a hundred acres, all right. Even more."

"Well, that's great, Raleigh," Buddy said. "It really is. So this little dog will have a place to play, and you'll have a reminder that you met someone your mom knew."

"Well, I don't know," Raleigh said.

"Your mom will let you have a dog, won't she?" Buddy asked anxiously. "I mean, kids are supposed to, aren't they?"

"It isn't actually up to her," Raleigh said.

"Well, how about you?" Buddy asked. "You want to take a look at him?"

"I guess I could do that," Raleigh said. "I'll just go tell my mom."

"Nah, don't do that," Buddy said. "We'll be back in a couple of minutes. She won't even know you've been gone. And, say, Raleigh? Could I ask you something? I know you're a big star and everything, but I'd really like it if you'd let me hold your hand on our way, just like I'm taking care of you."

∗   ∗   ∗

Raleigh was already thinking that maybe this wasn't such a good idea even before they got to Buddy's apartment. In the first place, it wasn't as close as he said it was. It was three blocks, which took them more than a couple of minutes right there. Then it was around in back of an empty store which had a FOR RENT sign in its window. And there were a lot of stairs. Four flights. It was dark, too. Raleigh could barely make out Buddy's blond head as he bounded ahead of him. Maybe there wasn't even a dog, Raleigh thought as Buddy fumbled with his keys and threw open the door.

"Come on, Raleigh," he called, outlined in the doorway by the sunlight filling the room behind him. "Shake a leg, Raleigh."

Tentatively Raleigh stepped into the apartment. Trotted after Buddy as he pushed open another door. "I keep him here in the kitchen," he said, smiling beatifically. "And you know why that is, don't you? It's because he's not housebroken yet, and I can't have him peeing on the rug, and all, not that it's much of a rug."

He stepped aside, gestured to Raleigh to come and take a look. There it was, Raleigh thought happily, just as Buddy had said. A little dog sitting there, his head cocked as he looked at them, his hind end wiggling around, his tail wagging. His fur was tan and gray and some of it hung in his eyes.

"That's some dog, isn't it?" Buddy asked proudly. "More of a puppy, though. Cute as a button, I'll say that for him."

"What's his name?" Raleigh asked, looking at the little dog.

"Well, I don't know," said Buddy, perplexed. "I guess that's up to you, if you want him. Do you want him, do you think?"

"Oh, yes," breathed Raleigh, kneeling in front of him, feeling the little dog licking his fingers as he petted his silky fur. "I'll need something to lead him, Buddy. Do you have a leash for him, and a collar?"

"Let me see," said Buddy, frowning. "I've got a ball of

twine in a drawer somewhere, as I recall. That'll have to do."

"Well, thanks very much," Raleigh said, standing. "I'd better get back now. They'll be looking for me, and I don't want my mom to worry."

"Oh, you can't go yet," said Buddy, a pleading note in his voice. "You just got here. How about a soft drink? I've got a couple of Cokes right here in the refrigerator. And you know what else? I've got a new camera I just bought where you take the picture and, presto, it comes out the end all developed and you don't even have to take the film to the drugstore. It's called a Polaroid. Isn't that a wonderful invention? So I thought I would just take a few pictures of you and the dog here. So I'll have something to remember you by. Okay? And you've got to take a look at the rest of my apartment. Okay?"

"Buddy, I've got to go," Raleigh said firmly.

"I can make you stay, you know," Buddy said after a couple of seconds. "I'm a lot bigger than you are, Raleigh. You can see that. And don't worry. I'm not going to hurt you any. I just want to talk to you for a while. That's all. I just want you to be my friend."

CHAPTER 33

He was a talker, all right. It seemed to Raleigh that all Buddy did was talk. At night, after the bars closed, he would wake up to the sounds of Buddy in the other room, stumbling around and cursing under his breath. Then he would hear him trying to get the key into the padlock on the bedroom door and there Buddy'd be, shaking him awake, saying his name in that pleading voice, while Frisky, clasped tightly in Raleigh's arms, gave a low, warning growl. Probably because Buddy was stinking of booze, as usual.

"Go to sleep, Buddy," he would plead. "We can talk in the morning."

"Now, Raleigh," Buddy would whisper. "Please, okay? I'm lonely, Raleigh. So do me a favor, okay? Just this once."

"Just for two minutes, Buddy," he would say.

And Buddy would be so grateful that he would be on the verge of tears, which he usually was, and he would talk and talk. And, of course, it was more like two hours than two minutes. Raleigh just couldn't understand it. After all, Buddy had all of the doctors at the Veteran's Administration to talk to, and they were really interested in what he had to say. About Korea, for example. Well,

Raleigh hadn't even wanted to hear what had happened to
Buddy in Korea because he was sure it would be really horrible to make Buddy so sick. But nothing had happened to
Buddy in Korea. He'd never heard a shot fired. In fact,
he'd never even been out of Seoul, which Buddy said was
the big city they had over there.

"Then why did you get sick, Buddy?" Raleigh asked.

"I knew it was happening to my friends," he said, getting
a frightened look in his eyes. "I wouldn't let myself go to
sleep because I'd see them at the instant they were being
shot. I'd hear their screams. I just couldn't stand it. It was
killing me."

"Buddy, all you were doing was sitting, typing in an
office. That's what you told me. You didn't really know
what was happening to your friends."

"I did," Buddy said, his eyes getting wild. "I could imagine it. That's how I knew, and I couldn't take it. I just
couldn't take it."

"All right, Buddy," Raleigh said, patting him on the arm.
"I'm sorry I said anything."

And Buddy wanted Raleigh to tell him all about himself,
everything he was thinking, everything he could remember,
just the way Sir George Dean always did. He didn't know
what to say when it was Sir George Dean, and now he
didn't know what to say when it was Buddy. Also, all the
questions were embarrassing, coming from a grown-up.
They should have better things to do with their time than
spend it quizzing a five-year-old. Why, Sir George Dean
was always kidding Raleigh about actually coming to live
with him. Here he had this wonderful house, and all of
those Oriental boys running around, doing whatever he
wanted, sometimes before he even thought about it himself. So why would he want someone to move in and dis-
rupt absolutely everything? And Raleigh knew that was
what happened, because now that he was here with Buddy,
everything Buddy did, or even thought about, was to try to
keep him happy and amused.

Some of it was fun, too. Buddy would heat up these

wonderful beans from a can, and he'd cut up hot dogs into it. Raleigh had never tasted anything like it, and it was really great. Or they'd have spaghetti with meat sauce, and that was really good, too. Or frozen chicken dinners, which Raleigh absolutely loved. They'd have soft drinks, which Raleigh had never tasted before. There was a choice of Coca-Cola or Pepsi. Raleigh liked them both, but maybe the Pepsi just a little better. Well, that was all Buddy needed to hear. At one point, Raleigh counted fourteen bottles of Pepsi in the refrigerator.

Buddy brought him clothes, shirts, a couple of pairs of jeans that were almost as good as new, which he'd gotten in a secondhand store near one of the bars where he'd drink with the other vets who spent a lot of time at the hospital. He brought Raleigh stacks of comic books which Raleigh just loved, especially the ones with Superman, Captain Marvel, and Prince Valiant. And the games. Monopoly. Almost as soon as Buddy told him the rules, Raleigh was beating him every time. Checkers, which was really easy compared to chess. A deck of cards. Buddy taught him how to play War, but it was so simple Raleigh's mind kept wandering.

"I'm going to teach you how to play football," Buddy said one day. "It's the best way to learn how to be a team player, Raleigh. I used to be a quarterback, you know. That's why your mom liked me. All the girls did. Everybody screaming my name, my letterman sweater. They go for that."

"No, Buddy, I don't want to learn," said Raleigh. "Paul says that only individual sports teach you that you can only count on yourself. Paul says they're just the way it is in real life. No substitutions. That's what he says."

"So why do you call him Paul, anyway?" asked Buddy. "Isn't he proud to be your dad? Is that it?"

"He doesn't believe in it," Raleigh said.

"But you call your mom mom, don't you?" he asked, getting that puzzled look in his eyes.

"She likes it," Raleigh said. "That's why."

"Well, I respect the way you're being raised, Raleigh,"

Buddy said. "After all, you're a big star, so it must be right. But just try it once, okay? I'd consider it a personal favor."

"No, Buddy. I don't want to."

And then Buddy was crouching, one hand spread on the rug, grunting, "Hup-two-three-four," or something, and Frisky was barking his head off, and Raleigh felt himself tumbling head over heels. He lay there, sprawled on the floor.

"I hate this, Buddy," he said querulously. "Now, don't do it again or I'll be mad."

Then Buddy got that pathetic look in his eyes that made Raleigh feel guilty, and he patted Buddy on the arm and told him that everything was all right.

Then there was the camera. Buddy was always popping up, shooting away. Even when Raleigh was in the bathtub.

"Now I know all your secrets!" he chortled, that crazy grin on his face as he watched, fascinated, as the photograph printed itself.

"I can't stand this anymore, Buddy," muttered Raleigh, shaking his head. "I've got to go home."

"Not yet," said Buddy. "We're having a good time, aren't we? Say we are, Raleigh. Come on, say it."

When Buddy was out, Raleigh would pace around the bedroom, Frisky at his heels, trying to figure out how he was going to get out of there. If only the apartment faced the main street he could just open a window and scream for help. But that would probably be even worse. Buddy would tie him up and gag him when he went out, Raleigh thought grimly. It wasn't that Buddy wasn't a nice guy. He just had a screw loose somewhere. Take this latest theory of his.

"Tell me your birthday again, Raleigh," he said.

"I've told you ten times," Raleigh said irritably. "August 22, 1952."

He watched Buddy, the frown on his forehead, as he counted on his fingers, concentrating as hard as he could just like a little kid.

"Raleigh, I've got something to tell you," he said solemnly. "I know you're not going to believe me, but it's the truth, the whole truth, and nothing but the truth."

"What's that, Buddy?"

"I'm your father," he said. "What do you think of that?"

"That's great." Raleigh sighed. "Just great."

Raleigh stood by the open window, his elbows on the sill, looking at the faded asphalt four stories below, at the slender blades of grass sprouting from its cracks. At the end of the lot, there were a few rows of tomatoes and lettuce that Buddy was growing. Behind the little garden was a wooden fence. And behind the fence, nothing. Just the endless, weed-choked, vacant lots. He leaned out, examined the rusted fire escape snaking up the side of the building. It was at least ten feet away. He squinted, considering his trajectory. What he was going to need was something he could use to swing over to it. That, and somewhere to attach it. Maybe this doorknob to the closet, he thought, pulling it open. No, the rod for the clothes. That was better. It was going to be really hard to do, he decided. What was going to make it even harder was taking Frisky along. But he wouldn't leave without Frisky. Raleigh leaned over and rubbed Frisky's pink stomach, and the dog wiggled with pleasure.

That was another thing, he reminded himself. He was going to need a leash. He'd have to find that ball of twine that Buddy used to tie up his tomato plants.

"Raleigh," called Buddy from the other room. "I'm home, son. And guess what I've got for you?"

Raleigh rolled his eyes as Buddy unlocked the padlock and opened the bedroom door.

It was a television set that Buddy had bought for ten dollars from someone he knew who was about to go into delirium tremens, whatever that was, if he didn't get a drink in the next thirty seconds. So that was fun. The two of them would sit there, watching cartoons. Popeye, and his girlfriend, Olive Oyl. Wimpy and his hamburgers made Buddy so hungry that he jumped up right then and ran down to the market for some meat and buns. They were absolutely great the way he fried them, and then toasted the buns in the oven, slathered them with mayonnaise and added tomatoes and lettuce right from the garden. They'd wolfed them down while the two of them giggled over Daffy Duck and Porky Pig and a lot of other funny characters Raleigh had never seen before. He had to admit it. Living with Buddy was very educational.

Raleigh awoke with a start around three in the morning at the sound of Frisky barking. Buddy had unlocked the padlock on the bedroom door and had gone into the bathroom adjoining it. He was leaning over the toilet, Raleigh saw, retching his guts out.

"Buddy, are you all right?" Raleigh asked anxiously, trotting to his side, trying to shush Frisky at the same time. "Can I get you something?"

"I went with a man tonight," Buddy said with a groan, turning bleary eyes toward Raleigh. "They come sometimes for the cute ones. I couldn't help it, son. I went. For the company. To hear somebody say something nice to me, you know what I mean?"

"Sure, Buddy," said Raleigh, wondering what he was talking about. "How about a glass of milk? Shall I get it for you?"

"Do you hate your dad for doing something like that?" Buddy asked in that pathetic voice that always made Raleigh feel sorry for him.

"Buddy—" he began.

"I'm not really that way, though," Buddy said. "I tell them that, but they don't care. Some of them even like it better. Your mom, well, she was the love of my life, son. And you're here to testify to that. Then in Korea, well, there were some girls there, too. But since I got back I just haven't been able to do anything about it. About finding someone, I mean. What's important is to get well, son. To make you proud of me. But when somebody comes along with a kind word, with a nice car, with some money in his pocket, well, I just can't help myself, son."

"You should go to sleep," Raleigh said. "Here, I'll help you."

"He told me I look just like Troy Donahue," murmured Buddy. "Do you know what Troy Donahue looks like?"

"Sure." Raleigh nodded.

"Do I look like him, do you think?"

"Not Troy Donahue," said Raleigh, trying to decide. "More like Tab Hunter."

"Tab Hunter," said Buddy. "Well, that's good, isn't it? Tab Hunter, he's a good-looking guy, too."

He pulled himself up with a groan, his hand on Raleigh's shoulder as he gingerly let himself be led to the living room. Raleigh watched as Buddy sank to his knees and rolled onto his sleeping bag. Raleigh sat on the sagging sofa, his heart beating faster, Frisky next to him, until he heard Buddy start to snore. Cautiously, he tiptoed over to the front door. Turned the knob. It was locked from the inside.

All he could do was shake his head in disappointment as he gazed at Buddy's sleeping form.

CHAPTER 34

$\mathcal{A}$s soon as he got a chance, the bedsheets were going to have to be what he would use to get out of here, Raleigh decided. They were so worn and threadbare that he was only going to need to get them started with the scissors Buddy kept in one of the kitchen drawers. Then he would be able to tear them into strands long enough so that he could swing to the fire escape.

He was getting his strength up, too, doing a hundred push-ups twice a day while Frisky rushed around and barked and had the best time. Frisky would have to ride in a pillowcase tied around Raleigh's neck.

"The first step in problem solving is to determine what the problem is," Paul was always saying. "Once you're reasonably sure of that, you can evolve a strategy to solve it."

What he was doing now was making Buddy think that he accepted the situation. He didn't ask Buddy to take him along to the market anymore. He didn't ask Buddy when he was going to let him go. Oh, he felt bad about it. He really did, because Buddy loved him, and Buddy was a sweet man. What Raleigh told himself was that making Buddy think something that wasn't true was just like playing a role in a movie or a commercial. You did it because you had to, because that was what people were depending on you to do. And he knew what he had to do the day after Buddy had bought the television set, when he'd flipped it on just before Buddy was going to padlock him in the bedroom and go out for the evening.

There was a newscaster looking very worried and solemn, and he was introducing two people to the audience, and it was Mommy and Paul.

Raleigh was so happy to see the two of them that he felt as if he were going to burst with joy. He stood there, fascinated, listening to them make an appeal to the kidnappers who were holding their son, half hearing Buddy, who was humming to himself in the bathroom while he shaved.

"Please let our little boy go," whispered Mommy, while the tears streamed down her cheeks.

"We promise you'll be treated fairly," Paul said in a funny, choked voice. "The FBI, the local authorities, everybody is standing by. Please call. Please."

Raleigh looked from Mommy to Paul, and back again. Mommy looked so miserable he could hardly bear it, and Paul was so angry with her that Raleigh could almost feel his rage quivering through the television set.

"Look at her," Buddy was saying reverently from behind him. "She's so beautiful, isn't she? She has the whole world at her feet."

"Listen, Buddy—" Raleigh began.

"And all I have is you, son," Buddy said, tears glistening in his eyes. "That's only fair, isn't it?"

He really was a nut case, Raleigh thought, staring at him. A real looney.

Before he padlocked Raleigh in the bedroom, Buddy got a meat cleaver from the kitchen and hacked the plug off the cord to the television set. And he started to babble about moving soon. To another state. Utah, maybe. They'd blend right in. Or maybe Alaska would be better, because it was so far away they probably had never heard of Raleigh Barnes.

Once he had the sheets tied together as tight as he could, Raleigh decided he would soak the knots and pull them tight.

The problem was that he was going to have to jump really hard to the right when he went out the window to generate the momentum to swing far enough to the left to catch hold of the fire escape. The sheets were so worn that there was a possibility they would disintegrate. He'd kill himself if he fell four stories onto that asphalt, and he'd kill Frisky, too. Worse, he thought unhappily, he wouldn't kill himself. "Measure the risk you're taking against your possible gain. Keep in mind the percentages," his father had told him.

In the next room he heard the door slam, Buddy's footsteps. This can't be, Raleigh thought. He's only been gone ten or fifteen minutes. That's never happened before. He's always out for hours, until after the bars close.

But that was before he saw Mommy and Paul on television, making their appeal, Raleigh decided, sinking onto the bed, absentmindedly petting the little dog. Maybe it had taken Buddy these ten or fifteen minutes to realize what he'd done. That he'd kidnapped Raleigh Barnes, and that there were probably stories about it on every television station in the world, in every newspaper, and that it was only a matter of time before his whole fantasy of the two of them living happily ever after shattered into a million bits.

"Aren't you going to the hospital, Buddy?" he asked the next morning, as Buddy sat at the kitchen table, staring moodily into space. "You've got to be there in a few minutes, you know. You're going to be late again, and you know how mad they get at you."

"It's okay, son," Buddy said. "Don't worry about it."

"But it isn't okay," Raleigh said. "You told me so."

"I called them when I was out at the market," Buddy said. "I told them that I had to go home for a few days. I told them I had a family emergency, okay?"

"Why'd you do that, Buddy?" he asked, feeling really scared for the first time.

"I've got to think, son," Buddy said, shaking his head. "I've got to think, okay?"

○ ○ ○

Something had to break, Raleigh decided after a couple of days. Buddy never left the house for more than a few minutes now, and Raleigh could tell from the different name on the brown paper bags that he wasn't even going to the same supermarket anymore. He said he'd told the vets he drank with that he was going home, too, so he was covered everywhere he was known. Maybe he'd dropped a hint somewhere, though, Raleigh thought, his mind churning. Maybe whoever had sold him the kids' clothes at the secondhand store, say. Maybe somebody, somewhere, would feel there was something wrong and come to check. In the meantime, Buddy just paced around the tiny apartment, his thoughts far away, while Raleigh anxiously watched him. Waited for a knock on the door. The FBI, or the police. Even the landlord. Anybody.

"You keep the home fires burning, son," said Buddy one evening. "I'll be back in a couple of minutes, okay?"

Raleigh sat there, in the bedroom, counting the seconds, then the minutes. Maybe Buddy just couldn't hold out anymore, and he'd decided to just pop into one of his favorite bars for a quick one. And he couldn't stop at one. Raleigh knew that. If he had one, he'd have to have six. Ten. He almost cried with disappointment when he heard Buddy's footsteps on the stairs, the key turning in the lock on the front door.

"I wasn't too long, was I, son?" Buddy asked brightly, when he unlocked the padlock, opened the bedroom door. "A couple of minutes was what I said, and that was exactly what it was."

"That's right, Buddy," said Raleigh, trying not to look at the paper bag he was carrying, and knowing at once that it was a bottle of booze, big enough to put Buddy out for the entire night. Except it didn't. Raleigh spent the night sitting on the floor, his ear pressed to the door. The only sounds he heard were Buddy's heartbreaking sobs.

By the third evening, though, Buddy was staggering and

bleary-eyed even before he went out to buy another bottle. Raleigh stood next to the door, listening, as Buddy cursed while trying to get the front door locked, groaned as he fell against the sofa. Raleigh hardly breathed during the silence that followed. And then, there it was. Finally. Buddy was snoring the way he always did when he'd been on a whooper-dooper binge, as he always called it afterward, looking ashamed and miserable. Raleigh had until morning, he estimated, judging from past experience with Buddy's drunks. But there were other factors this time. Maybe the light from under the bedroom door might wake him. Maybe the sound of the water running through the antiquated pipes. Maybe even the sound of Raleigh himself moving around.

He pulled the sheets off the narrow bed, frowning as he thought about the worst thing that could happen. Buddy could wake up and stop him. That was all. Still, he worked as silently and as quickly as he could, gritting his teeth as he tore the sheets into strands, panting with exhaustion as he trickled water from the faucet in the discolored bathroom sink over the knots he had made, and pulled them as tight as he could. Frisky knew something was going on, and he didn't like it one bit. He was cowering, shaking, and gazing at Raleigh with stricken eyes.

Raleigh's pulse quickened when he heard the chair he was moving scrape across the wooden floor. He stopped, listened. Heard nothing for a moment, and then Buddy, honking or something, then starting to snore again. Standing on the chair in the closet, Raleigh looped one end of the sheet across the rod, tied it as tight as he could. He was huffing and puffing as he moved the chair away. He sprang up, grabbed the sheet. He dangled there, jerking on it. It was holding. That was good, he thought, pleased. The little dog gave an agonized squeak and was quiet.

One more thing, Raleigh remembered, grabbing the pencil and the pad on which he'd been practicing his handwriting. *Good-bye*, he wrote slowly. *Love, Raleigh B*.

This part is going to have to be fast, he told himself as he reached for Frisky, who darted frantically away. Raleigh crouched on the floor, held out his hand, wiggled his fingers temptingly until Frisky took a step toward him, then another. In a single motion, Raleigh picked him up, stuffed him into the pillowcase, wrapped a length of sheet around it, around himself, as the little dog wriggled and clawed at him, yipped as if he were dying of fright.

Raleigh grabbed the end of the sheet and flung himself out of the window at an acute right angle, as close to the side of the building as he could manage. For a second, he felt as if he were suspended in space. Then he was flying through the arc he had calculated, straining with his fingertips for the fire escape, able to touch it firmly enough to push himself off again, to describe with his body a broader arc. He was swinging nearer, nearer, close enough now so that when he jumped he could grab the railing and pull himself onto the platform.

He lay there, his arms wrapped around the pillowcase, feeling the little dog quivering inside. His lungs were straining for air, his eyes were closed. There wasn't a sound in the pitch-black night. Raleigh sprinted down the fire escape, jumped, rolling himself into a ball around his burden as he felt himself land on his side. Gingerly he pulled himself to his feet, shook out his arms, his legs. He untied the pillowcase, looped the twine around Frisky's neck. For a second, he stood there, looking up four floors at the rectangle of light streaming through the window. Then he turned and trotted briskly across the empty lot, his heels clicking against the asphalt, the little dog trotting after him.

At first Raleigh stayed out of sight because he didn't want to be found where he could be traced back to Buddy's apartment. Then, when he started to hope that somebody would notice him, nobody did. There wasn't anybody walking on the sidewalk. And the cars streaking past never seemed to pick him up in their headlights. He had just passed the WELCOME TO BEVERLY HILLS sign when he heard a car slow next to him, found himself caught in a searchlight, and felt limp with relief when he realized it must be the police.

"Aren't you out a little bit late, young fellow?" asked the policeman who was standing over him.

"I'm Raleigh Barnes," he said, putting out his hand.

Then he and Frisky were in the backseat, and the other policeman was talking into the two-way radio in a high, excited voice. With a squeal of tires, they were off in a blare of sirens and flashing lights. It seemed to Raleigh that it was only a minute or two before they were pulling up in front of the Beverly Hills Police Department. There were all sorts of uniformed policemen, policewomen, and men in plain suits streaming down the stairs to meet them. It was pretty exciting, he thought, his eyes wide, as he and Frisky were hurried into the station, their feet barely touching the ground. Everybody was asking if he was all right, and he kept smiling and saying he was fine. It was like a party with everybody happy, and relieved, and thrilled to see him.

He looked around the station at all the people, the desks and typewriters, the file cabinets. And some of the people were on the phones, talking into the receivers, and what they were all saying was, "We've found him. Yes, he seems to be just fine. He was just walking down Sunset Boulevard with a Yorkshire terrier puppy on a leash."

Raleigh must have met a million people—FBI men, policemen, even the Beverly Hills police chief, who was still buttoning his shirt when he dashed into the room, his tie hanging loose down his shirt. And everybody was asking Raleigh if he was hungry or thirsty. Somebody brought a bowl of water for Frisky, so that was good because he and Frisky had really walked a long, long way, and Raleigh was sure that Frisky was as tired as he was.

A very nice man in a suit who said he was a child psychologist with the police department smiled at him and said why didn't they go somewhere for a few minutes where they could have a little chat, and he asked Raleigh if that would be all right with him.

"Actually, I'd like to go home now," Raleigh said.

"Why don't we just talk for a few minutes?" the man suggested. "Then you can go home."

"Well, all right," Raleigh said doubtfully. "But it can only be for a few minutes."

And the man was saying that was fine, and policemen of

all sizes and shapes were crowding in the room with hamburgers and hot dogs, chocolate malts, ham and cheese sandwiches, big glasses of milk, a piece of apple pie that made Raleigh's mouth water, and even a hot fudge sundae. He was really hungry, he realized as he tasted the first delicious bite of the pie. At the doorway, the child psychologist man was arguing with the police chief, telling him no, no, it would be better if he talked to the child alone, and he was waving away a lady with a steno pad, too.

The man told Raleigh he could sit behind the big desk, and the man sat in the chair across from him, while Frisky bounced around for a couple of seconds and then settled down.

"That's a cute pup you have there, Raleigh," the man began. "Active little fellow, isn't he?"

"He sure is," Raleigh agreed, trying to talk through the apple pie. "His name is Frisky."

"That's a very nice name," the man said, smiling. "Where did you get him?"

"Oh, a friend of mine gave him to me," Raleigh said eagerly.

"That's a wonderful present," the man said. "What's your friend's name?"

"Just someone," Raleigh mumbled.

"Well, everybody is certainly happy you're back," the man said. "Do you know how long you've been gone?"

"Not really," Raleigh said. "I did at first, but then I lost track of time."

"Fourteen days," the man said, and Raleigh could see by the expression on his face that he was really, really happy that Raleigh was back. "You're a lucky young man, and a brave one, too."

"I had a pretty good time," Raleigh said shyly. "We watched cartoons and played games and things. That was fun, kind of."

"That sounds like fun," the man said. "Now, Raleigh, who were you with, son?"

"I can't tell you that," Raleigh said. "I don't want him to get into trouble. He's a very nice person, but he drinks a lot, and sometimes he comes up with things . . . well, I just don't want to get him into any trouble."

"We'll see that he doesn't get into any trouble," the man assured him. "Just tell me who he is. You see, we have to tie up all the loose ends when something like this happens, and we can't do that without talking to him. But he'll be all right. I promise you."

"I don't believe you," Raleigh said, smiling across the desk at him.

"All right." The man sighed. "Now, when the police officers spotted you, Raleigh, you were walking along Sunset Boulevard just inside the Beverly Hills city limits. "How did you get there? Did he drop you off from a car?"

"No, I just walked there," Raleigh said.

"You mean you escaped?" the man said.

"Sort of," Raleigh admitted.

"That's wonderful," the man enthused. "You were being held captive, and you actually escaped all by yourself. That's very brave. I want to hear all about it, Raleigh."

"I just left," Raleigh muttered.

"You mean he told you you could go? Or he wasn't there, and the door was unlocked?"

"Sir, you said a few minutes," Raleigh murmured. "It's more than a few minutes."

"Well, you understand that we have to find out as much as we can," the man said in a wheedling tone. "We need your help, son."

Raleigh sighed.

"Now, let's go back to the beginning, in the parking lot of the market in Brentwood," he continued, glancing down at his notes. "A woman noticed you talking to a tall, blond man, and then you were gone. Did he use force in any way to get you into a car?"

Raleigh shook his head.

"During the time he held you, did he touch you in any way?"

"No."

That was the way to do it, Raleigh realized as the questions kept coming. No, no. I don't remember. I can't tell you that. I don't know where I was. No, no. I don't remember. There was the sound of voices outside the door, a light tap.

"They're clamoring for him," a man said, poking his head in. "They've got their deadlines."

"Okay," the child psychologist man said as Raleigh glanced up at the big, round clock over his head. The hands had moved some more, so he'd been here, what? Almost twelve minutes, he thought indignantly.

A couple of policemen hustled Raleigh down the hallway, slipped Frisky's lead into his hand with Frisky on the other end of it, pushed open a door, and ushered Raleigh through it. He squinted, blinded momentarily by the hundreds of flashbulbs, heard the applause, the cheers, his name being called. A thousand questions being shouted as the television cameras turned.

"Here he is, boys," the man who was holding his other hand announced. Raleigh tried to remember which one it was. The FBI man, he saw. "The bravest boy in the world, Raleigh Barnes. Now, we're going to start with the wire services. Everybody agree?"

There were murmurs of assent, the first question from a man in a blue jacket, gray pants.

"How do you feel, Raleigh?" he asked, his pen poised over his notebook.

Raleigh stood there, looking at him, at all of them, a mass of humanity crowded against each other, straining to see him, to reassure themselves that he was really standing there.

"I want my mommy," he whispered, the tears trickling down his cheeks. "I want to go home."

Behind him, there were frantic whispers.

"Did anybody remember to call his parents?"

"I thought you were going to do it."

"Oh, shit."

Raleigh winced as another round of flashbulbs popped away and the television cameras rolled on.

CHAPTER 35

$\mathcal{B}$eth Carol trailed along with the public relations
girl Paul had hired while Raleigh sauntered ahead on the
gently rolling, manicured lawn, holding hands with the
reporter from *Life* magazine. The photographer, three
cameras dangling on his chest, was pointing off toward a
stand of eucalyptus trees near the lake. It was the most
beautiful day, Beth Carol saw. The sky was a bright blue,
and there were a few little puffy clouds. But then, every
day was a beautiful day now that Raleigh was back home.
She felt her eyes fill with tears as Raleigh stooped over and
wrapped his arms around his puppy, who was dancing at
his feet.

   Where had he been during those ghastly two weeks, and
why wouldn't he talk about it? Beth Carol wondered again.
How she had beseeched him, cried, pleaded with him to
tell her. Nothing. Paul had talked to him about it for hours.
Then it was Darby's turn, who pointed out to Raleigh that
with the kidnapper at large other children were at risk. As
for the FBI, the detectives from the Beverly Hills Police
Department, well, they had just about thrown up their
hands. Even the child psychologist couldn't get him to say a
word about it.

   "Tattling isn't nice," Raleigh said firmly.

"This is different," the child psychologist said.

"No, it isn't," Raleigh said.

Oh, those awful, awful weeks, she thought with a shudder. She'd spent them sobbing hysterically, blaming herself for everything. Going back over every minute, every second from the time he had disappeared. She had been standing at the front of the store, chatting with Brad, her eyes never leaving Raleigh, though, as he sat there signing autographs. She had literally never taken her eyes off him, and yet he had vanished into thin air. The guy from the client had been talking with some of the store executives. When he was finished, he had come up to the two of them, mentioned how well everybody thought it had gone. Asked where Raleigh was, so they could leave. They had all nodded understandingly when he had added that perhaps he would still have time to get in nine holes on the golf course.

Beth Carol had gotten more and more hysterical as they searched the aisles of the store, the storerooms, the offices. Checked the parking lot, every car in it, just in case Raleigh had crawled into some backseat to take a nap. But, of course, Raleigh would never do any such thing, and Beth Carol knew that it was a waste of time to even check.

Then the phone call to the police, all the black and white cars, sirens screaming when they converged on the store. The anxious looks of the shoppers, their excited buzz while they wondered what terrible thing could have happened, and then their looks of dismay, terror, as they somehow realized a child was missing.

Beth Carol sat in a chair in the manager's office, her face buried in her hands, gulping for breath, tasting the salt of her tears as the detective tried to question her, with Brad on the phone, trying to track down Paul in his meeting with the money people in some office on Sunset Boulevard. Vaguely she heard the siren of a police car start to wail as it was dispatched to the estate to pick up something Raleigh had been wearing so the dogs could get his scent.

The house-to-house search, the questions asked of everybody, kids bicycling by, elderly ladies watering their front lawns, all the people coming into the market or going out. And only that one lady remembered seeing a little blond boy with a tall blond man. But there wasn't anything specific enough to say that it was even Raleigh. It could have been any little boy, shopping with his dad. It was amazing, Beth Carol thought wildly. Really amazing. Raleigh surrounded by his handlers, executives, assistants, Raleigh jumping off a building, performing gymnastics, and they were all ooohing and aaahing, every one of them in love with him. But take away the entourage, the performance, and he was just another cute little kid.

And then Paul was there, holding her, telling her not to blame herself, not to feel guilty. For appearances, because Beth Carol knew he was ready to kill her because she had been given the responsibility, just this once, to look after Raleigh and she had lost him.

The next few hours were a haze of alcohol and pills and hysteria, and it seemed to Beth Carol as if a doctor was there, giving her a shot so she could sleep. The magnitude of the awful thing that had happened didn't even begin to sink in until the newspapers with their funereal black headlines started to come in, until she turned on the television set and saw the market parking lot over and over again, shots of the police as they questioned people, the news conferences with the head of the Los Angeles office of the Federal Bureau of Investigation, the detectives from the Los Angeles Police Department. They were encouraged by the cooperation of the public, they said. Switchboards in all precincts were jammed with calls, reporting that Raleigh had been sighted. In Torrance, Long Beach. San Diego. As far away as Las Vegas. Portland, Oregon.

The next few hours were crucial, they said. They were expecting a ransom note. They appealed to the kidnapper to turn himself in. Clips of Raleigh from his movies were played over and over, as if he were already dead. Fern came to sit with Beth Carol and hold her hand while she cried and moaned. Paul, of course, couldn't even face her, couldn't look at her as he started to formulate a plan for the management of the crisis, tried to handle the calls that were coming in from all over the world. Beth Carol wouldn't even talk to that awful Brad from the advertising agency when he called to say how sorry he was about what had happened, to ask if there was anything he could do. What a hypocrite, she thought, furious with him. If he hadn't been flirting with her, distracting her, she would have been able to keep her eye on Raleigh and none of this ever would have happened. What a nerve he had to think even for a second that she would talk to him.

"I'll kill you if Raleigh isn't returned unharmed," Darby told her.

"You won't have to bother," she murmured, sobbing. "I'll kill myself, Darby."

But there was so much to do, with the investigators from everywhere swarming through the house, questioning her incessantly, the calls from the press, the television crews and reporters, the gawkers, the sightseers in their tour buses all ringing the property, that Beth Carol hardly had time to think about Raleigh, about the kidnapping. It was almost as if the story of the kidnapping was more important than the kidnapping itself.

And the calls of sympathy that came in from all over the world. It was incredible. One of the first ones was from the secretary to Mrs. Eisenhower, setting up a time that Mrs. Eisenhower could call Beth Carol to express her sympathy and her hopes for Raleigh's safety, as one mother to another. And that was when Paul had hired Maggie Edwards to handle the public relations aspect of the kidnapping because just that one phone call from the First Lady took all kinds of coordination with the press—who would get to be there while Beth Carol took the call, and who should be in the picture with her, things like that.

"We shouldn't have a girl, Paul," Beth Carol said. "We should have a guy, shouldn't we? I mean, nobody takes a girl seriously."

"She's the best in the business," Paul snapped.

And Beth Carol had to admit that once Maggie was in the picture things did seem to calm down. Maggie was very businesslike, of course. A real career girl in her tailored suit, her neat, honey-blond hairdo, her glasses with the flesh-colored frames. She was even married, to a reporter at one of the television stations. So Beth Carol figured that was why she was so respected in her field. Because she could get her husband to do stories on things her clients wanted publicized.

Mrs. Nixon called, too, and she told Beth Carol that all she could think when she heard the terrible news was that it might have been one of her two little girls, and that her heart went out to her. Beth Carol was really surprised, though, when Maggie popped her head in one afternoon and said that Queen Elizabeth was going to call as one mother of young children to another, and Beth Carol was going to have to pull herself together. The idea had started in the public relations office at Buckingham Palace, which had suggested it to the British ambassador in Washington, D.C. He had discussed it with the State Department. State had to clear it with the public relations people at the White House. When they said it was all right, arrangements had to be made with the British consul general here in Los Angeles. The British consul general, his wife, and a couple of members of his staff would be at the mansion when the call came in. And selected members of the press, of course, from England, Australia, and Canada, as well as some of the local and national newspapers, magazines, and television stations.

"I won't know what to say," Beth Carol whispered.

"Just say, thank you," Maggie said.

Her father called, too, and her sisters, asking to speak to her for the first time. Oh, Beth Carol wanted to talk to him, to all of them. She really did. But she knew it would just upset her even more than she already was. Paul took the call instead.

Then there was Paul, rushing down to the clipping service

every morning to pick up whatever had come in from all over the world, not even waiting for them to mail the clippings the way they did when things were normal. Paul would spend hours every day pasting the clippings into those big, leather scrapbooks he kept, shaking his head as if he couldn't believe all the coverage, and muttering that Raleigh was the most famous child in the world, even more famous than Prince Charles. It was the break they had been waiting for, he said, assuming that Raleigh was alive, of course.

Honestly, Paul was so buzzed by the whole affair, Beth Carol decided, that if she personally hadn't been there, right on the spot where Raleigh had disappeared, and if she hadn't known for a fact that it was her own fault that it had happened, she would have bet any amount of money that Paul had arranged to have Raleigh kidnapped for all the publicity it would get so he could improve his equity position in the production company with the investors. It was just the sort of thing Paul would do.

The coverage was absolutely spectacular. *Time* and *Newsweek* both had stories, each of them using the same color still from one of Raleigh's movies on the cover, with lots and lots of black and white pictures inside. The English magazines all ran cover stories, too, and *L'Epress* from France, and *Stern* from Germany, and from everywhere else in the world, too. And there were front page stories in all the newspapers, even from places Beth Carol had never heard of, in languages she didn't even recognize. And there were so many requests for interviews with her, with Paul, with anybody, that Maggie was working ten, twelve hours a day just processing them.

So Beth Carol didn't have time to think about killing herself that first week because she'd let Raleigh be kidnapped. She didn't even have time to think about Raleigh.

Everybody was really getting worried when a week had passed and there hadn't been any communication about how much ransom money would get Raleigh back. Beth Carol could see the strain on the faces of the guys from the

FBI, the cops, when they were interviewed on television. It was a bad sign, they would say cautiously, and Beth Carol felt her heart sink because if Raleigh hadn't been taken for money, there was only one other reason. And that was so horrible that she couldn't even say it to herself.

After that, the hullabaloo about Raleigh seemed to die down. Oh, there were still reporters asking for information, all right, but it was almost as if they didn't want to hear what the FBI guy or the cop had to say. And instead of leading the news every hour on the hour, the item would be buried somewhere in the middle of the program. It was as if everybody was thinking the same thing. That there was no hope. The phones stopped ringing in the mansion and Maggie moved back to her own offices, only calling in a couple of times a day.

That was when Beth Carol started to realize the enormity of it all, that Raleigh had been kidnapped. Even with all the pills she was taking, the drinks, to blot everything out, she would lay awake night after night, staring up at the ceiling. And she knew she looked as bad as she felt, too. Not that it mattered. Nothing mattered.

She was still awake toward dawn that morning when Raleigh had been gone for two weeks. She was tossing and turning, too exhausted to cry anymore, as the first rays of light colored the room gray, then a pale pink. Her heart nearly stopped when she heard the faint ring of Paul's phone in his room down the hall. Bolting out of bed, she flew down the hall, fumbled with the doorknob, threw open the door. Paul was sitting on the side of his bed wearing his striped pajamas. He was just hanging up the phone, and his face was white with shock.

"That was the Beverly Hills Police Department," he had said. "They've got Raleigh. He's fine."

CHAPTER 36

*R*aleigh was sitting in the child-sized, red, two-seater Thunderbird convertible that was just like the real one that Egyptian prince Bobby had gone with for a while had given to Bobby. The child-sized version had been presented to Raleigh by the regional manager of the Ford Motor Company a couple of weeks ago, just after he'd gotten back. When Beth Carol was looking through Paul's scrapbooks, she had seen a picture of the presentation on the front page of the *Detroit Free Press*. Raleigh loved the little car. It had a two-horsepower engine, and he got a real kick when he chugged around the estate in it.

"Smile, Raleigh," the *Life* photographer called.

Beth Carol's heart swelled with love as she saw Raleigh's smile, heard his gurgling laugh. Oh, it was such a miracle that he was back. She still couldn't believe it, couldn't stop touching him, gazing at him. What she'd decided was that she'd never let him out of her sight again, no matter what. Of course, even she had to admit that wasn't really practical with all of Raleigh's obligations. And he didn't really need her now, not with the security guard service Paul had hired, the bodyguard/chauffeur Paul had hired to drive the new limousine after he'd gone to court to get the expenditure approved. Raleigh's expenses were a fortune. They really were. But thank heaven for Paul, for the astute way he managed all the money. That was one thing Raleigh could count on. He was set for life.

Still, what if there was some slip in this four-picture deal that Paul still hadn't signed, Beth Carol worried. Furthermore, she didn't know if she agreed with the public relations plan he, Darby, and Maggie Edwards had decided to follow. There had just been that one press conference on the grounds at the mansion right after Raleigh had gotten home. Now there wouldn't be anything until this *Life* cover story appeared in two weeks, and, the same night, the television special in which Sir George Dean would be interviewing Raleigh for the first time about the kidnapping, and everything. Just the two of them, for an hour.

"If he hasn't said anything until now," she said to Paul, "why would he say anything to Sir George Dean?"

"Maybe he won't," Paul agreed.

"Well, won't that be boring?" she asked. "I mean, he's only five years old."

"It'll be okay," Paul said. "He'll do some stunts. There will be the film clips. Sir George Dean will talk about the new movies, the new company. Raleigh Barnes Productions."

"I hope you're right," she said. "You know, when I've heard him talk about Raleigh on his show, I've gotten the funniest feeling. As if what he's really going to announce that night is that Raleigh is going to quit making movies."

"That'll be the day," Paul sneered.

"Well, I don't know," she said, shaking her head.

"Look, baby," he snapped. "Every television set in America will be tuned in. This show will get the highest rating in history, and Sir George Dean knows it as well as the network. Everybody wants to see that Raleigh's okay. He could just sit there and suck his thumb, and it would still be fine."

And he was probably right, she decided, catching a glimpse in the distance of a couple of security guards walking together around the lake. After all, if she still couldn't believe it, maybe nobody could. She thought about how shaky Brad's voice had been, how relieved he had been to hear from her when she had finally called him back at the advertising agency after Raleigh was safely home.

"He was never out of my mind," Brad said. "I kept thinking about him and what we could have done. Beth Carol, I've got to tell you. When that news bulletin came over the radio when I was driving to work, I actually cried. So help me. I had to get off the freeway."

"Yes, it's wonderful," she said, and she could just see him there, sobbing, his head on the steering wheel. He was really sweet, so compassionate. And so attractive, too. "It's a miracle," she added solemnly.

"Well, all's well that ends well," he said, his voice still trembling a little. "We should get together and celebrate. What do you think?"

"Well, I'm having my hair done this afternoon," she said doubtfully.

"Where will you be?" he asked.

"At Secrets. On Sunset, right near Doheny."

"Well, how about Scandia?" he asked. "We'll break out the champagne and toast the kid. I'll tell you, there was hell to pay around here. I've never seen anything like it."

"Well, I don't know," Beth Carol said.

"Five o'clock okay?" he asked.

"Six would be better," she said. "A lot of the time Bobby runs late."

Brad was already there, jumping up from his stool at the crowded bar and coming to meet her just as the doorman ushered her into the restaurant.

"Beth Carol," he said, admiration in his voice as he took both of her hands in his. "You look beautiful, just the way I remembered you."

"It's nice to see you again," she said stiffly, liking what he was wearing. The navy blazer, double-breasted with gold buttons, the gray trousers with their sharp crease, the paisley tie in shades of red and blue. Liking the way he looked, too. The fair hair, the clear blue eyes. The way his mouth curved as he smiled at her.

He led her to the table in the bar he had reserved, helped her into her chair, looked around for the waiter in his little red jacket, who nodded and hurried over to them with the ice bucket, the bottle of the best champagne. She held Brad's hand as he lit her cigarette, looked up into his eyes from under her lashes and saw him flush under his tan.

"Here's to Raleigh," he said, his glass ringing against her own.

"Here's to Raleigh," she echoed.

"And here's to us," he said, lowering his voice, looking into her eyes.

"I don't know if I can drink to that," she said shyly.

"Did you bring your diaphragm?" he asked.

Slowly she nodded her head.

That first time, they drove over Laurel Canyon with the rest of the commuter traffic in the gathering dusk. She sat in the car in the parking lot of the Sportsman's Lodge while he went into the office and checked them in. Once they were in the large, silent room, Beth Carol felt his fingers trembling as he touched her hair, her face, pulled her into his arms and kissed her mouth. He was already hard, she thought triumphantly as he took her hand, led her to the bed, and began to undress her.

"You're beautiful," he said reverently. "I've dreamed about this moment."

"So have I," Beth Carol whispered as she drew his head down so that she could meet his lips with her own. Oh, it had been so long, so very long, she thought to herself as she felt his mouth sucking on her nipples, his fingers groping between her legs. Oh, it was so wonderful to be appreciated again, to have a man touch her there while he panted with lust. Oh, that felt good, she thought dreamily, trying to remember the last time

Paul had gone down on her. It had been such a long time that she couldn't even recall the year.

She gasped when he thrust his thing into her, held him tightly with her arms and legs while he pushed deeper and deeper, murmuring into her ear how pretty she was, how feminine, how good she smelled, and, again, how he had dreamed about her like this, in his arms, with his cock deep inside her soaking cunt, her legs wound around his waist, her mouth open for his tongue.

She cried out when she came.

Later, they showered together and drank the martinis he had ordered from the bar in the restaurant downstairs. Then they made love again, slower this time.

"Christ," he said, looking at his watch. "It's after nine. I've got to get home."

The other time, he'd picked her up after she'd had her hair done and they'd driven all the way out to Malibu to the Holiday House, where they'd had drinks on the terrace overlooking the ocean before they'd gotten their room.

She thought about him all the time. About how he was going to be made a vice president the next year. About how he'd gone to Thatcher, and then USC, which had the best marketing curriculum of any university in the country, and how he didn't care what anybody said. She loved it that he told her all the time how he loved to be with her. That he could really talk to her because she really listened. That it was an art to be able to do that. She dreamed about him, too. In her dreams, they were together. She even loved his name. Bradley Noonis. Mrs. Bradley Noonis. Beth Carol Noonis. I think I'm falling in love, she realized.

"Okay, Raleigh," the photographer from *Life* was saying, "now I want you to jump in the air. As high as you can."

Raleigh jumped. Higher and higher. Frisky got all excited, and he jumped, too. A yellow butterfly floated by on the gentle breeze.

The photographer clicked off frame after frame,

crouching, changing his position, dashing here and there, changing cameras. Without even looking at the reporter, he reached out a hand and she dribbled new rolls of film into it. Beth Carol sighed. The two of them had already been here for more than a week, and the reporter hadn't even started to interview Raleigh, to interview her and Paul. All it was was pictures, pictures, pictures. Everywhere on the estate, in the mansion. At the beach where Raleigh and Frisky played in the waves as they trickled onto the sand. In a fencing outfit, gym clothes, every way imaginable.

"Is it always like this?" she asked Maggie.

"This is a rush job," Maggie said with a laugh. "Usually they're around for months."

At last the light in the western sky started to fade. The reporter bustled around, loading camera cases, backdrops, tripods, lights into the trunk of the rental car while the photographer stood chatting with Maggie, making arrangements for the next day.

"They'll be here at ten," Maggie said to Beth Carol. "Is that okay?"

"It's fine." Beth Carol waved to them, said good-bye to Maggie as she climbed into her car, waved as she started down the long, winding driveway.

There'll probably be a million calls, she thought wearily as she dragged herself into the mansion, dialed the number of the answering service, gave her name and code number to the cultured voice that came on the line on the first ring. Of course, there was only one call she cared about, she thought dreamily. Brad. Oh, he was so wonderful. She could see his face, his smile, as if he were there with her.

"Mr. Noonis called."

"Did he leave a message?" Beth Carol asked, her pulse quickening.

"Just that he's checking in, that he would be in meetings all day, and that he'll call you in the morning."

"That's all?" Beth Carol asked, smiling, knowing that Brad wouldn't be indiscreet, wouldn't say anything to a girl at the answering service, but hoping, anyway.

"Miss Darling called. It's some sort of an emergency. Let's see. One, two, three . . . six times. And Mr. Fournier. He has meetings all evening and he won't be home for dinner."

"Go on," Beth Carol said, her mood darkening. Out again. Like last night, and the night before. And a couple of other times this week. How many meetings could he possibly have, if that was really what he was doing? I. Magnin called saying the dress she was having altered was ready, and did she want to come in and try it on, or should they send it, and would she please let them know.

"One moment," the operator said as Beth Carol heard another phone ringing in the background.

"That's Miss Darling again," the operator said, coming back on the line. "She's very upset and has to talk to you. Shall I cross-connect?"

"Okay," Beth Carol said, and there was Fern's breathy little voice on the line. Incoherent. In tears.

"Fern, I can't understand you," said Beth Carol, feeling her body tense, the fine hairs on her arms stand on end. "What is it? What's happened?"

"You've got to come, man. Right now."

"What's happened, Fern? What's going on?"

"It's Sir George Dean," she said. "He's dead, man. Murdered."

Beth Carol stood there, trembling, listening to Fern's sobs on the other end of the line.

CHAPTER 37

*E*ven before she got up the nerve to ring the bell, Beth Carol thought she could feel a brooding evil emanating from Sir George Dean's house. The door was answered at once by one of the Oriental houseboys. His face was drawn, white with shock.

"Miss Fern in drawing room," he muttered hoarsely, gesturing down the hall.

Beth Carol's glance was tentative and frightened as she looked around. A console table with a splintered leg had been pushed against a wall. A Braque painting that Sir George Dean had adored was slashed in its frame. She closed her eyes tight, covered them with fluttering fingers, and took a couple of deep breaths before she was able to move on.

She gasped as she stood in the doorway of what had been one of the most charming drawing rooms she had ever seen. Balls of stuffing from the upholstered pieces of furniture lay scattered on the carpet. Chippendale chairs, their seats slashed, stood at odd angles. Paintings hung crazily on the walls. The words *fag* and *queer* were painted in red among them, and there were dark stains near the fireplace. Shards of glass and dead flowers everywhere. Fern sat huddled in a corner of what was left of the sofa in front of the French doors. She was drinking a martini and her face was pinched and unhappy under her tower of blond hair.

"Have a drink," she whispered, pouring with shaking hands from the pitcher sitting on the coffee table in front of her.

I'm going to faint, Beth Carol thought vaguely as she sank into a chair, took the martini, spilled some of it on her lap.

"I'd been out really late, you know?" Fern said in a complaining voice. "Like, I'd only just gotten to sleep and Charlie comes pounding on my door and saying that I had to come at once, that when he'd gone in to open up the house, start the coffee and stuff, that he'd come in here, and that Sir George Dean and the kid he'd had around for a week or so this time were just laying on the floor. That they weren't moving, and that they were all bloody.

"So I jumped up and I threw on a robe, you know? And I come running in through the French doors, and it's, like, a disaster, man. There's blood everywhere, and the tables are all knocked over, and the chairs. And the sofa's slashed, broken glasses. Bottles of booze. It's wanton vandalism," she added, looking desperately into Beth Carol's eyes. "There's no other word for it, man."

Beth Carol gulped the drink, poured herself another one.

"So I go over to where Sir George Dean is laying, and I'm really scared, man, and I don't want to do it because I've never seen anybody dead before, and I hate the idea. I just hate it." She closed her eyes and sighed as she lay her head on the back of the sofa. "Well, I thought I was going to pass out right on the spot, you know? I mean, the back of his head is all smashed in and the blood's soaked his coat, and the rug. And the kid's laying there next to him, deader than a doornail, too, and all covered with blood.

"I say to Charlie, 'Don't just stand there. Call the police,' and he just looks at me, and he's really scared. I can see it. So I say, 'Okay, I'll call them.'

"So I'm in shock, right? I start to look around, and there's all this debris, and everything is broken, a shambles. But stuff's been taken, too. All the silver is gone, and those little gold boxes, the filigree ones, remember them? And the assholes slashed the Braque and the Modigliani. Smart, huh? Those were worth more than everything else in the house put together."

"Oh, Fern," Beth Carol whispered. "How awful."

"So the police are coming, and I'm there in a pink peignoir and I'm barefoot, you know? So I run back to my place and I throw on a pair of capri pants and a blouse, and I put on some lipstick, and I'm back. And they were already knocking on the door, the homicide guys. They were real fast. It couldn't have been more than ten minutes. Really.

"And they're looking at the bodies, Sir George Dean, and the kid, and asking a lot of questions. Making all these notes, and these photographers are there, taking pictures of the bodies, and everything. These other guys are dusting for fingerprints, checking the locks on the French doors. The coroner's office shows up, too.

"Like, it's time for the secretary to get there, right?" Fern said, looking at Beth Carol now as if she knew that, of course. "So she does, and she walks in in the middle of all this, and she starts screaming and screaming.

"'Pull yourself together,' I say. 'Have a cup of coffee, man. We have to get out a press release.'" She glared at Beth Carol as if disappointed with her. "It's been on television and the radio all day," she said querulously. "I was really surprised that you didn't know about it when I finally got hold of you, man."

"I didn't have anything turned . . ." Beth Carol murmured apologetically.

"That's blood," Fern said. "Those words on the wall are written in blood."

"Oh, no," Beth Carol gasped.

"So I was feeling kind of funny, really upset, you know?" Fern said in a mechanical voice. "So I started to call you and I called and called, and I couldn't reach you. So you know what I did? I decided I would fix myself a drink, that if I had a drink I'd feel better. But you know what? I don't feel better. I really don't feel any better at all." She stopped, a puzzled expression on her face.

"You should have something to eat, Fern," said Beth Carol. "You probably haven't eaten all day, and that's not helping. Let me ask one of the boys to get you something. All right?"

"No, no," Fern said, shaking her head angrily. "I don't want to eat."

"Fern, you're in shock," Beth Carol said miserably. "You are."

"I didn't think it would be like this," Fern wailed. "I mean, I didn't think anything in the world could make me feel this bad. I thought I was tough, man, and here I am, falling apart this way."

And then she was crying, big tears running down her stricken, pale face, her whole body shaking with gulping sobs as Beth Carol held her and said, "There, there," wondering what she could do for Fern as she slowly realized that Sir George Dean was dead, and how terrible that was because he'd really loved Raleigh. Gotten Raleigh's career started, in fact, with those first little mentions that made the people who could give Raleigh work realize that he had powerful friends who could help them, too.

Somehow she half dragged, half carried Fern out through the French doors, getting her away from that ruined room, the soft scurrying of the houseboys that had been coming from the back of the house, while Fern gulped for air and babbled away about how they had taken all of Sir George Dean's jewelry, a lot of his beautiful clothes, too, and how there had been no indication of forcible entry.

Beth Carol was panting herself, the scent of orange blossoms perfuming the cool, tranquil evening making everything that much worse for some reason, as she lugged Fern through the door to the perfect little house where she lived among the pretty things Sir George Dean had assembled there, cared for by Sir George Dean's servants.

Well, she wouldn't be living there long, Beth Carol thought with a giddy surge of triumph that made her feel ashamed. Some of those cousins, their children, the aunts, uncles, maybe, would inherit all of this and Fern Darling would be out on the street, out on her own. Oh, she'd get another job, of course. Probably right away. Somebody else's leg girl, an embarrassment to be kept unseen in some back office for anybody except Sir George Dean, and everybody knew how perverse he was. Beth Carol could just see the shrugs, the winks when everybody in town had heard the news earlier in the day. The only surprise was that it hadn't happened sooner. That would be the consensus.

But still, she thought, the tears welling up in her eyes, he had been so nice to her and Paul. That beautiful wedding he had given them. All the things he had done for Raleigh. He had been so devastated when Raleigh was kidnapped that it was as if Raleigh were his own child. And now he wouldn't be in their lives anymore. And to be murdered. It was awful.

"He gave me my first real break," Fern was muttering as she sloshed gin into a pitcher at the tiny, elegant bar. "Like, he taught me the ropes, introduced me to everybody who was anybody, you know? Oh, I had complaints, man. Like he never gave me any credit for anything. And I was, like, doing everything except actually writing the crap and what was he doing? Playing around with his little boyfriends, that's what he was doing. So it wasn't all rosy, man. Not by a long shot."

Beth Carol poured herself a martini, watched as Fern wove her way over to the sofa, nearly fell as she plopped down.

"But this is too much," she muttered darkly. "Nobody has this coming. Nobody."

Beth Carol sat on one of the stools at the little bar, smoking a cigarette, sipping her martini, watching helplessly as Fern started to cry again. After a while, though, she just sort of faded into unconsciousness, slumped there, her head against a cluster of decorative pillows.

I'd better get her a blanket, Beth Carol decided, as she stumbled toward the bedroom, flipped on the light switch, and saw Fern's king-sized bed with its lilac, quilted spread, the matching headboard, the dainty pillows in eyelet, silk, embroidery, all in shades of whites and ivories, the highly polished antique bedside tables with their lamps fashioned from Oriental vases, their shades an off-white silk. There were good prints on the white walls, a couple of lithographs, signed. Only her desk was a clutter of papers and files.

She was amazing, Fern was, Beth Carol thought groggily, a blast of perfume surrounding her as she pulled open the closet door, saw Fern's gowns, her furs, all of the peignoirs with their ostrich feathers, vulgar stuff like that. And there, on the top shelf, a quilt. That would do, she thought, stumbling as she reached for it, shaking her head at Fern's reaction. To be so upset at what had happened, to be so . . . well, human. Like a real person with real feelings. That was the big surprise. Maybe she had been all wrong about Fern. Maybe all of that tough talk and callous behavior was just a front. Maybe there was still something left of the little girl she had cried with on the Greyhound bus, the one who had said how scared she was, and all.

Fern could even have had love in her heart for Sir George Dean in spite of the fact that he never gave her credit in his columns or on his television shows. Wouldn't give her credit once again on his big one, the hour special he was going to do with Raleigh Barnes. But he wouldn't be doing the show, she reminded herself, a sinking feeling in her stomach as it dawned on her. All the careful plans that Paul had laid. The *Life* cover, and then the television special. A double whammy, he called it. And now it wasn't going to happen. But they wouldn't just cancel it, she realized. They'd get someone else to do it. Jack Paar, maybe. Or Steve Allen. No, not Steve Allen. He was at another network. But they'd get somebody.

A sound from outside made her stop in her tracks, tense

with fear as she strained to hear what it was. Footsteps, light and surreptitious. They've come back, she thought, her mouth dry, her pulse racing. They'll kill us both.

She stood in the doorway to the bedroom, watching in horrified fascination as a key was inserted in the front door, the knob turned, and Fern snored on the couch, blissfully unaware of what was about to happen to the two of them, the grisly horror of what was about to be repeated here.

It took Beth Carol a few seconds to comprehend that it was Paul who was standing there, Paul who had opened the door to Fern's house with his very own key. He looked haggard and terrible, she saw, as if some hideous, unspeakable thing had happened to him, too.

"You bastard," she said.

"It's you!" he blurted, his eyes wide with surprise and dismay.

CHAPTER 38

*Y*es, yes, he admitted to her in the car as they were driving home. All these years. Yes, on their wedding night, too, just as she had thought. "But I'll be better," he vowed, his jaw set as he drove. "I'll never touch her again. I promise you that, Beth Carol. I love you. You know I do."

"How can you expect me to believe you?" she asked.

"I'll make you believe me," he said. "I know I've been a lousy husband to you. But I'll change, baby. It was just lust. A lark, at first. It's over now. The best thing that could have happened was that you were there. It brought me to my senses. It really did."

Beth Carol sighed and shook her head.

"Watch what I do," Paul said, trying for a cocky grin, not even coming close. "Not what I say."

He was savage that night as he made love to her, if that was the way to describe it. He was biting her lips, her ears, just on the verge of really hurting her as he sought her nipples, took her clitoris between his teeth as he prodded her sex with his fingers. She screamed when he drove into her with his thing. She just couldn't help it. And once he started in her, he was superhuman. He'd never been this way before, never wanted to fuck her hour after hour, or never been able to. She squirmed out from under him, lay panting, trying to catch her breath. He pulled her back to him, thrust into her again, hurting her because she was sore from him now. It was really thrilling in a way to have him fuck her this way.

"I love you," he said.

"I love you, darling," she said, winding her legs around him again.

The team from *Life* was already there when she came downstairs the next morning, her nipples sore, and her hips aching in that good kind of way from all of their lovemaking the night before. Through the window Beth Carol saw Raleigh sitting cross-legged on the grass, talking to the reporter near the swimming pool. Maggie was standing, gesticulating as she talked with the photographer. He was wearing jeans today, the usual three cameras dangling down the front of his shirt.

Usually Beth Carol would pour herself a cup of coffee and grab the paper, turning by rote right to the society pages to see who was doing what with whom, what balls they'd been to, what tailgate parties. All the things she loved to read about and longed to do herself. This morning, though, she started on page one, looking for the story she knew she'd find about the murder of Sir George Dean, and not really wanting to find it. Wanting the whole thing to have been a bad dream. Even Paul was shattered by the news. When he'd gotten up this morning, she'd mentioned it. He'd shaken his head and said he didn't want to hear about it. Please.

She found it on page three, two columns in the lower right-hand corner. The picture was a smiling head shot, cropped so it was apparent he was wearing a tuxedo. The headline read, PROMINENT TELEVISION PERSONALITY SLAIN. The subhead read, ROBBERY MOTIVE SUSPECTED.

Tears welled up in her eyes, blurring the words as she tried to read them, saw in the first sentence right after his name that he had been thirty-eight years old. That was a surprise. Somehow he had seemed ageless in his elegance, but if she'd had to bet on it, she would have said he was older.

. . . was found murdered this morning, along with a male companion in his Hollywood Hills residence by representatives of the Los Angeles Sheriff's Department, who had been called to the scene by his assistant, Miss Fern Darling, who resides in a guest house on the property. Questioning of Miss Darling revealed that many items of considerable value were missing from the premises.

Beth Carol had to stop reading for a moment because her hands were shaking so much, and her tears were a flood now, dotting the page. Her gaze wandered to the garden, to Raleigh. She heard his gurgling, mischievous laugh, saw the reporter throw back her head and laugh with him. Oh, how was she going to be able to tell her poor, innocent baby that Sir George Dean was dead? she wondered, wiping her eyes with the back of her hand. How could she be the bearer of news that she knew was going to make him so unhappy? Darby would have to tell him, or Paul could do it.

Golly, that had been wild with Paul last night, she remembered ecstatically, but frowning, too, because it had given her such a jolt to have her suspicions about him and Fern confirmed. Because she didn't believe Paul when he said it was over between them. Because she wouldn't believe Paul if he said it was sunny at twelve noon on the Fourth of July. So she'd just have to wait and watch, hope he meant it, she guessed, which would make it kind of awkward, what with her relationship with Brad. She hadn't felt the least bit guilty about it because of Paul and Fern, but now, well, she just didn't know. Still, she was very civil, very concerned, when the phone rang and it was Fern, thanking her for being there, and everything. Then Bobby called, very excited, wanting to dish the whole thing, so they gossiped about it for over an hour, and she told him every single thing she remembered, and somehow, when she hung up, she felt a little better about it.

Well, she was ready to read about it now. Quickly she finished what was on the third page, turned to the page where the story was continued toward the rear of section one. It went on for quite a while, and there were other pictures, too. Three of them. Sir George Dean laughing with Humphrey Bogart and Mike Romanoff. Sir George Dean at the opening of Disneyland with Lana Turner and Lex Barker, and there was Fern in the background. Beth Carol could just make out the top of her blond head, the curve of her cheek. Sir George Dean signing autographs himself for a crowd of fans in front of Ciro's. Quickly she scanned the details of the rest of his career, including a couple of lines about the upcoming television special with child star Raleigh Barnes in his first appearance since his safe return from being kidnapped. "A particularly violent, brutal crime," a highly placed official in the department was quoted as saying. "As there was no forced entry into the residence, investigators are proceeding on the assumption that the assailant or assailants may have been known to Sir George Dean or to his companion, Elroyd "Buddy" Hatcher, twenty-two. Mr. Hatcher, a recent acquaintance of Sir George Dean, according to sources, made his permanent residence at the Veteran's Administration Hospital in Brentwood. When asked to comment, sources at the hospital confirmed that Mr. Hatcher had been in psychiatric treatment at the facility since his return from service in Korea several years ago.

This can't be, Beth Carol thought, reading it again. It's just a coincidence, the same name. But how many people are named Elroyd "Buddy" Hatcher, who are twenty-two years old? she asked herself as she glanced again through the window at Raleigh, standing there, listening to something the photographer was explaining to him.

Automatically she picked up the ringing phone.

"Hello," she said.

"Hi, dream girl," Brad purred. "Guess who I've been thinking about night and day?"

"I'll have to talk to you later, Brad," she said. "I've just had a shock. A big, big shock."

She hung up the phone. Lit a cigarette. Read the article

carefully from the beginning to the end. Buddy and Sir George Dean, she thought, amazed. It just couldn't be, but it was.

So there was that, and Beth Carol knew she would never, never say a word about it to anybody as long as she lived.

Then later in the day, Fern called again and said that Sir George Dean's will was going to be read at his lawyer's office, and that Raleigh should be there, so would Beth Carol bring him. It was going to be the next day at four o'clock, she said, and she gave Beth Carol the address. The fifth floor of some office building on Wilshire, midway between Crenshaw Boulevard and Western Avenue. They could park in the underground garage.

Beth Carol was so curious about what Sir George Dean had left to Raleigh that she even forgot to be scared when they were in the elevator with Paul, who had come along, too. Fern was already there, wearing a low-cut dress that showed everything she had, and a black hat with a veil that covered her forehead. She wore black gloves and dabbed at her nose with a little lace hankerchief. Her nose was red, and her eyes looked as if she'd been crying. Beth Carol glanced at Paul, trying to read his face as he nodded to Fern, then took the chair the lawyer was offering him. His face was a blank. But with Paul, that didn't prove anything.

The Oriental houseboys were there, too, and so was Kato, the chauffeur. Everybody on the staff got a small bequest that seemed to have been determined by the number of years each of them had worked for Sir George Dean. Fern inherited the house in the Hollywood Hills and half of all of Sir George Dean's investments, which included stocks, municipal bonds, and two apartment buildings, one with eight units, the other with ten, in West Hollywood.

How could he have done such a thing? Beth Carol asked herself indignantly. Leaving his money and stuff away from his own family. Well, she just didn't believe in that. Not at all.

"I bequeath the remainder of my estate to Raleigh Barnes," the lawyer read as Beth Carol just sat there, gasping with shock.

Then he went on to explain that based on what the stocks had been worth that morning on the stock exchange, the current value of the bonds, and the prices being paid for similar real estate in the West Hollywood area, Raleigh's share was worth around $120,000. It was to be held in trust for him until he turned twenty-one. The lawyer himself was the executor of the trust fund.

Beth Carol looked over at Raleigh where he was sitting, wondering if he understood any of it. He didn't seem to be paying the slightest bit of attention. When Paul had told him as gently as he could that Sir George Dean had died unexpectedly, Raleigh had just gone into shock. He had cried as if his heart would break, and even coming here, Beth Carol had been dabbing away his tears as they trickled down his cheeks.

Now he was starting to cry again, she saw with dismay as she leaned over, patted his arm. Thought about the $120,000. The market she didn't know about, and this was the first time she had even heard of municipal bonds. But everybody said that real estate was a great investment, so those apartment buildings were bound to go up in value. That was great for Raleigh, really great. And so sweet of Sir George Dean. It really was.

CHAPTER 39

*T*he background was grass, trees, all lime green and glittery, bathed in sunlight. In the foreground of the cover photograph was Raleigh, caught in midair. He was wearing his white fencing outfit with the red heart on the chest. His arms were flung out, the sun kissed his blond hair and the expression on his face was ecstatic, so joyous that it was almost hard for Beth Carol to look at it, to be reminded how close she had come to losing him. Frisky was in midair, too. A yellow butterfly floated at the tip of the outstretched fingers on one of Raleigh's hands.

Anxiously she flipped through the copy of *Life*, almost burst with joy herself when she saw the color photograph of the three of them that had been picked out. She loved the way Bobby had done her hair with just that little bang over her forehead, the suggestion of a flip. She looked so pretty, and her smile said everything about how happy she was that Raleigh was safely home. The decision about the dress had been perfect. Pale peach with a scoop neck and pearls. The matching shoes. And Paul, the perfect, young father, smiling, for a change, in his black polo shirt, his chinos, the highly polished penny loafers. And Raleigh, sitting between them in his shorts and T-shirt and his brown and white saddle shoes, looking uncharacteristically serious, as if he had realized just that minute that he had escaped, that he was home.

And the other pictures were so cute, too. Raleigh playing with Frisky, the one in the little Thunderbird. Another of Raleigh in midair, somersaulting this time. Working with Darby on the rings. Frowning as he puzzled out the words in one of his Dr. Seuss books. And this one, when he was a baby. Crawling across a rug, the one he had done for the carpet cleaner way back when. And here was one from the first rehearsal for the television special, sitting on the sofa on the set with Fern, who was pretending to interview him.

"I don't believe it," she had said when Paul told her Fern would be replacing Sir George Dean as hostess of the television special. "They could have picked anybody, and they pick Fern? She's never even been on television, Paul. You're kidding, aren't you?"

"No, I'm not kidding."

"Well, why did they do it?" she asked.

"Because I said so," he told her. "Either it's Fern, or the deal is off. That's what I said."

She just sat there, staring at him blankly for a couple of seconds, and then she started to understand.

"You'd ruin Raleigh's program just to promote your girl-friend?" she asked, her voice trembling. "How could you do such a thing?"

"She's not my girlfriend," he said wearily. "I've told you a hundred times that I'm not seeing her anymore. And I don't do favors when it comes to business. Even you must have noticed that."

"You don't have to be sarcastic," she said indignantly. "All you have to do is tell me why you did it. I don't think that's too much to ask."

"Just drop it, will you?" he had said, stalking out of the room.

The network had gotten behind it as if it were the best idea in the world. She had to admit that. They were running promos showing Fern and Raleigh at nearly every station break, full-page ads in all the local newspapers, papers across the country. And there was something cute about the two of them together with Fern saying to him, "You know, Raleigh, I've never interviewed a five-year-old before," and Raleigh just grinning at her, with Frisky wiggling in his arms.

Still, it wasn't any fun to think that Paul was still seeing her, that he had gone this far to do something for her. It seemed to Beth Carol that it was practically all she ever thought about these days. That and Brad, of course.

Poor Brad. He could be so soppy and treacly that being with him was sort of like eating a whole pound of sugar. Oh, sure, she liked being told that she was pretty, and everything, but the way Brad went on, you'd think she was a cross between Venus de Milo and Helen of Troy on their best days. And the way he couldn't wait to get at her whenever they were together. After all, his wife was expecting another baby, so it wasn't as if he were starving to death sexually. But there he was, pawing at her all the time, putting his hand under her dress, under her panties, even his finger into her right when they were driving. As if they wouldn't be at the motel in a few minutes. There were other things about him she didn't like, come to think of it. The way he had of jumping out of bed after they were through and taking a shower, cleaning his teeth, as if he couldn't wait to rid himself of her scent. Couldn't wait to wash away the evidence of his adultery. Not even cuddling for a few minutes. And there was the time she'd seen him empty the ashtray from the car right onto the street because, God forbid, that his wife would see cigarette butts with lipstick on them. Beth Carol hadn't liked the way seeing that made her feel.

Also, she didn't think he was very smart. She didn't think he was going to be made a vice president next year. In fact, she thought he was more or less as far along in his career as he was going to get.

So it had been fun in the beginning. Exciting and dangerous, too, because at any moment somebody might see them, and there would be hell to pay. But now, well, she was getting kind of bored with the whole thing. And she certainly wasn't starving for sex now that Paul was making it with her almost every night, no matter how late he got home. And, face it, he was fantastic in bed and Brad was only a little better than adequate.

Her dilemma was that it didn't make any sense to cheat on her husband when she was getting everything she wanted from him, just to have an affair with somebody who was really boring, and who wasn't even that good in bed. As she kept telling herself, she would tell Brad she didn't want to see him anymore in a minute if only she knew for sure that Paul really wasn't seeing Fern.

What she would do, she decided, was ask Bobby when she went in to have her hair done. Things were going so well for Bobby, and Beth Carol was really happy he was back with Sandy now that the prince was out of his life.

"Great fun, but just one of those things," he had said when it had ended.

"But Bobby, he's a guy," she said.

"But he's royalty," Bobby protested. "How often does that happen to a person?"

So that, in essence, was Bobby's philosophy about relationships. Whatever came along, as long as it was amusing, and, most of all, at the right level.

"Well, I really don't know," he said after a couple of minutes of thinking about it. "I mean, I was never even officially told that Paul and Fern were seeing each other in the first place. I just happened to see them together. Now, where was it?" he murmured, frowning at his reflection in the mirror. "Oh, well. Somewhere."

"Well, is Fern seeing anyone?" she prodded.

"Look, Beth Carol, don't ask me," he said, and, well, that was no surprise. That he said that. Bobby wouldn't say anything about Fern because Beth Carol was almost certain he was still putting it to her himself when both of them happened to be in the mood.

The only one she would never ask was Fern herself, she realized later that afternoon as she sat in the control booth above the set at the television studio, while down below, the last rehearsal was about to begin. It would be pointless.

All those items of hers were always true. Stars had been suing Sir George Dean for years now over things she'd told him, and they always lost in a big way with their stories splashed all over the papers. But when it came to her real life, Fern was the biggest liar Beth Carol had ever met, right up there with Paul himself, and so many other people in this town. She shook her head, wondering how all of them could survive on a diet composed entirely of hope, dreams, and illusions.

The director who was sitting a couple of chairs away from her with headphones on was talking into his microphone to the assistant director down on the set. The camera guys were rolling all that heavy equipment into place. One of the set decorators was fluffing up the pillows on the sofa, another was straightening the posters from Raleigh's films that were framed on the wall. Raleigh was working a yo-yo with one of the lighting guys. In a director's chair off to the side, the makeup girl was hard at work on Fern, while Bobby sat beside her, smoking a cigarette and waiting to touch up her hair. She noticed Paul, way over at the edge of the set with Maggie and a bunch of publicity guys from the station, some reporters and photographers.

Finally they were ready. They all were taking their places, and the announcer was watching the opening commercial as it came up on the enormous screen, waiting to introduce Fern, while the assistant director checked his stopwatch and the director murmured orders into his microphone as if he were moving a small army around. Beth Carol had seen it so many times she barely paid attention to what they were doing down there. It was all so boring, all this rehearsing.

"We're on the money," the assistant director called at last as he flipped off his stopwatch. The director in the booth nodded and made an okay sign to him with his thumb and forefinger. And the interesting thing, Beth Carol decided, was that all during the rehearsal Paul had never looked at Fern. Not once.

He slipped into the chair next to Beth Carol just as the

ushers were opening the doors to let the audience pour in, the men in their suits and ties, some of the ladies in hats and gloves.

"I love you," she whispered, leaning toward him.

He looked startled, but then he smiled at her and patted her shoulder.

The buzz from the audience ended as the announcer came out to welcome them, to thank them for coming. They were silent, expectant, as the announcer introduced "Miss Fern Darling, our hostess for this evening." There was a lot of applause as she strutted onto the stage in those stupid shoes she was always wearing. Then, when the audience realized that the little boy she was leading by the hand was actually Raleigh Barnes, in the flesh, they broke into cheers. Raleigh looked so cute in his little jacket, the short pants, the socks that reached to just below his knee, the striped tie, his white shirt, that Beth Carol felt overwhelmed with love for him. The assistant director was putting up his hand, trying to get the audience to quiet down because it was going to throw the timing off, and finally they settled down.

Fern made her opening remarks about Sir George Dean and how he had been a friend to her, as well as a mentor. She was a little teary as she spoke of him, and so was Raleigh, despite the fact that she had said those very words in rehearsal about a thousand times. Then she introduced Raleigh and said how happy she was to have him sitting there beside her, safe at last, and the audience started to clap and cheer, stomp on the floor, and the assistant director was waving his hands at them with a panicked look on his face.

"I've never interviewed someone who's only five years old," said Fern, and the audience made appreciative noises as they recognized the line from the promos the network had been doing all this time.

"Well, now you are," said Raleigh with a big grin as he kind of punched her playfully on the arm. He really liked Fern.

"So you're glad to be back, huh?" Fern said. "What are you working on now?"

"I'm going to do four movies," Raleigh said, not even glancing at the TelePrompTer, even though he was reading almost everything these days.

"Yeah, I hear," said Fern, and she was going to have to do better than this, Beth Carol decided. She could hardly hear what Fern was saying and the way she was licking her lips and moving her legs around, it was obvious she was nervous. "*Zorro*, isn't that the first one? And you'll be able to wear that great cape with the Z on the back, won't you? I mean, that's going to look terrific."

"I like the cape," Raleigh pronounced solemnly.

"So, what do you like best about being a movie star?" she asked.

"Well, I like it a lot when they clap when I'm through, when I've done a good job."

"Yeah, I guess what you do takes great timing, right?" she said. "I mean, you must practice all the time, huh?"

"A lot," he said, nodding. "But I don't worry about it anymore. That I'll make a mistake, I mean. I've been doing it as long as I can remember."

"Don't you sometimes wonder what it would be like to have a normal childhood? Like other kids?"

"Well, I'm used to this," he said shyly. "It's normal for me."

"But how about if you didn't have to work, and all?" she prodded. "How about if you could just play like other kids do? You're just about ready for school, too, aren't you? I mean, you're never going to be able to go to a regular school. What do you think about that?"

"Gee, Fern," said Raleigh, frowning a little. "I like it the way it is. I really do. It's all I know, you see. I don't have anything to compare it to, and I'm happy all the time."

"Does it bother you, Raleigh," she said, "that all of these people are depending on you? That you're supporting your whole family? Paying for everything?"

"A lot is put away for me," Raleigh said as Beth Carol

pursed her lips angrily, thinking that was a mean question that Fern had asked. "I'll have money to go to college."

"Yeah, yeah. College," said Fern. "So what do you want to learn, what do you want to be when you grow up, man?"

"The best," Raleigh said with a glowing smile. "I want to be the very best."

"So what does that mean to you?"

"I don't know yet," he said. "After all, I'm only five years old."

The assistant director cued the applause, and then there was a cut to a commercial. Then the fifteen-minute montage of clips from Raleigh's films, which gave him time to change into gym clothes and the crew the time to set up his rings, bars, the wire he would descend in order to make his next appearance on the set.

Just as the commercial following the montage appeared, Fern sauntered back on the set, wearing a different dress this time. Even lower than the last, Beth Carol thought with disgust. Looking more than ever like a streetwalker, a caricature of Marilyn Monroe, although Marilyn was pretty much of a caricature, too. Fern was becoming more relaxed, more confident as the minutes passed. Beth Carol could see it from her stance, the "us guys together" way she was whispering with the assistant director.

"And now, Raleigh Barnes!" she shrieked, leading the applause as Raleigh made his dazzling dive down the wire, did a somersault, and bounded onto the bars, almost in a single motion. Beth Carol had watched him during the dress rehearsal, felt him holding back. Now he was pulling out all the stops, flipping and twirling in the air, as the grandmoms in the audience tittered with terror. He leapt through the air, aloft for what seemed like an eternity, before he caught the rings, turned himself upside down, stood on his hands up there in space. Even Beth Carol surprised herself with a scream as Raleigh pushed up from the rings, twirled in the air, and fell, fell, just catching one of them at the last moment while the whole audience heaved a collective sigh of relief.

A few quicks turns through the air, a one-hand stand on a bar, and Raleigh was tumbling across the stage, arching his back as he pulled himself to his feet, throwing out his arms, grinning, his dimple dancing as the audience screamed and applauded with delight.

Then the filler, the brief interview with the legendary photographer from *Life*, while the stills from the article appeared on the screen. Right on cue, Raleigh slipped into his chair just as the second-to-last one flashed on the screen to the audible gasps of pleasure from everybody in the studio.

They applauded vigorously as the giant screen went blank and Fern turned to the photographer, a big smile on her face.

"Say, you're great," she said, admiration in her voice. "Like, I could use a couple of new snapshots of myself, man. What do you charge?"

"You couldn't afford me," he ad-libbed good-naturedly. "But thanks a lot for having me here today, Fern." And turning to Raleigh, he reached out his hand. "It's a great day, kid. I'm happy to have been a part of it."

"Say, don't go yet," Fern said. "I've got a little surprise for everybody, and I want you to see it, too. So just sit down for a minute, okay?"

The photographer dropped back into his chair, Fern motioned to the assistant director, and Paul leaned over to Beth Carol.

"What the fuck is she doing?" he whispered savagely.

As he spoke, a giant blowup of an amateur's photograph of Raleigh filled the giant screen on the set. He was sitting on a nondescript rug, the arm of a shabby sofa visible next to his blond head. He wore a shirt and pants that Beth Carol had never seen before. He had a big smile on his face, and in his arms he held Frisky, who was clearly younger than he had been on the night Raleigh had led him into the Beverly Hills Police Station.

"Oh, my God," Beth Carol gasped as she realized what she was seeing.

"Don't you wish you had a snap of that?" Fern was asking the photographer, who was gaping at the screen. "That's where Raleigh was when he was kidnapped. He's having a good time, too. Look how he's smiling."

Beth Carol looked at Raleigh. His face was bright red, and he was making himself small in his chair. She thought she would die for him on the spot.

"That's what it is, isn't it, Raleigh?" Fern asked, affectionately tousling his hair.

Slowly he nodded.

"And the guy who took you there . . . so tell us all about him, okay?" Fern drawled. "What was he like, and everything?"

Raleigh sat there for a couple of moments, looking doubtfully at the picture on the screen. At Fern.

"He loved me," he said at last in a small, choked voice. "He wanted me to be his friend."

"So how did he show you that?" Fern asked, leaning toward him. "Did he hug you, and stuff? Did he kiss you?"

It was almost as if a curtain of disapproval fell over the audience, Beth Carol realized, her hand to her throat. The director must have known it was coming, but now he seemed to be in shock. As for Raleigh, he just sat there for a couple of seconds, trying to decide how he felt. She watched his face, saw his eyes narrow, the set of his jaw. He was really mad, she saw.

"You're doing it wrong, Fern," he said, jumping up, trotting off in the direction of the green room. "You're supposed to follow the script. It's the way it's done."

"Ah, sit down, Raleigh," she muttered.

But he was already gone, and the director was waving his arms around, screaming something into his microphone as all of the monitors went to black while Fern gave a delicate little shrug of her shoulders as if she hadn't had a thing to do with upsetting Raleigh, hadn't been responsible in any way for the fact that the last three minutes of the program showed nothing except the network's logo and a printed message that said, PLEASE STAND BY.

CHAPTER 40

*F*ern wouldn't tell anybody where she'd gotten the picture. It was all over the afternoon papers the next day, Beth Carol saw, when she sat down to read them. Fern said that she couldn't reveal her source and that, as a reporter, it was her First Amendment right. And this coming from someone who moved her lips as she read and who could barely write her name. Beth Carol shook her head and lit another cigarette.

A grand jury was going to be convened. They'd ask her again. If she wouldn't tell them, she'd be in contempt of court. They could send her to jail.

On the news later, there was reaction from all over the country. The reporters' groups were coming out to say they would stand behind her, and all of these judges were being interviewed about what they thought, and everything everywhere was Fern, Fern, Fern. The bombshell she'd dropped when that picture had flashed into nearly every home in the country had eclipsed the show itself and the debacle it became. Still, the ratings had been extraordinary, and Raleigh hadn't seemed to be too bothered after a couple of hours of being really mad at Fern. Now that he could pretty much read everything, he was spending a lot of time with his Dr. Seuss books, and he was even starting *Winnie The Pooh*.

Beth Carol had never seen Paul so happy when he got

home that night, and in time for dinner, too.

"We signed the deal," he said, lifting her into the air, swinging her around. "I got everything I wanted. Four percentage points, that's what all this has been worth. We started out at forty-eight percent for us. Now it's fifty-two percent. That's control, baby. Oh, God, I'm so happy I could cry."

That night they made love for a long time. It was wonderful, just wonderful. When Brad called the next time to arrange a meeting, she told him she wasn't going to see him anymore. Because of the new baby he and his wife had on the way, and everything. It made her feel too guilty. She hoped he understood.

Beth Carol thought it was sweet when he cried and begged her to change her mind.

"Well, just one last time," she said.

The phone was ringing when she got home, and she was really surprised when she heard an operator's voice who asked her if she would accept a collect call from Fern Darling.

"Where are you?" she asked anxiously.

"I'm in the clink." Fern chortled. "Isn't that hysterical?"

"You mean jail?" Beth Carol asked.

"Yeah, the girl's jail downtown. And, man, you should see some of these girls. They'd make your hair stand on end. All this whistling, and catcalls. Like I felt like Queen of the May. I could have my choice, I tell you."

"Aren't you scared?"

"No, they keep me in a different place. I'm a celebrity, right? You know how bad it would look for them if some of those dykes in there held me down and put it to me? Well, they're not going to risk that. You better believe it."

"Fern, what are you doing there?"

"It was the grand jury, man. Boy, you should see that scene. You've got these twenty-seven assholes, and they're all in tiers, and I'm sitting there all by myself while they ask me all these questions. You can't even have a lawyer. Boy, talk about the Inquisition."

"I didn't think they'd actually do it," Beth Carol whispered.

"Yeah, well, we didn't, either, but we were hoping. You know what I wore? You know that white dress with the black polka dots? That one. And a black cartwheel hat, and a black patent leather bag, and matching shoes."

"You mean you wanted to go to jail?"

"Well, sure," said Fern condescendingly. "That was the point. To get the publicity, everybody up in arms. It's been terrific, man, just the way I planned it. The newspaper syndicate is drawing up the contracts right now so I take over the column, and they're giving me the television stuff, too."

"You can't write," Beth Carol said.

"I'll hire somebody to write." Fern laughed. "They're a dime a dozen, writers."

"Where did you get the picture?" she asked.

"You'll know soon enough," Fern said. "As soon as I'm off the front pages, say, in a week or so, I'll tell the grand jury everything they want to know."

"And meantime, they could be looking for Raleigh's kidnapper," Beth Carol whispered furiously. "Right now, while we're talking, he could be picking up some other child, and you sit there, holding out for the publicity."

"Yeah, well, listen," Fern said, "what I'd like from you is a little favor, okay? I need you to bring my makeup case and stuff. One of the boys at the house will show you where it is. And when you come, bring Raleigh. I'll arrange to have the press there. Can't you just see it on the news, in the papers? Raleigh coming to visit me in jail?"

"I'm not going to let Raleigh be a party to this," Beth Carol said.

"Oh, yes, you are," Fern said. "Just check it out with that darling husband of yours, man. See you."

Beth Carol sat there, listening to the dial tone, so angry she could feel the tears in her eyes. Fern was the worst person she'd ever met in her life. She was ice, all the way through the place her heart should have been.

Somebody had mailed the picture to her anonymously, she told the grand jury a week later when she had milked the situation for all it was worth. The envelope had been thrown away before anybody in the office realized it was important. So she really didn't know anything about it and what she had been doing when she wouldn't answer in the first place was making a point that was her right.

The photograph had passed through so many hands by the time it was given to the fingerprint experts that they couldn't lift anything but smudges. Nobody responded to the pleas when the photograph was shown on television, in the newspapers, asking if anyone knew where it might have been taken. And there were all of the big close-ups of Fern again, Beth Carol saw with annoyance, plastered all over everything.

"This will kill you," Fern purred one morning when Beth Carol answered the telephone. "So I get a call from none other than the mayor of Crescent City himself, you know? And they're planning this big do at the Rotary Club, and they want to honor me, give me the key to the city. Do you believe it, man?"

"What did you say?" Beth Carol asked.

"I told them to go fuck themselves," Fern said with a breathy little laugh.

CHAPTER 41

The clattering of the rotors of the helicopter was so loud that Raleigh couldn't understand what the pilot was trying to tell him. He leaned toward the pilot, cupped his hand to his ear, and shook his head. The pilot pointed past him south to the Santa Monica Mountains outlined by a full moon in a blue-black sky.

Fifteen minutes, he mouthed. Raleigh nodded.

Ahead was the city itself, a blanket of lights as far as Raleigh could see. Way off to the left, a cluster of skyscrapers dwarfed city hall. In front of them, a few lonely towers stood on what had been the back lot of Twentieth Century-Fox, where Raleigh had worked a lot. Century City. They'd shot there once. It was all so new, so empty, as if the bomb had dropped and this was what was left. Way, way off there were blinking red lights in the sky as the jets descended into Los Angeles International Airport.

A few minutes later, Raleigh could just make out a winding ribbon of lights jammed with cars. The Sunset Strip, open for business on a fine summer night. And farther along, the blue, red, white klieg lights over the swimming pool, the mammoth billboard on top of Raleigh Barnes Productions. Leave it to Paul, Raleigh thought with a smile. As soon as the major studios and the record companies had started erecting those big painted billboards, Paul had started to think about putting up one of their own. It would be bigger, of course, better. Animated. It had to do something besides just sit there.

Finally Paul had hit on what he thought they should do. There would be a continuous tape of information spelled out in lights the way they used to print the news on a sort of enlarged ticker tape in Times Square.

It would be for that underwater movie they were going to shoot down off the coast of Puerto Vallarta in Mexico, where John Huston had made *The Night of the Iguana.* So there would have to be water. Voilà, said Paul. A swimming pool. And a big billboard advertising the movie, and the ticker tape in lights would count down the days until they started to shoot, then the production days. Then the days until release. That sort of thing. All of which was fine, except when Paul had started to plan the thing they had been just about to begin a remake of *David Copperfield,* and after that they were still committed to *Peter Pan.* There wasn't a title, a script, a starting date, or financing. Still, once Paul got something into his mind, it was as good as done. The scaffolding had gone up on top of the building, a high wall that said WATCH THIS SPACE, and the whole thing was finished before the Board of Commissioners could even start sputtering that he hadn't gotten a building permit. So they'd brought a lawsuit, and so had all the neighbors, but all that aside, there it was. A swimming pool that seemed to be hanging in midair right in the middle of the Sunset Strip.

He had the big picture, Paul did, but he had follow-through, too. That was a neat combination, and Raleigh hoped it had been passed along to him. Of course, Paul could be petty sometimes. He fretted about the littlest things, worried them to death. The freckles, for instance. It had been a couple of years ago, Raleigh remembered, so he would have been ten. They were shooting way out at the end of the San Fernando Valley at the Corrigan Ranch, where nearly every Western was made. They had been rehearsing a stunt in which he jumped off the roof of a building right onto the saddle of a horse, and then he was to gallop off in a cloud of dust.

He, Paul, and Darby had been in the backseat of the

limousine that morning around four o'clock, rolling through
the gates of the estate, making a right onto Sunset and hitting
the San Diego Freeway going north. It was neat at that time
of the morning, Raleigh thought. Theirs was practically the
only car on the road and there was something so secret and
wonderful about that. By the time they merged into the
Ventura Freeway the sky was turning gray with little hints of
pink. The traffic was getting heavier, too, with trucks, mostly,
but some other cars, too. Paul was studying sheets of figures,
Darby was studying the day's setups in his shooting script, and
Raleigh was just sort of looking out the window, daydreaming,
enjoying the lack of activity for once.

Once they pulled in, though, everything was hustle and
bustle. All the gaffers and lighting people and assistants
were drinking coffee from paper cups, eating donuts, and
all the trailers that had been hauled into place at the beginning of the shoot were jammed with people rushing in and
out, getting ready for the day. Raleigh waved to his co-star,
the big-time cowboy actor whose sidekick he was playing,
and the actor waved back. The makeup girl said hello and
his dresser was there. Everybody. Over at one side, some
cowboys were dealing with the horses.

Raleigh, in his jeans and boots, his cowboy shirt, his hat, a
bandanna tied around his neck, was ready to go as soon as the
light was right. Darby was standing near the building where
he was going to do the stunt, talking to the cinematographer
and a couple of his assistants, and Paul was just standing
there, frowning, his hands jammed in his pockets, probably
worrying that something might go wrong. There had been
the time Raleigh had broken his wrist on *Robin Hood* when
his horse spooked and threw him. He'd had a cast for a
month, and therapy after that for another six weeks. Well,
Paul had practically gone nuts, with the production shut
down all that time and the insurance company screaming and
insisting that somebody else had to do the stunts because
Raleigh was too valuable a property to risk.

But nobody else could do the stunts, because Raleigh
was so small, and there wasn't a midget in the business who

was good enough to do the stunts that had to be done. So the insurance premiums were absolutely staggering and everything had to be done in the four hours a day that Raleigh could work because, under California law, he had to work with his tutors the rest of the time.

But the broken wrist was just one of those things, a hazard of the trade. This time Raleigh was going to do an easier stunt. The horse was well trained, and Raleigh had gotten to know him and they liked each other and trusted each other. They practiced the stunt over and over, and finally, just before they broke for lunch, it was a take.

There were long, wooden tables set up under the trees by the catering company and one of the gofers went off to get Raleigh's lunch as he slid onto the bench next to Paul.

"What are those spots on your face?" Paul asked with a horrified look as he leaned forward to examine Raleigh.

Measles, Raleigh thought, dismayed. He'd never had them. Chicken pox. Oh, no.

"What spots?" he asked.

"Those little brown spots all over your nose," Paul said, as if Raleigh had suddenly turned up with creeping leprosy or teeth that were falling out, which they had, of course, but the false teeth, flippers they were called, from the dentist to the child stars had solved that one. Or the time Paul was watching the rushes and he had realized that Raleigh's hair wasn't as blond as it had been. That it was, well, turning brown. So the call had gone out to Bobby, who touched it up all the time now, so Raleigh was still blond, even blonder than he had been when he was a little kid.

And now this. Little brown spots on his nose. Freckles, for God's sake. It shouldn't have been a big deal, but it was.

Paul called Darby over, and they both peered into Raleigh's face. Then they had called Maggie in her public relations office in town. They shut down for the day so they could all decide whether the freckles were good and should stay, or whether they were bad and should be covered with makeup.

Appeal was the question. Was Raleigh more appealing, more the all-American boy, with or without them? On the one hand, freckles had been great on Butch Jenkins. But then, not so good on Darryl Hickman. They'd worried it back and forth far into the evening, and finally they made their decision. No freckles.

It was mind-boggling, really, all of this attention to detail, and he was the center of it all. Sometimes, when Raleigh thought about it, he felt almost as if he were the sun, and everything in the world revolved around him. Oh, sure, Paul would keep reminding him that he would be nothing, just another little kid, without the management, the publicity, the whole package. But the truth was that he was Raleigh Barnes and they weren't. It was as simple as that.

Oh, he knew he wasn't an actor, not really, the way somebody like Marlon Brando was an actor. He was too young. He was more like a parrot, actually. Darby would tell him what he wanted, and Raleigh would do it. Smile. Laugh. Look concerned. Cry. He wasn't a singer, either. He'd proved that with *Peter Pan.* Everybody had really been worried, too. All of the hours working with the voice coach, and he could just about carry the tunes. What a shock it had been when the reviews were all raves, but Raleigh guessed it was because little kids didn't have to sing well. It was enough that they sang at all. It was sort of like dogs that walked on their hind legs.

So he wasn't an actor and he wasn't a singer. It didn't matter.

He was a movie star.

He was the one whose handprints and footprints were etched in cement in the courtyard in front of Grauman's Chinese Theater. He was surrounded by Rita Hayworth, Charles Boyer, Jeanne Crain, and Henry Fonda. He'd taken the stick he was handed and laboriously scratched, *For Mr. Grauman, Thank You Very Much. Love, Raleigh Barnes. August 10, 1961.*

And the fans were all screaming and cheering, crowding around him. Just wanting to look at him, get his autograph, touch him if they could. And they wrote to him, too, thousands of them every week. There was a whole shift of people that did nothing but send out autographed pictures, three people who did nothing but coordinate his fan clubs which were in every state now, except South Dakota and Tennessee.

There were death threats, too, although Raleigh wasn't supposed to know about them. They would come in the mail, written on pink notepaper in purple ink. Cut out of newspapers and pasted on lined paper from the dime store. Sometimes they would be phone calls at the mansion, whispers in the night. Paul would call the police when that happened, and they would change all of the phone numbers again. And for a couple of months the security guards patrolling the grounds would be doubled, too.

Sometimes, when they were driving somewhere, or during one of the interminable waits on the set, Raleigh tried to figure out what he meant to these people, the ones who loved him and the ones who wanted to kill him. Old ladies, for example. They really, really loved him. He figured he was the perfect grandson they had never had. A little boy who was very brave, but vulnerable, too. So that was easy. They wanted to mother him. The little girls who liked him wanted him to be their boyfriend, somebody to show off, to make them envied and admired by their girlfriends. Grandfathers liked him, too. But the one thing he never told the interviewers was about the most enthusiastic group of his fans, the homosexuals. Wow, how they loved him! It was amazing. They would gaze at him hungrily, as if they wanted to eat him up alive. That look, when he saw it, always gave him a start. It was the way Sir George Dean had looked at him when he was a little kid. It had made him so uncomfortable then because he hadn't been able to figure it out. He hadn't even known that there were men who only liked other men. Of course, when he thought about girls, he guessed he still wasn't old enough to figure out why anybody liked them, either. In the first place, they didn't seem to do anything. Everything scared them. The only thing they seemed to do, in the movies, anyway, was put a hand on your arm when you were going off to slay a dragon or do battle, or something, and say, "Oh, please be careful." That happened every time there was a girl in a movie with him. Or they wanted you to stop whatever it was you were doing and keep them company while they sat around. Take Mom. She was a perfect example. Oh, she was pretty and sweet, and all, but she was always on the sidelines of everybody else's life. Raleigh just couldn't figure out why she didn't want to be part of the action because it was so much fun and it made you feel so good to try something out to find out that you could do it.

Why, Mom wouldn't even get in an elevator alone. She wouldn't learn to drive. As for getting in an airplane, there wasn't a chance. What did she think would happen if she did those things? Raleigh wondered. The worst thing that could happen was that she would die. But she was going to do that anyway. They all were. No, he had to go along with what Paul was always saying. If you're going to do anything, you might as well try to do everything. Raleigh figured that started with breathing. Everybody did that. Then you just took it from there.

Maybe it was because Mom was so scared of everything that she took those tranquilizers all the time and drank too much. Maybe they stopped her from thinking about how scared she was. Still, he didn't respect her. He loved her, but he didn't respect her.

Sometimes he wondered about the relationship she had with Paul. It didn't seem to Raleigh that Paul was very nice to her. A lot of the time he was just this side of condescending. Other times, he was flat-out contemptuous. Then Mom would look as if he'd hit her, and her face would sort of cave in, and she'd start to cry. It tore Raleigh apart to see her like that. It really did. But still, what could she expect if she was zonked out of her mind on pills, or lurching around because she'd had a few too many?

And Darby never acknowledged her presence. But then, Darby was another matter. What was Darby doing living with them, for instance? Oh, Raleigh had heard the stories over and over about how it had been in the beginning. That right away they had all seen that Raleigh was special, and that they had all decided to devote their energies to seeing that Raleigh got to the top. But that was then, and this was now, and Darby was still there, living with them. He'd finally taken off that stupid, phony eye patch of his, but there was something strange about Darby, something Raleigh couldn't quite figure out. A possessiveness that brought back memories of that guy who'd kidnapped him. Gee, he hadn't thought of him in years.

Buddy, that was his name. He was a nice guy in his own ding-a-ling way. Still, it was all so long ago. If it weren't for the fact that Buddy was the one who had given him Frisky, it was just as if it had never happened. Once, he'd had the car take him down the street where he thought Buddy had lived, but if it was the place he thought it was, it had been torn down. There was a shopping center there now, with a Tiny Naylor's restaurant, a shoemaker, and a beauty salon.

Down below, Raleigh saw the blue rectangle of the swimming pool, the thousands of people crowding the street, the police cars with their red and blue lights flashing.

Darby leaned over the front seat, adjusted the buckles on the shoulders of his wet suit, handed Raleigh his swim fins. The helicopter inched lower as Raleigh put his foot into the loop at the end of the heavy rope, opened the door, and clung to it as it was lowered on its winch. For a moment, he swayed violently as the rotating blades of the helicopter churned the air. Then he was lower, lower, out of its sphere, hanging there. The night touched his face as he looked down.

The pool, lit from below, looked cool and inviting. The people on the roof, the celebrities, the press, the money people past, present, and future, were a sea of upturned faces. Waiters in red jackets had stopped in their tracks and were looking up at him, too. So were the musicians in the band. The tables on the roof were covered with green tablecloths, centerpieces of flowers. There were four bars.

As he swung closer, Raleigh could almost see all of them holding their breath. It was a great feeling, this, he thought exultantly as he swung closer and closer to the pool, almost low enough to jump. He couldn't get enough of doing things like this and he tried to keep himself from thinking about the time when it would end. Oh, it was fine for now because he was still a cute little kid. He was small and he looked a lot younger than he was. But what would happen when he was older and not so cute anymore?

Sometimes he thought that maybe he'd take acting lessons and really learn the craft. That was a possibility.

Or maybe he'd become a screenwriter and create new worlds right out of his own mind, and direct the movies, too, so it would be his own vision locked in place forever.

What he really thought he'd like to do was to become an explorer. That time he'd had his arm in the cast he'd read the lives of a lot of them. Sir Richard Burton. Lawrence of Arabia. Sir Edmund Hillary. He really liked the idea of doing that, of conquering new worlds.

He wished that he had a thousand lives so that he could do a thousand different things.

It's time, he thought, as he kicked out of the loop, clung with one hand to the rope, to a chorus of audible gasps from below. He positioned himself carefully and dived toward the pool below, feeling a heady freedom that was near to bliss as he knifed into the water, which was icy, like a slap on the face.

Just a couple of times across the pool for effect, they had decided. No big deal. After all, how interesting was it to watch someone else swimming? The dive had been the thing. That was the only time something could have gone wrong.

Raleigh broke to the surface, gulped air into his straining lungs, heard the cheers, the applause as he swam slowly over to the edge, pulled himself out. On the street below, it sounded as if there were a riot.

People were there, the aides, handing him towels, asking him if he was all right, clearing a path through the throng for him. They were all so deferential, so obsequious, even. Oh, stop it, he wanted to say to them sometimes. Just because I'm a movie star, it doesn't mean I'm not a real person. But he wondered if that were true, that he was a real person anymore, or if he ever had been. Maybe not. Maybe he was just the sum of all of their dreams, hopes, illusions, and he really didn't exist at all.

CHAPTER 42

*I*t had to be about that vulgar swimming pool, Beth Carol decided. It was an eyesore. So many tourists were coming to see it that as an attraction it was right up there with Disneyland. Traffic was impossible because of it, and on top of everything else, it was illegal and had to come down at once. She was sure that was what it was, because there wasn't any other reason on the face of the earth that Mary Lou Fernandez-Walters and Bitsy Horton would have invited her to have lunch with them at the Los Angeles Country Club.

Just the thought of driving through those gates at the Los Angeles Country Club was intimidating enough, but Mary Lou Fernandez-Walters was right up there among the social leaders in town, an heiress to one of the big Spanish land grant families, which was why she always used her maiden name along with that of her husband, who was someone important in aerospace, or something. And Bitsy Horton was only the wife of the publisher of the most important newspaper in town, so she had everything to say about everything. Beth Carol blushed when she thought of those days so long ago and the circumstances under which she had met Mr. Horton. It had really been indiscreet of someone like that to, well, pay someone to have sex with him. After all, didn't he realize that he might be recognized?

She'd never told anybody about that, either.

What she did was tell Mrs. Fernandez-Walters's secretary when she'd called with the invitation that she'd have to check her date book and call her back in a couple of hours. That bought her a little time so that she could decide what she should do, decide whether she would even be able to sit at the same table with Bitsy Horton, when she'd been to bed with her husband. Decide whether she had the strength to go through hearing the awful things they were sure to say about the swimming pool.

It was her curiosity that finally made her call back and say she'd love to have lunch. Oh, how she'd yearned to see the Los Angeles Country Club. One of the things about the club was that it didn't admit anybody as a member who had anything at all to do with show business. The members thought show business was simply too flashy, and therefore beneath them.

And then Beth Carol had really gotten anxious because she didn't know what to wear with girls like that in a place like that. Of course, Fern was the last person in the world to ask, but Beth Carol called her anyway, waited forever as she was transferred from one assistant to another. All Fern had to say was that she didn't see why Beth Carol wanted to spend her time with a couple of snobs like those two girls, and besides, who cared about the downtown people? They were all past it. Everybody knew that.

And then, Fern being Fern, all she wanted to do was talk about herself the way she always did, and how maybe marrying that bodybuilder she'd picked up in the Bentley when he was hitchhiking on Sunset hadn't been such a swift idea because he was getting really, really possessive, and who needed that? Well, Beth Carol could have told her that marrying Danny Tosca was a big mistake. He was a real jerk and he'd never even owned a suit until Fern bought him one.

"He can go all night, man," Fern had told her, wonder in her breathy little voice. "And you wouldn't believe the size of his dick. I bet it's ten inches. Honest."

Still, you didn't marry someone just because he was

good in bed. And now Fern was finding that out for herself.

Bobby, though, was properly impressed and excited for Beth Carol. They'd go shopping, he said. She'd even asked Paul to let her have the limousine for the lunch date, but he wouldn't do it. "How are we going to get to the set if you have the car?" he'd asked her.

But it was all right, really, she saw as she pulled up to the entrance to the Los Angeles Country Club in her taxi. All of the cars in the parking lot were Buicks, Oldsmobiles, cars she'd never noticed before, station wagons. There wasn't one limousine in the whole place, so she sighed with relief as the parking lot boy opened the door for her, because that would have been a terrible faux pas, to turn up in a limousine with a chauffeur who looked like a bodyguard, because that was what he was.

Beth Carol's legs felt like wet noodles as she approached the hostess, smiled shyly as she told her who she was joining. The hostess was impressed. Beth Carol could feel it in the deferential way she said to follow her into the large dining room with its sea of windows looking out over the golf course, its tables covered in conventional white. And the people having lunch there looked so nice, so refined. Some of them were in golf clothes, while tables of men were in business suits. And the conversation was so genteel, just a gentle hum.

The two girls looked up with smiles as she approached the corner table nearest the window. Oh, she'd thought she was dressed so conservatively in an oatmeal-colored two-piece dress with black buttons and matching black earrings. But both of them were in print silk dresses and pearls, little hats on their curls. Then the worst thing happened. Her hand was soaking wet as each of them took it in turn and introduced herself. It was horrible, Beth Carol thought gloomily, that they knew how nervous she was to be there. And even though she had promised herself she wouldn't have a drink, both of the girls were drinking martinis straight up, and so she ordered a Bloody Mary.

"I'm such a fan of your little boy," Bitsy said with a smile. "You must be very proud of him."

"Well, he just loves it," Beth Carol said, her cheeks burning. "It all started as a lark, you know. Paul thought that it would be fun for him for a few months, but he was so good at it, and he loved it so much. So it's just gone on and on."

"Well, it's wonderful," Bitsy purred, patting Beth Carol's hand. "I don't think it's anything to be ashamed of, not if the child likes it. And look at the exposure to the world he's getting, for heaven's sake. It must be very educational for him."

"Well, yes," Beth Carol agreed doubtfully, "but it isn't very conventional. Not like your son."

"Oh, Toosie." She smiled. "Well, he's quite a boy, too. A couple of years older than Raleigh, but what he wouldn't give to be the athlete Raleigh is."

"Toosie?" Beth Carol asked as they all smiled and smiled at each other.

"He's Roger II," explained Bitsy, making a face as she sipped her drink. "And two Rogers in the house just didn't work. We thought of Big Roger and Little Roger, but then we decided that really wouldn't be good for Toosie's ego, so we decided on Toosie, for two. You see?"

"Oh, what a wonderful solution," Beth Carol said with shining eyes. Toosie. How refined.

"Yes, he's at St. Mark's now and doing very well," Bitsy said. "He's doing wonderfully well with his studies, and he's captain of the tennis team this year."

"You must be very proud of him," Beth Carol said.

And then they were moms together, just like the girls at Secrets, and Mary Lou Fernandez-Walters said why didn't Beth Carol just call her Mary Lou, and she was talking about her five, three boys and two girls, the girls at the Marlborough School, of course, two of the boys prepping in the East, and the oldest one already at Yale, and what a chore it had been to get him in, as he wasn't exactly academically inclined.

Pretty soon Beth Carol was feeling relaxed, she was even having a good time, and when the waitress came to take their orders, she asked for a salad and an iced tea, just the way the other girls did.

"It's too bad the swimming pool is causing so much traffic congestion," she ventured after a while.

"The swimming pool?" Mary Lou asked quizzically, squinting a little as she said it, the way she probably did when she was out on the golf course. She had a great tan, Beth Carol thought approvingly.

"On the Sunset Strip," Beth Carol muttered. "Over the offices, you know."

"Oh, I haven't been on Sunset Boulevard in years," Mary Lou said apologetically. "I know it's terrible not to use the whole city, but somehow we're so insular in Hancock Park, maybe too insular, but there it is."

So it wasn't the swimming pool, Beth Carol thought, nodding and smiling, but nearly mad with curiosity over why she was there.

"It must be such a lot of fun for you to have the old Kendall place," Bitsy said. "So much room, but such a lot of work, of course. We used to spend a lot of time there when we were girls. It's one of the showcases in town. So tragic about the plane crash, about the Kendalls being killed. And Howard, dear, dear Howard." She stirred her iced tea thoughtfully and turned to Mary Lou. "He was a beau of yours, wasn't he?"

"Oh, just the year I came out," Mary Lou said brightly. "It wasn't anything serious, but still . . ."

"Your husband went to school with Howard, didn't he, Beth Carol?" Bitsy asked, her voice casual.

"Yes, he did," Beth Carol said, feeling her cheeks burning again.

"Well, it must have felt wonderful for him to be able to buy the estate where he grew up. What a measure of how successful he's become," Bitsy said. "And Diana was delighted about the whole thing. What would she do with all that room, and who wanted to be bothered anyway? Do you know Diana?"

"No, no, I don't," said Beth Carol, remembering the pictures of her. A pretty, blond child, smiling into the camera.

"Well, of course, she's always lived in the East," Bitsy said. "With that aunt and uncle of hers in Connecticut. But

I see her whenever I'm back there. To visit Toosie at school, and for the theater, of course. I just love the theater, don't you?"

"Oh, yes," Beth Carol breathed.

"In fact, it was Diana who had the brainstorm about the house, the ballroom," Bitsy said.

"I'm sorry?" Beth Carol said blankly.

"For a benefit," Bitsy said. "You know, for the new performing arts center that's going up downtown. You've seen it, of course. Don't you think it's going to be impressive? The three theaters, the one experimental, the one for the symphony and ballet, the third for popular plays and musicals." She sighed, sipped her iced tea. "It's been hell," she added darkly. "We'll get a commitment from one man, but he'll only do it if his name is on the theater. And if we agree to that, somebody else drops out."

"I'm afraid I don't get downtown very often," Beth Carol said.

"Oh, that'll all change as soon as this theater complex is finished," Bitsy said, brightening. "Everybody will come. From the Westside, from Pasadena, from Hancock Park. It will bring the whole city together. You'll see. That's the vision that Mother has had in mind all along. Roger's mother, that is."

"I'm sorry, Bitsy," Beth Carol said, bewildered. "I just don't see what this has to do with me. Do you mean you want to have a benefit for the performing arts center at our house? Is that it?"

She saw Bitsy glance at Mary Lou with hard, glittering eyes.

"It'll be perfect," Bitsy said. "A tour of the grounds, a luncheon for two hundred in the ballroom. Everybody will want to come. We all had such fun in that house and it's been years since any of us has seen it. We'd be so grateful if you'd donate it for an afternoon. We really would."

Beth Carol's heart sank as she thought about all the work it would take, all the people who would be milling around for weeks. Why, it would be just like planning a movie premiere, and everybody knew how much work that was.

"We're prepared to offer you a story on the front page of the women's section on Raleigh, and an inside story later in the Sunday magazine section," Bitsy said.

Why, this is barter, Beth Carol thought incredulously as she sipped her iced tea.

"Well, I don't know," she said doubtfully.

"Of course, we'll understand if you don't want to do it," Bitsy said. "After all, a mob like that at the house means a big mess. But we thought about it and thought about it, and it seemed to all of us that Raleigh is nearly an adolescent, and that's certainly a time of transition in the career of any child star when he can use a guarantee of continued press support."

Not barter, Beth Carol corrected herself. Blackmail.

"Well, I'll have to ask my husband," she said at last.

Really, she'd never had a better time, she decided in the taxi on the way home. There was just something about girls like Bitsy and Mary Lou. Something so substantial. They were so sure of themselves, so secure about their place in the community and their responsibility to it. They were so wonderfully down-to-earth in their sensible clothes and their sensible cars and their sensible attitudes toward everything.

And now here was a chance for her to become one of them. Oh, it was all so exciting. Still, she had felt guilty sitting there with Bitsy because of Roger, and everything, way back when. Beth Carol felt a little tingle of anxiety at the thought of Roger. But he would never remember her, she told herself. She had just been a baby then, brand-new in town. A raw kid. Why, even she didn't recognized herself from those days, so Roger wouldn't, either. No, it just wasn't a problem.

CHAPTER 43

*T*his might amuse you, Beth Carol," said Bitsy, taking
her arm as they strolled along behind a straggly line of girls
in garden party dresses and hats, listening to the docent as
she pointed out all the different exotic plants. "This is the
first time I've ever seen the entire downstairs of the house
opened up, and I must have been here a hundred times
when I was growing up."

"Oh, really?" Beth Carol said, smiling a little to herself as
she realized she could say the same thing. She'd lived here
now for, what, thirteen years and some, and it was the first
time she'd ever seen the entire downstairs opened up, too.

"It was because of Mrs. Kendall," Bitsy was saying. "She
graduated from USC, in fact, and most of her close friends
were here. But she loved the opera, the theater and, well, a
road show of *South Pacific* wasn't her style. So she spent a
lot of time in New York, London, for the theater season."
Bitsy paused, looked reflectively at the lake in the distance.
Sighed. "It was a quirk of fate that she was on that plane
with Mr. Kendall, with Howard. It's funny how things like
that happen, isn't it? So random."

"What about Mr. Kendall?" asked Beth Carol. "What
was he like?"

"Oh, he was a dear," Bitsy said quickly. "When he was

in town, the servants would open up his study and his bedroom, and that was all. Somebody was always asking to use the ballroom for some charity thing, and Mrs. Kendall would always say yes, and we'd get here, and he would never remember we were coming. He'd open the door in his old slippers and a dressing gown, and we'd just go ahead and put on our event as if he weren't there. So it's wonderful to be able to use the ballroom again, you know?"

"Did you know his secretary?" asked Beth Carol tentatively. "Paul's mother?"

"Oh, Mrs. Fournier," said Bitsy, frowning, trying to remember. "She was a dear, so helpful. And Mr. Kendall thought the world of her. We all thought it was wonderful of him to send Paul off to school with Howard the way he did to show her how much he appreciated her, and now it's Paul with the estate, so you never know, do you?"

"I suppose Paul was very popular," Beth Carol ventured.

"Well, he was very attractive," Bitsy said, "a wonderful, attentive escort with beautiful manners." She narrowed her eyes as she looked at the girls ahead of them in their pretty dresses. "It must have given him a lot of satisfaction to be able to do this today," she added.

"Oh, yes, he was thrilled," Beth Carol said, remembering that night she'd suggested it, still wincing a little at Paul's reaction.

"Do you know what it's going to take to get this place organized?" he had demanded. "It'll take a crew six months."

"Oh, please," she had begged. "These are such nice girls. They're the kind of girls I've always wanted to know. Please, Paul."

"Well, they never wanted to know me. I was just dirt, the live body Howard dragged along. The secretary's son."

And then he'd gone all thoughtful, and she could practically see the wheels turning in his mind, see him thinking about how all those people who had snubbed him when he was a kid would owe him one. Oh, he didn't miss a trick, Paul.

"Well, just the downstairs," he said after a while. "I don't want a bunch of women going through my handkerchief drawer, for God's sake."

"Of course not, darling," she said, so happy she could have jumped up and down with joy.

"And I'll tell you what," he added, those wheels really turning now. "They'll want to do a raffle for a door prize. They always did. So let me see what I can come up with. Tell Bitsy I'll do the door prize, but she's got to get somebody to underwrite the party itself."

And that was funny, a new role, Beth Carol decided. Here she was, a negotiator between two powers. It was kind of fun. Bitsy had actually asked her to tea at the mansion in Hancock Park to discuss it, and Beth Carol had thought that it was like sitting there with a general considering a campaign, when she wasn't worrying that Roger might walk in and recognize her.

"It makes more sense for Paul to underwrite the party," Bitsy mused. "I'll take care of the door prize."

"Well, he has a trade-off he wants to do to get the door prize," she said, parroting what he had told her.

Bitsy said fine, she could understand that. In the end, she'd pressured some savings and loan guy who needed something to underwrite the luncheon and Paul had come up with the door prize. A new Cadillac El Dorado. Bitsy was really impressed, and so were all of the other girls.

Meantime, Beth Carol had been in her very first Hancock Park mansion and it was dowdy and everything looked as if it had been sitting there for two hundred years. On the walls were portraits of disapproving-looking ancestors and one of Bitsy herself when she was at Vassar, in riding clothes, leaning over a fence. The silver tea service looked as if it had come over on the Mayflower, and Beth Carol just loved the whole thing. Then the younger children, the two girls, had come home after school from Marlborough, which was just a couple of blocks away, in their little blouses and blazers, their pleated gray skirts. Such adorable children, so proper.

The girls loved the grounds, the tour of the first floor of the house. The luncheon in the ballroom was wonderful, and then there were the speeches from Bitsy, the others, even old Mrs. Horton, who said a few words. Was she ever a formidable lady. It scared Beth Carol just to look at the determined set of her jaw, the steely expression on her face. Beth Carol looked from Mrs. Horton to Bitsy, saw the steel there, too, and thought maybe that was why Roger had paid for it way back then, because he needed a little softness somewhere in his life. And then she just couldn't help it, she kind of wondered if he were seeing someone now. If he'd set her up to be a mistress the way Beth Carol had been so sure he was going to suggest for her all that time ago.

And, of course, the Cadillac El Dorado had been won by a girl whose family had three Chevrolet dealerships, but she had been so thrilled about it, and so had everybody else. She had screamed and jumped up and down as if she were on a game show, and all of the other girls had laughed and applauded.

Beth Carol almost fainted with joy a couple of days later when she got a note from old Mrs. Horton herself thanking her for giving the party and offering her a founding member-ship in the ladies' support group for the new center. It was only a thousand dollars a year. Paul had sighed when she'd told him, but he said that the contacts were worth it and more.

It had been Bitsy who called to welcome her to the group when the check got there, and she said why didn't they have lunch at the California Club to celebrate.

Well. The California Club was so exclusive that they didn't even let the girls eat in the same dining room with the guys. They had to use a different entrance, even, and a different elevator. And it was all so elegant, so refined, with its high ceilings and paneled walls, the waiters moving silently on the thick carpets. It was the world she had always dreamed about, and here she was at last.

And surprise, Bitsy loved to dish, and of course she knew everything about everyone, all of those names that Beth Carol read all the time in the society pages. Which girl from an old California family with a main boulevard named after it who started to drink at nine o'clock in the morning, for example, and how her husband was going nuts because of it, but wouldn't leave because of the money and the social position, and all. Then there was a guy who was really rich in a national kind of way and he had one son who killed himself and his daughter was married with kids of her own, but was a lesbian. And there was this other lady, very rich, very respectable, who was having a fight with her husband over something or other and she bit off the top of his finger. Well, he was really upset about that and he was bleeding all over the place, so what he did was rush into his study and get a gun. Then he shot her in the shoulder. So he'd had to go to jail over that for three months. It was the worst scandal, and everybody had talked about it for ages.

Then Bitsy got kind of thoughtful when she started to talk about this young couple who had met when he was at Harvard and she was at Radcliffe, and how he was the heir to a big fortune in, was it vegetable oil, something like that, and she was a fifth-generation Californian. Anyway, they had gotten married right after college and her family had given them a big house right on the Wilshire Country Club so the golf course was just like their backyard. And in time they had two kids, a boy and a girl. And somewhere a few years down the line, the wife decided to divorce him.

Well, all the society girls had stepped in and fixed him up with people, and everything like that, but in the end he had married the au pair girl from Mexico who had taken care of his kids when he and his wife were married. So he could go to his family's summer home on Cape Cod with the first kids, but he couldn't take the second kids, the ones he had with the ex-nanny. His family wouldn't even recognize her, in fact.

"It was terrible," Bitsy said confidentially. "Here was this perfectly eligible, acceptable young man, and all the girls in his own class, and that was what he did."

"Was he cute?" ventured Beth Carol.

"Oh, yes," Bitsy assured her. "He was very attractive."

So *cute* wasn't a word they used, these girls, and Beth Carol started to see a little bit how it was with Paul when he was growing up with Howard. Because even though Paul was educated the same way as Howard, and much more handsome, she had gathered that he didn't count as a prospect for any of these girls because he didn't have anything. No lineage, no money. So Beth Carol could really start to see it, why Paul was so bitter, and everything, and why he had so much to prove.

That was the difference between the westside people and the downtown people, she decided. The westside people had a lot to prove because they came from nowhere, and the downtown people didn't have anything to prove because they were the foundation of the city.

The guys had all prepped in eastern schools and had gone on to Ivy League colleges, and the girls usually had gone to Marlborough, where Bitsy's little girls went, and then east to Vassar or Radcliffe when the time came. And there were always summer places somewhere else where the whole family went for months at a time. Camps in the Adirondacks, enclaves in Nantucket. Stuff like that, all of it back East. In fact, the whole thing seemed to be about the East in some way or other, so maybe that was why it all had such a substantial feel. Because it was rooted somewhere, and there were rules. Like the girls taking a different elevator up to a different dining room right here in the California Club and nobody stopping to think that maybe that was kind of peculiar, but just going along with it because it was the way it had always been.

She thought of all the girls she knew at Secrets and what they would give to have something as simple as that to tell them who they were and what they were expected to do. As it was, everything they did was a shot in the dark. Maybe it would work, but maybe it wouldn't. They were always at risk, always dependent.

These girls, well, they were dependent, too. They were wives, moms. But it was all so different. Oh, sure, they all thought that what the guy they were married to did down at the newspaper, or at his investment banker firm, whatever, was the focus of everything, which was the same as the girls at Secrets, but most of these girls were strong as steel, and each of them had her own agenda. Like this performing arts center, or the new museum going up on Wilshire Boulevard, which some other girls from the downtown crowd had picked as their project.

But still, they had their tragedies and their scandals, their marriages of convenience and even their kids who had gone bad, since suicides and that sort of thing weren't exactly what anybody would want to have happen.

Once Bitsy had dropped her off and she'd fixed herself a cup of coffee, she thought about how the rest of the lunch had gone, when Bitsy had turned to her with that calculator look in her eyes and said, "Now, tell me all about yourself, Beth Carol."

She'd laid it on, the island, the house, the mines. All of it. The University of Idaho was her alma mater, she said—and what was Bitsy going to do? Call them up and check? She'd met Paul when she was touring Los Angeles with her family, and then he had come courting, begging her to marry him, until she finally did. And what was Bitsy going to do? Sit there and tell her she was lying? Well, of course she wasn't going to do that. She just had to sit there and accept every word Beth Carol was telling her as the gospel truth. And then Beth Carol thought about it a little more, and she thought that the downtown people were really taking quite a chance on the new people to get all this stuff built to make Los Angeles a major city. Because who knew who they really were, and maybe some traditions would fall by the wayside. Maybe they all would, and then there wouldn't be anything left for any of them.

Anyway, it was intimidating, but it was heady, too. And more interesting than listening to Bobby list all of the presents his latest love had given him, or to Fern complaining that Danny was so overwhelmed by how important she was that he couldn't even get it up anymore. So maybe she had kind of outgrown her friendship with Bobby, with Fern. After all, people moved on, didn't they?

CHAPTER 44

*B*eth Carol, her eyes shining with tears of pride and happiness, looked up at the granite and glass facade of the first theater in the performing arts center to be completed, the crystal chandelier inside the lobby a brilliant blaze of lights, the splashing fountain in the courtyard reflected in its soaring windows. Across the way, the two smaller theaters were still girds and angles, but they were on their way. Oh, how hard she had worked for this day, how hard all the girls had worked.

And everybody looked so beautiful, too. The guys strolling up the stairways from the restaurants already open on the lower level, the parking lots below. All wore tuxedos. The girls clinging to their arms were all in long gowns. She clung to Paul's arm, looked at him, saw his eyes darting around at the different clusters of people who were chatting with each other. He was the best-looking man there, she decided. Too good-looking, in fact. And his tuxedo was the best-looking tuxedo there, too. Too well tailored, looking as if it had just been bought yesterday instead of the way the others looked. As if they'd been around since college days. Raleigh, though, in his little navy blue suit, looked just right. Some of the other kids were looking over at him, whispering behind their hands. So were some of the grown-ups. But Raleigh didn't even notice them, hadn't noticed that sort of thing in years. He was staring up at the front of the theater, fascinated.

Beth Carol waved at a couple of the girls she worked with who were just coming up the stairs with their husbands, their kids. What a change in her life there had been since that first day at the Los Angeles Country Club with Bitsy and Mary Lou. Every morning now, she literally jumped out of bed, hit the phones, coordinating and cajoling with the best of them. And even though she was a Beth-Carol-Come-Lately, which put her at a disadvantage, she was proud to say that some of these girls were almost friends.

The mayor, the guys on the board of supervisors, even the governor, were fawning over old Mrs. Horton, offering congratulations. Well, that was only right, Beth Carol thought. Mrs. Horton had been the driving force behind it all, wheedling, bartering, begging. Blackmailing, too. The greatest fund-raiser since Al Capone. That was what somebody had said about her. Why, she had been on her way to her table at Perino's for lunch one day and just from the front door to the maître d'hotel she had run into two separate financiers, and by the time she sat down she had matching grants from each of them for $125,000. She was wearing a gown of beige lace, diamonds at her throat, and her face was glowing, flushed with her success.

And there was Bitsy, standing just behind her mother-in-law, looking so pretty in pale green, shepherding the kids. Toosie was wearing a suit, too, and the little girls looked so pretty in their party dresses. And Roger, of course, in the shadow of his mom. Oh, Beth Carol had been so worried that first time when she knew she was going to be meeting him again, but it was fine. He hadn't known her from Adam, just the way she had prayed it would be. He had lost a little more hair and he wore glasses now. And actually, if she hadn't seen his picture in his paper all those years ago and put the name together with the guy she'd been with, she wouldn't have known him, either. Just as she remembered, though, he was the nicest man with a kindly, intelligent look in his eyes that made her feel warm and welcomed whenever they saw each other now.

There was a blond girl in pale peach and pearls coming toward them, who looked so familiar that Beth Carol almost smiled and said hello, and then she saw that she didn't know her after all. But the girl was looking very expectant, and right at them, and then Beth Carol saw that she was wafting toward Paul, was touching his arm in a shy, charming little way. Beth Carol saw Paul start with surprise, saw his dazzling smile as he took the girl's hand in his, chatted with her for a second or two before he felt the thread of Beth Carol's impatience. His arm was lightly around the girl's waist as he turned, smiled.

"Beth Carol," he said with a note of wonder in his voice, "this is Diana Kendall."

"How do you do?" Beth Carol said coldly, taking the girl's limp hand, sizing her up. Feeling a giddy sense of relief as she saw the narrow shoulders, the total absence of boobs. Taking in the whole dowdy image that stood in front of her. Golly, she thought, she's nothing. Nothing at all. "Isn't this exciting, the opening and all?" she added condescendingly.

"It's thrilling," the girl agreed, and then they were all chatting together, and the girl was saying that when she was little she had had such a crush on Paul, and he looked just the way she remembered him, only better, and how she was so happy to see him again. And Beth Carol just nodded and nodded, and wondered how in her wildest dreams she had ever thought Diana Kendall appearing in their lives would pose any threat.

So she was feeling pretty good about everything, and Bitsy was coming toward her, her whole brood in front of her. They were all hugging and kissing, the little girls were offering hands to shake, tittering a little as they waited to be introduced to Raleigh.

"And this is Victoria," Bitsy was saying. "This is Gail. And this is Toosie, their big brother."

"How do you do?" Raleigh said, shaking hands with the kid, smiling at the little girls, which sent them into paroxysms of giggles.

"It's nice to meet you," Toosie said. "I've seen some of your movies. They're great."

"Thanks a lot." Raleigh grinned, looking up at him. He was probably fifteen, Raleigh decided, a couple of years older than he was. Toosie had a neat confidence about him, an air of command, a graceful posture like an athlete. "I hear you're at school in the East," Raleigh added.

"Yeah, St. Mark's," Toosie said. "Where do you go?"

"I don't go." Raleigh shrugged. "I'm tutored."

"Oh, I heard that kids who work in movies are kind of connected to a school, too," Toosie said. "So they can have a class to graduate with. That kind of thing."

"They didn't want me to be corrupted, or something," Raleigh said vaguely. "I never did quite follow the reasoning, but that's the way it is."

"Do you like it?" Toosie asked.

"Well, I don't have anything to compare it to," Raleigh said.

"Yeah, I guess that counts in a lot of things," Toosie said. "What are you working on now?"

"We're in preproduction on a movie we're going to shoot down in Mexico off the coast of Puerto Vallarta. It's kind of an underwater adventure thing."

"What's preproduction?" Toosie asked.

"Oh, it's where you get the script written, the financing in place, hire the crew, all of that," Raleigh explained.

"Gee, I'll bet you get to go to some great places," Toosie said. "Puerto Vallarta. Gee, that's wonderful."

"I guess it would be," Raleigh said, "if there was ever any time to look at anything. Mostly it's just work."

"That's too bad," Toosie said, glancing across the courtyard where his grandmother was beckoning to him. "I've got to go," he added. "Mrs. H. wants me."

"Well, nice to meet you." Raleigh nodded.

"Say, do you play tennis?" Toosie asked.

"Sure," Raleigh said.

"Well, why don't I give you a call and we can get together sometime? Have a few games," Toosie said. "I don't have to get back for a couple of weeks."

"Sure," Raleigh said. Toosie sprinted across the court-yard, joined his grandmother and all the well-wishers swarming around her. Tennis with a civilian. Raleigh had never done that before. Maybe it would be fun.

After a while, there was the ding-ding-ding of the bell calling everybody into the auditorium for the inaugural concert. It was really enormous, Raleigh saw, looking around as he took his seat next to his mother. There were three tiers of seats rising into the stratosphere, and all these lighted chandeliers. The walls were paneled in wood, and the seats themselves were a coral color. What was really neat, though, was the feeling of excitement in the air, of accomplishment. It was sort of like a screening of a movie when it dawned on everybody in the audience all at once that they had a hit.

Raleigh glanced over at his mother, who was leaning forward, talking to some friend of hers in the row in front of them. It had changed her life, this project. Given her a sense of purpose. He had never seen her so happy, or so pretty, either. She was wearing an evening gown in some shade of gray with a matching stole, he thought it was called. Anyway, it looked neat with her hair in that new soft way Bobby was doing it, her shining eyes. Paul seemed to be having a good time, too. He looked pretty neat in his tuxedo, the way he always did. Raleigh had wanted to wear a tuxedo, too, but Mom had said no, that she didn't want him to look like a midget, that the other kids would be wearing suits.

"I'm not the other kids," he said. "I'm a movie star."

But Paul had agreed with her, so Raleigh had worn a suit and he guessed it was just as well because Toosie was wearing one, and that sort of went with that old saying that when you were in Rome you did what the Romans did.

Behind the curtain, Raleigh could hear all the instruments tuning up over the buzz of conversation. When the lights went down, though, it was absolutely still. The curtain opened on a stage filled with maybe eighty musicians in white tie, and when the conductor strode onto the stage there was so much cheering and applause from everybody that Raleigh thought it would never stop. His name was Zubin Mehta, and getting him had been a big coup, according to Mom and what Raleigh had read in the papers. He looked like a movie star, Raleigh saw, with black curls tumbling down his forehead, and dark, liquid eyes. The soloist was Jascha Heifetz, whose records Raleigh had been listening to for as long as he could remember. It was different, though, with Jascha Heifetz in person. Inspiring. Raleigh felt his spirits soar, joined the applause at the end that seemed as if it would go on forever, and looked around, trying to find Toosie in the crowd, wondering when he would call.

CHAPTER 45

*T*he thing was, Raleigh concluded a couple of days later, he had never wanted anything. From the earliest moment he could remember, everything in his world was arranged to anticipate his slightest wish. As for other people, they were there to love him, adore him, or to wait on him. That was it for other people. So maybe that explained his feelings of annoyance, rejection, even hurt, because Toosie hadn't called him about their tennis game.

He sauntered along in the wildest part of the estate, where the old trees practically blacked out the sunlight, threw a ball for Frisky, and stood there, watching him sniffing around trying to find it. Well, maybe he'd just forgotten it, Raleigh thought, or maybe Mrs. H. had decided it wouldn't be appropriate for Toosie to have a friend who was in the movies. He'd heard his mother talk about that kind of thing to Fern or Bobby when he came to do her hair, or to do Raleigh's color. Too flashy, his mother said. No sense of values. Not good enough, somehow.

So he worried about that because he was a movie star and everybody else in the world loved him, so how could he not be good enough for Toosie to call, and why didn't he?

He knew a lot of his restlessness was because the movie was only in preproduction. Everybody who was going to work on the picture was being hired, and there were conflicts to be resolved, locations to be firmed down, props to be built to be carted down to Puerto Vallarta, the script being changed for the hundredth time. Everybody else was going crazy because there was so much to do, except for him. He worked out in the gym because he always did. But Darby was so busy with the preproduction that he didn't have time to work with him, so it wasn't as if Raleigh were being tested, or anything.

The tutors were there four hours a day, and sometimes he could inveigle one of them to stay around and play chess, but other than that he had time on his hands, so he pretty much spent it being disappointed that Toosie hadn't called. Even his mother noticed that he was moody and out of sorts, but she was away a lot of the time now, raising money for the performing arts center, which was apparently a never-ending project that would take all her time until she was well into old age.

Maggie down at the public relations office had set up a couple of interviews for him to do for some important European magazines, but he was so bored and his feelings were so hurt that finally he had the chauffeur take him down to the swimming pool on top of the production company on the Sunset Strip. Well, the tourists couldn't believe their luck that they'd actually hit it on a day when Raleigh Barnes himself was the swimmer performing, and they cheered, and a big crowd gathered, and they all screamed that they loved him. Still, it was just a lot more of the same thing they always screamed, and it didn't make him feel any better.

So what he was going to do was just play with Frisky and do what he usually did, and read the Russian novelists who were next on his list, and pretty soon the movie would start, and they'd all go to Puerto Vallarta and he'd be so busy again that he'd forget all about Toosie and the invitation he hadn't meant, and these awful, unfamiliar feelings Raleigh was having that made him feel bad.

When he was in the house, he jumped every time the phone rang and ran for it, and a couple of days later, when he picked it up, there was Toosie on the other end. Toosie was all apologies and said he'd been busy with the family, and Raleigh knew how that was, didn't he, and Raleigh said sure.

"So do you still want to play?" Toosie asked.

And Raleigh said sure, and asked Toosie if he wanted to come to the estate because the courts were pretty good. Some guy named Bill Tilden who was a major, major tennis champion had played on them and said they were the best courts he'd ever seen at a private residence. That's what he'd heard from somewhere, anyway. And Toosie said why didn't Raleigh come down to his grandmother's and use her courts, and when did he want to do it, and could his mother drive him. Raleigh said his mother wasn't around and she couldn't drive anyway, but the chauffeur would bring him, and that he'd see Toosie in an hour or so, and was that okay.

"Great," said Toosie. "Come for lunch, too."

"See you," said Raleigh, and he was all smiles when he got off the phone. He called the chauffeur, and then he ran around to find his rackets and balls and his tennis whites.

Lunch was neat. Mrs. H., Toosie's mother, and a few of the other volunteers from the performing arts center who had been working out in the pool house came in. The staff had laid out a buffet on the sideboard in the dining room, and everybody took their plates outside to sit under umbrellas at the tables set up beside the swimming pool. The little sisters were there, too, looking at Raleigh with awe, and Toosie was terrific and poised, talking with the grown-ups as if he were already one of them about his time off from school, and stuff.

Raleigh was sitting next to Mrs. H. and he really liked her. She told him how she liked his spunk and courage. Said that he was an asset to the city. Added that she expected a check from him.

"I'll have to talk it over with my business manager," Raleigh said with a laugh.

It was all right on the tennis court for the first few minutes while they were just lobbing balls across the net, warming up. Toosie was dancing in place, getting loose, and the easy way he was returning the ball made it look as if he knew what he was doing. Raleigh won the toss, smoked an ace right down the center line while Toosie just stood there, his mouth open. Raleigh moved to the other side, smoked another. Toosie just got his racket on it and hit it way off to the side.

And this kid was supposed to be the captain of the tennis team? thought Raleigh, unintentionally hitting a soft one into the net. It seemed to him as if it were going to be more like mercy tennis if this was the best Toosie could do. Oh, well. It wasn't the final at Wimbledon, after all. Take it easy. Have a nice time. That would be a change right there. He served an easy one right at Toosie's feet and crouched behind the baseline as it came streaking back.

"Nice shot," he called, a thumb in the air.

"Thanks," said Toosie. "But listen, don't try to go easy on me, okay? It's insulting."

After they felt each other out for a while, got each other's rhythm, it was closer to a match. Toosie had his superior height, his greater reach, and Raleigh had his focus, his fine-tuned natural athleticism. And besides, he was still taking it easy on Toosie. He just didn't make it obvious.

The next day, Toosie came to the estate, and they played on one of the two courts there while Frisky jumped around, barking his head off, running for the ball, and Beth Carol, home for once, called them in to a perfect little lunch for Raleigh and his first friend. That was neat, he decided, looking at her in her little apron as she bustled around, getting to be a real mom, for once.

They rode their bikes, with the chauffeur trailing after them in the limousine. The people in the tour buses lumbering past them shrieked and called Raleigh's name, but he knew none of them really believed it was him. Two kids riding along on bikes? It was too out of context. No, in their minds they knew it was just some look-alike.

They worked out together in Raleigh's gym. They played chess, in which they were evenly matched. Raleigh ran a couple of his films for Toosie in the projection room, the ones that hadn't been released yet. One really neat day, they went down to the paper, watched the printing presses whirring, the roar of the machinery making conversation impossible.

It was Toosie who was the young prince of the realm here, Raleigh saw. Oh, sure, everybody was excited that he was with Raleigh Barnes. Some of the secretaries asked Raleigh for his autograph as they did the rest of the tour. But Toosie was the main attraction. His dad took the time to have lunch with them in the cafeteria, which Toosie wanted Raleigh to see, and Raleigh could feel the furtive glances in their direction. The people were excited at the thought of Raleigh and his celebrity, but more interested in the sight of the heir apparent, with his fair good looks and patrician manners.

They went for a long walk along the beach just as the day was congealing into gray dusk, the little dog rushing busily ahead of them.

"I guess you'll be running the paper someday," Raleigh said. "Gee, it goes how far back in your family? Way into the last century?"

"I guess," Toosie said, and nodded. "The paper, it's all I've ever heard. Responsibility, commitment, duty to the family, duty to the community. You know."

"Have you ever thought that you might want to do something else?" Raleigh asked, his hands in the pockets of his shorts, the sand wet between his toes.

"Not really," Toosie said. "I mean, I'm the only boy. My sisters, oh, they'll get married and maybe their husbands would be all right, but it wouldn't be the same. The family expects it of me. So probably it's the family business." He paused, looked ahead to the curve of the coast, where the blazing orange sun was just sinking over the horizon. "What about you, Raleigh?"

"I guess I *am* the family business," Raleigh said with a laugh. "Come on," he added, "let's run."

* * *

The dining room at Toosie's house was long and rectangular, with bare hardwood floors. On the antique table were curling silver candlestick holders. Another pair stood on the matching sideboard along with a cut crystal bowl filled with flowers from the garden. The curtains were tied back to show the garden, and on one wall there was a portrait of Toosie's mother in English riding clothes painted when she was still at Vassar. What was different from eating at home, though, was that every member of the family was there. Toosie's father sat at the head, and his mother was at the foot. One of the little girls sat on each side of her father. Raleigh sat on Mrs. Horton's left, and Toosie sat on her right. It was something they tried to do every night, Toosie explained, having dinner together. It was served by a housekeeper who had been with the family for years.

So this was a family dinner, Raleigh thought, watching the housekeeper pouring wine for the grown-ups, milk for all the kids. He looked at the portrait of Toosie's mom, and then at the real thing as she picked at her salad, her mind a million miles away. She had been a pretty girl, he decided, with a firm chin and intelligent brown eyes. But still, there was something about her even then that said she was somebody to be reckoned with, and that hadn't changed. And Toosie's dad, well, he was softer, somehow, but still the one who got the deferential treatment by a long shot. Raleigh could feel it in the tone of voice the little girls used when one of them answered a question, the deferential attitudes they all showed. Toosie showed it, of course. But his mom, too.

He thought of his own home, of the ebb and flow of their life there, which all depended on how busy everybody was with work. If they ate together once a week when they were in town, it was an oddity. And complicating the family picture, of course, was the presence of Darby, solemn and removed, always off with his own thoughts even though he might be sitting right there. Well, that was odd, Darby living with them. Raleigh knew that didn't fit into any family picture that he had ever heard about.

And there was the way he felt about his own father, Paul.

Oh, how he respected him. Paul was brilliant, a true original as a businessman, always able to see a bigger picture than anybody else. Do I love him? Raleigh wondered, watching the proud, loving way Mr. Horton was looking at Toosie. Well, sure I love him, Raleigh told himself. It's just different, that's all. With Mr. Horton and Toosie, well, that was a father guiding and directing his son, while with him and Paul, they were more a team.

And Toosie's mom, looking at everybody else at the table as if she were a general directing her troops, maybe that was what moms really did. Managing the kids, managing the dad. And in her case, second-in-command to Mrs. H., as Mrs. H. decided how the city itself was going to look and be over the next few decades.

It was all pretty oppressive, Raleigh decided, having everything laid out for you with never a thought about what you might want. Take Toosie, for example. What if he decided he wanted to do something else instead of going to work at the paper? They wouldn't let him, that's what would happen.

In fact, the only situation Raleigh could think of at the moment that was more oppressive than Toosie's was his own. He was the one who was really stuck. At least Toosie didn't have that responsibility. At least things would go on without him, one way or the other.

How powerful that made him feel, Raleigh thought triumphantly. Was there anything better than being right at the center of one's own universe?

So there were positive and negative aspects about every situation, Raleigh decided, glancing across the table at Toosie, who was looking very serious as he spoke in a hushed voice to his mom. His first friend. And they had, what, a couple of days left before Toosie went back to school. Then Raleigh would be off to Mexico to finally start the underwater movie. That was going to be a long shoot, too. Four months, if they were lucky. It would be a long time before he and Toosie could see each other again. I'll bet I'm really going to miss him, Raleigh thought. I hope he'll miss me, too.

CHAPTER 46

*I*t was worse than he would have ever thought possible, this missing Toosie, thought Raleigh grimly as he tossed and turned in bed while Frisky slept in a nearby chair. It was more than friendship, much, much more. He was wildly, crazy in love with Toosie, and Raleigh didn't know quite what to do, how to get comfortable with it.

Maybe it would help if he wrote Toosie a letter and told him how he felt. Told him that it was all right because Raleigh was a girl and not a boy. That his father and his father's best friend, Darby, had decided to try an experiment, to raise him according to all of this stuff that Darby believed about Sparta and Athens, and that Paul had said, sure, because he had been a psychology major and it would be interesting to see how it all worked out. And that his mother had gone along with it all because Raleigh had really seemed to like it and if Paul wanted it, that was all right with her, like everything else.

And later, when they'd gotten cold feet, had a few doubts that what they were doing was the right thing, it was too late because Raleigh was already so well known, and everybody knew that Raleigh Barnes was a boy. It wasn't the worst thing that had ever happened in town, Paul had pointed out when Raleigh had gotten old enough to notice the difference and had started to ask about it. Everybody lied.

And how would it look if they just changed? Well, they couldn't very well do that. People would feel used, cheated. Their credibility would be shot, the illusion they had created shattered. And besides, nobody would be comfortable seeing a girl do the athletic feats that Raleigh performed. They wouldn't accept it.

So it was the secret that all of them guarded with their lives.

Raleigh Barnes was a girl.

But I can't tell Toosie that, Raleigh agonized. It would blow everything into a million pieces, and I can't be responsible for that. Maybe this was why everybody was so skittish about love. Because all your defenses evaporated into thin air and you were open—skinless, even. If there was ever going to be a test of character, Raleigh thought bleakly, it was right now. It had come.

Toosie wrote, just as soon as he got back to school. It had been a rough flight, he said, with a lot of turbulence over the Rockies, and a lot of people had gotten sick. It had been a great two weeks, and he had enjoyed the time they had spent together. Even the first day back, everybody was saying how much his tennis game had improved, and he knew it would be that way the first time somebody was dumb enough to ask him to play chess.

He asked Raleigh to write to him about how she liked Mexico when he got there if he was just sitting around, waiting to be called by the director. And he said to give Frisky a pat for him.

Oh, God, Raleigh thought. This is the worst thing that's ever happened to me in my life. But really, there was only one thing to do about it, and that was not to answer Toosie's letter. To just forget they had ever met, and to put everything she was feeling about Toosie out of her mind permanently.

It was a relief when the shooting script was finally ready, and they were on the plane, on their way to Puerto Vallarta at last. Darby and Paul were happy to be going, too. As the little plane climbed into the flawless blue sky, they kept laughing and joking about getting out of town in the nick of time.

CHAPTER 47

There were only a couple of taxis in Puerto Vallarta. The pilot of the two-engine plane flew low over the dusty village with the river coursing through it, so the drivers would come out to the airport to pick them up. Raleigh felt as if she could almost reach out and touch the cross on top of the cathedral adjacent to a pretty green square with a bandstand in its center, a flock of pigeons that rose in fright at the roar of the engines. Shanties dotted the rolling hills, and along the winding cobblestone streets burros loaded with burlap bags plodded along next to men in sombreros, loose trousers, and shirts. A cobblestone road followed the curve of the bay with its waves lapping at a white beach. There was a hot sun shimmering in the white sky.

All the way down as they hopped from one small airport to the next, Raleigh had been trying to sort out how she felt about things. Images of Toosie's face playing in her mind as if they were on slow-motion film. His sudden smile on the tennis court when he won a point. His grace at losing. That slight frown of his when he was talking about the future, his responsibility to the family. He was sweet, so kind, and, face it, the first person she had really had a little time to get to know all on her own. And yes, she was crazy about him, a real first crush. But it was more than that. It was a glimpse of the future when her life as a boy would be over. And that was more frightening than throwing herself off the Empire State Building without a net.

She looked down, saw the enclave of trailers on the beach, the generators, the makeshift shelters against the blazing sun, the guys in the crew who had been driving down over the last few weeks. There must have been a hundred of them milling around down there, getting everything organized. Looming over everything was the galleon that had been built that was to be sunk a few hundred yards offshore. It had fallen off the trailer truck on the San Diego Freeway on the way down just before it got to Newport Beach. The freeway had to be closed down for an entire day, and pictures of it lying there had made the front pages of the papers, the wire services, spots showing it led all of the television news programs. Of course, Paul had been thrilled at all the exposure.

He sure didn't seem too thrilled now, she saw, looking over at him. Neither did Darby. There had been the fragments of sentences. Something about their major foreign distributor defaulting, and how they had carried him now for nearly a year on his promises that new financing was just about to drop in place. Raleigh heard Paul say that maybe they were just going to have to sell the entire library of Raleigh's films outright to raise cash. Then there was more silence, and Darby was wondering aloud if even that would be enough.

She felt a pang of alarm at that, wondered how so many millions of dollars could pour in for so many years and just not be there. "I'll think of something," Paul muttered, frowning, and he always thought of something, so it would be okay. Like always.

So here she was, wrestling with all of the agonies of her upcoming life as a girl, and there they were, wrestling with all of the financial stuff, and the preproduction on this movie had taken weeks longer than they had scheduled, and a lot of people sitting around and waiting had to be paid. And the stunts this time were so dangerous that the insurance premiums were so high they'd all had to go to court so that Paul could get approval for the mortgage on the estate he had to take out just so that they could go on with the project. Another mortgage. The third, or was it the fourth? The fourth, Raleigh decided. Anyway, that brought the amount owed on the estate to just about what it was worth, as the judge had pointed out when he had asked Paul if this was a judicious move. And the production company on the Sunset Strip was mortgaged to the hilt, too.

So there was a whole lot riding on the success of *Treasure Hunt.* Everything, in fact. Well, it had better be good, Raleigh thought morosely as the pilot started his descent into the airport, the runway a dusty strip of earth, the terminal a low structure of some sort with a corrugated iron roof.

The engines of the little plane roared, the pilot cut them, and there they were. A handful of locals sauntered across the field to help unload the luggage as Raleigh and the others jumped down from the plane.

They bumped along in the taxi along a dusty road. In front of them an ancient truck spewed black clouds of smoke. Burros trudged along with their burdens beside their solemn, weathered owners.

In the village, the shanties were jammed haphazardly against each other, open to the dusty street. Hordes of children played in the gutters. It seemed to Raleigh that nearly every woman was pregnant, with a baby in her arms, other kids clutching at her skirts. Shoots of grass pushed through the cobblestones. Ahead of them was the Oceano Hotel. It didn't look so hot, she thought, her heart sinking.

It was worse when the boy led her to her room, and pushed open the door. There was a single bed with a tired chenille spread, a table next to it with a lamp. A bureau spotted with cigarette burns. A dusty mirror over it. Heat hung in the air.

"You movie star?" the boy asked, flipping on the overhead fan, which groaned, caught, started to lazily turn.

Raleigh nodded.

"Elizabeth Taylor stay here," the boy said. "She big movie star. Richard Burton. They make movie. Sit in the bar downstairs, hold hands, and drink. You know them?"

"No," Raleigh said, handing him a dollar.

"You make movie here, too, no?" the boy asked. "You very pretty boy. You have nice time here. You see."

"Yeah, well, adios," Raleigh said firmly, walking him to the door, closing it behind him.

She wandered over to the window, pushed aside the limp curtains, and looked across the esplanade to the beach, to the sea. It was gray now, the last rays of the sun just sinking below the horizon.

Oh, God, I'm miserable, she thought, sighing. But pretty soon it'll be tomorrow and I'll go to work. And then I won't have to think about Toosie anymore. I won't have time to think about anything.

One of the assistant directors came for Raleigh when she was needed on the set. They bumped along for a while until they came to a ramshackle gate held together by rope a few miles north of town. It was another couple of miles along a lonely dirt road before they got to the beach. Then there was activity as far as Raleigh could see. Way off, Darby, a script in hand, was beckoning to her. Most of the crew had all worked together before, picture after picture, year after year. Everybody was saying hello, welcome to hell. That John Huston must have been crazy to come to this place. And they were all joking around with one another, with Raleigh. She started to feel a lot better. It was all make-believe, this business they were in. So she was make-believe, too. So maybe it didn't matter.

They worked like dogs from dawn until well into the evening. Every evening, the little plane flew the dailies back to the laboratory on Cahuenga Boulevard in Hollywood to be developed. The next evening, another little plane would return the film for them to look at, bring supplies they would need. Mail for all of them.

Raleigh loved getting the little notes that her mother sent. She wrote in a round, schoolgirl hand on pretty paper with her monogram at the top. It was mostly about how things were going with the fund-raising, of course. Now they had these little brown bags to collect money in, and Walt Disney himself had designed them, and wasn't that wonderful. Frisky was moping around the way he always did when Raleigh was on a shoot. And did Raleigh know that Fern was going to be coming down with a television crew to do a story on location. She hadn't had time to talk to Fern because she was so busy, but Bobby had told her about it when she'd gone to have her hair done. And, of course, Bobby would be coming down, too, to do Raleigh's color, and she thought it was all going to happen at the same time, so would Raleigh please say hello to both of them for her.

So Paul had gotten a commitment from Fern, too. That was a plum, even with all the journalists already swarming around the place from all over the world. Paul was really pulling out all the stops this time, building up excitement. It just had to work, Raleigh thought. Every time the mail came, all she had to do was look at Paul's face as he opened one official-looking envelope after another to see how bad things were. He got a panicked look, and those little white spots that appeared at the corners of his mouth.

"It's going to be fine," she wanted to tell him, and she really believed it, too. Things seemed to be going very well. The underwater set, once the galleon had been sunk into place and dressed to look as if it had been there a couple of hundred years, was really startling. Schools of brightly colored fish swam by, and the whole thing had an eerie, disembodied quality that Raleigh thought was really going to have the audience gasping. An ingenious, watertight room designed to house the cameras, the director of photography, his assistants, and Darby, was lowered into the water when they were shooting. Raleigh loved it all, loved to be swimming in her wet suit, her fins, her scuba diving gear.

But, wouldn't you know it, even though Puerto Vallarta

was right on the beach, they never ate fish. All they ever seemed to serve at the hotel or on the set was gray pork that tasted of nothing at all, or stringy chicken, rice, and beans. Some of the crew forgot that the water had to be boiled, and they were ill with dysentery, away from the set for days.

Once in a while, she wouldn't be needed on the set, and the chauffeur/bodyguard would drive her in one of the jeeps to neat waterfalls that cascaded into pools over black rocks. The tropical plantings everywhere were the same as what they had at home, but bigger, lusher. They drove fifty or sixty miles into the mountains, where it was cool and crisp, and where a horse standing in a pool of water looked over at them as they passed.

Raleigh's heart sank one evening when one of her letters was from Toosie. It was nice and chatty, all about school and sports, what he was reading and what he was doing.

I wrote you before, it said. But I guess you get so much mail that you never saw it. I hope you get this. Please write when you can. Yours, Toosie.

She closed her eyes and winced with the pain of missing him, wanting to be with him. It was so late when she finally fell asleep that night that somebody had to come and knock on her door to wake her in the morning. And when she got up, she felt kind of funny. Dizzy, sort of, with an awful feeling in her stomach, as if she had eaten something she shouldn't have. Paul would really go over the edge if she came down with Montezuma's Revenge, she told herself grimly as she dragged herself to the bathroom. That would be a catastrophe because she was in almost every scene that they had left to do. She felt all sticky between her legs, and when she dropped her hand to the inside of her thigh, she stared at the blood on the tips of her fingers with horror.

CHAPTER 48

*T*he television crew came first and then Fern, standing at the top of the stairs of the plane waving, with Bobby looming just behind her. She was an unlikely sight here in this dusty village in her orange sheath dress, her breasts pouring out of its low-cut neckline, her brassy blond hair piled on top of her head, her long, gold earrings that glittered in the sunlight.

"Hey, Raleigh," she called as she posed at the top of the stairs as if there were a circle of photographers surrounding her instead of just Raleigh, the driver, and a couple of people from the set who had come to pick up some supplies.

"Hi, Fern," Raleigh called back.

In an instant, Fern was right there, giving her a hug, bending to give her cheek a sloppy kiss.

"So how's everything?" Fern asked in her little, baby voice. "You still a virgin, man?"

"God, I hate little planes," Bobby breathed as the color slowly came back into his face. He was looking great, Raleigh saw, in white linen trousers, a white shirt with no collar, a gold Rolex. He wore white patent leather loafers without socks. Over his shoulder there was a pale brown leather traveling bag, hanging at exactly the right angle. He patted Raleigh's shoulder and looked at her intently.

"God, your roots," he said. "They're black."

"I know," Raleigh said. "That's why you're here, Bobby." She trotted ahead, motioning to the two of them to follow. "The vehicle's over here," she called.

"This place looks like a real dump," Fern said.

"It is." Raleigh grinned.

"What is there to do?" Bobby asked.

"Nothing," Raleigh said.

"Oh, God," said Fern, rolling her eyes.

"The people are nice," Raleigh said. "And there's the mariachi music. That's neat, too."

"So, the Oceano," Fern said, crawling into the jeep next to Raleigh. "That's where Liz and Dick fell in love. You know, man, I feel like I'm going to visit a shrine."

"You're not," Raleigh said.

"Well, they do have a bar, don't they?" Bobby asked, looking really anxious.

"Don't worry, Bobby," Raleigh assured him. "They have a bar and it serves Dewar's, Beefeater, the works."

"Thank God," said Bobby, a serene smile flickering across his face. "Because that would have been the limit, if there wasn't a bar. It really would."

This is the limit. Paul had said something like that the night Raleigh had told him she had gotten her period. She had found him in the makeshift editing room he had set up in the hotel, watching the developed dailies that had come in that evening on the little plane. For a few minutes, she had watched them with him. They looked good, she could tell it. Lots of action, great quick cuts. A sense of energy, and surprise.

"I've got to tell you something, Paul," she had said.

"Can I finish these?" he had asked, exasperation in his voice. "This is the first time I've been able to sit down the whole goddamn day."

"Now," she said.

He snapped off the projector, stopping her on the screen just as her whole face in its mask was filling the screen.

"What?" he'd asked, grinning at her.

"I got my period this morning, Paul," she said. "I thought you should know."

And he'd looked so shocked it was as if someone had shot him in the heart. She thought he was going to die right there.

"Well, you knew it was going to happen," she said crossly. "After all, I'm a girl, as you may remember, and I'm the right age."

"I don't know," he said, running his hand through his hair the way he always did when he was upset. "I just thought, well, with female athletes, sometimes they never get a period."

"Yeah, well, this one did," Raleigh said.

That's when he'd said that this was the limit on top of everything else that was going wrong. Something like that, anyway. Raleigh couldn't quite remember how it had gone. It had been a very emotional few minutes.

"I've got to think of a plan," Paul said.

"Thirteen years, and you don't have a plan?" she had asked, surprised. "You've got to be kidding. I know that most of the people in that town live in a dream world, Paul, but it never crossed my mind that you were one of them."

"Maybe you overestimate me, Raleigh," he said, flushing unhappily.

"I know you too well to overestimate you, Paul," said Raleigh. "After all, like daughter, like father."

What would Fern say if Raleigh passed on that little bit of gossip? That would sure titillate her readers, her viewing audience. They would probably get up and adjust their sets, positive they were hearing things. Bobby was gazing vaguely at the peons straggling along the road, the burros with their heavy loads. And Fern was going on and on with news from home as if she hadn't even noticed she had left it. That was Fern, all right. Very focused, and always on herself.

"So finally I told Danny to take a hike," Fern said, her arm around Raleigh's shoulders as they strolled into the shabby lobby of the Oceano Hotel.

"That's too bad," Raleigh said. "I always liked Danny."

"Yeah, well, onward and upward," Fern said, looking

around. "Shit, this place is really a dump, man. Liz really must have been in love with Dick to even put her foot in a joint like this."

"It's terrible," Bobby agreed, a dazed smile on his face. What is he on this time, Raleigh wondered, and why? Doesn't he ever wonder what his own life is really like?

"Did you notice my cameraman, the one who got off the plane first?" Fern asked. "Well, that's what I'm doing at present. Oh, I know, I know. Never shit in your own nest, and all. But what the hell, I said to myself when he came on to me. You only live once."

Once as a boy and pretty soon as a girl, Raleigh thought, staring at her, thinking about Paul's plan, how many elements it had, how everything could fall apart if just one person in the chain even breathed a word. A couple of days after Raleigh had told him her life as a boy was nearly over, Paul had flown to Los Angeles to put all of the pieces together.

On the day when they were to shoot the last of the underwater exteriors, the end of the principal photography, she would be swimming through the galleon and out the other side. And Paul would be in the speedboat waiting a couple of hundred yards away. Nobody would miss Raleigh in that short a time, and they would be on their way, up the coast to Mazatlán where the chauffeur/bodyguard would be waiting with a car. An hour's drive to a deserted airport, and a small plane would fly Raleigh and the driver into the United States, to the isolated ranch in the mountains of New Mexico that Paul had found. The driver would be there to take care of Raleigh's needs until her hair grew longer and returned to her natural color. Then she could come back to Beverly Hills, a young niece of Beth Carol's who had come to live with them.

"Golly, Paul." Raleigh frowned. "I don't know. My driver, well, okay. But a little plane, a pilot . . ."

"Well, what do you want?" Paul flared. "I can't fly a plane, for God's sake. I don't know how. I have to be here anyway, to manage the hysteria, the press."

"Maybe if my driver and I just drive all the way to the

ranch," Raleigh suggested. "Then it's just the two of us. How about that?"

"What about the border?" Paul demanded, pacing now, looking really worried.

"I'll wear a scarf over my hair, girl's clothes," Raleigh said. "All they ever ask you is where you were born. And they won't be looking for me there."

"Yeah, yeah," Paul said. "That might work. It'll save a couple of steps, too."

"I don't want Mom to be worried," Raleigh said.

"Oh, I'll tell her," Paul said. "Of course I'll tell her."

"And I want Frisky with me at the ranch."

"Fine."

"And books, lots of books. And my gym equipment."

"This is going to save our lives, kid," Paul said, nodding. "You don't know how close we've come to losing everything."

"I've picked up a little," Raleigh said. "When you've been talking to Darby."

"Yeah, well, the one thing I didn't want to lose control over was your library," Paul said. "The rest I couldn't care less about, even the house. But the insurance money will take care of everything, and then some. And it's double indemnity, too."

"Oh, golly," Raleigh said, dismayed. "I hadn't even thought about that. That's fraud."

"Okay, it's fraud," Paul said. "Do you have any other suggestions?"

And, of course, she didn't have any other suggestions. There just wasn't anything else for them to do. And that was why he kept putting Fern's location story off, and putting it off until the last minute. So she and her crew would be right on the spot when Raleigh Barnes was lost forever at sea.

When the luggage finally turned up at the hotel, there was a surprise picnic basket from Beth Carol and a note. Raleigh sat in her room reading it, listening to the groans and screams from Fern's room next door. Well, that meant her cameraman must have turned up, too, Raleigh decided. What did it mean, all of that screaming that Fern was doing? Did it hurt, what he was doing to her? But she must have liked it or she wouldn't have been doing it. I'm not going to like this, Raleigh thought gloomily. Being a girl didn't seem as if it had much going for it as far as she could see. She turned up the staticy radio, tried to block out the sounds next door. Munched on an apple from the picnic basket as she read her mom's note.

The big news was that Toosie's mom was going to law school.

> Of course, she would prefer to go somewhere with real prestige like Harvard [Beth Carol wrote], but she doesn't want to be away from Roger and the children. Maybe that's why they don't take many girls, because what we care about the most are our families. Anyway, they don't take many girls at USC, either, where Bitsy is going, but because of who she is, there wasn't any problem getting in.
>
> Personally, I can't see it. After all, she has everything. A wonderful husband and children, the best social position in town next to her mother-in-law, a beautiful home, and the wonderful work she does as a volunteer for the performing arts center. You'd think that would be enough for anybody. And I think her family life is going to suffer, even though she says she intends to see that it doesn't make any difference. But you can't just go to law school in a casual way. You've got to give it your all. That's why I think she's making a mistake.

At the bottom, she had drawn a paw print and added the words, Frisky sends his love, and can't wait for you to come home.

Raleigh sighed, tossing the note onto a table. It was all so normal, all so nice. She could just see her mother's sweet, shy smile. Beth Carol was so anxious to do the right thing, so eager to please. How Raleigh wished she were at home with her, that what lay ahead didn't have to be done. And, of course, it wasn't the stunt that was worrying her. It was afterward, when she started her life as a girl. That scared her so much that she could hardly bear to think about it.

CHAPTER 49

$\mathcal{E}$ven as Raleigh rose and broke the surface of the water, she could make out the speedboat a couple of hundred feet away. It was rocking a bit, barely visible in the moonless night. Swiftly she swam toward it, grabbed the rope ladder hanging over its side, and pulled herself on board.

Paul gave a start when he saw her step onto the deck.

"How did it go?" he asked.

"Like a charm," she said cockily.

"There's coffee in that Thermos over there," he said. "We'd better get going."

The roar of the engines shattered the night.

Raleigh detached her oxygen tank, shook off her swim fins, wiped her face, and toweled her blond hair. It was too noisy for them to be able to talk. Raleigh sat at the stern, watched Paul's back as he stood at the wheel, looked at the foaming tail trailing after them. It was an hour or so before Paul cut the engines and dropped the anchor over the side.

"Okay," he said. "It's time."

Raleigh peered into the night, but didn't see anything except water all around them. She had the craziest idea that all this time they had been heading out to the open sea, but that was impossible. The shoreline had to be there somewhere. It was just that it was such a dark night. She leaned down to pull on her swim fins, felt a stab of foreboding at a sound above her. She looked up and saw Paul, looming over her, something held high in both hands. A rock.

Why, he's going to kill me, she thought, amazed. He never loved me at all.

She tried to slip away from him, dive over the side. Anything. But it was no use. Everything went black, and then there was nothing.

CHAPTER 50

*B*eth Carol knew something was wrong when the doorbell rang at seven o'clock in the morning. When she opened the door, she saw that it was Maggie from the public relations office. But Bitsy was there, too, and so was Mary Lou, and that didn't make any sense. That those three girls should be there together.

"It's Raleigh," she said.

"Yes," said Bitsy as she moved toward Beth Carol and took her in her arms.

Fern and Bobby turned up that evening, and Beth Carol didn't quite know what to do about explaining Fern to her new girlfriends, who were still there. Oh, they knew who Fern was, she decided. They'd probably just think she was there as a television personality wanting a story. Not as a friend, because it would never cross their minds that somebody as proper as Beth Carol could ever have a friend as vulgar as Fern. And Bobby was her hairdresser. The society girls must have hairdressers, although sometimes she wondered about that. But they'd understand Bobby.

The television set was on pretty much all the time, with the latest film the news teams had put together. They rehashed all of that old kidnapping stuff, of course. And there were regrets from the mayor, interviews with Raleigh's co-stars. The usual.

She saw Paul when he arrived at the airport, surrounded by all of these reporters. His voice was all choked when he said that he held himself personally responsible for the accident. And then he was so choked up that he couldn't go on, and he just bowed his head and hurried on down the aisle. So he'd be along in a while, she thought indifferently. At most it was half an hour from the airport.

Frisky was upset by all the excitement, everybody coming and going. The doorbell ringing incessantly. Beth Carol took him onto her lap, felt him quivering as she put her arms around him.

The funny thing was that none of it seemed real to her. Maybe that was because a doctor came by and was giving her shots of a really strong tranquilizer. And, after all, they still hadn't found Raleigh, so it wasn't as if anything was final. But according to what they were saying on television, there wasn't much hope. It had been a couple of days and the ocean down there off Puerto Vallarta was really kicking up. The surf had never been so high, they said. It was practically like a continual tidal wave.

Another funny thing happened. Darby came back and moved out. Just like that. It was the day Beth Carol had been waiting for nearly as long as she could remember, and it had finally happened. Paul didn't even mention it. He was just so worried about how she was feeling. All sweet and solicitous, and looking so stricken and guilty, even though he hadn't even been on the set the night it had happened, according to what he said and what they said on television.

Everybody was calling about when the memorial service was going to be. The mayor's office and everyone, because all of the flags in the city had been flying at half-mast out of respect, but that couldn't go on forever. They had to get on with things.

Fine, she thought. Whatever.

Bobby came by the morning of the memorial service to do her hair, and Fern came by, too. So they all went together, in the Bentley. It was a beautiful day, of course. It always was. There were so many fans who had turned up that they could hardly get through in the Bentley. The police controlling traf-

fic had to clear the way for them. Paul was holding her elbow
tightly as they walked up the steps of the church in Beverly
Hills. It was strange, she thought, that so many people could
make so little noise. Of course, people came up to her in the
front pew to offer their condolences, even Diana Kendall, who
looked as dowdy as she had that other time, and who was still
in town, it seemed. Everybody important in the world had
sent flowers, and the church was jammed with a lot of important people, too. The only surprise was a contingent of Boy
Scouts, sitting way up front. But then Beth Carol remembered
that Raleigh had been made an honorary Boy Scout as part of
the promotion of some movie. Bitsy's son, Toosie, had flown
in, and he was so sweet and on the verge of tears. He'd gotten
so tall in such a short time that Beth Carol hardly recognized
him. Or maybe that was just the tranquilizers, the way she was
feeling, as if she were underwater, too.

The eulogies were very nice, very inspiring. A lot of stuff
about courage, the youth of America. Setting an example of
the best kind. That sort of thing.

Finally it was over, and it all looked very nice that night
on television.

You've got to keep busy, that was what everybody told her.
So a couple of days later, she made herself get up, get dressed,
go to the office where she worked with the other volunteers.
All the girls were so nice, so sweet. And, yes, so brisk, too.
Trying to distract her. It was dear of them. It really was.

"The worst thing in the world is to lose a child," someone murmured.

"Yes," Beth Carol said, but she didn't really mean it. Yes, it
was awful to lose a child. But to lose *the* child, that was worse.

So a few days passed, and she kept showing up, but then
one day it wasn't all right anymore. It wasn't that she felt dizzy,
exactly, when she tried to get out of bed, but it was something.
Strange. She just couldn't. In fact, she could hardly bring herself to even make the call to say she wouldn't be there.

It was an odd sort of day. For a few minutes she would feel
pretty good, almost her old self, considering the circumstances. And then all her nerves would start to scream, and she

would feel as if she were going to jump out of her skin. And then she'd feel better, and it just went on like that.

When the doctor called to see how she was feeling, the ringing of the phone was so jangling, so upsetting to her, that she just wanted to scream at him to leave her alone.

"I'm feeling very strange," she said.

"Well, that's natural," he said, and he told her to increase her medication.

That made her feel even worse, so then he suggested she cut it in half. That didn't make her feel any better, either. She just sat around, automatically petting Raleigh's little dog. But not thinking about Raleigh. Not really. Not thinking about anything. And not sleeping at night, and not eating, either. I can't go on this way, she told herself. I have to try.

The next morning, she forced herself to get up. Take a shower, and get dressed. She even put on a little makeup. It was all a terrible effort, as if she were pushing a boulder up a steep hill, and she was panting when she finished, but she had done it. She called on all her strength and made herself a real breakfast. Scrambled eggs, bacon, toast. A glass of orange juice. But it was no use. Even the feel of the food in her mouth made her sick.

What she did was sit with Frisky and watch television all day. Sometimes she was so weary that she felt her eyelids closing—slept, even, for a few minutes at a time. But that was the worst of all, because she would have her water dreams again. Not about Raleigh. The ones she had had when she was a little girl, the ones about the lake back home, all black and terrifying and, yes, enticing, too. At four o'clock in the afternoon, she would start to drink. And that helped, because it obliterated everything, and she didn't have to try to think. She couldn't anyway, because when she tried, it was as if all of her thoughts were just these bits of smoke that didn't have any meaning.

"There are a lot of business matters to be attended to," Paul kept saying to her. "I'll need your signature, Beth Carol. You've got to pull yourself together."

"Oh, Paul," she would say. "I'm not up to it yet. I'm sorry. Maybe tomorrow, okay?"

"Are you eating?" he would ask.

"Of course I'm eating."

"You've got to start eating, Beth Carol," he would say.

"I know."

When enough time had passed, it would be better, she kept telling herself. Distance, that's what would do it. But it was three months and it was worse. Frisky was pining away, too. His eyes were dull, and so was his coat. She brushed him for hours as she watched television. The cooking shows she had always liked. Game shows. The soap operas that were on every network from twelve noon until three o'clock. They were just little figures moving around on the screen and the plots were so complicated that she couldn't follow them.

Paul was there sometimes, but he was out of the house a lot, overseeing the postproduction on the movie, which was bound to make a fortune since it was Raleigh's last one. The only other person she saw was Bobby, who turned up every week to do her hair even though she had told him not to bother. That she didn't want him to come. But he did anyway, and he whispered the current gossip to her, which she didn't even hear, and by the time he was through, her nerves were popping through her skin and she was so exhausted that she wanted to scream.

People called all the time. Her girlfriends. Fern. Even that Diana Kendall, who asked her if Beth Carol wanted her to drop by. Beth Carol thought about that, thought about the fact that Diana had lost her entire family and that maybe it would be a comfort to see her. That Diana could understand what she was going through. But finally she decided she didn't care if anybody understood what she was going through, or if they didn't. Besides, that Diana Kendall looked like a whiner if she'd ever seen one and the last thing Beth Carol wanted to do was listen to somebody whine and feel sorry for herself. She had her own problems, after all.

After that, she stopped answering the phone.

One day, though, it rang and rang until she thought she would lose her mind. Fifteen rings, twenty. And then it would stop for a while and start again.

Angrily she grabbed the receiver, thought about flinging it against the wall.

"Hello," she said at last.

"Beth Carol? This is Roger Horton."

She waited, started to pant with anxiety into the receiver.

"I've been wondering how you are," he said. "We all have. Bitsy says she hasn't been able to reach you, that nobody has."

Her heart started to jump around in her chest, and she wondered if it meant anything. A heart attack, for example.

"Beth Carol?" he said again, really worried now. She could hear it in his voice.

"Yes," she said.

"Is there anything I can do for you?" he asked.

"Well, no, Roger," she managed. "I mean, I haven't been feeling very well. I can't seem to concentrate on anything. I think it's natural, though. I mean, it's almost as if it's nature's way of protecting me. You know, if I can't think about anything at all, then I can't think about it. About what happened, I mean."

"Maybe if you saw someone," he said. "Maybe if you saw a—"

"Oh, I have a doctor," she said with a weak laugh. "He's one of the best in Beverly Hills."

"Well, what does he say?" asked Roger.

"Well, you know, Roger, I don't know what he says," Beth Carol murmured, frowning. "I mean, it's so hard for me to concentrate, as I told you. It's going to take time, though. It always does. Something like that. And, meantime, I'm just going to have to try to be strong."

"Well, we've all been concerned—" he began.

"It was sweet of you to call personally, Roger," she said. "I mean, I know how busy you are with the paper, and everything. So I appreciate your taking the time. I really do. And give Bitsy my love, will you? And tell her I'm looking forward to seeing her again. Really."

"Beth Carol," he said, his voice dropping to a whisper. "I remember when we met before, all those years ago. When you were Jane, and you used to come to my hotel room."

"I don't know what you're talking about, Roger," she said primly. "You must have me mixed up with someone else."

"I was so excited every time I was going to see you," he said. "It was as if I were alive for the first time."

"Roger . . ."

"I want to be your friend, Beth Carol," he said. "I know you need one, and I'm there for you."

"Well, that's sweet of you, Roger. It really is," she said desperately. "And, of course, you are my friend. And Bitsy, too. She's been wonderful through all of this. So support-ive, and I'm so grateful."

"Why don't we go for a drive this afternoon?" he said. "You don't even have to speak, Beth Carol. We can drive down to Newport Beach. How about that? Then we'll just turn around and come back. You'll just have to sit there. It'll be a change of scene for you."

"Oh, I can't," she blurted, hysteria in her words. "I mean, I told you—"

"Why not?" he asked gently. "What will happen?"

"Well, I don't know," she said, trying to collect her thoughts. Trying to find the words to tell him that she didn't want to be anywhere else, even though she didn't want to be at home, either. But she couldn't say that. It would make her sound as if she'd really gone around the bend.

"Well, let's give it a try," he said cheerfully. "If you're uncomfortable, we'll just turn around and come back. I'll be there to pick you up around two o'clock. That's just about three hours from now. So you put on your prettiest dress, and I'll see you then."

"Roger, this isn't necessary," she said in a tired voice. "I'm fine, really."

"Well, you're not, you know," he said. "But you will be. All you have to do is let me be your friend."

"All right," she said. "I'll try."

CHAPTER 51

$\mathscr{R}$aleigh's eyes fluttered open, saw a fan on the ceiling slowly turning. It looked as if it were a mile away. It was hot and very humid and somewhere in the distance thunder was crashing around. Or maybe it was just sound effects for a stunt. She seemed to be lying in a narrow bed in a long, dim room with a couple of other beds, some medical stuff for sterilizing up at the front where there didn't seem to be a wall. It was just green, sort of jungly or something.

So what is this? she asked herself, frowning as she closed her eyes again. A movie, maybe, or a dream? She tried to sort out her thoughts.

"You're awake," said a voice.

Raleigh looked up and tried to focus on the girl who stood there. She had dark hair, high cheekbones. She was tall and slim and wore a loose, cotton dress.

"Where am I?" Raleigh whispered. "How did I get here?"

"Some fishermen found you on a piece of flotsam," the girl said. "You were pretty much out of it, almost gone. They brought you here because I'm a doctor. Ann Vincent is my name."

Raleigh frowned, closed her eyes. Opened them again.

"You had a nasty blow to the head," Ann said. "You've been in and out of consciousness for days, mostly out. I'm glad you're feeling better, I really am. You've been a very sick girl."

Raleigh squinted up at her, feeling kind of annoyed. She wasn't supposed to know that, this stranger. That she was a girl. After all of the careful planning and everything, and now, just like that, you've been a very sick girl. Boy, this was going to ruin everything, she thought woozily.

"What's your name?" asked Ann, holding Raleigh's wrist now, counting her pulse or something.

Raleigh Barnes, she wanted to say, but of course she couldn't say that because of the plan, the plan that she couldn't remember just now. This girl who said she was a doctor was fading in and out, too. And how could that be, anyway? Girls weren't doctors. Everybody knew that. She tried to speak, managed a sigh.

"We have a shortwave radio," Ann said. "We didn't pick up anything about a boat going down anywhere. What happened? Did you fall overboard?"

"I don't remember," Raleigh said, shaking her head.

"Well, we can talk about it later," Ann said, patting her shoulder. "You've had a bad concussion. Sometimes it takes a while for everything to come back."

Raleigh closed her eyes, concentrating hard now. It seemed to her they were shooting a scene and that it was underwater. Was she supposed to meet somebody? But that didn't make any sense. Who would it be, after all? Neptune? Davey Jones?

"Where is this?" Raleigh asked, fighting to keep her eyes open. Boy, she hated feeling like this. All weak and out of control.

"We're in Mexico, about halfway between Puerto Vallarta and Acapulco," Ann said. "We're pretty isolated, though. The only way to get here is by boat."

"No, no," Raleigh said, shaking her head. "That's the wrong way."

"What's the wrong way?" Ann prompted.

"I don't know," Raleigh admitted, hating it that she didn't know. Trying, trying to clutch at whatever that meant.

"What's the last thing you remember?" Ann asked.

"I was swimming," Raleigh said after a couple of minutes.

"Well, that's a start," Ann said with a quick smile. "I'll go tell the others you're all right. Everybody has been so worried."

"Yes, they're always worried," Raleigh muttered. "Like the time I broke my wrist. It was six weeks. Paul, the insurance company . . . everybody was worried."

"Who's Paul?" asked Ann, her eyes bright. "Is he a friend of yours?"

Well, that was a dumb question, Raleigh thought groggily. Everybody knew Paul was her father, so of course he was much more than a friend of hers. But there was something that she couldn't quite grasp, that tickled the corners of her mind, hinted that maybe she'd been wrong about that.

"I think I'll take a nap now," Raleigh said, feeling herself drifting off.

"Yes, that's a good idea," Ann said. "You sleep. And don't worry about anything. You're going to be all right. You made it."

They came later, the others, when it was dusk and Raleigh was awake again. Eleanor Fisk, the woman's name was, and Charles Fisk. That was her husband. And she was an important philosopher of some kind. Yes, Raleigh had heard of her, read about her. She was bone thin in her colorful caftan, with blue eyes that were quite beautiful and bright with intelligence. She had a regal head, silver hair piled on top of it. She was seventy, Raleigh thought, maybe even older. Raleigh tried to smile at her.

And Charles, he was, what, maybe twenty years younger than she was. A handsome man with thick, white hair curling down the back of his neck, a lean, aristocratic face, a great tan.

And there were a lot of other people, too. Younger. The ages of, say, college students, grad students. And Raleigh was really feeling anxious about it all and wondering what all of them were doing here in the middle of nowhere. Ann explained it to her later, when the others went off to have dinner, when she was sitting with Raleigh so Raleigh wouldn't be scared. Not that she ever would be scared, but there wasn't any reason to make a big issue of it, to insist that Ann go eat with the others.

So what they were, the younger ones, were students who came from all over the world to help Eleanor and Charles with their research for the history of philosophy, the books they were writing. So in a way they were interns and in a way they weren't. They didn't get college credits for the time they put in here, but what they did get was an enormous amount of prestige, which counted for even more. To be picked to come by Eleanor Fisk, that was really something, Ann said. It could virtually jump-start your career.

"What about him, the husband?" asked Raleigh, just making conversation now, her head throbbing like crazy all of a sudden.

"It's a wonderful love story," Ann said with a smile. "He was a grad student in one of her seminars at the University of Chicago, and he was absolutely dazzled by her. Well, she was flattered because he was so smart, and handsome, too, and after a while they fell in love. He comes from Illinois, from Decatur. An old family there that makes a line of furniture. They were furious because of the age difference, and all. And then there was her family. They come from Arcadia in Southern California, and they have something to do with that racetrack there. Santa Anita. And they were furious, too, because they thought it was unseemly. And there was such a scandal on campus, but Eleanor and Charles didn't care. They got married anyway, and here they are. Eleanor even gave him cowriting credit on her last book."

And then Ann went on to say that there was always a doctor there because they were so isolated. And that it was

going to be good for her own career to have put in a year
down here. That she really loved it. When her year was up
she'd go back to the States to start her residency. At Mass
General.

"I thought you were kidding me," Raleigh said. "When
you said you were a doctor. I've never met a girl who was a
doctor."

"Well, why shouldn't I be a doctor?" Ann asked.

"I guess there isn't any reason," Raleigh said, frowning
again, wishing that her head would stop doing whatever it
was doing.

"Now, what about you?" Ann asked, leaning toward her.
"Can you remember anything at all?"

Most of it, Raleigh wanted to tell her. All of the movies,
the stardom, the entourage that went everywhere with her.
The fans grasping at her, hoping that a little secondhand
stardust would rub off on them. The mansion and all the
other perks. Her little dog. Frisky, she remembered after a
couple of seconds. That was his name. And he always
moped around when she was away working, but there
wasn't anything she could do to make it all right for him
now. After all, she couldn't very well send him a postcard
saying she would be back soon.

"Are you all right?" Ann asked.

"I'm fine," Raleigh murmured, almost able to taste the
anxiety welling up in her. Realizing that she wasn't going to
be back soon, but that it would be all right because Frisky
was going to be with her somewhere. Because that was the
plan. It would come back to her. It had to come back to
her.

"We're going to have to call you something," said Ann
with a little laugh. "Until your memory comes back, that is."

Raleigh nodded miserably.

"Now, what's the first name that comes to mind?" she
asked brightly.

"Leigh," said Raleigh.

"Do you think that's significant?" asked Ann. "Do you
think that might really be your name?"

"No," said Raleigh, shaking her head, smiling to herself as she thought about how in one of her movies she had had amnesia and couldn't remember anything, and how this was kind of just the opposite. Now she could remember nearly everything but she just couldn't talk about it, couldn't just come out and say that she was Raleigh Barnes, movie star, and get on with things. She couldn't because everything was different now.

"If only we could tell your family that you're all right," Ann seemed to be saying as Raleigh drifted off to sleep again. Her dreams were fragmented, confused. She saw her mother's soft, frightened face. Toosie, across from her on the tennis court. She remembered her feelings as she eased up on him, even let him win, the care she took so he wouldn't know she was doing it. Mercy tennis, the first time. And the last, she thought, awake for a second. That was what love did to you. It made you compromise your values. Better not to do it if it made you vulnerable, weak.

And then she was swimming again with slow, strong motions. On her way to meet Paul, to put the plan into effect, the plan that would make everything all right for all of them.

Paul, that was it. She was going to meet Paul. But something must have gone wrong or she wouldn't be here. And how could she reach him? Tell him she was all right? She moaned, flailed around, trying to sit up. Gentle hands pushed her back on the pillow.

"You have to be very still," said Ann in a low voice. "I'll give you something so you can sleep."

"No," said Raleigh.

After a few days, Raleigh's thoughts were still pretty much fragmented, elusive. She was eating, though, getting back her strength. Still sleeping most of the time, and when she was awake, Ann would be there, or one of the servants. There must have been a dozen of them around the place. There were a lot of their kids, too. They would pop their heads in to look at her and, late in the afternoon when it wasn't quite so hot, Raleigh could hear their squeals of laughter as they played outside.

It was in the middle of the night, though, when it was cool, the sounds of crickets singing, a dog barking somewhere, that Raleigh felt her thoughts coming together. Realized what her position was. One minute she was the most famous child actor in the world, and the next she was nobody. Literally. Just a girl who had been rescued from the sea.

And oh, how she hated feeling the way she did. She had no strength to speak of, no energy. A couple of days later, she sat up on the bed, nearly fell back as her head swam. Her legs felt like water as she tried to stand, and she would have fallen flat on her face without the quick hands of the dark, silent woman who had been sitting with her. The woman held her as she showered under the sputtering drops of water warmed by the sun. Looking in the mirror, she saw that a chunk of her hair had been chopped off. Gingerly, she touched the raw, ugly wound. Thought of Paul and wondered why. She barely made it back to the bed, sat on its edge, panting, while the woman helped her into a loose cotton dress. It really felt strange, the dress. She felt so exposed in it. Like an imposter, too, as if she were in drag. Barefoot and shaky, she stepped out of the infirmary and looked around.

The compound was a series of low, adobe buildings open to the banana trees, the palms, the tropical flowers. A couple of horses stood looking at her over a ramshackle fence. A rooster crowed, and three or four kids crouched over some game they were playing looked up at her with curious dark eyes. She walked carefully toward the sound of laughter a couple of hundred yards away. There was music, too. Mozart. The sun blazed down on her, and the air was humid.

There they all were, Raleigh saw, having lunch at little tables under a *palapa,* it's palm-frond roof shading them from the sun. Fans sat on the tiled floor, and servants scurried around. Everybody clapped and cheered when they saw her standing there. One of the boys—the one from Sweden, she thought—jumped up and helped her into his chair. Somebody brought her a plate heaped with rice, beans, chicken covered in some sort of a chocolate sauce. A bottle of Coca-Cola. And everybody was asking her how she felt. It was sort of like old times, being the center of everything, except for the look in their eyes. Pity, concern. She winced, turned away, as if she had been slapped.

I'll show all of you, she vowed as she thrust back her shoulders, kept murmuring that she felt great. Really. She dribbled Coca-Cola into a glass of ice, tasted it. It was the best thing she'd ever tasted in her life.

Eleanor Fisk, of course, was at the head of one of the tables, laughing heartily at something the boy on her right had just said. She was chain-smoking, Raleigh saw, taking a bite of something, then a drag. And Charles. Every time Charles looked over at his wife, Raleigh got the feeling he still couldn't believe his good fortune, that she had actually married him, even taken his name.

Some English boy was flirting with Ann, and she was being all demure and everything, batting her eyelashes. Strange, Raleigh though with a frown, you'd think someone who could get to be a doctor would be above all that. Why, it was just like looking at her mother when she was putting on that act she had. Unconsciously, Raleigh's lip curled with contempt, with a twinge of the pity she always felt for the weak.

Somebody changed the record and it was Scarlatti this time, something she always played at home. She swallowed hard, thinking about it. Images of her mother, her little dog, Darby, Paul, floated through her mind. And there was something that bothered her about Paul, even more than the rest of them who didn't know she was okay, who must be beside themselves by now. And there wasn't a thing she could do about it. Not for the moment, anyway.

She toyed with her lunch, brooding and miserable.

CHAPTER 52

*R*aleigh wandered around the compound a couple of days later wearing a loose shirt, her fists jammed into the pockets of a pair of loose, white trousers, looking around, trying to get a sense of the order of things here. The research assistants and the swarms of servants that it took to run the place lived in the clusters of adobe houses here and there.

There were a couple of libraries with shelves and shelves of books in every language, long tables where the research assistants worked on yellow pads or old typewriters dating back to the twenties. Fans powered by the generator whirred incessantly and there were silent Mexican women sweeping up the fine sand that always seemed to cover the tile floors.

A sanctuary to get some work done. That was why they had come here, Eleanor had told Raleigh during one of the long conversations they always seemed to be having these days. To get away from the infighting at the University of Chicago, the eternal tea parties. The visiting scholars who turned up every hour on the hour, it seemed.

They'd been coming to Mexico for years, she and Charles, whenever they had a few weeks. And then Charles had inherited a little money, and they had been so gleeful, Eleanor said, her eyes sparkling, and they had said to each other that it was the time to go. That they could do it now. And so they had, but it hadn't helped all that much. First, a couple of grad students had volunteered as research assistants. Then the thinkers of the world had started to arrive on their own holidays. After a while, being asked to the compound developed its own cachet, and they were rather back where they had been.

The questions came gradually, gently, about who Raleigh might be and where she had come from. Eleanor would try to help. And Charles. Ann. Raleigh cringed under their pained sympathy, hating it, hating them for feeling sorry for her.

Give it a rest, she wanted to snap, as she wondered how she was going to get out of here and where she would go when she did. But she didn't have any way to think about it yet, because she still couldn't remember everything. The end of it, the part just before this.

Raleigh stood in the doorway of the main house, feeling a little dizzy now. There were vivid Mexican rugs on the tiled floor. Chairs with leather seats and backs. Primitive art and tribal masks decorated the walls. There were a couple of good English antiques that Eleanor had inherited from her mother. A few handsome modern pieces, a couple of Knoll chairs, a chunky glass table that had moved with the Fisks over Eleanor's long career. There was even a Brancusi sculpture.

The Mexican woman sweeping away the film of sand covering the floor glanced up at Raleigh as she strolled past on the way to the room she had been given there, one of the big ones usually reserved for world-renowned scholars, former ambassadors, writers.

Raleigh dropped onto the bed, put her hands behind her head, closed her eyes tight, and tried again to reconstruct how it had gone. Yes, she had been swimming. She was sure of that. But after that everything was a blank. Outside, great globs of hot rain splattered the white beach and everything was still.

Finally something was happening in this godforsaken place, Raleigh saw the next morning. Down at the corral, horses were being saddled and people were sort of milling around, watching them. Ann was in the middle of it all, giving orders.

"What's going on?" Raleigh asked.

"I'm going up into the mountains to one of the villages there," Ann said. "I'm going to give the kids their shots."

"Can I come?" Raleigh asked.

"Do you know how to ride?" Ann asked, frowning.

"Sure," Raleigh said.

And that felt neat, to be on top of a horse again, to savor its smell, the smell of the saddle beneath her, the reins in her hands as they climbed into the mountains, picking their way through the lush growth along the narrow dirt path. It was a village of shacks and *palapas* alongside a river fed by a rainbow-painted waterfall. Raleigh looked at the women watching them, the children with their frightened eyes as Ann set up her stuff.

And Ann seemed so competent now, so in her element, murmuring words of encouragement to the kids as she deftly inoculated them. Patted a shoulder and said in perfect Spanish how brave one of them was. Soothed an indignant baby who started to scream. And later, all the women were crowding around her, thanking her. Insisting that they had to give her lunch, that they had been waiting for her, preparing a fiesta.

Why are they making such a fuss about her? Raleigh asked herself crossly. Don't they know who I am? But of course they didn't know who she was, she thought with a sinking feeling. Nobody would ever know who she was again because she wasn't that person anymore. Wasn't Raleigh Barnes, movie star. She wasn't even a boy, for God's sake. She didn't even have a name, and worse, she was just a girl.

Well, she'd show them, she thought blindly, running over to where she'd tethered her horse, doing a circus jump onto its back. She grabbed the reins in her hands, pulled it into a canter, kicked it into a run, tore through the village as fast as she could make it go. Ran and ran until the jungle was so thick and the path so narrow again that she had to slow down. Picked her way down the mountain until there was some open space again. Ran and ran along the sand right at the edge of the sea until she realized her horse was getting tired and pulled him up. It was night now, with a full moon. When she got back to the compound, everything was dark, everybody asleep. She slipped into bed, a smile on her face. Slept without dreaming for the first time.

"We should have a little chat about the rules here," Eleanor said pleasantly the next morning at the breakfast table on the terrace overlooking the sea.

"Fine," Raleigh said.

"Ann said you left by yourself yesterday afternoon.".

Ann talks too much, Raleigh thought scornfully, keeping her expression interested as she looked at Eleanor.

"You just can't do that, dear," Eleanor said softly. "Ann was beside herself with worry. You were her responsibility. What if something had happened to you?"

"Well, nothing did," Raleigh said stubbornly.

"That isn't the point," Eleanor said. "Do you see?"

"No," said Raleigh.

"You're a child," Eleanor said. "You're just a little girl."

Raleigh's head jerked.

"What's the matter?" Eleanor asked, alarmed.

"I'm not," Raleigh muttered.

"Well, please don't do it again," Eleanor said, a puzzled look on her face. "We have to have a little consideration for others, you know."

"I want to leave here," Raleigh said.

"But where will you go?" Eleanor asked.

"I don't know," Raleigh said, shaking her head.

Raleigh was on the dock when the boat pulled in, and she helped to moor it as it rocked on the water. The servants unloaded cases of books, back copies of the *New York Times*, newsmagazines, stacks of mail. A couple of guests had arrived, too. A British psychoanalyst, and a historian from Cornell. Everybody was crowding around, saying hello, grabbing for their letters. The newspapers, the magazines.

Raleigh read about her death, the elaborate memorial

service at the fashionable church in Beverly Hills. Her stomach lurched at the picture of her mother's face, numb with shock and disbelief. And there was Paul next to her mother, holding her arm, a solicitious smile on his face. The picture didn't look right to her somehow, Raleigh realized, frowning. She looked again at Paul's face. Felt a stab of something. Fear? No, come on, she told herself as she glanced around the *palapa* at the others who had come drifting in, reading their letters. The boy from that writer's workshop at the University of Iowa had gotten a big box of oatmeal cookies from home that he was passing around. And now some of them were grabbing at the newspapers, the magazines, greedy for news.

Any second now, she thought with a slight smile, one of them would look up from the cover photographs of Raleigh Barnes, look over at her, compare the two. She sat there, watching them, waiting for the first look of incredulity that was sure to come. Why, it's the same person, one of them would be thinking. That girl is Raleigh Barnes. And then they would all realize it, and everything would be back in place again.

But it didn't happen, she saw with wonder. Nobody got it. Raleigh Barnes was a boy, she was a girl. There just couldn't be any connection.

Raleigh took a swig of Coke from the bottle, opened *Life* to its centerfold, felt a jolt of recognition. It was a gorgeous underwater shot from the film she had been making, and there she was, swimming, just the way she thought she had been. And she was at the gaping hole in the galleon they'd hauled all the way down from Los Angeles. The galleon looked great, as if it had been sitting there for a couple of centuries, just the way it was supposed to look.

She closed her eyes, started where she was in the picture and went on from there. Yes, she swam right into the galleon, out the other side. That had been the plan. She remembered now. She would be picked up, disappear for a few months. Paul was the one. He would be waiting there for her in a speedboat.

She saw him, looming over her. Saw the rock in his hand. Raleigh clutched the side of the chair as she felt her shock again, her terror.

"Oh, my God," she whispered to herself. "So that was it."

She started at a hand on her shoulder. Ann's hand.

"You went dead white," Ann said solicitously. "Are you all right?"

"I've never been better," Raleigh said coldly, shaking off Ann's touch.

She rode that night for hours along the beach, barely aware of where she was. Paul, her own father, trying to kill her. Nearly succeeding, too. It was so incredible that she thought she had to be wrong. That it was just the concussion, playing tricks with her mind. But again and again, the same scene played in her mind. Paul, standing above her, the rock held over his head. Her own terror and disbelief.

And who else was involved? she wondered as she urged the horse forward, felt the cool air on her face. Darby? Well, sure. And what about her mother?

Raleigh sighed as she thought of the way her mother always looked at Paul. That hopeful, frightened look, her eagerness to please him. So, yes, she thought. Her mother would agree to anything if it pleased Paul.

It was nearly dawn, a rooster already crowing as they walked slowly toward the compound. So where does this leave me? she asked herself. She slid off the horse's back, uncinched the saddle, and heaved it onto the floor of the stable.

Nowhere, she realized as she removed his bridle, rubbed him down, working methodically with the curry brush.

And what am I going to do about it? she asked herself as she closed the door of his stall and gave him an affectionate slap on his neck.

Well, that was easy, she realized. She would do just what he had taught her. Avenge her honor. Kill him.

CHAPTER 53

*R*aleigh stood in front of the mirror over the sink in her big tiled bathroom, looking at her hair. The roots were coming in brown, she saw. She thought of Bobby with a smile, thought how horrified he would be at the sight. He was a kick, Bobby. She'd grown a few inches, too. And she was getting breasts. It was all so horrifying, these changes, that it was actually fascinating in a weird kind of way. And it would be great when the time came. When she was old enough to go back, fight for everything that was hers and get it. Take care of Paul. She raised her head a little, noticed her clenched jaw, her glittering eyes. Eleanor Fisk's reflection behind her. Eleanor was wearing one of those caftans she liked and she was smoking a cigarette, as always.

"Hi, Eleanor," she said breezily as she turned to face her. "This is an honor, huh?"

"I thought we could have a little chat, dear," said Eleanor.

"In my bathroom?" Raleigh asked, raising her eyebrows.

"Well, somewhere," Eleanor said with a smile. "A little private chat."

So they tried to decide where, and Eleanor said how about the dining *palapa* because nobody would be there at this time of day. And they sauntered over there, sort of like chums, while Raleigh wondered what this little chat of Eleanor's might be about. It started out all right. About how Raleigh—Leigh—was coming along with her studies, and how pleased everybody was, and how Eleanor was sure that in a couple of years she would breeze into the University of Chicago just on equivalence exams and Eleanor's recommendation. And that was good to hear because she had to get her education, after all. Her life wasn't just going to be about revenge. No, she was going to do something major, something important. Realize everything she had been trained from birth to do. Complete the circle.

"We're a little worried, though, about the way you're adjusting," Eleanor said, smiling, lighting another cigarette. "You don't seem to be getting along very well with the others. Of course, we realize the difficulty of your situation. That you must feel very insecure."

"I've never felt insecure in my life," Raleigh said indignantly.

"Well, dear, that may well be true," Eleanor said with a little shrug of her shoulders. "But the point is that your behavior leaves quite a bit to be desired."

Never apologize, never explain, Raleigh reminded herself, her eyes narrowing.

"You've been told several times that you're not to go riding alone late at night," Eleanor said. "You do it anyway."

"I can take care of myself," Raleigh muttered angrily.

"You're only thirteen years old, and we consider you our responsibility," Eleanor said. "If we don't think it's appropriate, then we have to insist that you go along with what we decide."

Raleigh slumped in her chair, sighed.

"Several of the research assistants have reached out to you, tried to be your friend," Eleanor continued. "You reject every overture they make."

"I don't know what you're talking about," Raleigh said coldly.

"Stefan asked you to play chess," Eleanor said. "You

played two games with him and then you flounced away. You said you don't do mercy chess."

"Well, what exactly was I supposed to do?" Raleigh asked. "Sit there and beat him another ten times in three moves? Let him win and tell him he's great?"

"Of course not," Eleanor said. "It's just that you didn't have to go out of your way to hurt his feelings."

"I didn't go out of my way," Raleigh protested.

"That's just it," Eleanor said. "You know, really, dear, I've never met a child as arrogant as you are. You did the same thing when you were fencing with Claude. Just took off your mask, put up your foil, and walked away without a word."

"He doesn't know how to fence," Raleigh said.

"All right." Eleanor sighed. "He doesn't know how to fence. But why handle the situation with utter contempt? Why look down on him because he isn't as good as you are? Did it ever occur to you that you could help him to improve?"

"No," Raleigh said. "If he took lessons for the next six years, he still wouldn't know how to fence."

"It isn't the fencing," Eleanor said. "It's just the way you relate to other people. You don't seem to have the vaguest notion of what it means to share. It's as if you're the center of the world and everybody else is just there for your convenience."

Well, aren't they? Raleigh wanted to say, a little smile on her lips.

"You're a brilliant child, my dear," Eleanor went on, "and a beautiful one, as well. But there's more to life than that. The people here, well, they tell us that they go out of their way to avoid you. They can't stand to be around you, and I can't believe that's the way you want it."

"They don't like me?" Raleigh said slowly, feeling something awful welling up inside her. But that couldn't be. Everybody loved her, everybody in the world.

"I'm afraid not," Eleanor said gently. "And that's why I thought we should have this little talk. All I want to suggest to you is that you make the effort to show a little generosity of spirit. Do you think you could do that?"

Slowly Raleigh nodded.

"You'll thank me for this one day," Eleanor said, patting her arm. "Oh, I know. I was a brilliant child, too, and I thought as much of myself as you do. But I must tell you, I'm happy I was able to grow, happy I was able to appreciate the humanity of others, their goodness. And yes, the bad things about them, too."

"I'll try," Raleigh murmured.

"We're all human beings," Eleanor finished. "We're all in this together, you know."

Oh, who cared anyway? Raleigh thought later as she sauntered through the compound. The only thing that really mattered was that she wasn't going to be able to go riding anymore at night. Still, Eleanor had really gotten to her, hurt her feelings in the most awful way. In fact, it made her feel kind of naked and alone to know that nobody liked her, that in the real world it was a two-way street. That you had to do something back. She didn't even realize that she was on her way to visit Ann until she looked up and saw that she was at her door.

"Come in," Ann called at her knock.

"Hi," Raleigh said gloomily.

Ann was on a chaise, her legs crossed at the ankles. "What's the matter with you?" Ann asked, putting down her book.

"Oh, nothing," Raleigh said. "Eleanor just had a little chat with me. That's all."

"About what?" Ann asked, a smile in her voice.

"Oh, things," Raleigh said vaguely, slumping in a chair, one leg over its arm. "She says I don't know how to share. Stuff like that."

"And what did you say?" asked Ann.

"Oh, I don't know," Raleigh said. "What do you think?"

"I think you're the worst pain in the ass I've ever met." Ann said, laughing. "The most self-absorbed, spoiled brat . . . well, there aren't words."

"I guess I'll have to change," Raleigh said gloomily.

"I guess you will," Ann said.

And it wasn't so hard, actually. It was kind of like playing a part. It was even kind of neat to be friends with Ann. Most days they spent the hour before dinner in Ann's place, talking and talking, the way Raleigh imagined it must be like with an older sister. There was the reason she had decided to go to medical school, for example. It was because of her brother who had died of tuberculosis of the kidneys when he was eleven years old. That was what had made her decide to go.

Ann said it was really hard to get in, even though she had perfect grades and was a Phi Beta Kappa at the University of Minnesota. But the thing was that there were quotas for girls, and so a lot of guys whose grades weren't half as good as hers got in. Finally, though, she'd been accepted at two medical schools, Johns Hopkins and the University of Louisiana, and she'd picked Johns Hopkins because it had more prestige. And her internship had been hard to get, too, and she'd nearly died with joy when it turned out to be Mass General, and now she'd be doing her residency there.

"So what do you want to do?" Raleigh asked lazily, watching Ann as she sat at her little dressing table. She had a lipstick in her hand and she was frowning at her reflection in the mirror.

"Brain surgery," Ann said.

"Really?"

"Sure, why not?" Ann asked.

"Well, guys do things like that," Raleigh said.

"Well, if I can do it as well, or better, why shouldn't I do it?" Ann asked.

"I don't know," Raleigh said. "It's just that all the girls I've ever met, well, all they seem to care about is how they look and what they're going to wear."

"Well, that's just the girls you've met," Ann said. "But you can care about how you look and what you're going to wear, and what your career is going to be, too."

"I guess," Raleigh said.

So that was fun, spending those hours with Ann, talking about things. About Ann's family, and her parents back in Duluth, who had a big house with a porch. And about her older brother who was a chemical engineer, and how Ann was already an aunt. And then Ann said how insensitive she felt talking about her family when Raleigh had no past that she could remember and how terrible it must be. And Raleigh thought, Oh, I have a past all right. Boy, do I have a past.

"I worry about my dog," was what she actually blurted out.

"Leigh, this is fabulous," Ann said. "You remember that you have a dog."

And she really did look happy about it, Raleigh saw. Her face was radiant, and it was as if she had been given the Hope Diamond or something.

"What's his name?" she asked.

"Frisky," said Raleigh, deciding what could it hurt to say it, and thinking that it was kind of nice to say Frisky's name, a link with the past. The only good one, she thought wryly, considering how everybody else had worked out.

"Frisky," Ann said. "That's a nice name."

"Well, I was a kid when I got him," Raleigh said. "It's the kind of name a kid would give a dog, you know?"

Well, Ann was all over her after that, asking what kind of dog it was and making Raleigh close her eyes while she said to concentrate and who else was in the picture with Frisky? Did she see her parents, and where was it? All of that stuff that Raleigh wasn't about to tell her.

"I just don't know," she said, shaking her head.

"Well, it's a start," Ann said, still very pleased about the Frisky revelation.

It wasn't a start, though. Every time Ann got around to the subject again, Raleigh started to talk about something else. "Gee, that's a pretty dress," she would say to Ann. So they'd talk about dresses, and did Raleigh notice in the newspapers and magazines that came in that skirts had gotten very short—miniskirts, they were called—and Raleigh really had to try to listen to what Ann said and to be pleasant, because it all seemed like a lot of nonsense to care about such dumb things. And the way Ann put on her makeup. It was the worst. Amateur night in Dixie. How she could think she looked better with it on than with it off was amazing.

"Here, let me do it," Raleigh said, and on went the foundation and powder, the rouge. Then the shadow and mascara, and finally the lipstick.

"I don't recognize myself," Ann said, looking in the mirror. "I look like a model."

"You look good," Raleigh agreed.

"Where did you learn to do that?" Ann asked.

"You wouldn't believe it if I told you," Raleigh said with a laugh.

Ann was really a hit that night when they went in to dinner, and that cute English boy she was always flirting with just about came out of his chair. So Ann felt good about that, and feeling good made her look even prettier, but still, Raleigh wished she wouldn't get all demure like that with him. She was a doctor, after all. It just wasn't dignified.

Raleigh started to hang out in one of the libraries, too, and she taught herself to type on an old broken-down typewriter. After a while the research assistants started taking her for granted, and then they started asking her to look things up for them. That sort of thing. So pretty soon she had her own projects to do, and that was really neat.

CHAPTER 54

What Raleigh liked most was when everybody was in the living room at the main house. It would be after dinner and everybody else would be sloshing down wine, and chain-smoking and screaming at each other about the meaning of life, not that Raleigh thought that was anything to get all exercised about.

What she figured was when she was born it was as if she had been given one of those maps where it said, "You Are Here." Then Paul and Darby, and maybe her mother a little bit, had given her values, told her by their reactions how she was supposed to think about herself. And what they had told her to think about herself was that she was the best, that she could do anything. And when she was a little older, all the attention she got, all the adulation, reinforced that.

Then the reading. Well, her mother, all of them, thought it was great that she was always reading when she wasn't doing all of her physical stuff. What they didn't seem to realize was that she was reading something, other ways to look at things. So she had her own experiences, what other people told her about theirs, and all of the ways to think about life that she read about in books. Out of that, she could decide what suited her. Plus what turned up, like how she hadn't really thought about other people, how she was totally self-absorbed. But that was how she'd been trained, after all. She'd changed. She really had.

Anyway, those were really neat evenings and they always seemed to happen when somebody came from the outside. Because they were just starved for new faces, new people to talk to. John Kenneth Galbraith came. William Buckley, Jr., came. Marietta Tree came—she was a socialite from New York. Georgia O'Keeffe came with this Juan Hamilton person, and that threw Eleanor into a dither. "Are they or aren't they?" was what she kept saying, so what she did was put them in adjoining rooms so they could work it out themselves.

Alain Robbe-Grillet came. He was this oblique writer from Paris, and that was interesting because he didn't speak English and Raleigh got to try her French firsthand. And she was really upset—ashamed of herself, even—because she had thought she was pretty good and she couldn't understand what he was talking about, except for the prepositions. But, it turned out to be okay, because when she discussed it with some of the others over the next couple of days, they were having a hard time figuring out what he was getting at, too, and they were a lot older and better educated than she was.

Henry Kissinger came. He was a confidant of Governor Nelson Rockefeller of New York. Everybody was very impressed with him and Eleanor was saying that it was too bad that he couldn't be president, but he'd been born in Germany, and under the Constitution, you had to be born in the United States, so that was the way it went sometimes.

A guitarist named Bob Dylan came. He and Ann had a lot to talk about, since they both came from Minnesota. His name had been Bob Zimmerman, but he'd changed it in honor of Dylan Thomas. And that was interesting because Raleigh got interested in reading Dylan Thomas and thought he was very powerful. She got chills just reading him, and that was hard to do, since it was always so hot where they were, and so humid that she never felt as if she were really dry. This Bob Dylan played and sang for them, and Raleigh thought he was really good. Knew that he'd be a star. He had the quality.

Jessica Mitford came. She was this English person who had written a big best-seller about how funeral directors, people like that, really ripped off the families of people who died. But what she really talked about all the time was how she came from this crazy aristocratic English family, and how wild they all were, and how one of her sisters was this great friend of Adolph Hitler's. Then she went on and on about how she had run away when she was in her teens with this boy and how he had died, or been killed, or something. She was kind of middle-aged, and that was being polite about it, Raleigh thought, so it was kind of strange to her that Jessica Mitford was still talking about this boy she had known. And with her husband right there, too. Well, he'd probably heard it a million times by now. Probably didn't even hear Jessica Mitford anymore as she went on and on about this first love of hers.

When Tom Kelley came, that photographer who had taken the nude photograph of Marilyn Monroe with the red velvet background, Raleigh was really interested to see what would happen. Because Tom Kelley had photographed Raleigh, too. It would have been when she was around eight years old, a big color and black and white session that had gone on for over a week. It had been for the studio, Raleigh remembered. A cover take that they could distribute to media all over the world when it was needed.

She couldn't believe how happy she was to see him when he gingerly stepped off the boat onto the dock. A face from home. It made her feel all funny and warm. Connected, in a way.

"We've met before," he said when she was introduced to him.

"I don't think so," Raleigh said.

"No, I know you," he said, his expression puzzled. "In fact, we've worked together, haven't we?"

"No, no. We haven't," Raleigh said.

"Your hair was different," he murmured. "You were blond. I can almost see you."

Later that evening over dinner, every time Raleigh happened to glance over at Tom Kelley, he was staring right at her. He looked so frustrated that Raleigh wouldn't have been surprised to see him tearing at his hair. But there was something else in his expression, too. Sympathy. So Eleanor, or somebody, must have filled him in with her story.

"Have you ever thought of modeling?" he asked her the next day when they were sitting next to each other at breakfast.

"No, I haven't," she said.

"You'd be great at it," he said. "God, you've got a look about you. And your bones, you've got great bones."

And that was fun to hear, the admiration again. Boy, she'd really missed it.

Then Tom Kelley said that he had a great idea. That why didn't they knock off a few rolls, see how the camera felt about her. And Raleigh said sure.

So that was neat, working with Tom Kelley again. Sitting cross-legged on the sand, her hands at her chin, three of the horses grouped behind her. Strolling out of the ocean in a swimsuit. Just standing there, her legs apart, her hands thrust into the pockets of her trousers. And then they started to get into a rhythm, and he was the choreographer and she was the dancer, running toward him, leaping into the air, sommersaulting on the beach, thrusting upward at the end for a double. She felt exultant at using her body again, so alive that she almost felt reborn.

"I know I've worked with you before," he said, a hand on her shoulder as they sauntered back down the beach toward the compound.

"I know how you're going to move before you do it, I know just what your dimple is going to do before you smile."

It was such a temptation, Raleigh thought. Yes, yes, she

wanted to say. I'm Raleigh Barnes. Let's get out of here. Let's go back. Home. And that was what stopped her, of course. Because she couldn't go home. Not yet. Not until she was older, with a little more control over how things would go.

"It's just driving me crazy," Tom Kelley said with a laugh. "But I'll tell you one thing, kid. You're a real pro. There's a lot of work behind those moves of yours."

During the weeks before the large envelope came from Tom Kelley, a critic named Lionel Trilling came. And a Nobel Prize winner named Linus Pauling. And then there it was, that big manila envelope with his name, the address of his studio in the upper left-hand corner. Raleigh was so excited she could hardly wait to tear it open. Here were the contact sheets, each with its thirty-six frames.

And here was his edit, the eight shots he'd picked out, blown up. She looked into her own blue eyes, saw the way she held a hand, the curve of her shoulder. The toss of her head. Boy, do I look hot, she thought gleefully. I'm really great as a girl.

Eagerly she scanned his letter. He'd gone through his files, he said, in hopes that he would find her there. He was so sure that he'd spent hours with a loupe, scanning every contact sheet he'd ever shot of young actresses. Models. But there was nothing.

"As you can see from the enclosed shots," he added, "you're a natural with a major career ahead of you. Whenever you're ready, just let me know."

A major career ahead. A major career behind.

The thought made Raleigh smile.

Not yet, she thought.

Then there was this terrific evening when some zoology professor from UCLA came, a young guy with an Armenian name, and they were all drinking a lot of wine and shouting at each other about males and females, especially females, because he'd written a controversial book about how females were superior to males, and all the newspapers had picked up on it and some of the magazines, too.

"The more evolved, the less body hair," the guy said. "Let's start right there. Look at the difference." And Raleigh thought that was really generous of him, because he sure was furry with all this black hair on his arms, the back of his hands and on his toes in his sandals.

"Take kids in school," he said. "Oh, sure, there are a few brilliant boys. But the girls are always more advanced. And if you were going to admit students to the major universities just on the basis of grades and achievements on entrance exams, nearly eighty percent of them would be girls."

So why was it like it was? Raleigh wondered.

But he had the answer to that. On an unconscious level, he said, men think women are magic. They bleed and they don't die. They create life where there was nothing.

And Eleanor was laughing and chain-smoking, nodding her head and saying something about Freud, and penis envy, and how she never had been able to figure out how he'd managed to slip that one by. That a woman could possibly envy such a pitiful, ugly thing when it was she who could create life.

And Charles was grinning and drinking and saying how he didn't have to be convinced. He'd always known that Eleanor was the superior one. Just look at their relationship, at who had the power.

"Would you have come all the way down here just to see me?" he asked the professor, and the professor said, well, he didn't want to be rude, but no, not really.

But still, almost all of the time it was the guy who had the power and it was the girl who went along with it, Raleigh had to admit, and why do that? Well, it had to be because guys were bigger and stronger. If somebody could beat you up, he got respect.

"Man's true victory," Eleanor was saying, "is woman's willing recognition of him as her destiny."

And somebody said what a great line that was, and Eleanor said it was a quote from Simone de Beauvoir.

All of the things that were said that evening gave

Raleigh a lot to think about, sort of turned the way she had thought about all of that upside down. When she had been living her life as a boy, well, she sort of had contempt for girls. Thought that they didn't do much. In fact, that had been her one big regret when she'd started her life as a girl. That she'd had to give up first prize in the lottery of life for second prize. But now it didn't seem that way to her anymore. You didn't have to giggle and bat your eyes and wait for someone to open the car door for you. It wasn't a law of nature. What those girls were doing was creating an illusion, playing a part, just the way she had done in the movies.

So you could just live your life any way that satisfied you, brought out the best in you. It was going to be okay, being a girl. Better, even, the best of both worlds. As for that man as destiny stuff that Eleanor had quoted, well, Raleigh didn't believe for a minute that she was serious. No, it must have been some kind of bad joke that she was just too young to understand, because nobody could be that dumb.

Raleigh had the most awful feeling in the pit of her stomach as she watched Ann carefully fold the last cotton skirt into her suitcase and close it. She winced at the click, at the finality of it. Don't go, she wanted to say. This is all a mistake.

"Well, that's it," Ann said with a quick smile, a sigh.

"I'm going to miss you," Raleigh said, and, boy, she would, she really would. All the girl things they had done together, the gossiping, the giggling, the friendship and love that had developed between them over these months they had known each other. And there were all of the things that Raleigh had learned from Ann, her kindness, her compassion. Raleigh thought of Ann getting up in the middle of the night to ride to some distant village to deliver a baby, to set a broken leg. To sit with an old person who was dying. And there were the classes she taught the kids around the place. In English, simple mathematics, all kinds of stuff it would be useful for them to know. Why, she'd been a kind of one-woman peace corps until Raleigh had had a little time on her own hands. Had started to help out. Sort of a teacher's aide, in a way. And now Raleigh would be taking over, the teaching of the little kids. She'd really been surprised in the beginning because it made her feel so good. Probably better than it made them feel to be learning these things, to be getting all that attention.

A couple of the servants were there, picking up Ann's bags, hurrying them out of the room, down to the dock. Slowly Raleigh pulled herself out of her chair, put her arm around Ann's waist as they sauntered out of Ann's quarters for the last time. Raleigh felt the tears in her eyes, realized what the awful feeling in her stomach was. She felt empty, bereft, missing her friend already, and here Ann wasn't even gone yet.

Everybody was waiting to say good-bye. Eleanor, Charles, the research assistants. Most of the little kids. The servants. It was a beautiful day, not so humid, and whitecaps lapped at the dock. Ann grabbed her, gave her one last hug, a quick kiss on the cheek.

"This is funny," Ann said with a little laugh. "I can't believe it. You're just as tall as I am."

"That's right," Raleigh said with a shaky smile. "So I am."

"I'll write," Ann called as someone reached out, helped her into the boat.

"So will I," Raleigh called as the motor kicked in, roared, and the boat turned, gathered speed.

She stood there, waving with the rest of them, until the boat was out of sight. Charles, she saw, had tears in his eyes. So did some of the others. She wiped away her own with the back of her hand.

CHAPTER 55

*R*aleigh felt so strange after Ann was gone that she figured maybe she was getting sick, coming down with something. One of the kids in class would suddenly understand something, and all Raleigh would want to do would be to run, tell Ann about it, share the victory. But no Ann.

Raleigh sighed, feeling empty. Lonely for her friend. That's it, she thought wonderingly. I miss her. I care about her. And she couldn't believe how happy she was, how connected she felt, when Ann's first letter came with all of her news about settling in, about the work load she would be carrying in her residency. About the other residents, the hierarchy, and stuff.

And there were always the new people who came, the research assistants, the celebrated. And while it was true that Eleanor was at the top of her field, it seemed to Raleigh that there was something else about the situation that brought everybody there. It was Eleanor's warmth, the way she nurtured them, appreciated them. Nurtured Raleigh, too. Getting her ready to get on with her own life, her education at the University of Chicago.

And what a major hassle it had been to get her to Chicago in the first place, Raleigh thought. Eleanor and Charles and the trips to Mexico City to the American

Consulate there, the weeks and months of dealing with the Mexican authorities. Eleanor and Charles declaring Raleigh their ward, with all the lawyers, the paperwork on that transaction that stood a foot high.

And then Chicago, just after her sixteenth birthday, with the energy, the raw power the city seemed to generate. The buildings that were extraordinarily beautiful, all of that expensive real estate along Lake Shore Drive. There were the equivalence exams to take, Eleanor exerting all of her pull, wheedling and cajoling to get Raleigh's scholarship.

"After all," she had pointed out imperiously, "there is a chair named for me at this university."

So it had all worked out, and they had had a great time, the three of them, for the week they had been there together. They had stayed at the Ambassador East. Sauntered up the stairs past the lions guarding the entrance to the Art Institute, spent two entire days there.

They'd spent a lot of time on the campus, too, and at the homes of Eleanor's friends and admirers, who entertained for them. At the home of one of them, Raleigh met Saul Bellow. They'd gone to Marshall Field to buy her winter wardrobe. A heavy coat, a pair of boots. Boy, it had been a long time since she'd worn a pair of boots, and she couldn't remember that she had ever owned a winter coat. Not in Los Angeles, where there hadn't been any real weather that she could recall. Much like the place itself, she thought wryly. Not much real anything.

They strolled along Promontory Point, glancing at the picnickers, the bicyclists gliding by. Stood at its tip and gazed across the endless blue of Lake Michigan. There was a view of the city itself, an impressive skyscrape.

Even before they'd found the little studio apartment for Raleigh on one of the narrow, tree-lined streets in Hyde Park near the university, Raleigh had answered an ad in the paper, gotten a part-time job in the evenings teaching exercise classes at a gym, gymnastics to little kids on Saturday mornings.

It had been neat, the transition back to life in the

United States. Being on a campus, for one thing. She'd never even been to a school at all, much less a university with its thousands of students, the professors, some of them Nobel Prize winners. The teaching assistants, all of the administrators, the secretaries, the maintenance people. There were even the campus dogs, loping along beside their masters.

There was something almost magical about opening the front door in the morning and finding the *Chicago Tribune* sitting there, the newsmagazines on the day they were published instead of two weeks later, the way it was down in Mexico. She bought a portable radio and carried it around with her. Listened to the news almost all the time, and the Chicago Cubs, the baseball team. A television set was next, she decided, as soon as she'd saved up the money from her job.

It seemed to Raleigh that she'd been in Chicago maybe ten minutes, and all at once summer was gone. There were flurries of snow, quick and surprising and wet on her face. And it was a holiday weekend. Thanksgiving.

She sat on the train, looking out the window at the tired beige fields, the leaden gray skies that made the farmhouses, everything, look as if they'd sort of had it, for this year, anyway. When it was time for lunch, she ordered a club sandwich and a cup of coffee in the dining car. Ignored the scattering of guys cruising the aisle who would lean over and give her the "Where have you been all my life, you beautiful thing?" line that had surprised her at first when she'd gotten to Chicago.

Pretty soon, though, they were in Duluth. And she could see Ann, who was waiting for her on the platform. Raleigh was so happy to see her after three years of only letters and a snapshot now and then that she threw her arms around her. Cried a little with joy, and so did Ann.

Ann drove them out to the big house with the enclosed front porch and the big old trees in front that she had told Raleigh all about when they were down in Mexico. And it was all so familiar that Raleigh could have picked it out of a million houses if she had to. There were flurries of snow as they got out of the car, and Ann had to help her with all the presents Raleigh had brought along.

Ann's mom was medium height with a nice figure and she was pretty, like Ann, too. The father was a nice guy, a little thick around the middle, with a hearty laugh. And the chemical engineer brother was kind of quiet, with a soft, chattery wife—Denise, her name was. And there were their kids, little ones, a boy and a girl.

So it was great with all of them, in that big, old house with the furniture they'd all grown up with, and good smells coming out of the kitchen the next morning.

The guys sat in the front room watching football on television and the little kids played. Raleigh and Ann sat in the kitchen, chatting with Ann's mom and Denise while they rushed around putting together the turkey dinner. It was all very Norman Rockwell, Raleigh decided, only in a way it wasn't. Ann's mom, for example, had gone back to school and was just finishing her master's degree in social work, so she'd be in the work force for the first time in a couple of months, and she was talking about adjusting to that and seeing that the house was kept up. And Denise was saying that as soon as the baby was old enough for day-care, she was going back to work, too. Because sitting around the house was driving her out of her mind after the years she had spent teaching the third grade. So that wasn't exactly Norman Rockwell, Raleigh decided. As Bob Dylan would have it, the times they were a-changin'.

"That was a fantastic dinner," Raleigh said later that night as they crawled into the twin beds in the upstairs corner bedroom looking onto the backyard with its apple trees, its beds of tulips waiting for spring. "That was the best stuffing I've ever tasted. What does your mom put in it? Chestnuts?"

"Yes," said Ann. "Chestnuts and celery. Onions and pork sausage. It's the pork sausage that makes it so good. That's what Mother has always said."

"Well, it was the best," said Raleigh. "And that pumpkin

pie! I've never tasted homemade pumpkin pie."

"I've got some news," Ann said, and when Raleigh looked over at her, she saw Ann's shining eyes, knew exactly what she was going to say.

"What's he like?" Raleigh asked, and the two of them looked at each other and started to giggle the way they had sometimes back when they'd first met.

Larry Newman was his name, and he was a surgical resident at Mass General, too. The best-looking thing on two feet, Ann said proudly as she reached for the snapshots. He was, too, Raleigh saw. Tall and dark, with an aquiline nose, a narrow mouth. That arrogant expression guys seemed to have when they knew they could have anybody they wanted.

"All the nurses practically faint when he walks by," Ann said, wonder in her voice. "You should see it."

"When are you going to get married?" Raleigh asked.

"Oh, it'll be after we finish our residencies," Ann said quickly. "And then I'm going to go on staff for a while, teach, while Larry sets up his practice. You know, so much of that is referrals. There's a lot of politicking. He'll have to have a beautiful office, the right car. We'll have to join the country club, that kind of thing."

Raleigh examined Ann's face, saw her blissful expression, really felt happy for her.

"Oh, the way we met, it was so cute," Ann said dreamily. "We were in a seminar, and there was a surprise quiz. And I was sitting there writing away, and he touched me on my shoulder, and do you know what he said?"

"What?" Raleigh asked.

"He said, 'Would you mind moving your hand a little? I can't see your answers,'" said Ann with a joyous little laugh. "Isn't that adorable?"

"Is he smart?" Raleigh asked.

"Oh, yes," Ann breathed.

"Is he as smart as you are?" Raleigh asked.

"Well, maybe not," Ann conceded. "But that's my little secret."

Raleigh thought about that, chewed on her lower lip.

"Look, it could be a lot worse," Ann said. "After all, we could have met in med school. Then I would have had to quit, gone to work so that he could finish. At least I'm almost through with my own training."

"Would you have done that?" Raleigh asked, her tone incredulous.

"Well, I don't have to worry about it now," Ann said with a little laugh. "All I know is that he loves me and I love him. I'd do anything for him. I'd go to the end of the world to make him happy."

Raleigh wondered about how that going to the end of the world to make somebody happy worked. Whether it worked both ways, for example.

"You'll understand when you're older," Ann said, and Raleigh said, well, yes, maybe she would. But she thought about it after Ann had turned the light out, and actually she thought she understood it pretty well right now. That for some reason there were girls who were willing to take second place to a guy, but that she wasn't one of them.

CHAPTER 56

*R*aleigh trudged along the campus, her head down. The wind sucked the tears from her eyes, stung her cheeks. Oh, God, she thought, with dismay. It's starting to snow again. Hard, too. She could hardly make out the students gingerly walking ahead of her, and Mitchell Tower had disappeared in a shroud of fog.

All this to get to a class she didn't even know if she liked. Didn't even know anymore if she wanted to do philosophy. That was for Eleanor, and whatever Raleigh did, she didn't want to disappoint Eleanor. Or Charles, either. They were depending on her. Proud surrogate parents of their ward, Leigh Fisk, née Raleigh Barnes, the only one who didn't leave like the research assistants. They'd done so much for her, too. Sacrificed for her, because even though a lot of money came in from the books, there was the compound to support, and most of the research assistants only had partial grants. And there was all the money the Fisks spent to help the people down there. Down there where it's warm, Raleigh thought wistfully. Oh, to be warm.

And all of the papers she had to write, the homework she had to do for these classes she didn't even know that she wanted to take. And then the job. Minimum wage.

Even that dowdy little apartment. One bedroom, one

bath. A tiny kitchen with a hot plate and refrigerator. And here she was, a millionaire several times over. And her real home was a mansion so large she still wasn't sure she'd explored its last hidden corner, its grounds luxuriant with the lake, the gardens, statuary. It was outrageous that she should be living like this. Raleigh Barnes, Poor Student. Talk about miscasting, she thought grimly.

Still, it wasn't forever. In only a few more years she could go home, get what was coming to her. All of those trust accounts in her name. All of the real estate in her name. And the other thing, too. Revenge. She licked her lips, a mistake in that cold. With her mittened hand, she rubbed them vigorously to restore circulation.

Her spirits lifted at once as she thought about what it would be like with Paul. About how she would do it.

Raleigh figured that Paul had made two mistakes. The second one was trying to kill her and not getting the job done. The first was teaching her about honor and revenge. That was, what, two strikes on Paul. So he had one left and he was out.

Still, she felt some odd kind of longing when she would see his name in the entertainment section of the Los Angeles paper she got every day. Paul Fournier, announcing plans for some new multipicture deal, always with a couple of major stars attached. Which might or might not be true, Raleigh reminded herself. People got nervous when they didn't see their names in the papers every couple of days. Wondered if they were still alive. So out would go the press releases and they'd be reassured for a few days more. Paul Fournier, president and chief executive officer of Raleigh Barnes Productions. Of course, he'd kept the name. All of those films she'd made, well, they were worth a fortune. Millions and millions of dollars. Still, it sent a little shiver up her spine as she read her name.

And then, in the society section, mentions of Mrs. Paul Fournier. At a tea to raise money for some disease. As one of the chairs at a luncheon at the Huntington Gardens. Her mother, one of the ladies, just what she had always wanted to be. But what kind of a price had she been willing to pay for that? Raleigh thought, tears squeezing out of her eyes. My life?

And then, finally, a picture of her mother one day in a row of five smiling matrons, as Mrs. Paul (Beth Carol) Fournier entertained at a garden tour of her magnificent Beverly Hills estate. Raleigh felt a surge of love at the sight of her that almost knocked her back in her chair. It took her a couple of minutes before she could pick up the paper again. Look more closely into her mother's face.

"Oh, Mother," she murmured aloud as she leaned against the wall next to the window, held the picture up to the light. "Let's go back. Let's start over."

She looked so pretty, Raleigh thought wistfully, almost able to remember the smell of her mother's perfume, the way it had felt to be held in her arms when she was small. There was her soft face, that look in her eyes that pleaded to be liked, accepted. That self-effacing way she stood. She was blond now, which somehow made her whole look even softer, even more vulnerable. She wore a sleeveless dress, with a chiffon scarf around her neck, held something in her arms.

It was Frisky, Raleigh saw with astonishment. She grabbed her magnifying glass to look again. It really was. His eyes were bright and his topnotch was tied with a bow. Raleigh was so happy that she laughed aloud, tears streaming down her cheeks.

And then there was the half hour she spent five nights a week with Fern Darling, sprinting into her apartment from her job just in time to flip on the television set. Fern, looking just the same as she had when Raleigh had first become aware of her. Fern, with her bouffant hair towering over her little face. The long, dangling earrings. Those décolleté dresses she had always worn that defied gravity. The pudgy little fingers, dripping now with diamond rings, turning the pages on the desk in front of her. Fern, talking in that breathy little voice of hers about places Raleigh could remember as if it were yesterday. Talking about people whose names Raleigh knew as well as she knew her own.

What is missing from this picture? she asked herself.

I am, she answered.

I don't know if I need this much character building, Raleigh thought one Saturday morning as she looked out the window, about to dash out the door to go to work. All she could see was white. It was the blizzard that had been predicted the night before on the local news. She had never been so happy when the phone rang and it was the receptionist from the gym. Saying that the city was shut down. That she didn't have to come in.

Raleigh got back into her flannel pajamas, made herself a cup of coffee, flipped on the television set, and crawled back into bed. There was Bugs Bunny. Daffy Duck. The Saturday morning cartoons, she thought with a smile. And oh, how good it felt to be snuggled up in bed, dozing, reading. Dozing again. She sat bolt upright as a new one came on. *The Adventures of Raleigh Barnes,* said the title. And there was that fabulous little boy she had been, animated this time, foil in hand. Achieving impossible feats of derring-do. Unconsciously she fingered her dimple, the match for the one that played in and out of the rounded cheek of the little cartoon character on the screen.

Raleigh looked up gratefully as she picked her way along. The flurries of snow were dissipating now. Just ahead of her was a boy hunched into a kind of a baseball jacket. On the back it read RALEIGH BARNES FAN CLUB.

Now, what's all this about? she wondered, smiling to herself as she carefully increased her pace, tried to catch up with him.

"Pardon me," she said, touching his arm with her mittened hand. Startling him. He jumped, turned, and looked down at her. His eyes were watery with the wind and cold. His fair skin was blotched. Together they stood there, bracing themselves against the wind.

"Oh, my God," he gasped, his eyes widening. "It's you."

What have I done? Raleigh asked herself, taking a few steps away from him. He couldn't know that she was Raleigh Barnes. She was so bundled up that it was impossible. So he was a nut case of some kind.

"It's you," he repeated reverently. "You're Leigh Fisk."

"Well, yes," she said, frowning. "So what?"

"Don't you recognize me?" he asked, his look pleading.

"No, I'm sorry," she said. "I'm afraid not."

"From calculus?" he said. "The one who tries to sit next to you all the time? The one who moons over you? The one who thinks you're a goddess on the earth?"

"Look," Raleigh said, "I just wanted to ask you about your jacket. The Raleigh Barnes Fan Club."

"Do you know who he is?" the boy asked, swaying in the wind, pulling his watchcap down with gloved hands. "The kid movie star who drowned?"

Raleigh nodded warily.

"Well, he's our hero," the boy said. "We watch his cartoons on Saturday mornings. And we get together and watch his old films."

"What for?" Raleigh asked, puzzled.

"Well, it's kind of a fad," the boy explained. "It's going on at campuses around the country. He really was great, you know."

Well, it was kind of nice to hear that, Raleigh thought as the wind screamed by them. It made her feel connected to herself in a way, to her life as a boy.

"Say, I'm Craig Alexander," he said, thrusting out his shaking hand to take hers. "We have a lot of fun at these things. Would you like to come along some night? Are you a Raleigh Barnes fan?"

"I should be president," she said as the wind carried her words away.

"What did you say?" he shouted.

She shook her head, as the two of them stood there, bracing themselves to keep their balance.

Raleigh never would have recognized Craig Alexander when he opened the door for her at the two-story house where he lived, a couple of blocks away from her apartment. His russet-colored hair curled on his shoulders, and without his jacket he was kind of thin, narrow-shouldered in a turtle-neck sweater, faded jeans. His three roommates, who were drifting around with beers in their hands, nodded to her. They all had long hair, too. So did their girlfriends, who kind of scurried in later like little mice. And the other kids who came along later, with their offerings of cheap jug wine, six-packs of beer. Raleigh hadn't even thought about what she would wear when she was getting dressed. She was in jeans, too. A shirt, with a bulky sweater over it. In the dim light in the living room with its shabby furniture, its stacks of books, magazines, newspapers everywhere, it was really hard to tell the boys from the girls. Sort of disorienting, Raleigh realized, and smiled to herself at the thought. She should be the last one to talk about that, considering.

The Stones were on the stereo, then Bob Dylan, as Raleigh wandered around the room, looking at all the posters of herself from some of her films that hung, framed, on the dingy walls. Here she was as *Zorro*. As *Robin Hood*. And this one she knew was very rare: *Peter Pan*. That was on stage in Los Angeles. And here was that big blowup from the last one, *Treasure Hunt*, where she was underwater, swimming toward the galleon. The last movie. The last picture ever taken of Raleigh Barnes, movie star.

She felt a little shaky, frowned as she turned away from it, the memories flooding back in waves. Maybe I can't do this, she told herself, and countered with, Oh, come on. I can do anything. Smiled at Craig, who was standing right in front of her, adoration in his eyes as he offered her a glass of wine.

There were about twenty of them, finally, sprawled on the couches, the chairs, on pillows on the floor. Somebody dimmed the lights, the projector hummed, and the first of the two movies Craig told her they had rented for the evening flickered on the screen. It was one of the adventure ones, *Captain Blood*.

Raleigh took a big gulp of the wine, felt the interest from the kids around her, smelled the marijuana.

They clapped and cheered when Raleigh's credit came on the screen, scattered their applause through the rest of the credits, especially for Darby, when his director's credit came on at the end.

And then there was Raleigh Barnes, seven years old, the most famous child star in the world, in a shirt with puffy sleeves, a leather vest, trousers thrust into boots, a foil in her hand. Her chin was up, her blue eyes glittered with arrogance, energy.

"En garde," cried Raleigh Barnes, and all around her the kids were clapping and cheering. Saying the lines of dialogue a beat ahead of the characters on the screen.

Raleigh stared, fascinated, as the child on the screen flew through the air. Gasped along with the others at the sheer improbability of some of the stunts. But they weren't that hard, she remembered, frowning. Weren't even that dangerous. It was Darby, his direction, that was making Raleigh Barnes so daring, so splendid. Bigger than life, just the way a movie star was supposed to be.

What a beautiful child she had been during her life as a boy, Raleigh realized. But it was more than the shape of the blue eyes, the narrow nose, the full lips, that dimple, the mop of blond hair. That little boy on the screen had a jaunty insouciance about him and, yes, a vulnerability. A sweet innocence.

So odd to look at that little boy, to think of the teen-aged girl she saw when she looked in the mirror in the morning as she pulled a comb through her long, shining brown hair. To even be able to entertain the notion that the one had transmogrified into the other.

Out of the corner of her eye she watched the faces of the others as they stared, transfixed, at the screen. Thought of them going through their own baby snapshots and wondered if, on some level, they couldn't figure it out, either. How some adorable little creature with zip written on its baby face had mysteriously become one of these kids sitting here with all of the problems, the hopes, the dreams that being in college implied.

And, there were plenty of them. The Democratic convention and its riots that had taken place a few weeks before Eleanor and Charles had brought Raleigh to Chicago. Civil rights. The Vietnam War. They all talked about the sexual revolution, too. How it was all going to be different because all of that stuff that had been sold to the girls was just a bunch of nonsense. How they could go to bed with anybody just the way the boys could. All of that. Still, Raleigh noticed that when one of the boys wanted another beer, it was one of the girls who jumped up and went to get it. And when the pizza was delivered from the Italian place at the corner, it was the girls who pooled their money to pay for it. Big sexual revolution, she thought with a shrug.

The second film was a compilation of the commercials, the films, even the stills, from the early years. There she was, her very first appearance on the screen, a wide-eyed baby, her mouth open, looking up into Susan Hayward's face. And the others from the catalogs. Dazed with delight over the formula. The softness of the carpet she was crawling over. Amazing, she realized, to have her entire life at hand. All she had to do was crank up a projector and let it roll. For the first thirteen years, anyway.

"Wouldn't it have been terrible if he would have grown up and sold insurance or something?" someone said after the lights had come up. Another joint was being passed around, the record on the stereo something by the Beatles.

"Maybe he would buy a restaurant," someone else said. "Go around, shaking hands with the customers. A lot of them do that."

"Get fat and old," someone else added.

"A lot of them commit suicide," someone else said. "They can't take it when all of the attention isn't on them anymore."

"God, what it must have been to live like that," someone said with a sigh. "To have everything, to have the whole world in love with you."

And now Craig was saying something. That it was probably just as well that it had happened. The accident, the early death right on the brink of adolescence. Because this way Raleigh Barnes was stopped in time, would never change. He was utterly perfect just as he was, and they would have him forever.

"I've got to go home," Raleigh said, standing abruptly. In a moment, she had found her coat and was out the door. It doesn't get any stranger than that, she thought. Vaguely aware that her hands, thrust into her pockets against the cold, were a little shaky. She thought of the cans of her films that could be rented or bought. Of the compilation of commercials that was available only through mail order. Of the Saturday morning cartoons. And the Raleigh Barnes Fan Club, well, there were others on nearly every college campus in the country right now. A little light relief in these times of upheaval. That little boy who somehow represented stability, a commitment to excellence.

And all of it, even the fan clubs, directed by Paul. Raleigh Barnes the person might be dead, but Raleigh Barnes the product could go on forever. With the right marketing plan, that is. My father, she thought grimly as she unlocked the door to her apartment and closed it behind her. Cutting his losses. Keeping his eye on the main chance.

It seemed to Raleigh that every time she turned around, Craig Alexander was standing there with that dumb, lovestruck expression in his eyes. It was really getting annoying to have her privacy invaded like this. And there were all these other guys who were always hanging around her, too. Asking for her phone number, asking her to go to parties, films. And it wasn't just students, either. It was older guys on the street, a couple of photographers who said she could have a big career in modeling. Well, she considered it. She really did. It would be a lot more money than she was making with her exercise classes at the gym, get her well financially. But finally she decided to take a pass. How good could they be, after all? If they had any real talent, they would be where the real action was. New York. Los Angeles.

Yes, Los Angeles.

She could hardly wait.

CHAPTER 57

$\mathcal{E}$ven before she was fully awake, Raleigh could feel something different in the early morning noises around the compound. Oh, there was the distant chatter, a rooster crowing, even the sounds of the kids playing at this early hour in the morning. But there was something else, too. A sense of excitement.

And then she remembered. Bruno Bettelheim was coming for a couple of days, and it was going to be great. It had already been great even without him as they all sat around in the evenings, arguing and screaming at each other about his theories.

It was a few minutes later as she stood under the shower with the lukewarm water trickling over her that she remembered the other thing about today. It was August 22, 1970, her birthday. She was eighteen years old.

Well, here's looking at you, kid, she thought to herself as she stood there, the water dripping onto her shoulders, curling under her breasts, over her slender hips. Happy Birthday, Raleigh Barnes, Dead Movie Star. Happy Birthday, Leigh Fisk, Junior at the University of Chicago. Because that was what she would be when she went back to school in a few weeks. God, two years already, and what a lot she'd learned. Not just in her classes, either, that was for sure. A lot more being on her own, taking care of herself. She really felt good when she thought about it. Yes, she thought. I've grown up a lot.

It was probably just as well, too, she thought sadly as she remembered the quiver of dismay she had felt this time when she had seen Eleanor and Charles among the others who had come down to the dock to greet her when she got there. Eleanor was so thin now that she was almost transparent, hardly there at all when Raleigh threw her arms around her, kissed her bloodless cheek. But it was Charles who had changed the most. His face was gray under his tan, his beautiful white hair was lifeless. Raleigh felt her heart sink as she saw the black circles under his fine eyes. As he walked, his steps were tentative, and all of his ebullience, his vitality, seemed to be slowly draining out of him.

"Why didn't you let me know that Charles isn't feeling well?" she had asked Eleanor one morning when she found her sitting alone in the library, an open book on her lap.

"We didn't want to worry you, dear," Eleanor had said, patting a place next to her on the sofa, inviting Raleigh to sit down. "You have enough to think about with your studies."

"Oh, Eleanor," said Raleigh with annoyance.

"And it was the correct decision," Eleanor said firmly. "We went to Houston, to the hospital there. They gave Charles a million tests and they couldn't find a thing."

"Well, why does he look so bad?" Raleigh demanded querulously.

"He'll be fine," Eleanor said soothingly, patting her hand. "Now, tell me. How's school?"

And it had taken Raleigh a couple of minutes of talking around the issue, but then she told Eleanor. How she didn't think philosophy was for her. That it seemed to her that most of the great philosophers were commitable lunatics. But she loved astronomy. Why, when she'd walked into that first class, she felt as if she'd come alive. And she loved physics, too. So what she was seriously thinking about doing was changing her major. Becoming an astrophysicist somewhere down the line. And Eleanor had said that was great. That everybody should do what she liked best in life. That was one of the best things about going to a great university. To find out what was available.

And over the days that followed, Raleigh told her about all the guys who were always hanging around her, how besieged it made her feel, as if she were being stalked, hunted down.

"Why do they do that?" Raleigh asked unhappily.

"You're a beautiful girl," Eleanor said.

"But I don't do anything to make it seem as if I'm interested," Raleigh said, exasperated. "I don't wear makeup. I don't dress to attract them. I just plow along, with my head down. I mean, this being a girl, you really can't be yourself, can you? It's like, going in, everything you do has to be a covert operation."

"That's one way to put it," Eleanor agreed with a smile.

"And all those dumb things they say," Raleigh complained. "'I want to take care of you.' This one boy, Craig, he's always saying that. I mean, why would I want anybody to take care of me? It's insulting, his saying that."

"Well, it's the way they're brought up, dear," Eleanor said. "If they love somebody, they want to protect them. It's traditional."

"Well, maybe it is," Raleigh admitted. "But I'm not. I'll tell you that. And you're not, either. How did you do that, Eleanor?"

"It was a matter of deciding my priorities," Eleanor said thoughtfully. "My work was always first, of course. Then Charles came along, and I had to decide if I could make the fit. The intellectual with a commitment to another person. It was very difficult. For the first few years, I didn't think I was giving my best to my work, or to Charles. But it turned out to be just a matter of adjusting. And it's worked out for me," she added. "For Charles, too, I think."

Raleigh watched her as she lit another cigarette, felt a pang of anxiety as she realized the wafting smoke seemed more substantial than Eleanor herself. Thought of how ill Charles looked and imperceptibly shook her head.

"What about you, dear?" Eleanor prodded. "After all, you're eighteen years old. A lot of girls are interested in boys when they're younger than you are. Don't you find any of the boys you meet to be attractive? Interesting?"

"Once," Raleigh said. "But that was a long time ago."

Maybe it was because of that particular conversation she'd had with Eleanor, but it seemed to Raleigh that she had been thinking about Toosie a lot over the next few days, even remembering some of the feelings she'd had about him back in the waning days of her life as a boy. So at first she thought she had to be wrong when one of the three new research assistants who arrived at the compound on the same boat that brought Bruno Bettelheim turned out to be Toosie Horton.

It didn't make any sense, after all. A guy who was being groomed to be a major newspaper publisher in Los Angeles wasn't going to turn up down here. And then he didn't look the way he had looked when she knew him. He was so tall now, way over six feet. There had been something unformed and sweet about his face, but now his cheekbones were defined, his skin taut, tanned. How she knew it was him were his ears, well shaped next to his head, and his hands, with the long, slender fingers she had wanted to touch her even then. And there was that same interested, open look in his gray eyes when he took her hand, introduced himself to her.

"I'm Toosie Horton," he said.

"I'm Leigh Fisk," she said, watching the puzzled expression on his face now, sensing him trying to remember where, when. "I'm Eleanor and Charles's ward."

She could feel him straining, trying to keep himself from blurting out something silly. Oh, how I've missed you, maybe, because that was what she was trying not to say. And then there they were, all those old feelings flooding over her again, drowning her with happiness, with the joy of seeing him again.

∘   ∘   ∘

Maybe Bruno Bettelheim was brilliant that night after dinner as he talked about symbolism in fairy tales, or something. You couldn't prove it by me, Raleigh thought, slumped in a chair, a glass of wine in her hand, along with everybody else. He could have been talking in Sanskrit, for all she knew, her head swimming with visions of Toosie, of what he had meant to her when he was her first crush. And now here he was, just across the room. Looking at her. She could feel it.

Almost without realizing what she was doing, Raleigh rose and drifted out onto the terrace overlooking the sand, the sea. He was right behind her, as she had known he would be. She could feel him standing there, hear his breathing. She turned, looked up at him as he stood in the moonlight. It's really you, she thought. I could reach out and touch you.

"It's a beautiful night," she said.

"Yes, it's great," he said, a note of wariness in his voice. "You know, it's the strangest thing. I know we've met before."

Raleigh smiled. The same old line. Well, this time it was true.

"You've probably heard that one before," he said with a little laugh.

"I have the same feeling about you," she whispered, putting out her hand, taking his.

They sauntered along, holding hands, their bodies close together, the foam from the ocean trickling unnoticed over their sandals. And he was making college chitchat about Harvard and how much he liked it there. How it had opened up worlds to him that he hadn't known existed. And she was telling him about the University of Chicago. And about how she'd been in Boston the year before when her best friend had gotten married.

"She's a doctor and so is he," Raleigh said. "I was in the wedding, a bridesmaid."

"Maybe I know them," Toosie said. "Maybe that was it. What are their names?"

"No, I'm sure it wasn't," Raleigh said quickly. "Look, let's not force it, okay? It'll come to us."

"Okay," he agreed, his hand tightening on her own. "It wasn't that recent anyway," he added. "I know I sound like an idiot, but it's almost as if it were in another life."

Oh, yes, Toosie, you're right, she wanted to say. Smiled instead. Said nothing.

"That's really something, a line like that coming from me." He laughed. "The most practical man on the face of the earth, after all. Practically a mathematician, all but standing in front of my first class in some university somewhere."

"You're going to be a mathematician?" she asked.

"I sure am," he said. "And believe me, it's been a fight with my family. You see, my family has a newspaper in Los Angeles. We go way back. And my great-grandfather was the publisher, and his son, and his. My father. And I'm next up."

"But you don't want to do it," she said.

"I'm not going to do it," he vowed.

"So what happens to it?"

"Well, there's my sister, Gail," he said. "She loves it, hangs around down there all the time. She'll be great."

"How about your family?" she asked. "What do they think about that?"

"They were shocked. Really. But why not? Everything's different now. Take my mother, for example. I'm sure that when she was growing up, she thought she'd get married, raise her kids. Do a little volunteer work. And do you know what she's doing now? She's a lawyer. That's what she's doing now."

"How do you feel about that?" Raleigh asked.

"How would I feel about it?" he asked. "It's her life, not mine."

"What about your father?" she asked.

"Oh, I don't know," Toosie said unhappily. "I think

maybe it hurt his feelings, that their marriage, the family, wasn't enough for her. I think he has a girlfriend."

"That's too bad," she said.

"Maybe for the girlfriend it's too bad," he agreed. "Because he'll never ask for a divorce, never break up the family. Set the old example for the community, you know. Above reproach, at least in public."

"What about you?" she asked. "Do you have a girlfriend?"

"Well, I want to talk to you about that," he said, putting his arm around her shoulders, pulling her close to him as they wandered along the edge of the sea, the laughter and music from the compound faint in the distance.

And then everything had to be about her. About what she wanted to do with her life. About how she saw herself at the moment, in the future. And what about the past? he asked her. Who are you? Where do you come from? Those things were difficult to talk about. She trotted out the same old story about her loss of memory, got his sympathy without wanting it.

The gray dawn was turning pink when they spotted the compound ahead of them. "I have to get to sleep," he murmured, "because that way I can be with you again as soon as I wake up."

Is he going to kiss me? Raleigh wondered, frowning. Will I let him? Do I want him to?

"Promise me you'll be here when I wake up," he begged her, holding both of her hands, looking down into her eyes.

"I promise," she said.

That evening he called her darling for the first time.

"I feel as if I've known you all my life," he whispered, his lips touching her ear as he stood behind her, his arms around her waist.

"Yes." She sighed, her hands on his.

"I've never felt like this before," he said, thought about it for a moment, then added, "Well, maybe once."

"Oh, tell me about that," she said, pulling away, facing him.

"I was just a kid," he said with a dismissive motion of his hand. "I was only fifteen."

"What was she like?" Raleigh teased, a little surprised at what she saw in his face. A flush of guilt under his tan.

"I've never told anybody this before," he began, looking away. "But it wasn't a girl. It was another boy. I'd never been so attracted to anybody in my life. I was nuts about him, but I couldn't believe it, couldn't believe it was happening to me. I mean, if you came from my family, you couldn't be a fag, after all. It just wasn't possible. And then I told myself that it was just a phase. That I'd get through it."

It was all right, she wanted to tell him as she stood over him where he'd slumped in a chair. I felt it, too. She knelt at his feet, took his hand in hers.

"And then I figured out what it must have been," he said. "This kid, it was Raleigh Barnes. Do you remember? The movie star that drowned? Well, we had sort of been hanging out when I was home for a couple of weeks from prep school. And I think what it was, well, I think I was just dazzled by all of his fame and the attention he got. The stardust. It was pretty impressive, I can tell you."

"So you just went on," she said. "We all do."

"Well, I wrote him all of these dumb, whining letters," Toosie said with an embarrassed little smile. "I don't know what he must have thought. That I was coming on to him, or something. It was really sick."

"But in the past," she murmured.

"Yes," he said, stroking her hair. "It's in the past. Thank you for that."

Raleigh reached up, took his face in her hands, brought it down to hers. His open mouth on hers was hot and sweet, made her whole body shudder with the pleasure of it. He was pulling her toward him now, clutching her against his chest, his arms locked around her as he covered her face with a flurry of desperate little kisses. Groaned aloud as he licked her parted lips, kissed her again. Softly at first, then harder, as if he wanted to suck her into himself, absorb her. And she wanted that to happen in a funny kind of way, she thought wildly, panting as she pulled away from him. That was the magic, she realized slowly. When you cared. And that was the downside, too. Oh, God, she thought. What have I done?

"Forgive me," she said, jumping up. "I can't do this."

"Darling, we can do it," he said plaintively. "We belong together."

Oh, he was so sweet, she thought miserably. He was nearly on the verge of tears she realized with a start as she looked at the pain in his gray eyes, the longing. And it had felt so good to be in his arms, would feel so good to just give herself up to him. Go the emotional and physical places that she knew her feelings for him would let him take her.

"Good night," she said abruptly, then turned and hurried away from him, her sandals clicking on the tiled floor.

CHAPTER 58

$\mathcal{I}$t had been a horrible night, Raleigh thought, shaking her head as she pulled open drawers, started to stack some of her things on the bureau. One of the worst. She was so angry with herself that she had barely closed her eyes. What had it been about? she asked herself grimly. Love? Nostalgia? Curiosity? Whatever. And when it came down to it, was she just another wimp with the same amount of character as a wet tea bag? Well, she wasn't, she told herself. She was the same person she had been raised to be. Strong. Self-reliant. Focused. And don't forget, she thought. A kiss is just a kiss. Swell.

At the door of her bedroom there was a tentative tap.

"*Bueno,*" she called.

Slowly the door opened, and there he was. Toosie. What a silly name for a grown man, she thought crossly as she looked at him. He looked so fresh and clean in his shorts, his loose shirt, his sandals, as if he had just stepped out of the shower. And, golly, he was big. He nearly filled the doorway.

"I came to apologize for last night," he said slowly.

"Why?" she asked. "I was the one who kissed you."

"Well, I'm sorry anyway," he said. "I didn't mean for you to run off that way."

"It doesn't matter," she said indifferently, folding a shirt. Then another.

"What are you doing?" he asked.

"I'm packing," she said. "I'm going back to school."

"But it's weeks before you have to be there," he protested.

"But I'm going now," she said, reaching under her bed, pulling out a suitcase.

"So I'm driving you out of your own home," he said. "That's great, isn't it?"

"You're not driving me anywhere," she said. "This is a decision that I'm making because I think it's the best thing to do."

"Look, don't be like this," he said, his voice exasperated. "Will you stop clattering around for a minute? Will you sit down and talk to me? Please."

"Oh, all right." She sighed, wondering, when he was next to her, why he had to smell so good. Why it had to be this difficult to keep herself from reaching out, touching him. There should be a law, she decided, smiling to herself as they strolled onto her terrace, settled across the table there in a couple of rattan chairs. Some of the kids were hooting and laughing, playing in the surf, and the morning sun was bright in the sky.

"What you do is your own business," he said quietly after a moment or two, "but aside from my presence here, I don't think you're being responsible when you say you're going to leave."

"And why is that?" she asked, leaning back in her chair, her legs crossed, her arms crossed in front of her.

"Oh, come on, darling," he said impatiently. "It doesn't take Albert Schweitzer to see that Charles is very ill, that Eleanor is fading away. You're their ward. You're responsible for them. You could take off a year, be with them here. After all, what difference does it make? You've got plenty of time."

"Go on," she said pleasantly, wanting to give him a smack across his pompous, self-satisfied face.

"And then, you know, when the time comes," he said,

picking his words carefully, "well, I thought you could transfer to Radcliffe, finish up there."

"Why would I do that?" she asked.

"So that we could be together," he whispered. "I love you. I want to marry you."

He can't be saying this, she thought, a shock running through her. He's only twenty years old, and I'm eighteen. This is ridiculous.

"I have trust funds," he said. "Lots and lots of trust funds that go way back. I'm rich, darling. I can take care of you."

She sat there, looking at him, tapping one of her sandals on the tiled floor.

"Gee, this is exciting," she said at last. "My first proposal. But is this protocol? Aren't you supposed to get down on your knees? Ask Charles for my hand? And where's the ring? There's always a ring, isn't there?"

"Please—" he began, his voice agonized.

"Well, I just think it's so wonderful that you've got everything figured out," she said sarcastically. "We've known each other, what? A couple of days? And on the basis of that, you really think I'm going to give up everything that matters to me and that we're going to settle down and live happily ever after?"

"I just want to do whatever I can so that we can be together," he said unhappily. "I'm not presuming anything. Really I'm not."

"Well, good," she said. "I'm glad to hear that. Really. Because when the boat leaves tomorrow at noon, I'll be on it."

"Okay," he said. "I'll come with you."

"I thought you'd made a commitment to do an internship here for a year," she said coldly. "That is why you've come, isn't it?"

"Oh, God," he said. "That was the worst decision I've ever made."

"Oh, you'll like it," she said airily. "Everybody does. It'll do your career a lot of good. And where else can you sit down and get to talk to somebody like Bruno Bettelheim?"

"Don't do this to me, darling," he begged.

"I don't see what I'm doing to you," she said. "After all, you're the one who plotted out my whole life for me, if I remember correctly."

"Can I ask you just one thing?" he said.

"Sure," she said.

"And, will you tell me the truth?" he said.

"Yes, yes," she said impatiently. "What is it?"

"Do you love me?" he asked, his voice breaking.

She sighed, sat there for a few minutes looking out at the ocean, thinking about it. Glanced over at him and reflected on the slump of his broad shoulders, the pleading look in his eyes.

"I can't think about things like that," she said. "There are a lot of things I have to do first. And getting through school is the first one. I've talked it over with Eleanor and Charles. Of course I know how ill they are. But it's what they want. They want me to finish school, to be prepared."

"These things you have to do," he muttered. "What are they?"

"I have to find myself," she said with a laugh.

"I just can't believe you would say something like that," he said, shaking his head, a flicker of contempt in his gray eyes. "You know what you sound like? Some earnest freshman who's just left home for the first time. Nobody else would say a thing like that."

"It is funny, isn't it?" she agreed, laughing. "But you see, this time it's true. Literally."

Eleanor didn't even seem surprised when Raleigh told her, during the hour they spent together just before dinner, the way they did each day, that she was going back to school. "It's too soon for you to have someone in your life," she said. And Raleigh had nodded, said that maybe it would never be the right time. That she had done balancing acts in her life, but that she didn't have a clue about how to manage this one. Worse, she didn't even know how to start to practice to be able to do it somewhere along the line. And when she was standing on the deck of the boat the next day, looking back at the cluster of figures on the dock as they grew smaller and smaller, it was as if a piece of herself had been torn out of her, left behind with Toosie.

"I'll write to you every day," he had said.

And she had told him, "No, don't do that. I won't open your letters. Promise me."

"I want to kiss you good-bye," he had whispered, putting out his hand.

"You just don't understand," she had murmured, shaking her head.

He seemed to be with her all the time, always in her thoughts, her dreams. It was like being possessed, she thought, irritated with herself, as she worked harder and harder in her classes. Astronomy, physics, all of it. The theory was easy enough. The details were excruciating. And always there were the wraithlike figures of Eleanor and Charles, so ill, both of them. Soon to be dependent on her the way for years she had been dependent on them. When would they start to need her? she worried as she would snap awake over her books. Because it was going to happen. Everything now was a race against time.

CHAPTER 59

*W*ould you like anything else, senorita?" the dark-haired stewardess asked. "Another cup of coffee?"

"No, thanks," Raleigh said with a weary sigh, vaguely aware of the woman as she pulled the heavy cart up the aisle. She still wore her apron, Raleigh noticed. And some of the other passengers were roaming around, leaning over a seat here and there, chatting in that subdued way people had on planes. Still, it wouldn't be long before they landed. She could feel it. The jet was at the point in its flight where it seemed to be suspended in the sky, just dawdling around for a while until the pilot was told he could start his descent.

Well, she'd gotten to be an expert on the various sounds made by a jet engine, she thought gloomily, looking out the window at the rectangular patches of farmland way below. Looking at nothing, really. Not even a road. And when all of these trips had started, well, the timing couldn't have been worse, since she had been right at the beginning of her senior year.

It had been that letter of Eleanor's, the first one she had gotten when she was back at school after her summer at home. Oh, it had been so strange, Raleigh half expecting Toosie to still be there, although none of the research assistants stayed more than a year. And Eleanor, so sensitive as always, not mentioning his name, not volunteering anything about his year there, how it had gone. Waiting for Raleigh to ask. Waiting in vain.

They missed her already, Eleanor had written in a handwriting suddenly fragile. When Raleigh got a moment, they would appreciate it if she would send the following list of books. And the afterthought. That Charles hadn't been feeling at all well. That they were going up to Houston, to the hospital again. Just some tests, Eleanor added. Raleigh wasn't to worry.

That had been the first time. The dash out to O'Hare, the flight to Houston, trying to study on the plane. The four days sitting in hospital corridors, holding Eleanor's hand. The doctors didn't find anything that time, either. And then the next time, and the next. Somehow she was doing just fine in her classes between trips. Making Phi Beta Kappa. Oh, Eleanor had loved that. She was so pleased. And then the time when they thought they had figured it out. Some blood disease, they said. They were going to try a few things, see if something would work.

And finally Raleigh's senior year was over. She was a graduate at last. Magna cum laude, too, and accepted in the master's program at Caltech.

Eleanor had been so thrilled, Raleigh remembered, tears moistening her eyes. Why, they'd even gone out to a restaurant there in Houston that somebody at the hospital recommended. Ordered a bottle of champagne to celebrate. And it was almost as if that had been all Eleanor had been waiting for, because it was only a week or two later that she was a patient, too. Drifting in and out of consciousness. She was just worn out. That's what the doctors said it was. And nothing that they tried with Charles was working, either.

So that was what it was like, those last couple of months. It seemed to Raleigh that she was living in the corridors of that hospital, living for the few minutes each hour she could spend at Eleanor's bedside, at Charles's. Former students, kids who'd interned down at the compound came. Even some of the celebrated dropped by when they were on their way through town. And the flowers. There were thousands and thousands. Telegrams, too. Elegant handwritten notes, hoping for the best.

Ann came from Boston, stopping off in Minnesota to leave the twins with her parents. The two of them sat together in silence on brightly colored plastic chairs in the hospital lounge, the television set mounted overhead a soothing drone, their coffee cold in Stryrofoam cups, the pizza they had ordered forgotten in its cardboard box.

Charles died first, Eleanor a few hours later.

"Thank God it's over," Ann said through her tears. "And how blessed they were, that neither of them knew the other was gone."

Raleigh nodded, too emotionally exhausted to speak. Or to cry.

And what a darling Ann was, Raleigh thought gratefully in the days that followed. To just put her classes, everything, on hold, to let Larry fend for himself without even giving it a thought so that she could be there for her. Nurture her, support her while she dealt with the things that had to be done.

Ann went along with her to the lawyer's office for the reading of the will. The compound and an endowment to maintain it had been left to the Mexican government to be used as an international study center. Trinkets, rare books, all kinds of treasured personal effects went to former students, research assistants, distant relatives. The copyrights on all of the early books and the bulk of the estate were left to the University of Chicago. The copyrights on the three most recent books were left to Raleigh. So was the rest of the money in the estate. Raleigh's eyes widened at the staggering sum. I can do it, she thought. I can go home in style, even my score with Paul. Reclaim what's mine. Thank you, my darling Eleanor. Thank you, dear, sweet Charles.

Ann had flown with her back to Mexico to help with the

inventory, to get everything in order for the new administrators. But it was Raleigh alone who had stood on the deck of the boat a few miles out to sea under a blazing sun and who, with shaking hands, tossed handfuls of the ashes that had been mixed together in the urn into the air, watched as they drifted onto the blue-green waters, and whispered her good-byes to Eleanor and Charles Fisk while tears trickled down her cheeks.

There was a stream of Spanish from the intercom in the front of the plane as the stewardesses, in their uniforms now, hurried down the aisle, collecting plastic glasses, napkins. And then the same words in softly accented English. The usual stuff about seats, trays in upright positions. FASTEN YOUR SEATBELTS, directed the overhead signs as they pinged on throughout the plane. EXTINGUISH ALL SMOKING MATERIALS.

"Thank you for Flying Mexicana," the voice said. "The entire crew joins me in hoping you've had a pleasant flight. We are now beginning our final approach into Los Angeles."

Raleigh felt her heart beat faster as she looked out the window, saw the ribbons of freeways looping around each other, the streams of cars on them glittering in the sun. A mountain range was hazy in the distance, tall clusters of buildings jutted into the sky. Below was a sea of red-tiled roofs, the swimming pools in the backyards a string of sapphires. And everywhere the green of the trees, every conceivable shade.

She reached under the seat in front of her and found her elegant new tote bag, feeling funny in a way, as if she had been living in a state of suspended animation for all the years she had been away. Feeling as if she were only now, this minute, coming alive again. She dug around for the makeup case she had also bought in Texas at Neiman Marcus. Turned to the page in *Vogue* that showed the model painted with the acceptable mask of the moment.

The eye shadows, lots of them, blue, gray, lavender. Tons and tons of black mascara. Blusher. Not much mouth these days, she saw. Pale pink, an overcoat of shiny gloss. She ran a brush through her shiny brown hair that fell below her shoulders. Gave herself one of those phony, smoldering stares that all the models in the magazines affected. Laughed out loud as she snapped her compact closed, stuffed it back in the tote.

The plane was rolling up to its terminal now, stopping. The stewardesses were pulling open the door. Raleigh stood, hiked up her tight jeans, and adjusted the handkerchief in the breast pocket of her navy blue cashmere blazer.

Just outside the door to Customs, she spotted the black-clad chauffeur who was waving a sign that said MISS FISK. He had the bland good looks of a second lead on a daytime soap. Probably an out-of-work actor playing the role of the perfect chauffeur, she thought with a smile as she waved him over. He was good. He even touched his cap as he smiled deferentially at her, picked up her bags, and indicated with a small motion of his hand that she should follow him. She felt almost as if she would burst with joy as she strode briskly along, heard the clicking of her high-heeled boots. The door slid open as he approached, and with the suggestion of a bow, he stood aside. Raleigh stepped out into the California day, felt the slight breeze, the sunshine touch her face.

Welcome home, Raleigh Barnes, she said to herself.

Raleigh sat right next to the open window in the back-seat of the sleek, black limousine as the chauffeur joined the flow of traffic and swung out of the airport. The streets were so wide, so clean, the palm trees so tall, weaving slightly in the delicious breeze. And everything was so familiar, so right. Just ahead was MGM. Oh, she could almost see herself sitting in front of her makeup mirror in her dressing room again with the makeup woman working on her, the hairdresser, the wardrobe woman waiting their turns, could almost see herself on the set there when the last light had been adjusted just as Darby would bark that it was a take and the camera would start to roll.

And there were all kinds of new apartment complexes behind discreet wrought-iron gates, a golf course that went on and on, where foursomes in bright clothes took their turns as they teed off.

Here they were, right across the street from the entrance to Twentieth Century-Fox. And there was the winding street from the turn of the century, a permanent set with its quaint apartment houses, cozy neighborhood shops, just beyond the gate where a uniformed guard was talking to someone in a blue Alfa Romeo.

Oh, the days, the months she had spent inside those gates when the Raleigh Barnes Production Company had been renting space there while they were shooting. She could almost feel the old juices rising, smiled at the thought of being in there, throwing herself around again.

Now the chauffeur was cutting through Century City, joining the heavy traffic, the great-looking cars, the UPS trucks, the messengers on their motorcycles. A fountain splashed on the island in the middle of the boulevard, and all around there were all kinds of new skyscrapers. There were a lot of people strolling on the sidewalks, waiting to cross at the red lights. Men in business suits, women in pretty dresses with short, short skirts.

They inched their way north on Whittier Drive in front of the grammar school with its red-tiled roofs, graceful arches, as a cadre of crossing guards held up signs and glamorous young mothers hurried their beautifully dressed children into sleek Jaguars and Mercedes-Benz convertibles with the tops down. And then they were moving north past elaborate homes, a profusion of flowers. Graceful jacaranda trees rained their lavender blossoms over lawns so green it was hard for Raleigh to believe they were real.

"I'd like to make one quick detour," Raleigh said to the back of the chauffeur's head.

"Certainly, Miss Fisk," he said.

"It's 11607 Summit Circle," she said. "It's off Benedict Canyon."

"Oh, sure," he said. "The old Raleigh Barnes estate. A lot of people want to see it. It's great, isn't it, what the Academy is doing for him?"

"What's that?" Raleigh asked. "I've been on a plane all day."

"Oh, giving him a special posthumous award," the chauffeur said. "It was in the *Hollywood Reporter* just this morning."

She frowned, felt a sudden chill.

"Are you in the business?" she asked.

"Well, I'm trying to be," he said.

"How's it going so far?" she asked.

"Pretty well," he said hesitantly. "I've only been in town for three months, and I've got an agent already. She's sending me over to meet the casting director on one of the soaps."

"That's wonderful," Raleigh said

"Are you here on vacation?" he asked politely.

"No, I'm not," she said. "I've always lived here. I'm coming home."

Raleigh remembered every curve of the winding road, noted the new mansions that stood on what had been vacant lots choked with weeds. And then there it was, the high brick wall painted white, bright flowers at its base. And just around this bend was the front gate. The chauffeur would get out of the car, buzz the house. Those high gates would swing slowly open, and they would be on the curving drive, skirting the lake. She closed her eyes, could almost see the house coming into view. Stately, imposing, all three stories of it, with its nests of chimneys on the roof. The front door would open, and it would be Paul, telling Raleigh to come into the library for a minute, there were some people he wanted her to meet. Or Darby saying that he had some time, and why didn't they get in some serious work in the gym. Or maybe it would be her mother with a fluttery kiss on the cheek, surreptitiously patting her shoulders, her arms, making sure she was still in one piece. And, of course, Frisky, yapping, wiggling around.

"It must be something," the chauffeur said wistfully, "living in a place like that."

"Okay," she said. "We can go to the hotel now."

Even before she had finished tipping the bellboy and closed the door to her bungalow behind the Beverly Hills Hotel, the phone began to ring.

That's odd, Raleigh thought as she answered it.

"Leigh?" said a hearty male voice.

"This is Leigh," she said, puzzled.

"This is Buzz Gilbert," the man said. "I thought we could have dinner tonight if you're free. I know Jimmy at the Bistro. It's late, I know, but I think he'll probably be able to work us in."

"Do I know you?" she asked.

"Well, not exactly," he said with an embarrassed laugh. "I was just giving the kid my car outside when you pulled up in your limousine. I'm staying here at the hotel, too. I'm with a big ad agency in New York, and I'm out here all the time. And, listen, I'm an all right guy. You just ask the guy at the front desk. He'll vouch for me."

"Well, look," Raleigh said, "it's very nice of you, but I've been flying all day. I'm just going to stay in, order from room service."

"Well, how about a little company?" he asked.

"No, no, thanks," Raleigh said. "Maybe some other time."

"Would you mind if I called again?" he said.

"Why don't I call you?" she countered, keeping it easy, pleasant, as she said good-bye, just in time to answer the tap at the door. It was the bellboy again, carrying a vase with a couple dozen long-stemmed red roses. Those were from another guy who had seen her in the lobby when she registered, giving his room number, asking that she call.

So maybe the first part of the plan she'd started to form was going to work out, she thought, tapping the card on top of the bureau, looking at the roses, thinking how pretty they were. To look as hot and sexy and gorgeous as she could, to turn up in a limousine to establish the level. To cast the net, start to get around a little, see what was going on. Figure out in time how to get to all of those people who had been so important in her past, what to say to them when she did so that she could prove who she was. That was the most important thing. And she knew it wasn't going to be easy, never dreamed for a minute that it would happen overnight. It was going to take patience, hard work, focus, and, in time, the way to do it would reveal itself.

And then she could get on with the second part of her agenda. Dealing with Paul. She thought of the posthumous award the Academy was going to present to Raleigh Barnes, knew the lobbying and pressure that must have gone into that decision. That had all been Paul, of course, keeping the product viable, making sure the library of Raleigh Barnes films kept on generating income, making money for him as he slept, as the old saying went.

She could see it, she really could, how he just had to have her out of the picture. Dead and gone. What a potential disaster it would have been if she had been here all along. Getting angry with him, perhaps, trying to prove who she was. Making a big fuss in the press. Destroying everything. She thought again of that awful night on the boat for the first time in a couple of years. Remembered the shock, the fright as she looked up, saw the rock he was holding just as he started to bring it down.

She slid open the glass door leading onto the patio, breathed the perfumed air. Thought how sweet it was to be home at last.

CHAPTER 60

$\mathcal{E}$verybody in the Polo Lounge at breakfast the next morning looked up when Raleigh walked in. The out-of-town businessmen in their gray suits, sitting alone at tables covered with pink tablecloths. The *New York Times* and *Wall Street Journal*. The well-dressed tourists with their subdued children at the tables in the middle of the room. The people in the pink leather banquettes edging the room who looked as if they were in the industry, agents, maybe, producers, directors in their open-necked shirts, their hairy chests dripping with gold chains. The odd publicist, perhaps. And there was Lloyd Bridges, Raleigh saw as the hostess led her to a table. God, he never changed. He looked marvelous.

Oh, she'd been at meetings at every one of those banquettes in her life as a boy, dragged along by Paul when he wanted to impress someone. She'd been so bored, sitting there, kicking at the booth, being cooed over by the motherly waitresses. Signing autographs for the tourists who would shyly offer their books. Leaping up and rushing over to the window to try to get a glimpse of one of the cats who lived on the patio. It was beautiful, Raleigh realized again, looking out. One of the most beautiful patios in all of Beverly Hills.

A busboy brought her coffee, the waitress brought her a business card from one of the agents at one of the banquettes. *Call me if you are an actress,* it said, scrawled on the back. Raleigh smiled across the room at him, saw his hopeful, calculating eyes. Thought about all the things she had to do.

When she was finished with her scrambled eggs, sliced tomatoes, and whole wheat toast, she wandered out to the portico at the entrance to the hotel, sat in one of the chairs, and watched the parking lot attendants in their green uniforms. There were a couple of Corvettes, she saw, the people in them looking like rock stars. A few Rolls-Royces with business executives, expensive-looking wives with good jewelry. Cadillacs for the older, more sedate crowd. The people getting out of the Jaguars had just about the right look. Expensive, with it, but tasteful. When Warren Beatty arrived, he was driving a brown Mercedes-Benz convertible. A few other people were driving the same model. What finally convinced Raleigh to rent the Mercedes-Benz was when Natalie Wood also arrived behind the wheel of one of them.

She'd have to go over to Caltech, make arrangements for her master's classes a few months down the road. Arrange to use the gymnasium, its bars, rings, all of it, meantime. Most important, though, was the hairdresser. The very best, the one who was so hot everybody went to him.

The woman working in the flower shop said Bobby Prise. So did the woman in the boutique right at the entrance to the hotel, and all the salespeople in the jewelry shop after a short conference.

"That's incredible," Raleigh mused. "He's been around for years."

"Well, I wouldn't know about that," one of the women in the jewelry shop said. "I only transferred out here from New York two months ago."

So it was Bobby, thought Raleigh, shaking her head, and with his own place, of all things. She wouldn't have believed it, remembering him, that half-glazed look of his as if he were on a number of controlled chemical substances that didn't necessarily mix well together.

Mary Tyler Moore was just getting out of Bobby's chair when Raleigh was led through the salon to his station. Maybe it hadn't been such a good idea to come, she decided. She realized how raw and vulnerable she suddenly felt at the sight of him, as if a wound long healed had been torn open. Oh, it was such a long time ago when Bobby would stop by to lighten up her roots. And that last time she had seen him, in Mexico, the day it had happened. And he looked so good now, as handsome as ever, his hair to his shoulders. A black silk shirt, open at the collar. Black jeans. A silver belt buckle adorned with turquoise.

Another thing she hadn't considered crossed her mind. That her mother still came to him, and that she might be here. And oh, Raleigh wasn't ready for that. Not yet.

"I'm Bobby Prise," he said, putting out his hand to take hers, that same bemused look in his eyes, that same dopey smile that had always made it seem to Raleigh as if Bobby weren't playing with a full deck.

"I'm Leigh Fisk." She smiled tentatively.

"I'm sorry I'm late," he murmured. "I had an emergency. They just had to come in right now, for a comb-out. And I just did them last night, before they went out to dinner."

"Well, I'm really happy you could work me in," Raleigh said. "You're very popular."

"We started to do that when we opened, accommodate guests from the hotel," Bobby said vaguely, looking around at all the stations, all the mirrors, the operators cutting, setting, combing. The manicurists, the wash boys and girls, the kids sweeping up, pouring coffee. The massive flower arrangements everywhere. The marble floors, the pale, suede walls. The soft rock coming over the loudspeakers. The customers. A horde of women, some men, too. "I didn't think it would be like this, you know," he said, wonder in his voice. "This wasn't my plan. I thought by now I'd be somewhere on a beautiful, expensive island with lots and lots of servants and things. I never thought I'd still be a hairdresser. I mean, I'm forty years old. It's so unattractive."

"You're more of a businessman, aren't you?" asked Raleigh, smiling at him in the mirror, thinking how good it felt to see him again. "After all, it's your name over the door."

"Well, I guess so," Bobby agreed. "But I didn't do it. I mean, I could never put together an operation like this. It's all Debi, actually. She was a manicurist at a place I used to work called Secrets. And she thought I had a lot of talent, and she had a good head for business, and so she said why didn't we become partners."

"And it worked," said Raleigh.

"Oh, this is just the beginning," he said mournfully, as if he were going to cry. "She's raised all this money, and we're coming out with our own line of shampoos and conditioners. She found this chemist making the stuff in his garage, and it's great. It works. She checked around, found the best marketing and distribution people, the best advertising agency. Everything."

"Well, that's wonderful," Raleigh said.

"All of those people, they all talk very softly when I'm at the meetings," he said. "It's Debi. She told them that loud noises upset me."

"Do they?" Raleigh asked.

"Oh, I don't know," he said, shaking his head. "It just all seems like so much responsibility. I tell you, it makes me just want to get on a plane, go somewhere. Never come back."

"But you won't," Raleigh said.

"Walk away from all this success? All this money?" he murmured to himself. "No, no. I never would. I have everything I've ever wanted. But I never thought it would happen. I mean, I'm not the type."

"I guess you are the type," Raleigh said with a little laugh.

His eyes met hers in the mirror, widened as if he were only then realizing that she was sitting there. Realized that he had been saying all these things to her.

"This is crazy," he said abruptly. "I feel as if I've known you forever."

"I feel that way, too," she said.

Then his mood brightened and he was all sunny again, grinning at her in the mirror with that look of dazzled appreciation she remembered so well. Telling her that she was glorious-looking. Exquisite. That she was really going to knock them dead. That she could be a model. An actress. A movie star, the biggest. He knew. He'd seen a million of them come and go, and he could tell.

And all Raleigh wanted to do was say, Bobby, it's me. I'm home. I need you to help me. But she couldn't, of course. Couldn't take the chance of sounding like some lunatic, not until she had something, anything, that would back her claim. If there *was* something. Anything. But she couldn't let herself think that. Couldn't even entertain the notion.

Where was she from? he wanted to know. And when she said she was from Chicago, he said, well, then, they hadn't met there because he'd never been in Chicago, and wasn't it very cold. That's what he'd heard. But still, she reminded him of somebody. She really did.

"I need to buy some clothes," she said. "Where should I go?"

"Rodeo Drive," he said. "It's all boutiques."

He started to tell her about his belt buckle, and how he had known exactly what he wanted. Looked everywhere. Spent weeks. But nothing. So a friend with a plane, a Learjet, had said, well, this is getting so complicated, and why didn't they just run over to Santa Fe, New Mexico, and they did.

"It's a great belt," she said.

"Do you think so?" he asked.

"Oh, yes. Really."

He smiled at her again in the mirror, and said that he

knew a couple of places where they could start. That he'd go with her, that he knew exactly how she should look. And there were other places he would take her. The "in" restaurants. Stuff like that. That it would be fun to show her everything if she wanted him to. That it would make him feel young again, maybe. No strings. He didn't go in for that sort of thing.

"That would be perfect," she said to his reflection in the mirror. Saw a short, redheaded person closing in fast, her face pinched with fury.

"Do you know how late you're running?" the woman said. "Do you know who you're keeping waiting, Bobby?"

"Oh, Debi." He sighed. "I'll be through in a minute."

Bobby watched her stride away, a tendril of Raleigh's hair curled around his fingers.

"She scares me to death," Bobby said, turning back to her. "She absolutely terrifies me."

Raleigh looked into his face, saw only amusement.

"It's just fine," he said with a smile. "It's gone too far, this business thing. She's created me and now she can't do without me."

And he was right, Raleigh saw, as she nodded.

"So let's go," he said, taking her elbow as the two of them strolled out of the salon into the bright morning sun.

It seemed to Raleigh that there couldn't be this many charming shops, so many wonderful things for sale. The silk shirts, the perfect belts. Just the right scarf. The tiny miniskirts, the dark stockings, the shoes with their high, high heels. And always there was Bobby's voice, the murmured fragments of gossip as they sauntered from boutique to boutique.

They strolled among the tourists in their Bermuda shorts, summer dresses, cameras slung around their necks, down the street to Van Cleef & Arpels where Bobby stopped, gazed reverently into the window at a magnificent diamond and emerald necklace, matching earrings.

"I can see those on you," he said, smiling shyly at her. "That's the only jewelry you'll ever need."

Raleigh stood next to him, admiring the necklace, the earrings. Leaned forward to read the price. $495,000.

"They're beautiful," she said with a laugh.

Then he was taking her arm, whispering another little bit of gossip into her ear as they walked along, this one about Henry Kissinger. He's the Secretary of State, Bobby said, and Raleigh said, well, yes, she knew. "So, anyway," Bobby said, "he met one of my clients, this really pretty actress, at a cocktail party, and he asked her to dinner. Well, the Secretary of State. She was really thrilled. She got all dressed up, and I went up there myself, did her hair. She waited and waited, and he didn't come. Finally there was a phone call. It was the Secret Service. They were in a phone booth. They'd gotten lost and they were asking for directions.

"You just have to laugh," Bobby said solemnly.

Raleigh smiled, nodded at him, then frowned as she wondered how long it would be before the stories Bobby would tell her would be about her mother, about Fern. Little revelations that might point her in the right direction. This was awful, she thought, wincing. Here was Bobby, so sweet, so guileless, only trying to amuse a pretty girl he'd never seen before, and here she was, a phony, a user, exploiting him.

"It's time for lunch," Bobby said.

"Oh, I don't know," Raleigh said hesitantly. "You've been so nice, but I've taken a lot of your time."

"Who cares?" he said insouciantly, helping her into the driver's seat of her smart little Mercedes-Benz.

Well, I'll just have to make it all right somehow, she thought gloomily as she drove, following his directions. I promise myself I will, she resolved as she glanced over at Bobby, silently promised him, too.

CHAPTER 61

I don't have to listen, Raleigh told herself. I'll just say I don't want to hear about my mother or Fern, she decided, feeling better as they drove along in the bright sunshine. And, what luck that Bobby had gone along with her while she did her shopping. He had such perfect taste, knew just when something was a little bit off. She had been smart to just pick up those few basic things at Neiman Marcus in Texas, because there were subtle differences in style here. Yes, everything was going to be all right. She could feel it.

"Ma Maison is just up there," Bobby said, waving a langorous hand. "On the right."

Raleigh saw a bunch of parking lot boys in blue jackets racing around, driving off in expensive cars. A string of Rolls-Royces, Mercedes-Benzes was already lined up in front of what looked like a shabby, middle-class bungalow. No sign anywhere, Raleigh noticed as the two of them got out of the car and followed some people down a passageway cheerful with great terra-cotta pots filled with blooming flowers. Heard the hum of conversation, laughter, music, upbeat and happy, drifting over the terrace.

The sallow-skinned maître d'hotel at the door in his pinstriped suit, a carnation in the buttonhole, was shaking hands with Bobby, bending over her hand, kissing it. Leading them to a table.

So this was the "in" place, the one restaurant in town where everybody came to see and be seen, Raleigh thought, looking around. The umbrellas over the tables advertised Cinzano. So did the ashtrays on the tablecloths which looked like those flowered sheets she'd seen advertised on sale by Sears. The fake grass on the floor was dotted with cigarette burns. Even the shield over the terrace was only corrugated plastic. It sure didn't look like any nice restaurant she'd ever been in before, she thought, disappointed.

Still, the waiter in his striped jacket, his bow tie, was perfect as he took their order for drinks. A glass of white wine for Bobby, a tomato juice for her. And the menu sounded terrific, with all sorts of things to order that made her mouth water.

And the people in the place, well, they were miraculous-looking. Really. The women with their long, long legs, their long hair, their short skirts. The men, impeccably dressed, exercised, tanned, so at ease in their power, their position.

"You see?" Bobby said proudly. "Everybody in the place is looking at you."

"Bobby, everybody in this town looks at everybody," Raleigh said dismissively. "It's just that they don't want to miss anybody."

"No, it's different," Bobby insisted. "I can tell."

And maybe he was right, Raleigh thought. There did seem to be a lot of attention directed at them, at her. Stares, murmured conversations. It was the oddest thing, this being a pretty girl. Not that different, really, from the way it had been during her life as a boy. Only then she had accomplished something. She was a movie star. Now, all she seemed to have to do was show up.

And Bobby was having the best time, she saw. Smiling vaguely, waving to his clients who were scattered around the terrace. Pointing out celebrities. "There's Orson Welles," he said. "He eats here every day."

He was enormous, Raleigh saw, her eyes widening as she watched him waddle in. Why, he must have weighed four hundred pounds. She sipped her tomato juice, thought what fun it was to be sitting here, hanging out with Bobby, what fun it was to see a legend like Orson Welles, feeling tense again, wary, as she felt someone's eyes stabbing at her. Trying to compel her to turn. She concentrated on the menu, wondered about the warm duck salad.

"Oh, look," said Bobby, his voice excited as he touched her arm. "There's Paul Fournier, the producer, and he's looking right at you. I do his wife, or maybe she's almost not his wife anymore, now that they're separated. And he's with Sue Mengers, the agent."

Well, this is it, Raleigh realized, her eyes fixed on Bobby as she tried to smile at him. Felt her mouth go suddenly dry. Nearly seven years, and the moment she had been waiting for had finally arrived. She swallowed, slowly turned. Saw him sitting a couple of tables away.

He looked terrific, she saw. A little gray at the temples now, but he was tan. He hadn't gained an ounce. He wore a blazer, a striped shirt with white collar and cuffs, a muted tie. A lazy half smile as his eyes met hers.

She shuddered, felt herself recoil. No recognition in his expression, of course. Just a sort of free-floating lust.

My father, she thought blankly. The man who tried to kill me. And he'd use me now, kill me again. Without a thought. She could see it in his face.

"She was the sweetest thing when she came to town," Bobby was saying. "So scared. Of course, we all were. We were just kids."

Maybe I'm not up to this, Raleigh realized, all the little hairs on her arms standing on end as she fought to look away from him. I've got my own life. A career down the line. Friends. Even a man I think I'll love someday. Maybe it doesn't matter, what I'm trying to do. I can't sit here, she decided. Not with Paul only a few feet away. But I have to, she told herself.

"They're separated?" Raleigh said in a shaky voice.

"It was such a surprise," Bobby murmured, a puzzled expression in his eyes. "That they stayed together so long, I mean. You know who their child was, don't you? Well, no, you wouldn't. Raleigh Barnes."

"Raleigh Barnes," she said to herself.

"I was there, in Mexico, when it happened," Bobby said, his hands shaking as he lit another cigarette. "It was terrible. Ghastly. The worst thing that ever happened in my life."

"Yes," Raleigh said.

"And Beth Carol, well, she almost died, too," he said. "Raleigh was her whole life."

Raleigh sighed, shook her head.

"So that's when I thought it would happen, when Beth Carol felt a little better. That they would separate. Because it was Raleigh who kept the marriage together."

"But they didn't," Raleigh said.

"No, they didn't," Bobby said, "and everybody knew that Paul was involved with somebody else, that he wanted to marry her. Diana Kendall. Some society girl." He stopped, signaled to the waiter to bring them another round. "And not even attractive," he added. "I'd see them places together."

"Why did she stay?" Raleigh asked.

"Where could she go?" Bobby said. "She was seeing somebody, too. But he was married. So it was a standoff."

"So Paul finally had enough?" Raleigh asked.

"No, it was Beth Carol," said Bobby with a laugh. "The thing that was never going to happen, it did happen. The guy, the married guy, he was getting a divorce."

"That's terrific," Raleigh said, relaxing a little, feeling a surge of warmth for her mother.

"Paul practically had a heart attack when he finally got it," Bobby said, a note of malicious glee in his voice. "Here he is, the world-class striver, and who's the big winner in the end?" He sipped his wine, the hint of a smile on his lips. "Beth Carol. The guy she's going to marry is not only so rich that he makes Paul look as if he should be standing in line at the Midnight Mission, but he's at the very top of the social stratosphere. Plus he's so crazy about her that he can.hardly stand it when she's out of his sight."

God, so all's well that ends well, Raleigh thought, shaking her head as she tried to absorb what Bobby was saying. "Does she love him?" she asked at last.

"She's absolutely nuts about him," Bobby said. "That's the best part."

"It's nice to hear things like that," Raleigh said. "It really is."

"Well, it's all so complicated," Bobby said, frowning. "The money, and everything. Paul was in such a fury that the first thing he did was change the locks. Beth Carol couldn't even get her clothes. And he said, fine. She'd get her divorce. Gladly. That he never had been able to stand the sight of her. I didn't believe that for a moment. I always thought he was mad about her in his own neurotic way, just the way she was about him for a lot of years. But she was going to walk away with nothing, he told her. Not a cent. And this is a community property state. She's entitled to half of everything."

"Well, he can't do that," Raleigh said, realizing with a smile that she had vowed she wouldn't listen to a word Bobby had to say about her mother and here she was, eating up every word.

"Oh, Beth Carol would let him have all the money in a minute," Bobby said. "Anything to get away from him at this point. Roger won't let her, though. She's legally entitled to half of everything, and that's exactly what she's going to get. That's what Roger says."

"Roger?" asked Raleigh.

"That's the married boyfriend," Bobby explained. "Roger Horton. The publisher."

"Roger Horton?" Raleigh blurted, staring at him.

"You know him?" Bobby said, taken aback.

"No, no," Raleigh murmured. "It's a familiar name. That's all."

Around them, more people were being seated, the hum of conversation grew louder. So did the music overhead.

The maître d'hotel stopped by, leaned over them, asked if everything was all right. Added that it was a beautiful day.

"Oh, look," said Bobby, "they're leaving. And Paul is coming over here. I told you he was looking at you."

And then he was there, shaking hands with Bobby, who half rose from his chair, murmuring pleasantries. Taking her hand in his as Bobby made the introductions. She looked up at him, saw him looming over her. Saw his eyes. Cobra's eyes. Oh, Chicago, he was saying. Terrific town. Used to stop there to pick up the Twentieth Century into New York. Back when there was the time to take trains. And was she an actress. And how he hoped she was. She was such a beautiful girl. And she had the quality. Something different. Special.

His hand holding hers was like a band of steel, she thought, her eyes narrowing, adrenaline rushing through her. No, no. Just visiting, she murmured. Smiling. Wondering how she would do it when the time came. It would have to be very personal. A knife. Right across his throat. Then he was moving away, saying it was nice to meet her. That if there were anything he could do for her, to give him a call. That Bobby knew where to find him. And she was still smiling. Nodding, watching his back as he sauntered away. Watched him at the entrance to the restaurant, shaking hands with the maître d'hotel, laughing with him about something.

"Why did you come here to Los Angeles?" Bobby asked with a puzzled look in his eyes. "Who are you?"

"I told you," Raleigh said.

"That Paul Fournier? The guy at lunch?" Bobby told her that evening on the phone when he called her at the hotel. "He was on the phone when I got back to the shop, asking for your phone number. He said he hadn't been able to get you out of his mind."

"What'd you say?" Raleigh asked, shuddering. Almost able to see Paul looming over her again.

"Well, first of all," Bobby said with a soft little laugh, "I reminded him that he was engaged to be married."

"And then what?"

"And then I said I didn't know. That you were just a pretty girl on vacation who had come into the shop."

"Thank you, Bobby," she said.

But her dreams that night were confused, almost nightmares. Paul, standing over her. On the boat again as it rocked on the black ocean off the Mexican coast. And then her mother's face. Devastated at the loss of her. So she hadn't known, hadn't been in on the plan, after all. Hadn't gone along with it because it was what Paul had decided must be done. Oh, she was so soft, her mother. So vulnerable. Forgive me, Mother, she said to herself as, unconsciously, she rubbed her right hand with her left, erasing Paul's touch. Forgive me for even thinking you could have gone along with such a terrible thing.

CHAPTER 62

*R*aleigh figured that the only things that could cross her up were those she didn't know about. Decided to start at the beginning, at the Hall of Records. She roared along the Santa Monica Freeway in the hot little convertible, the sun on her face, her hair whipping around in the breeze. Truck drivers in eighteen-wheelers honked their air horns, grinned as she waved, passed them by. Palm trees fringed the freeway. Ahead was downtown Los Angeles, new skyscrapers pushing into the blue sky.

She parked in an underground garage, hurried up into the daylight, joined the steady stream of pedestrians, a lot of the men in suits, carrying briefcases, women dressed for a day at the office, too. So many of the faces were Mexican, Asian, a scattering of blacks.

In a couple of minutes, she was crowding into one of the elevators in the lobby of the Hall of Records, lurching slowly upward. A few minutes later, she stood, holding her birth certificate in her shaking hands.

Barnes, Raleigh, she read. *Father, Paul Fournier. Mother, Beth Carol Barnes Fournier. Sex, male. Length, unknown. Weight, unknown. Date of birth, August 22, 1952. Recorded at Los Angeles, California, April 17, 1953.*

Raleigh sighed, so disappointed that she could have

cried. What did you expect? she asked herself angrily. Well, little baby fingerprints. Little baby footprints. Just compare them, she would have announced. I'm Raleigh Barnes. A piece of cake. A walk in the park.

Sex, male, she thought bitterly. And why had they waited so long to record her birth? God, April. She would have been eight months old by the time they bothered to get around to it.

No marriage license issued to Paul Fournier and Beth Carol Barnes in 1951. Nor in 1952. 1953.

Well, she knew they had gotten married, she told herself as she walked slowly back to her car. Her mother had shown her the pictures often enough, all neatly organized in Paul's scrapbooks. Her mother, looking so pretty in her dress with the full skirt, her hat with its ribbons. Paul, looking so handsome and scared. And the friend who had given them the wedding. It seemed to her that he had something to do with Fern. Oh, yes. It had been the Englishman that Fern had worked for, the columnist with the television show. The one who died so suddenly. God, what was his name? she wondered. She hadn't thought of him in years.

They could have taken out the license right in Beverly Hills, she decided. Or maybe Santa Monica. After all, why go all the way downtown? But still, somebody had come all the way downtown. To register her birth, eight months late. She drove slowly west on Sunset Boulevard, the longest street in the city, thinking about her mother. About how wrong she had been about her mother, about how wonderful it was going to be to see her again. That it had to be very delicately done. Thinking about Paul, his glittering cobra's eyes. She shuddered.

Raleigh hurried through the lobby of the hotel, stopped at the reception desk to pick up a message, a letter. The message was from the guy she had been chatting with that morning when both of them were waiting for their cars. A nice guy, an investment banker from New York. Did she want to have dinner with him that night at Le St. Germain. It was very hot, very new, he'd heard by asking around.

Well, that would be fun, she thought, smiling to herself. She'd call him as soon as she got to her bungalow. And it was part of her plan, after all. Get around. Be seen. See what led to what. The letter was from Ann. She smiled, shook her head. God, that handwriting. How anything Ann sent ever got delivered she would never know. Quickly she tore it open, scanned it as she strode out the back door next to the Polo Lounge, along the path among the flowers, the lush banana palms, to her bungalow.

The twins had been so happy to see Ann when she picked them up at her parents' house that they had been perfect angels on the plane all the way back to Boston. Of course, Larry was sulky because she had been gone so long and there hadn't been anybody to take care of him. He'd won a trophy at a golf tournament at the club, though, and finally the thaw came because he just had to tell her.

I know you must be exhausted after this miserable last year when things were so grave for Charles and Eleanor, she continued. *At last they are at peace. I hope your vacation in Beverly Hills is everything you had wanted it to be. And ahead, all of those great projects you'll be involved with when you start at Caltech. Write soon. Much love, Ann.*

Raleigh sighed, read it again. Yes, it had been an exhausting year, a great idea to come here, no matter what. Her tennis lessons with Alex Olmedo on the hotel's championship courts. Sunning by the pool with all the movie people making their deals on the phones. The starlets shrieking as they splashed in the pool. The tourists taking it all in. And this little bungalow was so pretty with its chintz-covered furniture, its sliding glass door onto its own little patio. And those roses were certainly holding up. It was, what, now, five days that she had been in town and they still looked good. And somebody else had sent something, she saw. She walked over to the bureau and looked at it. It was a single orchid, some exotic variety that she'd never seen, with fleshy white petals striped in red. Exquisite, she thought, opening the card.

Your secret admirer, she read, smiling.

*   *   *

She was going to have to come in, look up whatever she wanted herself, she was told when she called Records at Beverly Hills. Santa Monica. Nothing at either of them, she found, getting back in her little car. Heading north on the Pacific Coast Highway in the light afternoon traffic, the radio on loud, blaring rock and roll.

Nothing in Oxnard, or Ventura. By the time she got to Santa Barbara, it was after five o'clock and the county offices were closed. Well, first thing in the morning, she decided, checking in at the Biltmore. Thinking how great it had been just to drive up the coast that afternoon. How beautiful it was, and how free she had felt. She was at the county courthouse the next morning at eight o'clock when it opened. There was nothing there, either. What was all of this? she worried as she hurried down the steps, slid behind the wheel of the little car. Hit the road again. Somebody had certainly gone to great lengths, literally, to see that nobody could check on that marriage license, she thought, dismayed.

Raleigh yawned, thumbed dispiritedly through the file in front of her. Foster. Foulger. God, she was in Paso Robles, not that far south of San Francisco. Maybe she had gone in the wrong direction in the first place. North instead of south. She could just see herself, wandering in and out of county courthouses all over California. Because it had to be California. That was one thing she knew for certain. Fountaine. Fouquet. Fournier, Paul.

She felt every nerve in her body in a rush of adrenaline, peered at it again to be sure she wasn't just willing it to be there. Fournier, Paul. Barnes, Beth Carol. The groom was twenty-three years old, born in Los Angeles. Occupation, producer. The bride was only seventeen, Raleigh saw, her eyes widening. Born in Coeur D'Alene, Idaho. Occupation, none. The marriage license had been issued on April 12, 1953. And there was Paul's scrawl, her mother's neat, girl-ish signature.

April 12, 1953, she said to herself. Five days before my birth certificate was recorded. And I was eight months old. I'm illegitimate, she realized, sitting down suddenly. Feeling as if the wind had been knocked out of her.

"Are you all right?" the woman behind the counter asked.

"I could use a glass of water," Raleigh said weakly.

"You looked a little pale there for a moment," the woman said, handing it to her.

"It wasn't the way I thought," Raleigh murmured.

Raleigh drove slowly south on Pacific Coast Highway, only vaguely aware of the roar of the ocean as it splashed upon the beach in the red-tinged dusk, of the little car shuddering as the semis screamed by. In the rearview mirror she saw a beautiful young woman with large, expressive blue eyes, high cheekbones. A narrow, patrician nose, full lips. A dimple. A cascade of shining, brown hair. She frowned at herself, feeling disconnected, displaced. I don't know that person, she said to herself miserably.

Funny how she had never wondered about what had happened before she was born, never thought that the world was less than perfect with Raleigh Barnes, movie star, at its center. And now this. Illegitimate. It made her feel diminished somehow. Sixteen years old. That was what her mother had been when she was born. She could almost see her. Pregnant. Unmarried. And she couldn't have had any skills. She was too young. Oh, God, she must have been so scared, Raleigh thought with a stab of pain. And then, finally, they were married and she was safe, respectable. But why then? Raleigh asked herself, catching a glimpse of her frowning face in the rearview mirror. Why did they get married a few days after April 12, 1953, when she was eight months old?

CHAPTER 63

*T*he Gerber's contract, Raleigh decided. The dates fit.
That must have been the reason, so that Paul would be on
record as her father. Have control of the money. Raleigh
glanced over the clips again. The paragraph in *Variety,* its
headline TINY THESP INKED TO PACT. A short item from *The
Daily Journal,* evidently a legal publication, noting her
appearance with Paul and her mother in court to have the
contract ratified, laying out what amounts were to be paid
on what dates, half of everything to be placed in a trust
fund for the minor in question, the trust to be adminis-
tered by the court. A stack of duplicates from newspapers
across the country, all headed, SIR GEORGE DEAN'S HOLLY-
WOOD. That had been his name. Fern's boss who died. She
remembered now. And what a rave he had given her in the
column. The most beautiful child ever born. Gorgeous
eyes, a dimple you could move into. And so bright. Raleigh
Barnes was already talking at eight months old. It went on,
listing those first appearances, virtually all of the small
roles, the commercials. It went on and on, every word
dripping with adoration, love.

Raleigh sighed, leaned back in her chair, looked around
the library in the Academy of Motion Picture Arts and
Sciences. Film students at the long tables, file folders

stacked in front of them, made notes on yellow pads. Here and there, people were typing on manual typewriters. And everywhere, shelves and shelves of books on every aspect of film. The entrepreneurs who had come west to found the business in the first place. The writers, directors, cameramen. All the books written on all the studios. The actresses. The actors. The child stars.

She glanced back at the stack of files the librarian had pulled out at her request that must have stood over two feet tall, she calculated. And there were books, too. *Raleigh Barnes, Child Star. Kidnap! The Mysterious Disappearance of Raleigh Barnes.* Exploitation books, put together in five minutes, pieced together from old clips, hurried into the stores.

She opened one of the early files at random, found herself looking at a picture of herself sitting on her mother's lap. She must have been about a year old, she decided, a beautiful, exuberant child, a headful of blond curls, the sense of squirming energy even on that gray page. And her mother. She was as dark-haired as Raleigh was now. And so heartbreakingly young with frightened eyes. "The most important thing to both of us is that Raleigh leads a normal life," the article began.

Sure, just your average kid next door, Raleigh thought wryly, turning the yellowed pages. Here she was with Darby, the start of the acrobatics, caught by the photographer in midair, a look of glee on her face as Darby waited with open arms. She would have been, what, about two years old, she thought, looking more closely at the picture. Looking into Darby's face. He was still wearing the eye patch then, she saw with a smile. But there was the determined jaw, the wide face, the tight, fair curls, the icy, self-contained expression she remembered so well. Darby, who had lived with them for as long as she could remember, and she never had been able to figure out why he did it. Still couldn't. Well, she would ask him when she saw him. Because he was high on her list of people she had to see. Maybe in just a few weeks, when she got through all of this stuff, found out what she couldn't remember because she had been so young when it had all happened. After she had done all of the preparation she could do so that she could ask the right questions. Get the answers so that she could prove who she was.

God, here was that opening at Disneyland, and here she was, holding Goofy's hand, smiling, in that little Peter Pan costume. What a day that had been, the most exciting she had ever had. And here she was with Walt Disney himself. And, this one with a handsomely dressed man who was gazing at her with wet-eyed love. *Sir George Dean, prominent television personality . . .* she read below the picture. Yes, she thought, nodding to herself. Yes, that was the way he had always looked at her, and there was something else, too. Yes, it had embarrassed her in a funny kind of way, as if he were mutely asking her for something she didn't have to give. Here was one of the fans trying to get at her, the security guards around her. And here was Fern. Well, she hadn't changed at all, with her towering blond curls, the low-cut dress. The picture could have been taken the night before on her television show. Fern. That had always been part of her plan, to start with Fern. The disinterested party, the gossip columnist with the television show. The one who would know all the secrets, would tell her all the secrets, too, if she could come up with something she could barter for them. Her own story, of course, with every nasty detail. Raleigh Barnes is alive and well and living at the Beverly Hills Hotel. And guess what, folks? She's a girl! Yes, Fern would kill for a story like that when the time came. When Raleigh could prove it.

She felt a presence behind her, started.

"We're closing now," the librarian whispered.

Now, what to wear to dinner with Bobby at that new place he was taking her to? Le Restaurant, he said it was called. Absolutely divine. All of these little, bitty rooms. So intimate. Almost no light. Just enough so you could see who else was there. Bobby. She just had to smile whenever she thought of him. She'd called, what, six, seven times, and always it was the same. "I'm sorry, Mr. Bobby isn't available just now."

And finally the phone rang after a few days and it was Bobby's whispery voice. It had just been awful, he had said fretfully. All he'd done was go to dinner with this friend and the next thing he knew they were on their way to a villa in Acapulco. "I was hijacked," he said. "And, after all, I couldn't come back until they were ready to come back. Could I?"

The black Valentino, she decided. The sleeveless one with the shawl sort of thing. And slit up to here. He'd love it, she told herself, whipping it off its hanger, holding it up in front of the full-length mirror. Black stockings, high, high heels. No jewelry. She was still trying to decide when there was a tap on the door.

"Just a minute," she called, hurrying across the room, pulling it open, smiling at the bellboy who stood there.

"Hi, Chico," she said as he handed her an orchid in its crystal tube, gave her a big smile back. "Hold it a minute," she added as she grabbed her purse, reached in. Handed him a tip.

This one was yellow, she saw, its fleshy petals tipped with brown, flecked with brown. The card read, *Your Secret Admirer.*

Raleigh turned it over in her hand, saw that it didn't come from the florist in the hotel. A shop on Sunset Boulevard. David Jones. She made a mental note to give them a call in the morning, try to find out who was sending the orchids.

She looked at the pretty bouquet in pinks and whites, sent by that nice guy from San Francisco after they'd had dinner the other night. Looked at the tiny yellow roses, still tightly furled, in their brandy snifter. Another thank you for a pleasant evening. All she'd felt when they had been delivered was a little surge of pleasure. That was it. So why was it different with this orchid, the third one she had gotten?

Why did it fill her with a sense of foreboding?

You're just being silly, she told herself firmly as she slowly walked toward the bathroom, turned on the shower, started to get ready for her dinner date with Bobby Prise.

Of course, he wasn't ready when she got to his house to pick him up. She hadn't expected that he would be. And then there was the guided tour. It was old, Mediterranean. Not much furniture, but every piece there was exquisite. Signed. And the art was great. Stella. Bill Jack. Andy Warhol, a series of repeating portraits of Bobby himself. The master suite was all in black and silver. There was a Jacuzzi, a sauna. The other four bedrooms were decorated like restaurants. Mexican. Italian. French. Chinese.

And Le Restaurant was everything Bobby had said it was. They sat at a little table for two in a room with tiled floors decorated with hanging baskets of ferns and flowers, listening to the water splashing in the fountain outside, the soft jazz drifting overhead.

"Listen, Bobby," said Raleigh, leaning toward him, putting her hand on his arm. "You're not sending me flowers, are you? Orchids?"

He looked at her blankly, thought about it for a moment, then looked concerned.

"No, I'm not," he said. "But I will if you want me to."

Raleigh smiled, shook her head.

"I just wondered," she said.

The girl who answered the phone at the florist's shop when Raleigh called the next morning said she was sorry, but she wasn't permitted to give out that information.

"Well, would you just tell me one thing?" Raleigh asked slowly. "This guy, is he all right?"

"Oh, sure," the girl said. "He's rich, powerful. A looker, too. It should happen to me," she added wistfully.

"Well, thanks anyway," Raleigh said.

CHAPTER 64

$\mathcal{G}$od, this kidnapping stuff, Raleigh thought. So much of it, and from all over the world. Paul must have thought he'd died and gone to heaven to get all this publicity.

And the timing couldn't have been better, she saw as she thumbed through the tear sheets, the transcripts of television and radio mentions, caught a fragment of a sentence here and there. Just when that first four-picture deal was about to be signed. What a bargaining position to be in.

And it wasn't as if she had ever been in any real danger, she remembered. She hadn't even been scared. Oh, maybe she had been scared a couple of times. Right at the beginning, when she had realized he wasn't going to let her leave. And then after he brought the television set home. When he finally realized what he had done, started talking about going somewhere else with that trapped, desperate look in his eyes. Poor, dopey Buddy. The problem was that he was such a space cadet that anything could have happened.

Cover stories, duplicates. More of the same.

And here were the first stories after she had been found. Headlines on newspapers all over the world, the front page picture of her and Frisky. God, Frisky would be old now. It was hard to believe so much time had passed, hard to believe that she had ever lived the life of a boy.

And here was the stuff from that first press conference they'd had at the house. Frolicking with her puppy. With her mother. With Paul. Sitting in that little Thunderbird. It seemed to her it had been red. She'd had a lot of fun with it, puttering around the estate.

PROMINENT TELEVISION PERSONALITY SLAIN, she read, frowned as she decided the clip must be in the wrong file. ROBBERY MOTIVE SUSPECTED. The picture, a smiling head-shot. It was Sir George Dean, she realized as her stomach lurched. Murdered. So that was what had happened. God, now she could remember as if it were yesterday when Paul had sat with her, explained how their dear friend had died so suddenly, so unexpectedly. What had he said it was? A heart attack? Well, she couldn't remember what he had said. Just that she had cried and cried because she knew how much he had loved her. Murdered. How ghastly. Well, Paul had been right to keep it from her. She wouldn't have known how to handle it. Not at five years old.

Still, what was the clip doing here? she wondered, scanning the article. Spotting the reason. A couple of lines mentioning the upcoming television special he was to do with child star Raleigh Barnes. The television special that Fern had done instead.

She flipped rapidly through the clips. Came to the buildup for it, with all of the pictures of her and Fern on television pages in newspapers across the country. And the stuff that had come later, after Fern dropped her bomb-shell. The picture of Raleigh and Frisky that Buddy had taken. The spate of stories that covered the days Fern had spent in jail when she wouldn't reveal where she had gotten it. And here were the pictures of the two of them when Raleigh had gone down to visit her. And finally the disappointing revelation that the picture had come anonymously through the mail.

Those pictures Buddy was always taking of her with his Polaroid that he was so proud of. Popping up all over the place, even when she was in the bathtub. "Now I know all your secrets." That's what he had said. Something like that.

She flipped back through the pages, came again to the story on Sir George Dean. And there it was, a couple of lines that hadn't quite registered when she'd looked at it before.

> . . . investigators are proceeding on the assumption that the assailant or assailants may have been known to Sir George Dean or to his companion, Elroyd "Buddy" Hatcher, 22. Mr. Hatcher, a recent acquaintance of Sir George Dean, according to sources, made his permanent residence at the Veteran's Administration Hospital in Brentwood. When asked to comment, sources at the hospital . . .

Raleigh closed her eyes, sighed. Put her fingers to her throbbing temples.

Sir George Dean. Buddy. The picture Fern had shown on television. All of the rest of the pictures Buddy had taken of her. The one in the bathtub which showed that her life as a boy was a sham. Both of them dead. Murdered.

She glanced at the clipping again. "*A particularly violent, brutal crime,*" a highly placed official in the department was quoted as saying.

Her legs were trembling as she walked up to the front desk, asked the librarian for the file on Sir George Dean.

A ton of stuff up until the time of the murders. The clipping cross-indexed in her own file. A minor story on a back page. TELEVISION PERSONALITY LEAVES ESTATE IN EXCESS OF HALF-MILLION.

She scanned it quickly, started with surprise when she came to her own name listed among the beneficiaries. Stocks, bonds, real estate, all to be shared equally between Sir George Dean's assistant, Fern Darling, and Raleigh Barnes, the child star. She tried to remember, couldn't. Made a note of the name of the law firm mentioned in the article in her notebook.

And then a smattering of clips over the next few weeks. Investigations were continuing. Pawnshops had been provided with descriptions of the jewelry taken during the robbery at the time of the murders. Solid gold cuff links with Sir George Dean's initials. A gold Philippe Patek watch. Family silver with Sir George Dean's family crest, a running griffin, three stars above it. A lot of other trinkets as well. And then nothing. No suspects taken into custody. No resolution.

The conclusion that didn't even have to be spoken. A rich, epicene homosexual and a cute young boy who wasn't playing with a full deck. Just another gay murder. You pick up rough trade, you've got to know there's a downside. It happens all the time. Well, she would have thought about it that way, too, if she hadn't known the people involved. Poor, sweet Buddy with all his crazy ideas who meant no harm. And Sir George Dean, her biggest booster, who had loved her as if she were his own child. Not this time, though. No, this time there was more to it, maybe a lot more to it. She knew it as sure as she was sitting there.

If only she had somebody she could talk to, she decided, somebody to sit with, bounce around ideas. Well, it couldn't be Bobby. He would just look at her with that dazed, blissful smile of his and agree with everything she had to say. And besides, she felt bad enough about Bobby, not being able to tell him who she really was.

And not Toosie, either, she thought, an image of him in her mind for the first time in weeks. No, she didn't want to be around him until she understood her feelings for him. Was able to handle them.

Well, there was always her secret admirer, she thought, smiling to herself. Rich, powerful. A looker, too, the girl at the florist's had said. She could just hear what she would say to him.

So, listen, Mr. Secret Admirer, I think I've come across a couple of murders that were covered up about fifteen years ago, and how would you like to help me figure out who really committed them, and why? And, oh, yes, another thing. I'm Raleigh Barnes. You remember, the movie star who died. The one the Academy is honoring posthumously this year.

Sure, she thought wryly. That'll be the day. What you really have to do is pull yourself together. Get on with things. Alone. The only one you can count on is yourself. Just the way Paul had always told her. Funny, how right he'd been about so many things.

Still, she found herself waiting. For the phone to ring, a tap on the shoulder. Something.

CHAPTER 65

*W*hat a perfect day, Raleigh thought lazily. And it felt great to be lying next to the swimming pool, wearing the smallest black bikini she had picked up in Beverly Hills one of the times when she and Bobby had gone shopping. She was getting a nice tan, she saw. Her hair was in a single, thick braid. She glanced around through her big sunglasses.

There were some kids splashing in the shallow end of the pool, the lifeguard watching them. Women in cover-ups and sandals, men in swim trunks and open shirts, were already strolling toward the sheltered tables for an early lunch. Others baked on their chaise lounges. Waiters in white jackets scurried around with drinks on trays. Phones to be plugged in. "Mr. Zanuck, please," one of them called. "Mr. Richard Zanuck." "Mr. De Laurentis. Mr. Dino De Laurentis."

Still, she was thinking hard. There were so many things to consider, to try to sort out. She reached over to the table next to her, sipped her iced tea, breathed in the pungent scent of mint. Sighed as she grabbed her notes.

Leave it to Paul, she thought, shaking her head as her eyes flickered over the pages. He had been back from Mexico for, what, about ten minutes. He'd just about had enough time to give those maudlin interviews about what a tragedy it all was. How stricken he was. It was so soon after she had disappeared that they were still searching for her body. And where was Paul? At his attorney's office, arranging to petition the court for the dispersal of the Raleigh Barnes estate. Well, the insurance companies fought him on that one. No body, no money. Not for seven years unless the body was recovered in the interim.

Well, it was almost seven years.

Paul must have really gone up the wall when the courts ruled for the insurance companies. He had really been counting on those millions. All of his appeals denied. Everything was to be held in trust except what was necessary for the actual maintenance of the estate. That money could be paid out, and the completion bond so that the movie could be finished, distributed, advertised. To satisfy the investors. And it had made millions for them. And for the Raleigh Barnes Production Company. It had been the most successful film in history with a child as its star, according to the grosses reported in the trades and the entertainment sections of the newspapers.

And the Raleigh Barnes film library was a gold mine. Every one of the films she had made was distributed in countries worldwide. The mail order business. Another bonanza. The merchandising. T-shirts, beach towels, lunch pails. A Raleigh Barnes doll, its wardrobe replicas of costumes she had worn in the films. Even the fan clubs made money what with dues, newsletters, pins. The satin jackets.

A lot was written off against the estate, of course. The mortgages on the production company. Paul's salary, a half a million dollars a year, plus bonuses. A Rolls-Royce every other year. The other perks. The rest of the salaries, operating expenses. And the mortgages on the mansion, all of the expenses connected with running it. It had given her a funny feeling when she had gone over all of the early petitions to the court on her behalf in the Hall of Records downtown. The limousine with the bulletproof glass after the kidnapping, the chauffeur/bodyguard. The cadre of security people patrolling the estate twenty-four hours a day.

And the little stuff. The flippers, those false teeth the dentist had made for her when her baby teeth had fallen out. Bobby's bills for all those dye jobs over the years. Florist's bills for flowers sent to Fern, bills that stopped after Sir George Dean was murdered. And Buddy.

Still, the value of the Raleigh Barnes estate had increased by a factor of ten, according to the records she had dug out downtown. And this posthumous, honorary Academy Award, well, that would mean another quantum jump in its worth.

There had been another item that was tugging at her memory. A couple of paragraphs in an unlikely place. *The Wall Street Journal*, that was it. A rumor that Paul Fournier was going to make a bid for one of the major studios. Maybe that had something to do with the award, too. Make that library so attractive that he could sell it for the money it would take to buy a major studio.

Fern had petitioned the court, too. Asking that assets left in trust for Raleigh Barnes be distributed to her under the original bequest in Sir George Dean's will. It was denied. Not for seven years without a body.

Finding that item had taken forever, Raleigh recalled. God, the files in the Academy library on Fern Darling. They topped four feet. Easily. All of the columns she had written over the years, of course. The television transcripts. Details of the many times she had been sued for slander, defamation of character, the outraged sputterings of whoever was doing the suing. Fern's response. And, inevitably, the picture of a smiling Fern, the story underneath it reporting that the case had been dismissed for lack of evidence.

Her marriages, three so far. The first was that Danny Tosca. He'd been nice, Raleigh remembered. A bodybuilder. He'd even taken Raleigh along with him to Gold's Gym down in Venice a couple of times. That had been fun, all those big, muscled guys tossing her around on the beach while the photographers clicked away.

Danny and Fern had been married in a wedding chapel in Las Vegas, Raleigh saw from the single paragraph that had run in *Variety*. And here was a line that a final divorce decree had been granted. Only two years from the beginning to the end.

And the second, here she was in a picture with him on their wedding day. A big smile on her face, a corsage on her dress. He was a dark, beefy-looking guy. Owner of the biggest chain of dry cleaners in Southern California, according to the caption. *"This time it's for keeps,"* she was quoted as saying. *"I've never been happier."*

And then, eighteen months later, the separation. A routine mention of a final divorce decree being granted.

Here was the third. A little older, slicked-back hair, secretive, hooded eyes. The co-owner of a hotel on the Las Vegas Strip. *"We'll both commute,"* the new Mrs. Antonioni was quoted as saying. *"I'll go to Vegas weekends, or Ducky will come here. After all, it's pretty easy when you've got your own Lear jet."* Another two years, another final divorce decree.

There were feature interviews with Fern, too. In newspapers, the women's magazines. She was all in pink, smiling, holding a big, white Persian cat on the cover of the *Ladies' Home Journal*, several years back.

Inside, the story opened with a full-page shot of her standing next to Burt Reynolds, an open notebook in her hand as she gazed suspiciously up at him. NEW MEDIA STAR RISING, read the splashy headline over the story on the next page.

With old-time Hollywood gossips such as Hedda Hopper and Louella Parsons out of the picture now, a new star, Fern Darling, has imperceptibly arrived on the scene to not only fill the vacuum left by them, but to carve out a niche larger and more powerful than the ladies in question would have dreamed possible.

"You should see this place at Christmas," she says in that

breathy little voice so familiar to viewers of her week-night television shows and her countless television specials. "Like, you can't even get in here, there's so much stuff. And I mean serious presents, man. Jewels from Cartier, Van Cleef, Tiffany. And luggage. Gucci. Vuitton. And I mean those big steamer trunks. The ones that cost a bundle. I've gotten cars, too. Somebody even sent me a Shetland pony. Can you believe it, man? I mean, what would I do with a Shetland pony?"

Shetland ponies aside, Fern Darling, a small blond woman who looks larger than life, lives in a jewel box of a house high above the Sunset Strip with a view-to-die-for of the twinkling lights of the city below. As she points out various important pieces of antique furniture, signed lithographs, priceless objets d'art in her drawing room, there is a sense of excitement about her, an incomparable zest for life, the qualities, no doubt, that brought a major New York publisher knocking on her door.

"Like, it was a big surprise when they wanted me to do my autobiography," Fern confides. "First of all, I find out stuff about other people. Second, I've had a very ordinary life, so what is there to tell? Besides, I'm only thirty years old. I mean, hey, man, who even has an autobiography when they're only thirty years old?"

And, certainly in the beginning, Fern Darling is right. She was raised as an only child in a small town in Northern California which she refused to name. ("I don't want people sniffing around up there, man," she explains.) Her father was the local banker and her mother devoted her time to a number of local charities. "I was real pretty when I was little," she says. "And people were after my mom to enter me in contests and stuff. She wouldn't, of course. She didn't want me to just live off my looks. She wanted me to get an education, make something of myself."

Sent to her mother's alma mater, Vassar, as a precocious fourteen-year-old, Fern decided to major in communications with a possible career in television journalism as her goal. After she graduated, her ambitions were helped along by her uncle, Sir George Dean, who invited her to become his assistant in London, where he had already made for himself a major career. It was under the auspice of Sir George Dean, a cousin of Queen Elizabeth II, that Fern made her debut and was presented at court. "It was the most exciting thing that ever happened to me in my life," she declares.

When Hollywood beckoned to the illustrious television personality, he invited his little niece to come along as well. From there, it has been pretty much a matter of keeping up with her burgeoning career.

Not that Fern's life hasn't had its dark side, most notably when Sir George Dean was brutally murdered in 1957. "I found him, man," she says in a voice choked with emotion. "It was right in this very room. I still dream about it at night."

And, too, there are the three failed marriages which also haunt her. "I tried, you know?" she says. "But there's no way to get around it. Guys eat up a lot of time."

Meantime, Fern lives alone with her beautiful Persian cat, Princess, and a housekeeper who attends to her needs. There is also a chauffeur who maintains her classic Bentley, a legacy from her late uncle. A staff of five assists her with her syndicated column, and a fluctuating staff too numerous to count produces her television shows and specials.

As busy as she is, Fern finds the time to contribute both time and money to her favorite charities, Children's Hospital and the ASPCA. "You've got to give back, man," she points out. "That's what life is all about."

Does anybody believe this? Raleigh wondered. Does Fern believe this is what her life has been about so far? Well, maybe she does, Raleigh decided, smiling to herself as she closed the file. Make yourself up, and dare the world to say otherwise.

Raleigh was in most of the pictures in the early interviews in Darby's file. Window dressing, performing some stunt with him as he talked about whichever one of the films they were shooting. Explaining what he had in mind,

what effects he was going for. Not a personal word anywhere, not even who his parents were or where he was
born. Yes, that was Darby. So distant, so secretive. The B.
Traven of directors, she thought. His work though, so visible over so many years. Two Academy Award nominations
just in the last three years. No sense of the man there.
None. Interesting, too, that he'd never again worked with
Paul after the film in Mexico. He hadn't even been around
for the postproduction. The editing, the music. The titles.
She'd have to ask him about that, she decided. Maybe it
meant something. Darby suspecting that Paul had had
something to do with the accident. Maybe it didn't.

No more interviews after the Mexico film, either. Oh,
sure, there were location stories in the national press, the
international press. But not another word from Darby
Hicks. Not one.

In the morgue of the newspaper downtown, she sat with
her mother's file, examining the handful of pictures of her
that had appeared over the years. At garden parties, charity
balls. The one she'd already seen with Frisky. Her hair getting lighter and lighter as time passed. A few mentions in
the lists of those present at luncheons. This is the one that's
going to be the hardest, she thought. For me. For her. Oh,
God, how am I going to do it? she asked herself, anguished.

On an impulse, she hurried over to the Hall of Records
again. Said hello to the woman behind the desk, who greeted her now as if she were an old friend. The divorce
records. Felicity Cunningham Horton from Roger Horton.
Dissolution pending. Her mother and Toosie's father. It
still gave her a jolt when she thought about it.

In the underground garage, she got into the little
Mercedes Benz, started the engine.

"Well, I'm as ready as I'm ever going to be," she murmured to herself as she started up, out of the garage, into
the beautiful, sunlit day.

CHAPTER 66

*D*irectors Guild of America," said the voice on the phone. "Good morning."

"I'm trying to reach Darby Hicks," Raleigh said as she sat at the desk in the living room of her cozy bungalow, her hands shaking a little, now that she was actually starting. Taking that first baby step past the paper trail.

"One moment," the woman said. "I'll transfer you."

And then another voice. Directory.

"I'm sorry," the woman said when she came back on the line. "He doesn't have an agent or a publicist. We're not permitted to give out his address or his phone number."

"Well, there must be some way to get in touch with him," Raleigh said.

"You can write to him here," she said. "We'll be happy to forward it."

"Thanks anyway," Raleigh said, hanging up.

She thumbed through the phone book, found Fern's number. A West Hollywood prefix, no listed address.

"Yes, I'd like to speak to Miss Darling," she said to the woman who answered the phone.

"May I say who's calling?"

"She wouldn't know my name, but it's very important," she said, taking a deep breath. "It's about Raleigh Barnes."

"What about Raleigh Barnes?"

"I have some new information that I think will be interesting to Miss Darling."

"I'll be happy to take it," the woman said.

"No, listen," Raleigh said unhappily. "I've got to talk to her, see her. Just for a few minutes, whenever she can work me in."

"I'm afraid her schedule is full," the woman said.

"How about next week?" Raleigh said. "The week after? I just have to see her."

"All I can suggest is that you drop her a line with your information," the woman said. "Then she'll be able to decide."

"But—"

"I'm sorry," the woman said before she hung up.

What am I going to do? Raleigh asked herself anxiously, standing, starting to pace. Where do I go from here?

She stopped for a moment, touched the orchid that had come that morning. It was exquisite, its outer petals a hot pink, the ones at its center almost white. I'll bet you would know, she said to its unknown sender. I'll bet all you would have to do is flip open your Rolodex. Make a couple of calls. Fern, baby, there's somebody I want you to see. Darby, I'm sending somebody over. Have the coffee ready, okay?

Even if she got to Fern, to Darby, she was still tip-toeing around, she thought to herself as the hostess led her to her usual table in the Polo Lounge, where the waitress was smiling, already pouring her morning coffee from a silver pitcher. If there was any proof that she was Raleigh Barnes, it would be in the mansion, among Paul's important papers. The ones he kept in the vault. The vault with the combination that only he knew.

Oh, she could kick herself for falling apart the other day when she was right there with him at Ma Maison. Shaking hands with him. And she'd been so relieved, so grateful, when Bobby hadn't told him her name or where she was staying.

I could have used myself as bait, she realized, shuddering as she knew she couldn't have done it. That she was too frightened at even the thought of her father's hands on her, his mouth. Oh, God, she thought miserably.

"I saw you sitting over here," a voice said, "and I thought I'd come over and say hello."

Finally, the orchid man, she thought, her heart beating faster as she looked up. Saw a young guy with all-American good looks, so familiar, but where had they met? At a restaurant, maybe? At a party?

"I'm sorry," she began, "I don't—"

"You don't remember me," he said, flushing. "I drove you here from the airport two weeks ago. When you got back to town."

"Of course," Raleigh said, smiling at him, motioning for him to sit down. "It's nice to see you."

"I told you about that part on the soap my agent was sending me out on, remember?" he asked. "Well, I got it."

"That's great," Raleigh said.

"I can hardly believe it myself," he said, his voice full of wonder. "It's a continuing featured role, too. I've got a contract for a year. They had me back three times before they finally decided." Gesturing across the room, he added, "That's the woman who does publicity for the show. I'm telling her all about my life so she can decide how to promote me."

"I'm really happy for you," Raleigh said warmly.

"Say, I was wondering," he said, "would you like to go to a party tonight? She got me invited. She thinks I should be seen there. It's at Allan Carr's. He's that personal manager who handles a lot of important people, she says. Ann-Margret. Marvin Hamlisch. The party's in honor of some guy named Rudolf Nureyev. He's a ballet dancer."

"I know," Raleigh said. "I'd love to go."

"I don't have a very good car yet," he said with a little laugh.

"That's all right," she said. "We can take mine."

"Gosh, I'll have to rent a tux," he said. "It's black tie, she says."

"I have something long," Raleigh said.

"I'm Grant Martin," he said, holding out his hand.

"I'm Leigh Fisk," she said.

"Yes, I know," he said. "I remember from when I picked you up. It's just like a fairy tale, isn't it? One minute I'm driving you from the airport, and the next I've got a great part on a show and we're going to a party together."

"Yes," Raleigh said. "It's just like a fairy tale, being in this town."

Her gown was crimson satin, low-cut, with a matching stole. Bobby had wound her hair into a chignon. She wore diamond earrings, her only jewelry.

"You take my breath away," Grant said when he picked her up just before midnight.

"You look wonderful in your tuxedo," she said. "So handsome."

"I've been thinking that maybe it's a good idea to buy one," he said as he helped her into the car. "An investment, that's what it will be."

And now they were waiting patiently in the line of cars and limousines while the parking people, an army of them, opened doors, helped the women in their beautiful gowns, while horns honked in the night. The angry drivers who just wanted to get over Benedict Canyon, Raleigh realized.

"That's Loretta Swit," Grant whispered into her ear as they crowded into one of the station wagons that was to shuttle them up the steep incline to the house. "Gosh, I can't believe this," he added.

It was another hundred yards, maybe, to the house itself, the brick steps illuminated by candles in hurricane lamps. Raleigh heard the music, the laughter, even before they approached the open front door.

"Where's a photographer?" shouted a chubby little man

above the din in the capacious entry hall. He wore horn-rimmed glasses, a bejeweled caftan. "Where's a photographer?" he demanded again, holding tightly to the arm of Alexis Smith. "Here's a legend! Here's a legend!"

People jostled against her as Raleigh found herself in front of him, murmuring her name.

"Take a picture of me with this beautiful girl!" Allan Carr screeched at the photographer, holding her hand. Nikons clicked. "I can make you a star," he said to her. "Give me a call tomorrow. I'm in the book."

Grant took her elbow and the two of them worked their way through the swirl of guests, the waiters in white gloves with their jeroboams of champagne. There were open bars all over the enormous drawing room with its high, vaulted ceiling, long tables with mounds of caviar in silver bowls, chopped onion, chopped egg, paper-thin slices of rye bread, impossibly ornate arrangements of exotic flowers.

People were really nice, introducing themselves, smiling as she nodded and murmured her own name. "Have you met Rudolf Nureyev?" someone asked, and her hand was in his, as he, too, nodded, smiled. Turned to Grant, shook his hand, too. Vanished into a crowd of admirers.

"Have you met Rudolf Nureyev?" Grant said with a laugh. "Do you believe this?"

Raleigh laughed with him, eagerly scanned all of the familiar faces, tried to put names to them, heard him say that he'd be right back, that he saw somebody he knew just across the room. The music started to play again, and couples were dancing on the terrace outside.

"Raleigh?" said a hesitant little voice. "Raleigh Barnes?"

My name, Raleigh thought, startled, unable to believe it. She turned, saw a tower of blond hair, Fern's stricken face, her blue eyes bleary, puzzled.

"Like, I thought you were someone else, man," she slurred, taking a step away. "Sorry."

"I am Raleigh Barnes."

"Like, don't put me on," Fern said hoarsely, weaving a little.

"I've been trying to reach you, Fern," Raleigh said. "I've just got to talk to you. Please."

A heavyset woman in a beige lace dress, her sparse gray hair in tight curls, was pushing her way toward Fern, possessively clutching at her arm. Muttering something in her ear that Raleigh couldn't hear.

"This is my mom, Mrs. Miller," said Fern, clinging to the older woman for support. "She's living down here with me now. She's just saying it's a little late for her, that she wants to go."

Raleigh nodded at the woman, smiled.

"Come on, Fairalea," she said, acknowledging Raleigh with a tight smile.

"So, sure," said Fern as her mother pulled her away. "Come by tomorrow night. We'll have some drinks. Get to know each other, right?"

"Right," Raleigh said.

CHAPTER 67

A white silk shirt, tight jeans, the high-heeled boots. A buttery suede coat that hit around mid-thigh. Raleigh looked at herself in the mirror, tried to concentrate long enough to see if she looked all right, went back to what she had been obsessing about ever since those moments the night before with Fern. At first, Fern had been astonished to see her standing there, alive. But then, she wasn't surprised to find that someone she would mistake for Raleigh Barnes was a female. And she was drunk.

The laughter, the music, had gone on for another couple of hours, with Grant so excited he didn't even notice that Raleigh's mind was elsewhere. When they got back to the hotel, he gave her a quick kiss on the cheek and sort of waltzed over to where he had parked his car. "I'll call you tomorrow," he said, and waved, a blissful smile on his face.

Astonished. Not surprised. Drunk. The litany ran through Raleigh's mind as she drove east on sunset, the lights of the city blinking on. Made the turn that was so familiar from her life as a boy onto Sunset Plaza Drive.

As she stood at the door, she could almost see Sir George Dean's face looking at her, those moist eyes, blinded by love.

Fern answered the door within seconds, wearing a gold lame top cut low on her enormous breasts, skin-tight, matching pants, high, high heels. Her gaudy gold earrings grazed her shoulders.

"So I wasn't that bombed, after all," she said with a smile, a calculating look in her eyes as she took Raleigh's outstretched hand in both of hers. "You're just as pretty as I thought you were."

Raleigh let herself be led into the long entry hall she remembered so well, breathed in Fern's perfume that she knew so well. And here was the living room. The Chippendale chairs, the sofa upholstered in a different fabric. The piano, in the same place. The French doors onto the terrace standing open.

"I'm having a martini," Fern said. "That okay for you?"

"That's fine," Raleigh said.

"The cook fixed us a little supper," Fern added. "All I have to do later is heat it up. And my mom, Mrs. Miller, lives out back, in the guest house. I never hear a peep from her in the evening. She just puts in a frozen dinner and watches her favorite television programs."

"You used to live in the guest house," Raleigh murmured.

"Yeah, a long time ago," said Fern, handing her the drink, fluttering her eyelashes as she touched Raleigh's glass with her own. "Here's to the beginning of a beautiful friendship, man."

"Thank you," Raleigh said.

"I had a word with Allan last night at the door, when my mom and I were leaving," Fern said, undulating over to the sofa, gesturing to Raleigh to come and sit beside her. "He said he really meant it, that you should call. That you have a quality about you. Very unusual. Like a young Katharine Hepburn, only prettier."

"Fern, I really need a friend," Raleigh said.

"Say, how about some music?" Fern said brightly. "You like Sinatra?"

"Fine." Raleigh watched her as she sauntered over to the stereo, dropped on a record. Felt something rub against her leg, heard a purr.

"Princess," she said, leaning down and picking up the cat.

"Yeah," Fern said, looking at her curiously as she sat down next to Raleigh again. "Princess."

"I read it in an article about you," Raleigh said. "The cat's name."

"Well, that's flattering," Fern said, patting her leg. "So you went to all that trouble and looked me up, right?"

"This is such a pretty room," Raleigh said. "It's so good to be here again. And it's almost exactly the same."

"Yeah, it was the cover they used with the article," Fern said amiably. "I'm sitting here on this sofa, and I'm holding Princess. You would have seen the room on the cover."

She doesn't believe I'm Raleigh Barnes, she realized with a start. Sipped the martini and wondered why Fern had invited her over anyway.

"That was the darnedest thing, though," Fern murmured, "seeing you there at Allan's last night. It was like seeing a ghost, you know? I was sort of disoriented there for a sec. It was scary, man." She smiled at Raleigh, ran her hand lingeringly over her shoulder. "So what are you trying to pull?" Fern asked pleasantly as she stuffed a cigarette into a holder and lit it with a silver lighter from the coffee table. "Who are you, and what do you want?"

"I'm Raleigh Barnes," she said.

"Sure." Fern snorted. "And I'm Sonny and Cher."

"I'll prove it to you, Fern," she said. "I'll tell you all about that night in Mexico. After I swam into the sunken galleon and disappeared. What happened then. Where I went. Where I've been."

"Why are you doing this?" asked Fern with a frown, moving away from her. "I mean, who cares? The kid's dead. It was all so long ago."

"It'll be the biggest story of your career," Raleigh said. "You've got to help me, Fern. You've got to help me prove who I am."

"You don't need this, man," Fern said placatingly. "You're a beautiful girl. You can make it on your own. You don't have to go in for this poor man's Anastasia stuff. It's unattractive, you know?" She moved closer to Raleigh, reached out to touch her chin with a red-tipped finger, as Raleigh flinched. "Tell you what," she whispered. "Let's just have a couple of drinks, a little supper. See if we can ignite some sparks between us, okay?"

"He was there, in a speedboat," Raleigh began, pulling away. "He was waiting for me when I came out the other side."

"Look, whoever you are," Fern said, sitting up straight. "I was there that night, right there, watching when the kid disappeared."

"I know," said Raleigh. "I went to the airport when you got there, you and Bobby. You were having an affair with one of the guys in your camera crew. You had the bedroom next to me. I could hear you."

"Oh, look," Fern said wearily. "Everybody knows everything like that about me. They know it about everyone in this town. You could have read that stuff anywhere."

"It was Paul," said Raleigh with an imploring look. "He was the one who was waiting for me."

"Paul was in the editing room he had set up at the hotel," Fern said. "He was there when we left, he was there when we got back. So don't give me this crap, okay?"

"You've got to believe me," Raleigh muttered.

"Look, man," said Fern, standing up. "This is, like, getting real old. I think you'd better leave."

"The picture," Raleigh said desperately, "the one you showed on the television special, the one you took over after Sir George Dean was murdered. The one that showed where I was when I was kidnapped."

"What about it?" said Fern in a shocked whisper.

"Where did you get it?"

"Just where I said," Fern said. "It came in the mail. We didn't know who'd sent it. They couldn't pick up any prints from it. Nobody recognized the room. You've been doing the sleuthing, man. You know all this. It was in all the papers." She gave a harsh little laugh. "It made my name, that picture. I went to jail for it, and when I came out, I was famous."

"I'll have another drink now," Raleigh said.

Fern stood there, looked at her for a moment, scowled, thought about it.

"Sure," she said. "I mean, why not?"

"That wasn't the only picture," Raleigh said, watching her at the little bar. "There were all kinds of pictures. He'd gotten a Polaroid camera. It was his new toy. He'd follow me around, snapping away."

"Go on," Fern said, handing her the drink, her blue eyes narrowed, speculative.

"I was outside the market in Brentwood," she said. "He came up to me, started to talk to me. He said that he knew my mother, that they'd been sweethearts back home. He knew that I'd been named for my grandfather. He couldn't have read that anywhere, so I believed him. He said he had a little dog he wanted to give me, so I went with him."

"I'm listening," she said, sipping her martini, trying to look indifferent. Not succeeding, Raleigh saw with an inward smile. I've got her now, she told herself.

"It was Buddy Hatcher," she said. "The boy who was killed with Sir George Dean."

"Yeah, well, I wouldn't know anything about that," Fern said, pale now, her mouth working in a funny way. "Sir George Dean, he'd have a million of them. They'd come for a night, a couple of weeks sometimes. I lived out back, after all. I never even noticed them."

"I was in the bathtub in one of those pictures," Raleigh said. "I was nude. It was obvious I was a girl."

Fern sucked in her breath.

"And you knew that," Raleigh said. "You were surprised last night at the party that I was alive, but you knew I was a girl."

"He told me," she said. "Paul."

"Paul told a gossip columnist that I was a girl?" she said, her eyes widening in disbelief. "He told a gossip columnist something that could have ruined him?"

"Yeah, well, we were pretty close at the time." Fern snorted. "Very good friends, as they say."

"That night in Mexico," murmured Raleigh, "I was supposed to disappear. It was just a matter of time before everybody would have known I was a girl. And there were big financial troubles, too. He needed the insurance money. Then, after a while, I was to come back to live with them. My mother's niece. That was what the story was going to be."

"Beth Carol," said Fern, slurring the name as she drained the pitcher, picked her way carefully back to the bar, made a new batch. "That was the worst of it, when Raleigh disappeared. I mean, Raleigh was dead, right? There wasn't anything to be done about that. But Beth Carol, she might as well have been dead, too. That kid was her life. It was all she ever wanted, right from the beginning. From the time we met. A husband, a nice house. A kid." She poured herself another drink, a faraway look in her eyes. "So when Raleigh died, it was like she was nobody."

Raleigh felt the tears stinging her eyes.

"So why didn't you get in touch with her, man?" Fern demanded fretfully, weaving now as she crossed the room. "Like, didn't you think she'd be upset? Crazy with grief?"

"I thought she was in on it," Raleigh whispered. "She always did what Paul wanted."

"Yeah, she always did what Paul wanted," Fern said bitterly, "and Paul always did what he wanted, so that made two of them, didn't it? But not that time."

"I want to see her, Fern."

"Well, don't look at me," Fern snapped. "I'm not going to be a party to this."

"But you'll help me," said Raleigh.

"Look, just tell me one thing," said Fern, slumping down on the couch, taking a couple of tries at her cigarette before she got it lit. "Just for the sake of argument, let's say that you really are Raleigh Barnes. I mean, what do you want?"

"My identity," said Raleigh, startled. "My past."

"That's a laugh." Fern snorted. "Everybody comes out here to forget their past, to make their own identity. And you? You come back here to *find* yours, man?"

"And my share," Raleigh added. "My share of all of the money."

"Now, that surprises me," Fern said, frowning. "I

wouldn't have thought that the money would have mattered to you. Like, you're the high-minded type, I would have said. So, why do you want the money?"

"Because I earned it," Raleigh said. "It's a matter of principle."

Raleigh looked at Fern, saw her narrowed eyes, the speculative look.

"Well, this has all been very interesting," Fern said, after a moment, staggering to her feet, "but I think it's beddy-bye time for Fern here."

"Are you going to help me?" Raleigh asked again, realizing that Fern had closed her off. She rose, grabbed Fern as she teetered on those high, high heels.

"Oh, look," said Fern, as they moved unsteadily toward the door. "You can't prove any of this, can you? As far as I'm concerned, you've just got a fixation of some kind."

She fumbled with the doorknob, flung open the door. Stood there, weaving, holding on to it.

"It's too bad, too," she muttered, reaching up to touch Raleigh's cheek. "Because you light my fire, man. You really do."

She believes me, Raleigh told herself, as she drove slowly back to the hotel. It's the money, though. She doesn't want me to have my share of Sir George Dean's money. It must be nearly a million dollars by now. Even a story this big isn't worth it to her. Well, how about if you relinquished your share of Sir George Dean's estate? Put it in writing? But Raleigh knew she would never do that, knew that she would never settle for any less than exactly what her share was. Of everything.

At the desk in her little bungalow, she opened the drawer, took out a piece of the hotel's stationery, the telephone book. *Mrs. Paul Fournier,* she wrote, *C/O Mr. Roger Horton.* The name of the paper, the address. *Personal and Confidential* at the bottom of the envelope.

Dear Mrs. Fournier . . . she began to write.

Fern, making a pass at her, she thought with a smile as she licked the envelope, pressed it closed. Now, really.

CHAPTER 68

*T*he voice was soft, tentative. There was hope in it, but doubt, too. "This is Mrs. Fournier," it said. "You sent me a note a few days ago."

Raleigh sat down abruptly, opened her mouth, tried to speak.

"Are you there?"

"Yes, yes," she stuttered. "I'm sorry. I'm happy that you called. I really am."

"Well, I didn't know whether I should," said the voice. "I mean, back then, when it happened, well, there were all sorts of calls. And they all said the same thing, what you said. That they had information about Raleigh. Of course, I never talked to any of them. Mr. Fournier did that. Raleigh's father. And it always turned out the same way. None of them knew anything. And sooner or later they would want money for something or other."

"Well, thanks so much," Raleigh said, putting out a hand, looking at it. It was steadier now.

"But it's been years since anybody has gotten in touch with us, said that they had information on Raleigh," the voice continued. "But the thing is, Mr. Fournier and I are separated now. And it's been very unpleasant. So you see, I had to think about it, decide what to do."

"Well, as I said—" Raleigh began.

"And somehow it didn't seem to be the sort of thing that I could bring up with my fiancé, Mr. Horton," the voice continued. "He can be impatient."

I might as well just let it run, Raleigh thought, making an encouraging noise into the phone.

"But finally my curiosity just got the better of me," the voice said, a little laugh in it. "I mean, after all, you're staying at the Beverly Hills Hotel. And what I really had to ask you was how you knew that a letter sent through Mr. Horton would reach me. I mean, we've tried to be circumspect. I mean, neither of us is actually free yet."

"Bobby mentioned it," Raleigh said. "He's my hairdresser, too."

"Oh, you go to Bobby!" the voice said, delight in it now. "Well, that explains everything."

"I'd be very grateful if you would give me a few minutes of your time," Raleigh said. "Whenever it's convenient, of course."

Well, she had to have an evening dress altered. There was just a little something funny about the way it hung at the shoulders. And her legs waxed. She had to do that. There was a full schedule of luncheons, teas. Then, of course, she had to go to see Bobby, too. And while she was there, get her manicure. Her pedicure. They were planning a little trip, too. She and Mr. Horton. To Santa Barbara. So she had to decide what to pack for that.

"Maybe Thursday," she said, her voice doubtful.

"Shall I come there?" Raleigh asked.

Well, maybe that might not be such a good idea, the voice said as Raleigh decoded the subtext. The Beverly Hills Hotel, Bobby, whatever. This person was still a stranger. Possibly a dangerous stranger. You never knew these days.

"Why don't you come here?" suggested Raleigh. "I'll take you to lunch at the Polo Lounge."

"Well, no," she said. "I don't think so. I mean, what if what you have to tell me about Raleigh upsets me? And there I'll be, in front of all of those people."

"Fine," said Raleigh patiently. "I have a bungalow here. We can order lunch and have it out on my little terrace."

"I guess that'll be all right," she said.

Negotiating what time she would arrive took several minutes more. I can see how she spends her days, Raleigh thought, smiling, as she hung up the phone. Oh, she just couldn't wait to see her mother. Couldn't believe how desperately she had missed her until she had picked up the phone and heard her voice again. Thursday, at one o'clock. Oh, I can't wait. I just can't wait, she thought blissfully.

But it wasn't Thursday, and it wasn't one o'clock, Raleigh read on the message in her box when she got back from a couple of hours working out in the gym at Caltech. And would she please call?

"I've been thinking about our little meeting, dear," Beth Carol began when the housekeeper put her on the line.

Oh, no, thought Raleigh.

"You might as well come here," she said. "I asked Bobby about you when I saw him yesterday. I must say, he's becoming very difficult. I mean, waiting is one thing. I've always waited for Bobby, ever since I started going to him. But sometimes he isn't even there. He could have somebody call, after all. I mean, it's so rude, don't you think?"

"Yes," Raleigh said.

"At any rate," she continued, "Bobby says you're a perfectly nice young person and that you grew up in Mexico. So come for tea, all right? On Tuesday, I thought. Around four? I just love tea, don't you? I mean, it doesn't interfere with what I have to do in the morning, and there's still time afterwards to get ready for whatever I'll be doing in the evening."

"Fine," Raleigh said. "I'll see you on Tuesday at four o'clock."

The thing was, she was so nervous about it, she realized as she drove down Wilshire Boulevard on Tuesday afternoon. It was a splendid day, bright and clear with a little breeze. She stopped for a red light in front of the Los Angeles County Museum of Art, for the people in the crosswalk in front of her. On the steps of the museum itself, tourists were taking pictures of each other. How much should she tell her? she worried as the light turned green. Oh, sure, about the Fisks. The University of Chicago. She glanced over at the tall, white Carnation building, its swaying palm trees, the playground of a school. But what about Paul? That he'd tried to kill her? Could her mother take that? Maybe it wasn't fair to her. Maybe Raleigh should edit Paul out of the scenario. Just an accident of some kind, but here we are, Mom. Together again, at last.

Raleigh drove her little car through the gates at the entrance of Fremont Place. Gave her name to the uniformed security guy in the gatehouse. Sat there while he called to see if it was all right for her to be there. Nodded, raised the arm so that she could drive in, and told her to have a nice day.

It was all mansions in here, she saw, one next to the other on large lots with green lawns, bushes of white and pink hibiscus, oleanders. It was different, though, from the ones in Beverly Hills with its jumble of architectural styles as if everybody had decided all at once to live in a favorite fantasy. No, these were stately, subdued, a lot of them in faded brick as if they belonged somewhere in the east where protection was needed against freezing winters, snow and sleet.

Turn left at the second corner, the guard had said. The third house, the one with the white birch trees in front. There it was, she saw, pulling over to the curb. Parking the car. It was brick, too, painted white, two stories with dormer windows. A gardener was clipping the orange bougainvillea that arched around the front door. She looked at the house, swallowed hard. Sat there for a few more minutes, wondering what it was going to be like to see her mother, before she slowly got out of the car. Walked up to the front door, which was painted an emerald green. Nodded to the gardener, who nodded to her. Rang the doorbell and heard it chime somewhere inside the house.

Fascinated, Raleigh stared at the doorknob as it started to turn, heard her mother's voice, its note of gaiety, as she said, "My dear, I thought you'd gotten lost. . . ."

She looked into her mother's blue eyes that were just like her own. Saw the look of welcome change to one of confusion. And then, almost at once, to comprehension.

"Raleigh," she gasped, her hand flying to her throat. "It's you."

"Mother," she said, the word almost a sob as she opened her arms to her.

"You're so beautiful," her mother kept murmuring as, clutching at her arm, she led Raleigh through the capacious entry hall with its polished floors, its graceful, winding staircase, through the large, formal drawing room with its heavy draperies, Oriental carpets. "My baby, my baby," she murmured as, arm in arm, they entered a cozy library, its walls lined with books, the furniture, overstuffed, covered with a chintz in apricot, pale green, lilac. Antique occasional tables, lamps with parchment shades. The perfume from the roses in their crystal vases. "You're so beautiful," she said again, gazing at Raleigh with tear-filled eyes. "I've never stopped believing this day would come," she said.

"I love you," Raleigh kept saying over and over. "I've missed you so much."

"You're all grown up," her mother said, gazing at her, not able to get enough of looking at her. "You make me feel so old."

Raleigh gazed at her mother, taking her in. Touched her arm, her shoulder. Caressed her cheek. "I love you," she said again. "I've missed you, Mother."

"I've made tea," her mother said with a little laugh. "Little sandwiches—scones, even. There's an English shop close by, on Larchmont. Maybe we should have a drink instead. To celebrate. Champagne." She took Raleigh's hand, wound her fingers in Raleigh's fingers. "I love you, my baby," she said. "I've missed you so much."

"It doesn't matter," Raleigh said. "All I care about is being here with you."

"It was Paul, you know," her mother said. "He was the one who did it. For the money, of course."

So she knew, Raleigh realized, the hairs on her arms standing on end, a chill running down her spine.

"Oh, I was such an innocent," Beth Carol murmured, tears in her eyes, as she stroked Raleigh's arm. "He was the first man in my life, the only man in my life. He just swept me off my feet. Before I knew it, we were man and wife. It wasn't the way it is with girls now. All of this promiscuity, this free love. The pill, that's what it is. That's why they think they can get away with it." She paused, shook her head as she gazed at Raleigh. "Oh, my baby," she said. "You're really here."

"Yes, Mother," she said, tears on her cheeks.

"I didn't even know there was such a thing as contraception," she said. "I thought babies came from the belly button. I really did. It was our wedding night, darling. That's when I got pregnant with you."

Raleigh thought of the date on the wedding license hidden away in the Hall of Records in Paso Robles, the date on her own birth certificate downtown. Oh, well, she thought to herself, and smiled at her mother.

"Paul knew how much my father wanted a grandson," she said. "Well, with five daughters, maybe it's understandable. The family name. That kind of thing. 'We'll tell him it's a boy,' Paul said when you were born. 'He'll never know the difference. He's up there, we're down here. It's not as if you have a close relationship with him, after all. We'll name it after him. He'll send us money.'

"It was wicked," her mother said through her sobs. "And I went along with it, darling. I was so ashamed, I never saw my father again as long as he lived. I just couldn't bring myself to face him with a child who was his grandson in name only. I couldn't even talk to him on the phone. And Paul, well, he wouldn't even let me talk or write to my sisters. 'You'll blab something,' he said. 'I know how you are.' But you, my baby, how could I have done such a thing to you? To myself?" Dabbing at her tears, she turned imploring eyes to Raleigh. "All of the things I couldn't do for you. Your proms, your debut . . ."

"Mother, don't do this to yourself," Raleigh begged as Beth Carol's voice faded away, her shoulders slumped.

"I think I will have a little drink," she said with a shaky laugh. "After all, it isn't every day my only child returns from the dead."

"I don't remember what happened." That was what Raleigh decided to tell her as dusk started to settle into the pretty little room. "I just woke up and I was in an infirmary in a village on the coast of Mexico. The Fisks lived there. Eleanor and Charles Fisk, the philosophers. Some fishermen took me there because they had a doctor."

"The couple who just died," her mother murmured. "I read about it in the paper. What a wonderful love story."

"They took me in," Raleigh said. "I was such a spoiled movie star brat that there were probably times when they wished they could throw me back. They thought I had amnesia. I didn't know what to do, so I just went along with it. After a few years, they made me their ward, sent me off to college in the States. In Chicago, where Eleanor had taught."

"It was the worst time of my life," her mother said grimly as she poured more vodka over the ice cubes in her glass. "I was paralyzed with grief. I could hardly get out of bed. I just sat there, brushing your little dog. Frisky. Such a sweet little dog. He lived to a great old age. But I wanted to die, I might as well have been dead."

"I didn't know what to do about getting in touch with you," Raleigh said lamely, her cheeks burning.

"And your father, Paul, well, he was a big help, as usual," she said in a tight, bitter voice. "He was going his own merry way, running around on me just the way he always had. Oh, he was always unfaithful," she said, patting Raleigh's hand. "Right from the very beginning. And do you know what he had the nerve to say to me when he asked me for a divorce a year after you disappeared?

"He said that I had failed him," she said with a harsh, disbelieving laugh. "He said I hadn't been there to comfort him in his grief. That all I thought about was myself. He said that he had turned elsewhere and that he had fallen in love with someone else." She sat there, shook her head. "And do you know who it was? Do you know who it is to this day? Diana Kendall," she said, a sneer in her voice. "You remember, it had been her family's estate. Paul's mother was Mr. Kendall's secretary. He grew up there with her brother, with her."

Raleigh entwined her mother's fingers with her own.

"Well, you should see her," her mother said, contempt in her voice. "Plain as mud. Skinny. I tell you, Raleigh, it doesn't matter what that girl puts on, how she does her hair. It doesn't make any difference at all. I'll never believe it, that he's in love with her, that he has been all these years. No, it's the social position. It's his way of getting even. Because his mother was a secretary, a servant. He hated that."

"You must have been very hurt," Raleigh said.

"Hurt!" her mother exclaimed. "Darling, I was stunned. Absolutely stunned. And there he was, standing there, with that smug look on his face. 'I'll give you alimony,' he said. 'Twenty thousand dollars a year for five years. By then you'll have found somebody.'"

Raleigh tried not to smile. All of those millions of dollars in assets and that was his offer. God. Paul.

"So, you were seeing Roger back then?" Raleigh asked.

"If it hadn't been for Roger Horton, I never would have made it," her mother said. "We'd met at a couple of charity events, the opening of the performing arts center. I was on a committee with his wife. He would come once a week to take me for a drive. At first, I would just stand at my bedroom window upstairs, watching him down below. He'd just sit there in his car, waiting. And after a while he would leave. Finally I got dressed one day, and I was ready when he pulled up."

"A nice man," Raleigh said.

"Yes, yes, he's very kind, a wonderful man," her mother said, nodding.

"So Paul wanted a divorce, you wanted a divorce, and the two of you just went on living there together? For how long? Nearly seven years?"

"Oh, darling," her mother said. "I didn't want a divorce. Roger was married. I wouldn't have been one of those women for anything. They always seemed so pathetic to me, trying to make the best of things. Always looking for the next husband."

"So it was a standoff."

"We hardly saw each other." Her mother smiled. "It was a very large house, you know. And Roger bought me this one. So we would have a place to be together."

"Does he live here?"

"Oh, no," her mother said fervently. "It wouldn't be discreet. Bitsy wouldn't like it, either, not until their divorce is final. And I haven't even filed yet. I can't file until the property settlement is worked out with Paul. I'd give him everything now that Roger and I can be married, but Roger won't hear of it. I'm entitled to half of everything, and that's what I'm going to have. Paul, well, Paul won't budge."

Raleigh heard the catch in her voice as her words trailed off. Studied her face and absorbed for the first time the circles under her eyes, the strain written on her face.

"You're a blonde now," Raleigh said, reaching out to touch her mother's hair.

"Yes, Bobby has been taking me lighter for years." She laughed. "It's softer when you get a bit older, he says. I tell you, it was so gradual I didn't even notice it."

"Well, I like it," Raleigh said.

"Oh, Raleigh," said her mother, her eyes shining with tears again. "You're so beautiful, darling. I'm so glad you're finally home."

CHAPTER 69

*I*t was getting dark now, and Raleigh watched her mother as she scurried around the room, turning on lights, plumping up pillows. She was so pretty, Raleigh thought, in her little silk dress, a scarf tied around her throat. Her spectator pumps with the two-inch heels. On her left hand, she wore an enormous diamond ring. Ten carats, maybe. Diamonds in her earlobes. Listened to her giddy chatter. "I'll make us a cheese soufflé, a wonderful new recipe. Roger says it's the best he'd ever eaten. Really. And a green salad with just the best dressing I've learned how to make. Essentially just oil and vinegar, because, well, I'm watching my weight now, but, darling, you'll never need to. You have the most beautiful figure I've ever seen. But with a tang of lemon, to make it a little interesting. And, oh, that wonderful French bread they serve at Musso's—you know, that place that's been there on Hollywood Boulevard for a thousand years. The housekeeper runs up to pick it up three times a week. Oh, my darling, it's as if you've never been away. And there's probably something for dessert in the freezer," she said with a little frown.

"Come on, darling," she said gaily, putting out her hand, taking Raleigh's in her own. "A son is a son until he takes a wife," she added. "A daughter is a daughter all of her life."

"Golly, I missed you," Raleigh said as she followed her

mother through the dining room with its gleaming mahogany table, eight matching chairs, roses from the garden in a crystal vase on the sideboard, a crystal chandelier, into the kitchen, all warm and cheery in blue and white, butcher's block counters, a cozy table, four chairs at the corner windows looking out onto the garden.

"I was resigned to things as they were," her mother said as she started to take ingredients out of the refrigerator and line them up on the counter. "Oh, I'll admit it, I did think that Roger might ask for a divorce once all of the children were in college. But I knew in my heart that it wouldn't happen. People like Roger don't get divorced. Ever. Because of the family's position, and all." Twirling, she smiled broadly at Raleigh. "And then, out of the blue, guess what happened? Bitsy asked him for the divorce. She's an attorney with a big entertainment law firm in Century City. She's going to marry one of the partners. Of course, they hadn't had a marriage, not really, for years. But she was the one who was just waiting for all of the children to be in college."

"How are the children?" Raleigh asked, trying to sound nonchalant.

"Oh, that's right," her mother said, looking over at her, nodding. You knew them, didn't you? The oldest one, the boy, he was a friend of yours. He used to come to the house. You used to play tennis together."

"I saw him again in Mexico," Raleigh murmured. "He was a research assistant for them, for Charles and Eleanor."

"Well, then you know." Her mother giggled. "He certainly has turned out to be a handsome young man, hasn't he?"

Raleigh nodded, felt her face burning.

"Oh, I think my little girl has a crush," her mother cooed, dancing over to her, bending to kiss her hair. "Oh, this is so much fun, having you here. I've never been so happy in my life."

"He told me he was going to be a mathematician," Raleigh said.

"Oh, that's what he's doing, all right," her mother said,

concentrating on the eggs she was breaking into a bowl. "He's at Harvard now, working on his doctorate. Roger is so proud of him." She stopped, turned abruptly to face Raleigh. "You didn't tell him, did you?" she demanded. "Who you really are, I mean?"

"No, I couldn't," she whispered. "Not then."

"And Bobby?" she asked, her voice tinged with fear. "Does he know?"

Raleigh shook her head.

"And your father, Paul. Well, it would be the last thing in the world he would want to be known." Turning to Raleigh, she said, "Oh, darling, you're not going to run right back and tell him everything we've said, are you?"

"I haven't even seen him," she said. "The one I wanted to see was you. I wanted to be with you."

"I felt so excluded all those years," her mother said.

"I did see Fern, though," Raleigh said. "I ran into her at a party."

"Fern," her mother said contemptuously. "She was one of your father's little floozies, too. For years. Years." Grabbing her drink, she drained it. It was her fourth, Raleigh realized. She was holding it a lot better than she used to.

"Do you know when they started their little dalliance? On our wedding night. He came to our bed reeking of her perfume." Her blue eyes were like ice, her mouth set. "How one girl could do that to another amazes me," she said. "But there was nothing I could do about it. I had to be nice to her. For you. For your career." Reaching into the cupboard above her head, she took down a bottle of vodka, filled her glass again. "Even after they broke up, I still had to be nice to her. 'Call her,' Paul would say. 'Take her out to lunch. I've got this to publicize. That to publicize.'"

"When did they break up?" Raleigh asked.

"You know, I really can't remember," her mother said, frowned a little, narrowed her eyes. "It would have been, let's see . . . yes, just after Sir George Dean was murdered. So you would have been . . ." Turning, she looked at Raleigh with wide, horrified eyes.

"You're not giving anything away," Raleigh said gently. "I've been doing some research in the library at the Academy. I came across the clippings. I know he was murdered."

"It was horrible, ghastly," her mother said. "It was Paul who told you. Sir George Dean loved you so much, and I just couldn't face how upset you would be."

"I had a drink with Fern," Raleigh said. "She knows who I am."

"Oh, no," her mother whispered.

"She didn't want to believe me," Raleigh said. "But I convinced her after a while. Because I knew things that only Raleigh Barnes could know. About the boy who was staying there, the one who was murdered, too. Buddy Hatcher."

Her mother swayed, put one hand on the counter to steady herself as she said in a shaky voice, "Yes, that's right. There was someone else. I'd forgotten that. It was such a long time ago."

"He was the one who kidnapped me," Raleigh said. "He took that picture that Fern showed on the television special, the one that got her all that notoriety. There were other pictures, too. One of them taken in the bathtub. It showed that I was a girl."

Her mother's face was white, her mouth moved. No words came.

"He told me that he knew you from back home. That you had been high school sweethearts. He knew that I had been named for my grandfather. So I went with him."

Raleigh sipped her wine, looked at her mother.

"Well?" she said.

"I don't remember, darling," she said with a helpless, little gesture. "There may have been some people at home named Hatcher. I just don't know."

"Fern isn't going to use the story," Raleigh said. "It's because of the money that Sir George Dean left to me, the money that she gets if I predecease her. So it's up to you."

"What's up to me?" her mother asked blankly.

"Well, you're my mother," she said. "You know I'm Raleigh Barnes."

"Oh, sweetheart," her mother said imploringly, sitting down next to her at the table, taking her hands. "Don't you think it would make more sense to let sleeping dogs lie? After all, here you are. A beautiful young woman with a wonderful career ahead of you. Not that I even quite know what an astrophysicist is." She tried a little, tremulous smile. "We'll have our relationship. We'll see each other all the time."

"You mean you're not going to acknowledge me?" Raleigh asked angrily.

"Oh, it's not that, dear one." Her mother sighed. "It's just that I think it's going to take some discussion. You know, it was all so tacky, what we did. Why not just go on with things?"

"Are you serious?" Raleigh demanded. "Do you really expect me to let my whole life go? Just forget it ever happened?"

"Oh, Raleigh," her mother said miserably. "It'll be such a scandal. Everybody will be laughing at you. At me. And I don't even want to think what it would do to Roger. To our relationship."

"If he loves you enough, why would he care about what anybody says?" she asked.

"Just promise me you won't do anything right now," her mother begged. "Let me think about it. All right, darling?"

"I can't do anything," Raleigh snapped. "Without you, I don't exist."

And then, somehow, there were a lot of things that just had to be done at once. A phone call from Roger to be answered, for one thing. "Oh, yes, darling," she heard her mother purring into the receiver. "I'm making a little supper for one of my girlfriends. No, no. You don't know her. Eleven o'clock? Oh, darling, I hate it when you have to work so late. Yes, yes. I miss you, too. I love you." And then her mother was rushing around, setting the table in the little dining room with her pretty china and crested silverware. Serving the soufflé, the elegant little salad, as Raleigh uncorked another beautiful bottle of white wine. Two more phone calls. A couple of girlfriends. The housekeeper, back from her day off, popped her head in to say good night.

"This is Miss Fisk," her mother said, not daring to look at Raleigh.

And then she was up, kind of hopping around, bringing in dessert. Looking at her watch. It's time for me to go, Raleigh realized. She doesn't want me to run into Roger. Not tonight. Maybe not ever.

They were walking together toward the front door, her mother's arm around her waist, and she was saying that she still couldn't believe it, that this was the happiest day of her life. "I love you," Raleigh said. And that other matter, well, her mother said, they'd discuss it further, when things weren't quite so emotional. When it could be approached calmly. Rationally.

"Raleigh, when you see your father," her mother began hesitantly, "when you see Paul . . ."

Raleigh stood on the front stoop, holding her mother's hand. Waiting.

"I don't know how to say this," her mother said desperately. "Oh, Raleigh, back when we were young, when we were kids, I made a movie . . ."

"What kind of a movie?" Raleigh asked.

"A movie that Paul produced, that Darby directed," she muttered. "It was to make some money. We were all so broke."

A porno movie, Raleigh realized.

"Oh, they didn't do anything with it," her mother said. "They didn't want to be associated with it. But now Paul is threatening me with it. Threatening to show it unless I give him my half of everything. 'You're set for life now,' he said. And Roger, well, Roger is a businessman. Everything that's mine has to come to me. He insists on it."

Raleigh clutched her mother's hand, stared into her tortured face.

"If you could just talk to him, darling," her mother pleaded. "Maybe if it's you, he'll give it back."

"I don't have any plans to see him," Raleigh said hesitantly. "Not yet, anyway. It was something that happened in Mexico . . ."

"This is killing me," her mother said, sobbing.

CHAPTER 70

*F*ragments of their conversation floated in Raleigh's mind as she looked into her rearview mirror and saw her mother standing in the doorway, waving good-bye. The porno movie Paul was holding over her head. "I had to do it," she had said. "He would have thrown me out. I had nowhere to go."

"But couldn't you have gotten a job?" Raleigh asked.

"Doing what?" her mother said. "I wasn't like you. I had no education, no skills."

"There must have been something you could have done," Raleigh began, and then she stopped. Realized that all her mother had wanted to do was to be with Paul, that she would have done anything to be with him. That somehow she was playing her proper role back then, no matter what the cost.

And the way she had reacted when Raleigh had told her about her own career plans. First, the master's at Caltech, working on some of the programs they were developing there to explore the farthest reaches of space. Then her doctorate.

"When you were little, you always used to talk about being an explorer," her mother remembered, her eyes shining. A pause, and then, "But, dear, what about a husband, children?"

543

"What about them?" Raleigh asked.

"Well, don't you want them, darling?" her mother had asked. "A nice home, a family?"

"All I want is to be the best I can be," Raleigh said, frowning. "I want to use myself up as I go along. It's my life. It's my adventure."

"I can understand that," her mother said. "But doesn't your adventure include love?"

"It depends on the price." Raleigh smiled.

Her mother took that as an insult, as if Raleigh were implying that Beth Carol had wasted her own life in devoting it to her husband, home, and child. And now to Roger. God, every other sentence out of her mother's mouth started with the words "Roger says," or "Roger thinks," or "Roger feels."

And the way she had reinvented her own life, Raleigh pondered as she sat there at a signal in the little Mercedes-Benz. Paul, the only man in her life. I got pregnant on our wedding night, she had said. Had she told these things to her girlfriends, to herself, so often that she really believed them? What was wrong with the truth? Raleigh asked herself as the driver in the car behind her honked her horn when the light turned green.

But still, there was such a sweetness about her, just the way Raleigh had remembered it. And it had been so thrilling to see her again, to feel her own rush of love, her mother's rush of love toward her, that thread of continuity between them taut again, binding them.

Ahead, she saw the hotel, pink and green, in the still, black night. She turned up the curving driveway, drove past the beds of purple, white, and pink flowers. At the entrance, the parking lot attendants in their green jackets were rushing around, delivering cars to the waiting people, the men in dark suits, the women in cocktail dresses. Yet another party, Raleigh saw. She stepped from the car, realized how emotionally exhausted she was.

She picked up her messages at the desk, read them as she strode through the lobby, and stepped out into the fragrant night on her way to her bungalow. Grant had called. So had Bobby. Mrs. Fournier had called to see if she had gotten home safely, and would she please call the moment she got in. Raleigh smiled at that one as she opened the door. Saw the orchid that had been delivered while she was out. Heard the phone start to ring. Mother, she thought, as she picked it up.

"This is your secret admirer."

It was Paul.

Raleigh froze at the sound of his voice, then took a deep breath.

"Thank you for the orchids," she said. "They're beautiful."

"You like them?" he said, pleased. "Well, I spoke to David himself about them. He always has the most beautiful orchids in town."

Raleigh sat there, could almost see the way Paul looked when he was deciding how to put something, what to say. The expression in his eyes, reflective. His brow furrowed. Moistening his bottom lip with the tip of his tongue.

"We have been introduced," he said with a little laugh. "I'm Paul Fournier. You probably don't remember me, but I met you at Ma Maison a couple of weeks ago. You were having lunch with Bobby Prise."

"Of course I remember you," she said, lowering her voice seductively.

"Well, that's very flattering, coming from a beautiful young woman like you," he said.

"How did you find out where I was staying?" she asked.

"Oh, that was easy." He laughed. "A beautiful young woman with all the style in the world? On vacation? There was only one place you could be staying. I just called reception and described you."

Raleigh laughed, too.

"Look, I'm really embarrassed to be calling you so late," he said with that boyish sound in his voice that she remembered so well. "I've been out of town on business and I just got in a few minutes ago. I'd like to take you to dinner. That is, if you'd like to go."

"I'd love to," she said, feeling the pulse in her temple start to throb.

"Let's see," he said. "I've got a business dinner tomorrow night. How about Thursday? We can go to the Bistro, to Chasen's. Tell me where you haven't been yet."

"Why don't you come here tomorrow night when you're through with your business dinner?" Raleigh asked. "You can ring me from the lobby. I'll meet you in the Polo Lounge."

"No, I don't think so," he said apologetically. "I've met with these people before. It'll go on and on. Way after midnight, at least."

"Well," Raleigh said. "I haven't been to Chasen's yet."

"Great," he said. "I'll have my secretary make a reservation. Is eight o'clock all right?"

"Eight o'clock is just fine."

"I'm really looking forward to seeing you," he said. "I can't tell you how often I've thought of you."

"Now you're flattering me," Raleigh said, curling a lock of hair around one finger. "I'm looking forward to seeing you, too."

Well, keeping her voice steady during *that* conversation was as hard as anything she had been doing lately, she thought as she said good night and hung up the phone. It was going to have to be tomorrow night, she realized with dread. Oh, God. So soon. She started as the phone began to ring again.

"Hello," she said.

"Raleigh," said her mother's anxious voice. "I've just been frantic. You know, dear, it would have been considerate if you would have called when you got in. After all, it doesn't take this long to get from Fremont Place to the Beverly Hills Hotel. You just can't imagine what I've been going through. Anything could have happened to you."

"I'm sorry, Mother," she said, smiling. "The phone was ringing when I got in. I was going to call you in a minute. Really."

"Well, you know how I worry," her mother fretted.

"Listen, what's the security like on the estate these days?" Raleigh asked. "Are the security guards still there? The dogs?"

And her mother said no, that the court wouldn't permit that kind of expenditure after Raleigh had disappeared. That what was there now was just a service that came by every hour or so, a burglar alarm that connected the house to the Beverly Hills Police Department.

"Is there a way to switch it off?" she asked.

"Oh, yes," her mother said. "You know how those silly things are. Sometimes they go off for no reason at all, and you can lose your mind before someone comes."

"What about the vault in Paul's office?" she asked. "You wouldn't happen to have the combination, would you?"

"Yes," her mother said.

"That's wonderful, Mother," Raleigh smiled. "I'll call you first thing in the morning. I promise. Now, you get back to Roger, all right?"

"Raleigh," her mother said in a wary voice, "what are you planning to do?"

CHAPTER 71

*J*ust after dusk the next evening, Raleigh dialed the number at the mansion and listened to the phone ring four times before the answering machine picked it up.

Okay, she thought as she slipped her suede coat over her black body suit, locked the door of the bungalow behind her, and cut through the lobby of the hotel to the front entrance. A couple of tourists were marveling over a slinky peignoir, the jeweled evening bags, displayed in the window of Helft's and, just checking in, was H. L. Hunt, whom she recognized from pictures of him she had seen in the newspapers. He glanced in her direction and she saw that he had the bluest eyes she had ever seen.

So maybe this meeting won't go until after midnight, she thought. Maybe it only goes until eleven, or even ten. At least she knew that it was on. She'd called Paul's office, checked with his secretary, to be sure of it.

Smitty, the head of parking, was helping somebody out of a Cadillac. He turned, saw her standing there. Smiled in recognition, touched the bill of his hat as he beckoned to one of the tanned, blond kids who worked there to bring up her car.

She'd thought about the car, whether it was right. Whether she should rent something a little less conspicuous. But actually there wasn't anything less conspicuous than the little Mercedes-Benz. Everybody drove them. It was the perfect getaway car if you were, say, robbing a bank in Beverly Hills, or breaking into the Raleigh Barnes estate.

It was only a few minutes before she was turning up the curving road she knew so well. She didn't even glance at the entrance to the estate as she drove past it, wound around the back to the narrow dirt road where the trees hung over the brick wall, to the farthest point of the property that she had discovered so many years ago during her life as a boy when she would pretend she was an explorer at the end of the world.

She cut the engine, pushed her hair into the black knit cap she'd brought along. Remembered her mother's words when she'd seen her earlier in the day. "I'm not going to let you do this, Raleigh," she had said, her blue eyes panicked as she kneaded her hands. "I absolutely forbid it."

"What would you suggest?" Raleigh had asked.

She crawled onto the hood of the car, leapt, caught one of the overhanging branches on the first try. Dropped onto the cushion of dead leaves on the other side. She started to jog slowly in the direction of the mansion, got her rhythm after a couple of minutes. She wasn't even breathing hard a half an hour later when she finally saw the lake, the mansion itself, looming in front of her, outlined by a full moon in a misty gray sky. She kept in the shadows, darted from tree to tree until she was right in front of the eight-car garage. She flicked on her flashlight, played it over the gleaming hood of a Jaguar roadster from the fifties, an XKE. A station wagon. Several empty spaces. She started at a sound outside. An owl hooting. Dropped the beam of light to the used brick floor, counted them until she came to thirty-seven west, sixteen north. On her haunches now, she played the light over the bricks until she saw the catch her mother had told her about. She lifted it, saw the coil of wires, turned off the burglar alarm. As she stood, she took a deep breath and wiped her forehead with the back of her hand. Stood and listened for a moment. There wasn't a sound.

She hugged the outline of the house, keeping close to it until she came to the back garden with the swimming pool, the statuary. The little sun room. The French doors leading into the ballroom. With her glass cutter, she carved an arc, heard the glass tinkle as it fell in pieces into the room. Reaching in, she turned the handle and stepped inside.

In a moment, her eyes adjusted to the darkness of the room. The magnificent chandelier, the crystal sconces on the walls, sparkled in the moonlight the way they always had. I'm trembling, Raleigh realized, taking a couple of tentative steps. I'm frightened. But what I really am is sad. So sad about the way it really was. The manipulation, the betrayal.

She glided across the parquetry floor, the scene of so many parties, the women in their gowns, the men in their dinner clothes, the orchestra playing there on the stage. She opened the door to the ballroom, stepped out into the hall, closed it behind her. The moonlight beamed on the marble floors as she raced soundlessly up the wide, winding stairway.

Something Ann had once said came back to her. It was about how when she went back to Minnesota the first time after she had gone away to college her house seemed to be so much smaller than she remembered. Other people had said that, too. About going home for the first time. But this, this seemed enormous, even bigger than Raleigh had remembered it. She pushed open the door to her mother's room, saw vague shapes there in the dark, the impression of paintings on the walls. Remembered how it had been when she was a child, when Diana's dolls had still lined the shelves, been displayed in glass cases. Closing the door, she moved on down the wide hallway. Opened the door to the gymnasium, where she had lived during her life as a boy. The bars, the rings, everything was still in place. There were a couple of new pieces of equipment, she saw. A rowing machine. A stationary bicycle. Of course, she realized. Paul still used it. And right through that door was his suite, his office, the projection room he'd had built where she'd shown Toosie her movies so long ago. She sauntered over to where the films were cataloged, played her flashlight

over the titles. All the movies she'd ever made, the movies
Paul had produced in the last six years, nearly seven, since
he'd tried to kill her. Thought he had killed her.

He'd redecorated his living quarters, she saw as she let
the beam of the flashlight play around the room. Vertical
blinds and draperies now covered the windows. The bedspread was in a black and white pattern, big pillows also in
various patterns of black and white. In a corner there was a
freestanding fireplace with a white, lacquered hood. On a
wall there was an orange and yellow lithograph that read
"Dreamboat." A small Picasso that she recognized. A
Manet. She moved quickly through the room, threw open
the door to his office. Automatically flipped on the light,
realized simultaneously that the office faced the back garden, that it couldn't be seen from the front of the house.

There were the scrapbooks, stretching out along the
shelves. The mammoth antique desk, piled with scripts and
neat file folders. The potted plants with their shiny, green
leaves. The door to the vault.

Five left. Two complete turns to sixteen right. Fifty-
three left. A click. Raleigh swung open the door. There
were the rows of file cabinets, the negatives to all the films.
Quickly she scanned the early titles. Found it almost at
once, "Wood Nymphs," read its label. The only one with a
print next to it. Promise me you won't look at it, her mother
had pleaded, her eyes averted.

In a moment, Raleigh was threading it into the projector, pushing the switch that turned it on. There was blank
film for a few seconds, no titles, no sound. Then a wood,
grass, a girl in a diaphanous gown, her arms outstretched,
teetering toward the camera with tiny little steps. A
close-up of her face filled the screen. That soft, young
face, the Cleopatra makeup framing frightened blue eyes.
That long, blond hair that made her mother look exactly
the same as she had looked when Raleigh saw her earlier
in the day. She hit rewind, flipped it off. Bingo, she
thought as she hurried back to the vault, yanked open the
first file cabinet with her name on it. Slowly and meticu-

lously started to examine paper after paper.

The court documents again, this time with the actual contracts attached to them. Department stores, movie companies, food companies. Here was the actual Gerber's contract, around twenty pages. She thumbed through it, flipped to the last page. TINY THESP INKED TO PACT. That had been the headline in the mention of the deal in *Variety*. She hadn't, though. Not literally. No little fingerprints here, either. Just the judge's signature, the representatives from the company. Paul Fournier on behalf of Raleigh Barnes. She felt a little disappointed, as she glanced at her watch, saw that it was almost nine o'clock. Listened for a moment to the whispering of the mansion, opened another file. Her mother's, dated 1952. Scanned the amounts, the initials, cross-referenced payments to other initials. Raised her eyebrows as she realized what they must mean. Beauty salon bills. Clothes. Even mileage when he'd driven her to an assignation. That bastard, she thought, wondering if what he'd done to her mother would cross her mind when the time came. When she evened the score with him.

And here were more court documents, bills supporting expenditures made on her behalf. The security, the payments on the various mortgages. Food, clothes. And here was one from that dentist to the stars who had made the false teeth, her flippers, when her baby teeth had fallen out. She scanned the file, stared at her x-rays for a couple of seconds before she realized what she had found.

My dental records, she thought. Now I can prove I'm Raleigh Barnes.

She was hurrying now, knew that she was running out of time as she picked up another file, opened it, felt the shock run through her as she saw the stack of Polaroids. Three or four of them with Frisky in the front room of Buddy's apartment, eating a big plate of spaghetti, sauce ringing her smiling mouth. A couple of her, sitting reading comic books. One in the kitchen, drying dishes. The one in the bathtub that showed she was a girl, looking annoyed.

What are they doing here? she asked herself in astonishment, heard at the same time a different sound. Footsteps in the hall that stopped at once. He'd seen the light, she realized, darting out of the vault to switch it off. And she couldn't even go out of the window. There wasn't a tree, not even a crawling vine.

Raleigh's mouth was dry as she pasted herself against the wall next to the door. I can push his nose right through his brain, kill him now, she thought calmly as the door slowly opened.

"Who's there?" he demanded hoarsely. She saw a glint of silver in his hand.

She sprang at him as soon as he entered the room, tried to get her arm around his neck, heard the gun as it clattered to the floor. He flailed wildly around, managed to get a grip on her. She slid out of his grasp, dropped to her knees, drove straight up with her clenched fist, caught him hard, right in his Adam's apple.

He couldn't even scream as he toppled over backward clutching his throat. Even as she stepped over his body, she could hear his gagging coughs, a horrible gurgling sound, see him outlined by the moonlight as he writhed in pain.

Well, there are worse things than being dead, she reminded herself as she replaced the files in the vault, closed the drawers, took one long look around to see that everything looked exactly as it had when she'd gotten there, pushed the door closed behind her, and raced out of the room, down the hall, the stairs. Sprinted out of the French doors in the ballroom, and broke into a run.

She could hear the distant sirens even as she sat in the little car, gasping for air, pulling her fingers through her hair. She glanced at the film cans on the seat next to her, the files with her dental records, the Polaroids. Two police cars, their sirens wailing, their red lights flashing, were just pulling up to the entrance of the estate as she drove sedately by, her long hair blowing in the gentle evening breeze.

As soon as Raleigh got back to the bungalow, she called her mother, who answered on the first ring. Her voice was slurred, anxious.

"I've got it," Raleigh said, surprised at the tremor in her own voice, her hand on the receiver which seemed to have developed a life of its own. "The negative, and a print. I ran a couple of frames, just to be sure it was the right one."

"You've got it," her mother said, disbelief and wonder in her voice.

"And my dental records," Raleigh said.

"Well, that's probably the right thing," her mother murmured. "You sound awful, dear."

"I'm just exhausted," Raleigh said, closing her eyes, letting her head drop back against the chair.

"If you only knew what it's been like, sitting here, waiting for you to call," her mother moaned. "I've been beside myself."

"I'll talk to you in the morning," Raleigh said.

"I love you, darling."

"I love you, too."

Tentatively, she stood, unzipped the body suit as she dragged herself to the bathroom. A bruise was spreading on her right thigh, she saw. God, where did that come from? The corner of the desk, maybe. Whatever. She looked at her face in the mirror, ran her fingers over her cheeks. A little sore, she thought, wincing at her own touch. But she looked all right. A little flushed, but that was all. Turning on the shower, she stepped in, felt the hot stream pelting her shoulders, her breasts. Soaking her hair. She steadied herself with a hand on the tiled wall, closed her eyes, and lifted her face to its flow. Saw Paul writhing on the floor, heard those awful noises he was making. Wondered for the thousandth time, the millionth, how he had gotten those Polaroids that Buddy had taken of her.

It was nearly dawn before she was able to will herself to sleep. A few hours later, she felt herself being pulled back to consciousness by the ringing of the phone. She groped for it on the table next to the bed, found it. Groggily said hello.

"Miss Fisk?" said a woman's voice.

"Ummmm," she said, burying her head in the pillow.

"This is Mr. Fournier's secretary," she said. "He asked me to give you a call. He's afraid he isn't going to be able to make it this evening. He's come down with rather a nasty case of laryngitis."

"I'll bet," Raleigh muttered.

"Pardon me?" the voice asked politely.

"Too bad," Raleigh said.

"He'll call you as soon as he feels better, if that's all right," the woman said.

"It's fine," she said. "Just tell him I'm looking forward to seeing him soon."

She smiled to herself as she hung up, picked up the phone again, and asked reception to hold her calls. It was midafternoon when she woke up, and the sun was beating on the drawn shades in the bedroom.

CHAPTER 72

Raleigh drove along Sunset Boulevard, the top down, humming along with the radio, which was playing "The Way We Were." She rounded a bend past a wall dripping with hot pink bougainvillea, saw what she was looking for at the signal just ahead. A sign that read, MOVIE STAR MAPS, with an arrow that pointed around the corner. She made the turn, saw the Map Lady's old Ford station wagon with a sign propped up on its rear bumper: MOVIE STAR MAPS HERE. She drove slowly past a couple of big American cars with out-of-state license plates and parked in front of them. Business was brisk, she saw as she got out of the car. There were a couple of men, one in Bermuda shorts and a straw hat. A couple of women who were the men's wives, she supposed. A few kids running around.

And there was the Map Lady herself, sitting in a camp chair under a big, old tree, her maps, her crossword puzzles on the table in front of her, a big Thermos on the grass beside her, looking just the way she had for as long as Raleigh could remember.

"We have the most accurate addresses in town," Raleigh heard her saying as she approached. "We update every three months. Liza Minnelli. Jimmy Stewart. Everybody." Raleigh stood there waiting, watched the Map Lady as she pointed, giving directions, watched her making change from the gray metal cashbox in front of her.

"Good afternoon," she said, smiling at Raleigh. "We have the most accurate addresses in town. We update every three months. Liza Minnelli. Jimmy Stewart. Everybody."

"I'm trying to find an address for Darby Hicks," Raleigh said. "The director."

"Oh, yes," the Map Lady said. "I know where that is. It's not on the map, though. Most people, they don't care about directors. Just movie stars. Frank Sinatra. Julie Andrews. She's just rented a house in Malibu Colony, but we know it already. That's how current we are."

"What about Darby Hicks?" Raleigh said.

"Well, it'll cost you the same as a map," the woman said dubiously. "Five dollars."

"That's fine," Raleigh said.

She watched as The Map Lady consulted some little pieces of paper in her big handbag and wrote it out for her.

"He's up there on Mulholland Drive," she said, handing her the piece of paper. "You know where it is?"

Raleigh nodded.

"Well, there's Warren, and Marlon, and Jack," she said. "The next one, the one that's farthest west, that's Darby Hicks."

"Thank you," Raleigh said as she handed the Map Lady a ten-dollar bill and told her to keep the change.

It was great winding along Mulholland Drive, Raleigh thought exultantly, feeling the warm sun on her face, the wind in her hair. It was just like being on top of the world. On one side was the city. The office buildings downtown. In Century City. The jets at LAX, the ocean beyond it. On the other side was the Valley, stretching as far as she could see, the San Gabriel Mountains. And up here, fields of wild flowers. A motorcycle roared by her, and she fleetingly saw a deer bounding in the distance. The rest of it was mostly private roads, gated estates. But not all manicured the way they were everywhere else on the west side of town. Wild. That was the word. That would be it, she saw from the address. She stopped the car at the gates, looked at the dirt road beyond it, the eucalyptus trees, their leaves littering the ground. Parking the car, she hurried up to the gate. It was padlocked. There was no bell. It all looked abandoned somehow.

All I can do is wait, she decided as she got back into the little convertible, moved it around a curve where it couldn't be seen by anybody using the gate.

Raleigh awoke the next morning as the eastern sky over the Santa Monica Mountains turned white. A paneled truck slowly drove by and she heard the sound of newspapers as they plopped onto the pavement in front of the gates. Boy, this sleeping in a two-seater leaves a lot to be desired, she thought, sitting up, yawning, feeling how stiff she was as she stretched. The birds were waking up, too. She could hear them as they started to sing.

And then, out of the corner of her eye, she saw movement behind the gate that led to Darby's house. Saw the gate open, even heard it creak. Her heart raced as she saw that it was Darby himself. His hair was more gray than blond now and even from where she was watching him, she saw the look of maturity, the feeling of substance. He wore gray sweats, running shoes. As she watched, he broke into a slow jog, got his rhythm, increased his speed.

And here I am, in high heels, she thought, disappointed. She checked her watch. It was six o'clock.

She was still smiling when she got back to the hotel that night after dinner with her mother. "Raleigh, I know all the girls are wearing those short, short skirts now, and I don't want to imply for a minute that your legs aren't absolutely beautiful, because they are. But, darling, fads come and go, as you know. You should really have a style all your own." That had been one of the themes of the evening. "Darling, I know you're brilliant, and I can't tell you how proud that makes me. But do you have to be quite so obvious about it? People aren't used to it, you know. It just throws them off. Makes them nervous." That had been another one of the themes. There must be a mother book, Raleigh thought as she walked up to the reception desk to see if she had any messages. They all read it. Nothing, she saw, looking at her box.

"I'd like a five o'clock call, please," she told the clerk.

Raleigh, wired from all the coffee she'd brought along in a Thermos, was waiting for him the next morning when he stepped through the gate. She was out of the car in seconds, calling his name as she sprinted after him.

"I've got to talk to you," she called, gaining on him, almost even. "Darby, it's me, Raleigh. I can prove it."

He was running now, didn't even glance at her.

"You were right," she cried as she ran alongside him. "Paul did try to kill me in Mexico. He had one of the speedboats, he was waiting for me . . ."

It was almost imperceptible, but he was slowing down. She slowed with him, stopped when he did. Watched his expressionless face as he turned to look at her.

"He took me out into the ocean and hit me over the head with a rock," she said, panting. "Some fishermen picked me up."

"Raleigh," he said.

"And you suspected it," she said. "That's why you never worked with him again. You didn't even do postproduction on that last movie."

"Nobody saw him leave the editing room," Darby said. "He was there when we got back."

"You still thought he'd done it," she said.

"Yes, I thought he'd done it," Darby said.

"I went to the house the other night," she said, walking along beside him as the first rays of the sun softened the sky. "I found the Polaroids that Buddy Hatcher took when he kidnapped me. I figure that the only way Paul could have gotten them was if he had something to do with the murders. That's the only possible explanation."

"Yes." He nodded. "We killed him. We killed them both."

Raleigh stopped in her tracks, felt her whole body stiffen.

"It was so different from the way we thought it would be," he said, a puzzled tone in his voice. "We went there, and Sir George Dean was really confused to see us. I guess he thought he'd missed a signal somewhere. But then he was all smiles, and he was even introducing us to this poor kid. And then we were hitting them, hitting them . . ." His voice trailed off. "It was hideous, ghastly. Real blood, real screams. We hadn't expected that, somehow. But we'd started it, you see. We couldn't just stop, say we were sorry, that we weren't up to doing this, killing them. We just had to go on. There wasn't anything else to do."

"But why?" she whispered.

"Because of the Polaroid, the one that showed you were a girl," he said. "It would have ruined everything. The audience wants to be entertained, enchanted. They won't be conned, though." He sat on a curb next to a field of goldenrod, motioned for her to sit beside him. "Sir George Dean picks up this dumb kid at some bar near the Veteran's Administration in Brentwood. And the kid's following him around, waving these pictures at him, and saying, 'I'm not a fag. I've even got a kid, and here are the pictures to prove it.'"

"Yes, I remember now," Raleigh said. "He was always saying that he was my father. Of course, he was pretty crazy. He had a lot of other peculiar ideas, too."

"He's following Fern around, too, saying the same thing," Darby continued with a mirthless smile. "And Sir George Dean, Fern, they're saying, 'Sure, sure,' and then finally Sir George Dean looks at the pictures to placate the kid. And who does he see? Raleigh Barnes, the movie star. Only Raleigh Barnes is a girl."

Raleigh just sat there, her arms locked around her knees, staring at him.

"Sir George Dean calls Paul," said Darby. "He says, 'Raleigh retires and comes to live with me. That way you can still exploit the library. Otherwise, I blow it wide open and you're over.'" He gave a tight little smile as he met her eyes. "He was crazy about you."

"I know," she said.

"We certainly couldn't have that half-wit wandering around like that, showing off those pictures of his kid to anybody who would look at them. So we didn't have any choice," he said. "Then there was Fern. She and Paul had been having an affair for years."

"My mother told me."

"Fern was always complaining about being the one who did all the work and never got any credit for it," he went on. "She went along with us. She left the French doors on the patio unlocked." There was a faraway look in his eyes as he added, "But when she walked into that room the next morning, saw all of that real blood, those real bodies, it dawned on her that she had been the one who had set it in motion. She was beside herself.

"Of course, she wasn't so upset that she didn't insist on the original plan. That she replace Sir George Dean as the host of the television special. 'You make them do it,' she told Paul, 'or I go to the cops, and we all go down.' She had no experience. The network didn't want to do it, but Paul had all the cards. 'It's Fern and Raleigh,' he told them, 'or you've got an hour of dead air.'

"But that was the end between them," he said. "She couldn't face Paul, couldn't face what she'd done. And he couldn't face her, either. None of us could deal with what we'd done."

"But nobody believed Buddy," Raleigh said slowly. "Nobody could believe that Buddy was my father."

"Well, Paul had blood tests done just after you were born," he said. "There was no possibility that he was your father. Even Beth Carol thinks that Buddy was your father. She told Fern that it must have happened when she was still at home. That the boy was Buddy Hatcher."

Raleigh felt the blood drain from her face, felt a little giddy, as if she were going to pass out right there. She saw

Buddy's face in front of her as if it were yesterday. That sweet, dopey face. Those pleading eyes. "Talk to me, Raleigh," he would say when he would come in after he'd closed the bars where he drank with the other vets. "I'm lonely, Raleigh. Do me a favor. Just this once."

Buddy Hatcher, she thought, frowning. Her father. Not in a million years. And it would be easy enough to prove it. All it would take was a call to the Veteran's Administration. They would have a record of his blood type. She'd bet her life it wasn't true.

"So we killed your father to cover our asses," he said. "But maybe even that wasn't as bad as raising you as a boy. You know, people come out here to get into the movie business, it doesn't have a whole lot of reality about it. They think they can make the whole thing up, reinvent themselves. Make up their own set of rules. That's what we did. Such egomaniacs. You were our grand experiment. And before we knew it, you were famous. A star."

"So it worked." She laughed.

"I guess it did," he said sheepishly.

"And my mother," she said. "She just went along with whatever the two of you decided."

Darby nodded.

"You hated her for it," Raleigh said. "I could see it in your eyes when you looked at her."

"I couldn't hate anybody that pathetic," he said to himself. "She was just some little kid he'd picked up. She was weak, clinging. She was so malleable that she would do anything he said so that he wouldn't throw her out. Even go with anyone he told her to."

"She's come a long way." Raleigh smiled. "She's got everything she ever wanted. An elegant life. Respectability. A place in the community."

He looked at her thoughtfully, glanced at his watch, slowly stood up. "I've got some people coming for a breakfast meeting," he said, reaching out a hand to Raleigh, pulling her up.

"Did you ever go to bed with her?" she asked as they

trotted along. She glanced over at him and saw him nod.

"Did you ever think that you might be my father?" she pressed.

"That's what kept me around all those years," he said. "I thought about the timing, and it always seemed to me that there was a pretty good chance that I was. So I decided to stick around, be your mentor."

She glanced at him again, thought about how much alike they were. The focus. The discipline. Well, a blood test would prove it somewhere along the line, Raleigh decided as they reached the gate in front of the road leading to his house, stood there facing each other in the crisp morning sunlight. "Darby, don't blame yourself for the way I was raised, okay?" she said, putting a hand on his arm. "As a boy, I mean. Brave, reverent, true. All of it. I thought it was just great. Really. I wouldn't have had it any other way."

"You're sure?" he asked hesitantly.

"I'm sure," she said.

She looked into his eyes, saw that he wanted to believe what she was saying. That he didn't. Not completely. Well, she'd have to convince him.

"I want you to have my telephone number," he said, "in case you need anything."

"Well, there is one thing . . ." Raleigh began.

CHAPTER 73

*T*he gown itself was wool crepe, strapless, avocado green with a matching satin band across her breasts. What turned it into a magnificent costume, though, was the hooded cape, yards and yards of billowing copper-colored satin. Raleigh turned, looked at multiples of herself in the mirrored doors of her mother's capacious dressing room. Turned again, admiring the gown.

"Now, darling," her mother said as she stood next to her and gazed at Raleigh's reflection with starry, tear-filled eyes. "You have to admit it was worth all our work."

Raleigh squeezed her mother's shoulder, smiled at her as she thought about the past few days, the hundreds of boutiques her mother had dragged her through, the specialty shops, the designer departments at the major stores. The lingerie, the shoes, the gowns that were a blur. It had taken days just to find the right evening bag before her mother decided it would detract from the outfit. And no jewelry, either. And all of the dainty little sandwiches they had eaten in the tearoom at Bullock's Wilshire, places like that. It was shopping as an art form, Raleigh decided. Mars could have been colonized with the time and effort it had taken from the moment Raleigh had phoned to ask if her mother wanted to go shopping with her until this moment as she stood examining the final effect.

And Bobby, well, that had been a major effort, too.

"I'm just not going to do it," he said, sulking, when she outlined what she wanted him to do with her hair.

She'd begged, pleaded, cajoled, until finally he said, well, okay, but she was to keep in mind that he was on record against the whole crazy idea. And then when it was cut, bleached, colored, and he had started to comb her out, the look of recognition on his face in the mirror.

"Oh, my God," he whispered.

As the doorbell rang downstairs, her mother hurried across her pretty, flower-filled bedroom and looked out the window.

"It's the car, darling," she called.

At the front door, Raleigh hugged her, kissed her cheek, felt the tears.

"This is the happiest day of my life," her mother whispered. "You look beautiful, darling."

"So do you," Raleigh said, touching her hand again as she turned and saw the long, black limousine sitting there in the brilliant afternoon sun.

"Thank you," she said to the chauffeur as he helped her into the backseat.

"You look fabulous, kid."

"Thanks, Darby," she said, looking at him, thinking how handsome he was in his dinner clothes, the pleated dress shirt, the cummerbund, the patent leather shoes. Then, the terrible confession he had made to her flickered across Raleigh's mind. There wasn't a shred of evidence on the face of the earth to link him to those brutal murders so many years ago. Or to link Paul to them, either. But Paul was another matter. Paul had tried to kill her. She was the witness. A charge of attempted murder would hold up in court.

"It's really nice of you to do this for me," she said.

"Anytime," Darby said, shaking his head.

She sank against the seat as the limousine pulled silently

through the gates to Fremont Place and turned onto Wilshire Boulevard. It was only about ten minutes before the towers of downtown Los Angeles were visible in front of them, a few minutes after that before they were pulling into the stream of limousines in front of the performing arts center.

"Aren't you Darby Hicks?" a fan asked as they stepped from the car.

"No," he said as he took Raleigh's elbow, propelled her up the flight of steps, joining the other women in their gowns, the men, a couple of them straightening their black bow ties.

Even before she saw them, Raleigh could hear the fans in the stands set up in the plaza, screaming. "Barbra." "Dustin." "Cher." And then the nominees as they approached. Marsha Mason. Robert Redford. Jack Lemmon.

Raleigh looked at the splashing fountain as it sent a fine spray over those who passed. Looked over at the theater-in-the-round, the larger theater beyond it. Remembered that evening when she had come here for the first time when the main auditorium was inaugurated. They paused for a moment in the crush at the door, then moved through the magnificent lobby with its glittering chandeliers. An usherette led them to their aisle seats just behind Faye Dunaway and her escort, a man with a beard. Raleigh glanced around. A few stragglers hurried down the aisle as the house lights blinked and dimmed. The tension, the excitement crackled through the theater as a voice said, "Ladies and Gentlemen, welcome to the forty-fifth annual Academy Awards!"

The applause began as the curtains started to open, grew in intensity as the voice boomed, "And, here's your host for the evening. Johnny Carson!"

There he was, slim and dapper in his tuxedo, jogging down a curving, sparkling stairway. Taking the mike, seguing into his monologue as everybody in the audience responded appreciatively. The Nixon jokes. The McGovern jokes. The jokes that were so in that Raleigh figured only his writers knew for sure what they meant. The dancers streamed onto the stage for the first big production number. Raleigh swallowed because her mouth was dry. Unconsciously she rubbed her wet palms together.

Best supporting actor. The screenwriting awards. Best original score.

"And now, ladies and gentlemen," Johnny Carson was saying, "we come to a very special part of our program tonight, a tribute to a child star who gave the people of the world not only pleasure as the committed professional he was, but who set a standard of excellence, of courage, of bravery, that many young people reached into themselves to emulate." Stopped for an instant, smiled. "Heeeere's Raleigh!" he said to the applause, the cheers, as the house lights dimmed again and the montage of the films she had made during her life as a boy began to roll on two giant screens, one on either side of the stage.

Raleigh sat there, licking her dry lips, her body tense. Listened to the delighted laughter of the people around them, the oohs and aahs at some of the seemingly impossible stunts being performed in front of them. A close-up of her smiling face, the tousled blond hair, from the last film froze on the two screens. The applause swelled, tapered off as Johnny Carson motioned for silence.

"And now, here to present this posthumous, special Academy Award to Raleigh Barnes is one of the most successful child stars our industry has produced, one who has gone on to make a name for himself in other aspects of our industry. Ladies and gentlemen, please welcome Jackie Cooper!"

He was warm, self-deprecating, spoke for three or four minutes about the role of the child actor in the industry. Said something about how all the attention was a true test of character. That sort of thing.

"And now, accepting this award posthumously on behalf of Raleigh Barnes," he said, "is his father, Mr. Paul Fournier!"

Here goes, Raleigh thought, standing, starting up the aisle as the applause burst around her. Felt eyes upon her as she took a step, then another. Heard the questioning buzz as she glanced across the auditorium, saw Paul striding purposefully ahead, a big smile on his face. She reached the bottom of the steps at one side of the stage just as he reached them on the other side. He was aware of the titters behind him now, the whispers. The smile on his face faded as he saw her there, turned to a puzzled frown as he slowly started his ascent. Raleigh matched him, step by step.

"Hey, what's going on?" asked Jackie Cooper, the Oscar in his hand, as Raleigh let the hooded cape slide off her shoulders onto the stage, stepped forward, took the award from his hand.

She held it to her breasts, met Paul's eyes as he stood a few steps away from her, saw his face go white with shock. Heard his gasp as he rushed into the wings.

She stepped to the podium, ran a hand through her short, blond hair, tousling it to match the pictures still on the screens, felt the shock radiating from all thirty-five hundred people filling the tiers of the auditorium.

"I'm Raleigh Barnes," she said. "As Mark Twain once said, 'The news of my death has been greatly exaggerated.'" And they didn't like it, the audience, she realized as she stood there. They didn't know what to make of it, didn't want to think that it was anything other than an elaborate joke. But she could sense them accepting it, almost seeing them nodding as they looked from her face to the pictures of her.

"I want to thank the Academy . . ." she continued, as she wondered if Toosie were watching. He probably was, she decided. Everybody watched the Academy Awards.

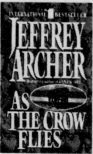